KINGDOM

I hope you enjoy
reading my book
Susan 2023.

KINGDOM

KINGDOM

SUSAN PENNOCK

Matador
9 Priory Business Park,
Wistow Road, Kibworth Beauchamp,
Leicestershire. LE8 0RX
Tel: 0116 279 2299
Email: books@troubador.co.uk
Web: www.troubador.co.uk/matador
Twitter: @matadorbooks

ISBN 978 180046 470 4

British Library Cataloguing in Publication Data.
A catalogue record for this book is available from the British Library.

Printed and bound in the UK by TJ International, Padstow, Cornwall
Typeset in 11pt Adobe Jenson Pro by Troubador Publishing Ltd, Leicester, UK

Matador is an imprint of Troubador Publishing Ltd

FOR:

MUM, CHRISSIE, LEE

AND

THE JUMBLY BUMBLY BOYS

PROLOGUE

Now its strength was returning, it needed a new host. Hearing the bell, it manoeuvred its mirror to the front of the Glasserium. Swelling in size, its glow dazzling, it blocked all others from view, making sure it was the first to be seen.

As the banishing spell was cast, fear and terror ripped through Monis, his pleas to his father ignored. Thick black tendrils began pushing into his body. He banged on the glass, mouth stretched wide as the Darkness claimed him for its own.

PART I

PART I

Chapter One

'Margaret,' said Dalil, as he grasped her hands, 'you may at first feel a bit disorientated.'

'How is this even possible?' she replied, in wonderment, 'if I turn back, it's gloomy, in the distance, dark. If I look this way; bright sunshine.'

'It's the natural barrier between our realms. If someone should accidently stumble through, all they would see is an indistinct landscape.'

Excitement at being in another realm threatened to overwhelm her. As they approached the first buildings, eager to see the difference, her disappointment that they looked remarkably like the houses at home was acute, before noticing the strangest shaped tree she had ever seen looming skywards, stumbling in shock as what looked like hands waved at her.

Dalil laughed.

The leaves of a large branch ruffled her hair, tickling her under the chin. A warm breath caressed her cheek.

'Welcome home.'

Confused, she looked around expecting to see someone standing next to her. A booming sound vibrated through her feet travelling up her entire body.

'What's that?'

'Fingerling laughing,' chuckled Dalil.

Sweeping her gaze across the room, Margaret noticed although bright inside, no obvious lights were visible. It certainly wasn't coming from the windows, where not even a pinch of light appeared to show. Considering this was supposed to be a magical place, she couldn't help thinking how plain and dull it actually appeared to be. Many of those gathered looked as equably unimpressed as she felt.

'Guido,' said Dalil, untangling himself from his brother's hug. 'This is Margaret.'

'It's good to meet you at last. May I, introduce Penny.'

Grasping Margaret's hand, holding it tightly between her own. She barked questions out like a sergeant major.

'Are you going to stay? Do you find it strange?' peering at the brothers, she announced loudly, 'you look exactly the same,' all said without drawing breath.

Margaret laughed, which set Penny off. Unable to stop, her laughter turned into a bout of coughing, then into hiccups. Passing her a glass of water, catching a glance pass between Dalil and Guido, Margaret noticed how as she gulped it down, Penny's hands shook.

'Are you okay? You look pale.'

Locking eyes, the intensity of her gaze was making Margaret feel uncomfortable.

'Do I know you? You remind me of someone,' she snapped out sharply. Unsure of what to say in reply, Margaret smiled.

Watching them leave, Dalil knew Penny would not be allowed to attend any more meetings. She was too unstable. Instead of her picture being a portal. It would now become a watcher. Having magic in her or having been touched by it she would need monitoring.

'I thought the point of being in Kingdom was for us to leave our unhappiness behind.'

'Sometimes a person's sadness is so deep, even here, it is impossible for them to rise above it. Her thoughts are muddled, she talks about searching for someone. At the same time she gives the impression she is talking about herself. Forever looking for something she cannot define. Penny doesn't give herself a chance to actually see what or who is around her.'

'What happens to her now, does she go back to her normal life? Aren't you worried she may tell someone about Kingdom?'

'Penny won't remember her time here. Her memories will be wiped. Guido has had to step in several times when she has cross examined magicals. Demanding to know who they are? What realm they live in? What can they do? Even asking, if they remember her. You saw how she fired questions at you, her manic laughter. Penny has been doing it more and more lately. After consultation it has been decided even though her life in Novia may not be the best. At least there, she appears to be holding onto her sanity.'

Noticing the other greeters making their way towards the door. Margaret's anxiety levels began to rise.

'Don't look so worried,' said Dalil, 'Elfrad will take you to the meeting. Then I will return and escort you back to your picture.'

Disappearing before she could form a reply. Glancing around it was apparent she wasn't the only one feeling confused.

'If you would all follow me,' said Elfrad, smiling in reassurance as the portal took shape.

Pulsating with a ghostly blue glow the cold leeching from it felt by all, no one moved. Then, as if a collective agreement had been voiced. They all moved as one to enter the unknown.

A group of ladies chattered with excitement, Margaret followed in their wake, no excited feelings for her, instead the cold penetrated her clothes making her shiver as her stomach rolled. Funnelled into a straight line, they followed Elfrad. Passing through a long endless corridor one moment it opened out, then narrowed. The floor underfoot rolling slightly as they walked. Like being on a boat, she thought. The darkness inside the tunnel made her stumble into those in front. The chatter dying down as everyone concentrated on staying upright. The corridor finally started to become brighter as light began to penetrate it.

Shielding her eyes against its glare, unseen hands pushed her from behind, once again apologising as she fell. They were now in a chamber resembling a large round cavern with chairs arranged in a semi-circle. Taking their seats as directed she noticed like the house at the gateway, the walls appeared at first glance plain. Studying them more closely she discerned letters forming. Her eyes widened to see them chase each other across the surface, reforming into a word before jumbling up again. Tension filled the air as everyone strained forward wondering what was about to happen next.

Just as the meeting was getting interesting, Dalil and the other greeters appeared and began shepherding their charges towards a portal.

'Why can't we go back via the gateway?'

'There seems to be some sort of emergency happening. Please don't be concerned. I'm sure it's something and nothing. You need to get your affairs in order before letting me know when you're ready to cross.'

'Talking to a picture, is a bit weird, even you must agree?' giggled Margaret, at the madness of it all.

Dalil waved goodbye, breathing a sigh of relief to see her cross the beach and leave her picture. Hurrying away he passed the gateway at a trot, turning off into a side alley he headed towards a plain box like building tucked back as if in hiding. A door appeared as he walked towards it, stepping through, he felt the change in the air as it closed silently behind him.

'Did Margaret get back okay?' asked Elfrad, as they headed towards the meeting room.

'Yes, safe and sound.'

'Eldora has taken a special interest in her. Who will be her picture carer? I take it she is fully aware of the importance of who she chooses.'

'She is going to ask her son Sam.'

'When you go to speak to him check your surroundings thoroughly before entering the beach.'

Using his wand to get everyone's attention, Elfrad ignored the Wakanda's muttering at being used to rap the table.

'I wish I had better news. Everyone returned safely through their pictures except for those using the west gateway. The stragglers at the back were causing such a fuss at the meeting being cut short. By the time they were all through the wraiths had massed enough to snatch them as they exited the portal. It happened before we could react.'

'How many did we lose?' asked Dalil.

'Thirty.'

All knew to mount a rescue would be near impossible, hampered by how quickly the wraiths managed to hide them. Elfrad knew his next words would bring them even less comfort to hear.

'The wraiths appear to be on a free for all, everyone a potential victim. Stronger and much more daring in their raids. Targeting who they abduct. Many able to leave their mirrors. Free to roam; undetected and without the encumbrance of using someone else's body.'

Shock and alarm flew around the room, the situation worse than any thought. For some magicals in the Glasserium the haziness of their appearance earned them the name; Wraith. To change both the construction of the mirrors and the abilities of the magicals incarcerated. They knew only dark ancient magic could be in play. Wraiths, with or without their mirrors help, had for many years used the opportunity of anyone peering into a mirror to cajole and entice them in. Offering wondrous adventures. Once pulled through, the wraiths changed into the nightmare they really were. Those taken, too stunned to do anything.

Graphic accounts of what it felt like were the stuff of nightmares.

Described as if pricked with millions of small needles. Then a sharper stabbing pain as the wraith forced its way into their bodies, swapping places. Leaving them inside the mirror, while it took over their life. Only snapping back into its wraiths body when the strain became too much to sustain. Those used, pushed back through the mirror to experience the needle like pain once more.

Many never recovered, often finding their magic mixed up. The spell cast, giving them the opposite result. To clean a house; instead filled it with dirt. Detoxification, the only remedy to get any residual wraith out of their system. A period of spell checking, to make sure their magic had returned to normal. Not all recovered. Some, continually plagued by headaches, aches and pains even a magical doctor couldn't cure, only alleviate the suffering.

'Has anyone noticed their powers diminishing?'

The flood gates opened, all having a tale to tell, either about themselves or someone else.

Elfrad caught Dalil's eye and steeled himself for what he was about to say next.

'The Shimmers magic is also fading, because of this and everything else that is happening they have requested a gathering. Fingerling is opening Verlimusa. Eldora also picked up the scent of ancient magic surrounding a norm and has requested that once in Kingdom, Margaret be guarded at all times until she can figure out why it is so.'

The greeters turned as one to look at Dalil, whose face showed equal amounts of shock and surprise at the news.

Chapter Two

Sam hesitated, he still found it astonishing to think that his mother was somewhere in a different realm. When she had first mentioned Kingdom, he thought she had lost the plot, refusing to leave the room, waiting for her to enter the picture, wanting to see the evidence with his own eyes. Telling him that it wouldn't happen while he was there made him worry even more. When she mentioned a friend would be coming to meet him and explain further, he expected someone to knock at the door, not emerge from a picture.

'Keep watching, this is the way Dalil will come.'

Sam stared, feeling unnerved that she obviously believed what she was saying.

'Look. Here he comes now.'

His mouth fell open, someone was striding across the beach heading straight towards them.

'Mum, I don't…'

Dalil appraised Sam, tall, slim and a bit gangly, as if still coming to terms with the length of his body. His hair military short, made the colour hard to discern. His blue eyes mirroring the tension his body was emitting. Aware he had to tread carefully. Margaret had been building up to this moment for a long time, whereas for him it was all still new.

'Here we are,' she placed the tray down, oblivious to the tension in the room.

Sam's voiced squeaked. Coughing to cover his embarrassment, he asked, 'so where is this place exactly?'

'I come from a realm called Kingdom, similar to yours except it is magical. It senses unhappy norms and sends out a picture. These can only be found in Emporium's. A pairing can happen quickly, or take years for a match to happen, in some cases it doesn't happen at all. Once matched, the process of drawing them in begins. I should also add, time spent in Kingdom isn't always in sync with your realm, which we call Novia. Eventually, a meeting is suggested to find out what can be expected if a move to Kingdom is made. This is why a picture carer is so important. A norm can only return home using the picture matched with them.'

'Surely, you cannot take every norm as you call us, who is sad,' exclaimed Sam.

'I have magic in me, or been touched by it. That's the selection criteria Kingdom uses to find us.'

Sam looked dazed. Margaret unsure if he believed anything he was hearing.

'So what happens now?'

'Are you going to be the carer of your mother's picture?'

As Sam nodded in agreement, Dalil glanced at Margaret.

'It's now up to you.'

'Once everything is straight in my own mind, and we have had a proper discussion. Then as silly as it still sounds, I will tell my picture that I want to come.'

'But who will hear?' demanded Sam.

'Kingdom,' stated Dalil.

Seeing his mother's dazed look, Sam smiled, asking, 'good trip?'

'The best yet. I'm glad you're here. I need to talk to you about…'

'You've made up your mind?'

Pulling her towards him, he hugged her tight as tears pricked his eyes.

Sitting across the table from each other, how to deal with the fall out, was now much more of a concern. Margaret sure that Sam would take the full brunt of his father's wrath.

'When do you go?'

'A week from today,' she replied, unable to keep the excitement from her voice. 'When your father goes away that will be my opportunity to leave. I can prepare without fear of being stopped. He will be mad at first. Then will turn on me. I know he has never...' Stopping her thoughts, she added, 'I'll leave him a letter explaining.'

'Take my St Christopher.'

'Why?'

'Humour me it will make me feel better,' countered Sam, feeling near to tears with worry. He wanted her to be happy. If it meant going away for it to happen, then he would support her. The thought of life without her though, made him feel uneasy, sad, and fearful of both their futures.

Placing the necklace around her neck he kissed the top of her head.

'I love you mum. I shall miss you dreadfully.'

Hugging him to her, she reached into the pocket of her cardigan.

'I also have something.'

Undoing the clasp she released what looked like a small ball of rope. Holding it out for Sam to take, the rope unravelled and a gold ring emerged.

'This, like you, means the world to me.'

Margaret's thoughts flew back to when Balin gave it to her. Both happiness and sadness intertwining the memory. Such a long time ago, bumping into him, knocking his files to the floor. Like a classic movie bending down to retrieve them, they knocked heads.

'Hi, I'm Margaret.'

'Balin,' he mumbled.

A shiver run down her spine. Finally, when she'd nearly given up, he asked her out to dinner. Hardly able to contain her exictment, she tried on everything in her wardrobe at least twice. Each time they met she fell deeper in love. When he left, her world fell apart.

'Please, sit down, listen... listen, calm down. I have a family problem. I have to go.'

'I'll come with you; I want to meet your family,' she pleaded, holding tightly to his hands.

'I cannot explain, please trust me. I will return, it may not be for a while. But I will come back.'

'How long do you mean? Please don't go, I love you,' wailed Margaret.

'I love you too, but I cannot take you with me. I wish I could.'

Remembering even now, how she had cried and clung tightly not wanting to let him go. Seeing the worry on his face made her realise that she would have to trust him.

'This is my most precious possession. If you doubt my return. This will remind you that I will.'

Finding out that she was pregnant, the ring quickly lost its charm to bring comfort. How she got together with Barry was still a mystery, finding him brash, disliking his innuendos. It seemed though, after Balin left, everywhere she went, he turned up. When he proposed in front of her parents, she still cannot remember actually saying yes. Her sense of fair play though wouldn't allow her to deceive him into marriage.

'I know what you're going to say. I don't mind, in fact. I am not even bothered. I've known for a while.'

'Surely you're not desperate to be lumbered with someone else's child?'

'Correct. I do however want your father's business. What do you say? Do we have a deal?'

Pulling her thoughts back to the here and now, determined she wouldn't let the memories spoil her happiness. Kingdom had called her and she was more than ready to answer. The thought of leaving Sam, impossible to contemplate. Staying with Barry though, was not an option, she had to get out.

Hesitating, Margaret turned to take a last look, a feeling of sadness overtaking her.

'I love you Sam, please don't hate me,' she whispered, hoping her words would somehow be carried to him.

'We are going by portal to meet Sensie where sadly I must say my goodbyes,' said Dalil.

Drinking in what she thought may be her last sight of him, feeling she owed him so much. Wrapped up in her thoughts, she didn't notice the bright aura which surrounded the portals blue haze.

Eldora worked hard to hold it in place. She couldn't risk any part of Margaret's entrance into Kingdom being noticed.

The cold enveloped her, the portal swaying as they travelled through it. This time though, she didn't feel sick. Dalil held tight to her arm as they exited. The blue haze flickering.

They were standing in front of a typical chocolate box cottage, the type a child would draw, and a grown up would break the bank to own.

'Welcome,' said Sensie, enfolding Margaret in a hug.

'I must go,' interrupted Dalil.

'But you can't, not yet, surely you have time for...'

He took her hands in his.

'It has been a pleasure getting to know you, Sensie will keep you safe and help you to integrate into Kingdom.'

'Why do I need to be kept safe? Is there something that you're not telling me?'

Dalil felt uncomfortable, he didn't want to lie to Margaret, yet at the same time, he couldn't tell her of Eldora's interest, and therefore the possible interest of the wraiths. Sensie seeing his dilemma jumped in.

'All he means is that magic can seem unsettling and scary for those not used to seeing it used every day.'

Sure she was being fobbed off in some way, yet sensing Dalil's eagerness to leave, she kissed his cheek.

'Thank you, for everything.'

Turning quickly, she walked away, tears coursing down her face. All the emotions of the last few days shuddering through her body.

Sam felt drained, every time he'd closed his eyes and tried to sleep, he could only think about tomorrow, the last time he would see his mother. Now the day had arrived, he only wanted to sit down and cry. As they prepared for her leaving, he'd never seen her smile or laugh as much. While inside, he felt utterly miserable. Trying to put on a brave face had taken its toll.

Opening the door he knew she'd gone. Gathering himself together, he walked unsteadily towards the sitting room. Feeling bereft, fighting hard to hold back his tears. Spotting an envelope lying on the table, his hands trembled as he opened it...

My Darling Sam,

I know how upset and hurt you will be by my leaving without saying a proper goodbye. I realised last night, if I waited for you, there would be a good chance I wouldn't leave at all.

Forgive me?

Live your life to its full potential, don't waste any opportunity. Find love, and when you do, keep it safe. Cherish it every day. Though we may literally be realms apart, never doubt that I love you.

Mum xxx

Finding it impossible to hold back the tears, he let them have full reign, sobbing as if his heart would break. Come on, man up, pull yourself together; he told himself.

'Did you know about this? Where is she? I won't stand for it.'

Sam reluctantly made his way back to his parent's house, hoping his father having got the rant off his chest on the phone, may have calmed down enough to talk sensibly.

'WELL? WHERE IS SHE?'

'Dad, can you at least let me get my coat off.'

'Always mummy's little favourite.'

'If you're going to be sarcastic. I will leave, and you can wallow in your own self-pity.'

Gulping down his drink, his father poured another one, equally as big.

'What has she got to be unhappy about? I've given her everything, haven't I?' he shouted, tearing up her letter.

'More like the other way around, you treat her abdominally.'

With each word uttered, Sam could see the situation getting worse, happy for his mum, but also angry she had left him with this sorry excuse for a man.

'Get out. You're not welcome here anymore.'

Shocked at his father's vitriol tone, he replied, 'look dad…'

'I'm not your dad. Your sainted mother got herself pregnant by someone else, keeping it quiet until after the wedding, leaving it too late for me to back out.'

Barry knew this wasn't true, but he enjoyed seeing the shock on Sam's face.

'She never told me who he was. A loser probably,' he offered up, with a smirk.

'Dad, please don't talk…'

'I AM NOT YOUR FATHER.'

Stumbling outside, Sam's head reeled with the feelings of betrayal that were overwhelming him. Questioning in his mind over and over why she'd never told him? Leaving, she'd had the perfect opportunity to come clean. Trust that he would be okay with the news. Shocked, yet deep down glad that he wasn't in anyway related to Barry. Now she had gone he would never get the chance to ask her about the identity of his real father.

CHAPTER THREE

Margaret turned her face up to the sun enjoying its warmth. Thoughts of Sam never far away. Making friends with Dandelion had made leaving him bearable. They'd met on one of her many walks. A pack of dogs surrounded her. Sticks dropped in anticipation, throwing them, making her laugh at their obvious delight.

'They like you.'

Startled, she'd nearly tumbled into the river. After that, whenever she went for a walk, Dandelion and her dogs would usually appear.

'How much of Kingdom's history did Dalil tell you?'

Dandelion's voice, pulled her back from her thoughts. The enormous lunch they'd eaten, lay heavy in her belly. The dogs curled around their feet snored gently their bellies also full, drowsiness filled the air.

'Only in general terms, nothing in depth.'

'All good things I suppose, no mention of dark magic.'

Margaret thought back to their conversations, it was true he had always portrayed the realm in a favourable light.

'Why did you want to come?' Dandelion opened one eye, staring at Margaret. 'You don't have to tell me if don't want to.'

She didn't know what to answer, her feelings and thoughts were all over the place. Cowered by Barry at home, since entering Kingdom she'd gained something of her old spark back. Is that enough? Often flashed through her head. If it hadn't been for Dandelion and Qiao, a young boy she had taken under her wing. She might have already returned home.

'Kingdom's history is the age old story of the fight between light and dark. Settle back, and be warned, light doesn't always triumph.'

Closing her eyes, she let Dandelion's hypnotic voice draw her back into Kingdom's past...

Tassach, the king's brother craved power, he sought out those steeped in dark magic and persuaded them to use all their combined magic to create a black mirror and call forth the Darkness.

Preparations were at last complete. The mirror hovered above the ground, its frame etched with the faces of demons, snakes and clawed hands. A rolling mist appeared, wending its way through the mottled branches of the trees. Clinging to the mirrors back like a rider astride a horse. Watching as it moved down the mirrors surface, the witches and magicians knew the time had come to cast their last spell.

Fanning out in a circle they waited for Tassach to arrive. Dressed in black, no markings adorned their robes depicting who they were, or what they could do. Hoods pulled low covering their faces, dim lights flickered as they moved.

As he entered the clearing every witch started a low humming, the sound turning the candle flames red. Taking his place in the centre Tassach faced the mirror, once he stepped inside there would be no going back. The last spell would conjure the Darkness, bonded, he would emerge a Dark Lord, his transformation complete.

The dark magicals thought Argonorth dead, the trees burnt and killed during the last battle. Unknown to them it had become the home of the Trip Trees. Unlike most trees they loved to be mischievous. Tangling their branches across the ground, tripping unwary magicals, laughing as the more they tried to get up, the more entangled they become. The old burnt trees with their bent and gnarled trunks gave the land an eerie feel. The Trip trees constantly moved around them none knowing where they would appear next.

Those who couldn't avoid crossing the land held themselves ready, their eyes roaming for any signs of their appearance. Often caught out by their roots trained to yank them off their feet, before the trees themselves burst through. Branches shaking in laughter at the magicals lying tangled on the ground.

Since the forest had been invaded by the dark magicals, the Trip trees had shown their true metal, making Fingerling aware as soon as they'd spied them at work. He knew the time had come to act, even in Verlimusa he could smell the evil being created.

More and more reports were being brought to the king's attention. The clans were all in agreement. He had no choice but to order the death of his brother.

A magician shuffled forwards, her hands clutched her staff as she strained to stay upright.

'This is Eshe, please listen carefully to what she has to say,' said Conan.

'Once Tassach is dead. We must secure the Darkness in a tomb. The Alvie's forester nets are to capture and hold it while the Fae cover it with fairy dust. Shimmer from the king will bind the magicians and wizards spells. Using only the purest gold, a pentagram covering the tomb and an outer circle surrounding it needs to be constructed. Making sure that the Warra cleanse everything once complete.'

As Eshe's words sank in. Heads nodded in agreement, all relieved that a solution may have been found.

Conan watched as a hand emerged to place a pebble carefully onto the ground. As he picked it up the eye opened and turned in the direction they were to follow.

Walking through the forest, branches bent back out of their way. Small lights flickered on the path like sparkles of rain, enough to see; but not enough to give them away. Bracken and twigs sunk into the ground, their footsteps remaining silent. The camouflaged skin of the Alvie making them hard to detect; even the moon hid her face, doing her best not to give them away. All aware, the nearer they got the less chance the spells woven to hide them would work. The dark magicals had used the forest thinking it dead, and not able to thwart them. Instead, the forest used their arrogance against them, fighting back in any way it could.

Tassach braced himself, waiting for the sign he should grab the sides of the mirror and climb inside. The witches were drawing towards the end of their incantations; ready to cast the last words.

Conan struck, flinging himself at Tassach, pulling him away. As each sentinel brought down a witch, the Alvie flung their nets, while the Fae's dust hovered ready to fly, all alert for any sign of the Darkness. A witch managed to break free, flung her hands towards the mirror and cast the last spell. Everything stopped.

Tassach shook off his brother's arms. A sentinel stepped forward. Conan's face aged in the seconds it took for his brother to die. Gently laying him onto the ground, the warrior turned and bowed. Everything around them erupted in uproar. The witches and magicians fought to get away from the sentinels who were in the process of gagging and binding them. Their minions rushed about striking anyone who dared come in range. The madness in their eyes, froth foaming at their mouths, showed how far they had succumbed to the dark magic.

Conan knelt over Tassach and closed his eyes, bending to kiss his forehead. The witches including their minions were taken away. The sentinels and the Bomani rounded up the last of the magicians who had tried hiding amongst the trees. A mistake soon realised, as the Trip trees penned them in with their branches cutting off their escape.

A loud bang echoed as the mirror started to undulate and bulge outwards. Everyone left in the clearing, gathered themselves ready to fight. Out of the forest poured more sentinels, their swords at the ready. As the Ambrogio removed their collars releasing them from their containment, all hoped in the furore of battle, they would be able to control their natural instincts and focus only on attacking the Darkness if it should escape. The space around them grew bigger as everyone inched away. Even the trees seemed to lean backwards, as if afraid to be touched. The Fae's skin, started to glisten and move, their fairy dust lifting, causing small puffs of it to float in the air, as the Alvie readied their nets.

Puddles appeared at the base of the trees, as the Warra arrived. Their forms taking shape bringing the sound of cool water as it fell around them. The Kaimi were keeping watch high up in the trees for any lingering dark magical still hiding in the forest. The Lobes and Lens were straining to hear and see into the mirror, for the first signs of the Darkness. They knew it would come. Seeking a host, something they were all determined wouldn't happen.

'It's coming.'

Everyone watched in horror as a dark shape started to grow. Twisting and turning, growing bigger until it filled the whole of the mirror. Everyone strained forward. It started with a small bead of black tar like substance suspended from the mirrors edge. Joined by more and more beads, until a continuous river of black fell down onto the ground, curling around like a snake. Everyone waited, knowing the exact timing essential. The Darkness had to leave the mirror completely for them to be able to capture it with no part left inside. Time seemed to stand still.

'Alvie ready,' cried out Lens. 'The last drop will be, NOW.'

Rushing forward the foresters threw their nets over the black mound. The vampires stood beside them ready to unleash their fury and power, should the Darkness start to move. The mirror exploded outwards before folding in on itself and disappearing. The Warra poured in to wash the ground clean, tumbling over each other in their haste to cleanse the earth. Once the nets were secured, the magicians and witches cast holding spells over the now small black bundle.

To make sure nobody came in contact with it, the Warra used a path to create a river, using just enough current to keep pushing it forwards to its journeys end. On either side, everyone else kept pace as the bundle floated on the surface of the water. The journey back to the castle happening in silence. Everyone wrapped in their own thoughts; hoping all the safeguards in place would be enough to contain the Darkness, and what the outcome would be if they didn't work.

Tassach's body lay on a stretcher guarded by sentinels. Conan stood in front, his sword ready as if to repel anyone who should draw near.

'Even though my brother was stopped,' explained Conan, 'we will all be living with the consequences of his actions.' Indicating the magicals standing behind him he continued, 'these are to be my personal guard. While another guard endowed with my magic will take care of the tomb. All future royals will take part in an Ashbala, to determine if they are pure of heart. Should the Darkness ever escape and find a new host, the Fadia will hold a weapon that can destroy it.'

Dandelion nudged Margaret, 'keep awake, I haven't finished yet. You need to hear the rest.'

Faolan our last King had three sons, under his rule Kingdom was a peaceful place. Magic flourished and life was good. Until his brother Botolf had a son with a witch. Her family had long been suspected of dabbling with dark magic and as such he wouldn't allow them to marry. Deeorna planted the seed of hate into their unborn child where it festered and grew, coming to a head when his cousin, was due to take part in his Ashbala.

Trying to placate Abaddon, Botolf knew wouldn't work, always volatile if he didn't get his own way. His tantrums as a child legendary. He tried to explain. In the end he had to be blunt.

'Due to your mother's links with dark magic, you are not allowed entry into the Osias. I have though found a way for you to attend,' seeing the hope flare, Botolf added quickly, 'only to watch. You will have to change places with a book carrier. I cannot stress enough that no matter what you see or hear you mustn't draw attention to yourself.'

Positioned at the back, partly hidden in the shadows suited Abaddon fine. He let his mind wonder, wishing he was the one taking part, being given a special skill.

As the pentagram slowly moved upwards, the Darkness peered out at the gathered throng instantly feeling a small surge of discontent. On the outside, the black column appeared still, while inside the Darkness raged in frustration, before realising that the anger came not from the magical standing on the golden circle, but from someone else.

The mass unable to leave its prison, had found a way to cling to the clothes of anyone in its vicinity. Once they stepped off the circle its finest tendrils began to probe and search the chamber, unseen and unknown. If no dark thoughts found, they faded.

Uncertain; hesitant, its tendrils crawled towards their prey. At the back of the chamber the Darkness found what it sought. The nearer it got, the stronger the pull, as its tendrils moved upwards, it drank in the feeling of envy and hate flooding out from the magical.

The pentagram lowered, the black column disappearing into the ground. A prisoner once again, the mass hunkered down, while outside, its tendrils anchored themselves tightly inside its new host.

Envy scoured Abaddon's insides, feeling watched, his hostility built, he wanted to rip something apart, kick out. Lose himself in pure violence. Over the next few days, his thoughts were in turmoil, keeping his anger in check was becoming difficult. His decision to visit Novia only made possible by the accidental sight of his family picture. Finding an old invisibility cloak. Thinking to put it to good use, he wandered his father's rooms. Hearing him enter, Abaddon stayed rooted to the spot. When his father pressed against the bed post, and commanded, "Arjun," he watched intrigued to see a draw slide out.

The deaths were mounting up. The outrage against Abaddon's killings, gaining support in every picture he passed. Turning blank, if Botolf so much as looked at them. Even his own picture, wouldn't let him enter, somehow managing to place itself back under his bed.

A commotion made him look towards the window to see Faolan had arrived home early.

'What has happened to Abaddon? The destruction he's causing, lives taken. From all the accounts I've received, revelling in the mayhem caused, including the blood spilled.'

'Faolan please, if I could...'

'Go and get him. We are way past that.'

Noticing how the Baldassare had arranged themselves around his room, for the first time Botolf felt afraid. The look on his brother's face telling him, Abaddon could expect no mercy.

'Get your picture.'

Two Baldassare detached themselves to stand on either side of him, drawing their Quillan's holding them crossed in front of him. Botolf couldn't stop the tremors running up and down his body. Their black swords had never looked so deadly.

'Kedja, Abaddon,' commanded Faolan.

Botolf groaned, the thought of his son being bound and chained for all to see, brought tears to his eyes.

Faolan's clothes began to move as the thread from the pattern woven through the cloth started to unravel. Moving down his body towards the floor growing thicker as each part joined another. The last of the thread to fall making the chain complete. Like a living entity it crept up the wall, leaving a thick black stain in its wake.

In Pictures, everyone knew their significance. No one impeded their travel, all life inside had come to a stop. They knew that when the Kedja caught Abaddon, he would be dragged through. Like a collective unspoken agreement, everyone would turn their faces to the walls and not acknowledge his passing.

Abaddon woke to see what appeared to be black snakes working their way up his legs. He tried to stand, shake them off, but they held fast. Peering closer, he could see they were in fact chains, laying heavy across his legs, his feet had all but disappeared into their curled mass. Struggling only bound him tighter. Creeping nearer to his face he felt something inside him wake and struggle. A drum beat in his skull thumped out the word; No.

Finally, the Kedja finished. Its chains bound him head to foot, his eyes looked out through the links. The malevolence leaching had no place to go. Instead, it turned its anger inward, his eyes glazed over with pain, from the chains on the outside; and the Darkness within. Yanked from his chair, Abaddon blacked out, totally unaware of his passage through Pictures. Silence reined, the only sound from the chains as they dragged him through.

Botolf daren't move a muscle. When he thought he couldn't stand it any longer. The Kedja fell out dragging Abaddon along with them.

'Take him,' commanded Faolan. 'He is never be released.'

'Have mercy, he is my only child.'

'Has he shown any? The only boon I will offer him is for you to do the casting.'

The Glasserium stretched back endlessly. Constantly changing, like Pictures, an entity in itself. A place in Kingdom, yet separate from it. He rang the bell summoning the mirrors. Abaddon lay before him, the chains mostly gone. His body still, as if dead. Botolf started the incantation. It felt strange to allow someone to enter his head, like an echo of his own voice, as Deeorna's brother Mael, added a clause to the spell.

Chapter Four

Locked away in his mirror, Abaddon allowed his hate for everyone and everything to build. Coiling like a snake growing in the pit of his belly. The Darkness hadn't left him; it was waiting for the furore around him to calm down. What at first seemed like the end of its plans, had actually turned out for the best. It now had a ready source to feed from, with the ability to garner many more. Leeched by the Kedja, it needed to get its strength back.

In one of the darker halls it felt a faint pull. Old, ancient, and definitely dark magic, the sort it needed. A flinch, had been enough. Homing in, it pounced, sending its tendrils to weave their way around the mirror.

The Kai opened his eyes, why had he awoken? Unable to see out, he moved around his room, the feeling of being watched growing.

'Open the door.'

Tendrils swarmed, flicking against his body making him shudder, he remembered what these were, but couldn't understand how they were here.

'It is forbidden.'

The tendrils tugged him to the floor.

'OPEN THE DOOR.'

The Kai lay panting trying to breathe over the pain.

'I'm waiting,' the voice like a knife, scraped across his scalp.

He started turning. Picking up speed, becoming a blur. When it seemed his body couldn't go any faster. It disappeared in one last furious whirl. A shining golden key appearing on the floor where he'd stood.

From the dark depths of the Glasserium, the sound of a door being opened was heard. The air shifted, mirrors reared back, fearing it would not herald anything good. Tendrils flew towards the sound curling around the open door sensing movement.

Inside stood several large mirrors covered with flowers woven around their frames. A strong pungent smell rose up, as if every sewer had poured into this one room. Once it registered, it made Abaddon gag. The Darkness didn't care about the smell, pushing him out of his mirror to the back of the room and the largest one.

The flowers on this had almost all fallen off. They lay on the floor curling black at their edges. The petals shrivelled, their smell not as pungent as the others, more like rot and decay than raw sewage.

Arms pulled Abaddon through the mirror. Witches and magicians were everywhere, he couldn't believe his eyes when as one they fell to their knees.

'My name is Meridian; I cast the last spell. Your host was killed before he could enter the mirror. The ancient protection spells in place, meant when caught, they couldn't kill us.'

'From now on you will deal with this new host. If you fail me again. Nothing will save you, entry into the Soul Lost land will be guaranteed.'

Meridian watched the Darkness settle back down into Abaddon. His features once more returning to normal.

'Gilda,' she instructed, 'forge a link between Abaddon, his father and you, work on him to convince his father to kill his family. Only summon the Iwatoke to burrow under Botolf's skin once the seed is planted.'

'Uncle,' cried Valko, 'it's so good to see you,' as he and Phelan grasped Botolf's hands it initiated the Iwatoke.

In two strides he pushed them away and grabbed Bardolpf transferring another. The binding snakes began pulsating with a green light, faint at first, getting stronger as they gained more of a hold. Now started, they couldn't be stopped.

Faolan had been listening to music, lying back with his feet up enjoying the moment, when his books began generating an almighty noise. Once they had his attention, a face appeared telling him his sons were in the library in grave danger.

Hearing his brother's voice, Botolf turned and made a grab for his hand, a Baldassare stepped to block him, the snake meant for Faolan, transferred to the guard.

Pushed out of the way, as Botolf stumbled his heart exploded awakening his Iwatoke.

Faolan's gaze kept returning to his youngest son, kneeling down he leaned as close as he dared. Suppressing his look of surprise, he covered the bodies with sheets. His gaze swept over his brother's body, unaware that now dead, his nephew would be free to leave his mirror.

'Your majesty, I've received word. It's Abaddon; he's in the process of turning into a Dark Lord.'

Snapping his fingers a warrior held up a cat like creature hanging from his hands as if dead. The cat's eyes opened.

'Devil's gap. The black mirror has been called.'

With a twist of its body it sped away. Faolan's rage pounded through him. So this was why his sons were dead. Understanding now, that he would have been next.

Impatience evident in each part of his body, the waiting making him even more on edge. Time was slipping away he wanted to act now. He knew what he had to do. None would be happy with his decision. Waiting wasn't an option.

'I'm going to kill him. He may look and think he is a Dark Lord, but until he bonds with his mirror. He's still Abaddon.'

'Sire,' said Aurelien, 'you must wait for the Maia.'

'Abaddon as good as killed my sons, not a Dark Lord. My own nephew. It may have been my brother's hand that passed the snakes, it was his son though, that made it possible.'

'I understand your anger. It's not only the killing that you would have to undertake, his mirror also has to be dealt with.'

'Enough talk. I've made up my mind. Get me there and I will do the rest.'

No one knew what to say, they could see he had a sort of madness about him. Faolan swept all their concerns aside. Beyond reason and waiting, he roared.

'Cast the spell, NOW.'

Grasping the sides, he hauled himself inside, even a black mirror couldn't stop him from entering. Vibrating; humming; shaking one minute dark then light. A pull, a push sometimes even a caress, all aimed at his senses to throw him off balance. Faolan's anger held in check in Kingdom, poured out, his eyes blazed with light from the shimmer flowing inside him and the sword he held. His breathing speeded up, while his heart raced.

Flexing his hands; wanting, needing to hit something. He would have one shot to kill Abaddon, the Dark Lord, whichever visage the Darkness chose to wear. Whoever stepped through the portal must be killed, if the bonding started, strength would be drawn from the mirror.

Becoming aware of Faolan, the face started to morph into Abaddon's. Launching himself at his nephew, he struck his sword through his belly, shimmer flowed down his arm into the metal. He struck again and again his fury finally at full power, blood poured from the many wounds he was inflicting. Knowing he had to strike now and strike hard, before any dark magicals followed their master. Still in transmission, Faolan's shimmer was starting to weaken it.

'Uncle, what are you doing?'

Time seemed to stand still as his features became clearer. His nephew crouched before him his eyes pleading for mercy. Rather than make him hesitate, Faolan lost all control, striking out, whirling his sword Abaddon's head hit the floor. With the wail of the witches echoing through the portal, without hesitation, he burst through the glass of the black mirror turning as he landed, striking it with all his might. The full blast when it came, tossed both him and the Baldassare to the ground. The mirror burst apart, the glass hovering above the ground, trying to reform. Once again he struck, each time it tried to reform he continued to chop and hack until at last the mirror fell to pieces.

Pulling its tendrils around itself the Darkness once again hid within a mirror, thwarted this time by shimmer. The sword entering Abaddon's body struck the heart of the Darkness. Feeling the cold heat of it burning still, its tendrils tried to consume the damage. Meridian had made it possible for it to leave Abaddon's body and escape. Keeping the portal open, it fled, draining dry the witches and magicians she had pushed through. The Darkness settled down to plot and plan, knowing that with her help on the outside, it would have an army ready to rise. This time it would leave nothing to chance, it would take Kingdom and crush anyone that stood in its way.

Faolan's fever raged through his body. When the doctors examined him, they found a small cut on his neck where a sliver of the black mirror had entered. The skin surrounding the wound turned black spreading outwards covering his body. Seeing the Baldassare leave, all knew the king was dead. The doctors, now able to remove the sliver were all aware that it couldn't be kept in Kingdom. Passing through his body, made it even more dangerous. Embedded in a ring it was taken to Novia. The ring bearer given strict instructions that it was never to return to Kingdom.

CHAPTER FIVE

Dandelion smiled as she laid the table. She had enjoyed telling Margaret about Kingdom. It was a long time since she had spoken at length about the old days.

'Let's have some breakfast then we'd better get you back to the cottage.'

She placed a large plate of bacon and eggs, a pot of coffee and toast dripping with butter onto the table. Sighing with contentment, they both tucked in.

'Sensie came round last night to see if you were here. I sent her away with a flea in her ear. No doubt your reception when you get back will be frosty.'

'To be honest having heard your epic tale, I'm even less sure that I want to stay somewhere so dangerous.'

Margaret felt tears pricking her eyes, this was not what she had left home for. She didn't feel part of this realm, with its threat of wraiths and dark magic. The first time she'd been allowed to pick up a magicians Wakanda, the wand hadn't stopped shaking until she put it down. Handed his staff, they both jumped, as it shouted.

'Don't hurt me.'

A few days later she was then stuck on a broomstick and had to be rescued. Feeling star struck when several witches landed in the village square. As she drew nearer, a witch wearing a large hat, a bat clinging to the brim, cackled in her best witchy voice.

'Hello my dear.'

'Are they real brooms?'

The witch grabbed Margaret's hand pulling her up. As soon as she was on, they were off, and in a flash, so was the witch. Luckily they hadn't gone too high before the witch hit the ground with a thud. Several witches took flight to bring her back. She'd clung on terrified. The broom dodging away each time they came near. Until finally, its games finished, it swooped down tipping her off. Conscious of the witches staring, she, like them, had heard the broom snarl.

'Get off,' to its own witch.

Awaking to a stomach growling with hunger Margaret made her way downstairs to hear raised voices coming from the study. Careful not to stand on the middle of the third step, she crept quietly along the hall.

'I know you mean well, but I cannot allow you to take her off to who knows where.'

Dandelion and Sensie turned as she opened the door.

'I want to see more of Kingdom, give me hour to freshen up and I will meet you at your house,' she announced firmly.

'Can I come too?' asked Qiao, sneaking up behind her.

Dandelion strode ahead, little puffs of dirt floating up each time her staff hit the ground. Although they had left early, the heat of the day was beginning to gain ground. Margaret felt hot, and could see Qiao also feeling the effects of the heat. Dandelion though, looked as fresh as a daisy.

So far, their surroundings appeared familiar, except the landscape was all jumbled up. What they had taken for a ring of mountains and rugged countryside, turned out to hide at its centre, a beach with what looked like a sea lapping at its shore. Both she and Qiao had stared in wonder. She because it messed with her senses, and him because he'd never ventured far from the confines of the village. Therefore everything they saw drew raptures, be it a rainbow or the flowers that sprung up everywhere they walked.

'Come on, we're nearly there.'

Dandelion pointed her staff at them to hurry up, approaching a large lake both hers and Qiao's attention was diverted by the land on either side of them filling up with flowers, all waving, as if saying hello. They bumped into Dandelion, whose glare made them both step back.

'Be quiet, stand still and do not react, or at least try not to.'

Turning to face the lake, she banged her staff hard onto the ground.

Ripples formed at the edge, getting bigger as they moved towards the centre. Margaret and Qiao grabbed each other, amazement reflected on their faces, as the shape of a man started to form.

'Good day Pelagias, my old friend. I take it by the noise we heard earlier, you are playing water fall?' Turning, she told them, 'I do wish you'd close your mouths. I've told you Margaret about the Warra, and you Qiao surely must have seen one before?'

'I have, but only in the distance,' he stuttered, amazement reflected in his voice.

Margaret stood mesmerised, she could now see that instead of clothes, water fell to merge once again into the lake. The colours reflected in the water were like looking inside the rainbow they had seen earlier.

'Before I escort you, would you be interested in seeing the waterfalls?'

'Can we?' they both asked, sounding like children wanting a treat.

To their astonishment, Dandelion stepped onto the water.

'Come on, you won't sink and no Qiao, you won't get wet either.'

Holding hands, both still not convinced, they gingerly stepped onto the surface of the water. Their amazement evident, at finding it felt solid. Their mouths gaped in awe as before them a boat rose from the lake. Hauling herself inside, Dandelion patted the seat beside her, making a small splash as she indicated they should sit. Still unsure, Margaret lowered herself slowly down, still expecting to sink into the water. Qiao had no such doubts, plonking down, making the boat rock to and fro as it settled on the water.

'Hold tight.'

Pelagias stepped in front leading the way as the boat followed in his wake.

'We're in time,' he pointed to the cliffs soaring high above them, seeming to touch the sky.

They all turned at the same time as four shapes rose from the lake, to Margaret, they looked like old faded sepia photographs, making her want to rub out the gloom covering them and show the brightness hiding underneath. Pelagias pulled the boat up next to a pile of stones, belying her age, Dandelion jumped out.

Still amazed they hadn't got wet, they laughed as several cushions jumped from her bag spreading out onto the ground. They had seen this trick often enough not to be fazed by it. Both equally fascinated, in would go her hand, and out would come plates of food. As for drink, it was like she had a tap inside it. In would go a glass, out it would come, full to the brim and not a drop spilled.

Hearing the bell toll, they all strained forward, where before the Warra had shape and form, their water now fell in a blur of speed. Suddenly, they all shot up into the air, water falling hitting the lake then bouncing up again. They flew over the top of the cliffs, each one arching high above, catching the light. The sound was so loud Margaret covered her ears. The water thrust itself from the lake as if powered by an unseen engine hidden below. Seeing water tumbling down was magnificent; but this she thought; was truly a wondrous sight. A cheer went up, as from depths rose a great column of water.

'Varun's the winner,' shouted Dandelion.

Pelagias smiled as they stepped back onto the boat, Dandelion's cushions following, dropping into her bag with a satisfied sigh. This time they zoomed across the lake. Standing on the shore they waved goodbye, Margaret suddenly felt tired, her senses shaken to the core, realising for the first time she was beginning to believe Kingdom truly was a magical place. As if copying her thoughts, Qiao yawned.

'We will have to sleep outside tonight,' said Dandelion, 'we need to find shelter, Pelagias, said a storm is coming.'

They hurried to keep pace, feeling the air around them begin to change into something heavy. The flowers, which had followed them all day, had finally disappeared, as if they too were seeking shelter.

'This will do nicely,' looking up, Dandelion called out, 'we seek shelter for the night.'

This time, they didn't even bother wondering who she was talking to, sure all would be made clear before too long.

'Qiao take my bag and shake it out over there,' pointed Dandelion.

Three trees which had been standing apart moved closer together. Bending their branches to make a bower. Qiao shook the bag, out fell blankets, pillows and thin mattresses. Holding it up above his head he tried to look inside.

'Nosey parker,' a voice shouted, nearly trapping his nose.

Snuggling down, Margaret felt cosy and full, once again Dandelion's bag didn't disappoint, soup, crusty bread, all washed down with a large glass of wine, coffee for them and hot chocolate for Qiao. What a day, she thought, I've ridden in a boat made of water, seen water go upward and have ended the day being sheltered by trees, only Qiao's snoring marring the silence.

'Wake up. Come on sleepy head, the flowers are back and there are hundreds of them.'

Margaret dragged herself up from a lovely dream, to see Qiao's excited face peering down at her. The trees had gone, she wasn't going to ask how, but when she sat up, she couldn't believe her eyes she was surrounded by flowers. Hesitant at first, she stroked the petals of a rosy red one that seemed to be larger than most, surprised how silky soft the petals felt. Snatching her hand back when it giggled.

Darting forwards, Qiao went to snatch the one that she had been stroking. As soon as his hand closed around it, he was flung through the air, landing several feet away, the air forced from his lungs with the impact. Margaret cried out.

'He's only winded,' chuckled Dandelion. 'The Calmans when under attack can draw strength from every flower in Kingdom.'

Giggles could be heard as one by one they disappeared. Picking up her bag she banged her staff, with a great whoosh, their bedding disappeared inside.

Following a well-worn path under the trees, Dandelion made sure to say good morning to each one they passed. They in turn, returned the greeting, much to the delight of Margaret and Qiao. Both jumping, as a figure detached itself from a sapling, which was peeking from behind a larger tree, as if a child hiding from strangers.

'Hello Dandelion, and…?'

'Hafren, Tairlaw. These are my friends Margaret and Qiao.'

'Good day to you both.'

Before Margaret could think, she spluttered, 'you're Elves? Why is your skin a funny colour?' clapping her hands over her mouth she mumbled, 'I'm so sorry, that was rude of me.'

'You think us Elves?' spat Tairlaw, screwing her face up in disgust.

Margaret felt ready to cry, they stood like a tableau. Disturbed only when thin branches rained down, scooping them all up.

'Now then, now then, what's all this,' said a voice, sounding like a sergeant major on a parade ground.

The foresters crossed their arms the colour of their Alvie skin changing from green to brown at an alarming rate.

'No need to get cross, no harm was meant. Magic has gone from Margaret's world, they make up stories to frighten themselves. Sometimes elves are good, sometimes bad, one thing for sure though. Whether made up or real, you all have the same ears,' his laughter echoed around the tree canopy with others joining in, making a rich pleasant sound.

'That's as may be...'

'I didn't mean to insult either of you. Seeing stories come alive in front of me, is unnerving. I'm truly sorry if I have offended.'

Silence greeted her apology. Then the clapping started. It seemed that every branch was applauding. Then whistling blew through the trees.

'Alright, alright, we get the message,' they chorused.

With that, the oak tree placed them all back onto the ground.

'Thank you,' said Dandelion, straightening her hat and adjusting her bag, ready to be off.

'Would you like to come and watch the Tournament?' asked Hafren, nudged by a branch to speak.

Pointing through the trees at a great wall of granite, towering above everything in sight. Margaret was at a loss to see how they could have missed it, even before they had entered the forest. It dominated the landscape

Taking them towards a small hill, Tairlaw told them 'if you climb a bit higher, you'll get a better view. Don't be tempted to come down, it may seem friendly, but once the competition starts, all bets will be off.'

Dandelion's bag once more came into play, cushions jumped out, eager to escape. Bottles and glasses clinking together, followed by plates of hot food, their aroma's rising with the steam. Fully replete, they plumped the cushions, which always fought back, until Dandelion clicked her fingers.

When they'd arrived earlier, the inner part of the triangle had been nearly empty, while they were eating it had filled up with trees. The Alvie moving around each one, psyching them up like boxers in a ring. The clash of a cymbal rang out, the trees all turning to their nearest neighbour began to wrestle, branches wrapping around each other making the ground shudder as they fell.

Two got so tangled together they had to be prised apart. The cymbal crashed again, those trees caught on the ground were dismissed. Then off they went again, slamming into each other with such force even the hill they sat on shook.

Finally, the only two left were both mighty oaks, their trunks enormous, gnarled and knotty. Their branches appearing to be curling inwards, making them appear as if full of tiny fists. Squaring up, they faced each other. The clash when it came made the hill shudder. In a matter of minutes it was all over. The winning oak scooped up his Alvie for their victory walk as cheers and whistles bellowed out.

Thinking it was all over, Margaret watched in astonishment, as another band of trees entered the triangle, this time brandishing swords. Qiao was practically jumping up and down with excitement. Dandelion smiled to see him so happy. Once again the trees all set to, their swords flashing in the sunlight. As each bout was fought, a true winner began to emerge, this time a tall willow appeared to be becoming the star attraction.

Suddenly, Qiao was up on his feet cheering and clapping, he shouted, 'look, its Hafren, his tree is the winner.'

'That was so… Fantastic,' laughed Margaret.

'I take it you are enjoying your trip through Kingdom?'

'Enjoying it, Dandelion, that expression doesn't even come close, to how I feel.'

Poking the fire, and covering Qiao over with another blanket. Dandelion turned to Margaret and asked, 'why were you sad at home? You don't come across that way, the opposite in fact.'

'Being on this trip has given me back my zest for life. I lost that, when someone I loved, disappeared.'

'What do you mean?'

Margaret drank her coffee, watching Dandelion, watch her, she placed the cup down.

'I met the love of my life. Then I lost him, he doesn't know it, but he is the father of my son, Sam.'

'Does this love have a name?'

'He's called Balin. He left me before I knew I was pregnant. Some emergency to do with his parents. He told me he would return, but never did. Not even to collect the ring, the keepsake he gave me.'

'Did you ever try and find him?'

'I thought I could trust him to find me,' exclaimed Margaret.

The name Balin had conjured up a memory. Dandelion tried to clear her thoughts to bring it to the fore.

'His name sounds familiar.'

'Do you think he might be here in Kingdom? Perhaps that's why I never heard from him again. But that doesn't make sense, he knew where I was and could have contacted me. You have to remember where you heard his name mentioned.'

'Slow down. If Balin is from Kingdom, then you would certainly have been touched by magic. Plus, as his father, your son may have inherited magic from him.'

Margaret came down to earth with a bump; Sam, magical.

Now on their way back to the cottage with more time to think, thoughts of Balin had taken her over. Sure now, he was from Kingdom. Margaret wracked her brains trying to imagine what could have stopped him from getting a message to her.

'We have one more night and then we will be home. It looks as if another storm is on its way. Up ahead there are caves we can use. Once settled, please don't stray too far, the land round here is a bit tricky. It likes to move and confuse.'

Searching in her bag, Dandelion handed Qiao some chalk.

'If you do go exploring mark your way from the caves. Like I say, this is a tricky place.'

'But surely,' said Margaret, 'if where we have marked moves, we will be in the wrong place.'

'She can find us though, can't you Dandelion,' exclaimed Qiao.

'Yes, lad, I will be able to find you,' she answered, ruffling his hair.

Once the bedding was in place and their bellies full, they itched to explore. Always their favourite time, pretending Dandelion didn't know what they were up to, sneaking off like naughty children. Margaret knew she should know better. After all she was a grown woman, but then Qiao was not exactly a child. Although, because of his childlike ways it was easy to forget when he lumbered along, chatting away at ten to the dozen, walking with a swinging motion, as if his arms and legs were loose, while his head bobbed this way and that, trying to take in all his surroundings in one greedy gulp.

'Wait, I keep slipping, it's alright for you. You're like a monkey.'

Finally, as she pulled herself up over the top, looking back, she found it hard to believe that she'd actually managed to climb the rock. Her sense of achievement made her feel pleased with herself. Smiling like a loon, she walked towards Qiao.

'I've walked all round it and there are no openings, what do you think it's for?'

'Even you should know in Kingdom, something doesn't actually have to have a purpose, things appear and disappear in a trice. By tomorrow this will probably be gone.'

Close up, Margaret could see how it had been made using large blocks of stone set at different angles. The more she looked at it the more she didn't like it, the feeling of being watched growing by the minute. Qiao meanwhile was busy running his hands over the stone work hoping to find a secret door.

'There's a crack here, I bet I could get my hand in.'

Before she had a chance to answer, in went his hand and he followed. She banged on the stone in a frenzy, calling his name, panic setting in. She ran around the structure, praying for a doorway they'd missed. A grating noise broke the silence.

'Come see, I've found a door,' shouted Qiao, his excitement evident in every word.

Running towards the back again, she was relieved to see his grinning face and wild hair peeking out.

'It's full of pictures painted all over the walls.'

'How can you see? Isn't it dark in there?' she asked, relief in her voice at finding him.

Stepping inside, she was surprised to see how big it was, the walls soaring, with a small piece of sky still visible. Dim lights lit their way as she followed Qiao, still feeling as if watched.

'Taa-lah.'

The walls appeared to tell the history of Kingdom laid out in pictures.

'This is brilliant, we must tell Dandelion, I'm sure she would like to see it.'

'Look, there's more.'

As he rounded the corner, the air shifted and the walls moved. Margaret screamed.

'Qiao, can you hear me? Are you alright?'

The door, she thought, which side is it on? Hearing a faint noise, she looked up.

'I'm here I managed to climb up.'

'Be careful, is the door on your side? Can you get out? If so go and get Dandelion.'

Margaret winced as she heard him fall, frustration making her cry.

'Qiao, please answer me?'

'I'm okay, well apart from my ankle. Ouch, that hurts.'

'Can you still see the sky, is it still daylight?'

Looking up, he could see a faint blue, he cried out as something landed on his face.

'What's the matter? What's happening?'

'It's raining, the storm must be getting closer, Dandelion will be wondering where we are. Do you think she'll come to look for us?' asked Qiao hopefully, his belief in her ability to save the day, knowing no bounds.

'The rain, call for the Warra, ask them to help get you out of there.'

'How will they do that?'

'I don't know, but it's worth a try, perhaps they can whoosh you out like when they went over the cliffs.'

Feeling slightly silly, calling for someone he couldn't see, he placed his hand in the puddle.

'I seek help, thank you.'

He waited, nothing happened except more rain fell making the puddle larger.

Margaret couldn't bear the silence. Forgetting she was even more stuck than Qiao, at least he could see the sky, whereas, she was effectively now in a box.

The puddle moved, becoming solid.

'Someone's coming.'

She didn't know who he meant, the worry making her heart pound so much it was in danger of jumping right out of her chest. Feeling the coolness seeping through the stone, even though she couldn't see, she knew the Warra had arrived. Relief flooded through her.

'Margaret, are you okay?'

'Yes, I'm fine.'

'I've hurt my ankle and cannot stand,' moaned Qiao.

'Rather than push you up by your feet. I will fill the room with water and you can float to the top.'

'How will I get down?'

'My friend will come and get you. Have you ever flown before?'

Before he could ask what he meant, Pelagias disappeared and the water began rising.

Margaret sat down to wait, something had changed, she checked to see if the door had appeared, but the walls were as smooth as before. Her senses were on high alert, something, or someone, was in here with her. She called into the gloom.

'Why don't you show yourself? I'm only a norm. I cannot hurt you.'

She didn't expect laughter, a good belly laugh at that. Emerging from the gloom, a tall figure made its way towards her, appearing to float above the ground rather than walking across it. Surely he must be at least seven feet tall; she thought, her eyes widened as she caught sight of his black hair swept back from a widow's peak, eyes flaming red.

'Vampire,' she blurted.

His fangs lengthened, fingers turning to talons as his eyes turned black.

'You can't kill me, so stop pretending you can. You wear the golden collar; it will stop you. My friend has told me about Kingdom, including its vampires.'

'Perhaps she has also told you that I may not be able to kill you, but I can hurt you.'

'But you won't, you would have done it by now,' taking a moment to really look at him, she held out her hand, 'my name is Margaret, what's yours?'

'Cian,' he replied, surprised by how calm she was. 'Why are you not afraid?'

Before she could answer, light flooded in and Dandelion stood in the doorway.

Qiao bombarded her, 'I flew Margaret, a giant eagle called Acillino, picked me up from the top of the mausoleum, and brought me down. You should have seen Dandelion's face.'

CHAPTER SIX

Entering the village, Margaret looked at it with fresh eyes, it was easy now to see how run down it appeared. Even Bilberry's house decked out with bunting couldn't mask the drabness surrounding it. On their travels Kingdom had appeared bright, colourful, lush and alive. This village, and others surrounding the cottage all had the same thing in common, they had no real colour and what they did have, appeared to be washed out. Unless in their finery, even the magicals looked grey and worn down.

One thing all the villager's made sure of though, was the flow of food and drink. She found it hard to imagine anyone in Kingdom starving, even without using any magic. Grabbing a drink from a tray hovering near the door, they went to pass through into the garden where bunting hung from the trees and every available post. The smell of roasting meat making their mouths water. In his eagerness, Qiao bumped into a rather portly magician in the throes of telling a story to his avid listeners. Shouting at him to watch where he was going. Margaret placed her hand on his arm, saying sorry on Qiao's behalf. When all hell was let loose.

The magician's staff which had been leaning against the door jamb flew at him, striking his legs and arms, crying in a loud voice, 'be off with you, we don't want your sort here.'

Everyone turned to look, Margaret felt mortified, thinking how nothing had changed while she'd been away. Fortunately, Dandelion chose that moment to make an entrance and with one swipe of her wand, the magicians staff and him, were propelled unceremoniously out of the door.

As the chatter died down to normal levels, Margaret came out of hiding. She had removed herself to Bilberry's study, ignoring a Bodleian who kept asking her what she was doing. Finally getting the message, he'd left her in peace, though not before he'd ruffled all the pages of Bilberry's books. Another one throwing a tantrum; she thought.

The party eventually drew to a close, magicals shouted their goodbyes, all slightly worse for wear. She laughed to see Qiao trying to describe to a group of bored witches, how the Warra played water fall.

As more left, the mess they had created became apparent. Tables that had groaned with food, now looked as if an army had trampled all over them. While a pile of bottles argued over who had poured the most drink.

Bilberry plonked herself down in her favourite chair, a riot of colour and pattern, sighing, as she took off her shoes, flexing her feet as if she had walked for miles. She smiled as the last guests waved their goodbyes, most unable to stand, they stumbled home.

'Shall we have a little tipple?' she asked Dandelion and Margaret. 'Now that lot have gone.'

Clapping her hands, a large bottle of brandy appeared, three glasses landed on the table, clinking together in their haste.

Once the drinks were poured and Qiao had been given his hot chocolate. They all settled back.

'So what's this Dandelion tells me, about you and a vampire,' smirked Bilberry.

'You never asked. I never said anything. How do you know?'

Qiao's eyes were practically out on storks, flicking between the three women, knowing that the tension in the room, meant he'd best stay silent.

'You were in a mausoleum, it's were dead things go. I know from past experience that they like to enter them.'

'His name is Cian. I think I surprised him when I mentioned his collar and shook his hand. Then you opened the door. I'm glad you did, but how did you find it so easily?'

Ignoring the question she peered over her glass at Margaret.

'You're turning out to be a real conundrum. Adored by the Calmans, friends with a vampire.'

Qiao winced, knowing what it was like to be spoken to in that tone of voice.

A few days after the party, still stung by the way Dandelion had spoken to her. Recalling again their adventures, gave Margaret the idea that they needed some more. Deciding, with the possibility of meeting more Alvie that they should head to the forest near the bottom of Sandy Hill. Although appearing small, she knew from past experience looks can be deceiving. Dandelion hadn't wanted to take them there, making it the perfect place for them to go. Qiao suggested they set off at night to make it even more daring.

It all went wrong right from the start. Qiao had little or no magic and his lights wouldn't hold, they had to fumble their way along the path waiting until the moon showed her face. Progress was slow, their packs were full to bursting, with no resource to Dandelion's bag they'd tried to be prepare for every eventuality.

'I think, we'd better find somewhere to stop for a while Qiao, or at least until it gets a bit lighter. If it means someone comes looking, so be it. It's getting dangerous to navigate, the path keeps veering off. I thought, we would at least be at the edge of the forest by now.'

'I agree. To be honest it feels a bit creepy. I thought earlier, I heard someone following us.'

Margaret had also gotten the feeling that they were being followed. Not wanting to mention anything, she was beginning to feel that they had made a mistake in thinking they could cope by themselves. Huddled together they shared a sandwich. The hoots of several owls unnerving them, making Qiao spill his drink.

The feeling they were not alone continued to grow. Not much of an adventure, she thought. Not wanting to worry him anymore than he already was, deciding, once it got light enough to see where they were going, they should head back before anyone noticed their absence.

'Someone's here.'

Trying to stay calm even though the same feeling had been creeping over her, she went to reply and stopped. Someone was moving with some form of light, which swept the ground as they walked. Even though all her instincts were to run, she knew they had to stay still. After what seemed like ages, they realised the light had gone and daylight was coming. Relief lit up both their faces, their limbs cramped from sitting still for so long.

'That certainly started our adventure off, do you want to continue? Or would you prefer to go home?' she asked.

Watching fascinated as he stretched his long limbs making the joints snap, happiness written all over his face, he pranced about, swinging his arms, as if trying to fly.

'I was a bit scared last night. Now we have all day to explore and tonight we can prepare a proper camp.'

The eagerness on his face washed away her doubts, repeating to herself like a mantra; it will be fine.

They packed up and moved deeper into the forest. The trees like sentinels, their branches stretched up to form a canopy that offered shelter, but also cast shadows hiding the light. Both thinking something was wrong with them. Unlike the other trees they had come across these didn't talk or move. Their leaves dead. Brown and curled at the edges, ready to fall. Looking more closely at their trunks, sap oozed in places as if they were crying.

Touching one, Margaret wanted to shout, 'hello,' like Dandelion had, but once again the feeling of being followed, clung. Both were averse to advertising their presence more than they had to.

The silence of the trees felt unnatural, especially after their last encounter. This forest felt dead or in the process of dying.

'Somethings wrong, that funny smell is back again,' whispered Qiao. 'I'm sure we are being watched.'

'I think you're right, perhaps we should turn around and go home after all.'

Putting his mouth close to her ear, he again whispered, 'we can't, it's gone.'

As she went to turn he held tight to her arm.

'Keep walking, the forest is not the same behind us anymore. The light we saw last night is back. Much brighter now, it's blocking out the trees and the path.'

They could do nothing except keep walking. Frightened to stop, in case whatever it was caught up with them. Glancing to the left the decision made for them, that path had also disappeared. A layer of fog and mist swallowed the ground, blurring the edges. Margaret feared they were being herded. Feeling the air getting cooler she thought they must be near water.

'We need to keep moving and find some shelter,' she muttered.

Not wanting to be boxed in, she knew they both needed some rest. How far and how long they had been walking for was anyone's guess. The tree canopy effectively blocked out the light the further they went, as if they were also in on the hunt.

'Look,' she pointed, 'there's a sort of dip with a bit of an overhang. We'll head for that.'

Fat drops of rain began to fall through the trees. The dip was just enough for them to sit with their backs against the wall and legs out in front. Eating the last of the sandwiches, washed down with cold tea, a sleeping bag tucked over his legs, Qiao at last looked rested. Margaret was worried it had all been too much for him.

She, like Dandelion knew little of his history. Bullied because he couldn't do magic no matter what the provocation. Thought of as an oddity, desperate to fit in, he'd tried all ways to cast, all it got him was a red face from the effort.

'Wake up. Its back. The light.'

Margaret surfaced feeling groggy, Qiao's face showing his distress.

'Where are you going?'

'We can't stay here.'

'Okay, calm down, let me think.'

What the hell could they do? She had no idea where they were, let alone how to get home. Qiao was visibly shaking, the tremors making him look as if he were in the throes of a mad dance. Ignoring his impatience, she studied their surroundings, above them she knew was a hill awash with stones. The trees in front were dense, their branches clasped tight to block out the light. Once again she felt they were being herded, their path shrunk to the dip they were in and the forest in front. No choice, she thought; through the trees it is.

Trying to sound decisive, Margaret stood up, folded her sleeping bag, sorely tempted to leave everything and make a run for it. Common-sense took over, hoisting her pack, helping Qiao with his, she smiled to reassure him as they stepped onto the path so obviously laid out for them, the silence acute and heavy. Nothing stirred, everything waited.

When it came, for a moment both felt some relief, that at last they could face their foe. Only it wasn't what either of them expected, if Dandelion hadn't told her about them, Margaret wouldn't have known what she was actually looking at. Floating above the ground was a wraith, its eyes looking as if rimmed with kohl. The black slash of its mouth as it tried to smile, both frightening and fascinating. Its teeth, gleamed brilliant white as if a dentist had polished them. Within the ghostlike appearance could still be seen the remnants of its clothes. Tattered, faded, hanging over its body, making it look like a bag of bones. No time to wonder where its mirror was, her only thoughts of escape. She tried recalling what Dandelion had told her. Before the thoughts could form, Qiao was off.

The wraith whirled, watching his progress as he crashed

through the trees and ended right back beside her. Panting, tears of frustration rolling down his face he buried his head against her shoulder. The wraith watched with a comical lift of his eyebrow.

'What do you want?'

The answer she got was another flash of white teeth, the smile now more of a grimace. We can't stand here; she thought. In the distance she heard cries and shouts. The wraith turned distracted. Without really thinking about it she grabbed Qiao and ran.

A banshee like wail could be heard behind them, they could feel the rage peeling from the wraith, as it flew after them. A great whoosh of air descended, she fell, shaking her head to clear her thoughts, confused to find her hands buried in sand.

'Are you alright?'

Looking around Qiao wondered where the trees had gone. Answering with a question.

'Where are we? More importantly, where is the wraith?'

Her eyes widened as she realised she knew where they were.

'How did we get here? That's my hut over there the one I came through when I entered Kingdom. When we ran, all I could think about was home, and that is my door to it. You must be a Transporter. I remember Dandelion telling me about magicals who have the gift. It's rare.'

'But what does it actually mean?' demanded Qiao, the pleasure in his voice apparent.

'Dandelion said that they could move themselves or others by thought alone to the place where they wanted to go. With me thinking so much of home, and holding onto your arm, meant that you took us here.'

'Then surely if we both think of Dandelion, we can get back.'

Holding tight to her arm he scrunched his eyes up in thought. Nothing happened.

'I'm not sure we can, when you brought us here we were in danger. What if your skill only works when that happens? Anyway, now I'm here, I'm not sure that I want to go back.'

'Kingdom called you because you were sad. If you go back, will you go back to being sad?'

Feeling torn. She wanted to stay, especially after their trip with Dandelion, now though, so near to home she felt unsure. As she stared into the distance her breath caught in her throat, sure she could see a white mist like cloud coming towards them. In fact, now that she really looked there were several spreading out in a fan, their banshee wail instantly recognisable.

'I don't have any choice now. I'll have to go home. If you cannot transport, then we must hide you.'

'Where though?'

He cannot hide inside the beach hut, it wouldn't accept him, she thought. The only place she could see was for him to hide behind the open door and hope he could keep still and quiet enough not to be noticed.

'Listen, we haven't much time, thank everyone for me. When they've gone, make your way home. When Dalil took me to the gateway, we turned near those tree stumps. Thank you Qiao. Your friendship has meant a lot to me.'

Taking a deep breath, she stepped inside and strode towards the door that would take her back to Novia.

'Where do you think you're going?'

A wraith peeled itself away from the wall, cracking its knuckles in anticipation. Terror broke over her, both for herself and Qiao. Without thought she flung herself towards the door leading to the beach, the wraith grabbed her legs bringing her down with a bump. The air pushed from her lungs. Shaking her head she got onto her knees, thinking; I'll crawl if I have to. Unfortunately, the wraith had other ideas, wrapping its arms around her, it hauled her upright. The fetid smell emanating from it, made her gag. Its laugh making her skin crawl. With a super human effort she wrenched herself from its grip, home a few strides away. Tripping, she fell half in and half out of the doorway, banging her head making her woozy.

'Will you stop,' shouted the wraith, getting annoyed.

Slinging her over his shoulder he loped away.

Terrified, Qiao listened, wanting to help, too frightened to move. Once he was sure all the wraiths had gone, he started the long walk home.

Dandelion read the note, Sensie asking, 'do you know where they would've gone?'

'They never mentioned anything to me. To be honest, I haven't seen much of them since Bilberry's party. They both see Kingdom as an adventure. With me, to a certain extent they were protected, by themselves, well…'

'Hello, hello. Anyone home?'

Dandelion turned, as Elfrad walked into the garden.

'Is something wrong?' he asked. 'Where's Margaret, has she settled in?'

As the silence stretched out, Dandelion stepped forward.

'It's so good to see you again. It's been a long time my old friend.'

Wary that his questions had been ignored, he looked for an explanation.

'Margaret has gone off on an adventure. She's left a note, none of us though, have any idea where she may be.'

'You let her go by herself?'

'She is with a young lad called Qiao, who she has made friends with,' answered Sensie. 'But he has no magic,' she added.

Furious, he shouted, 'how could you have let her loose without a proper magician or witch in tow.'

Dandelion watched the play of emotions wash over his face. She needed to speak to him alone. Knowing, that when she told him her news, it would make him even more upset about Margaret's disappearance.

'Please sit. I will get some food and then we can talk.'

'I'm disappointed. Eldora will not take kindly to what's happened,' he muttered.

'Margaret told me about the love of her life, who left her

because of a family crisis. Shortly afterwards she found out she was pregnant with their son Sam,' she paused, 'the father is called Balin.'

Elfrad sat up straighter knowing instantly who she meant.

'This is incredible, how on earth did she meet him?'

'That doesn't really matter, what does though, is before leaving her, he gave her a ring.'

He stood up, his whole body shaking.

'Please tell me Dandelion, that she hasn't brought it with her?'

'No, but she has given it to Sam, which could be as bad. After she told me about Balin, I racked my brain for days, trying to figure out where I had heard his name before. No wonder Eldora is interested in her.'

They both sat for a while as the implications sank in. Never believing, but knowing if true. Kingdom was in mortal danger.

'Why would he have come back to Kingdom? I always understood, although the family could live here, the ring bearer had to stay in Novia.'

Elfrad was stunned, he had only called in on his way to the gathering, hoping for some good news to pass onto Eldora.

'If this is true, it is even more important that she be found.'

'Coming back he knew wasn't allowed. The family crisis she mentioned, what could that have been about? Not only do we need to find Margaret, we also need to discover Balin's whereabouts in Kingdom.'

Sensie looked up, to see a horse and cart trundling up the road towards her. An old witch held the reins, her horse looking nearly as ancient. Drawing near, a face emerged. Qiao burst into tears, the sobs wrenching from him, unsettling the horse.

'Where have you been? Where's Margaret?'

With that he started making a keening noise, sounding more like an animal in distress.

'I found him wandering haven't been able to get much sense

from him. Only the name of the village where he lives, and that he has lost someone,' said the witch.

With a flick of the reins, she turned the cart around making her way back towards the road.

'Come on, let's get you inside. I expect you're hungry, how about a hot chocolate? Then you can tell us what happened.'

Dandelion and Elfrad arrived at the cottage to see Qiao wrapped in a blanket sitting by the fire, still visibly upset. Seeing Dandelion brought a fresh bout of tears.

Elfrad could see the boy's distress was going to be a hindrance to getting to the truth. Before anyone could react, he stepped forward and placed his hand onto his head. Instantly he calmed.

'Open your eyes, you are among friends, there is nothing to worry about, all is safe. Now slowly and clearly tell us everything that has happened to you since you left the cottage.'

Dandelion and Bilberry sat together watching the sun go down, jumping, every time Qiao appeared and disappeared practicing his new skill of transporting.

'Do you think she is still alive?' asked Bilberry.

'I hope so. If though, she's been taken by a wraith. Perhaps death would be preferable.'

Chapter Seven

Elfrad left the cottage, his thoughts in turmoil, they had tried to find the local Lobe and Lens, but they were on a sabbatical to Novia. He felt everything was conspiring against him as he tried to get word to Eldora about Margaret. Dandelion remembering that one of the Kaimi had been seen in the area thought they could send word through her. She though, had flown away minutes before they arrived.

Striding along, his staff banging the ground announcing his presence, most he passed waved and greeted him. The odd few, that didn't like the look of him, turned their backs and continued with what they were doing. He may dress and look like a greeter, but he still smelt like a Bomani.

Pausing for a moment, he scanned the landscape; Kingdom's appearance was definitely changing. In the past trees would spread themselves out creating mighty forests. Now seen in only small clusters, huddling together for safety. Leaving the land looking barren.

Sniffing the air, he caught a tang on the breeze that made him shiver, pulling his cloak tighter, feeling the ache in his legs, he thought; enough meanderings.

Snapping his wand open, the Wakanda crackled with magic as he muttered a spell.

With a flash and bang a pony appeared, its large brown eyes blinking furiously.

'Where to?'

'Verlimusa,' he announced with a smile as he climbed aboard.

The rhythm of the trap soon lulled him into sleep. A sharp retort from the pony startling him awake.

Hearing his name called, he turned to see Aurelien appear.

'I've come to escort you.'

Opening a portal he bade Elfrad forwards. In moments, they were through into a completely different kind of landscape, desolate and devoid of magicals. The trees even from a distance he could see weren't the same usually found in Kingdom. Drawing nearer a loud crackling rent the air, once passed, each tree drew together forming a barrier behind them. Approaching the end, he looked to see that the trees had gone, in their place a large solid wooden door.

Aurelien raised his hand and knocked. As the door swung back, a face peered out and waved them inside. Light poured in, the air felt fresh. They stepped out and made their way towards Eldora.

'Did you manage to speak to Margaret?' she asked as they approached.

'It's not good news, she's been snatched by a wraith. Unknown to Dandelion, a young boy called Qiao turns out to be a Transporter. While under attack, before either knew what had happened, they were outside her hut. Unfortunately, a wraith was waiting inside for such an opportunity. Qiao got away, Margaret was taken. That's how we know what happened.'

'And the other matter?'

'In Novia she met a magical called Balin. We think he has come back to Kingdom. More importunately though he is the ring bearer.'

The silence between them stretched, she had not expected this turn of events. With her shimmer practically non-existent it was easy for Elfrad to see the play of emotions cross her face, this was the worst news, with everything else happening in Kingdom, the last place the ring should be was anywhere but here.

Breaking into her thoughts, Elfrad continued, 'that is not all, her son Sam, is Balin's child.'

'This means that the old magic I sensed is because she's been close to the ring bearer.'

'And the ring?' asked Aurelien.

'He gave it to Margaret for safekeeping. Before she entered Kingdom she left it with their son. He doesn't know Balin is his father.'

Aurelien snapped, 'we must bring him here. If wraiths or dark magicals find out where it is. They will go after him with a vengeance. We cannot protect him, or the ring properly in Novia.'

Elfrad took his seat, nodding to several magicals he recognised, all like him eagerly waiting for the clans to arrive. Everyone turned their heads as if pulled by a piece of string.

The ground to the left of Fingerling started to bubble and pop. Water flowed across the surface slowly at first before gaining momentum, while all around it the earth began to move, sinking down in the middle to accommodate the water and rising at the sides to form a wall. Arising from the centre water droplets coalesced into shapes, firming up, until before them sat the Warra. Their chairs also made of water, continually reformed as the water drained downwards. Pelagias and his brothers nodded to the gathered throng.

Lens and Lobes strained to pick up signs of other clans arriving. The first to hear and see were the Bills, announcing in unison.

'The Fae are coming.'

Verlimusa started growing outwards, as if pushed by unseen hands. A breeze, slight at first, made several magicals remove their hats when it changed to a mad flurry. The sky grew darker, the sun blocked out by the beat of wings. As they came into view the dragons opened their mouths and blew, fire belched and the air smelt of ash, their landing hardly making a sound. Everyone craned forward, Elfrad felt as excited as a child, this was a rare sight indeed.

Leaving their dragons, the Fae made their way forwards, Zekia and her clan nodding at the Shimmers as they passed. Small in stature, their gossamer wings seeming to float behind them as they walked, delicate looks, disguising their fierce temperament. Their fairy dust lay upon their skin, ready to be deployed, if attacked or threatened.

Elfrad felt queasy as Verlimusa kept moving, his vision would blur and the boundaries change. The only constant was Fingerling like a teacher overseeing a classroom full of students. Another set of hands were raised, this time the Gates announcing loudly.

'Kaimi.'

All manner of birds large and small flew in formation landing almost silently. Shaking their feathers, before changing into their magical forms. Gawain, leader of the seekers, was the largest hawk Elfrad had ever seen, still unsure how he managed to take flight, let alone stay flying. His clan quickly took their seats glancing around to see who else had arrived.

'Picture Players next,' shouted the Buds, as their eyes and ears returned to normal.

This time, the air could be seen to bulge and shift. Several frames emerged, hands appeared, in perfect synchronicity out jumped the players. Straightening their clothes before running their hands through their hair. With a flip and a bang the pictures disappeared. Not sure what to do they looked around at the gathered throng.

Yox-All thrust his hand towards the Shimmers and in a high voice said pompously.

'Thank you for inviting us to this auspicious occasion.'

Taking their seats, they twittered like school children, eyes widening as they spotted the dragons scales reflecting in the sunlight.

Two sets of hands shot up, the Watts just piping the Hicks.

'Bodleian on their way.'

Books started to rain down in front of the Shimmers, each one thumping into the next as if deliberate. An urgh sound, accompanying each one as they dropped to the ground. The books disentangled themselves, with one heave they stood upright as if sitting on a shelf. Elfrad was fascinated. Usually, the Bodleian don't like to leave their books, preferring to emerge from the spine. Sometimes, only a face will appear, at others, their whole body, their preference to stay attached in some way. Here though, they would be expected to wholly emerge from their shell.

Eldora bent down and tapped each spine in turn, asking, 'we welcome you, will you show yourselves?'

Nothing happened, knowing how fickle the Bodleian could be, Elfrad was keen to see how long they would take to appear. Surely, he thought; even they wouldn't turn up, and then not make an appearance. After what seemed an age, movement could be detected.

Hands appeared, then a head, before the rest of the body popped out. Reaching forward they grabbed their books, in a blink of an eye, reduced them in size and placed them into their pockets. They each held a piece of paper, placed glasses onto their noses and started to read. All speaking at once and over each other, no one could make out, let alone understand what they were saying. Always in a state of constant rivalry with each other, this however, thought Elfrad, was neither the time nor the place to show off.

Never one with a lot of patience, Aurelien interrupted telling them.

'Thank you, for your kind words.'

Elfrad hid his smile behind his hand, they wouldn't be happy to be stopped in mid flow.

'I'm Gerringong the leader of the Bodleian.'

'No you are not. I, Narrabri am.'

Before they could start squabbling, a lady stepped forward, her face, wreathed in smiles.

'I'm Barraba, unfortunately married to Flinders, who is, the leader. Not that you would ever know it.'

'Alvie,' shouted all the Lens and Lobs together, allowing the glee in the voices to show at the forester's arrival.

All around the perimeter, trees started popping up, stretching their branches, saying hello to Fingerling. The oaks taking up much of the room, their roots could be seen running through the earth snaking out, heading towards the water. As the first ones appeared at the edge, a mighty oak, nearly as tall as Fingerling, boomed.

'Pelagias, may we drink?'

Once the trees had settled, the Alvie put in an appearance. Their camouflaged skin changing colour to match the surroundings, Elfrad smiled as they walked with confidence towards the Shimmers, Mercia and her clan nodding to their friends the Fae as they took their seats beside them.

A fanfare of trumpets and drums started up, cymbals joining in. The witches flew in formation astride their bright red broomsticks. Not to be outdone, the magicians used their staffs to join in the acrobatic display.

Peasey, leader of the Quiryn, waved his hand somewhere in the vicinity of the Shimmers direction before he and his clan claimed the seats at the front in an effort to push the witches to the back. The Hecate's bowed to the Shimmers while laughing at their antics, as Verlimusa once again shifted to accommodate.

Elfrad sighed with relief, unless the Ambrogio decide to turn up, the roll call should be nearly finished.

The constant refrain from all quarters of, will they come? To get the introductions over with, he hoped they wouldn't, but if honest, like everyone else attending, the main attraction apart from the dragon's, were the vampires. The stuff of legends even to other magicals.

Verlimusa shifted once again, everywhere now ringed by trees and sentinels, the warriors drawing their swords as the Lobes and Lens hurried to their seats, the look on their faces telling everyone who was coming.

The sentinels stood straighter, the trees lengthened turning their branches into clubs. Fingerling had flowers appearing and disappearing all over his trunk and the ground surrounding it. The Warra, the first to arrive had sat patiently through the role calling, now though even they were agitated, water falling from them pounded the lake, rather than fell.

When the Shimmers stood up, Elfrad knew they were here. Everyone craned forward, they heard them before they saw them. The ground shook. At first, he couldn't make them out, dazzled when sun hit their golden collars, binding them to Kingdom. Even with these in place though, a fission of fear flowed through everyone, hoping they would be enough to keep them in check. At the back of everyone's minds was the question; what if they took them off?

The Ambrogio stood in a line as if on parade, their skin glowed with luminescence, while their eyes shone red. Hands flexed, talons curled, fangs lengthened. Everyone could see them grow taller, bigger, the violence emanating from them palpable. To say they're a formidable sight; would be an understatement; thought Elfrad. Like everyone here though he was glad they were on Kingdom's side. The alternative didn't bare thinking about.

Everyone instantly became quiet as a pounding could be heard in the distance getting nearer. The dragons raised their heads and bellowed, releasing fire in a wide arc. Elfrad was stunned, before him was a sight he hadn't seen in years. Hell Cats, their striped coats glowing in the sunshine. Giant fangs, giving the vampires a run for their money, glistened, as they pulled their jaws back in a snarl. Large paws padded the ground, their tails swishing to and fro, like house cats getting ready to pounce on their prey. Even with his own history inside him, he couldn't help the thought that these were a sight to put the fear into anyone, the magicals sitting on top of them adding to the formidable sight.

For once even the Shimmers appeared lost for words, invitations had gone out, but in reality, no one thought they would respond. Sliding from their mounts the wizards held onto the reins, taking a good look around.

'Look who we have here. If it isn't poor old Elfrad himself. Look at the state of you, have you no pride in representing your clan,' they chorused, ignoring the Shimmers.

He felt everyone's eyes turn towards him, wishing he could disappear in a puff of smoke.

'Aren't you going to come and say hello? Surely, you're not afraid of little old us?'

Realising, he had no choice. Knowing they wouldn't give up, conscious that everyone including the Shimmers were still waiting acknowledgement by them. The sooner he got it over with the better. Making his way down, as he passed, several magicals patted his arm, he didn't know if this was meant in comfort, or in sympathy.

'Hello Beadu, where are the men?'

Ignoring his question, she looked him up and down and by the look on her face, obviously found him wanting. Elfrad stared back.

'Welcome,' said Aurelien, seeing his discomfort.

'We are pleased to have been invited. We are of course not only warriors, her eyes flicked to the sentinels spread around the perimeter, we are also wizards of the highest calibre.'

As each of their names were called, they nodded to the Shimmers, letting their eyes skim over the vampires. Standing as tall, referred in the past as Amazon's. They liked to fight, often starting, always finishing. Dressed in leather tunics and trousers covered in symbols denoting their warrior status, two swords held in sheaths across their backs, knives strapped to their legs, they were armed and dangerous.

Elfrad in his flowing white robe and cloak felt decidedly dowdy in comparison.

'Where are your men?' he asked again, addressing Beadu.

Her scowl, not putting him off in the least, suddenly, her hell cat lunged towards him.

'Down,' he commanded.

'So you do remember,' she smirked, tapping his chest. 'Once a Bomani. Always a Bomani. No matter what fancy robe you wear.'

'You haven't answered my question.'

'Our men won't come, they resent things that have happened in the past, but we are here. It's time we put our own likes and dislikes aside for the good of Kingdom.' Turning, she raised her eyebrows, 'well?'

Each Bomani tapped the nose of their hell cat. In a flash they were reduced to tiny kittens, placing them onto their shoulders they disappeared into their pouches.

Verlimusa shifted once again, Fingerling moving to the side, while Elfrad's seat moved at the same time as the others to face the Shimmers. Looking into the distance, he could still faintly make out the dragons belching puffs of smoke. He fixed his gaze forwards as Aurelien stood to address the crowd.

'Thank you all for coming. These are troubled times, not only for those of us living in Kingdom, but also for those who choose to live in Novia. Dark magic is on the rise, more prevalent in Kingdom as we would expect. Yet, Novia also is experiencing its share. The Glasserium, as you'll be aware has been out of bounds for a long time the wraiths having now taken it over. The dark magic allowing them to exit through any mirror, is also allowing them the freedom to live on the outside. We could spend aeons debating how this is even possible. But, what we are sure of is that it must be magic of the worst kind.'

'There is something else you should know,' boomed Fingerling. 'It was first brought to my attention about a month ago. Since then, my brothers and sisters have been on the alert gathering more information.'

A shift in the air and every tree in Verlimusa emanated fear, the feeling so strong Elfrad felt he could almost taste it. Fingerling moved his branches, his hands gently placing a magician onto the ground, nudging him forwards.

'Go on, tell them, they don't bite, well not all of them,' he chuckled.

The magician pulled his cloak tighter, leaning heavily on his staff; he swept off his hat, allowing an abundance of grey hair to fall down his back.

'I'm Nakos, a hermit. I live in the caves west of Finchwood. I couldn't understand why magicals and norms were being taken into the woods, spread out in groups and told to start searching.' Pausing to conjure a chair, he continued, 'because I know the area well, I was able to get close without being detected. They were on their knees moving the dirt with small trowels, looking under plants, even rubbing their hands down the trees, much to their disgust. They were searching for the black mirror. The ones wearing gloves were magical. I overheard them say if they picked it up it would burn them.'

The silence was acute, Elfrad like everyone else, stunned, it had always been a possibility that someone would try to gather the black mirror. Yet, no one really believed that it would ever happen.

Mercia stepped forwards, her skin a muddy brown, the colours shifting to show glimmers of yellow and green.

'This makes sense of what we have been seeing over the last few months, years even. As Alvie we patrol all the woods in Kingdom and have seen magicals many times wandering about as if searching for something. The only other thing which was noticeable about them was the smell.' Turning, she called Selwood forward.

'I first noticed it when patrolling the Herringwood. Thanks to Seymour Penge and the animals he conjured, we have to patrol in threes. We headed in and thought something had died, the smell of blood so strong. We spread out, on hearing raised voices came together to find a group of about twenty magicals busy scrambling around a small mound of fallen tree trunks. To say that they looked manic would be an understatement. Their searching was frenzied, the noise they made a result of finding what they were looking for. When they noticed we were there. As one they all stopped, this is when the smell was at its strongest, blood and sulphur. They reeked of it. When I asked them what they were doing, they stood in a bunch, eyes wide looking everywhere but at me, as if getting ready to bolt. Then, before our eyes they seemed to sag, the smell disappeared. They picked up their baskets smiled and walked away, they were all wearing gloves.'

Yox-All, stepped forward.

'Magic in Pictures still flourishes, nothing for us has changed. We have noticed though, especially in Novia, magicals talking about taking a journey and gaining great power. For us hearing conversations happens all the time. Norms like to hang pictures onto their walls, ensuring we're always going to hear even if we do not choose to listen. I only honed in when mention was made of searching for mirror fragments. The magician telling them it would give them access to unimaginable power. This type of conversation has been reported many times since.'

Elfrad felt the tenseness emanating from the crowd like a physical blow.

Before the players had sat down the Bodleian piped up, as usual, all talking over each other until a look from Aurelien stopped them.

'We were informed last week about a raid on one of our libraries, several old grimoire's were under attack, fortunately we were able to assist and wiped the pages before any damage could be done. Even so, after the furore had died down, it was soon ascertained a small grimoire had been taken. It was a targeted attack. If it wasn't for the traps we have in place, they would have gotten away with much more.'

'What did the grimoire contain?' demanded Eldora.

'Specific details on how to use dark magic against Kingdom and its magicals.'

'Are you telling us,' snarled Lefu, 'these type of books are kept outside of the realm?'

'Sometimes in plain site is the best defence.'

'Not this time,' he snapped in disgust.

Elfrad was surprised to see Peasey and Ruzgar step forward together. Indicating for Peasey to talk, Ruzgar leant on her staff.

'Together we speak for all magicians and witches, we are losing our powers to some degree or another. Groups of us have been gathering to discuss the problem, setting trials to see how we have been affected. Small magic seems to be okay, anything that requires real effort is more than a strain. At times even impossible, we can still do bigger magic, sustaining it is the problem.'

The day dragged on into the night, the more information shared by the clans, the horror of what was happening became clearer, dark magic was infiltrating every corner of Kingdom. All had been affected in some way, Elfrad's thoughts darted all over the place, trying to make sense of what he was hearing.

Aurelien clapped his hands, bringing the arguments to a close, indicating the banquet he'd conjured.

'Please enjoy.'

Elfrad leant against Fingerlings trunk, glad to get away from the chatter starting up as soon as the magicals left their seats. The only ones seemingly unconcerned were the Fae, instead of joining the throng, they went to check on their dragons.

'How come you were invited? Surely, not in your capacity as a lapsed wizard?' snorted Beadu.

Before he had a chance to say anything the rest of the wizards joined them. All looking at him, waiting for a reply. Ignoring the question, he asked.

'What made you come today? As for putting all your differences aside, even I know wizards thrive on being different. Your men would not miss this for the world. So what are they really doing?'

'Still the same wily old Elfrad,' Beadu sneered, as her hell cat pawed her shoulder, spitting and growling to be released.

'The men are not here because some have been taken, those who weren't abducted, are in hiding.'

'Have you told the Shimmers? When did this happen?' he exclaimed.

'That is the real reason why we came today, you may not practice as a wizard anymore. But you have not lost any of your skills even our cats can tell. Taking on the Bomani is not an easy task. The Ambrogio tried it once as a test, and were severely bested. Even with their skills of shadow they couldn't compete with our magic.

Whoever organised the raid knew the men would be together. They came at night and got through the defences destroying staffs and Wakanda's in the process.'

Elfrad felt the shock of her words run through his body. Taking on a lone Bomani would be a hard enough, but several at once, his mind couldn't take it in. He may not have practiced for many years the skills though were still in him. He would only have to bring them to the fore, his greeter persona would fall away subjugated by the warrior wizard he would always be. Aware that the gathering was about to resume, he stood up, the Bomani as one turned to him.

'Would you speak for us? We are still not trusted, judging by the dark looks being sent our way.'

They all looked up as Fingerling rustled his branches.

'Everyone be seated.'

Shooing the wizards back to their seats, Fingerling called the Shimmers over.

'Tell them.'

'Combined with Elfrad's news and everything we have heard today, it is imperative we bring the ring back to Kingdom. While the mirror is still being gathered we have time to stop it from being made whole. If however the dark magicals obtain the ring all will be lost. It's time for you to speak, you know what to say,'

'Me?'

Verlimusa began moving again bringing everyone round into a tight semi-circle, Elfrad felt like he was on a stage and they were his audience. After he spoke about what had happened to the wizards, he gave everyone time to ask questions and debate the issue. Waiting patiently for them to wind down, slowly the crowd quietened.

'We have heard today how Kingdom is being attacked. Everything points to the Darkness kidnapping magicals to search for the black mirror as well as leaching our magic, it seems to stem from the Glasserium where we believe it may have set up home. The taking of anybody is worrying, but the taking of seven warrior wizards at one time, is truly terrifying. The dark magic used must be ancient and of the darkest kind. One question that we must ask ourselves is, who can we trust? Because without help from inside the Bomani clan, the taking of them would not have been possible.'

Elfrad saw the shock register on their faces as they looked at their neighbours weighing them up.

'This is a difficult thought to entertain, think back to things that have happened, could they have been caused by someone inside your clan? I'm not trying to divide magicals, but we have to be more alert. Somehow, we have to stop the mirror from being collected. If we cannot do that, then we have to make sure it cannot be put back together. We have to find a way into the Glasserium, seek out the Darkness destroying it and its minions. Dark magicals and possibly untainted ones, are working to bring it forth. Battles are coming, ones we can see and other's we can't. We must all work together for the safety of our clans, Kingdom, and Novia.'

Elfrad felt his heart race, his hands grew sweaty. He couldn't help think about the risk of telling his fellow magicals about the ring. Out in the open, meant those who they'd rather not know about it could get to hear. Everyone strained forward as he took a deep breath.

'Unfortunately we also have another problem, the ring bearer is somewhere in Kingdom, while the ring is in Novia.'

Confusion swept across the crowd, for some, they knew exactly what he was talking about, others hadn't a clue.

'How did they become separated?' asked Lefu. 'I thought they had to stay together, has he been taken?'

Others shouted their questions, nerves evident in each enquiry. Elfrad waited for the furore to die down.

'Balin left the ring with a norm. We fear he may have been taken by wraiths. Margaret didn't know he was magical. She is here now after being called by Kingdom, she has since also been taken. Before leaving Novia she gave the ring to her son. Balin is his father.'

The crowd erupted, everyone shouting, fear written across their faces, even the vampires appearing unsettled. After they calmed down and said their peace, everyone wanted to know what the Shimmers were going to do. No one wanted the ring in Kingdom, especially with the black mirror being gathered. Yet, they all knew it wasn't safe left in Novia. It couldn't be taken from the norm and only he could bring it to Kingdom. But how?

'May I speak?' asked Hib-Hob.

'A norm cannot come here without being called by Kingdom, or dragged through a mirror by a wraith.'

'We know this,' sneered Henty, an impatient Bodleian at the best of times.

Ignoring her, Hib-Hob continued, 'there is a way into Kingdom, but it won't be easy. He would have to travel through several Pictures, enter the Nether and pass through the Red Caves.'

Elfrad, could feel himself want to close his eyes and go to sleep as the debate went on long into the night and into the next day. Some magicals were up in arms at the thought of a back door into Kingdom. Never common knowledge, even those that did know, thinking it more of a myth. His head hurt with all the thinking. It would all depend on Sam and whether they could get him to want to attempt it.

'Elfrad,' opening his eyes he found himself surrounded by Bomani.

'We are going now, we will be in touch. Eldora has opened up a channel for us, hopefully because the wraiths have targeted only our men, they will be unaware we are as powerful and ferocious. It may help give us an edge.'

Before he could answer, they placed their kittens on the ground, tapped their noses, the ground shaking as the cats appeared. Snarling and pawing, eager to stretch their bodies after being cooped up. With one leap the wizards mounted, their cats yowling in delight at being on the move.

The Bodleian were still arguing as they disappeared back into their books. The witches and magicians jumped onto their broomsticks and staffs, peeling away to their exits, waving to the

Fae as they mounted their dragons. Joined by the Kaimi, for a few moments the sky was full, the next instant empty.

The Warra were the first to arrive and the first to go, only a small puddle left, showing they were ever there. The Alvie returned to their trees who were now also in the process of disappearing, the sound of their voices ringing out as they said their goodbyes. Elfrad noticed how tired the Lobes and Lens looked, they had been constantly on alert, scanning Verlimusa as the gathering proceeded. Bowing to the Shimmers they turned and made their way towards their exit.

'So,' said Lefu, 'what happens now, why did you ask us to stay behind?'

Eldora answered, 'we are going to send an Enabler to visit Sam's home, his task to guide him into wanting to come to Kingdom. We hope that if he thinks his mother is in danger, he will want to rescue her.' Addressing Yox-All, she said, 'we will need the help of players, preferably those who don't mind danger. Could you make a start in sounding them out?'

'Hib-Hob, would be my suggestion, unpredictable at times, it may however be what this situation needs.'

'I take it they are also able to navigate all, including some of the more…'

'Hib-Hob can run rings around most pictures, and if truth be known even a few mirrors, not that they will admit to any of it.'

'Lefu, my thanks to your clan for their patience. I'm sure you know what I'm going to ask.'

'It can't be done. Besides, Pictures will only allow us to move straight through them even with our collars on.'

'There is one of you though who doesn't wear a collar and hasn't hunted.'

Elfrad was sure the vampires grew taller in an instant. The wash of violence falling from them as fangs lengthened and talons grew. Eldora continued to wait for an answer not put off by their show of strength and anger.

'You are talking about Aeryissa,' said Lefu. 'I don't know where she is. The last sighting of her was in Novia. At the same time a rumour said she was still in Kingdom.'

'Maybe she won't want to do it, or can't. But would you ask?'

'A message will be sent, there is no guarantee that she will hear it, or even be willing to rally to its call.'

Chapter Eight

Margaret opened her eyes. Moving her head, pain shot through it like a knife. Painful memories returning, sitting up she found herself in a cell like room, with no discernible windows or doors, only smooth walls. Apart from bruises and small cuts she was relatively unscathed. Dizziness, took hold as she got to her feet. Holding onto the wall, she waited for her senses to realign themselves and for the lights going off in her head to stop flashing.

She felt her way around the walls as high as she could reach trying to detect any sign of an opening. Exhausted by the effort she slid down on to the floor aware now of how thirsty she felt, even as her stomach pitched and rolled. She shuddered to remember the feel of the wraiths body, the coldness of it and the smell of sulphur clinging to him. Closing her eyes she let herself succumb once more to sleep.

The first thing she became aware of was the noise, where before she had woken to silence. Now, the hubbub of magicals talking and moving around felt like an assault on her ears. Pulling herself up, she could see many like herself dazed and a bit battered.

'Hello? Sleepy head. Drink this it will make you feel better. If you can keep it down, I'll get you something to eat.'

Margaret grabbed the bottle as if her life depended on it the cool drink soothing her parched throat instantly making her feel better. Wiping her mouth with the back of her hand, she looked up to say thank you, the words dried up. Her mouth fell open in shock. A wraith hovered before her, a white fog like substance clinging around the body of a man.

'Your, a wraith,' she croaked. 'Get away from me,' shooing him, as if the action would disperse him.

A hand grabbed her arm, 'it's alright dear. He's one of the better ones. Taken a shine to you he has.'

Margaret turned her head to see a witch, her pointy nose and black eyes too big for her small crinkled face.

'I'm Anglas, and this is Jeel,' she indicated the wraith, who bowed in acknowledgement.

'Why don't you go and find us something to eat. I will explain why you are not such a monster, as she thinks you are.'

The wraith disappeared the crowd moving swiftly out of its way, Margaret could feel tension across her chest like a tight band.

'How do you know my name? Why would I trust a wraith? It's because of them that I'm here.'

Anglas smiled, the wrinkles lining her face making her resemble a walnut.

'Because you told me the last time you woke. Wraiths usually cannot be trusted. Jeel for some reason likes you. It's because of him we haven't been taken, although he won't be able to hide us much longer. You've been drifting in and out of consciousness since you were taken from the box.'

Her anxiety levels rose as memories flooded back. Anglas could see the emotions play out across Margaret's face. The box so far had been the worst part of this ordeal, she decided not to mention that some hadn't made it.

When Jeel appeared this time she didn't flinch. Kneeling down, he laid baskets on the floor filled with food, their mouth-watering smells, making her tummy rumble. It cost her, but her good manners one out.

'Thank you.'

Jeel drank her in.

'It will be in a few days. Make sure she eats and drinks plenty, shield her. When it's your turn, stay in the middle and avoid wraiths with black mist surrounding them.'

Anglas passed her a basket, 'eat, we don't know when we'll get a chance to do so again.'

For the last few days she'd been in a dream like state, at one point even wondering if the food Jeel brought had been drugged. Yet, Anglas didn't seem to be affected. She also wondered if she ever slept, every time she woke she was beside her, eyes scanning the crowd making sure magicals kept away. Jeel marking them out as different, made others curious as to why this norm should have special treatment.

Anglas whispered, 'it's time, hold my hand and don't worry about being polite.'

With that, they were off; pushing their way through the crowd, muttered oaths following their progress. She barrelled her way through, dragging Margaret along with her. As they slowed down, her senses picked up the atmosphere of fear. Anglas's hand giving her some degree of comfort. What had been a cacophony of sound with everyone talking, turned into total silence, as if a switch thrown had turned them off. With no choice, but to follow those in front, they set off.

Cocooned as they were in the middle, when the screams started, it took a while before they realised who'd made them. Margaret stumbled, but was soon pushed along by the magicals behind. She could see Anglas was struggling to keep up the pace, worried they would fall and be trampled, thinking it might be easier if they moved over to the side. Shaking her head, Anglas mouthed the word, 'no.'

At last, the march came to a halt, Margaret still couldn't make out where they were or what had happened to make magicals scream. When the crowd dispersed, she wished she'd stayed ignorant for longer. They were in an encampment surrounded by wraiths all holding long spear like rods which they poked at anyone getting too near, burning them as if branding cattle.

Several witches and magicians had already been singled out and herded towards a large cave. The wraith taking great delight in prodding them, one witch grabbed the end of the spear-rod pulled it from his hands and thrust it into the wraiths body. The screech that rent the air made everyone shake. Several wraiths descended upon him. The screams of the witch the only sound heard as a blur of bodies wove around him.

As suddenly as it started, it was over, the wraiths pulled back. Apart from the black mist, gaining more ground around their bodies, they showed no ill effects of the fight. The witch lay on the ground, "shredded," would be the word she would think of later. The body, now hardly recognisable as a magical as blood seeped along the ground looking for a new owner. Cowed by the violence, the rest followed like sheep, disappearing into the cave, swallowed up by the dark.

As night descended, the air turned cooler, Margaret pulled her jumper tighter, tucking it into her trousers and pushing her arms up into the sleeves. Everyone sat in stunned silence. If the earlier violence had not been enough to quieten them, then the beating of two magicians certainly had. They lay discarded in the corner no one allowed near, their moans, a backdrop to their fear.

'UP,' a voice shouted. 'Everyone up, you are to collect pieces of glass. You will not speak to each other, if you disobey in any way you will be killed.'

Margaret looked at Anglas, wanting to ask, but daring not to. They fell in line, drawing comfort from still holding hands. Herded together with a group of twenty others, each was given a basket, conscious she the only norm, the only one not to be given gloves. They entered a wooded glade everyone stood with their heads bent, defeat in every line of their bodies.

The stiffness radiating through her knees and back made Margaret sigh deeply as she moved towards the centre of the circle, so far finding nothing. Sweeping her hand under a clump of flowers as if waiting especially for her light glinted on several large pieces of glass. Lost in her thoughts of the Calmans, remembering her travels through Kingdom, comparing it to scrabbling in the dirt, she stopped working. Without any warning, a wraith plunged his spear-rod into her side, the pain more than she could bear. Before the wraith attacked again, Anglas quickly pushed aside the flowers so he could see the hidden cache.

Margaret was so engrossed in what she was doing, it took her awhile to realise, the voice she could hear, was one she recognised. Desperate to look up, aware though, of the many wraiths surrounding them; she continued searching. Finally, she had filled her basket, holding up her hand, calling out to show that it was full. Waiting for the wraith to take it from her, she took the opportunity to glance at the magicals nearest to her.

As their eyes met, there was no mistaking each other, even after all these years and in their dishevelled state. Margaret looked into Balin's eyes, which widened when he realised who she was. They'd no chance to do any more, another basket was passed to her and once again she bent to her task. All the while conscious that a few inches from her Balin worked. Anglas had caught the look between them, she knew from Margaret's description and reaction that this must be Sam's father. Happy for her, but at the same time worried that it would make her careless in her need to see and talk to him.

She couldn't sleep, jumbled thoughts cascaded through her, she was hot, she was cold, she wanted to go and find him. So many questions she needed to ask, and so much to tell him, not least about Sam. So eager to get to work anyone would have thought she enjoyed digging in dirt. Anglas tried to talk sense into her, telling her not to make it so obvious. Making her aware for the first time there were snitches in the camps, magicals willing to sell out others, she could tell by her face that she wasn't listening.

Each time Margaret raised her hand and called for another basket, she could see how every time Balin handed his basket over he was working his way nearer to her. By the afternoon he'd finally gotten beside her. Reaching for the same piece of glass their hands touched, shock waves moved up her arm. She tried to suppress a smile; Anglas dug her in the ribs, shaking her head. Balin emptied her basket into his putting his hand up calling a wraith. While they waited, he inserted his self between them as if they were all in the same work gang. The wraith swooped down picked up the basket and gave another to Balin, they all held their breath. Either he didn't notice he'd moved or didn't care.

As the day continued they were constantly aware of their hands reaching for the same piece of glass. Anglas felt like piggy in the middle, ignored by both of them. When they left the wasteland, Balin made sure he stayed in between them. Others, who noticed, held their own council, not wanting to get involved. Once inside they fell into each other's arms tears streaming down their faces. Anglas tutted, pulling them over to their corner away from prying eyes.

'However are you here? In Kingdom. How did you end up being captured?'

Anglas interrupted, 'keep your voices down, you never know whose listening.'

'I've plenty of questions of my own,' whispered Margaret. 'Not least why you never came back to see me.'

'I had every intention to do so, that's why I gave you my ring as a token. Why are you not wearing it? Where is it?' he demanded, his voice strident.

'I left it in Novia with our son,' snapped back Margaret. 'I didn't know I was pregnant. I had no way of contacting you. When you didn't return. I married. To my regret, I never told Sam about you, he believes Barry is his father. If that's all you're worried about. I hope he throws it away, I wish I had,' sobbing, she turned away wishing he would leave.

'I'm sorry, it's all a bit of a shock, finding you, learning I have a son.'

Once sure that Margaret was asleep, Anglas nudged Balin, and moved closer.

'There are snitches in this group. If the wraiths or their masters find out about you, or where the ring is, it will be Kingdom's doom.'

'Surely, it will be safe in Novia, especially as Sam is unaware of its history or of me?'

'The ring and its whereabouts has been a closely guarded secret. Unfortunately some will talk about things they shouldn't. The wraiths haven't got us all searching for the fun of it. You more than anyone know that without your ring it can never be complete. They may not be able to take it from Sam. I'm sure though,' she nodded at Margaret, 'they can use ways to make him give it up voluntarily.'

With her last comment ringing in his ears, Balin closed his eyes. As sleep eluded him, he thought back to his return to Kingdom, and the despair he'd felt at leaving Margaret.

Contacted, by a Lobe and Lens friendly with his family, they told him that his brothers had gone missing. His parents, fearing they'd been taken by the wraiths, caused his father to collapse and his mother wanted him home even though she knew it was something he wasn't supposed to do.

A few months later his father died, his mother inconsolable, tasked Balin with finding his brother's. As the years went by, his memory of Margaret was pushed to the back of his mind as he searched for any news of their whereabouts. Returning home from another fruitless mission he'd let his guard down.

Like her, he woke in what he now knew of as a box cell. Remembering how sore he'd felt and how his head hurt, luckily he had retained his pack. Surprised it hadn't been taken from him, grateful for the water bottle still inside. Days went passed, the water run out, he couldn't keep awake.

Finally, he found himself in a room filled with magicals, shocked at how they looked. Starved, dirty, the mad look in their eyes offering no comfort. He thought back to all the years lost in the relentless pursuit of glass, his hands sore, his back aching form all the bending.

Finding Margaret helped put thoughts of his family behind him, too painful to share he locked them away. Instead they shared their stories of Kingdom and Novia, Sam, a subject they both found painful. Margaret because she missed him and Balin because he'd never met him.

Smiling at Anglas, Margaret was pleased to see her integrating more with everyone else. Since Balin arrived, she was conscious how they always had their heads together, making plans for when this was all over, never entertaining the thought it might not be. A movement near the door made her look up, her mouth gaping open as she stood. Sure a mirage was coming towards her. His smile split his face, wrapping her in a bear hug, oblivious to Balin's stare.

'I can't breathe. How? Are you even here?'

As he released her Anglas cuffed him around the ear, raising her voice.

'Where've you been? I've been worried sick. No respect for your mother.'

Looking totally baffled. Margaret pulled him down, rebuking Anglas loudly.

'Don't scold him so, I'm sure he didn't mean to stay away so long.'

Qiao looked mystified as to what was going on. Anglas sat down with her back to the room,

'Keep smiling,' she mouthed, before crowing in a loud voice, 'isn't this nice. All together again.'

Once everyone had settled down for the night, Qiao told them how he'd managed to gain entry into the camp.

'Remember when I transported us? It wasn't a fluke, it's what I am, a Transporter. I've been practicing since you were taken, so that I could come and bring you back.'

'But how did you know where I was? There are hundreds of camps, how did you find this one?'

'You're my best friend. I kept thinking of you over and over. Although you must have been moving around a lot. Because, every time I've honed in on you, by the time I managed to circumvent the wraiths security, you'd gone.'

'Does that mean you can get Margaret out?'

'I can get you all out of here. In fact, with a bit of effort, I might be able to get the whole camp out, but obviously that would alert them to what was happening.'

Always one to get straight to the point, Anglas demanded, 'when can we go?'

Taking Qiao's hand, Margaret smiled, 'you can do this. This is what you were born for. You saved me once, without realising you could. You have to believe you can again.'

Balin whispered, 'what will you think of to get us out of here? It will have to be somewhere safe. Otherwise we could be back inside a camp again.'

'Dandelion,' they said together.

Margaret spoke about their adventures in Kingdom. Qiao had his own memories. They got Balin and Anglas to repeat the things they said, fixing Dandelion in their minds. Nothing happened, all they got was a headache and clenched hands from thinking about her so much.

CHAPTER NINE

Eldora waited for everyone to take their places, noticing for the first time how drained they all looked. Finding it more and more difficult to shake off the listlessness that in the last few weeks had taken them over, all aware the shimmer held inside them was fading.

'Kingdom is once again under threat from the Darkness. Confirmation was received this morning. As suspected, it's inside the Glasserium. Unfortunately, the cost of getting this information meant, several witches lost their lives in the process. Pesah is the only one to survive whether he will make it remains to be seen.'

'Are the wraiths still searching for the mirror? Shouldn't we be stopping them?'

'It's time to take the fight to the enemy, not sit back waiting for the axe to fall. We have to get the ring into Kingdom. That is our priority,' explained Aurelien. 'Without the last piece, the mirror cannot wake. We should open the Akiva and make use of the war room. It is still the best place to bring everyone together to gather information. The Plotters were effective before, this time their skills will be even more crucial. I propose we ask Dandelion to step forward one last time, as hard as it is to say, reliance on us is futile.'

Everyone waited outside their entrance as the Lobes and Lens relayed information back and forwards between the clans busy sweeping the tunnels. So far, only the vampires had found anything amiss. Gork's had set up a den, quickly cleared, they had enjoyed the unexpected hunt, still wiping the blood from their faces as they reached their entrance.

Each clan chanted the spell revealing their door into the Akiva, the instruction to turn the keys given. Cogs moved in protest. The faint sound of a bell, echoed along the tunnels.

The doors shifted, bulging outwards. Settling down as lines appeared covered with shimmer. Tumbling into words spelling out the name of each clan. When they stopped, the doors opened, a musty damp smell wafting out as everyone moved inside.

All waited expectantly to see if the room would once more come alive. Pinpricks of light started to appear, shapes emerged from the gloom, a faint breeze, wove itself around the room, bringing with it the smell of rot and decay. The room lightened the seated figures becoming clearer.

A fine layer of dust had settled over them giving them a ghost like appearance. While in stasis, their hair and nails had continued to grow, turning their hands into talons. Their heads shrunken, hair sparse on some, others retaining their flowing locks. Some had closed their eyes at the moment of stopping. Others left open, stared at their visitors as if surprised to see them.

Aurelien touched each forehead.

Nothing happened, the impatience in the room a physical presence. Slowly a twitch of fingers, a fluttering eye, a slight shift of the shoulders, the lights flickered, sighs could be heard and movement felt. In the blink of an eye they woke.

As the Plotters became fully awake, so did the room, expanding outwards to accommodate everyone. Tables and chairs appearing in readiness. In the centre the main consul started to glow. Maps detailing Kingdom rolled out covering the walls. Sconces flooded the room with light, happy at last to be of use; getting in the way in their desire to help. One minute the Plotters were relics, the next, having shook off the dust retracted their nails and hair they waited hands poised for instructions. As more magicals appeared the room grew bigger with only the consul staying in the same place. The clan stations lit up as they were linked to their magicals ready for information to be fed to the consul.

'Clans,' said Aurelien, 'we need all the details of where you have seen, or believe wraiths are operating. Plotters mark the maps with the information.'

The consul started to hum, from the middle rose a tangled ball of information. The Plotters hands flew over their controls, drawing the information down until the ball had disappeared. The information sent across to the maps filling them with coloured dots denoting known and suspected sites of wraith activity.

Elfrad had never been inside the Akiva and was eager to see how it worked. As more information came in his eyes travelled from the consul to the dots. Expanding to cover more and more areas, so many, they came to resemble a living entity, rather than a map. A dull thud brought him to his feet, the clink of metal on stone brought his knife into his hand. Turning, as the door behind flew open to hit the wall, revealing a figure swathed in robes, face hidden by a deep cowl.

Pushing back the hood, Dandelion's face emerged wreathed in smiles.

'Hello everyone, sorry I'm late, had a bit of bother,' glancing at the nearest map, she laughed, 'I see you noticed.'

Releasing herself from the containment of her robes, she sighed in relief, letting the weight of them fall to the floor. Necessary she knew as part of her disguise, but uncomfortable to wear.

Before Elfrad could comment, Aurelien claimed her attention, leaving him feeling even more confused and isolated. As night wore on, he busied himself helping out where needed feeling like a spare part. Dandelion had been locked in conference since she'd made her appearance. Apart from him, no one else seemed interested, all busy with the process of getting their clans into place ready for the next stage, whatever that may be. The maps constantly changed to reflect the information they were adding.

He found it unnerving the way the room moved to accommodate magicals as they came and went. The glow now muted allowed the consul's vivid blue light to sweep the room.

The picture in the middle, getting stronger and more defined. Showing Kingdom and its inhabitants be they good or bad, while a smaller model of Novia hovered beside it, equally filling up with information sent from those choosing to remain there.

'Elfrad.'

'Sorry, I must've dropped off for a moment.'

'It's been a long few days my friend. Before I brief everyone on what is going to happen, I need to speak to you about why you're here.'

Drawing him through the door appearing behind him she led him into the resting room. Although empty at the moment as the battle's commenced, it would soon fill up with weary magicals.

'I am to be the coordinator. My role to direct the clans on what they need to do. In the past, the task has not been easy to undertake alone. This time I've asked that you be allowed to help me.'

'What can I do? I could help with the norms, but that is about the extent of my usefulness.'

She tapped his chest above his heart. 'You chose to be a greeter, but in here, you are still a wizard and a Bomani to boot. Your skills are dormant, not gone. Everyone believes you are, as you say, "just a greeter." In the past the Akiva has been infiltrated, how, is still debatable. I need you to be my eyes and ears. I cannot spare any Lobes and Lens for this task. I need their focus on finding where the black mirror is going to be placed. Your fellow Bomani's role is to patrol the tunnels. Casting spells continuously as only they can do to change the tunnels appearance. If fighting should break out as warriors they will also be able to deal with it.'

He still doubted he could be of help, he'd spent so much time in his greeter persona even he believed it to be his true self.

Dandelion watched his thoughts play out across his face. She, couldn't force him. Like everyone in the Akiva he had to want to be there and want to help. Otherwise, they were in danger of being influenced by the dark forces ranged against them. She would prefer not to have to think that someone may sell them out. Past experience though had shown her it was always a possibility. Best on the lookout for it from the start than allow it to creep up taking them all by surprise.

'The maps are all drawn and awake, they will of course keep changing as things happen,' said Dandelion.

The Bodleian appeared, all cursing as they landed on top of each other, all trying to leave their books at the same time.

'Your task,' she told them, ignoring their arguments, 'is to find a way into the Glasserium.'

'That's impossible,' cried Baillieu, shaking her head, expecting the others to agree.

'Impossible, is all you ever say,' snapped Dorrigo, looking scornfully at his wife. Noted for their long standing arguments, if left unchecked, they could easily go on for days.

Gerringong interrupted their spat, asking, 'are we looking for a physical presence to enter, or magically?'

'Aren't they both one and the same,' muttered, Kurri, flicking her long hair over her shoulder, while the eye that was awake scanned the room.

Fearing they would start debating the subject, Dandelion stepped in.

'We have ascertained that the Darkness is present in the Glasserium. Is it enough to take the form of a Dark Lord? We have no idea. Whoever is behind it, must think so, otherwise, they would not have been searching for the black mirror. We have to find its lair, the Darkness cannot be killed, the only option is to capture and contain it again.'

'Surely, the Maia is still our best defence,' suggested Elfrad.

'It will only be activated when a Dark Lord enters Kingdom. For now we must put thoughts of it aside. We need to gain entry into the Glasserium not only to capture the Darkness but to clear out the wraiths. They've been allowed to come and go as they please for far too long.'

Gerringong announced to the room, 'we will try our best. Our books are arriving as we speak. If you're happy for us to leave we can get started.'

Elfrad looked up to see the wall in front of him bulge outwards; a Plotter's face appeared

'Players on their way.'

As the face withdrew, a picture frame took its place. Seconds later out stepped Yox-All.

'Mr Culpepper is in the process of closing all the Emporiums,' he explained. 'The one which held Margaret's picture will stay open for as long as it takes her son to find it. Vidya has granted her permission for the courtyard to be opened. If a large scale evacuation of Kingdom is called for, it is one of the few places which can accommodate a large number of magicals at any one time. It would take too long to get everyone through their own pictures. For those who go there, they'll not be the most comfortable of places to be. Everyone will need to keep their wits about them, they are still haunted. So far, they haven't been seen, only their presence felt.'

'Surely, after all this time, the clown's antics would have abated, especially, without an audience to motivate them.'

'If, we have to evacuate Mercia, they will have that audience. Hopefully, it won't come to that. The thought of magicals having to flee for their lives, only to find themselves locked inside with clowns bent on making them laugh every minute of the day and night doesn't bear thinking about.'

Elfrad felt the mood in room plummet. The courtyard clowns were a relic from the past. Thinking, he would rather face an angry wraith than be subjected to continual pointless jokes and games. Also sensing the change in mood Dandelion suggested they take a break, she'd noticed the vampire's fangs extending and retracting, a sure sign they were getting hungry.

Before taking their seats again everyone's eyes were drawn to the maps and pictures, filled now with an ever changing myriad of information.

Addressing the Kaimi, Dandelion told them, 'your first task is to locate any wraiths who are scanning for the mirror.'

'Shall we start in the northern wastelands?' suggested Gawain. 'They have only now started to work there above ground. Usually this means they will be out in force. If we spread out and stay high we should be able to pick up their signatures, plus the sound of their machines even from a distance.'

'Would it help if we cast a holding spell to cover the air underneath each of you, it would then enable you to take a rest and fly for longer?' suggested Vayu.

'Is your magic strong enough?'

'Have you forgotten that we are elemental witches?'

Gawain laughed, as they floated upwards.

'I meant with everyone's magic less than it once was. It's a lot to ask you to do.'

Turning to the Alvie, Dandelion told them, 'once we have the locations, we will need you to use your nets to scrap the ground and move the mirror somewhere else.' Glancing at Mercia, she told her, 'if you have time, release the trees. Do not jeopardise the operation by staying in the area.'

'But,' cried Hafren, his skin a multitude of colour reflecting the turmoil of his feelings. 'We cannot just leave them.'

Dandelion felt the weight of their anger pressing down, waiting for her answer.

'Most of you have been here before, you know the risks and you know the sacrifices that will be made. I understand how important the trees and forests are. You will however have to leave some trees still wrapped. Those in areas that have already been mined can safely be released, those that have yet to be searched will have to stay bound.'

'We will do as you ask,' replied Mercia, the strain in her voice evident.

'Once we have the location of where the wraiths are searching, and how many are on guard. The next part will require cooperation between each clan, allowing our grab and snatch approach to happen. Timing is everything. Elfrad, could you find out, if the Warra have been in contact yet?'

Grateful to stretch his legs, even if it was only into the next room. His admiration for her had risen as the day wore on. Not sure he would be able to keep hold of each clan's attention in such a fraught situation. He noticed the water in the jug move slightly.

'I believe they may already be here.'

As the words left his mouth, the water rose towards the ceiling, spreading out to fall down the walls. In the blink of an eye four Warra stood in each corner of the room. As laughter filled the room Dandelion rapped the table, drawing their attention back to her.

'Once located the Ambrogio will attack the wraiths, please note, they will be removing their collars. Permission has been granted.'

Cian and Harsha couldn't stop the release of their fangs or their eyes turning a flaming red. Elfrad noticed they quickly retracted them when Lefu threw them a dark look. For once, even the Fae seemed to be taking notice of what was going on.

'Make no mistake,' explained Lefu, 'we will be killing them. As strong as their magic may be, even they cannot withstand a bite from us. Anyone else we deem to be, "on the other side," we will also kill. Magicals don't have to watch, but must understand. Do not, try and stop us. Once in a frenzy, and if the fights are anything like the last time anyone trying to intercede may be killed. Those of us who won't be removing our collars will be targeting wraiths for capture.'

'Magicals and any norms must be taken to safety. None of us know how they are going to react,' explained Dandelion. 'Too far down the path of conversion, they may not want to be saved. Rather than take a chance of any escaping to give the game away. The Fae have come up with a variant of their fairy dust which can instantly calm a crowd and make them amenable. Spread over them it will work instantly. Once it has taken effect the witches will fly them to meet the magicians who will then move them into Pictures. Vidya has made available portable frames the safe word only known by those in charge. Once through, they will be dispersed to a holding area checked over and moved on as appropriate. Wind witches are working on spells as we speak to enable all their brooms to fly faster.'

For the first time all day Zekia actually spoke, 'we have adapted our fairy dust to show those who may have been contaminated. Their skin will have a particular colour to it, undetectable by anyone else. Any magicals or norms found with the taint will be moved away and held under quarantine until they can be dealt with.'

'We don't know how long it is going to take for the ring to come back to Kingdom,' said Dandelion. 'Once it has arrived, the real battles will commence, the Darkness will know that it's here. I've asked Melock, to take a contingent of sentinels and patrol where we believe the exit may appear. Several trees are already in position, their roots burrowing as we speak while the Alvie are mapping where they go and where they are stopped. I would like to thank you for your cooperation and patience. Food and drink has been laid on, apart from the Ambrogio, obviously. The wizards have left your tunnels. I believe Gork's are on the menu, make sure to let them know when you have left so they can return to their posts. Take advantage of the sleeping quarters, there is plenty of room for everyone. Most of you will remember how the Akiva will grow to accommodate us all. Now please go and relax, it may be the only chance we'll have for a long time.'

'You look exhausted,' said Elfrad, 'I don't know how you've managed to keep going for so long.'

'I am, but also relieved that we are actually doing something. This should have happened a long time ago, unfortunately, the situation has to some extent been left unresolved. Entombing the darkness, creating the Maia, was thought of as the problem solved. No one expected that part of the Darkness would find a way to escape. Many magicals now want or believe they deserve more, turning to dark magic to get it. Add in wraiths who resent being locked away. Throw in the possibility of a Dark Lord waking, means a battle of some kind; has been inevitable.'

Passing through the tunnels, the Kaimi never saw the wizards even though they walked right between them.

'How many teams are already in flight?' asked Orev.

'Twenty at the moment, another fifty are being prepared. They have been given the coordinates for each raid and will meet us for a briefing at the nest,' explained Gawain. 'From there we'll take flight fanning out to cover as much area as we can. We will probably hear their machines before we see any wraiths. Once we're sure they've scanned the area and left, the Alvie can take over. Two teams of wraiths have been seen near the edge of the Cato ravine, one team is overseeing work near to where it drops down into the valley, the other near the burnt Elm. By the time we get to the nest we should have confirmation.'

In one swift movement they changed into their bird form, enjoying the freedom of movement flying gave them, all eager to be taking the fight to the enemy at last.

The noise from the nest, hit them like an assault. Everyone milling around, talking excitedly about what was to come and how they hoped to play their part.

'Gather round. Listen,' commanded Gawain.

As the silence grew, they could all hear in the distance a faint high pitched whine.

'Usoa and Yanah, I want you to take your teams and find where the wraiths are searching. Stay and observe, only return once they've completed their survey and the Ambrogio have moved in. Keep high and make sure you take enough rest, the witches spells should help.

Falk, Orev, you are both with me, we are going to check out what Haiwee saw on her way over here. Paloma can you get everything ready for when the other teams arrive. As soon as they have rested, send them out in groups of ten. By the time we return the others should be back from their recognisance.'

Gawain, Falk and Orev returned to their bird forms, happy to be leaving the noise of the nest for the silence of the skies. Flying in their usual formation the two hawks either side of the raven, their eyes constantly scanned the ground below

Haiwee had been right, there were two groups of wraiths both overseeing large numbers of magicals bent over searching for the mirror. The wraiths hovering with their spear-rods ready to jab. To the right of the searchers were a clutch of bound trees they watched closely to ascertain if any more wraiths or magicals would appear. After an hour of watching they all agreed the area must have already been searched as no one had entered or left. Falk broke away to advise the messengers.

Everything done so far had been recognisance, once the Ambrogio were released from their collars they all knew there would be no going back. As the groups started to set out, the mood inside the Akiva became more sombre. All were conscious the next few days would show if they even had a chance. The real fight for Kingdom was about to begin.

Dandelion's first order had been for the vampires to snatch the survey teams and pass them along to the Warra. Next, the Alvie were to move in, release the trees and cleanse the ground. If the wraiths or anyone else showed no interest in what had happened, the search teams would be next. As her orders were relayed to the stations, Elfrad watched the Plotters draw down the information making it appear on the maps, overlaying the information already noted. Whereas before, this had been shown as different coloured dots, now they were also covered by a black cloud.

Following the coordinates the vampires didn't take long to come across the survey area. Afanas, raised his arm signalling to his team, in one silent bound they took up their positions on either side of the wraiths.

Watching from the safety of the trees, the Alvie were glad these Ambrogio still wore their collars. Even so, they appeared terrifying, their mouths gaping wide, fangs extending, as their eyes turned black. It took a moment for the wraiths to understand what they were seeing. The element of surprise paralysing them enough to allow the vampires to hold them still.

Afanas licked his lips, leaning forwards as if to bite, when from the ground a small burst of water appeared, growing to become man shaped.

'If your team holds them steady my brothers will cover them,' said Pelagias.

Each wraith now had a puddle of water surrounding them. The water moved quickly up their bodies encasing them tightly, once their arms were secured Afanas and his team let them go. Fascinated to watch as the Warra continued covering the wraiths until completely bound by the water. With one coordinated motion they sucked the wraiths underground, dragging them in their water boxes for interrogation.

The Alvie so engrossed in releasing the trees, didn't notice the vampires leave. The trees bound with wire looked a sorry sight, with tears in their eyes they set about cutting them loose. Fortunately, they'd only been bound for a short while so no lasting damage had yet been done. Once they were all free and their wounds checked, as one they pulled up their roots and disappeared.

The wraiths had marked slabs of stone with yellow to show their survey boundary. Now the trees had gone, it made it easy for the Alvie to lay out their forester nets and drag the ground. Making sure to take several passes collecting any glass that had risen to the top. They then dragged the earth captured by the nets several miles away to a large hole created by the Warra, who then swept in drowning the hole in tons of water. The waters fury made the earth fly up in great columns turning it into thick mud, dispersing the mixture far and wide. Making sure that any glass collected was completely covered, nothing left to glint and feel the pull from its master.

Raising his voice, Lefu commanded, 'remove your collars.'

The vampires stretched, rubbing their necks, all enjoying the freedom. As if an invisible signal had been sent, their eyes turned black. Hands changed into talons, razor sharp and lethal. Fangs extended, blood dripping as they emerged, skin glowing, taking on an unearthly sheen. Tall and well built, unconstrained, they towered above everyone. The scent of prey, making their hearts race, the blood inside them pound with need.

Lefu told them, 'once blood is spilt, it will be hard to hold yourselves in check. When your kill is complete, put your collars back on.'

Acknowledging his words with a nod, each wondering if they would be able to do as he commanded. Moving stealthily forwards, the wraiths and those who searched for the mirror unaware of the predators in their midst. They pounced.

Screams rent the air, magicals fled thinking they would be next. Some ran towards the trees, others stuck out in the open curled themselves into a ball, keening in fear. The Fae, high up astride their dragons waited for the chance to sprinkle their fairy dust. The Alvie more concerned over the trees than the magicals, itched to release them from their bonds.

Cian and Delano stood either side of a wraith which was taking great pleasure in stabbing a witch with its spear-rod. From her position on the ground she had seen the vampires emerge as if from nowhere. Her eyes widening as she watched them clamp their talons on to each of the wraiths arms. Not used to being touched it couldn't make out what was happening. Cian opened wide his jaws, the wraith became aware of the movement, trying to pull away out of reach, instead, he fell into the jaws of Delano. With a satisfying crunch he bit down. The wraith struggled against the bite, screaming in agony. Delano released him and Cian took over. The witch watched mesmerised as her gaoler's life ebbed away. The miasma of white which surrounded the wraith started to break up, his head now hanging on his neck by a thread. The vampires weren't finished. Holding his arms, with one quick wrench, they split his body in two. His head fell to the floor, his mouth stretched wide in a world of pain. His hands twitched and were still. As they looked for more prey their eyes fell on the witch.

A voice in their heads, ordered, 'collars boys, the wraiths are dead.'

Their hearts still raced, their blood pounding inside their bodies, the smell from the wraiths blood washing over them. They both wanted more, needed more, their eyes moved again to the witch. Sensibly she stayed still. If she moved, she knew they would pounce.

Slowly they calmed down. Cian soon realised they were the only two who seemed to be having a problem. Everyone else now wore their collars even Lefu. This fact, more than anything, brought them to their senses. As their collars snapped into place they both sighed, the feeling of release had been good while it lasted.

When the vampires had attacked, everyone had ran away trying to find cover. The Alvie began the job of gathering them all together. Still frightened, some put up a fight, believing they were trying to feed them to the monsters. In the end Tairlaw had enough and ordered nets to be used. Gradually they managed to round everyone up, huddled together, some looked as if they'd already given up, staring into the distance, unaware they had been saved.

The dragons swooped down, the fairies holding tightly to their backs letting their fairy dust lift from their bodies and fall over the now silent crowd. Motionless in fear, waiting for death, sure it would follow. Still traumatised, they didn't even blink at the sight of the Fae astride their dragons. Once the dust settled they visibly began to calm down. The dragons peeled away climbing higher and higher, belching fire turning the air black and smoky. Unaffected by the dust, the Alvie waited impatiently to release their friends. The trees moaned in the background, calling out repeatedly for help, knowing they were near.

Scanning the skies, Hafren was the first to notice the witches appear, their Edom's red against the blue sky. Swooping down they jumped off just before they came to a halt.

Tairlaw joined Hafren, both fascinated to see them start to elongate, enabling each broomstick to accommodate up to ten.

'However are they going to get off the ground? Won't they fall off? Most look as if they can hardly keep awake, let alone hold on,' exclaimed Tairlaw.

Laughing, Hafren told his wife, 'I've seen this before, keep an eye on their familiars.'

The broomsticks were ready, the witches mounted, sitting astride with their cats perched on their laps. The Alvie moved forward, leading groups of ten. If it hadn't been a serious situation it would have been comical. Some didn't understand what was expected of them, and tried to pull away. The hissing and spitting of the cats frightening others, while some were too wobbly to stand, let alone able to stay on a moving broomstick.

Once everyone was on board, the cat's tails started to lengthen, snaking away along the broomstick until it had woven around the ten like a rope. Crossing the remaining tail under and over, knotting it firmly into place, checking everyone was secure, the witch gave the broomstick a twitch and they were away.

Tairlaw couldn't believe her eyes, Hafren laughed to see the amazement on her face.

After several trips, everyone had gone, now the Alvie could play their part and release the trees. The wire used by the wraiths had cut deep into their trunks, removing it was going to hurt, crooning to the trees they set to work. Using their nets they wove them into long lengths of fine rope before threading them through the wire. This was the part they dreaded, as the nets worked on weakening the wire, the Alvie got ready to pull it off. This would hurt the tree, they had to be sure that it had all been removed and this was the only way to do it. Hafren and Tairlaw's skin constantly changed colour, reflecting their worry at what they were about to do.

With one wrench they pulled the wire off, the screams emitted by the trees keenly felt by all. A riot of emotions flooded their bodies, making their skin turn into a kaleidoscope of colour. Tears streamed down their faces. With the sobs from the trees ringing in their ears, the Alvie set about tending their wounds, crooning quietly as if to frightened children before watching them uproot and return to Fingerling.

Everyone in the Akiva waited eagerly as the stations relayed the information received from the messengers into the central consul. The Plotters then filled in the picture and maps with the details. To look at the maps, made Elfrad feel dizzy, since the raids had started, the colours had been constantly changing. The earlier black overlay, gradually disappearing as the results came in. They appeared to be winning, or at least no reprisals or repercussions had so far occurred.

When hearing about the level of violence the Ambrogio had used on the wraiths, Elfrad blurted out, 'is that necessary?'

Dandelion's reply brooked no complaint.

'Once their blood lust is up and no collars to restrict them. This is how it will be. We can kill a wraith. Only vampires though, can get close enough to do it undetected. The level of violence used, is the price we pay. In the past, we have held back, now we cannot. Even from those things which we find hard to do or take. War isn't coming, it's here. Meaning that our sensibilities will have to take second place.'

Peasey was the first to spot the witches as they flew towards the clearing. In seconds the sky was full of broomsticks all eager to land. Tied up as they were, the witches had to wait for their cats to unravel their tails. The broomsticks twitched, returning to their normal size, dumping their cargo onto the ground. Some were now more aware of what had happened, others, still remained under the influence of the fairy dust. The Fae moved among them checking their colours. Only one stood out, he sat on the ground holding his head; the fairies could see that his hands were now a bright shade of green. The tell-tale sign of someone disguising their true nature. On the pretence of helping, each took an arm, pulling him up, groaning as he swayed on his feet. Lifting his head, his face, had also turned green. A sure sign, he really was on the other side. Catching the eye of Ettrick, Zekia beckoned the Alvie over.

'This man is really ill, he may need special treatment.'

'Oh dear, poor you,' placing his arm around his shoulders, Ettrick continued, 'come this way, we'll soon make you better.'

Leading him off behind a tree, he looked back to see if she had found any more. Shaking her head, Zekia mounted her dragon and with a wave to her sisters they took to the skies. Ettrick covered the witch with netting, ready for onward dispatch to the Akiva.

The magicians took out their small pictures, whispered the passwords and placed them onto the ground. The frames immediately started growing, lifting upwards. A face appeared in each, Hib-Hob leant out from the middle one.

'Send them through each frame in twos. Quickly though, we haven't much time.'

As the first pair were directed to grab the sides of the frames, hauling themselves inside, it acted as a wakeup call to the rest. Even those, who still appeared affected by the fairy dust were as keen to get inside. Making sure no one had wondered off and been forgotten, the magicians gave the all clear, gently tapping the sides of the frames waiting for them to collapse down to their smaller size. With a swirl of their cloaks, a flash from their staffs, they too disappeared. The Warra poured in to wash the ground clean, wiping away any trace of the magician's activities.

As night fell, the success of the raids filtered in and the last of the raiding parties returned, all tired, dirty, hungry and in dire need of sleep. Elfrad felt for the first time in days the tight band around his head, relax. So many had been saved and were now safe inside Pictures. The trees that had been bound were recovering back home with Fingerling. Many wraiths had been killed, those who'd been captured, had been taken by the Warra, covered and placed into their water boxes. Once in the Akiva they would be turned over to the Interrogators, none would survive. Over the coming weeks many successful raids were carried out, so far, apart from one wraith attack on a group of Alvie in the process of releasing trees. It had all gone as planned.

'Why are you worried?' asked Elfrad. 'Surely, its good news, we have only had a few bad injuries. A great many are now safe inside Pictures. Everyone is working together. What's wrong?'

'The Darkness, where is it in all this?' explained Dandelion. 'I don't want our magicals to be attacked. Yet, they should be. Something isn't right, I've a dreadful feeling, that it may be a set up.'

Astonishment washed over Elfrad, 'it's not the real black mirror.'

Dandelion rubbed her eyes, tiredness wanting to take her over.

'I think everything may have been a smoke screen to keep us occupied. Remember when you showed me the garden, and we sat for a rare moment of peace and you wondered how they knew what they are gathering was the black mirror? I didn't think about what you'd said, until much later. When it hit me, it is only black when being used. Scattered it would be clear.'

'But where would they get glass from? Even with every mirror in the Glasserium at their disposal, would it be enough? This has been going on for years.'

Sirens wailed, the noise making everyone's ears hurt, especially the Lobes. As the shock waves hit, the wizards alerted the Plotters to the breach. Busy collapsing the consul and hiding the maps, they were impervious to the shouts and call to arms each clan was sounding. All outer doors were now sealed effectively locking everyone inside. The breach had taken place in the sleeping quarters were everyone was at their most vulnerable. The clans followed by several sentinels, hurled themselves along the corridors, knocking into each other, in their haste to be first to engage the enemy.

Dandelion had fallen into a deep sleep, tired from the last few days, the problems they faced wiping her out. As her sleep fogged brain began to wake up, she became aware of the sirens blaring out their warning. Sitting up, she was in time to see and feel a great push of air that forced her up against the wall. The next moment, a pile of bodies filled the floor next to her bunk, tangled up and groaning as they started to separate. Dandelion was astonished to see Margaret's face smiling up at her with other ones emerging as they extricated their bodies. The sentinel appearing in the doorway drew his swords, others joining him, drawn swords now inches from the group. Feeling themselves hauled backwards, Cian pushed the sentinels out of the way, extending his fangs, talons growing, ready to pounce as he reached to remove his collar.

'STOP', roared Dandelion, 'they're friends.'

At the appearance of the vampire, Margaret grinned.

Cian's black eyes raked her body, reaching out to touch her face.

Balin drew in his breath ready to launch himself. Tilting his head slightly, Cian growled.

Retracting his fangs and talons, he took one more look at Margaret, then disappeared. The sentinels who had been pushed aside, once again thrust their swords forwards, indicating the group should stand up and follow them.

'Dandelion what's happening?'

'Go with them, I'll be with you shortly. Can someone please stop those sirens?'

The meeting room was crowded, Margaret drew her chair up close to Qiao, still upset at seeing Cian, jaws extended, ready to bite. Anglas sat with her eyes half closed as if falling asleep. Balin showed how nervous he was as his eyes roamed the room. Whereas she felt remarkable calm. Strangely, seeing Cian again, instantly made her feel better. Hoping he would come to the meeting, disappointed to see two others enter the room instead. Followed closely by a face she recognised.

Watching her as she gazed around the room taking it all in, Elfrad thought; this is not the Margaret I first met. Now she appeared confident and looked remarkably at home in a room full of magicals.

'Let me start by introducing our guests. Then perhaps they can tell us how they got here. This is Margaret, Balin, Anglas and Qiao. Margaret is a norm; Balin is the ring bearer, or rather he was. Anglas, is a witch. The transporter is Qiao.'

Not only did the magicals sit up and take notice, but so did Margaret. Hearing his name, Qiao smiled at Dandelion

'That's me, I practised and practised, now I can do it whenever I please. Although to be fair, we mostly got here because Margaret and I thought about you constantly. We would've been here sooner, but I couldn't get it to happen. It wasn't until the wraiths were coming to take us away, when I managed to make it work.'

'Slow down.'

He laughed in reply, 'sorry, I'm so excited, well not last night I wasn't, when the vampire tried to bite us. Then, I was scared. Now though...'

Stopping only when Margaret patted his hand. Watching her face, his eyes never leaving hers, he began to calm down.

'Sorry about that,' she addressed the room, 'if he stays excited for too long, he's liable to transport himself. Which, may not seem a problem, but he's so strong that he could actually take us all with him.'

They'd all relied on him to get them out of the camp. Qiao had worried at it like a dog with a bone. Each attempt and failure stressing him, and them out. They'd got out this time by the skin of their teeth. Even now, safe in the Akiva, she could still feel the rage of the wraiths as they'd lunged, the feeling of relief that had swept over her, as she looked up to see Dandelion peering down at her.

Everyone was leaning forwards except the vampires, every now and again out of the corner of her eye she would see them lick their lips. She hadn't seen any Fae before and was surprised how small and delicate they appeared, their wings gossamer like, while the fairy dust on their skin glowed and moved, making her wonder how it didn't get on their nerves. She had seen how the Alvie's skin changed when she'd met them previously, next to the Fae though, their colour changes seemed dull. Balin's voice brought her back from her reverie.

'Margaret, is unaware that I am or rather was, a ring bearer.'

Seeing her startled reaction, Elfrad moved to sit next to her. Smiling as he held her hand, he nodded to Balin to continue.

'I am supposed to stay in Novia. When I left home to move there. I didn't expect to fall in love.'

Gazing at Margaret no one seeing his look could doubt his words.

'My father was unwell, my brothers gone, my mother made contact with me. When my father died, I spent years searching for my brothers. The last time I did, I got taken, moved, from one camp to another collecting glass.'

'That's all very well,' snapped Gawain. 'Coming back to Kingdom has put us all in danger. You should have stayed in Novia as directed.'

'Balin gave me his ring before he left for Kingdom,' said Margaret defensively. 'I left it with our son. Balin has only recently become aware of his existence.'

'Surely that makes him now the ring bearer. Doesn't that mean the ring is safe, as long as he stays in Novia?' questioned Hafren.

'No I don't think it does,' Elfrad glanced at Dandelion. 'Tell them, perhaps they will think us mad and it will be the end of it.'

Everyone sat stunned, even the vampires peeled themselves away from the wall, pulling up chairs next to the Alvie who tried to move away, but thought better of it.

'If this is true, and the black mirror is being assembled in the Glasserium, and everything else has been a diversion. How does it help to bring the ring back? Surely this is the last place it should be,' spat Lefu, his eyes turning black in annoyance.

Margaret shouted, 'Is Sam in danger?'

'Why don't you go and rest, I'll let you know what is decided,' said Balin, gently.

Rearing back she pushed him away.

'I'm not a child. I don't need to be protected. If you're going to discuss Sam, I want to be here.'

'The norm has claws,' muttered Zekia.

Anglas spoke, quiet up till now, watching and listening to the magicals gathered in the room, some more opinionated than others.

'We have no choice other than to bring the ring here. Whatever we do is a risk. The real question is how are you going to get Sam to want to come?'

'An Enabler is going to try and encourage him to look for the Emporium, leaving clues in the hope that he will follow them. If successful, once inside Pictures, others will take over.'

'My necklace,' said Margaret, 'when the wraith grabbed me, I lost it. Sam gave it to me. It may still be in the sand.'

Chapter Ten

A noise brought Sam from his doze, realising he'd drunk more
than he meant to, in his haste for self-pity he'd forgotten its
effects. Standing up, made the room spin. Negotiating the stairs,
would be difficult, flopping back down again. Closing his eyes, his
last thoughts were; later, I'll look later.

The Enabler entered Margaret's picture, keeping his eyes on
the hut he walked across the beach. Senses on high alert, a glint
of something sparkled. Bending down, he brushed the sand away
placing the necklace in his pocket. The signs of Margaret's struggle
with the wraith clear to see.

Ready to climb out, he cast his mind outwards. Careful not to
disturbed Sam, he placed the necklace next to the whiskey bottle.
His next task would be to get him into Pictures.

Sam woke to a dry mouth and a sore throat, slowly sitting up
he gazed around unsure of his surroundings. Noticing the half full
glass, he groaned, the movement making his head spin and ache.
Standing took a monumental effort, rubbing his face he could feel
stubble and felt sure his hair would be sticking up all over the place.
Still wearing his suit, he looked down at the crumpled mess it had
become.

Showered and shaved, clean clothes and three cups of coffee, he felt himself start to return to normal. Unable to face cooked food, he made some toast. Moving the whiskey out of the way, his hand hovered in mid-air. The necklace he'd given his mother lay on the table. Not daring to touch it he ran up the stairs. Pausing for a moment, taking a deep breath, he barged open the door staring at the picture.

When did the door close? Scanning the picture his nose inches from the scene, placing his hands on either side of the frame, he willed himself to enter. Tears fell. Resting his head against the picture he looked down, his brain unable to take in what he saw. Sand, bending down he touched it, hesitantly at first before picking it up and letting it fall through his fingers.

'MUM, MUM, WHERE ARE YOU?'

Running through the rooms looking in cupboards under beds. His voice hoarse from all the shouting, he sat on the stairs too frightened to look inside the room in case he'd imagined it.

He hadn't slept for days, pacing his house like a caged animal. The same scenario going round and round his head. That she was in danger.

Tracking Sheila down had been the easy part she still frequented the same gym and spa, waiting for her to emerge, hadn't been. No idea of how long she would be, he could only wait it out. Sam jumped from his car trying not to squash the flowers or drop the champagne.

'Sheila,' he called, trying to sound cheery, thrusting them towards her hoping they would do the trick.

'Oh my, they are lovely, thank you.'

'Can I buy you a coffee?'

Sam weaved his way around the busy cafe, sidestepping a toddler, who suddenly broke away from his mother, right into his path.

'So where is your mum living these days? I have to say, I didn't believe her when she told me she was leaving your dad.'

'He's not my dad,' wishing his mum could see the look of surprise on Sheila's face.

'Your mum never said a word. I thought I was. Am, her best friend?'

'I only found out after she left. Barry threw it in my face, glad to tell me. Mum had already left home. I couldn't ask her anything about my real dad.'

'What did she say when you finally asked her?'

'She's travelling, making up for lost time. She didn't want to tell me over the phone.'

He hoped she would accept what he said at face value and not ask any more questions.

'Do you remember the shop where you found mum's picture, it was that which gave her the courage to leave him.'

'It's near the viaduct, there's a café on the corner.'

With no real plan on how to find his mother, Sam knew he had to at least try, before he could do anything, he had to find the shop at the moment he couldn't think any further than that. Asking directions all he got in return were vague answers. Fed up, he was brought up short, because there on the corner was the cafe. He daren't look to see if the shop had also appeared.

Approaching it as if a wild animal he slowly opened the door. His brain told him it was a cafe. His senses smelt the coffee percolating inside. He still expected it to disappear as he crossed the threshold. Only two of the tables were occupied. Picking up his cup he headed towards a window seat, unaware it was exactly where his mother had sat previously.

Finally, he dared to look, thinking, all I have to do is enter the shop and find my mother. He noticed one of the couples leaving were heading towards it. Hot on their heels. He knew he had to enter with them or he wouldn't get in.

Out of the gloom appeared a man wearing bright trousers and an even brighter waistcoat.

'Welcome, I'm Mr Culpepper and this is my Emporium.' Noticing Sam, he bellowed, 'who are you sir? What are you doing in my shop?'

The couple moved away.

'Why are you here?'

Annoyed at being spoken to as if he had done something wrong, Sam demanded.

'You gave my mother a picture. She's in trouble. I need to find her.'

The bell jangled in protest as the door was yanked open.

'You have to go, I can't help you.'

Sam dug his heels in; Mr Culpepper though, was much stronger than he looked.

'She's in Kingdom.'

'BE QUIET.'

Bundled out onto the street, Sam stood for a moment trying to make sense of what had happened. Trying the handle, the door stayed firmly shut. Peering inside didn't help much, the gloom so thick he couldn't make anything out.

Taking off his wet coat, Sam unwound his scarf, checking to see if the heat had come on. The snow had been falling since he'd left for work soaking him going and again coming home. His thoughts taken up with a hot bath and yesterday's leftovers he automatically went to place the junk mail in the bin, a flyer fell from his hand, bending to pick it up, he read; For the attention of Sam a meeting has been arranged at the theatre in Duke street.

'When would you like to attend?'

Sam's eyes widened in shock as a head emerged from the flyer.

'Well? I haven't got all day. Surely you must know when you can attend. How about this Thursday? Can you make that?'

He nodded in agreement. Paralysed, scared and if honest a little bit excited. Magic crackled around him, he felt as if he could reach out and touch it.

'That's settled, seven sharp, don't tell anyone.'

Loud laughter followed the face back into the flyer.

'There isn't a theatre in Duke Street,' he mumbled.

The head popped out again, the voice showing its annoyance as it sneered, 'it's big, with columns, stairs, a large wooden door, right next to the viaduct, even, a norm like you, should be able to find it.'

It took a good heave to push open the theatre doors, the silence putting him on edge. A cough drew his eyes to a tall thin man dressed all in black who sat on a deck chair in the middle of the stage. Candles floated above his head casting a dull light around him and the deck chair next to him.

'Please come and join me.'

Sam hated wooden deck chairs, having got stuck inside of one when younger, embarrassed as the whole class laughed at his distress. Gingerly sitting down, sure he heard a snigger from somewhere.

'So, you want to find your mother?'

Snapping his fingers, the candles became brighter, making it easier for Sam to see his face. Long thin, with extremely bushy eyebrows, a smile that reached his eyes, showing the whitest teeth he'd ever seen.

'You will have to enter Kingdom.'

'I can leave anytime, can we go now?'

'I am here only to help you get started on your journey.'

The Enabler could hear Sam's thoughts tumbling over each other, frustration and anger at the forefront. He wished he could take him straight to Kingdom, especially as he wore the ring. He wanted to wrench it from his finger. If only it was as easy as that, he would've done it in a heartbeat. Unfortunately though, only Sam could wear the ring, only he could take it to Kingdom.

The train station was as busy as a weekday, packed with holiday makers, all rushing for a train to take them away from their normal day to day lives.

'I'm late, things took longer than I expected, but I'm here now and we can get started.'

'It's you, but how? You're so...'

'Small? You must suspend all your preconceived ideas about what you think magic is, or what it can do. Take this card, it will allow you entrance onto Kingdom's train. Use it in the machine the same way as you would a normal ticket.'

Keeping his eyes locked on to the Enabler, ignoring the voice telling them to mind the gap, Sam walked into the carriage and fainted.

The room swam as he sat up, making him feel sick. Shaking his head to clear his thoughts, he remembered stepping onto the train, then nothing.

'Forgot to mention coming on board might make you feel woozy.'

The Enabler filled the doorway, his black clothes a stark contrast to the white room. Swinging his legs off the bed, Sam gingerly placed his feet on the floor, feeling movement underneath them.

'Would it be possible to get a coffee and something to eat? For some reason I'm ravenous,' covering his mouth he stifled a yawn.

A table appeared in front of him, laden with bacon, eggs, toast and a large mug of coffee.

'Remember, accept magic for what it is, and what it can do. Enjoy your breakfast.'

Fully replete, shaved and feeling fresh from his shower, Sam stood on the threshold of a large room filled with all manner of magicals. The lightness of air, the aromas wafting from the food, a musky scent emanating from them as they moved, made him once again feel lightheaded. Blinking away the feeling of dizziness, the Enabler blocked his view of the room.

'You'll soon get used to it, once your body adjusts to the air in Kingdom.'

'I thought we were on a train?'

'Correct, the train though is a part of Kingdom, it was created to provide shelter and help for those in need and can be accessed from any train station in Novia.'

The corridors they walked along, the rooms they passed, the magicals that seemed to be everywhere, gave Sam a real sense of how vast the train was.

Gradually, they left the main corridors behind, silence became more noticeable, the only sound their boots, slapping against the concrete floor. Coming to a halt in front of the tallest doors Sam had ever seen. Embellished in gold, intricate carvings stood out, making them appear alive. Sure that the warriors depicted, could at any moment step down and be ready for action.

Placing his hand into the lock the Enabler used it like a key. A ticking sound started. The noise from the doors opening made Sam wince, his ears still ringing as he gazed around the room. Weapons of all descriptions covered the walls. Most, he'd no idea how you'd even use them, wondering if they were for show rather than actual use.

The Enabler led him over to a side room, sitting at a desk was a lady with hair that moved about her head like a nest of snakes. Sam couldn't take his eyes off her as one of her long tresses made its way across the desk. Mesmerised, he stood totally still. The tress wound itself around his body stopping only to caress his face, before snapping back across the desk. Sam staggered. The Enabler laughed. He thought he must have dreamt it, the lady before him, did have long hair, but it was neatly tucked away in a bun at the back of her head.

Smiling at him she cooed, 'I'm Delilah, a lowly witch who guards the secrets.'

The Enabler laughed, 'there's nothing lowly about you. Now could you open the door, I need to get Sam kitted out.'

A door appeared, opening as they moved towards it. Sam's first thought; how small the room seemed compared to the others, then it started moving backwards. Shelves appeared covering every wall, held in place by batons of wood, rolled up cloth in various colours filled the spaces. Someone was shouting, although he couldn't make out the words. A banging began, like a drum getting louder with impatience. The Enabler looked astonished, as one of the batons started to bulge outwards and the cloth behind looked to be waving, the sound emanating from it, getting louder by the minute. He didn't understand what he was seeing let alone what was happening, seeing the Enabler also puzzled didn't help.

'Take the cloth and hold it in the palm of your hand.'

Sam reached forward, the cloth trembled and shook. The banging now muted turned into a low moaning.

'I've never seen one react to anyone like that before. Usually they only change colour when happy for someone to take them.'

The Narla wrapped itself around Sam's hand, squashing it tightly.

'What's it doing?'

'It's bonding, once it stops you will have to give it a name.'

'What is it? Why do I have to name a piece of cloth?'

'Remember what I told you about magic, trust in what you sense. There it's done, what are you going to call her?'

The cloth now a subtle shade of pink lay in his hand as soft and light as a feather.

'I'll call her Lois.'

The cloth rolled into a ball, spun around and disappeared into his pocket.

'She likes it. Come sit down and I will show you how to use her. A Narla's purpose is to be a safe place. Now bonded, she will only respond to your command. Take her out and make sure you use her name.'

Sam held the cloth in his hand.

'Throw it towards the ground.'

The Narla unfurled in mid-air turning into a single mattress, pinks, blues and greens fought to be the brightest.

'Sit down, it's solid.'

Hesitantly, expecting his weight to push it onto the floor, surprised when it didn't, Sam lay full length.

'Now say five minutes.'

The Narla wrapped itself around him and he disappeared. He knew he'd gone, he didn't know where, but he did feel safe. Suddenly he was back on his feet, in a whirl the cloth folded in on itself disappearing into his pocket.

Passing through a long narrow corridor they entered another room, this time filled to the ceiling with glass draws. A bell rang as a box near the floor slid out, a small doll like creature emerging. As the draw slid shut it began to grow. Looking like a small child, its huge eyes never leaving Sam's face. Scaly blue-green skin covered it from head to foot. A tail flicked behind its back. When it smiled, he was lost, thinking, she's so beautiful.

'Cat, as lovely as ever, let me introduce Sam.'

He stood immobile lost in her gaze.

'I take it you have never seen a Cactus before?'

'We have them at home, but they're prickly plants not…'

Cat giggled, the sound much like listening to his favourite song.

'When happy and calm we appear thus.'

She twirled, making her tail with its fluffy tip fly out.

'Sad and angry we appear like this.'

Her skin changed colour, razor sharp needles pushed their way out covering her like a cactus. In a flash they disappeared, as once again a smile lit her face.

'What do you need, Enabler?'

'Rope, the sort that can grow if required; an anchor watch, one that also keeps Novia time; umbrella, better make it one that can cover at least ten magicals; shoes, fast but lightweight; glasses, day and night wear as usual, can you include rain as well, you should have received authorised permission from the Scotts.'

'Let me check.'

Cat's eyes rolled to the back of her head only dark voids left. Her eyes snapped back.

'That's all in order, I cannot get you any more books the Bodleian have placed a veto on me. You can, however ask them yourself when you pick up the letter.'

'Sam will also need access to food and drink.'

'We've developed a new drinking bottle. Don't look like that, it's been vigorously tested. Pouring hot or cold drinks. It can be seen in the dark only by those using it, as to food, we have these beauties.'

Cat reached up and opened a draw that looked to be full of small white pebbles.

'Try one,' she offered.

Sam placed the disc into his mouth, immediately it flooded with the most marvellous taste of strawberries. He could feel it moving through his body energising him like a pick me up.

'Do they all taste the same?'

'They can be pretty random,' she chuckled, 'the Scotts have also agreed the use of a hearing aid and Pelagias has granted puddle permission.'

As each item was mentioned Sam got more and more confused.

'I will have everything prepared in time for when you have to leave. Before you enter the training room probably best if you talk to the reader first.'

The Enabler guided Sam into another endless corridor, telling him as they walked.

'We are going to meet a Bodleian. A tricky lot. I have to pick up your letter and they don't like them, they only like books.'

'Come in, come in,' called a grumpy voice from the depths.

Sam's eyes widened as each book turned to watch their progress. A magical sat behind an enormous desk of polished mahogany surrounded by books wrought in gold and silver with jewels embedded into their covers. The Enabler pointed towards the ceiling which was also covered by books, these ones though looked old, covered in red leather cracked and faded adding a strange contrast to the others shining out in all their glory.

'I suppose you're after a book for this adventurer?'

'Let me have the letter and yes Sam does require the use of a book. Before you pull a face Deakin, I'm not leaving here until we get one. So why don't you stop being awkward and hand it over and we can be on our way.'

'I wouldn't dream of withholding your letter, check your right pocket, it has already been dealt with. As to the use of a book, that is a different matter entirely. I'm still not convinced he will need one, besides as a norm he's hardly qualified to use it.'

'Why do I need one?'

'This is what I mean. Norms should not be allowed anywhere near books.' Deakin glared, making Sam feel like a fish on a hook, before handing him a small book, commanding, 'treat it with respect otherwise it may bite.'

Once again the corridor changed, bending away from them as they walked, Sam could still feel movement under his feet, like on a real train, but with added small vibrations that he found hard to place. The door opened as they stepped near, bare of anything except a table set up in the middle with various objects laid out for inspection. Placing the book and letter onto the table the Enabler indicated he should sit in one of the chairs appearing behind him.

'These items are the same as those you will be taking with you, please listen carefully as I explain how to use them.' Holding up the rope he let it spill over the floor. 'You can see this is not only strong but fine and flexible. It will adapt to the circumstances of its use so tell it what you're going to use it for.' Holding up the food, the Enabler chuckled, 'these you've already tried, always an adventure not knowing what you're actually going to get.' Picking up the water bottle he held it at arm's length. 'I don't trust these things. Cat assures me the kinks had been ironed out and that these new ones should work properly.'

Handing it to Sam, he put the bottle to his mouth and instantly felt cool water trickle down his throat.

'That is so good, where will I fill it up?'

'You won't have to, it's self-filling.'

'Moving on, this watch is called an Anchor, I've asked for one that can be set to your Novia time, allowing you to keep track of your days. Not only does the watch tell the time, but it also can be used to anchor you to whichever realm you are in. These glasses and this hearing aid are not the same as you will find in Novia. In Kingdom we have magicals called Lens and Lobes who have special skills regarding seeing and hearing. They have agreed for you to take these items with you on your journey.'

Sam put the glasses on and fixed the aid into his ear, immediately his ears picked up conversations and his eyes sharpened letting him see through the corridor into the next room. Holding onto the chair to steady himself, he sat down.

'The first time is always the worst. I've known magicals be sick afterwards. The aid will help if you need to zoom in and listen to someone without their knowledge. Once you have pinpointed the sound, the glasses will help you see them. Or you could use them in reverse, see someone and want to know what they're saying. It's hard to filter out everything else, but with practise you'll get better.'

Picking up the shoes, Sam gingerly put them on. With a quick flick the Enabler unfurled the umbrella.

'This is for single use but Cat is preparing one to accommodate up to ten. It folds down really small, but as you saw with a twist it opens out much larger when I place it over my head.'

The Enabler disappeared, in a blink, he was back.

'It won't keep you safe from a determined magical, but it will give you breathing space to plan your escape.'

The more Sam heard the less he liked, even thinking, he might be stuck in a dream a fantasy made real. Suddenly, his feet shot forward, he could feel heat radiating up from his toes spreading out and up his legs.

'What's going on,' he cried, trying to push the shoes off.

'Calm down, let them settle, now stand up,'

Sam felt as if his feet were standing in cement.

'Are you much of a runner?'

Still staring at his feet he answered, 'I've done a few circuits, nothing regular only when I have the time.'

'Good, you at least know what the sensation feels like. These shoes will be like any others to wear, unless you start running. Then they'll help you run faster and for longer.'

Sam grinned.

'A word of warning though, only run if you need to, and make sure you are running to something so that they let you stop. Don't practice with them there is no need.'

The Enabler handed Sam the book.

Flicking the pages, he asked, 'why are they all blank?'

'All the pages remain blank unless you want to read something or find information. The letter is similar, it will also appear blank. Yours is adapted to work only for you. We sometimes use your post boxes for travel, the map on the back details which ones they are.'

'How does that work,' Sam chuckled.

'You post your letter, when the door opens you enter, make sure you retrieve the letter, otherwise it's liable to smack you in the face as a reminder.'

Sam laughed again, 'sorry it all seems so farfetched.'

With a look of disdain the Enabler carried on, 'enter and the lights will come on as the door closes. Most have stairs; some of the older ones may still have a chute, whatever the arrangement, this is what you use. This is serious Sam.' Waiting for his laughter to stop, he added, 'the use of one may save your life, a quick way of getting from one place to another undetected.'

'What if someone else is in there when I enter?'

'They can take multiple entries without them ever coming in contact. I know you're going to laugh again; Puddle permission.'

Sam giggled, 'sorry, I am taking it seriously, but really, it sounds hilarious.'

This time the Enabler joined in.

'I'm all ears,' said Sam, going off into another fit of giggles.

Picking up the water bottle the Enabler emptied it onto the floor. Pulling Sam forwards he said, 'help,' and they both disappeared.

Disorientated, Sam knew he'd gone under water and downwards, he'd felt the sharp tug on his body. Surprised to see they weren't wet. Not sure he could ask how? Without breaking into hysterical laughter. It was all getting a bit too much.

'If you need to hide quickly, the Warra have given permission for you to create a puddle. Your permission has been extended to include others.'

'Look up,' said the Enabler, 'the next time you see stars, you'll be in Kingdom. Remember this moment, you'll be amazed at the difference.'

Sam's body felt as if it had folded itself in half. The Enabler marched off, muttering.

'I like places like this at night, come on, no one can see or hear us.'

Small points of light surrounded a large picture, before extending their range out to the entire room.

'That's the Hay Wain.'

'It's also your entrance into Pictures.'

Reaching forward he pressed his fingers onto the right side of the ornate frame.

'What are you doing?' cried Sam in alarm.

'I'm ringing the bell of course.'

The Enabler chuckled. Sam gave him a dirty look, before he could form a retort, hands appeared gripping the frame from inside the picture. A head emerged from the centre, followed by a long thin body. The man shook himself like a dog before straightening his clothes and addressing Sam.

'When we enter you're not to wander off by yourself. At all times you're to listen to what I say and act accordingly. Pictures can be a dangerous place. As a norm you are especially vulnerable to attack or manipulation.'

'Are you going to separate here? Or once you have entered,' asked the Enabler.

Confused by what he meant, Sam's eyes widened as the man separated into two magicals. Still looking exactly the same, except one had white hair and the other black, sticking out at odd angles from their heads. Looking as if they were the victims of a hairdresser gone mad.

'Still can't change it back? I'd have thought Vidya would have forgiven you by now,' grinned the Enabler.

'She says we haven't learnt our lesson and must keep like this until we do.' He turned to Sam, 'I'm Hib and this is Hob. While travelling, we'll stay split apart. I will lead and Hob will follow. You must stay in between us, unless we say otherwise.'

'Do you want to sit down, you look a bit peaky,' asked the Enabler.

'I do feel a bit lightheaded. I'm not sure I'm up to all this.'

'I know this is all somewhat intense at the moment, a lot for you to take in. Magic exists, you are now a part of it.' Placing a small rucksack onto his lap, he continued, 'in this bag is everything I showed you on the train. Have you brought your Narla?'

Sam nodded.

'The rucksack may disappear, it will however return when needed. Cat also said, she fixed your toy.'

Reaching into the bag, the Enabler pulled out a small silver plane not much bigger than Sam's hand. It was the broken one he'd found. He remembered putting it in his coat pocket. It must have still been inside when he entered the train.

'This isn't mine. It's useless without the remote.'

'Put the glasses on and hold the plane in your palm, now point it towards the end of the gallery.'

The plane started to vibrate, a small push against his hand, and off it went flying towards a picture. The landscape came to life in front of his eyes, highlighting the trees and fields. Sam thought sure he saw someone waving to him. Turning to the Enabler, breaking contact, he jumped when the plane landed next to them.

'Are you ready?' asked Hib-Hob. 'We shall be spending the night in the cottage. From there we will make our way to Long Meadow. When we enter the picture you may feel disorientated. Please tell us if you do and we'll stop. Don't speak to anyone, if the farmer calls out, ignore him. He'll be complaining again. Stand between us, place your right hand onto my shoulder and Hob will place his onto yours.'

Sam felt as if he was being squeezed flat before ballooning out again to fill his skin. Swaying, as if on a boat, he felt sure the floor was moving. Hib and Hob held onto his arms steadying him. They were standing in the lane opposite Valley Farm. Sam could remember visiting Flatford Mill as a child, throwing pebbles into the water, chasing the ducks and peering through the windows of the buildings. His mother had come to visit some old friends and had sent him off to explore.

As they walked the path towards Willy Lotts cottage in the middle of the stream sat a farmer on a cart, Sam could see his mouth moving unable though to make out what he said.

A voice called out, 'Who is it? What do you want?'

Both rolled their eyes, speaking together they answered, 'it's us Enda, Hib and Hob. We have brought Sam with us to spend the night. We spoke about this, last week, you gave your permission.'

They waited, nothing happened, then a large ginger cat appeared, weaving its way around their legs, the door opened, all ducking to pass underneath with the cat following to take up a position on the stairs.

Sitting beside a large brick fireplace, the logs crackling and hissing as they burnt, sat an old woman, long grey hair spilled over her shoulders pulled back to show her face. Wearing a dress patterned in yellows and greens with matching green cardigan. It reminded Sam of one his mother used to wear, calling it her, "Easter Bunny dress." An enormous stripped scarf grew from her knitting needles covering her lap pooling around her feet. The steady clack of them giving him even more comfort. Remembering many a time he'd sat listening to his mum knit as he told her about his day. He could feel a giggle bubbling up inside him, feeling as if he'd joined Alice down the rabbit hole.

'Sit,' she barked.

He felt a nudge behind his legs as a bench appeared behind them.

Hib asked, 'you do remember our conversation last week?'

'For us to stay the night,' continued Hob.

'I'm old, not senile, of course I remember. It's that old fool out there, his shouting is trying my patience.'

Turning to Sam, she asked, 'are you feeling more comfortable? Only I would prefer to get back to normal, if it's all the same to you.'

Hib and Hob laughed to see his confusion.

'Enda likes to present herself in a way that calms. Hence, reminding you of your mother.'

With a theatrical flourish, the room lit up with bangs and flashes, filling it with smoke. As the noise stopped and the smoke cleared, Sam couldn't believe his eyes. Before him was a totally different person. Sitting at a jaunty angle on her head sat a large wide brimmed black pointy hat. The floral dress had been replaced by a long black one with what could only be described as blobs of silver all over it. The knitting replaced with a wand, while a red broomstick lay at her feet.

Sitting in front of the fire, the bench now having been replaced by a set of comfy chairs, he could feel sleep wanting to pull him under. Feeling something touching his leg, he opened them to see Enda poking him with her wand.

'Mr Gibbs will show you to your room, mind your head,' she tittered. 'It's even lower up there.'

Enda pointed to the stairs and the cat that had followed them earlier.

'Follow me,' arching its back, stretching, as only cats can do, it growled, 'come on I haven't got all night, some of us have things to do.'

With his tail held haughtily in the air, it leapt up the stairs. The world of nonsense has just got bigger, thought Sam, as he followed a talking cat. Enda's words ringing in his ears.

'It won't bite, well, probably not.'

CHAPTER ELEVEN

Wishing he didn't have to stay in between Hib and Hob, wanting to explore, Sam sighed his displeasure.

'We are now at the boundary of the picture,' explained Hob. 'To enter another one we do this by going over the edge of the internal frame, when we drop down we'll be in a corridor. To enter the next picture we have to go over its internal frame, pulling ourselves inside. Like before, our bodies have to flatten out; or rather the forces we are trying to go through flatten them for us. To us it's normal, for anyone else though, it can be really painful, the best thing to do is to do it quickly, the slower you are the worse you may feel.'

Hib added 'the more you do it, the more your body will get used to it, although, some do say for them; it never does.'

'What about my rucksack?'

'It will also flatten, as will everything inside it,' laughed Hib.

'Ready? I will go first and Hob will follow. Put your hand out and feel the edge, that's where we're going to go over. Over time everyone gets to know where a picture ends. Normally we dive head first, as it's your first time, we'll go sideways, follow what I do and you'll be fine.'

Sam's heart rate sped up, sweat broke out across his body, making him feel clammy. Lying flat he placed his hand onto the hard edge. Inching their bodies sideways, he could feel the surface under him change. Instead of grass and dirt it was becoming hard and smooth. Thinking; this is not too bad, before feeling the first push against his body, as if someone stood on his back. The more he moved sideways, the more the feeling grew, the urge to go back overwhelmed him. Hob sensing his distress, grabbed his ankle while Hib grabbed his hand, smiling in reassurance.

As Hib flattened, the grin got pulled out of shape, looking more like a grimace than a smile. Tears pricked Sam's eyes, thinking he couldn't take any more, he fell over the edge. Hib and Hob were already standing, concern written over their faces.

'How do you feel?'

'It hurt to start with. If you both hadn't grabbed me. I don't know what I would have done.'

'Would you like to try head first? It's quicker and more fun.'

'Fun, is not the word I would use, but yes, let's give it a go, surely it can't be any worse?'

This time he stood behind Hib, the corridor where they'd landed had shortened. Facing the opposite wall, Sam took a few deep breaths, trying to stay calm. Hib bent down dragging his hands across the middle of the wall, stopping at nothing he could see. The next second he started to disappear inside. Sam took a leap of faith and followed. Once again he could feel the push on his body, this time though, he knew what to expect. They had emerged at the edge of a large field where he could see a cottage on the horizon.

'Where are we?'

'Long Meadow. Here you won't have to walk between us, as it's a safe sanctuary.'

'How is this possible? One side of my brain knows we are in a picture, but it's having a battle with the rationale side that is telling me, it isn't possible.'

'Every picture in time will become a representation only. The real pictures live here. Where we are now, is a picture hanging on someone's wall, when they look at it they see a field with a cottage in the distance, whereas we can see so much more. The scene in here has grown bigger even though the actual picture stays the same. We could talk about this all day Sam, and still not really scratch the surface of what, "being inside a picture means," by the time your journey through them is complete, you'll have gained more than enough of an insight, I'm sure.'

Meg and Dillon both frowned as the players drew nearer not noticing Sam, so agog at the state of their hair. Dillon the first to see him, nudged Meg. Gazing past Hib and Hob, she saw a tall thin man in his early twenties, wearing a puzzled expression. Holding his hand up to shield his eyes from the sun, he locked eyes with her. He knew it was unrealistic but he was smitten. Gazing at her madcap curly blonde hair, drinking in her baby blue eyes, noticing her strong chin and determined look, Sam had fallen in love. The dogs bark brought him back to his senses. Hib-Hob smirked, making him blush.

As his gaze fell on the dog, he took a step back, it was huge. The pads of its feet looking much bigger than even the splay of his hands, its fur thick and fluffy; black, tan and white all vying for a place in its coat looking more like a small pony than a dog. Rooted to the spot, he daren't move, having heard what police dogs do to criminals. Sitting down, the dog cocked its head as if listening.

'Don't fuss him with your right hand, he doesn't like your ring, use your left.'

They all looked trying to see where the instruction had come from, suddenly, a hazy white mist began appearing before taking the shape in the form of a woman. It kept fading in and out until after a few moments it settled. Now they could make out her outline, dressed in a smart red coat, with a hat of the same colour, feather placed at a jaunty angle. Black handbag and shoes completed the ensemble. While, her clothes could be seen clearly, her features were blurred.

'Hi, I'm Damala, this is my friend, Ammon,' her voice when it came was gravelly as if she had a sore throat.'

'I call him dog.'

'Dog, Ammon, whatever you call him, he speaks to us all.'

'He doesn't speak,' sneered Dillon, 'he's a dog.'

'Young man, mind your manners, otherwise, I will mind them for you.'

Throughout these exchanges the dog had sat, its brown eyes staring at Sam, making him feel equally privileged and scared. Kneeling down, holding out his left hand, he waited to see if Ammon would allow him to stroke his fur.

'You of course must be Hib and Hob. I see by your hair that the Froade haven't yet forgotten your transgressions. Never mind, I'm sure after helping Sam, all will be forgiven,' she chirruped, the throaty sound of her voice making her sound like a bird calling its mate.

'Why are you so hazy looking? Ghostlike,' asked Sam, intrigued as she wavered in and out.

'Grab a chair and get comfortable. Like Meg and Dillon I'm a twin. My brother Larc, jealous from the moment of birth. What I had he wanted, what I did he tried to do better. As we grew older he found it harder to rein it in, culminating, in my murder.'

'He killed you,' shocked, at her words; Sam couldn't understand how Damala sounded so casual about it.

'In the end I had to let him do it. Otherwise I would never have had any peace. Looking back with hindsight, I should probably have sought help sooner. I had to keep hiding what I could do. Until one day he caught me in the middle of a spell. After that, things went downhill. Larc would cast spell's binding me to chairs, to my bed, even to the railings outside the house. Eventually I would get free, but it began to happen so often, I couldn't rest. The only friend that I could trust, was Leystan. Battered and bruised, I told him that I would be better off dead. Leystan said if I truly wanted to get away he could make part of me die, while the other part hid.'

Horrified, Sam cried, 'why would you choose to do that, or him even suggest it?'

'Because then I would be free, and keep my magic,' explained

Damala, 'when a twin dies all their magic goes to the survivor. Larc killed me on a Sunday at precisely ten fifteen, he bound and drugged me. Then took me to an abandoned quarry weighted me down and left me to drown. Leystan's spell had made a living breathing other self. Effectively he split part of me away. The real me. Is the one you see before you, the other part of me that Leystan splintered off is the part which appeared to die.'

Dillon and Ammon ran ahead delighting in the freedom of the fields. Finally, after what seemed like hours, they came to a halt, a line of trees blocking their path, their branches low and dense, making it hard to see through them to what lay behind.

A face peered, the leaves rustling in complaint as a slight figure emerged climbing down the branches. Brushing herself down, she held out her hand.

'Hi, I'm Theora.'

'This is Ammon,' pitched in Dillon, before Damala could say anything.

Kneeling down she rubbed his ears, looking up at Hib and Hob, she asked, 'are you sure you want to do this? You're going to make a lot of magicals angry, plus it's dangerous. There is no guarantee that you will even be able to go over the cliff.'

Four pairs of eyes swung towards them in enquiry.

'To get onto the raging seas we have to cross a few religious pictures. Theora has given us a guide to the least likely ones to cause a fuss, although she can't guarantee it.'

'Which is the good news,' continued Hob. 'The bad news is that once past these, we will enter a picture, if seen we will be attacked, maybe even imprisoned. Those inside will do everything possible to stop us.'

Hib took over, 'in the pictures coming up, we must stay close to the bottom frame. Once though them we enter a picture called the Soldiers of Mott. In this we will have to run full pelt across its width and jump over the edge of the cliff and into the raging seas.'

They all looked equally stunned, not really understanding what Hib and Hob were saying, all focused on the part where they had to jump over a cliff.

'Don't make eye contact with anyone, don't talk to anyone and walk as fast as you can, don't run. When we enter, I will go in front, Sam, Meg and Dillon will follow next, then Damala and Ammon, while Hob will bring up the rear.'

Dropping down into the corridor Sam fell to his knees, finding it easier each time, he couldn't help wonder though, how Ammon managed to do it and land on his paws.

'Stay in a line, no deviations, ignore everything, focus on getting across to the other side,' Hib smiled, trying to relieve the tension.

At the end of the corridor he placed his hands on the wall and dived through. Sam took a leap of faith and followed. One by one, they emerged into a bright landscape, beautiful angels and fat cherubs filled the picture. A holy man sat in the centre, an expression of serenity on his face. His eyes trained on Hib, Sam caught a flicker of movement before Meg stumbled into him.

'Hold the line,' shouted Hib and Hob.

As soon as the words left their mouths arrows rained down. Although blunt, they still stung as they hit. Ammon whimpered as several struck his flank. Dillon picked one up and threw it back, hitting an angel in the face. All hell broke loose, the cherubs had the advantage of flight, hovering over the group their fury at full pelt. Arrows rained down from all sides, Damala pushed Ammon between her and the frame. Arms over their heads they walked quickly across the picture. The air changed, Hib dived for the frame, the others following, falling into the corridor in a heap. Checking over their bruises they all felt shaken by what had happened.

Meg muttered, 'that was like something out a nightmare.'

Landing in the next picture, they emerged into a scene bare of anything but rocks, the sky a dull grey, the small amount of sunlight weak. All wary after their last encounter, they kept silent, careful where they put their feet, trying not to call attention to themselves. Moving slowly they followed the path.

Half way across, a hermit emerged from behind a large pile of rocks, his clothes dirty and full of holes, eyes homing like lasers peeked from his wild hair. Banging his staff, he shouted, the words too jumbled to make out, easy to tell by his expression that he wasn't happy to find them there. They all heard the rumble before the rocks fell. Ignoring everything they had been told; they ran. The avalanche gathered pace, stones pinging off their bodies. Sam turned as one slammed into his cheek, making him cry out. Diving head first over the frame they landed once again in a tangle of bodies.

'I think we should take a rest before we venture forth to the next one. I for one need something to eat and a drop of something wouldn't go amiss. For medicinal purposes of course,' Damala tittered, brushing herself down.

Taking the chance to have a nap, Ammon stretched out with Dillon by his side as Hib-Hob took the opportunity to join together and give their separate bodies a rest. Meg's head grew heavy with sleep falling naturally onto Sam's shoulder. He closed his eyes in contentment, while Damala having polished off the wine, mumbled in her sleep.

Meg stretched her arms above her head, her movement waking Sam, his startled expression making her laugh and Dillon snort. Hib and Hob separated making them all chuckle as once again their hair stuck out at all angles. Ammon barked, waking Damala.

Hib disappeared into the next picture closely followed by everyone else, and were met with a scene of several women washing clothes in a stream, their laughter a welcome change from the group's earlier experiences. Dressed in flowing robes of various colours they stood out against the stark landscape.

Dillon tapped Meg on the back, whispering, 'I don't like them, they're creepy.'

The women appeared to be chatting and washing, they acted as if the group weren't there, yet managed to follow them with their eyes. Once in the corridor they all breathed a sigh of relief, still unsure why the women had unnerved them so.

Rubbing his hands through his hair Sam declared, 'I have to admit that was the most scared I've ever felt.'

'Even Ammon could feel their malice. The pictures are getting more intense. We cannot go back, only forwards. I'm going to enter the next one by myself before we all go through,' said Damala.

'Why not Hib and Hob?' asked Meg.

'Because I can disguise myself as a religious. They cannot.'

With a flick of her hand, flowing robes covered her from head to foot, the hood pulled low over her face, they all watched her push her way through the frame. As soon as she remerged, her clothes changed into overalls.

'What did you see?' asked Dillon and Sam together.

'It's not good. There's something wrong with the picture. It should be daylight yet it is night. I saw lights in the distance that were moving nearer. But it was the overriding smell of sulphur that worries me more.'

'It depicts a scene of good and evil. Somehow it must have been altered,' said Hib.

Hob's eyes widened in panic, 'surely they wouldn't have pulled the dark forwards. It would unbalance the picture and could be catastrophic.'

Everyone started speaking at once, Ammon barked and growled, stopping them.

'If I used my glamour magic,' chuckled Damala, and make us appear as dogs it would confuse those waiting for us.'

Stunned silence greeted her words.

'Anyone got any better ideas?' she flung over her shoulder before walking off in a huff.

Sitting down next to her, Sam asked, 'so how will it work?'

'To all intents and purposes we will be dogs. Which will allow us to see in the dark.'

Ammon leapt forward over the frame. Total darkness greeted them. The smell of sulphur even stronger as their doggy noses caught its scent, magnifying it, making them feel sick. Taking a moment to listen, Ammon stepped forward, ears cocked, eyes sweeping the path before him, his paws silent, senses on high alert. Moving slowly, they kept their eyes locked on him. All sharply aware of the danger which lurked around them as Damala's glamour started to fade.

Ammon growled low in his throat. Huddling together they tried to get their bearings. Damala gasped, the first to notice the figure outlined against a fire that had sprung up. As others appeared, the group shrunk in fear. Ammon's barking the only sound disturbing the silence.

Sam couldn't believe his eyes it was like a scene from hell. Several figures stood in a line, the fire behind throwing their scaly red skins and constantly flicking tails into sharp focus. Horns stuck out from their heads, eyes that were black pits and a grin that was the stuff of nightmares. The pitchforks they held dripped with blood.

'We have to move,' grabbing Meg's hand and pushing Dillon, Sam held onto Ammon's collar.

Ammon growled and barked. Getting louder as a figure jumped down in front of them, it took all Sam's strength to hold him back. The devil held his pitchfork ready to plunge, Dillon shot forward to stand in front of him. Meg screamed as the devil attacked. Sam threw himself between it and Dillon managing to grasp its arm. Barely had his hand touched, when it let out a loud scream and scuttled off, rubbing its arm.

'It's your ring, it doesn't like it,' cried Damala, the fear in her voice making it wobble.

Cornered, the devils slowly advanced. Meg, still shaking from the last attack held fast to Dillon. Even Ammon had quietened all accepting their fate. Sam decided that if he was going to die, he would look his killers in the eye and not cower as a victim. He turned to face them full on. As the others noticed, they also faced their enemy, unconsciously thinking the same.

'Hib-Hob. Am I seeing things, or is the sky over in that corner getting lighter?'

All turned to see where he was pointing.

'It is,' cried Dillon. 'Look along the top edge.'

The devils halted. As the light got brighter they looked even worse. The dark had hid much, now they could see how contorted some of them really were, truly a nightmare come to life. In the distance figures could be seen running towards them, the light becoming brighter as they got nearer. The devils along the ridge indecisive as to what to do, ordered to kill those in front of them. Aware, that if the light touched them it would be they who died.

'They're players,' shouted Hib and Hob.

Once more split in two they jumped up and down, waving like mad men, ignoring the devils between them and their friends. The players pulled the light with them as they ran, only a thin strip of dark remaining. Everything stopped. A brilliant flash lit the picture, the shockwaves knocking them all to the floor. Dazed, Sam sat up, a headache beginning to emerge. Dillon and Meg also held their heads moaning as their ears popped.

Getting unsteadily to their feet, as one they asked, 'what happened?'

'Only the Froade could have caused that explosion,' answered Hib.

'Not a decision taken lightly, killing the devils, kills part of the original picture,' explained Hob, walking off to greet the other players.

Having said their goodbyes and at Hib's insistence getting once more into line, they crossed the rest of the picture in silence, all glad to be leaving it behind.

'Once we have eaten, I suggest you use your Narla's to get some rest. Tomorrow will be another hard day,' sighed Damala in weariness.

'Good morning, did you sleep well my beauties?' laughed Damala, as Meg, Sam and Dillon all appeared from the safety of their Narla's at the same time.

'Breakfast is ready, but be quick, my lovely's, we have come up with a plan.'

'You seem in remarkable good spirits considering all that's happened,' said Sam.

'Probably because she's been drinking them.'

'Dillon…'

'It's okay. Let him have his little joke, it may be on him later,' she trilled. 'This time we are going to run. The next picture is our entrance to the raging seas.'

'You told us we cross them on a raft, and to get to it we go over a cliff,' said Meg, 'I take it there isn't a corridor in between. Which means, we have to land on the raft or end up in the water.'

Damala clapped her hands, 'clever girl. There are too many of us to hit the raft at the same time. Hib and Hob will merge back together, and the suggestion is, that we three join forces as it were.'

'What about Ammon?'

'He will be fine. My suggestion is for me to boost our running ability. Then stand between you and Meg linking us together by magic. Instead of three running separately we will be one person, separating when we land on the raft.'

Hib-Hob added, 'this way only three and a dog will go over the cliff.'

Remembering his shoes, Sam pulled them out.

'As long as I know where I'm running to. They should make me run faster.'

Hib-Hob dived through, everyone else hot on his heels. Landing, they took a moment to orientate themselves. Then they were off, feet skidding as they ran over the stones laid like marbles across their path. Sam wary of his shoes at first, soon loving the feeling of speed they gave him, outpacing even Ammon. Hib-Hob waved him back, nearly falling over in his effort to keep Sam in line. Half way and they all started to feel that maybe this time they would get across without any miss-haps.

It didn't take long to dawn on them that they may as well be running on a treadmill, they weren't actually going anywhere. As soon as they passed the half way mark they were back at the start. Bending forward, Sam had never felt so tired, his shoes may be able to run, but his body couldn't take much more of the pace.

'They must have placed a push back at the half way mark, we will have to go round it,' Hib-Hob sighed in annoyance. 'Listen, this time run towards that boulder, as you get near veer off to the…' A frown creased his forehead, 'not round it, over it. Someone told me that it has to be kept low to the floor.'

In a flash he was off, Sam quickly following, the others bringing up the rear, Ammon ran beside them. Pouring from all sides trying to head them off, their long robes hindering their progress the soldiers gave chase. Adrenaline pumping, giving them all added stamina, they clambered over the boulder, shouts ringing in their ears. Feet flying as they hit the ground on the other side, seeing the cliff coming up giving them another burst of adrenaline. No one hesitated, the shock of hitting the raft nothing compared with the wave that engulfed them.

Meg screamed; Sam grabbed Dillon's legs, throwing himself over him, anchoring him to the raft. The wave crashed down clawing at them trying to drag them over the side. Damala held tight to Ammon's collar burying her face in his fur, she hated the sea, her terror also felt by the dog. Hib and Hob had separated holding hands with Meg all cowering in the face of the waves that pounded down on top of them. Tossing the raft up, throwing it down like a toy. No one dare move from their position, each trying to steady themselves. The raft had a small rail running around the sides with poles at each corner. Meg watched in horror as Sam and Dillon started sliding towards the opening. The raft tilted up, pushing them away, bumping them into Damala. Letting go of Ammon she held onto Sam, Meg reached forward and held Dillon. Carolled together Ammon in the centre they rode out the storm.

The seas calmed; the raft settled, the sun even peaked to say hello before disappearing. Dazed, they looked about them, miles and miles of empty sea stared back, the water now gently lapping against the sides of the raft. Wet and stiff with cold they took stock, the bruises they had sustained earlier standing out in sharp relief. Scratches and scrapes covered them all, even Ammon hadn't escaped injury. No one dared move; until Ammon broke the deadlock. Standing up to shake himself water spraying everywhere, brought a smile to their faces.

Meg held tight to Dillon, exclaiming, 'what happens now? How do we get off?'

Hib-Hob looked at each other, 'the raft will eventually take us to the edge of the pictures frame.'

'I don't like the sound of, eventually.'

'We're in the eye of the storm,' they answered together.

Sam asked, 'and in the meantime, what do we do?'

'We wait.'

Damala changed her torn clothes for thick trousers and jumper, topping it off with a multi coloured bobble hat, bringing a smile to all their faces.

'At least you can change into dry ones.'

Sam glanced down at his clothes hanging from him in rags, clammy where they touched his skin.

'My dear, happy to oblige. You all look as if you could do with a makeover.'

Muttering a few words, rolling her hands for effect then touching each one in turn. In an instant they were dressed exactly like her, right down to the bobble hats. Laughing as they looked at each other. Dillon took Sam's blue striped hat swopping it for his own lime green and orange one.

'Hey, I like that one.'

Sam opened the rucksack, the food supplied by Cat sat on top of the rope, the water bottle peeking through its coils. Meg cupped her hands while Ammon drank as if his life depended on it. He worried that when the storm came back they may not be so lucky, taking the rope they wound it around one of the posts twice, placing Ammon in the middle as everyone sat with their legs facing outwards. Sam and Dillon pulled the rope along their bodies, crossing it over and passing it back until there was no rope left. What we must look like, he thought, trussed up ready to be sacrificed.

Tied together for what seemed like hours, they were getting restless. Hib thought they were only half way across the picture. Hob thought they hadn't moved that far. Arguments broke out as each person tried to predict where they were.

'Look,' nodded Sam, pointing to the horizon, 'it's coming back.'

Thick black clouds gathered, rolling angrily against each other. The air became charged, electrified, lightening flashed across the skies, thunder booming out its anger. Slowly the seas started to boil, gathering momentum they slapped hard against the raft pushing it upwards, before forcing it down, shaking them, determined to throw them from its back.

Every time a wave hit, the water got colder, stinging their hands and faces. Glad now of the clothes Damala had dressed them in. The raft started to spin madly in circles, Sam and Dillon held tight to the rope, their hands burned and sore. Sitting at the front, they both turned as the rail that ran around the side started to break up, splintering off, peppering the sea and them in wood. Realising at the same time that if the side they were lashed to broke, they would all slide into the water.

Detecting the panic in each other's eyes, they renewed their efforts to hold on. Once again they were lifted, falling back onto the water, submerged as the waves covered them. With one final mighty heave the seas picked the raft up and flung it. Crashing through the frame, bits of wood hit them as they fell. The force so great, they tumbled down the corridor only coming to a stop by banging into the far wall, a tangled heap of limbs. Everyone groaned, no one moved.

CHAPTER TWELVE

Sam woke refreshed from sleeping in his Narla. Lois had gone from a single bed to a small square in the blink of an eye. Besides Ammon he was the only one awake, sitting together in companionable silence, every time his brown eyes met Sam's he felt a wealth of experience hiding behind them. He'd never been much of a dog person, not that Ammon was much of a dog, more like a wolf. Outwardly, he was massive to look at. He could feel the dog's muscles rippling as he stroked him. When Ammon acted in defence of them, his body appeared to swell in size. While his razor sharp teeth glinted lethally.

Slowly, the rest of the group emerged. Breakfast was a quiet affair, everyone's thoughts turning to the next stage. Damala had once again supplied them with a change of clothes. Hib and Hob protesting, brushing their views aside she continued with her spells.

Getting naturally into line they all dived one after another over the frame. Holding up his hand, Hib stopped them going any further. They had emerged inside a cave, sunlight spilling in from its opening. Waiting for the air around them to settle, Hib strained his ears, Ammon nudged his hand and silently crept towards the light. He sniffed the air before venturing outside and disappearing. Hearing him bark, Dillon rushed forwards breaking the line.

'It's okay,' he called back, 'he's barking at birds.'

The mountain loomed, the air of menace it exuded making them all feel uncomfortable.

'What happened to their bodies?' asked Sam, unable to hide his disgust.

'They have been disposed of,' replied Damala. 'The mountain only wants faces, it has no need of them. Their bodies may be dead, their faces however are alive. They may speak. If they do, you mustn't answer or react.'

'Their purpose to lure and trap others,' explained Hib-Hob. 'This is a dangerous place. The faces don't like dogs, so Ammon will patrol beside us. If he thinks they are targeting anyone he will bark, if you feel mesmerised, hone on to the sound, use it like an anchor.'

Everyone's thoughts were on the next part. At least before they knew more or less what to expect, the mountain and its many faces now seemed the scarier option. Meg, the first to notice the faces staring at them, stopped as one particular one leered at her. She couldn't make out what he said, sure though it wasn't anything nice.

Pulling her arm, Damala muttered, 'look at the ground. Do not, engage.'

Hib and Hob scanned for the entrance. They knew the door was hidden by the faces that covered it. They would try to block their entrance. Even though, the mountain itself wanted them to step inside.

The noise when it came made them all leap back. All eyes turned, all mouths spoke at once, the cacophony of sound hurt their ears, making it hard to understand what any of the voices were saying.

'We need to find the door,' explained Hib, 'spread out and each check a section of the mountain. Ignore all overtures and don't touch the wall even if it appears bare, a face could be hiding, waiting to pounce.'

'Ammon will patrol around us, if you hear him bark stop and step away,' added Damala.

Meg felt Ammon brush pass her legs, giving her the strength to carry on. The part of the mountain she was checking appeared to be made up entirely of, "dirty old men," as her mother would say. The nearer she got the clearer their voices became, blushing, seemed only to spur them on to embarrass her further. Looking across at her brother he seemed oblivious to the chatter raining down on him. While Sam on her other side looked to be having as bad time as she was.

'Found it,' called Dillon, 'it's hidden by these ugly faces, look,' showing them by tracing in mid-air the gaps in between them.

'Come closer and say that, we dare you,' they thundered.

Dillon wagged his finger, 'you will have to do better than that.'

'Don't provoke them. Remember we have to go inside, finding the door is only the beginning.'

At Damala's words, the angry faces turned into shrieks of laughter, their eyes rolling in delight. Hib and Hob held their hands a few inches from the doorway, as they finished the incantation the door opened inwards, the dark flew out to greet them, a sour musty smell following close behind. Stepping through, it slammed shut, the darkness complete, the feeling of being watched felt by all. They were standing in a hall like chamber, two paths directly in front of them disappearing into the distance.

'Can someone magic some lights?'

'Not in here we can't Dillon,' answered Damala, holding tight to Ammon's collar.

'Then how are we going to see where we're going?' wailed Meg, drawing closer to her brother.

Chuckles could be heard reverberating around the chamber.

'Come over here, we won't hurt you, let us help you, show you the way, although you have to do is...'

Before they could finish Ammon's barking rent the air echoing around the chamber.

'You shouldn't have brought a dog inside, we don't like dogs,' they shrieked.

Ammon kept on barking. Stunned by the noise, they covered their ears, finally the voices stopped only a few hisses lingering.

'Which path do we take?' asked Sam, as he lowered his hands.

While Ammon and the faces had been having their standoff, Hib, Hob and Damala had been debating what to do.

Like a light bulb moment, he cried, 'my glasses.'

Putting them on he didn't know what to do next.

'Look around the chamber, can you see anything?'

'Faces, lots of faces and they are not happy that I can see them.'

Once again Sam delved into his bag, taking out the toy plane.

'If I set it off down each path I should be able to see where it leads.'

Holding the plane in his palm, Sam looked towards the left hand path, as the plane lifted, he smiled his thanks to whoever had lost it. Bending around to the right, the plane flew on. All the faces it passed, had their eyes closed.

At intervals, more walls appeared as if directing where the plane should go. Sam had given a running commentary while the plane flew. Now concentrating on the right hand path he let it fly.

'This path is wider than the other one. The faces still have their eyes closed and there are not so many of them. Another wall has appeared this one seems solid, not like the ones on the other path. This definitely goes on further; no other walls have appeared to herd the plane.'

Hib, Hob and Damala edged away talking in low voices, the others watched able to tell by their body language that they were arguing.

'We are taking the left hand path. Hib and Hob, don't agree with me,' sighed Damala dramatically.

'Although, I have never been inside the mountain. I know from experience that it likes to deceive. Most magicals would take the right hand path because it contains less faces. That is, precisely why we shouldn't go there.'

While she had been talking Ammon circled them nudging each person's right hand. Damala stared, willing them to understand. Hib and Hob gave a small shake of their heads, silencing Dillon's question.

'Remember, don't engage, look straight ahead,' ordered Hib, sounding like a sergeant major.

Hob added in the same tone, 'most importantly of all. Do not be tempted to run.'

Ammon placed a paw on each of their feet as he continued to circle.

'As you have the glasses, perhaps in this instance it may be best if you go first, Ammon will bring up the rear,' said Hib and Hob as they merged together.

Placing the glasses back on, this time Sam knew what to expect, waiting a few seconds to allow his vision to adapt, he shouted, 'GO.'

As one they sprinted down the right hand path, as Ammon streaked forward they came to a halt. Without exception they were all winded, Sam felt as if his lungs were on fire, his heart banged inside his chest, like an animal trying to escape. Dillon clutched his side, his face red from the exertion. Hib and Hob had fared the best, merging, gave them double the energy. Meg and Damala sat together taking deep breaths trying to slow their breathing down.

'It's much lighter in here,' noted Meg as she stood up and stretched, stumbling as a face near her opened its eyes.

'We don't like the dark, it's easier for us to see who is wondering around our domain,' said a deep male voice, his brown heavy lidded eyes making his face look sad.

'Meg,' shouted Hib, 'don't engage.'

'Mind your own business. If Meg, that's a lovely name by the way, wants to talk to me, then she can, come closer my lovely.'

She felt herself yanked away by Dillon, pinching her hard on the arm.

'Leave my sister alone,' he shouted, raising his fist, as the face sneered at him.

'Little boy, who thinks he's a man. I'm sure we could make use of you in some way, if only to fill a space on the wall.'

Laughter echoed around them as other faces opened their eyes, all eager, hoping he would react and step nearer.

Ignoring the jeers and catcalls from the faces, Hib said, 'now that it's much lighter and we can see where we're going, we should get back into line. Now that you've seen how the faces operate, it is imperative we all try not to react.'

Walking along the path in single file, told by Hib to watch each other's feet, while Ammon patrolled around them. The faces shouts and taunts were getting harder to ignore, sensing their anger, he quickly brushed passed, nudging them with his nose, breaking their thoughts.

One face in particular was being a nuisance, calling out incessantly to Meg, cajoling her, whiney to angry and commanding in an instant. Catching sight of Dillon behind her, his anger barely in check. Sam hoped he could hold it together.

From nowhere a wall appeared in front of them, a large face opened its eyes and stared, its tongue hanging from its mouth. When it licked its lips they all shivered, the menace in the action felt by all. Effectively they were at a dead end, as Hob turned to look behind them a wall was advancing, boxed in they had nowhere to go. Meg started to hum in panic, shaking as the voice once more called her name, telling her all the things it wanted to do to her.

Damala gathered her into her arms crooning as if to a baby, patting her back. Nodding at Sam to take care of Dillon.

'Keep it in, he wants you to react.'

Ammon weaved himself between them, he looked up at his friend, as their eyes met Dillon felt himself relax.

'What do we do now?' cried Sam.

The wall that had been advancing stopped. The face in front still leered, while the side walls had quickly filled up with faces, all calling, encouraging them to come closer. The one voice that cut through everyone, still aimed most of its vitriol at Meg, sneering at Dillon and generally being rude to the rest of them.

'It's a false wall,' said Damala, 'the face is too big, everyone on and in the mountain used to be a magical. We have to figure out which way to go.'

Hib and Hob stared at the wall in front, making sure to keep away from the side walls. Edging forwards they both said at the same time, 'we go left.'

The shouting from the faces grew louder. The large face leered, flicking its tongue. Holding onto Meg, Sam and Dillon followed Hib and Hob, Damala and Ammon brought up the rear. As soon as they got nearer to the face it was easy to see the path winding away to the left. Hib and Hob didn't hesitate even brushing against the face as they passed. Sam and Dillon crowded Meg, pushing her through, ignoring her moaning as the large face winked. Once again, the path laid out appeared to go on forever, this time though, the walls were at least bare of faces.

Believing the worst to be over, they hurried along, all focused on getting out, away from the evil that surrounded them. Meg still felt unnerved by all the attention she had garnered earlier. Spooked at every turn, even jumping when Sam touched her arm.

'Meggie… Where are you my love? You can't get away from me. You're going to be mine. Forever…'

The voice echoed around them, sounding even more menacing than before. Meg stood rooted to the spot, shaking and crying as Sam held her arms, worried she was going to run off.

'You must ignore it Meg,' shouted Hib over the noise.

'Easy for you to say,' shouted back Dillon.

'Everyone calm down, this is what it wants, divide and conquer. We must be nearing the exit. That is why it has renewed its efforts, be strong Meg, its only words.'

'Come on,' said Sam, pulling her along, 'I'll take care of you and Dillon won't let anything happen either.'

As if in a trance Meg let them each steer her along the path.

'This is getting out of hand,' Damala whispered to Hib and Hob. 'Surely we must be near the end?'

Meg screamed as the face of her tormentor appeared on the wall next to her. Shouting, whining, cajoling, wheedling every form of invitation used to get her to come closer. Breaking free she sped off, the voices cheered, shouting out their encouragement. Falling down she curled into a ball, Damala slowly approached, brushing back her tangled hair, wiping away the tears running down her cheeks.

'I can't take anymore; I've never been spoken to like that. Ever. I need a hot shower to clean away the words.'

Helping her up, Sam wrinkled his nose, 'it's not the only reason you need a hot shower.'

'That's the sort of thing I expect my brother to say,' peering over his shoulder, she cried, 'where is Dillon?'

Everyone became aware of furious barking. Racing back the way they came, they were confronted with the site of Ammon, hackles raised, snarling at the faces, making them hiss and swear. Dillon appeared to be suspended, his feet inches above the ground, pain evident on his face, hands balled into fists.

'Hello Meg,' said a voice over Dillon's shoulder, 'look who came back to, "sort me out." I believe were his words.' The voice sneered, 'by the time my friends have finished. The only sorting out he'll be doing will be to join us on the wall.'

'Let him go,' she screamed.

'Now, now Meggie, I don't like bossy women.'

Sam approached Dillon.

'Don't touch him, they are taking him,' cried Hib and Hob pulling him back.

Shrugging them off, he shouted, 'we have to do something.'

Laughter greeted his outburst. Sam stumbled back, the horror on his face making Meg whimper.

'Their faces are protruding from the wall and their tongues are attached to his back.'

'That's how they take magicals. They destroy the body by poisoning it. Once finished, it is discarded and you end up as a face on the wall.'

'You have magic Damala, can't you do something?'

'Not against this, I'm not sure anyone can.'

Dillon groaned, the pain in his back like a hot poker stabbing him over and over.

'Help me,' he cried, as his legs and arms began jerking.

Ammon leapt, clamping the tongues between his jaws he shook his head from side to side pulling them out as blood spayed across the walls. The hateful voice started up again telling them he would still die and Meg would still be his. Laughing and sneering at the shock on their faces when Dillon fell forward, his back a mess of blood and pus as he twitched in agony.

In one bound Ammon jumped, opening his jaws wide he closed his fangs over the face, everyone shuddered as they heard the crunch as he bit down. Not content, he worried it until only a bloody hole was left on the wall. Chaos reigned, the faces screamed their rage. Sam held Meg while Damala helped Hib-Hob hoist Dillon onto their shoulder. Following Ammon they set off back along the path, all shaken by what had happened.

'Let's stop here, before you say it Sam, I know we have to get out. But I need to assess the damage to Dillon.'

Hib-Hob laid him gently onto the ground, his exposed back still weeping pus. Feeling his forehead, Damala waited, counting to ten.

'He has a fever which is good. It means the poison is moving through his system and hasn't yet taken hold, if it does, he will turn cold.'

Gently she removed his shirt the extent of the damage clearer, large red circles covered his back, the skin inside flayed, blood and black pus seeping from each one. Damala felt at a loss, keeping the wounds clean was going to be a problem. Hib-Hob wouldn't be able to carry him much further. Catching Meg's eye, she smiled trying to reassure. She had really grown to like her. It was likely that Dillon would die, as his twin it would affect her greatly.

Everyone stilled as Ammon growled, all strained to listen, expecting the faces to have returned. A light appeared, faintly at first, growing stronger as it drew near. Hearing Dillon groan, Meg dropped to her knees beside him. Rubbing his hands, murmuring endearments, ignoring what was coming.

Ammon walked towards the light.

A voice asked, 'are you hurt? You're covered in blood.'

'Stop there,' commanded Hib-Hob, holding up their hands. 'Don't come any closer.'

Ignoring their command, she asked, 'is someone else injured? Can I help?'

Ammon stood beside a young girl, his size making her look even smaller. Elvin face, green eyes and red hair. In any other circumstances they would have thought how lovely she was. Instead they were wary of her intentions.

'I'm Fia, are you lost?'

No one moved or answered. The fact that Ammon seemed okay with her, making them wonder.

Her voice rang out, filling the chamber, 'you shouldn't be here. Go back to where you belong. They are under my protection now.'

Ammon barked.

She added, 'and his.'

They all gasped to see the walls covered in faces. All shouting what they were going to do to them if they ever came back. As suddenly as they came they went, the echo of their voices slowly disappearing bringing a welcome silence.

'Please follow. Let me help,' said Fia, walking away.

Ammon walked at her side, turning once as if to say, 'come on.'

'If she's good enough for Ammon,' muttered Damala, 'then she's good enough for me.'

The others nodded in agreement. Hib-Hob carefully picked Dillon up. Damala strode ahead, while Sam held tight to Meg's hand.

'Come in, you're safe now,' said Fia, smiling at their worried expressions. 'The faces are not allowed here. They shouldn't have followed you, they will be punished.'

'How would you punish a face?' asked Sam, looking puzzled.

'By taking away their senses,' said Fia, directing Hib-Hob to lay

Dillon on the table. They will not be able to hear, see or speak. A fitting punishment for how they behaved.' Feeling Dillon's forehead, she turned to Damala, 'he still has a fever, that's good, the longer it lasts the better.'

'Surely we need to get the fever down?' stated Meg anxiously.

Fia held her hands, 'normally yes, while this fever rages it means the poison hasn't found a weak enough spot to hold on to. He must be strong.' Leading Meg to a bench she knelt down in front of her, asking, 'what did you feel when the voices were talking to you?'

'I was frightened.'

Fia waited, looking deep into Meg's eyes and asked again, 'what did you feel?'

Sam, went to intervene, Damala shook her head and pulled him away. Meg glanced at her brother twitching and moaning, his back exposed, the red rings angry against his white skin.

Turning back, she retorted, 'angry. I still am.'

'But who are you really angry with?'

Meg blinked, unable to look away from Fia's eyes.

'ME,' she shouted, 'I'm angry with myself for reacting the way I did. They made me feel so weak.'

'I'm going to help Dillon, but he also needs your help. Think about your anger how it makes you feel, turn it into a ball of light and direct it at him. As his twin Dillon can draw strength from you. At the moment your strength, is your anger.'

'Sam, will you sit with Meg, she needs to focus. In helping Dillon we will hurt him. She mustn't break her concentration.'

Fia laughed to see Hib-Hob split apart, their hair springing in all directions.

'Perhaps you could look after Ammon, he needs cleaning up. There is plenty of hot water and towels, while Damala can help me with Dillon.'

'Don't pull that face, it's only blood,' said Damala, as both Hib and Hob wrinkled their noses. While Ammon rubbed himself against their legs.

'Alright, alright,' they cried, as he barked in response.

Sam felt the concentration coming from Meg in waves, the tension in the hand he held, making his ache. Her eyes never left her brothers body, if will alone could make him better, then, he would survive.

Ammon, clean of all the blood lay at Sam's feet, head on his paws, eyes locked onto Dillon. He still felt shocked at the sight of him ripping the face apart, the savagery of the act even now made him feel sick.

Damala and Fia sprinkled a powder like substance into the rings on Dillon's back. As he gave a blood curdling scream, Sam felt Meg's hand clench down on his. Ammon placed his head in her lap, whimpering in sympathy. Sam watched in horror as small tendrils of smoke appeared to be drifting from Dillon's wounds, all the time his screams getting louder. Meg's eyes didn't waiver, she stared at her brother willing him to survive. Hib and Hob retreated into the next room, both upset by what was happening, feeling they were to blame for not keeping a closer eye on Dillon.

At last he was quiet, everyone breathing a sigh of relief that the screaming had stopped.

'Good morning,' called out Damala, giving them a wide grin as they entered the room, 'you have visitors.'

Meg rushed forward, Dillon held up his hands to stop her hugging him. Both laughing and crying at the same time.

'As you can see, although much improved, he isn't out of the woods yet. I've decided to come with you,' Fia announced, 'that way I can keep a check on his wounds.'

With Meg's help Dillon shrugged off the thick jacket Fia had insisted he wear to cross the frame, worrying that the crushing they would experience would open his wounds. He winced as the last one fell to the floor.

'Let me see.'

Fia pulled up his shirt, apart from a small edge of one ring they all remained closed. Winding a scarf around her head and face, she pulled on a long sleeved top.

'You all need to cover up. When the sand storm hits it will be brutal.'

Making their way across the hard compacted ground, the tops of the Pyramids highlighted by the sun, it was hard to understand where any sand might come from. Relentless heat shone down, dogging their footsteps. Ammon, growled deep in his throat as a low thrumming noise came from all around them, building in intensity. Pulling up their scarf's, in moments they were engulfed in sand.

It whipped, driving them to their knees, Damala wrapped her arms around Ammon, protecting his head. Dillon joined her, trying to shield his friend. Fia and Meg held tight to Hib and Hob's hands, while Sam was being tossed and pushed further away from them. Each time he tried to stand, he was knocked down by the force of the wind. Giving up he crawled forwards, out of nowhere a twirling mound of sand surrounded him pounding down as if trying to wipe out all trace of him. The others could only watch, huddled together, they dare not move. As fast as it came, it went. Once more the ground was hard and bare, Sam groaned as he tried to stand up, feeling as if he had gone ten rounds with a boxer.

'Wow. Where did that come from? It didn't like you Sam, that's for sure,' said Dillon.

'Will it happen again?' asked Meg.

'It may even increase in intensity. It doesn't want us here,' said Fia.

'Perhaps we should stay in line for this picture,' added Damala. 'Use Sam's rope to tie us all together, then at least when it comes back. We could all brace each other against it.'

Threading the rope through their belt loops, Sam passed it under Ammon's collar and then tied it to himself, insisting that he should be at the front. If the sand attacked him again, then the others could crowd around and hopefully fend it off. They hadn't gone far before the ground started moving, little swirls of sand lifting and hitting them as they walked. With one almighty whoosh they were covered, the sand springing up from all around them, stuck, they huddled together, their arms clamped together protecting Ammon in the middle. He was the first to realise that it had stopped, barking to get their attention.

Taking off the scarf Damala had placed around his head, Dillon gently wiped his snout. Opening his rucksack Sam offered up his water bottle, all grateful as the cool water hit the back of their throats.

'What about this?'

Meg and Dillon laughed, 'it's not exactly raining.'

While Hib-Hob cried, 'why didn't you say you had one of those? Really Sam, do you know what's in that bag at all?' they harrumphed.

Meg and Dillon looked at each other puzzled how an umbrella was going to help them. As soon as Sam opened it and disappeared, they understood. Waving his hand telling them all to get under, Hib and Hob merged together to give them more room. The urge to run now they were invisible felt by all, keeping their inclinations in check, they slowly walked towards the edge of the picture. If any sand attacked them on the way they were blissfully unaware.

'You can put it down now Sam,' said Damala, we have reached the edge and are in no man's land.'

The ground beneath their feet shifted before giving way. Stunned and shocked by the fall they all lay where they fell, Dillon groaned loudly as Sam's foot caught his back on the way down.

'Everyone, okay?' called out Damala, brushing herself down, looking up she could see the hole they had fallen through already covered in. Turning to Hib-Hob, she asked, 'do you know where we are? I know it's not the void.'

'We are still in the picture, but underneath it,' they answered.

Having all searched the walls and floors for any sign of a way out, they slumped together. Even Ammon looked fed up, thought Sam; head on his paws, watching each of them in turn, for a sign of movement.

'Somethings different,' whispered Damala. 'Someone's here'

Picking up on her anxiety Ammon growled low in his throat, the sound both unsettling and comforting at the same time. Their mouths gaping open, as the walls suddenly turned into mirrors. Surprised to see the state they were in, sand still clinging to their clothes and hair, dried on in splodges, making their faces appear spotty. Even their boots looked as if they would soon fall apart the sand having worn down the leather.

'Not a pretty sight,' said a voice, coming from the mirror, 'we will soon have you ship shape again.'

A white face appeared, its eyes black, grinning at them as its hands pressed against the glass.

Hib-Hob stood up, pointing at the apparition, shouting, 'you shouldn't be here, you're a Wraith, this is a picture, our domain, not yours. Go back to the Glasserium where you belong.'

In answer, it stepped from the mirror.

'I'm not a Wraith.' The apparition abating as its magical form emerged. 'My name is Eadulf. I've come to help.'

'Take us over you mean, stay back,' they cried.

'I've never met a Wraith,' spoke up Dillon, as Meg shushed him.

'Why do we need your help?' asked Fia.

'Hib-Hob cannot take you any further,' holding his hand up as they went to interrupt. 'You have done a sterling job to get this far, Sam's adventures through Pictures stop's here. Vidya, has requested your return.' Seeing the horror on their faces, he added, 'not back the way you came. Oh no, special treatment for you. As I speak corridors are being moved, and pictures shifted, if you spilt apart you will see that the Froade have released you from your, "hairy sentence." Say your goodbyes and we can all be on our way.'

Long luxurious black locks spilled down their backs. Hib and Hob, shook their heads to make it swish, both sighing in contentment. Dillon and Sam laughed, earning them both dirty looks.

'When you get back up into the picture, go over the frame as normal, wait in the corridor, when it changes to red, follow it and you will emerge back home.'

CHAPTER THIRTEEN

'Before we go any further,' spoke up Sam, 'I for one would like to know where we're going and why you have to be the one to take us.'

The others all nodded in agreement. Dillon crossed his arms, planting his feet, 'how do we know if we can we trust you?'

Damala demanded, 'if not through Pictures, how are we going to get into Kingdom?'

'I have been living here as a gatekeeper to another lost soul. We have become friends, unlikely you may think, but needs must and all that. To meet the vampire who is going to guide you through the Nether means you will first have to enter a mirror. Dangerous places normally, mine though is not.'

Damala looked doubtful, saying, 'no mirror is harmless, you may not try and take us, but what about the mirror itself, can it be trusted.'

Sam listened, the talk about mirrors going over his head, unnerved enough by the word Nether and now with the word vampire thrown into the mix, his mind was in turmoil. Dillon hopped from one foot to another, excited to get going, while Meg hung back with Fia.

'Step inside, you will be surprised,' chortled Eadulf.

The glass disappeared, gingerly stepping over the frame they found themselves in a musty smelling room full of overstuffed chairs and tables covered in plants. Hackles up, Damala was ready for flight. Never having been inside a mirror, she was surprised to see it was being used as a home.

'We will stay here long enough for you to rest, freshen up and have something to eat and drink. Find yourselves a room. Dinner will be ready when you're finished.'

Leaving them looking bemused, Eadulf conjured a door and disappeared. By now, used to Damala kiting them out, they were pleased to see this time she had abandoned the idea of anything weird or wacky even for herself, dressing them all in standard tunics and trousers. Even Fia and Ammon weren't immune to her spell, ignoring Fia's protests, saying, 'with your colouring; green is definitely your colour,' while tying a bright blue piece of cloth around Ammon's neck, choosing to hear his bark as a sign of agreement.

Expecting to exit the mirror the same way they came in, all were surprised as Eadulf opened a hatch in the floor, ushering them down the stairs, small lights appeared on the walls glowing dimly at first getting brighter the further down they went.

'Upstairs,' he told them, 'we were underneath the picture, now, we are underneath the mirror. We shall be entering a tunnel, the lights will follow us, but even they may struggle to penetrate its gloom. You may find it hard to see me. Rest assured I will be at the front.'

Light began to spill out in front of them, a welcome relief from the dark. Candles burned giving off a faint vanilla scent. In the middle of the chamber sat a giant black coffin, golden symbols carved over its surface. Humming like an electricity pylon, thought Sam.

Dillon tapped the sides, 'anyone home,' he cooed.

Meg kept away; she didn't like to think what was inside it. Since they had entered the mirror. Fia had hardly said a word, walking around the coffin, she muttered to herself, tracing with her fingers the symbols etched upon it.

'How will we stop it from biting us?' asked Sam nervously.

'She is called Aeryissa, and she doesn't bite,' retorted Eadulf looking insulted.

'Of course she does,' spat Dillon, 'that's why they're called vampires.'

'The writing says she is an original, it also states that she doesn't wear a collar.'

'That's correct, Fia.' Leaning towards Dillon, Aeryissa grinned, 'I only bite if I want to.'

No one moved, all thinking, 'how did she get out?'

'You're not big enough to be a vampire,' sneered Dillon, 'this coffin is huge and you're not much bigger than me.'

Sam could see what he meant, not only was the vampire small in height but looked as if she hardly weighed anything either. Her features were plain but neat, large grey eyes and a small nose, expecting to see fangs; instead, when she smiled he could see like them, she had teeth. Dressed in black leather, she looked like a biker, only the motorbike missing to complete the picture. The only thing he could see which looked lethal were the spurs that covered her boots.

Eadulf laughed, 'I can tell by their faces Aeryissa you won't convince them.'

'I'm convinced,' stated Damala, a look of fear crossing her face.

'That's because you can see me.'

They all wondered what Damala could see that they couldn't.

'Has Eadulf told you what the Nether is and what you will have to undergo to get into it?'

'I thought it best I leave it to you to explain. I wasn't sure if you were going to tell them beforehand what you have to do.'

All eyes turned, faces expectant, fear etched on all.

'The Nether is a place beneath both Kingdom and Novia. Ambrogio often use it to practice their skills away from prying eyes,' explained Aeryissa. 'Some magicals who use dark magic are also drawn to its numerous levels. Hiding out waiting to trap the unwary to use them in their experiments. To get you into the Nether, I will need to compel you. We then catch a night bus which will only stop for vampires.'

Sam couldn't stop a giggle escaping, he blushed under her gaze. 'Sorry it's… How can somewhere called the Nether have a bus?'

'It's a mixed up place,' explained Eadulf. 'It has been used in the past to take things out of Novia, including norms. The purpose never made clear. It's a place little known or talked about. The name enough to conjure nightmares.'

Dillon stood up, flinging his arms out, shouting, 'no way am I letting you into my head. It sounds as if you're trying to turn us into vampires.'

Aeryissa snarled, 'you really are hot headed; aren't you? Perhaps you could let me finish.'

'Even if you are genuine in wanting to help. I can't go, Ammon cannot be compelled. I'm not leaving him behind,' he spat, flinging himself down next to his friend.

Ignoring his tantrum, Aeryissa told them, 'when we enter, we have to wait until the bus comes. Others may also be waiting, you will not be aware of them or they you. I will board the bus first, the driver will know that you are my, "find," and allow you admittance. I take it you still have your letter?' at Sam's nod she continued. 'We find the post box and enter before anyone realises you are awake.'

Aeryissa stared hard at Sam as he fought to suppress another giggle.

'It all sounds really straight forward,' said Damala, 'I'm guessing by the looks exchanged between you and Eadulf, that may not be the case.'

'You're perceptive, you may not like the idea of me being in your heads, that however is the easy part. The night bus is often used to gather magicals and norms who want to be changed. They will never become full Ambrogio. To do that you have to be born one.

Usually requests to change are dealt with on an individual basis, rather than in a group.'

Meg shivered, the more she heard, the less she liked, finding it hard to believe Aeryissa was an actual vampire, expecting her to be bigger and stronger wearing a black cape, white face and fangs that dripped with blood. Rather than someone who looked much like herself.

'Before we enter, you should all know this is also new territory for me, I have never compelled anyone before, or been inside the Nether. This means that I will be noticed and may generate more interest than we need. Compelled by me, you will be safe from other vampire control. They can however hold us up and that is what worries me. I have no idea if it will work and if it does, how long the spell will last.'

Sam asked, 'what about Ammon, Dillon's right, we cannot leave him here. Can you compel a dog?'

'I can use my glamour to make him appear as a man,' said Damala.

'Only I have to get to Kingdom, why don't you all go back. There is no reason for any of you to put yourselves into more danger.'

'No way, Sam. I may not trust them,' pointing at Aeryissa and Eadulf, said Dillon. 'But we are in this together. Meg feels the same. Don't you?'

'I'm going as well,' said Fia, the first words she had spoken since they had met Aeryissa.

Ammon barked in agreement, Damala chuckled.

'It seems we're all going.'

'There is one other problem. Me,' spoke up Eadulf. 'For reasons which I won't go into. I also need to return to Kingdom. To do that though, I will need to merge with one of you.' He asked hopefully.

Silence greeted his words until Ammon went and sat beside him.

'I will do it.'

'No Sam you can't,' shouted Dillon, he'll take your body and turn you into a wraith.' Turning to Damala, he pleaded, 'that's what you told us they do to magicals, tell him he can't.'

'Eadulf doesn't need to take anyone over. He fled his home in the Glasserium because it was taken over by dark magic. Eadulf is not the enemy. He is though, the last of his kind.'

'Thank you Aeryissa. It's true, I have no need to take, or want to have anyone else's body. Mine may be indistinct at the moment, but I do have one of my own. I'm as much a magical as the rest of you.'

Sam laughed, 'If only I were. I would have clicked my fingers and entered Kingdom long ago.'

'Then I cannot merge with you.'

'You can use me,' piped up Meg, ignoring Dillon's shout of protest. 'To be honest, having someone with me will help me get through it.'

Dillon grabbed her hand, 'please don't let him take you over,' he begged.

'I won't be, "taking her over," instead your sister will wear me like a coat. Once compelled, she won't even know I'm there.'

Dillon could see by the set of Meg's mouth, there would be no reasoning with her. Dirty looks was all he could throw towards Eadulf, mouthing, 'I'll be keeping an eye on you.'

When the side of the coffin opened they all jumped, Ammon barking his disquiet.

'It's a shell,' laughed Aeryissa, directing them to follow her inside.

They all shivered, the inside of the tomb like ice, the atmosphere dangerous, all sure something waited to pounce. Silently the door closed locking them in; still smiling at their worried expression's, Aeryissa led them down a flight of stairs and into a great hall. The walls covered in tapestry's depicting Ambrogio in battle.

'Damala if you could cast your glamour over Ammon, while Eadulf merges with Meg, then I will compel you all at the same time,' said Aeryissa, ignoring Dillon's sulky face.

Leading Ammon away, Damala knelt down and whispered

words into his ears, barking in return, his brown eyes followed her hands as she moved them over his body.

'Wow,' said Meg, forgetting her fear for the moment at the sight of Ammon as a man.

Sam, seeing her face as she admired his new appearance, made him feel a stab of jealousy that she had never looked at him in that way. Ammon's eyes roamed around the room. Dillon avoided his gaze, preferring his friend as a dog, rather than this odd coloured eyed magical he'd become.

Meg gasped as Eadulf surrounded her, feeling like a heavy cloak had been placed over her shoulders. She could feel him at the edges of her mind, but found it comforting rather than scary. Standing in front of each person, Aeryissa placed her hands against the side of their heads, as her eyes changed to black she looked deep into their eyes until the spell was cast.

'Follow me,' she told them, surprised, when as one they turned towards her, eyes white and vacant, no one at home.

Walking through the door; the group followed without thought. The atmosphere charged, Aeryissa could feel the weight of other vampires pressing down, trying to get into her head, find out who she was. Mentally shaking them off, she let her eyes turn red as they adjusted to the half-light. Her ears elongated, listening for the sound of the bus. Striding off she didn't look to see if the group followed, she had to act the part even if unsure of what to do.

She discerned others making their way between two tall buildings, the vampires leading, berating them for lagging behind. Seeing an area that appeared empty, she headed over, her senses on high alert to any threat. Realising her mistake, she decided to brazen it out, calling to her group to hurry up, while mentally telling them to only do as she commands.

'Well, well, look who's turned up, never thought we would see the likes of you here,' a large vampire shouted, his fangs extended. Letting the body he was biting fall to the ground, suddenly he stood in front of her, the blood dripping from his mouth, smiling, as he looked her up and down.

Ignoring the stench leeching from his body, Aeryissa side stepped away from him, her hands turned into talons, the spurs Sam had noticed on her boots, multiplied, their lethal blades shining in the gloom. Not allowing her fangs to show, knowing Mach would take it as a sign to fight, she smiled back, her teeth staying small and even.

They had both turned, hearing the buses engine getting louder as it drew nearer. The shelter had appeared while they had been squaring up to each other, three magicals already waited inside, muttering and wringing their hands, one man kept standing up and sitting down acting like a jack in the box.

Expecting Mach to bring his group over to the shelter, Aeryissa was surprised and relieved to see him disappear. As the bus drew to a stop she waited for the two men and the woman to enter first. The vampire driving, a bag of bones, ancient and desiccated the stench of him made even her flinch. He grinned at her showing blackened stumps, drool pooling and dribbling down his chin, one ear hung by a thread, waving about as he indicated to her to step on board. Downstairs was already full. Aeryissa had no choice but to take them upstairs.

Two old vampire's turned, glaring and hissing at her to go to the back of the bus. Fog covered the windows, like a rider clinging to a horse. The bus rattled and groaned as its cargo of souls cried out at each bump in the road. Her group joining in, she glanced at Fia, she alone was proving harder to control. It seemed to take forever before it was their turn to leave, the directions she had been given vague at best. Clambering down the stairs, she wanted to get off and away from the stares of the elder vampires, all taking much more interest in her and her group than she liked. Pushing them off the bus, Fia the last to leave turned as the doors closed, trapping Aeryissa, her voice blasted through their minds, 'RUN AND HIDE.'

Pulled off the bus in chains, she hung from a wall. Raising her head, Aeryissa could see four vampires seated on a raised dais. Their eyes, unblinking black chasms of pure hate, her senses had locked down as soon as she'd felt the weight of the chains, now they flew outwards bringing back the jumbled thoughts of those watching her.

'Why are you here?' boomed one, who she quickly identified as Mach. 'What's so special about your group to make you enter the Nether? Choosing not to answer isn't an option. We will make you,' he sneered, baring his fangs, pointing his hand, showing her his lengthening talons.

The smaller one approached Aeryissa, the wheedling tone of voice not matched by the violence in his eyes. With four quick slashes he cut her arms and legs, the leather peeling away, the skin underneath now flayed and bloody. Her fangs extended. Smiling at her reaction he reached up and stuck the knife into her belly, gouging her insides, as the others silently watched. She came awake to find several magicals lapping at the blood oozing from her wounds. Trying to shake them off, all she did was make the chains bite deeper into her skin.

Clapping his hands, Mach emerged from the shadows, kicking those too slow to leave her alone, he laughed, 'look at you now, bloody and weak, tell us why you're here and where you are going, and we will let you go.'

'You haven't caught them have you?' she muttered, trying not to breathe too hard. 'They don't really need me. You're wasting your time.'

He punched her hard in her chest, breaking ribs, knocking the wind out of her.

'Perhaps we should kill you and be done with it. You have always been a thorn in our side.'

Looking him full in face, she retorted, 'you're not brave enough to even try. Instead, I shall kill you.'

The next punch knocked her out, he slammed her head back against the wall for good measure. Mach wasn't worried about her threat, she hardly had the strength normally, let alone after all the torture she had undergone. Mempe always went too far, revelling in hurting others, especially women. Angry that her group had so far evaded all efforts to find them. This was their realm, anyone lost inside should be easy pickings. So far all the scouts had come up blank. Pen suggested they let her go, let her lead them to the group. One thing Mach remembered about Aeryissa was her stubbornness, letting her go would only allow her to lead them on a merry dance.

Meg tripped as she ran, banging into Damala and Fia knocking them down. As they fell, Sam, Dillon and Ammon tumbled over their legs. This more than anything saved their lives. Aeryissa was right, Fia had only been slightly compelled. As they ran, it wore off, by the time they fell, she alone was able to push and pull the group into the safety of the shaft they had fallen into.

Sam woke from his trance, eyes wide and startled to see the others sitting like zombies, while Fia gently patted their faces.

Hearing him moan, she called, 'help me wake them up, we must get further into the shaft. We can't move them like this.'

Dillon and Meg blinked and their eyes returning to normal, followed by Damala. Ammon the last to wake up, his bright blue eye a contrast to his paler one, the intensity of his gaze making Sam feel unsettled.

'What happened? Where's Aeryissa?'

'The bus disappeared with her inside. The last thing she said was to run. Compelling me didn't really work. I was able to keep us together, then we fell down here,' explained Fia.

'How are we going to find the post box?' groaned Meg.

'All we can do is hide until Aeryissa can find us,' muttered Damala, her worried expression making them all feel tense.

'What if she doesn't? We cannot stay here; we don't belong, they're all dead and we are alive,' spoke Meg, her eyes darting about, as if expecting someone to jump out at them.

Dillon wished Ammon would turn back into a dog, disliking the stare of his odd eyes.

'Wait,' Sam hushed them, as the shaft started to broaden out, a faint noise could be heard like hearing voices behind a wall.

'Taron, where are you? You shouldn't go running off. What have I told you?' shouted an annoyed voice, getting nearer.

'They're here,' she answered, as a tall long haired vampire emerged from the doorway. Her eyes like her daughters fell on the group.

'I'm Fald and this is my daughter Taron, we have been looking for you.'

'How can a child be a vampire?' blurted out Dillon.

Turning her eyes towards him, she asked, 'do you really not know?'

Blushing bright red, Meg hugged her brother. Thinking; he could always be relied on to say something stupid and break the tension.

Taron laughed, baring her fangs, letting her eyes turn black. Her skin glowed. She waved her talons, capering in front of him. Waiting for her daughter to stop her antics, Fald smiled indulgently.

The large room where they had gathered was surprisingly warm. Its granite stone walls rising up far above their heads, Dillon sat in a corner with Taron, their laughter a welcomed sound, as she repeatedly showed him her tricks. Damala whispered to Ammon who stared at the wall as if not listening. At one point Sam felt sure he saw Ammon's lips move in answer. Fia once again sat alone, still not talking, her silence was beginning to worry him. Not understanding what had happened to make her withdraw into herself. Happy though, to feel Meg's head resting against his shoulder, slightly unnerved to think that Eadulf also rested against him.

Fald had brought them through a series of shafts and tunnels keeping them away from the surface. Only once on their journey had it seemed they had been found. Raised voices and running feet heard in the tunnel they had left, sending all their heart rates into overdrive. Fald had swept them aside into an alcove as if made of paper, once safe, she bade them hurry and follow.

'Aeryissa is being held captive by a vampire called Mach. She knows him and his band of brothers from the past. In here they act even worse trying to lord it over everyone else. They are using the Nether as their "Kingdom," and have gathered together a large number of vampires who are also dissatisfied. He sees her as a threat and a gain. Now that he has her in his clutches he won't want to let her go. She should never have come.'

Feeling bad that because of him she was being tortured, Sam, nevertheless asked, 'what about us? How are we to get to Kingdom? Can you take us to the post box?'

Fald shook her head, 'it has to be Aeryissa she brought you here. The rules are clear. You are subject to her will.'

'What if Mach kills her?'

The same thought flashing through Sam's mind.

'Then anyone can take you.'

'We have to rescue her then,' piped up Dillon.

Taron laughed, 'you're funny. You're no match. They would drain your blood and eat you.'

Dillon paled, in his laughter with Taron earlier, he had forgotten what she was. She may only be young, but standing in front of him now, she was every inch a vampire.

'As soon as Aeryissa set foot in Nether, all would have felt the shift in the air. Unlike the majority of our kind, she is different.'

'So why did she agree to bring us here?' asked Sam.

'Why put herself in danger,' added Meg.

'That I do not know. Mach and his group have been waiting a long time to get their hands on her. They have a "past," they grew up together. Once it was obvious that her powers were more than his would ever be. He became unbearable, hating the fact that she wasn't scared of him. She ignored his threats. Laughed at his pursuit of power.'

'Why has it took her coming into the Nether for him to attack her, surely in Kingdom she was as vulnerable,' asked Dillon, 'she only had Eadulf for company and he doesn't seem up to much.'

'Don't be cruel Dillon, he can hear you,' Meg cuffed his leg.

'We can and are violent, more built for fighting than peace. Which is why Kingdom's law requires us to wear a collar. It keeps our natural instincts in check. Aeryissa is different. She has never worn a collar. Her skills are more enhanced than others of our race. She hasn't yet reached her full potential. Long before she left her family, fractions had been occurring in our clan. Not interested in petty squabbles she wouldn't get involved, preferring to walk away. Mach doesn't want to wear a collar or be governed by those in charge. He has been living in the Nether gathering others of his ilk. Spreading his vile credo. He loves and hates Aeryissa in equal measure and is arrogant enough to believe that he can break her. Capturing any of you as hostages, he would hope to use to force her to stand at his side.'

'So what happens now?' asked Damala, feeling weary, every twist and turn of the journey got more complicated the further they went. Like Sam, she was worried about Fia, even Dillon had quietened down, Taron obviously making an impression on him. The sly looks he gave her and Ammon made her feel uncomfortable. The sooner he could return to being a dog the better. Eadulf was managing to keep Meg calm, she had seen her with her head cocked as if listening to something no one else could hear, often bringing a smile to her face. Sam's response when he caught her doing it, made Damala smile, wearing his jealously like a coat.

'My husband Chronis and others are looking for her. But Mach knows the Nether inside out and has many hiding places we are not even aware of. So we wait.'

Aeryissa came awake, instead of chained to the wall, she was now anchored to the floor. Every bone in her body hurt, her ribs had mended and her cuts no longer bled, a thumping noise pounded inside her head, as if to the beat of a drum. Mach wanted her to stand at his side using words of love to convince her. Snarling at her in temper, when she dismissed the rumours of her powers as fantasy.

Although she knew no one could read her thoughts, she kept them firmly locked inside her head. Allowing only her low level senses to roam outwards to hear the workings of Mach's group, the constant chatter, punctuated by screams and shouts. Recognising their footsteps, she looked up as Mempe and Pen opened her cage. While Pen walked around her, Mempe stood in front, raking her body from top to toe, licking his lips as if looking at a plate of food.

'Still as ugly, I see,' she spat.

His leg lashed out, his boot connecting with her shoulder, from behind Pen also kicked her, his landing in the small of her back, making her crumple forwards, ready for Mempe's boot to hit her other shoulder. Rocked back and forwards by their constant kicking, both Mempe and Pen were sure that Aeryissa must be weakening. Although, Mach had told them to leave her alone, they hadn't been able to resist. Wanting, since their younger days to make her pay for always being much more adept than them.

'Let's bite her.'

Mempe raised his eyebrows at Pen, snapping his jaws at Aeryissa.

Hearing his words she struggled against her bonds, of all the things that could happen, that was the one thing she did not want.

'You must be mad,' Pen, backed away, 'Mach would kill us.'

'How will he know? We can cut her and let the newbie's suck her blood, hide the evidence.' Sneering at Pen's expression, running his hands around Aeryissa's neck, he asked, 'wouldn't you like a taste, she's never been bitten. The first time is always the best.'

Holding up his hands, Pen backed away, as he ran he heard Mempe's manic laughter follow him down the tunnel.

Her whole body quivered, feelings of disgust and revulsion bubbling over. The thought of Mempe, making her feel sick.

'If you do this. I will kill you,' the anger in her voice making him laugh.

'You are tied with chains and not any old chains, you can never break free. Already your skin is turning black where they touch your body, you will die, why waste a good feed.'

'Aren't you worried that Mach will kill you?'

'His power is waning, that's why he wants your help. He uses bluster and force to get what he wants. That isn't enough anymore.' His eyes raked her battered body, licking his lips to see her blood drip. 'I have never believed the rumours about you. You're a woman for a start. No woman is stronger than a man. Even before the beatings you hardly amounted to much. I will be doing him a favour, I can't understand why he hasn't done it already, something to do with "love," I expect. I'm going to enjoy this.'

Swooping down he clamped his jaws onto her neck and bit. As her blood filled his mouth, his whole being flooded with warmth, the transference of power making him sway, drunk on the nectar of her blood. His eyes, black pools of desire stared down as her body slumped sideways; barely breathing, blood dripping from her neck, she gave a shudder and was still.

She remembered wincing when she felt Mempe's jaws worrying her neck, the stench of him rising up, as he drank deep, his fangs scraping her bone in his effort to take it all. Flashes had gone off in her head, her heart raced, she accepted the bite, letting him drink his fill.

Withdrawing his fangs, he dropped Aeryissa like a piece of meat, unheard by him, she sighed in contentment. While she'd slept, the wound in her neck had closed. The ache in her shoulders and back just about bearable after the kicking she had sustained earlier. Glancing around her cage, she suddenly felt hungry and desperately wanted to stretch her aching limbs. Without any thought she reached her arms above her head, the snap of the chains making her smile. As she stood, she peeled her leg chains off like bracelets.

Shaking her hands, stamping her feet, laughing at the feeling of freedom. With one yank the cage door fell, listening for sounds of anyone near, she made her way along the tunnel. Each step she took making her feel stronger.

Standing in the shadows Aeryissa took in the scene before her, Mach arguing as usual with his henchmen, Mempe being the most vocal of the group. Pen leaning against the wall trying not to get drawn in, the first to feel a change in the air, looking around to see what had caused it, his eyes alighted on Aeryissa. Dismissing him with her hand, oblivious to the threat now in the room, he leant back against the wall.

As they squared up to each other she stepped forward into the light.

'Having problems?' she asked, laughing at the surprised expressions on their faces, while Mempe cringed.

'How did you get free?' they asked together.

She pointed at Mempe.

'He bit me.'

'What sort of fool are you?' shouted Mach.

Mempe sneered, 'tasted lovely by the way.' Licking his lips, he leered at Aeryissa.

Mach screamed in fury, his face changing instantly into the predator he was, black eyes blazing, skin shining like a beacon, fangs and talons extending, he leapt at Mempe. Slashing and biting they fought together. As the blood flew, everyone moved back to the sides of the room. Aeryissa watched the display a smile playing on her lips. With one last brutal thrust of his hands, Mempe spun Mach around bouncing him off the walls, kicking and hitting him each time he landed.

Chest heaving he turned to the group.

'I'm in charge. You will obey my command. As for you,' he pointed at Aeryissa, 'you will do as you are told.'

While the fight had been going on, Pen had made moves to leave the room, finding the door sealed. Feeling eyes on the back of his neck, he turned to see Aeryissa looking at him shaking her head. Mach groaned, Aeryissa moved towards him.

'How touching,' sneered Mempe.

She looked him in the eyes, with a quick twist she pulled. In one swift motion she laid Mach's head at Mempe's feet, licking the blood from her fingers.

The vampires reeled back, not understanding what they were seeing. She hadn't changed, she was still small in stature her eyes still grey. They knew she was a vampire, they could smell her scent, but she looked like a norm. Mempe's shocked face stared between Mach's head and Aeryissa's smile. If he hadn't seen it with his own eyes he wouldn't believe it possible. His brain was in a whirl trying to figure out what to do.

'You shouldn't have bit me. Thanks to you, I am awake and becoming.'

Backing away he bumped into Pen, the other vampires ranged behind them. Although they towered over Aeryissa, the power and strength emanating from her was like a presence in the room felt by all.

'Would you prefer me to look more like a vampire when you die? Will, it give you comfort to know that I can be like you?' she asked, staring into Mempe's eyes.

With a shake of her head and body, she grew taller and bigger. Muscles bulged like ropes across her arms and thighs. Her eyes blazed, pits of black, red and orange the colours fighting for dominance. The leather of her clothes covered with runes that chased each other across her body. Shaking her hands as her talons extended, the nails black and razor sharp. It was her shine though, which mesmerised them, all Ambrogio glow with a faint golden light, some more than others. Every part of Aeryissa's skin that showed glowed gold and silver. It sparkled and twinkled at odds with the rest of her appearance. Her fangs lengthened even more, sweeping her gaze over them she attacked.

They lay in heaps, like discarded meat. She had barely drawn breath. Seeing the destruction she'd caused, feeling the magic coursing through her body, made her realise, it wasn't Mempe's bite that had awakened her. It was the killing.

Hearing a commotion getting nearer, the group stood up, even Fald took a step back.

'You're safe,' cried a voice they recognised, if not the person it came from.

In the blink of an eye Aeryissa returned to normal, everyone including Fald drew a sigh of relief, until they realised her size and appearance may have changed. Menace and strength still rolled from her in waves, physically hitting them, making their skin crawl in fear.

'Sorry. There it's off now. You should all begin to feel more comfortable.'

No one knew what to say, relieved she was back, hopeful they could now leave, yet fearful of what had been unleashed and would walk beside them. Dillon fed up with all the waiting, not only did he want to get out of the Nether he also wanted his old friend Ammon back. Hoping Damala's glamour would have worn off by now and he would have been returned to his doggy self.

'Now your back, can we go?' he whined, as Meg frowned at him.

Leaving the tunnels they fell into line, Aeryissa walked with Damala closely followed by Ammon. Meg and Dillon linked arms chattering as only twins could do. Sam accompanied Fia, still worried about her silence, trying several times to engage her in conversation. Realising he was making her uncomfortable he fell back letting her walk alone.

'When we get outside we will be surrounded by vampires,' explained Aeryissa, 'Ignore them as much as you can. When the taxi comes I want Meg to drive, Dillon you are to place your hands onto her shoulders. Damala if you look after Ammon. I will bind Sam and Fia together.' Holding up her hands to still the onslaught of questions, she continued, 'the taxi will take us to the post box. Meg, do not stop for anyone. When we arrive get out as quick as possible. Sam, make sure you have your letter ready to post.'

Without further ado she turned and stepped out into the Nether. As the group emerged, once again they found it hard to see in the gloom. Seemingly from nowhere vampires rose up, the glow from their faces looking like small beacons of light. Aeryissa walked through the crowd which parted as soon as she drew near. The group hurried to keep up, only feeling safe in her slipstream.

Sam thought, seeing the night bus had been hard enough to take in. Waiting for a taxi to appear, topped even that. Damala telling him the Nether was a mixed up realm didn't really help, only making it all the weirder.

'Look,' pointed Dillon.

A taxi sign was getting closer, its orange glow penetrating the gloom. They felt, rather than saw the vampire's move, like a wave of air hitting them.

The taxi stopped, the driver jumped out saluted Aeryissa and took off. Meg jumped in, the others piled in the back. As soon as Dillon placed his hands onto her shoulders the taxi sped off. Aeryissa climbed onto the roof no one questioned how she was going to hold on.

They all concentrated on ignoring the vampires who were throwing themselves at the taxi. Baring their fangs, scraping the paintwork with their talons, thumps could be heard from the roof as Aeryissa fought those who were brave enough to take her on. Several stood in a line across the road, Meg made straight for them. Her foot flat on the accelerator, the engine whining in response, the nose of the taxi crumpled as she hit them. Everyone felt the jolt, flung about inside only Dillon stayed still, his hands firmly placed on Meg's shoulders, shouting into her ears. Sam didn't know much about taxi's back home, but he thought; surely this one couldn't take much more. Both the taxi and the night bus had been hard enough to take in, Sam couldn't help grin when he saw shining like a symbol of home, a bright red and black post box.

The taxi rocked to a stop, as soon as they all tumbled out it disappeared, hurtling down the road, its lights flashing on and off, its horn pressed down by unseen hands blaring out its progress.

'I'll take that,' hands shoved Sam, snatching his letter.

Their faces dropped, they had got so near to leaving. Several vampires had surrounded the post box, their eyes all falling on Aeryissa, some with fear, others with need. A stalemate, no one moved. Sam caught a glance between Damala and Ammon, in an instant he was back to being a dog, only this time much bigger and even more wolf like. With one bound he charged into them biting anything he came into contact with.

Those that hadn't been bitten, fled, those that had, writhed on the floor, clawing at their bites which were growing bigger by the minute.

Feeling his rucksack shift, Sam knew it wanted him to open it, there on the top lay his letter. As soon as he posted it the door opened, they all clambered inside, the door closing with a bang. They shot downwards.

The Enabler had warned Sam that the post box might contain a chute, but not how fast they would move. Ears popping from their descent, coming to a stop, the box literally pushed them out. Even Aeryissa felt its disdain as it slammed the door shut and disappeared.

The post box had dropped them into a bare set of rooms.

'The last obstacle to overcome is the Red Caves, then we will be in Kingdom.'

Aeryissa looked at the avid faces staring at her, hardly able to bring herself to tell them that their troubles were far from over. War had come to Kingdom. They would be stepping right into the thick of it.

'Dare we ask what these caves contain?' laughed Sam, eager to get the job done and find his mother.

'The caves are alive, as such they are an entity in themselves, and will not take kindly to us passing through,' said Aeryissa.

Aware of how exhausted they all looked, she hoped that this last stage would not be as fraught as the Nether had proved to be.

'How do we get in?' asked Damala.

'We checked the walls and couldn't find any doorways,' added Sam.

'Don't look for openings, look for any discolouration of the stone.'

'Do you mean reddish?' asked Meg, pointing into the corner where a faint stain on the lower part of the wall could be seen.

Placing her hands on top of the stain, Aeryissa pressed, at first nothing happened, then the floor slid backward making them all stumble, only she and Ammon able to keep their balance. The wall rose in front of them disappearing far above their heads. Reds of every hue covered everything, making it appear bloodlike. Sam shivered as they crossed the threshold, thinking; it feels as if they had stepped inside someone's body. Sure he could hear the beat of a heart.

They all looked to Aeryissa for guidance on where to go. Fia walked off not waiting for the others to catch up, as she disappeared around a bend in the rocks a wall appeared, banging on it proved fruitless. Hearing rocks sliding, they looked to see the wall behind them start to move downwards.

'Fia knew where she was going,' shouted Damala, 'She hasn't been the same since we entered the Nether.'

An avalanche of rocks began to fall, running away from the onslaught they were brought up short by a wall appearing in front of them. Both Sam and Meg slammed into it, Damala and Ammon skidding into them as another wall fell behind them shutting them in. Only Aeryissa chose to remain as the rocks rained down around her. Dillon hadn't been far of the mark earlier, she thought; divide and conquer, the caves motto. If like her you could read the signs it was written all over its walls. Aeryissa closed her eyes, she'd had enough. They were all exhausted and were in no mood to play the caves games.

'Release them,' she commanded.

Brushing themselves down, Meg grabbed Sam's arm.

'Look.'

Hearing the fear in his sister's voice Dillon looked up, his mouth dropped open. Ammon lay down and placed his head on his paws.

Gone was the small girl they were used to, in her place a magnificent creature of the night, her skin glowing silver touched with gold. Razor sharp fangs didn't detract from her beauty. Sam watched the symbols on her clothes chase each other making him dizzy, noticing how her spurs now adorned her boots back and front their lethal blades glinting with menace.

'You will not hinder our progress but show us the way.' With a flick of her wrist the walls bled as if she were raking her talons down its surface. 'Otherwise, I will destroy you.'

Screaming in fear the walls moved backwards, a path opened in front of them straight and true. The red walls gone, replaced with plain. Aeryissa closed her eyes and was back to normal.

'I'm glad you're on our side,' said Dillon in awe.

Meg and Sam nodded in agreement. Ammon barked. While Damala sighed with worry knowing that once they entered Kingdom, they would all have to take sides.

PART II

Chapter Fourteen

G ilda felt a slight push, a sharp stabbing pain invaded her head, the voice sounding like the scrap of a claw.

'He's here.'

Entering Meridian's quarters was always fraught with danger; her moods if anything had gotten worse. Opening the hall door she could hear her screaming at Katrina. Stepping aside as she came rushing out, the mark of Meridian's slap showing bright red against her pale skin.

'What's happened now?' she asked, more because it was expected, than out of interest.

'Everything.'

'The ring has returned.'

Meridian's hand stopped in mid-air. Smiling, she grabbed her glass downing its contents in one. Her bad mood broken, thoughts of the power she would soon wield, making her blood course faster through her veins.

The Darkness knew it had to keep a close eye on Meridian, her lust for power and dominance hard for her to contain even in its presence. When she'd sent word that the black mirror was missing one last piece; it had lost control, wreaking havoc on those nearest to it. By the time it had finished slaking its anger, the Glasserium looked and smelt like an abattoir.

The memories of its failure still sharp. Instead of ruling like a Lord, it had to hide like a fugitive. Having had a taste of what it felt like to move inside a body, weightless, without form, was something it never wanted to go back to being.

It chuckled, a sound not enjoyed by those working near, sending shivers down their spines. Using the ancient dark spells found by Gilda, Meridian had sent out the call, some pieces practically skipped home in their eagerness to return, others reluctant to be drawn back. As the mirror began to take shape, she put the next part of the plan into action. The appearance of small stones were altered to make them look and feel like glass. The wind and storm Meridian created showered them all over Kingdom, quickly sinking below ground, waiting to be found.

Having spies in the Akiva was an added bonus none of them expected. Informed that the Bodleian had been tasked with finding a way in to the Glasserium, wraiths were sent to destroy their libraries. So far, they had only been able to burn one and that by accident. The spells and incantations put in place, even Gilda and Meridian combined couldn't break. Lost in his thoughts he didn't see the mirror appear. Eyes blazing, his anger flared at the sight.

'Master.'

Meridian dipped her head in deference as she stepped out, closely followed by Gilda.

The mirror cringed, once a pure mirror, now shabby and dirty, tainted by use. It cowered in self-pity every time Meridian used it, wishing it was strong enough to reject her, knowing that if it tried, she would rip it asunder destroying it forever.

Gilda felt a squeeze in her mind as the Darkness turned towards them.

'Why have you come?'

'We wanted to...'

'I have already put plans in place to bring the last piece here.

You are to return to Novia until summoned. Continue the work of gathering magicals and norms turning them to my cause. When I step into Kingdom, the real war will begin. Between the army I have created here and the one you should be creating, Kingdom will be mine for the taking.'

Meridian sat in the dark, the light from the muted candles scattered about the room giving her an eerie glow. The dark magic she'd used for so long had taken its toll on her body. Her once good looks gone. Even she didn't recognise the hag she had become.

The Darkness always wanted more from her, happy in the past to oblige. She had slowly come to resent its requests. Wondering, what was in it for her? As far as she could see, she was doing all the work to make its emergence as a Dark Lord happen. Once these thoughts took over, the dark magic held inside her, started voicing her thoughts back to her. Telling her how she could rule Kingdom. Worn down with their constant refrain, she had started to listen. The Shimmers were the key said her dark magic.

It had taken her weeks of scouring old and dusty grimoire's, dark magic like a bird on her shoulder, constantly urging her on. Tired and fed up she swept the one she was reading onto the floor. It lay open, showing a picture which stewed at the back of her mind, flaring into thought, before other things distracted her. Spurred on to act by Gilda inadvertently picking up thoughts from the Darkness. Making her panic, when told that he planned to kill the Shimmers, destroy the Akiva before taking Verlimusa.

Since then her dreams had been full of black wings beating frenziedly, blood and betrayal. Waking, drenched in sweat, heart thumping, she summoned lights to push the darkness away.

Her call had gone out, from this point on, even if they didn't come; for her, there would be no turning back. The candles flickered, she shivered, trying to stay still and be patient. Opening her eyes she could see shapes emerge, hazy at first before firming up.

'Welcome, please sit.'

Meridian indicated the chairs that had appeared. The wizard's robes crackling as they moved. Pushing back their hoods to reveal craggy faces lined with age and wisdom, dark knowing eyes turned towards her. No one spoke, the silence stretched.

She held up her palms towards the wizards, telling them, 'the room is now secure, all exits sealed. We can talk freely.'

Each speaking in turn they introduced themselves.

'Why have you called us here? You are either brave or foolish,' asked Khalon

The other wizards nodded their agreement.

'If something should go wrong and once again the merging fails, then we have an opportunity to seize control for ourselves. None of us in this room can be trusted,' she cackled, 'that's why I think we can work together. We all want power, yet, we are all held back from taking it by others.'

'Carry on,' Khalon nodded, his interest piqued.

'We trigger the magma, killing the sentries, locking the Shimmers in the Osias, away from the Dark Lord's clutches. Those sent in will be kept by me in stasis. At my command they will either secure the Shimmers and the tomb or kill them and destroy it, should the merging be successful. Without access to either, the Dark Lord's power will be limited.

The wizards looked at each other and laughed. She waited, drawing dark magic around her like a cloak, desperate to blast them where they sat for their levity. The silence lengthened, the wizards shifted uncomfortably under her gaze.

'You want us to send wizards into the Osias, to be covered in magma and then at some later date; be released?' asked Khalon, his disbelief evident at her suggestion.

'Basically yes,' cackled Meridian.

CHAPTER FIFTEEN

'Sam has entered Kingdom,' smiled Elfrad, seeing the look of relief on their faces.

'What are you not telling us?' asked Balin.

Dandelion spoke up, 'the Darkness will want Sam's ring, or at least what it contains. As we speak a large contingent of dark magicals are making their way to intercept him.'

Margaret pleaded, 'why can't you magic a portal?'

Elfrad explained, 'those in league with the Darkness are powerful, they could easily highjack it, meaning we could inadvertently bring them here.'

The door burst open. Dandelion and Elfrad were instantly on their feet, wands drawn at the ready.

'Come quick, we are under attack.'

Rushing into the consul room, they immediately understood the threat. The Plotters had changed the map of Kingdom to show the area surrounding the Akiva. An army had arrived, they had to move fast or all would be lost before it began.

'Listen up everyone,' commanded Dandelion, send the codes, tell the wizards to seal the tunnels. Qiao, you need to go now, before we lock down, are you sure you will be able to get back in again?'

'After all the practice I've done, you're really going to ask me that?'

She smiled in return, 'once you've spoken with the clans, head towards the old collapsed mine. That's where Melock will bring them. The Finns will be honed into your signal, any problems they will relay it back to us. Once you have them come straight back here.'

'Tell Sam I love him,' pulling him into a hug Margaret pecked his cheek.

'I'm not kissing him for you,' he answered in disgust.

Laughing at his expression, she ruffled his hair; 'that was for you.'

Dandelion called out, 'shields up, Finns you concentrate on Qiao. Potts and Lasts take up positions, inform the Plotters of anything you hear or see, no matter how inconsequential it may seem. Let us know as soon as they hit the buffers, hopefully that will be as far as they get. If they manage to get passed them deploy the stars, use the ones to confuse. If they do not stop them, go lethal.'

Hearing a commotion, they all turned as Elfrad strode into the room dragging one of the Otley twins with him. Throwing him to the floor he told them, 'young Coot here was trying to escape, unfortunately his brother Amp managed to.'

'Hand him over to the interrogators. If he is twin linked, then we can use him to find out where his brother is going,' ordered Dandelion.

'It looks like they're making camp. Stopping before the buffers. From what I can see they knew exactly where they start.'

'Are they casting or conjuring?' she asked.

'Neither,' answered the Lasts together.

Fia drew her legs up and wrapped her arms around them, letting out a sigh of weariness as she rested her head onto her knees. Aware the ground around her was getting damp, she stood up. Water spread outwards from her feet, she braced herself for what was to come. Surprised, only to feel a slight tug on her legs before she disappeared underground. The cave dripped with water. As it pooled at the base of the walls, bodies started to emerge. Bowing low, a broad smile lighting up his face, a deep voice spoke.

'Hello, I'm Udadhi and this is my brother Varun. We are your escort.'

Fia smiled at their formality, she had never met any of the Warra before and was surprised to see how solid they appeared, even if they made her feel cold.

Standing either side of her, they explained what they were about to do, assuring her that there was no danger of her drowning. Yet, she couldn't stop the shaking that was running through her body. Eyes wide in fear she waited for the water to surround her. Locking arms together, keeping her in the middle, they covered her head to toe with water. Cocooned inside, she could make out small pin pricks of light filtering through as the water moved.

She tried to breathe normally and not pant for breath, as the next part really would knock her off her feet. Before the thought had formed, she felt the water tighten, filling her up. Swept along at speed, she tumbled and fell. The whooshing she heard, loudest when dragged deep underground. Marvelling at how her body felt so fluid, as it merged with the water surrounding her.

Sam, stepped gingerly outside for his first taste of Kingdom, Ammon, walked beside him, for once also being cautious. Meg, Dillon and Damala quickly followed, while Aeryissa brought up the rear. The noise hit them all, shouting and screaming making Meg cringe in fear. Before he could move forward a man mountain appeared.

'They're here.'

Through the undergrowth another large man appeared. The swords they held still dripped with blood. Making him take a step back.

'It's okay,' Damala told him, 'they're sentinels, warriors.'

'Captain Melock, at your service,' looking at Sam, he said, 'as you can probably hear we are meeting with some resistance, it seems a few others are also interested in your arrival. We have already lost someone from your group and have a long way to go. You will all be safer in the middle of the troop.'

'Wait,' shouted Dillon and Sam together, 'do you mean Fia? She ran away, we thought she was still trapped in the Red Caves.'

'That's how we knew where the exit was. We have been clearing foliage for days trying to find it. She came bursting through and ran into the arms of one of my men. She wouldn't tell us her name or who she was. At the first opportunity she took off, that was three days ago.'

Meg could still feel Eadulf like a cloak over her shoulders, comforted by his presence, yet wondering why he hadn't made himself known. Aeryissa she noticed was also acting strangely. She had seen the Captain give her a sharp look when first introduced, then his eyes seemed to glaze over and after that he ignored her presence. Like Fia, Aeryissa had gone quiet, she was also acting scared, jumping at the least little noise. If she hadn't seen her change into a vampire, thought Meg. She would never believe under the little girl exterior she was projecting; hid the heart and soul of a killer.

Ammon also appeared to be affected by being in Kingdom. Continually looking at Damala as if waiting for some silent instruction. Each time it didn't come, his tail drooped a bit lower. With her thoughts wondering, she nearly missed Eadulf's goodbye, a whisper in her head and he was gone.

The sentinels stopped, all around sounds began to emerge, whistles and clicks getting louder as they drew nearer. The ground shook, trees thrust themselves up from underground, a man and a woman stepped from behind them. Sam's eyes widened, as their skin changed so quickly he couldn't say what colour they actually were.

Dillon leant forwards telling him, 'they're Alvie, foresters who live with the trees.'

'Captain Melock, I'm Hafren and this is my wife Tairlaw.'

'I take it we cannot get any further this way?'

'If you do you will soon run into a contingent of wraiths and witches. At the moment the vampires are keeping them busy. But as fast as they put them down others are taking their place.'

Eadulf peered through the bushes, watching several wraiths pushing and prodding a group of magicals, laughing when they fell over, kicking them to get up. Taking a deep breath, he rushed from his hiding place and straight into the path of the biggest wraith he had ever seen.

'Where did you come from?'

Ignoring his question, he shouted, 'I'm sure they came this way. Why I was given the task of looking after children I don't know. More trouble than they're worth. Are you sure you haven't seen them?'

Eadulf reeled as the wraith cuffed him around the head knocking him to the ground.

Keeping his anger from showing in his eyes and voice, he cried, 'why did you do that? We're on the same side.'

A smaller wraith appeared, demanding, 'Omi do you have to hit everyone that speaks to you?'

Turning to Eadulf he reached out his hand to help him up, 'I heard what you said. I wasn't aware that we had collected any children in this area.'

'We found them by accident, one of them sneezed, they tried to burrow further in, but we managed to root them out.'

'You say we, are the other wraiths lost as well?'

Eadulf tried to look shamefaced.

'They set chase too soon, made them scatter. So like me they are probably out of luck,' shrugging his shoulders to emphasise the point.

Omi grunted, sending dark looks Eadulf's way.

'You had better come along with us. We can always do with more help. Our orders are to sweep up as many magicals in this sector as we can find, they're needed as fuel.'

Eadulf made sure to keep his face blank at the news, hoping that the Darkness hadn't yet merged with his mirror. He needed to get home before that happened.

He winced every time a magical was prodded, a random act committed by Omi. Many more magicals had joined them, the wraiths outnumbered, yet still able to instil fear in their captives. The more he walked through Kingdom's landscape the more it saddened him, colour had disappeared replaced by a dull grey dirty hue. Leeched away, barren and dry. The land shifting as they walked, hills appeared and in the blink of an eye flattened. Water had also disappeared, taken by the Warra. Bez and his cohorts had to conjure it to drink.

Lost in his own thoughts, he only became aware they had stopped when he heard shouting. Fights broke out as several magicals banded together and tried to escape. It seemed at first they may succeed, until Omi waded in enjoying their screams.

Eadulf felt a tremor run through his body. Recognising the signature call of the Glasserium, panic set in as he realised they must be near to an entrance. Moving slowly backwards he allowed the crowd to swallow him up.

'Where do you think you're going? I knew you couldn't be trusted,' sneered Omi.

Eadulf stood still. His mind in a whirl, he had to get into the Glasserium. He could see by the look on Omi's face that he wasn't going to let him go, he would kill him first. Realising he had no choice, he held up his hands in surrender.

The wraith raised his spear rod, before stopping; unable to move. His arm, where Eadulf had touched him, began turning into glass. His eyes frantic with fear, could only watch in silence as it crept over his body. As the last bit slid into place, Eadulf clicked his fingers, shattering Omi into a million pieces. Giving in to the pull of the Glasserium he let it wash over him, until he too disappeared.

Aeryissa melted away, cocking her head listening to the sounds of fighting, she wasn't aware of the trees slowly moving away from her. Sunlight hit her skin, for a moment she allowed herself to bask in its warmth. Hearing a gasp, she reacted, grabbing a witch that had somehow stumbled into her path. Admonishing herself for being lax in her defences, she held him at arm's length, eyes bulging; leg's kicking in protest at her hand around his neck.

'Who are you?' she demanded, letting him fall to the ground.

Panting for breath, he rubbed his neck.

'Perical, please don't kill me.'

Drawing a door symbol in the air, she dragged him through. Safe from prying eyes.

'Tell me what's happening.'

As his eyes clouded over, he chanted, 'friends are enemies. Enemies are friends; One last piece. The Norm has it. The Dark Lord will rise. Kingdom is lost.'

'Why were you running?'

Perical whined, 'Ambrogio, they attacked my group ripping them apart. I was lagging behind so I hid. I didn't want to come in the first place. I want to go home.'

Sitting in the quiet room she had created, she pondered how she was going to pass through Kingdom. If she used her skills or magic too much, remnants of her signature may be picked up. Different from other vampires it would stand out, inviting interest. Realising Perical had fallen asleep she nudged him with her foot. Waking, he backed away, rubbing his eyes as if unsure at what he was seeing.

'You're a girl,' he stammered.

Laughing, she flicked her hair over her shoulder. 'Well I should hope so, are you feeling better? I found you on the path. You don't appear to be injured. Do you feel okay?'

'My head hurts,' standing up made him sway, 'it's not safe around here. You should go home.'

'Can I come with you?'

'Why would you want to come with me?'

Allowing a smile to light up her face, a slight blush to form on her cheeks, Aeryissa looked up from under her eyelashes. Twirling a strand of hair around her finger, she cooed.

'I'm frightened. You are a strong witch. I'm not much good at even small magic.' Letting her lips tremble, she added, 'I don't have anyone to take care of me.'

Flummoxed by this turn of events, Perical pulled his shoulders back, thinking; he could always offer her up to save himself.

'What's your name?' he demanded.

'Aer. Can I come with you?' she pleaded, letting her eyes fill with tears.

Perical nodded, letting a superior tone enter his voice, he told her, 'you may, but you have to do as I say. Kingdom is a dangerous place.'

Brushing down his dirty robe and running his hands through his scraggly hair, his brown eyes glazed over as Aeryissa collapsed the room. Waiting for him to steady himself, picking up the nearby sounds of magicals. Wanting to hurry him along, she said the magic words.

'Someone's coming.'

Damala had seen Aeryissa slip away. Nudged by Ammon she knew it was time they also left. Sure though, if they went Dillon would kick up a fuss, exactly what they didn't need.

'Can I have a word? It's important,' she asked, waiting until the food had been cleared away.

Meg asked, 'what's the matter?'

Waving her hand, Ammon came and sat down next to her, much to Dillon's disgust, still jealous of anyone receiving his affections other than him.

Looking at each in turn, she told them, 'I have enjoyed our adventures. Well most of them. Now though, it's time for us to go and as such we leave together tomorrow,' she stroked Ammon, looking at Dillon so he knew what she meant.

Flouncing off before she'd finished speaking, he ignored Meg's entreaties to be reasonable.

Flicking her hand and muttering a spell, Damala changed into a dull brown robe. Wriggling, her toes in her soft leather boots she pulled her cape around her shoulders fixing the hood in place. Ammon peered up, his brown eyes speaking volumes. The next part of their journey together would be the most dangerous.

'Ready,' she asked.

Ammon bounded ahead, nose extended, ears alert to the noises of a new day. It didn't take them long to realise they were being followed. Damala waited, sitting on a pile of rocks as if she hadn't a care in the world. Believing he had lost them, Dillon came crashing through the undergrowth, taking no notice of his surroundings or who might be waiting in his eagerness to find them.

'I wondered how long it would take you to catch up.'

Brought up short by the sound of her voice, feeling a nudge behind his knees as Ammon barrelled into him making him stumble.

'I'm not going back,' he yelled.

Damala's annoyed look, made him cross his arms, plant his feet, defiance sweeping across his face.

'What about Meg? She's your twin as well as your sister, you can't leave without telling her.'

'I've left a note. Besides; she has Sam and Captain Melock, to look after her. If you send me back I will follow. I want to help with… Whatever it is you are going to do.'

'But can I trust you to do as I say? Kingdom is at war, tantrums will not be tolerated.'

Ammon's growl made the decision for them, frightened voices getting nearer drew them together. Squeezing between a dead tree and a rock fall, they huddled together with Ammon between them. Dillon shook, as the voices turned into blood curdling screams making his skin crawl in fear. Ammon pressed close, his warmth a welcome friend.

By the time they had eaten breakfast it was clear that Dillon was nowhere to be seen.

'What's wrong?' asked Captain Melock, hearing the commotion.

'Dillon's gone,' answered Sam. 'He must have left after we all went to bed.'

'We must go after him. He could be lost or injured.'

Catching the Captain's eye, Sam told her, 'we can't Meg, it's too dangerous. We don't know which way he or they went.'

'I'm afraid your brother will have to take his chances. Now, please gather up your things, we need to get going.'

Ammon lay down beside them head on his paws. Dillon sighed with impatience, knowing this meant more waiting. Their journey so far to get here had been a roller coaster ride. So busy blaming Damala for their predicament. His shouting had alerted the wraiths to their approach. Out of nowhere they wrestled him to the ground, knocking Damala over and kicking Ammon. Ready to deploy their spear rods.

They fell like skittles. A blur of movement, grunts, shrieks and horrible sucking sounds rent the air. Looking up they found Aeryissa covered in blood, staring down at them.

'They have set up camp in the valley between the two mountains. From what I heard they intend to stay there for a while. They are searching for something.'

'Not Cardew, I hope,' said Damala.

Ammon reacted to the tone in her voice with a low growl.

Standing inside the mountain, Dillon felt sick. The last time he'd entered one, it hadn't been the best of experiences. As soon as Aeryissa told them how they could bypass the camp, his back had started hurting. Even nudges from Ammon couldn't give him any confidence. Her assurances this was a mountain with only tunnels inside did nothing to a lay his fears. Especially when told she wouldn't be coming with them.

Ammon stopped, in a flash he ran between them, his barks echoing, bouncing off the walls. Frozen, Dillon stood in fear, while Damala smiled to see a large wolf emerge from the dark. As the light hit its face it stopped. Like a tableau they all waited, Ammon padded forwards, the wolf lay down.

'It seems we have another companion,' chuckled Damala.

Whereas Ammon's fur was dark, this new wolf's was snowy white with a few touches of brown scattered here and there. A she wolf, her eyes swept over Dillon, brushing herself against him as she passed. He automatically reached out a hand passing it across her soft fur.

They trudged for what seemed like hours, finally, they came to a large hill, as they crested the top; in front of them lay the Folded Valley, nestled between two large ridges. Used to the magic of Kingdom, even Damala gasped at the sight of it. Three layers sat one on top of the other. The bottom looked like normal scrub and dirt, clumps of misshapen bushes trampled as if by many feet lay scattered, tossed aside carelessly across its surface. The second layer's earth and roots hung down like a curtain above the first. This too looked bare of life. The third was open to the sky, its earth and roots red in colour hanging in a tangled mass. Silence held sway. A dead place.

Ammon sat on his haunches, with a flick of his tail he headed down the hill making for the lower fold. Following, the white wolf made sure to stay between Damala and Dillon. They waited at the entrance, Dillon the only one not aware of why they didn't cross it straight away. Impatience, made him step forward, Ammon growled, his fangs showing, stopping him in mid stride.

Damala whispered, 'the landscape may look empty but it isn't. Ammon is trying to dredge up from his memory a safe path. But it was a long time ago and the folds would have changed their structure many times since then.'

At last they were ready, all nervous of stepping under the upper fold. The earth looked as if at any moment it could fall down, smothering them. Halfway across things started to change, small clumps of soil began to fall like rain. Ruts appeared running across the ground like snakes on the hunt for prey. The dried up bushes had somehow coalesced together making a hedge, cutting across their path; halting their progress, swaying and bending. Their dry leaves crackling the sound both sinister and normal. Part of it shot out and grabbed a hold of Dillon, quickly wrapping itself around his arms pulling him towards its centre. Screaming in fear, the more he wriggled the more entangled he got. Damala tried to use her weakened magic. Instead, it bounced off knocking her from her feet. Dillon caught like a fly in a trap. Thrown through the air he narrowly missed careering into Damala. In seconds the landscape returned to its previous bare look. Shaken to the core they followed the wolves. Astonished as the valley folded in on its self, over and over. Disappearing, until all that remained was a flat landscape, nestling between two hills.

'Good sleep?' asked Damala, ignoring his raised eyebrows at her companions.

Looking directly at the man, Dillon demanded, 'why have you conjured him again?'

The woman laughed, her eyes raking his face making him feel uncomfortable.

'Who is she?' his anger making him snarl, which only made her laugh more.

'I'm Layla.'

He staggered in shock as they changed into wolves before reverting back to their magical forms. Dillon sat on his hands to stop them shaking, as three pairs of eyes watched him steady himself.

The voice when it came was rich, deep and musical.

'I am the King.'

Dillon couldn't help it, he laughed, making himself choke with the effort to stop.

'I hope everyone doesn't react like that,' retorted Bardolpf, looking affronted.

Safely inside the castle he could at last feel the tension leave his body. It felt strange to be upright, although his wolf and magical self were separate, parts of each over lapped. Bardolpf smiled to see Dillon flitting about the great hall, touching the armaments trying on helmets and brandishing the small swords that he could reach.

Damala felt apprehensive. Everyone had to be focused on getting the Maia near enough to be used against the Dark Lord. If Bardolpf was seen too soon, everyone would be distracted by his presence. Worrying at the problem, she didn't hear what Layla said.

'How strong is your glamour magic?' she repeated.

'Sorry, I was miles away. Why do you ask?'

'Would it be strong enough for you to make me appear as Bardolpf?'

'Even if I could, the Baldassare wouldn't follow you. Without them no one would believe that you were a king.'

'What if we used the sentinels? Do you think we could pull it off?'

Bardolpf left the great hall and made his way towards his father's rooms. He had mixed feelings about being back inside Cardew. Standing before his family pictures made him feel sad. Because his brothers had been killed by the Iwatoke, and his father subsequently died after fighting the Darkness, their portraits contained no life. Their dead eyes unnerved him, the weight of their deaths heavy in his heart. Laying down he closed his eyes, letting himself drift back, allowing the memories to flow...

Hugging the knowledge to himself, Bardolpf couldn't wait to leave the castle and try out the skill he'd been gifted. Finally, in desperation he had convinced his friend Isandro to swap clothes. They had a vague look of each other apart from their eyes. Tasking him with moving around the castle he hoped that everyone would assume that it was him.

The Shimmer had told him that to become a wolf all he had to do was believe that he was one. Visualise himself changed and it would be so. Screwing up his eyes bringing the image of a large wolf to mind, he imagined turning into one. After several failed attempts he gave up.

Opening the bag that contained his bread and cheese, Bardolpf sat with his back against a gnarly old oak, the shade from its branches a welcome relief from the hot sun beating down. He hoped Isandro was okay and not in any trouble, he hadn't expected to be out so long. He remembered falling asleep, when he woke it was nightfall. He immediately knew something was wrong. The forest was making a low moaning, the sound entering his body and mind making him unsettled. Fear made him stand, he had no weapons. His eyes raked the ground in front of him looking for a stick, anything he could use to defend himself.

As the ground split apart, a tree hauled itself up filling the sky blocking the sun. Bardolpf stood mouth agape.

Shaking his branches Fingerling sighed in distress, 'there is no easy way to tell you this. You cannot go home. Your brothers have been killed, and your father is dying.'

'How...? When...? I don't... I must get back.'

'You cannot. Everyone believes that you have also perished.'

'Isandro,' he whispered. 'I must, surely if my father dies I will be King. How did this all happen? I have only been away for a few hours.'

'You have been here over a month, sleep has been your saviour,' said Fingerling, his heart aching at the distress he was causing Bardolpf.

Anger pulsed through his trunk, spilling over to be felt by all the trees in Kingdom. He couldn't let him go back, dark forces were still at large, intent on murder and mayhem. Bardolpf was to be kept hidden until the threat had been dealt with.

A large tree gently scooped him up nestling him within its branches. The swaying of the tree soon sending him off to sleep, fit full dreams filling his mind. Calling his brothers names over and over, searching for his father, sadness filling his body, he cried in his sleep. His low moaning making the oak croon to him as a mother would to a baby.

Waking, he rubbed his eyes, for a moment forgetting what had happened. He found himself in a small clearing, the oak tree which had brought him, standing guard. Out of thin air a picture began to emerge, tiny at first, until the frame expanded and pulled it into shape. He had never met Vidya, the leader of the Froade, instantly though, he knew who she was. Beckoning him to enter he grasped the sides of the picture frame and immediately was pulled in. Landing in a heap, he smiled his apology for his unceremonious entry.

'Fingerling has told you what has happened?' enquired Vidya. Without waiting for his answer she continued, 'it was your cousin Abaddon who instigated their deaths. Those who worked with him have escaped. In Pictures you will be safe. But you will still have to keep hidden and not draw attention to yourself.'

Vidya watched Bardolpf, the news of his cousin's involvement something he couldn't grasp. Or how much danger he was in. Looking up, she pinned him with her eyes, letting her owl senses flood her body. She grew larger, towering over him, filling the room. Spreading her wings she enveloped him. The images of his brothers deaths by the Iwatoke made him rear back in horror. Watching his father's battle to kill Abaddon shocking in its intensity, his death from the shard of black mirror, slow and painful.

Sobbing, Bardolpf felt bereft, all his family gone, homeless and if known about, hunted. He had no idea what he was going to do.

Vidya knew what skill he'd been given, he had to find a way within himself to set it free.

'You must change into your wolf form before you leave this room.'

'I tried to change. But I couldn't. No matter how much I focused.'

'What does your mind conjure up at the thought of being a wolf?'

'Stealth and freedom.'

He knew he'd changed, even if he hadn't heard the gasp from Vidya. Seeing the world from the perspective of being on all fours he found the strangest. Ears pricking at the smallest sound, while his snout wrinkled at all the myriad of smells it could pick out. Heart thudding, Bardolpf could feel the power of his blood flooding through his body. His paws splayed ready for him to spring into action. His jaw opened wide as he yawned showing his fangs. Shaking his head to clear the last dregs of the inertia he'd been feeling. He barked at Vidya telling her he was ready.

When Bardolpf met Damala, he had been roaming inside Pictures for a long time. His ears pricked up as he twitched in his sleep, it was her singing that had awoken him, a nursery rhyme he remembered hearing when younger. Raising his head he sniffed the air, drinking in her scent. Nothing but goodness resounded back, she smelt like vanilla. Standing up he arched his back stretching the muscles.

'Hello my lovely, look at the size of you. Why don't you join me for a swim?' she asked, as her dress changed into a costume.

With one leap he landed. Laughing delightedly Damala splashed him in turn. Afterwards they went everywhere together, she found out he wasn't really a wolf by accident. In mid-flight his senses had picked up a scent he'd smelt before and didn't like. He landed badly, a sharp pointed rock stabbing into his pad, when she pinched the sides he growled low in his throat, not in warning, but in pain. She was at a loss as to what to do, or where she could take him for help. The magic she'd tried to use had appeared to be working. Then within minutes the wound was back looking exactly the same.

Changing himself back into his magical form, his hand bore the wound, the cut deep and oozing pus. Using his magic, he cast a healing spell over it, the pus fizzled and dried up, the wound drawing its sides closed. Aware of someone standing behind him Bardolpf slowly turned.

'Well this, I didn't expect,' said Damala, seeing his outstretched hand, the wound now sealed.

'It's a good job that in your wolf form your eyes are brown, even having seen you only the once, and that from a distance. With your odd coloured eyes it means that, it can only be you, Prince Bardolpf. Remembering what happened to his family she whispered, 'which makes you now my King.'

Holding out her hand Damala waited for Bardolpf to grasp hers.

'We are friends; we can look out for each other. When it is safe to do so, you can change into your magical form and we can chat. Obviously while you're in wolf form, I shall talk and you will have no option but to listen,' she chuckled to see the look on his face.

The tension he'd been holding dissipated.

'Damala, I would be happy to call you friend. It has been lonely without someone to talk to. Plus, like you, I cannot return to Kingdom. As you say, together we can watch each other's backs.'

Finding Dillon in Long Meadow had also been by accident. He had gone off exploring and found him lying in the long grass. Sitting on his haunches, mouth relaxed his brown eyes stared willing him to be friendly. He liked his smell, it reminded him of Isandro.

That was the start of their friendship. Everyday Ammon tried to visit, telling Damala, but not wanting her to come. Racing with Dillon made him feel free the pure joy in chasing and being chased, with no hidden agenda.

Meeting Sam had been the catalyst to where he was now. Risking his life to find his mother made Bardolpf ashamed of how he had hidden himself away. Determined to play his part in saving Kingdom, when he and Damala joined Sam's journey, they both knew he would have to one day shrug of his wolf form to become the king he was always meant to be.

After her conversation with Layla, Damala needed to speak to Aeryissa, inside Cardew no messages could get in or out. She had pondered the problem on how to go about it, finding a secluded spot in the garden she settled down to give her idea a try. Sitting quietly she slowed her breathing, and let her mind focus. A large silver coloured beetle with splashes of blue across its back emerged. When the beetle reached her hand, Damala opened it palm up.

Smiling, she bent forwards, whispering her instructions. The beetle folded back into its shell, scuttled back and burrowed back down into the earth.

'I've sent the message to Aeryissa. We will take it as read that she agrees.'

'Do you think it will work?'

'Truthfully, I don't know. If it does though, it will be a surprise not only for the dark forces, but for the magicals. I still see Meridian as our most lethal enemy. The Dark Lord, for whatever reason hasn't been able to reach his full potential. Even though he can only be killed by the Maia, he still doesn't feel such a threat as Meridian and her cohorts. No one knows about you. Imagine how everyone will feel when they find out, their King is alive. It will give everyone such a boost and our enemies pause for thought.'

CHAPTER SIXTEEN

Sam felt wretched, Meg wouldn't talk to him, following behind he could see that every line of her body exuded anger. The Alvie led the way, their bodies constantly changing colour to blend in with their surroundings, making it hard sometimes to see where they were. He kept glancing at the sentinels, at the least sound they were off, often coming back wiping their swords clean of blood.

Seeing the set of Meg's shoulders reminded him of his mother, not often stubborn, when she was though, then there was no changing her mind. Hoping that when they met they would like each other, surprising himself at how important it was that they did.

During their trek to Turtle River, trees appeared and disappeared so much that he had come to expect it. Now though, the landscape in front of them was empty, not a tree or bush in site. Barren, dry and so quiet he could hear the clunk of the sentinel's shields knocking against their breastplates.

Pulled from his thoughts, he sighed in happiness, as he felt Meg's hand slip into his. Like a mirage, water appeared out of nowhere, instead of dry earth, a river flowed.

So engrossed in saying their goodbyes, they hadn't taken any notice of the boat. Seeing the confusion on their faces, Captain Melock explained.

'It is made of water. Nevertheless you will remain dry, treat it like any other.'

As he stepped aboard, the boat rocked gently, holding hands for moral support Meg indicated that Sam should sit first, wanting to see if he got wet from the seat. Shaking his head, he pulled her down beside him.

They both nearly fell overboard when a large volume of water appeared and formed into the body of a man. With one heave he pushed the boat away from the shore disappearing under the bow as the boat picked up speed.

Melock watched them both. He had given Meg her assurances that her brother was indeed with Damala and Ammon. They had been sighted by a seeker as they entered a valley and disappeared amongst the trees. He couldn't help thinking though, that Sam may be in for a shock. Margaret was nothing like the mother he had said goodbye to, not only in looks but in her whole demeanour. From the conversation they had earlier he still expected to find her downtrodden and nervous. He also wondered how he will cope when meeting Balin and finding out who he was.

The boat began to slow down. He peeled his eyes away from Sam and scanned the water's edge. It wasn't far to the collapsed mine where they were to meet Qiao, however, a lot could happen to those who were not vigilant.

As soon as they touched the shore, Pelagias disappeared taking the boat and water with him. Once again the land lay before them dry and barren.

'Quickly, it's not far.'

'There you are.'

They turned to see a boy with hair sticking up all over the place, gangly limbs evident as he hopped from one leg to another.

'Your mother,' he announced, 'is my friend.'

Sam didn't know what to say in answer, feeling that he was being challenged in some way.

Meg broke the standoff, saying, 'I'm Meg,' laughing, as she added, 'Sam's friend.'

'I nearly forgot, Margaret told me to tell you that she loves you. I told her that there's no way I'm kissing you.'

Qiao grabbed their hands, Sam felt as if his body deflated and filled out again all at the same time, his head spun and his heart beat erratically in his chest. For the second time in his life he fainted.

Opening his eyes he smiled to see his mother sitting beside him rubbing his hand. Sitting up, he became aware of a man standing behind her reminding him of someone.

'Are you feeling better?' we have a lot to discuss.' Turning to Margaret, Dandelion added, 'I know you want to spend time alone,' her eyes flicked to Balin. 'Unfortunately the situation is getting urgent.'

Margaret felt torn, wanting to tell Sam about his father in private in case he took it badly. At the same time, he needed to know the part he was playing in Kingdom's future. She took a deep breath, blurting out.

'Barry isn't your father.' Looking him in the eye, she added, 'Balin is.'

The silence in the room wrapped around Margaret, fearful that he wouldn't forgive her deception. Surprising her when he laughed.

'Don't look so worried mum. Barry has already taken great pleasure in telling me that I am not his son.' His eyes flicked to his father, 'what I don't understand is why you couldn't have told me before you left.'

Margaret looked again to Balin and nodded.

'I'm sorry that we couldn't have told you privately. To cut a long story short, a black mirror is being reassembled, one piece is missing.' Pointing to his ring, Balin continued, 'the last sliver is embedded in that. I come from a family of ring bearer's, our task, to keep the ring safe in Novia. When I left, I gave it to your mother telling her that I would return.'

'He didn't know I was pregnant. He couldn't get a message to me, or I to him.'

'Because you are my son and are wearing the ring, you are now the bearer. The Darkness will want it. It cannot be taken from you. You have to want to give it up.'

Dandelion interrupted, 'in Novia you would have been vulnerable to attack from his cohorts. Here in the Akiva we can protect you.'

Sam raised his eyebrows and looked at Meg who seemed as stunned as him by what they were hearing.

'If getting me here was that important, surely someone could have found an easier way for me to travel. Meg, will agree it hasn't been a picnic.'

'So what happens now? Does it mean Sam can never leave here? Can I? Or am I also a prisoner? We thought we were going to find his mother and...'

Meg shrugged her shoulders as Sam snapped.

'Go home.'

'We're sorry that you are both being thrown in at the deep end. We are at war and cannot leave the safety of the Akiva,' explained Dandelion. 'Our forces are ranged far and wide across Kingdom, fighting is breaking out everywhere. The Darkness determined to make sure we are kept busy. False information is being spread. By the time we realise, we are either ambushed, or too far away from what is really happening to engage. The ring you wear is our last hope. We may be stuck inside the Akiva. But at the same time, the Darkness is stuck inside Glasserium, a stalemate. Both sides are relying on their armies of magicals to tip the balance.'

Qiao, staggered as he appeared, his voice breaking as he shouted.

'It's worse than we thought. The clans are not coming to help. All entrances are barred. Any clan members that are outside be they fighting or not, cannot now enter. The leaders ambushed and taken away.'

'What about the Ambrogio? Lefu is not only a vampire but higher magical, how have they managed to take or even subdue him,' demanded Elfrad.

'When I appeared I practically fell over a turned vampire, she was hiding, terrified at what she had witnessed and heard. It was a bloodbath. Many magicals lost their lives. A powerful witch appeared, casting a spell linking his chains and collar to everyone in his clan. If any tried to take them off, the silver inside would be released killing them.' With tears rolling down his face, Qiao continued, 'the Fae were next. I travelled on to their grotto. The news gets worse. Zekia's dragon died trying to protect her. They set it alight from within itself. It died in agony while they made her watch.'

'Why have we heard nothing of this until now? When I came in the Plotters and the clan stations were calmly coordinating the latest round of skirmishes. How come the Lens and Lobes are not picking up what is happening?'

'I fear,' answered Elfrad, that isolating ourselves to keep the ring safe, may also be stopping us from receiving information on what is truly happening in Kingdom.'

Dandelion brooded on the news received from Qiao, letting the chatter in room wash over her. The priority must be to keep the last piece of glass safe from being used. At the same time sitting locked inside the Akiva was no longer an option.

She stood up silencing everyone.

'Qiao, come with me. Elfrad I need you to speak to those members of the clans that are in the Akiva or out in the field. Find out what they know. Observe the Plotters, have they been compromised. Double the guard on Coot, and take our friends to the Sanctuary.'

Elfrad watched the Plotters at work. Information usually came into the stations from clan members outside of the Akiva. Once they had updated their system, it was drawn down by the Plotters, added to the picture hovering in the centre which then in turn updated the maps. Except that wasn't happening, a pattern soon emerging, the same information was being fed over and over. Once the information hit the maps for a few seconds it stayed before the new data would disappear.

In fact when he concentrated on watching the maps update, the details stayed the same. Making it appear the Darkness's cohorts were far away from the Akiva and the clans were still in play. It had been compromised, if he couldn't find out how, he would have to shut it down making them even more vulnerable. Clapping his hands to get everyone's attention he raised his voice and shouted.

'Anyone not working at a station please leave.'

Turning at the sound of his voice their blank eyes sought his. He hoped they looked tired and had not been taken over. Sentinels surrounded the room, snapping his fingers, Elfrad locked the door hearing mutterings behind him as the clans wondered what was wrong.

'We have been told that some of your leaders have been or are in the process of being taken, crippling your clans. The information you are receiving is the same each time. How are you unaware of this?'

Each clan member started talking at once, getting louder the angrier they got. Elfrad waited patiently letting them have their say. As they ran out of steam, he was convinced the problem wasn't with them. As the air moved around them, the sentinels drew their swords, sheathing them as Dandelion and Qiao appeared. Somewhere on her journey she had lost her air of defeat.

Striding to stand in front of Cian, she commanded, 'take off your collar.'

Even the sentinels blanched at her words. A vampire of Cian's power could decimate them all with one hand tied behind his back. Doing as she commanded, he allowed a smile to form, aware everyone had taken a step back. Holding his collar in his hands, Cian could feel his blood start to pound through his body. Immediately his eyes changed colour from the blue he kept them at, changing into a deep red. At the same time his fangs lengthened and his talons unsheathed. Dandelion and Qiao smiled, while Elfrad looked puzzled as she told Cian to put it back on. A sigh of relief went around the room.

'Do you mind telling me what that was all about,' he asked touching his collar.

Ignoring Cian's question, she turned to Rayna, 'see that chair can you destroy it.'

Raising her eyebrows in enquiry at the request, she waved her hand. Her fairy dust lifted and flew towards it. Falling like rain, it covered the chair breaking it into pieces.

Dandelion glanced at Haiwee, asking the Kaimi to change, confused as the rest of them she turned into her bird form. Flapping her wings, giving them a stretch before turning back.

'Thank you. The reason I asked you all to use your skills is because the Darkness must be capturing the leaders to neutralise them and subsequently their clans. I believe the only reason you have kept yours intact is because you are inside the Akiva. Our shields appear to be holding, the magic used on your clans hasn't so far affected you.'

'Unless of course you leave,' added Qiao.

'And the rest of you?' asked Elfrad.

Hafren and Tairlaw produced their nets, letting their skin change colour so that they blended into the room making them hard to see. Whampool flicked her wand, rising off the ground only stopping when she hit the ceiling. Drawing a symbol in the air, her staff rose up turned on its side allowing her to sit and float gently down. The Lasts joined in letting their eyes and ears grow, allowing the sights and sounds of the Akiva and beyond to wash over them.

The witches each held their hands palm up, producing a small dome. Inside fire, water and earth appeared. A swirling wind filled another, while a white feather floated in the air in the dome beside it. The last to appear a sun and a moon, enchanting everyone, making the domes look like small worlds all of their own.

Producing a small blue book from her pocket Dandelion opened it and tapped its middle.

'When we find something, we will let you know. Keep interrupting us doesn't help,' exclaimed Gerringong tetchily.

'Do you know where Flinders is? Have you spoken to him lately?'

Pulling himself further from the book he frowned, seeing their worried looks.

'What's wrong?'

'They are targeting the clans. Some leaders have already been taken. Forget about finding a way into the Glasserium. Concentrate on protecting the libraries at all costs.'

Not bothering to reply, he faded back into the book closing it with a bang.

While Dandelion had been talking, Elfrad kept glancing over to the Plotters. Catching her eye he nodded in their direction. Raising her hand she drew it across her throat. Silently the sentinels fell on them, their swords cutting a swath through the Plotters bodies. Everyone watched in horror as a thick black cloud unfolded. Hafren and Tairlaw quickly threw nets. It writhed and boiled as Rayna sent her fairy dust to cover it, losing power as they took effect. Stunned at the thought of what had been amongst them, Dandelion indicated everyone should follow her, leaving the sentinels to seal the room.

Chapter Seventeen

Margaret sighed in contentment, thinking, with Sam on one side and Balin on the other, sanctuary felt like a little taste of heaven. A calm space in a sea of mayhem. She looked up to see Anglas smiling at the three of them as she made her way across the garden to Meg.

Sam looked at his father, unsure how to address him, taking a deep breath, he asked.

'Balin, I know you said that I had to want to give up the ring. Surely though, it could be taken from me by force?'

'It cannot. When my father passed it to me, he told me that the magic woven into it is both ancient and powerful. So much so that even if I were to be killed, it still couldn't be taken from me.'

Digesting this news, Sam wished he had never put the ring on in the first place.

'Is there no one here who I can give it to? Then at least I would be able to go home. I know mum, you want to stay. Personally, I've had enough of Kingdom.'

Balin could see unhappiness crush Margaret on hearing Sam's words. All she had been able to talk about was how good it was to have the two she loved most, together at last. He'd told her that now he didn't have the responsibility of the ring anymore he wanted to stay. She had readily agreed, even with all the battles taking place she'd told him she had begun to feel more at home in Kingdom than she ever had in Novia.

He smiled, still surprised at how much alike they looked. Sam a younger version of himself.

'You can only give the ring to either a Shimmer or the Darkness.'

An ear splitting explosion rent the air, thrown onto the floor, bricks and rocks rained down. Sam could hear his mother and Balin groaning, shaking his head to clear the ringing in his ears, he pushed the debris off their bodies, shocked to see their faces cut and bloody. Balin the first to open his eyes.

'What happened?'

Before he could answer, strong arms grabbed him from behind. Seeing the look of fear on his mother's face, he quickly realised, he wasn't being helped, but taken. Balin launched himself at Sam's attacker. No match for the wraith who backhanded him, flinging him towards the wall, hitting it with a thud, his body dropping like a stone. Margaret screamed in fear and anger, grabbing the wraiths legs, holding on for dear life, making him stumble enough for Sam to pull free. Holding his mother's hand he pushed her towards the corridor, straight into the arms of another wraith. The one they made stumble, held tightly to Balin, once again grabbing Sam. Dragging them both through the rubble they were joined by a group of witches.

A boy stepped out from behind a large wizard and commanded, 'take them through the tunnels, if any one tries to stop you, kill them.'

Several explosions had rocked the Akiva at the same time. Dandelion had managed to contain most of the damage. Thinking at some stage this may happen. Spells had been cast so that any blasts would be sucked away. Not all had worked. Monitoring the army gathered outside, she found it strange that none of them made a move towards the Akiva. Expecting an assault team to arrive at any moment she had prepared everyone on what to expect.

The Lasts burst into the room.

'The wizard Einar has opened his tunnel. Dark magicals have taken the ring bearer. The explosions were a distraction.'

No trace of them could be found, only Meg cowering in fear, Anglas dead beside her.

Crammed into a small cell Margaret held hands with Balin and Sam. Tremors shook her body, her mouth dry with fear, Balin tried to smile, but it looked more of a grimace. Sam stood quietly as if accepting his fate. A witch glared at them through the bars of the cell. Told to watch, she stared, flicking from Sam's face to his finger.

The sound of many boots approached, a tall white haired witch, touched the bars which quickly opened, her eyes shone as they alighted on the ring.

Crooking her finger, Sam began to walk towards her, Margaret and Balin made a grab for him and were flung back into the cell unable to move.

'Give me your ring,' she commanded, holding out her hand.

'No.'

Making a fist of her hand she squeezed it tight, crushing his heart, his eyesight blurred as lights went off in his head.

Tears coursed down Margaret's face, unable to move, she could only watch as the witch killed her son. Sam fell to the ground, she screamed thinking him dead, while Balin shouted his name over and over. Seeing how emotional they were Meridian snapped her fingers and drew them out of the cell.

They dropped beside Sam feeling for a pulse. Both smiling as they felt it faintly move. Cradling his head Margaret looked up. Gilda heard her thoughts, glad that she was only a norm and not a magical.

'Bring them.'

Pushed and pulled along, held up by his parents, Sam felt dizzy. They entered a tunnel, the cold like ice cutting through their bodies. The rocks partly dug out from the cave were black and jagged.

Yawning open, it looked like the pits of hell, the air emanating from inside thick and cloying as if alive. Two wraiths manhandled his parents inside.

At first nothing happened, then rocks started moving, the sound loud and grating. Black dust burst forth covering the air around them before settling on the ground. Margaret and Balin clung together, the rocks either side of them got closer, scratching their arms and legs. Once the rocks were up to their knees they both realised that they were going to be buried alive. Panic set in, both tried to lift their feet but it was impossible. Sam watched in horror as the rocks moved up their bodies.

'The ring. Give it to me and I will let them live,' demanded the witch.

'I can't.'

Meridian let her fury unleash, the rocks whirled around the tunnel hitting Margaret and Balin covering them with dust. Their shouts getting louder as each assault hit. With a flick of her hand they were covered. The rocks stopped moving, the dust settled, Sam hung his head and cried.

Gilda stepped forwards, placing a finger under his chin she lifted his face. She heard the words; Shimmers or Darkness. The response was immediate.

Once more behind bars, they huddled together for comfort.

'You can't Sam,' whispered Margaret.

He looked at his parents covered head to toe in dust. He knew he couldn't lose them. He had no choice. Balin smiled, his teeth pearl white against the black of his skin.

'Whatever you decide to do we will support you,' glancing at Margaret, Balin smiled in reassurance.

'Either way you will die,' burst out the witch, staring at each of them in turn. 'Like the others incarcerated down here. In fact, most of Kingdom is going to die if Meridian has her way,' she added scornfully.

Stepping through the cell doors another witch indicated Balin and Margaret should move away from Sam. Reluctant, they sat with their backs against the wall, ready to jump to his rescue at the first sign of attack. Gilda smiled as she read their thoughts. She held out her hand. They all watched as a darker stronger face emerged. As her eyes turned red, the aura of menace and power fell from her like rain. The voice that emerged powerful, commanding.

'I am the Darkness. I ask for the ring. If you do not give it to me, I will destroy Kingdom and everyone in it.'

Sam stuttered in terror, 'without it you cannot become a Dark Lord. You won't be able to destroy Kingdom.'

Meridian flew at him, halted only by a flick of Gilda's finger. Hands extended like talons, ready to rip him apart.

Sam took a step back, he was scared of the Darkness, but the white haired witch was a whole other matter. She looked like a She Devil, her body physically shaking with the force of her fury as her eyes blazed with hate.

The voice of the Darkness drowned out her muttering's.

'If you give up the ring, I will guarantee that you will all live. Prisoners, but alive.'

The air in the room moved as if being sucked away, in an instant both witches were gone.

The Potts and Lasts, told the meeting the army that surrounded them was slowly moving away, other areas in Kingdom were also being abandoned. All appeared to be making their way to the Devils Gap.

Addressing the room Dandelion said, 'we can have no doubt with the snatching of Sam and his parent's, that the Darkness has the ring and therefore can complete the mirror. Because of the spells woven, clan members will be unable to leave the Akiva without losing their skills. Only those who are not affiliated will be able to go.'

'Go where? And do what?' asked Elfrad. 'Those of us still fighting are hampered by the spells that have been put in place. Once the Dark Lord rises all will be lost.'

'It's not like you, to sound so defeated,' said Naddle. 'It's true, we are all hampered in some way. But we cannot give up; we will have to find other ways to defeat him.'

'Outside the Akiva we may not be able to revert to the bird form of a seeker. But that doesn't mean we are not still Kaimi,' said Falk.

'If we leave, we'll lose our camouflage,' smiled Hafren, 'we may not be able to blend in anymore or use our nets, but as Alvie we still know how to hide and call the trees.'

Dandelion could see and feel how animated everyone was becoming, looking across at Elfrad they both smiled. Feeling the air grow cooler, a puddle appeared on the floor, in seconds Pelagius stood before them.

'We have been busy pulling all the water deep underground.' Hearing the gasp from the Alvie, he told them, 'don't panic, we are making sure all trees and plant life are taken care of. Magicals that need water have been given a code. If correct, we supply, if not we drown. I know it seems harsh but we cannot take the risk of helping the wrong ones.' Turning to the Alvie he added, 'the trees are safe, most are underground, not their first choice of a hiding place. The Ancient Wood of the Dead.'

'Oh no,' piped up Hafren, 'they wouldn't like that, big and strong they may be, yet they fear that place.'

Pelagias chuckled, 'that's not the worst of it, because there are so many of them, we have had to use the Tall Mountain and the Swampy Pasture, they may fear the wood but they hate the pasture. Constant arguing is breaking out as each take their turns in the Tall Mountain to give them some relief in standing upright.'

'How are you getting sunlight to them?' asked Tairlaw, a worried frown appearing on her face, while her colours changed from dark green to light.

'Another first for Kingdom, Seymour Penge and Professor Morley have put aside their differences and have both worked hard conjuring sunlight spells, which Narrabri found them and Ciro and Helio have boosted.'

The tension in room eased as everyone laughed at the thought of the two old enemies working together for the common good.

Elfrad asked, 'has anything been heard of where the Bodleian have taken the Libraries?'

Dandelion's pocket began to vibrate, reaching inside she lay her small blue book onto the table. Flipping over showing its middle, two hands appeared, then a face. Hauling himself out Gerringong was quickly followed by Monash. Both looking the worse for wear, their clothes dusty and torn, wild hair and eyes with a manic look added to their mad appearance. Usually, Gerringong pushed himself forwards always wanting to claim leadership, for once, he hung back letting Monash take the floor.

'Thanks to the quickness of the Potts,' he nodded in their direction. 'We managed to get Flinders away before he could be taken. The Libraries are safe; for now. How long before the Dark Lord or his cohorts start to seriously search, is anyone's guess. I cannot tell you where they are. Or details of the plan "B" that is in place should they be discovered. We will remain in the Akiva, access may be slow, but at least we will still have it.'

Hearing a commotion, they all turned as Beadu and Herwig were pushed through the door, quickly followed by Rayna. Fairy dust covered the wizards making their skin glow and itch.

'Leave them alone,' shouted Fianna, as she crashed through after them.

Rayna turned, her dust lifting from her skin ready to fly.

'They had nothing to do with it, we have been hiding,' she continued, readying her staff, to counter the attack.

'Stand down,' commanded Dandelion, 'please remove your dust from the wizards.'

'Now, Fianna, please explain what you mean?'

Moving to stand next Herwig and Beadu, she answered, 'Since Verlimusa some of the wizards have given their allegiance to the other side. I like many Bomani have been in hiding. Not wanting to get involved in their schemes and plans. An old witch called Meridian has taken charge, her power over the darkest magic, irresistible to many. All manner of magicals and norms flocking to her side with promises of the power they will receive when Kingdom falls.'

Dandelion and Elfrad looked across at each other.

'Surely it cannot be, I'm old, but she must be ancient,' exclaimed Cian.

'I fear it must be,' answered Dandelion, 'it makes sense of what has been happening. The Darkness is hampered by being inside the Glasserium. Kingdom and Novia have been having problems as long as I can remember. Everything is more organised and focused.'

'What really surprises me,' said Fianna, 'is that none of you seem to be aware, that most of the wizards who were guarding the tunnels have gone.'

'That's not correct,' spoke the Lasts. The Lobes and Lens let their ears and eyes grow, both searching the tunnels for the wizards. 'I can hear them. I can see them,' they choroused one after another.

Seeing the look on Fianna's face, Dandelion muttered, 'it's another trick.'

'Meridian is old and immensely powerful. We hid, because we believe in Kingdom, if we had shown ourselves, we may have been made to leave with the others and join forces with her.'

'Are you willing for us to look inside your minds and see for ourselves?' asked Cian.

The wizards all felt panicked by his suggestion, not because they had anything to hide. Rather the fact that if the vampire's didn't believe them. Even with all their warrior skills they would not be quick enough at such close quarters to avoid death.

Having decided the room they used earlier was not big enough to accommodate all those who wanted to attend, Dandelion and Elfrad opened one of the dormitories that used to hold the Baldassare when the old king used the Akiva. Unused for years on opening the doors a dank musty smell greeted them. Dark and uninviting, bare of any furniture, they both set about changing its appearance.

Dandelion asked the Warra to douse the room in water to cleanse it. Once it was dry she conjured tables and benches. With no access to the map room anymore, Gerringong searched the archives and found some ancient ones.

Now adorning the walls they gave the room a vocal point to focus on. Taking their seats, everyone glanced over at the old maps and smiled. Tattered and torn in places they showed a Kingdom long gone, when peace reigned and dark magic was only a whisper heard in the night.

'Perhaps a member of each clan could come up and note where their clan bases are situated.'

Addressing Fianna, she asked, 'I know you don't have an actual leader or clan base anymore, due to the split between warrior and wizard. But could you indicate on the map the likely hood of where they may gather.'

Standing back, Dandelion waited until Elfrad had placed markers for the Armoury, Osias, Akiva and Verlimusa, adding details of the trees whereabouts at a prompt from Pelagias. With a flourish he flicked his hand sending small drops of water covering the maps, drying quickly the small grey dots indicated where all the water was being stored. Dandelion finished by adding the Glasserium and the Devils Gap, the only known places that the Dark Lord may make his appearance from.

'We can now see visually how hard our task will be,' said Dandelion. 'If we could rely on the clans it would show a different picture. Unfortunately we have to act on the basis that apart from those here, everyone else is tied to their leaders and cannot help us. When the Dark Lord emerges he will want to take the key sites in Kingdom. I believe he will go after the Osias and the tomb first which may give us a bit more time. If by some fluke he manages to get in then the magma would be released.'

'Fingerling still has control of Verlimusa,' explained Elfrad. 'It will be hard for anyone to gain access, even someone of Meridian's capabilities. This though may change, when she has the added advantage of the Dark Lord's power to call on. This is the heart of Kingdom, we cannot let that happen. Once the Dark Lord steps from the mirror the Maia will be released, who will hold it, we have no idea. Whoever it is will have to go first to the Fadia for initiation. We have to empty Kingdom of every resource we can and that includes magicals. Getting everyone into Pictures has to be a priority. We also have to find out where Meridian and her followers are hiding.'

'As none of you can leave the Akiva, your job will be to patrol it. This will release the sentinels. Your first task is to check the tunnels, clear out whatever is making us think that the wizards are still there. Secure them and the sites of the explosions, if you should find anyone that shouldn't be here, interrogate them. If their answers are not satisfactory, kill them.' Hearing gasps, Dandelion frowned; 'There is no room for sentiment. Make no mistake we are fighting for our lives. We're all going to have to make tough decisions.'

Elfrad stepped in hearing the anger in Dandelion's voice. He knew how annoyed and hurt she had been at the betrayals they had already suffered.

'The more we can help move to safety the better, some magicals are going to be only too glad to leave. Others may take some convincing which we haven't got time for, another reason to use the sentinels.'

Seeing the eager faces around her, Dandelion felt more energised, believing that they may still have a chance. The more magicals and resources they could deprive their enemies of the better, making sure that the taking of Kingdom was an empty victory.

Eadulf stood for a moment savouring the feeling of being back in the Glasserium. He could hear and feel a thrumming coming from the main hall. The Black Mirror an abomination which should not be allowed to exist, its contamination of the halls evident everywhere. Pulling a small mirror from his pocket, he threw it into the air, as it snapped open and grew, he threw himself inside.

'Take me home.'

Waiting for the mirror to stop moving, he was conscious that he needed to be quick. As soon as he had entered the Glasserium, the process had started and he'd began to change, once his transformation was complete, no one would be able to detect him, not even a Dark Lord.

Utter blackness descended, he clicked his fingers, peering through the glass as the outside lights on the frame began to penetrate the dark. Sensing his mirror before he could see it. Then, out of the gloom it appeared, golden and bright, the glass clear, shining like a beacon welcoming him home. Jumping from the mirror transport, he tinkled as he landed on his feet. Glass had already made its way up to his knees. Soon he would be covered again.

Startled, as a voice cried out, 'at last, your back. It's been so long I thought you may have gone for good this time. We have a lot of work to do. It was bad enough when Abaddon tried to be a Dark Lord. Monis is even worse, he's sneaky and organised and has been using the Glasserium to build his black mirror.'

Eadulf, was lost for words, no one should be able to enter his personal chamber the magic used to safe guard it both ancient and secret. Calling for more lights, he couldn't believe his eyes, before him was the scruffiest mirror he'd ever seen. Its frame barely holding together, the glass pitted and streaked with so much dirt making it hard to make out anyone inside.

'Who are you?' he demanded. 'How did you get in here?'

A chuckle was not what he was expecting. The mirror fell down none to gently its bottom frame touching the ground. He watched as hands appeared, followed by the top of a head, with one heave a body fell at his feet. Muttering, the bunch of rags picked itself up.

'Guri, surely it can't be you?' astonished, Eadulf smiled at the old crone standing before him.

'Of course it's me, who else would wait this long for you to come back,' she sniffed in annoyance.

He recalled the last time they'd met. She in the process of getting as far away from the Darkness and Abaddon as she could get. Him, leaving the hall after trying in vain to stop them from taking control.

'How have you managed to stay hidden?'

'By hiding in the subterranean levels of course,' she chuckled.

'I did come back once before but the Darkness's hold was too strong.'

'So why now?' asked Guri, seeing her refection from the glass now covering him to chest height.

'The last piece of the mirror has returned to Kingdom, if the Darkness gets it…'

Clapping her hands in delight, she crowed, 'let the games begin.'

'Saving Kingdom, is hardly a game,' he snapped, as glass finally covered his face.

CHAPTER EIGHTEEN

Gilda held the sliver of glass like a precious jewel. Meridian hovered, muttering how it should be her. The Darkness waited, patrolling back and forth, impatience evident in every step.

'Master,' crowed Meridian, 'we have the last piece, soon Kingdom will be; yours,' she added reluctantly.

Ignoring her, the Darkness approached Gilda. Opening her hands the sliver lay in her palm. Pulsing, it called to its real master. Placing it into the gap, the Darkness stepped back.

At first nothing happened, then, thrumming burst out, filling the halls with its sound of triumph. The glass bowed inward then pushed itself out as if reaching for something. Before going totally silent. Finally it rippled, turned black and lay still.

'Bring the magicals, I need to feed before I enter,' commanded the Darkness.

Gilda caught a glimpse of Meridian's face as she turned away, jealousy and anger fighting for expression.

'I will see you both on the other side.'

Holding onto the frame the Darkness hauled Monis's body through the glass.

Meridian kicked the bodies littering the ground out of her way. Joining hands they began chanting the spell that would catapult the Dark Lord into Kingdom.

Inside the black mirror the Darkness waited. Something started to crawl over him, a fine black mist began to climb up his legs moving over his body making him shiver. More mist appeared, thicker this time, sinking into his skin. Moving like a snake looking for its prey. A numbing coldness penetrated his body. Slowly his skin began to slough off, until it lay in a heap at his feet, new skin quickly replacing it gleaming as if burnished. He felt his back bone lengthen, his chest fill out and legs grow longer. Flexing his now claw like hands, he imagined the damage they were going to do. When he'd first pushed through into Monis's body, his face had always been distorted. Now he could feel the contours of his jaw, hard like steel, catching site of his refection in the glass, his eyes flashed black and red. The power now flooding through his body felt immense. The mist left him and attached itself to the inside of the mirror, spreading out across the surface before making its way back to cover him once more. The process was complete.

Starting the chant, letting it build in power, Meridian threw her dark magic towards the black mirror. At the same time moving her pure mirror out of the hall and into Kingdom. Inside the hall every mirror began to thrum, rippling inwards, then, bulging outwards, glass filled the air. Their power sucked towards the black mirror, feeding on their strength adding to its own. The Glasserium stilled, as all its mirrors shattered, glass falling like rain. The black mirror bulged out into Kingdom, expelling the Dark Lord. Meridian snapped her fingers sending her pure mirror back, smiling at the thought that it would be the only one apart from the black mirror still intact.

Walking towards the Dark Lord she was amazed at his size. He really did look magnificent; Monis had served him well as a template, now though with his own features over laid his strength and power shone out.

Cheers rent the air. All the magicals that had been making their way to greet their new master saw it as a celebration. Meridian's cronies made their way to her side, chattering and sneaking looks at the Dark Lord. Everyone waited, since entering Kingdom he hadn't moved, or acknowledged their greetings. Head cocked as if listening to someone, he stared unseeing at the growing number of magicals and wraiths arriving.

Much to Meridian's annoyance the Dark Lord disappeared in a swirl of black mist.

She was incandescent with rage. He wouldn't be here if it wasn't for her efforts, the least he could have done was acknowledge her presence. Moving away, the black thoughts in her head whispered that she should never have brought him back. Her power was over. Now only a servant to his wishes.

Gilda warily approached Meridian, who twitched and scowled in equal measure, muttering as if in answer to a question only she could hear.

'He's gone to the Devil's Gap,' she said, 'to feed and kill.'

Landing, she was met by an eerie silence. Bodies lay everywhere, some intact, while others had been ripped asunder, tossed away like rubbish. The stench of blood, the low moans of the injured and dying, sounded like whispers on the wind as they faded in and out.

The decoy mirror that had been erected lay shattered, its frame bent and buckled by the forces used to make it appear real. Bodies lay in piles, friends and enemies joined together in death. A movement behind made her turn, the Dark Lord covered in blood and gore swept his eyes across her face, Meridian lowered hers, lest he saw her thoughts.

She waited for his acknowledgement of her place by his side.

'Kill any that are still alive. Then burn the lot.'

Gilda found her sitting on a mound of stones watching a pile of bodies burning. Bent and broken, her matted hair flowed over her shoulders. The stench of the fires made Gilda's eyes water, with a flick of her fingers the ground opened swallowing the remains, leaving small dust clouds in their wake.

'We should go.'

'Please be careful,' said Gilda, 'he has plans in place to take

Verlimusa, moving on to the Osias and Akiva. Each one will make him more powerful.'

'Is this you speaking?' demanded Meridian. 'Or is he still invading your mind? Because either way, if it hadn't been for me; he would never have been able to emerge in the first place. You need to think about where your loyalties lay. I won't be pushed aside.'

The castle sprawled, surrounded by high walls, turrets thrusting towards the skies, stone work blackened over the years through neglect and abandonment, yet still it looked formidable. Although cleansed of any remnants of royal life, the Dark Lord had felt their power as soon as he'd walked through the gate. The hill he decided was where he would make his camp, away from any royal taint.

Crowds had gathered. Those who had been outside the Glasserium, wary, after hearing what the Dark Lord had done at the Devil's Gap, their chatter muted.

Meridian made her way towards her cohorts. Many thought of her as unpredictable, scared of her power. Instrumental in getting the Dark Lord released, so far they hadn't seen them working together in the same place. Both powerful, both capable of taking over Kingdom. They had all at some time or other seen or felt Meridian's power, whereas the Dark Lord had yet to show his real strength.

It hadn't taken Meridian long to realise that for all his power the Dark Lord didn't really know how to harness it without her guidance. While he'd been hiding in the Glasserium she had been honing her skills of magic especially the ancient dark side. The dark voices in her head had gotten louder since he'd risen, repeatedly telling her that she should rule. Judging by the mess he was creating she was slowly believing them. Many magicals had fled to safety in Pictures. Gilda telling her that Kingdom had sent out the call to evacuate, both of them hadn't expected it to be organised so quickly. The trees had all but disappeared. The Warra had taken the water and hid it. Even using her darkest magic she hadn't been able to find any. Kingdom wasn't the land of riches she thought it would be. Being told by Gilda that she only had herself to blame, didn't help.

When Abaddon was killed and the Darkness fled, she had made it possible for the core of her dark magicals to escape into Novia. Since then she had worked tirelessly to undermine Kingdom. Ordering Gilda to use her talents and make magicals believe that their magic was dying. Concentrating on building a loyal army ready for the Dark Lord's return, neither of them had realised that their combined use of such powerful dark magic over so many years had taken on a life of its own. Seeping into the fabric of Kingdom. Leeching the core of its magic; strong enough to affect even the Shimmers. In her quest for power, Meridian had unleashed something older and darker and now it was impossible to stop.

Hearing talk about the Shimmers, made the voices in her head sing out noisily telling her it was now time to act.

'Katrina, will you slow down. What did he actually say?'

Having Meridian's full attention made her squirm, Gilda nudged her to answer.

Scowling, she told them, 'the witch kept on repeating himself about a magician that he was at odds with. Everyone got bored and moved away. I was jammed in the corner and couldn't escape so easily. He called for more wine, and spotted me, a captive audience.'

Meridian's impatience was starting to show, tapping her foot was a bad sign.

Another nudge from Gilda and she blurted, 'the Dark Lord has recruited a bunch of wizard mercenaries and is going to use them to force their way into the Osias. They are confident they can overpower the sentries allowing him access. They are working on spells that would enable him to drain the Shimmers of their power and kill them.'

Disappearing in a whirl, she left a startled Gilda and a thankful Katrina in her wake.

Yanking the cloth from her orb, Meridian sat down and placed her hands on either side of it. Old fashioned magic it maybe, she knew though, that many dark magicals had lost or ignored their skill to use one. Whereas, like all her other abilities once gained, she never stopped honing and refining them.

Concentrating, she sent her mind out to search for Khalon. She found the wizard in his garden, at first she thought he was talking to someone, but soon realised he was actually speaking to a plant. One lonely rose bush stood defiantly upright, while everything else had dried up and died. Calling his name, she waited for him to answer.

'Is it time?'

'We may have a problem. Wizard mercenaries are supposedly helping the Dark Lord to obtain access. Who are they? Can they do it?'

He chuckled. Meridian's face changed, her eyes flashed, power flowed through her hands into the orb. Khalon recognised the danger before he felt the blow.

Holding up his hands in surrender, he cried, 'it must be Lecah; he has been trying to win favour with the Dark Lord since he emerged. There is no way that he or any of his cronies are capable of taking on a sentry, let alone all of them. If they try and enter, the magma will be triggered and all our plans lost. We must act now.'

Chapter Nineteen

Eadulf walked through the hall, furious at the destruction of the mirrors. Glass littered the floor, frames bent and buckled lay where they fell from when the black mirror had blasted the Dark Lord into Kingdom. Guri's mirror also hung by a thread, he knew she was upset at the thought of losing it, begging him to save it. Ignoring her pleas as she followed him about, constantly muttering and moaning, a running commentary he could do without.

Standing behind Eadulf, Guri could see herself reflected in the glass which now covered him. A walking mirror, the glass shining through the darkness like a beacon. Highlighting even more the hall's destruction.

Several times he had stood watching and listening as the black mirror pulsed and throbbed, occasionally rippling as its power was being accessed. Eadulf focused his eyes on the last piece to be added. Having passed through Faolan's body this would be its weakest point. Already he could see a small pinprick of lighter glass near the corner of the frame. This would be his entry in.

Movement caught his eye, looking past the black mirror, a pure mirror cowered against the wall. It's frame warped and marked with dark magic, glass pitted and streaked with dirt. It trembled so much, its glass tinkled as if ready to fall out.

'That's the one Meridian used. You should shatter her before she alerts her to your presence.'

'Be quiet Guri,' he commanded, her constant buzzing like an angry bee in his ears.

Approaching the mirror he gently laid his hands onto her frame, her trembling immediately stopped. For a second her glass blazed with light.

'You're back. Please help me. I can feel Meridian's taint all over me.'

Eadulf considered what to do, unless the other pure mirrors had managed to hide. This could be the last of her kind. The mirror was right, Meridian's taint permeated the mirror, the dark magic she used still holding a link to it, which must mean that she still had a use for it. He may be shut away in the Glasserium, but like others in Kingdom he was well aware of the conflict that was slowly developing between Meridian and the Dark Lord. Weakening the black mirror would help towards stopping him. However, Meridian would still have to be dealt with, if she was keeping a link to this mirror then it must mean at some stage she expected to come back into the halls. If the Dark Lord was defeated, he couldn't imagine what use she would have for the black mirror. He only knew that it was even more imperative than ever it be destroyed.

Getting the pure mirror to follow him took ages, every time the black mirror made a noise she froze in fear. Guri had given up waiting and had retreated to her battered one. Eadulf couldn't help smiling at the sight of the two side by side. The pure mirror for all its usage by Meridian still retained a regal stance. Whereas Guri's really did look the worst for wear. He knew that she was ignoring its pleas to be put out of its misery, tired and worn out only her hope held it together. She had known no other and only this mirror would do. Overtime it had come to feel the same.

Decision made, he left them to their moaning and made his way to the furthest reaches of the Glasserium. As he passed through the tunnels and rooms the light from his glass body threw shadows high up against the walls. His feet crunched over broken glass from thousands of shattered mirrors their destruction weighing heavily on his mind.

'Hello old friend, you took your time. My, don't you look shiny,' laughed Aeryissa. Adding, 'not sure I like to see myself reflected so much. Can't you tone down the glass a notch?'

'Perhaps you should change back to "little girl Aeryissa," rather than a scary vampire.' He countered, laughing at the look on her face.

'I've missed you Eadulf. It's actually nice being "me" without worrying about who may see.'

Chuckling, he agreed. Giving her a twirl he asked, 'what do you think?'

'Glassy,' she answered, laughing at her own joke.

Aeryissa walked beside Eadulf conscious that she was breaking more glass as she trod on the shards scattering the ground.

'Can these ever be put back together?'

'The halls will be restored, first though, the black mirror has to be destroyed. I think I've figured out a way to do it. Which's why I need your help.'

Guri heard them approach her eyes widening at the sight of the vampire. While the pure mirror wailed and trembled in fear.

'Aeryissa meet my army. This is Guri, she has lived most of her life inside the Glasserium, as you can see by the state of her mirror and this frightened creature is possibly the last remaining pure mirror.'

'Not so pure now,' cackled Guri. 'She's well used,' she snorted.

Aeryissa eyes raked across her face, the rest of her words dying on her lips at the look she gave her.

Taking her over to the black mirror, Eadulf waited to see what Aeryissa's reaction to it would be. While they had been talking it had been rippling constantly, a sign the Dark Lord was accessing its power. As they approached, the silver under her skin glowed so bright she looked as if it had been polished. With the shine from his glass they were like a beacon of light in a dark world. The black mirror appearing to flinch as they drew nearer.

'Is that the last piece? I can make out a small dot of light,' she pointed to the corner of the frame.

Eadulf nodded, glad he had left her to find it herself. Now surer than ever that between them they could destroy it.

For once Guri was silent, watching in disbelief as Aeryissa scattered fairy dust over the forester nets she had cast earlier all over the halls. Desperately wanting to ask, how it was possible for her to be able do it? One look from Eadulf had silenced her, since then, she stayed beside the pure mirror, her own rag tag one barely able to hold itself together. Refusing to listen to its pleas for release, not out of cruelty but rather because she couldn't bear the thought of being without it. They had gone through so much together, no other mirror would have put up with her.

'Guri, it's for the best.'

'I know, it's hard though to see it destroyed in this way,' she answered, wiping away her tears.

Her old mirror lay at their feet, shattered into trillions of small pieces ready to join all the others in the Glasserium. The frame, a bundle of wood stacked against the wall.

The pure mirror horrified at the destruction, waited to see what her fate would be. Aeryissa was still inside, walking her rooms, running her hands over the walls and sniffing the air. When she had stepped inside, the dark magic which covered her every surface, recoiled at the vampires scent.

Popping her head through the glass, she told Eadulf, 'I'm going to start, keep well back both of you.' Patting the mirrors frame, she told it, 'soon be over, but it will hurt.'

Withdrawing back inside, she moved to the centre of the room. Standing still, senses on high alert, eyes and ears searching for any signs of Meridian's interest. Releasing the silver from her body, she allowed its shine to wash over the room. She knew it was working when she detected the mirror's moans. The pain would get a lot worse before she was finished. Ignoring its distress, she allowed nothing to distract her as she searched for the dark magic. Once her silver had searched each room and corridor there was only one place the dark magic could go, over the edge into the void. This was exactly what they wanted. It was important for Meridian to still believe that she could access the mirror.

'It's going over. NOW,' she shouted, as silver flowed from her into the void chasing it towards Eadulf.

He waited, his glass trap ready, open like the jaws of a hungry animal. The dark magic had nowhere else to go if it wanted to maintain a hold on the mirror. The cage snapped shut, the glass covered by Aeryissa's silver. Contained, it could never get out, but if Meridian were to cast her eye towards the mirror it would still appear to be under her control.

'Will you stop moaning, you're giving me a headache,' whined Guri.

Annoyed at having to watch the show from outside of the mirror, she itched to know what was going on.

'No arguments, in you go. Will you both stop? No one is boss of the other. Guri your task is to make sure the pure mirror stays pure.'

'How? If I live inside?'

'The pure mirror's task is to make sure if Meridian sweeps her, she still thinks she is the cowed mirror she left behind, and not this beautiful shining example of what a pure mirror should look like.'

'Please, you're making me feel sick. How come she gets a shiny new frame and glass? While my, poor old mirror got destroyed.'

Aeryissa's patience was being sorely tested, opening her jaws wide she growled deep and loud. Instantly the arguing stopped. Even Eadulf looked surprised to see her fangs and talons extend.

'Now that I have your attention, we still haven't finished. There is the small matter of a black mirror to deal with.'

To add even more of a contrast to her face, her eyes and ears started to widen and grow. Guri held the mirrors frame to steady herself, her thoughts a jumble, who is this vampire? Not only the skills of the Alvie and Kaimi, she now had those of a Lobe and Lens.

Turning to Eadulf, Aeryissa said, 'we need to do this now. I have to go.'

Guri climbed into the pure mirror, turning so they could both watch the proceedings. Eadulf approached the black mirror, Aeryissa by his side. Holding hands he placed his thumb onto the glass where the small dot of light could be seen. Aeryissa's silver flowed across their joined hands through his body and into the mirror. At the same time with her other hand she flicked out a forester's net. Snaking across the ground, when it touched the ones already laid on top of the glass, her silver mixed with the fairy dust. Shimmer and silver lit the hall, sending the dark away. The glass under the nets appeared as if on fire, ready for their journey into the black mirror.

They both smiled to see what had been when they started, a pin prick of light had now grown bigger. Anchored into the mirror, the old king's blood mixed with Aeryissa's silver waited ready to draw in the glass laying under the nets; fairy dust dancing above them, eager to cover its prey.

CHAPTER TWENTY

Meridian stared at each clan leader, her mind in turmoil, the Dark Lord's plan to enter the Osias worrying at her thoughts, like a dog with a bone. Waiting to hear from Khalon had driven her to new heights of anger.

Lefu stared at her through the bars of his cage, his eyes dripping with hate. She didn't need to read his thoughts to know what he was thinking. Her dark magic hadn't let her down, she hated the clan leaders with a passion, the loyalty they managed to incur, a thorn in her side.

'There is a messenger waiting to see you.'

She turned her back on the vampire's stare, hoping the message was from Khalon.

It would take her moments to activate the magma. How long before everything was covered she had no idea. If the sentries got to the wizards before the release, all would be lost. To be able to secure the entrance to the Osias the wizards must be covered by the magma yet stay alive in stasis for her plan to work. The spells woven into their bodies, the potions they had drunk, were all to insure that they would emerge alive, while the sentries would be dead.

Ignoring the rumbling coming from the depths, she cast the

spells. The air shifted, the rumbles stopped, replaced by a tearing, shifting sound. A couple of the wizards had stopped their eyes round in fear. The droplets of magma were slow to fall at first, gaining speed they splattered down, the wizards dropped to the ground, pulling their hoods over their faces wrapping their cloaks around their knees; they buried their heads waiting for the onslaught to stop and the magma to cover them.

Renewing her efforts the magma took on a life of its own; pouring from the walls it covered the wizards making them appear as lumps of clay waiting to be moulded. Pummelled with magma, it clung to the sentries armour weighing them down their pace slowing. Caught without the protection spells the sentries stopped like statues frozen in place. Satisfied the wizards would be safe, she closed and sealed the doors, disappearing into the night, the sounds of Khalon's diversion ringing in her ears.

When the Dark Lord heard about the magma being released, he assumed it was the wizard Lecah who had tried to enter, failure was not tolerated. Before giving him a chance to explain that he had nothing to do with it, he drew a claw across wizard's throat, he was dead before his body hit the ground.

Unable to enter Verlimusa, the Shimmers dead, he turned his attention to the Akiva. Even though they had crippled the clans, he wanted ownership of these key areas in Kingdom. All places where the old king ruled, where magic was at its strongest.

Flexing his muscles, he let his mind fly back to his mirror drawing on its power, recharging himself. Having to do this more and more meant he was weaker than he should be. A Dark Lord conjured from ancient dark magic should be all powerful. Instead as each day passed, he felt weaker, his magic sporadic. Whereas Meridian had gained power and knowledge which far outstripped his own. What to do about her had now become a problem. Even if he felt able to and he doubted he could; killing her was not an option, he still needed her dark magic. He had to find a way to reign her in. Like him, she also had an army behind her and like him, she ruled by fear. Who though, did they fear the most; him or her?

Meridian kept her eyes on the Dark Lord ignoring the twins flanking his side. Thinking, how she would like the opportunity of having them alone to turn their skin inside out and watch them suffer.

The Dark Lord's eyes raked over her, long gone was the beautiful women she had once been. Still tall, but stooped, she leaned heavily on her staff, her wild tangled mass of hair sat like a nest of snakes on top of her head. Skin wrinkled, lines running in deep ruts across her forehead, bags heavy under her eyes. Veiled now, her thoughts locked. He knew he couldn't trust her. Both were using each other for their own ends.

'They're in the tunnels. The vampires have them. They're dead. More coming through; we're being swamped,' cried the Potts.

Searching stars lit up the room before exploding, the smoke they emitted adding to the already noxious air.

'Tell Cian to pull back. We can close the tunnels from here. We have to keep the centre of the Akiva clear,' shouted Dandelion in reply. Turning to the Lasts, she asked, 'how many now?'

'Hundreds of them, our shields and spells are holding but they are taking a battering. Whatever magic they are using to gain entry is strong.'

'Send the Fae and the Alvie between them they may be able to do a patch using their dust and nets. Lasts, send a message to Qiao tell him only the elemental witches are to come through, all others are to stay away for now.'

'Grab him.'

Harsha pounced, pulling the magicals heart out of his chest. Amazement crossed his face, before he keeled over with a thud.

'How?' shouted Elfrad.

'Through the old map room, when they turned the Plotters they must have gotten them to tamper with our seals,' shouted Hafren, ducking as something flew past his head.

'Captain, send the sentinels to intercept them, show no mercy,' commanded Dandelion, shaken by her near miss.

'Surely Qiao should be back by now?' raged Elfrad, ducking as bits of wall and furniture rained down on them from an exploding star.

'I hate those things,' he muttered, his ears ringing from the impact.

The Lobes equally affected, immediately drew back their ears, shaking their heads to clear the noise.

'They have broken through near Sanctuary,' shouted the Lens.

While both the Potts and Lasts eyes swivelled, seeking out their prey. The Lobes once again let their ears grow out.

'They're in the corridors heading this way,' they all shouted together.

More stars fell, their explosions shaking the walls. Flung to floor Dandelion and Elfrad looked up at the same time to see Cian crash into the room a witch clinging to his back. Casting spells at him and anything she could see. Pulling back her fist, Harsha knocked her off, as the witch hit the floor, she reached forward and pulled out her heart, as a large wraith filled the doorway.

Emrys leapt across the bloody mess wrapped his hand around the wraiths neck and pulled. Everyone heard the sickening pop, chucking the head away in disgust, he kicked the body back out into the corridor, slamming the door shut.

'Is the Dark Lord with them?' shouted Dandelion, trying to be heard above the noise of explosion's going off like fire crackers.

'We cannot see him,' spoke a Lens.

'Wait,' cried the Potts together, 'Meridian is here, which means he won't be far behind.'

'Pull everyone back, release the traps. We go down. I know it's not ideal but there is nowhere else for us to go. We must keep fighting until help can arrive.'

The constant skirmishes had begun to wear them all down. Yet their enemies often gave up, running away in defeat, even when their victory was assured. In the first few months of his emergence, the Dark Lord caused plenty of havoc and mayhem, killing everyone he came across friend or foe. It soon became apparent that something was wrong with him. Like the rest of Kingdom he seemed affected by its lack of magic. Bursting through at times, sending him and his armies on the attack. Then fizzling out, wondering aimlessly, they became easy pickings.

Meridian was a different matter. Her dark magic hadn't waned, if anything it had gotten stronger. Fighting two enemies, both with different agendas, made everything much more difficult. Fortunately, some of those who fled into Pictures had returned, adding their strength to the fight. Without the Shimmers or the clans, power and skills, Dandelion had no idea how they were going to defeat their enemies.

Sealing the last hatch, everyone took their places, maps ready on the walls, without looking, everyone well aware how much the enemy forces now covered most of them. Only small pockets of resistance managed to flare every now and again, shining through the darkness; as battles were fought.

The underground part of the Akiva a secret known only to a few, Dandelion hoped that by completely sealing the upstairs floors hiding the hatches, creating a portal leaving a signature showing their flight, would be enough to keep them occupied long enough for her to figure out what to do.

Each battle they fought seemed to get them further away from defeating their enemies. Even though the forces ranged against them, appeared out of control, sometimes with no clear idea of what they were doing, luck still appeared to be more on their side. Her decision to send out only small parties to clear any magicals not fighting into Pictures, had been their only real success. Harassing the enemy to keep the main bulk of them away from the Akiva, allowing Qiao to ferry magicals back and forth unhindered, was now proving difficult to maintain.

When the magma had been released, trapping the Shimmers

inside the Osias, the news had rippled through the Akiva causing shockwaves. With the Dark Lord's mirror safe inside the Glasserium and no one able to enter and destroy it. She'd found it harder and harder to imagine how they were going to defeat those pitted against them. Pulled out of her reverie, she became aware of shouting.

'She made me Dandelion,' cried Qiao, as a small girl and a scruffy man stepped forward.

'We got here as they emerged,' said Elfrad, wand drawn ready to attack.

Cian had removed his collar, Dandelion waved at him to put it back on, never taking her eyes from the girl.

'Why and how did you make Qiao bring you here?'

Aeryissa felt Cian's eyes boring into her as he tried to reach into her mind. Ignoring the stares aimed at her, she drew out a chair and indicated to the witch to do them same, before calmly sitting down.

Elfrad couldn't help but smile, the girl looked around the room, taking note of each magical, unconcerned at the animosity being thrown her way.

'My name is Aeryissa. This is Perical, he's a witch.'

'You cannot be,' sneered Cian, 'Aeryissa is a vampire. We,' pointing at Emrys and Harsha, 'would know if you were her.'

Unfazed by his outburst, she continued, 'never the less, I am she.'

Cian snorted in disgust at her claim, if he remembered correctly the real Aeryissa hadn't even been much of a vampire, unwilling or unable to hunt, eventually outcast by her family.

'Where's Meg, she will vouch for me,' smiling at Cian, she added, 'as a vampire.'

No one spoke as they waited for her to arrive.

Elfrad couldn't help admire Aeryissa's calm demeanour. Angering the vampires was not something he would want to do. Not being able to leave the Akiva they were operating on a short fuse, taking any opportunity to unleash their anger. All turned to see Meg's reaction at the sight of their visitor.

Slinging herself forwards, she hugged Aeryissa, laughing with excitement.

'It's so good to see you. The Darkness has taken Sam. Dillon is off having adventures. I'm stuck here.' Bursting into tears, she put her hands to her face and sobbed, 'I want to go home.'

'She says she is a vampire and that you can confirm it?' stated Dandelion, ignoring Meg's tears, throwing a glance at Cian aware his fangs were showing.

'Aeryissa is the scariest vampire I have ever seen.'

No one around the table knew what to make of her claim, wondering how come the other vampire's in the room were adamant that she wasn't.

Elfrad told her, 'the vampires inside the Akiva cannot leave. Their clan leader has been captured and his collar linked to all the other vampires.'

'You want to know why I don't wear a collar and can move about Kingdom without being affected as they would be,' she answered, casting her eyes towards the vampire's collars. 'The answer is simple. I'm different, I always have been, now, even more so.' Telling the vampire's firmly, 'my family did not make me an outcast. I chose to leave.' Turning to Dandelion, she continued, 'who or what I am is immaterial. If you want to save Kingdom then you need my help. The Maia is being prepared.'

The room erupted, everyone shouting, throwing questions. Both Dandelion and Elfrad tried to calm things down. Eventually the room grew quiet. Aeryissa ignored the outbreak she'd caused, choosing to talk to Meg instead, adding to everyone's annoyance with her.

'How do you know this? How do we know that this isn't a trap and you are not one of Dark Lord's cohorts?' asked Dandelion, keeping her voice level and calm.

'You don't.'

Elfrad had been closely watching Aeryissa, without making it obvious he allowed his wizard senses to come to the fore. Rusty from non-use, nevertheless he knew that he could trust them a hundred percent.

'I'm not the only one with secrets.'

Startled, to hear her voice in his head he let his senses abate, nodding at Dandelion.

Aeryissa could feel that all the magicals were near breaking point. Even this far below ground her senses could easily pick up sounds of the enemy as they flooded the Akiva. The enmity emitted by Meridian stronger than from the Dark Lord, his was rage and anger. While hers was a dark ancient creature, snuffling, filling all the corners constantly looking for prey. They needed to hold on. They also needed a reason to do so. It was time.

Letting her true self emerge, mouths gaped open. Magicals drew back their chairs, even Cian gasped at the sight of her. On a primeval level he knew instantly, that she was much more than a vampire.

Meg laughed, 'see, I told you.'

Dandelion and Elfrad stared in wonder at the creature before them. Unlike, other vampires who glistened in the sunlight, Aeryissa blazed, silver moved under her skin with touches of shimmer. One minute a slight girl, the next an Amazon. Muscles rippled, teeth and talons lengthened, her eyes constantly changed from red, orange to black. Settling on a grey that was totally at adds with the rest of her. Taking it in turns to look at each magical, she let her thoughts enter their heads, amazement and disbelief, writ across all their faces.

'How can this be?' asked Tairlaw and Hafren together, others, repeating the same question.

Allowing her true self to abate, the room instantly becoming less tense.

Meg piped up, 'she got hurt protecting us. That was the trigger. She saved us, by sacrificing herself.' Looking downcast, she added, 'I wish you hadn't left. With you here they may not have been able to take Sam.'

'How does he fit into all this,' asked Elfrad, pointing at Perical, who through all the talking had sat immobile not even blinking.

'He is my master, or at least it's what I've told him to think. He is so inept at magic, as his assistant I follow his lead. It has helped us to move around. It's best to ignore him, even when not under a spell. He's irritating.' Glancing at the ceiling Aeryissa smiled, 'they are getting angry, each blaming the other for your escape.'

'How do you know about the Maia?' asked Dandelion, the others around the table nodding at her question.

'I have been tasked with bringing together the elements needed to defeat the Dark Lord,' explained Aeryissa. 'The Maia cannot be used on Meridian, we will have to find another way to defeat her. I intend to release the leaders and therefore their clans. With the help of the elemental witches, those of you unaffected by the binding spells will be able to heal the leaders. The clans will then form part of the guard that will escort the Maia here.'

Dandelion's thoughts like Elfrad's were in turmoil. Both didn't doubt the vampire's confidence, they couldn't see though, how one person could make it all happen. She heard all their thoughts and doubts. While she waited for the furore she had created to die down, she spoke quietly to Meg, assuring her that she would soon be seeing Sam again.

Over hearing her remark, Elfrad demanded, 'how do you know they are still alive?' he felt another slight push, a whisper heard only by him, 'you will see for yourself, you're coming with me.'

Waiting for the air to settle, Aeryissa held her hand against Qiao's mouth signalling with her eyes for him to be quiet. A contingent of wraiths were moving around aimlessly in the courtyard, while others on the battlements lounged against the walls. Elfrad hadn't been inside the castle for many years, saddened to see the damage done by the use of dark magic within its walls. Noxious weeds clung to them dripping their venom, the stone pitted and broken, holes gouged out where stars had fallen, bodies piled up like so much rubbish. This wasn't the result of an attack, rather of misuse.

They made their way towards a tall tower on the north side of the castle. Its sides smooth and unadorned with no windows or door to be seen. Standing at the towers base, Yue at Aeryissa's signal, called to the moon asking it to hide its face. Ruzgar lifted her arms high into the air, as she brought them down she asked the wind to blow across the battlements. Aeron summoned the rain to pound down on the castle and the hill opposite.

'Sam and his parents are in this tower, we must release them first before the leaders.'

'Can you?'

Grinning, she looked at Elfrad.

'Why climb?' chimed in Qiao, 'when I can transport you there.'

'If you do; you will never get out again.'

'Well Elfrad? We don't have much time.'

Before he could give it any more thought he allowed his wizard senses to flood his body. Raking the tower his eyes like lasers looked for places to hold onto.

At the top of the tower Elfrad's eyes widened as Aeryissa began a low humming. Cocking her head to listen she placed her hands on a square of stone that was a different colour to the rest and began humming again.

'Follow me.'

Silver flowed from her body blasting through the stone, as the rubble fell inwards, Aeryissa followed. Elfrad fell through steadying himself as adrenalin pumped through his body. Inside the tower was smooth, no windows or doorways only the hole they had come through.

They sat facing each other knees drawn up holding hands.

'Let your wizard self-fly, you find the norm, I'll find the magicals.'

Closing their eyes they entered the real room. Mist and fog swirled, wind howled like a wolf, tugging at their clothes. Both listened, trying to catch sounds which didn't belong in this landscape. Aeryissa heard it first, metal on stone, someone was in chains. Honing her senses towards the sound she tapped Elfrad on the shoulder and pointed, bent double they made their way across the stony ground.

They found the three of them chained to a wall, arms and legs spread, heads hanging down in defeat. Clothes tattered, feet and hands cut and scraped. Low moans heard from them all.

Letting his wizard senses come to the fore Elfrad linked his mind with Aeryissa's. She would search for the magic that bound them, while he searched for his friends.

'Sam, Balin where are you?' called Margaret, panic making her voice wobble.

Elfrad heard it, as Aeryissa sensed it. Ignoring the wind pushing against them, they both flew to the sound. Margaret was wondering around in circles saying the same sentence over and over; Balin and Sam nowhere to be seen. Aeryissa drew symbols out of the air until they were lined up in front of her.

'Start calling her name. Don't stop whatever happens. You will be her anchor.'

From Aeryissa's hand a thin thread of silver dripped onto the symbols, as soon as the last one was covered they joined together and began circling Margaret. The chamber which held her could now be seen. Flashes of dark magic fought to keep their hold as they were drowned by Aeryissa's magic. Elfrad chanted Margaret's name the image of her face sharp in his mind. Slowly, the dark magic was being squeezed out, the wall collapsing. With a final howl the dark magic fled. Margaret stopped walking and calling, like a zombie she stood, face vacant, eyes staring at something they couldn't see.

'We need to get her back to her body,' said Aeryissa, as the howl of the wind abated taking the mist and fog with it.

'How? If we cannot touch her.'

'Simple my friend, we become what she was looking for. Do you want to be Sam or Balin?'

'Margaret,' called Elfrad, 'there you are, we must get back.'

Like a light turning on, her eyes filled with joy.

They ran. Margaret's laughter chasing them. Stopping either side of her chained body, beckoning her to come near, Aeryissa wasn't certain if she could see herself hanging between them, or only saw the images of Balin and Sam they were using.

'Stand between us.'

'We used to do this, when you were small. To check how much you had grown.'

Laughing, she moved closer, instantly her body began to vibrate, Margaret unaware stood between them, like a cloak her chained body wrapped itself around her drawing her in. The smile still etched on her face turned to a shriek as her core and body joined. Pins and needles flooded her limbs.

Aeryissa felt Elfrad fidgeting beside her at seeing Margaret in so much pain. She had to be sure that she was completely back inside her body before releasing her. Her eyes rolled back, snapping open, she cried at the sight of Elfrad standing before her. Catching her as Aeryissa broke the chains, he rubbed her chaffed wrists. Expecting her to collapse with fear and shock, he was taken aback when she pushed him away.

'Where's Balin and Sam?'

Elfrad's eyes turned to their chained bodies. Aeryissa held Margaret back before she could touch them.

'Is this how I was?' she asked.

Seeing the answer in the look they shared. She squared her shoulders.

'You found me, so you can find them.'

Aeryissa and Elfrad once again linked their senses, Margaret could see by the tenseness of their bodies that they had not managed to find them.

Breaking their link, Aeryissa stood in front of Balin and Sam. She couldn't touch them physically, but perhaps...

'They are not in the same type of prison as you were. In fact, they may still be somewhere inside their bodies. I propose we link with you as the bond between the three of you is strong, you're the glue that holds them together.'

Standing between them holding their hands, looking up at the bodies of Sam and Balin chained to the wall, Margaret wished she had magical abilities that would enable her to kill Meridian, as the thought formed, a door inside her mind; opened. She imagined them all at home safe, happy and living together in Kingdom. Aeryissa used Margaret's thoughts as a beacon to stab through the dark magic. Elfrad let his wizard senses merge with Margaret's imagery, bringing Balin and Sam into sharper focus. They all reacted at once. Aeryissa heard them. Margaret felt them and Elfrad saw them.

Working together like a heat seeking machine, all their senses and magic flowed together. For few moments Margaret got to feel what it felt like to be magical. Under their chained bodies Balin and Sam started to appear, hazy at first, getting clearer as they honed onto their signatures. Dirty and unkempt they both sat hugging their knees completely unaware of each other or them. Like a shield dark magic surrounded them their bodies out of reach, hidden from view. Margaret gasped, both Aeryissa and Elfrad held tight to her hands so as not to break the link.

'Elfrad is going to change places with me, both his hands holding yours. When I break away, Balin and Sam may fade from view, don't panic, as soon as you are connected to Elfrad they will emerge again. You must stay calm.'

Nodding at Elfrad, he brought his other hand across hers grasping hold of Margaret's as Aeryissa let go. Balin and Sam remerged, Aeryissa drew symbols in front of their faces. Once again, writing over them with silver, this time though, she pulled them out of the air and gathered half in each hand before throwing them over Balin and Sam. They reacted as if burnt, Elfrad held tight to Margaret as she screamed. The symbols and silver coalesced before turning into masks, after a few seconds it began to spread over their entire bodies, comatose bathed in silver they looked like statues.

Aeryissa drew back her hands, two nets appeared, wrapping first around Balin and then Sam. Puffs of fine black mist pushed out through the mesh trying to escape. Held back by her magic, it began to hiss. Drawing the nets away she blew fairy dust over the writhing mass making it boil and dance as it was slowly consumed.

With a quick flick of her fingers the silver flew back, disappearing under her skin. At the same time she broke their chains, their bodies fell, with a loud ooh from both of them they were once again reunited; core and bodies together.

Margaret knelt down, opening their eyes at the same time they made a grab for her, tears of joy running down all their faces.

'Your reunion will have to wait, we still have to get you back to the tower. Elfrad will be your anchor and guide. I need the three of you to clear your minds. You must concentrate, don't be distracted by anything else. Only listen to his voice.'

Elfrad began his siren song, Balin, the first to hear it closely followed by Margaret and Sam. They walked as if they knew where they were going sure footed and happy. A wall of dark magic tried to insinuate itself between them, Aeryissa quickly covering it with silver and fairy dust. Burnt and smouldering, its howls of pain loud enough to wake the dead.

'I believe you have all been transported before?' she asked them.

Before they had a chance to say anything, they were at the base of the tower, and Margaret was being hugged by Qiao.

'If you can transport why did we have to scale the tower?'

Aeryissa grinned, 'because it's much more fun.' At his look, she added, 'besides, you need to start using your wizard skills more. They are a bit rusty to say the least. That siren song, I'm surprised they followed it. Bit old school even for a wizard of your years.'

'It's the only one I could remember,' chuckled Elfrad.

CHAPTER TWENTY-ONE

Aeryissa listened to the sounds of the castle, pushing away those of no concern, honing in on those of interest. Now that everyone had gone she let a moment's peace wash over her. After the witches left and the rain and wind had died down the wraiths once again emerged. Luckily the elementals had done a good job in making it seem a natural event and not anything magical. Sending her senses out towards the hill encampment it appeared they too thought the same, without Meridian or the Dark Lord to keep them in check it seemed their forces could be easily distracted.

Peeling away from wall she headed towards the dungeons, she felt the walls and floor with her hands focusing her mind turning her thoughts inwards, silver left her body followed by fairy dust. Tumbling together, the dark magic screamed as it felt their touch. Aeryissa's inner eye watched as it swarmed away from the wall trying to evade her magic.

Bracing herself for the impact, she ran turning her shoulder towards it, her silver and fairy dust followed her like a cloud, all three blasting through the stone. The dark magic howled in anger, throwing a net she smothered its fire. As it tightened it thrashed and whimpered, pain its only friend.

Rounding a bend in the corridor the sight which greeted her

made her stop, bodies were piled up everywhere, drained, discarded like rubbish. Anger flowed through her body, to rip apart Meridian and the Dark Lord a need she felt like hunger. Her silver hummed, a separate entity she held inside her, part of her, yet not. It too ached to let fly, wanting to kill.

Shaking her head to clear her thoughts, she decided to release the Fae. Wrenching away the bars to her cell she approached the fairy cautiously. Her fairy dust had been turned against her, instead of hovering over her body it covered it like a blanket. Zekia's eyes rolled, the excruciating pain burnt and itched her skin. Her mind near breaking point, thoughts of what had been done to her dragon at the forefront.

Looking deep into the Fae's eyes she smiled, 'I'm Aeryissa,' holding up her hand she let her dust dance above her skin.

Zekia's eyes widened, a vampire shouldn't be able to have or use fairy dust. She tried to speak, the sounds, grunts and groans, desperately wanting to get away scared of what was going to happen to her.

Holding out her hands, Aeryissa's mind spoke to the dust, a siren song from her wizard sense. Anyone watching would have wondered what she was gathering in, as her hands picked up speed until they were only a blur. Zekia could feel the change. Her skin was cooling, her mind clearing. Her fairy dust gone, taken by the vampire standing over her. Feeling life come back into her limbs she began to sit up. The vampire was still in thrall to whatever spell she was using. Moving slowly away she stood up, not taking her eyes from her tormentor. Aeryissa's talons retracted, her eyes went from red to black to grey as they sort her out.

'If you give me a moment, I will be able to give it back to you.'

'You're a vampire, how can you even take it from me. Let alone give it back,' she asked incredulously.

'Brace yourself.'

Dust lifted, hovering for a moment before it flew, like an old friend coming home, Zekia smiled as it dived beneath her skin before bursting out to hover. Sheer happiness flooded through her.

'Thank you, whoever you are. Whatever you are.'

She twirled in delight, no more pain, her fairy dust returned, the sacrifice of her dragon the only thing that marred the occasion.

They had heard and seen the vampire pass their cell. Meridian had closed off their abilities leaving them barely normal sight and sound, frustrated at not knowing what was happening, they both jumped as she appeared in front of them.

'Hello Scotts.'

Reaching forwards she touched the Lobes ears, Meridian had filled them up with her dark magic, like a stopper in a bottle.

'This will hurt. I'm sorry but there is no other way.'

She blew gently into his ears. The Lobe screamed, his Lens partner unable to see but hear, cried out at his distress. Like a fly caught inside his head Aeryissa's magic wormed its way in, seeking Meridian's. In such a small space the dark magic had nowhere else to go, tasked with only filling the ear canals. It couldn't escape into the Lobes body. Hemmed in, it tried to fight back, the Lobe shaking his head trying to release the pressure from the two warring fraction's fighting inside his ears.

Aeryissa ignored his pleas and the wailing of his partner, focusing only on the dark magic. Slowly hers was winning, pulling the dark into the light. The Lobe groaned, fainting as the last part was pulled free. Aeryissa quickly wrapped it in silver and fairy dust tossing it into the waiting foresters net. Leaving the Lobe to recover she turned her attention to the Lens. Before the she had a chance to say anything she blew on her eyelids.

The Lens whipped her head from side to side trying to shake the feeling out. Aeryissa waited for the dark magic to emerge, tossed into another net it writhed in anger, its sting taken.

Zekia watched in amazement as the Scotts eyes and ears started growing as their skills returned.

'Who and what are you?' she asked, fearful of the answer.

'My task is to release you and take you back to the Akiva.'

'That doesn't explain how you can use fairy dust,' retorted Zekia.

The Scotts exclaimed, 'you can also use your ears and eyes as we do. We can feel you. How are you able to have both our senses in your obviously vampire body?'

'I don't have time to explain, others are waiting to be released.'

Peasey sat feeling sorry for himself, his staff and Wakanda abandoned on the floor. He looked up thinking that Katrina had returned, like him she also felt hard done by, often spending time sitting outside his cell, moaning to him about Meridian's latest crimes against Kingdom. When he'd asked questions about the Dark Lord she had sneered.

'He doesn't count, she is the one in charge.'

By the time the cell door fell to the floor, he had backed himself up against the wall, shaking in fear at the apparition standing before him. No vampire in Kingdom looked like this, she had all the characteristics but so much more. The collar she should be wearing the first thing he noticed, the second that she glowed silver. Aeryissa picked up his wand and staff.

'Take them,' she told him.

'I can't, if I use them my clan will suffer,' his voice trembled in fear.

'I'm here to save you, not hurt you. My name is Aeryissa.'

Peasey didn't trust her, a vampire with no collar, able to walk into the dungeon unimpeded. No he decided this is where I make my stand. He wouldn't fall for her tricks.

'I can hear your thoughts, the only one of us here who is tricky. Is you. Take them.'

'What now?' he asked.

'We begin.'

In seconds they flared, his wand turning from red to black, the white of his staff falling away revealing the darker colour hiding underneath. Both began to vibrate, desperate to let go, stuck like glued to his hands they weren't going anywhere. Ignoring his pleas, Aeryissa focused her mind. Peasey saw a wand and staff while she saw their true nature. Creatures dragged from the depths of dark magic, writhing and hissing like snakes.

She waved the wand and staff she'd conjured, taunting the ones Peasey held, they flew out of his hands, she let hers fly, meeting mid-air with a bang. Like two magicals fighting a duel, they fought each other, each wanting dominance over the other.

Peasey was terrified, unsure of what was going on still not trusting the vampire. Fairy dust made them smoke, howling like mad dogs as they tried to pull away, silver appeared and began to wrap around them, for a few seconds they seemed almost beautiful, before they began to eat away the dark magic making it scream. Writhing together they melted, ending up as a puddle on the floor. Peasey's eyes widened further as the vampire covered the mess with a forester's net.

Wiping her hands as if wet, she passed him a new wand and staff.

'It's done, you need to join the others.'

Mercia heard the cell door open and fall. The net covering her, burning her skin making it itch, helpless underneath it, her camouflage gone. Her senses though, were still intact, she knew another Alvie was in the dungeon, friend or captive she had no idea. She also knew something magical was happening and that it was strong and old. She recognised the scent. Mercia's eyes widened at the sight of a vampire with camouflaged skin. Her colours rapidly changed into the greens and browns of the forest, teasing her with their appearance, flashes of silver like lightening in between the changes.

Aeryissa grabbed hold of the net tearing and ripping it apart. She snarled and cursed as it tried to wrap itself around her looking for new prey to cover. Mercia huddled on the floor as the vampire lost her battle with the net, covering her completely it began to pulse. Edging her way out of the cell she faltered when she heard voices.

'It's okay Mercia, follow the corridor you're in and turn left.'

'Where's the vampire?' demanded Peasey, the others looking behind her.

'The net attacked her, the dark magic too strong even for her.'

'It must feel good to have your camouflage back,' said Zekia, allowing small puffs of her fairy dust to dance above her skin.

Mercia looked down at her arms and legs. Once again her colours were back, flaring bright as they settled.

'We have to get out of here,' whined Peasey, impatient at their apparent lack of urgency.

Mercia threw him a dirty look, she didn't have much time for magicians at the best of times and he was one of the worst, always putting his self-first. He would be happy to leave them all if he thought it would save his own skin. As a movement caught her eye she cried out.

'I thought you were dead, how did you break free?'

Shocked at the sight of the vampire, Mercia's colours tumbled over themselves in distress.

Gawain had been sleeping, hearing footsteps he sat up stretching his arms above his head. Shouting at the sight of his friend's crowding into the chamber.

He scrabbled backwards in fear as Aeryissa wrenched his cell doors apart. Plucking a strand of hair out of his head before he could react.

'She can help you,' they all shouted at once.

Pulling one from her own head she proceeded to twine them together. Her words too low for the others to hear, they all watched fascinated to see what she would do. Gradually the hair was changing, feathers started to appear in their place falling in a heap onto the floor. Gawain stared mesmerised as more and more hawk's feathers started to appear. His eyes followed their progress, hungry to be wearing them once again. Everywhere was now covered, each time one of them moved stirring the air, the feathers rose and fell as if dancing.

'Did Meridian destroy your feather?'

Hearing the answer before he spoke.

'That's good,' she said with a smile.

Before he could form a reply, she rolled her hands over and over, then opening her arms wide, brought them together with a bang. The feathers took flight, whirling around the cell so fast they looked like snow. Gawain stood in the centre of the storm unable to move, fixed to the spot by the vampires eyes.

Sure he saw her change into a hawk, before the feathers flew at him attaching themselves to his body. Closing his eyes against the pain which was excruciating, like being stabbed with a thousand knives. Slowly the pain grew fainter; Gawain gingerly opened his eyes to find all the feathers were gone. The others had watched him become completely covered, also sure that the vampire had turned into a hawk. Peasey certain he saw giant wings open, fanning the air guiding the feathers to their target. Gawain could feel his hawk inside him, desperate to fly and stretch his wings he turned to thank Aeryissa but she had gone.

'Finally, I have sat here and listened as you released the other leaders, wondering when it would be my turn.'

She looked through the bars of the cell at the large vampire sitting with his back against the wall. His golden collar gleamed in the dark, the chains that held him clanking as he moved to get a better look at her. Meridian had obviously made sure that he had took several beatings, dried blood covered his skin, some cuts had started to heal, others too deep. Only blood would cure those. His eyes flamed as she pulled the cell door and bars apart, taking large chunks of wall out as she yanked his chains free. Bending down, she placed her hands onto his collar and kissed the top of his head.

'Hello father.'

Letting the silver in his collar flow into her, the dark magic entered her system, drowning in the silver contained in her blood, once drained she removed the collar from her father's neck.

'You don't need to wear this anymore.'

Before she could destroy it, Lefu took it from her, placing it back around his neck.

'Not yet, the time isn't right. Until we know who we can trust, let everyone believe that the collars are still necessary.'

Chapter Twenty-Two

Gilda, felt the Dark Lord's disappointment permeating the Akiva. Lashing out in anger at those around him, the bodies were piling up, once loyal magicals now discarded husks. Only Coot and Amp seemed to be able to navigate the minefield of his bad temper. Meridian had gone off to investigate the tunnels, muttering something about the portal and its signature.

Once close, she had gone too far down the path of dark magic to pull back. All magic for Gilda was just a means to an end, only using it never allowing it to use her. Whereas Meridian had allowed herself to be submerged into its dark heart, her inner self sacrificed for the use of its darkest arts. There would be no going back, death her only release.

Choosing to stay close to the Dark Lord had been seen by Meridian as a betrayal, Gilda knew at some stage she would want to make her suffer for her choice. All she could hope for was that whatever malaise had overtaken him, would eventually wear off and he would be the victor, otherwise Kingdom would be torn apart by their fight to be its ruler.

'They haven't gone,' shouted Meridian. Are you listening?' she snarled at him, 'the portal is an illusion, they're still here. Which means they must be underneath.'

She had wanted to use a more stealthy approach to gain entry. He had overridden her caution. Instead, ordering the use of hundreds of stars to blast their way in giving their enemies time to disappear. Only a few unfortunate magicals left behind had been found hiding under a cloak of invisibility. Meridian had watched in distaste as he sucked them dry, his eyes never leaving her face. She had finally turned away in disgust, this desperate feeding made him look weak. The voice in her head constantly whispering, he is weak, he won't last.

Since emerging, strategy had disappeared. Allowing his senses to take over, feeding was becoming his overriding want and need. The effort to calm herself was evident for all to see.

'They know we are here,' said the Lasts and Potts together as Aeryissa nodded in agreement.

Casting her mind outwards she honed onto an elderly magician and his apprentice, making them both jump as her command bounced into their heads. Pushing themselves towards the front, they stumbled against each other in their haste to be first. Like all magicians their pocket's bulged, odd things fell over the sides escaping the confines only to be scooped up again. Their action's so fluid they appeared not to be aware they were even doing it.

'These two are most adept at gaining unauthorised entry into the armoury.' Ignoring their spluttering denials. She added, 'Qiao, will transport them to their hidden cache. All the weapons and magical items that they have stolen will be taken to the tunnels under the Hift quarry. Sentinels will accompany them plus Harsha.'

Turning away in disgust Aeryissa nodded to Pelagius.

'Once we receive the command we are going to flood the lower levels taking everyone out and away from the Akiva. We intend to create many small pools to keep those above distracted. None of them have seen real water in months,' explained Pelagias.'My brothers and I will draw you deep underground and bring you up inside the quarry. To do this we will have to wrap each of you in water. Magicals should not pose a problem. Norms or half norms may, their body makeup being different. Therefore we are going to have to split you into two groups. Elfrad, could you look after the norms?'

'He's coming with me,' announced Aeryissa.

'I am?'

'No one is to leave the tunnels before Dandelion receives my signal,' commanded Aeryissa. 'Our focus is on getting the Maia near enough to kill the Dark Lord. However, Meridian, will be given the chance to escape.'

Everyone erupted at her words, killing her, all that many could think about. Aeryissa let her face change, as her eyes turned black and her fangs slid out, the quiet air of menace swept over the crowd.

'Killing the Dark Lord must take priority. Seeing him killed will give Meridian pause for thought, make her wonder how strong our magic is. She may not take the opportunity to flee, if she doesn't, we will have no choice but to fight.'

Elfrad felt out of sorts, Aeryissa hadn't told him why she'd brought him along. Only that he had to make the decision; Greeter or Wizard. As a greeter he was only useful for dealing with norms. Since Aeryissa had included him in releasing the castle's captives. His wizard side kept bubbling to the fore. He noticed magicals looking at him differently, even though he still wore his greeter's garb.

Crouching down Aeryissa let her senses fan out. She knew he was doing the same. More and more he was using his wizard skills, most of the time without even realising it.

'While I'm in the Speaking Cave, you need to make your decision. Kingdom needs a new leader and we are all agreed that it should be you. Dandelion is dying, that's why she retired to her village this was to be her last cycle.'

'Who knows?' asked Elfrad, the sadness in his voice equalled by that on his face.

'Only those who need to.'

Entering the Speaking Cave, meant for Aeryissa all the plans made, would now become real. Sitting down she braced herself for what she must do. Light from above began to fold itself over her, moving over her body, entering her bloodstream, making sure she was who she professed to be before allowing the images to wake.

'Hello father, how are you feeling?'

'Better thank you, the clan has also recovered and are ready to fight'

'It's time to take your forces and head towards the old Hift quarry. There is no need to hide your intent. Make sure you bring the war horses, fully kitted out in all their finery. Zekia, I see you have a new dragon. She looks beautiful. I haven't forgotten what Meridian did. One day she will pay for her cruelty. Make your way to the Gorge tunnels which cross over with the quarry. They at least have enough room for your dragons to stand up. Scotts, can you inform Yox-All, that the majority of magicals are only to leave Pictures when the Dark Lord is dead. I'm aware that many want to join the fight. But if they all enter before that, they may find themselves becoming his dinner instead. Mercia, you look so much better, that colour suits you.'

'Thank you. I have done as you asked, everyone is fully prepared. We leave at first light.'

'You have your orders Peasey, make sure you follow them.'

'Gawain, you certainly don't look any worse for your ordeal. Your feathers look immaculate.'

Preening for a few seconds in his hawk form, he changed back to being a magical.

'It's so good to be able to fly again. None of us can wait to get our claws into Meridian, so to speak.'

'You will soon have your chance. Are your nests ready? Is everyone in place?'

Nodding his assent, he let her see into his mind. Satisfied all was ready. Aeryissa closed their connections.

Waiting to make sure they were all gone, she asked, 'do you think we have a chance?'

Fingerling's voice boomed around the cave, making the light waver as his image became clearer.

'Everything is in place, Flinders and the other Bodleian are busy scouring the grimoire's for how to deal with Meridian. Eadulf is poised to destroy the black mirror. The Fadia have called the Maia. We cannot hope to defeat both the Dark Lord and Meridian at the same time. All know the parts they are to play, distraction is all we can do and hope that she is convinced enough to fall for the trap. I have added my voice to your request. We know that she has been searching. Bringing forth some of what she seeks, should pull her off balance. Those we captured, swear that she and not the Dark Lord, was behind the magma being released. If this is so, it means at some stage she means to return and claim her prize. Our main priority for now though, has to be killing him. The Kaimi have been tracking his movements both before and after their wings were clipped. All say the same, at times he stands and stares lost in thought, usually after a burst in power. He may not be the threat we had first thought him to be. He is though, still powerful. If in concentrating our efforts on him, means Meridian is given the chance to escape, then so be it. We will deal with her once all traces of him have been removed from Kingdom.'

'I have spoken again to Dandelion and she has assured me that she wants to go through with it. Elfrad is still debating on what to do.'

'Let us hope he makes the right choice. We will need him. When the true King is finally revealed. It will cause uproar and confusion, while also sending a message to Meridian. Once the Dark Lord is dead, our magicals will expect everything to return to normal. That cannot happen while she is still a threat. Send the signal to Pelagius, tell him to release the water and remove everyone from the Akiva.'

Exiting the Speaking Cave, Aeryissa's mind was taken up with the tasks ahead. The biggest Hell Cat she had ever seen blocked her path. Its fangs, more than a match for her own. Its claws raking the ground in impatience.

'She's magnificent.'

Lifting her hand to stroke the soft striped fur, the cat snarled, pulling back her jaw to show her teeth. Aeryissa growled deeply letting her eyes turn black and her silver shine. The cat immediately mewed like a kitten.

'Leave her alone,' laughed Elfrad, 'she's still only a baby.'

'You have decided then?'

She pointed at his body armour, crossed swords adorning his back, the much heavier staff and redder wand of a Bomani on display. Aeryissa smiled at him in return; glad he had come to his senses at last.

Chapter Twenty-Three

Pelagius and his brothers finished wrapping the last of the magicals. All the norms had made it okay, only Meg and Balin suffering after effects. Taking a last look round they gave the signal to leave. Like pulling a plug, all the water they had created drained away taking the last of the magicals with it. Only the chaos created by the witches still raging above them was left to disturb the Akiva.

The tunnels beneath the Hift quarry were a hive of activity. The weapons secured from the magician's secret stash were being put to good use. Even Meg and Perical were getting used to handling the smaller stars. Margaret had surprised them all when she had taken a weapon similar to a wraiths spear gun, wielding it with no problem. Balin still suffering from being wrapped, sat in a corner only able to watch as each time he stood up his head spun.

The Finns and Potts relayed back that the dark magicals were taking full advantage of the pools of water which the Warra had created, at the same time Meridian broke through their first layer of spells. At the rate she was going it wouldn't be long before she broke through completely. By then, everyone hoped that Aeryissa would be back. Even the norms had wanted to get involved. When suggested they stay in the quarry. Margaret had been the first to stand up for them, arguing how this was as much their fight as Kingdom's.

With no magic to defend themselves, they had taken the majority of the smaller stars and spears. Fashioning shields out of cloth and wood. Dandelion smiled with affection, thinking they may look like a ragtag army but she couldn't fault their enthusiasm for the fight. Even Perical had joined in, showing his skill at using a bow and arrow. Basking in the praise he wasn't used to receiving.

'Remember, as hard as it may be, this is not about Meridian. This battle is about killing the Dark Lord. You all have your orders. This is not a time for heroics, stick to the plan and we may have a chance.'

Lefu didn't need to push to the front, everyone moved out of his way. Like the vampires, the large horses they rode wore golden collars, these though were only for show. Snapping and snarling they tossed their heads, black eyes constantly looking for prey. Their razor sharp teeth putting everyone on edge.

'Nearly everyone is here.'

Aeryissa smiled in answer as her senses picked up movement from inside Viveca.

'It's time. Elfrad, come with me. Alvie fan out in front of us. Make sure the trees give us cover. Kaimi take to the skies.'

Two large golden doors appeared giving the impression that if you walked behind them nothing would be there. Magicals jockeying to see earnt themselves dark looks from the vampires. Fia rode through, apart from Aeryissa no one knew what to expect. All eyes were drawn to the sword at her side, one word spread through the crowd, "Maia."

The trees made a wide avenue for the magicals to pass through, keeping the overhead canopy tightly woven, hiding them from sight. The forest creatures below felt and heard the pounding of hundreds of feet above them. They scattered this way and that, excitement filtering through to even the smallest bug.

Damala adjusted the strength of her glamour. It was taking all of her years of training to hold it in place. She hadn't been able to use it on the horse Layla was riding. Instead, they had covered it in golden armour, making it appear every inch a horse fit for a king. The ground beneath them shuddered a warning. Trees sprung up on either side, shaking their leaves, while their branches stretched towards the sun.

'We are to be your escort. Stay on the path we have created.'

As they came to a halt she peered through the trees to a sight she had never expected to ever see in Kingdom, magicals of all abilities mingling together while in the middle sat Fia, looking like the young girl she was and not someone who was going to kill a Dark Lord. The sword strapped to her side, appearing too big to be wielded by someone so small.

Everyone looked up as hundreds of owls flew into view. Landing in the trees they ignored the stares their arrival and silver feathers generated. Three of the larger ones landed in front of Aeryissa.

'Vidya sends her compliments,' their voices high and strained from under use.

She inclined her head in acknowledgement. Turning to face the gathering, she held her hands up for quiet.

'You have all been given your orders. Fight, if forced to, but remember, this is all about distraction and confusion. Our main aim is to kill the Dark Lord. Many of you will want your revenge on Meridian. Today is not that day.'

She waited for the mutterings to die down. Knowing how hard it would be for them to see her escape. Aeryissa smiled, pointing to the sky.

A huge dragon flew over their heads. Its silver underbelly in sharp contrast to its black scaly body. Shrieks of fright travelled through the throng, used to the Fae's smaller dragons no one in Kingdom had seen one this big before. Swooping towards the crowd, in mid dive it changed into a magical, floating down the last few feet, his silvery hair and glowing skin making him shine. As he touched ground, he smiled on hearing the Fae's dragons roar in greeting.

Fafnir's eyes fell upon Aeryissa, drinking in the sight of the silver glistening upon her skin, sending her signal, the yews parted.

Damala and Layla followed by the sentinels rode forward. It was taking all her strength to keep them looking like Bardolpf and his Baldassare. The crowds stunned to silence. No one spoke as they moved towards Fia.

'I present to you, Bardolpf, son of King Faolan,'

Even though he hadn't been seen since a child, none doubted her claim. All knew the Baldassare wouldn't rise for anyone other than a true King.

'We march.'

The questions everyone was asking, the suppositions they were making. She could hear like a wall of sound assaulting her ears. Closing off their chatter, she and Elfrad began to lead the army forwards.

All heads turned, they could clearly hear drums and trumpets beating out a loud refrain. A sound not heard in Kingdom for years. The Dark Lord swayed, something about the sound was making him feel uncomfortable. Meridian caught the movement, the dark voices in her head telling her to kill him. As if he heard he looked straight at her, his eyes seeming to bore into her soul.

He looked away first, his magic and power were waning, his senses not as sharp, a pain in his head like the drum beat they could all hear, wouldn't stop. Day and night pounding through him. Nothing had gone right since he'd emerged from his mirror. In sharp contrast, Meridian's power seemed to be growing, as his faded.

Commanding everyone to ready their magic, wraiths run back and forth bringing more weapons. As more and more magicals appeared, they readied their selves for battle, the voices in her head gleeful at the fight to come.

The Dark Lord hadn't moved, the twins standing beside him. Exasperation made Meridian shout her annoyance at him. Turning his black eyes towards her she felt a squeeze to her heart, astonished that he still had the power to hurt her. They stared at each other, hate spilling from both their faces. Now though, they needed each other. The showdown between them would have to wait.

Dandelion nodded towards Aeryissa and Elfrad and took her place at the front of the army. The ground behind her shook as the Yorkus burst through, followed by all the other trees. The Alvie soon catching up, their skin changing to green and muddy brown, nets held ready. Once the ground had settled she moved off.

Everyone was making some sort of noise, singing, shouting and cheering. Margaret had organised all the norms into groups, hitting their homemade shields with spears and sticks, a continuous beat coinciding with the thump of their marching feet.

Gawain led the Kaimi, the sky filling with all manner of birds. Joined by the silver owls, they looked like an aerial acrobatics team.

The Ambrogio had removed their collars, those magicals nearest giving them a wide berth. Lefu hadn't told anyone that the collars were redundant, keeping up the pretence, letting them all believe they would keep their instinct to kill in check. Fangs lengthened, eyes black, they bellowed their release, their war horses joining in. Rearing up hooves flying, showing their approval.

Objects fell out of the magician's pockets making magicals trip. Cursing them, they kicked them aside only to be tripped again as the objects scrabbled for a new master. Unconcerned, the magicians led by Peasey banged their staffs as they walked, like everyone else their magic had weakened but with a group of them they could still manage a small show. Each magician conjured fireworks. Shooting upwards they popped up above their heads, going for noise rather than display. Happy when everyone jumped as they merged together creating a loud explosion. Determined not be last Peasey had disobeyed his instructions, forcing his clan to the front, ignoring Aeryissa's command to stay at the back.

Zekia's new dragon crashed into the trees in her excitement at seeing Fafnir flying. Only stopping when one of the Yorkus grabbed her tail. Zekia readied her dust. Apologising, when she saw who was holding it.

The atmosphere around them constantly changed as the witches played with the elements, also using their combined magic to project the singing and talking. A cacophony of sound rolled around Kingdom's land. Every now and again Sam threw a small star for Perical to hit using his bow and arrow, making the explosion fan out across the crowd. A full orchestra had joined the trumpets and drums; no one could hear themselves think.

The Potts and Lasts like other Lobes worked hard to block the sounds from penetrating their ears. Many had headaches from trying to keep the noise at bay. Dandelion walked with her eyes straight ahead, conscious of all that was going on behind her but not letting it distract her.

Drawing to a halt, no man's land stretched in front of them. Both armies checking out their competition, hers noisy and colourful theirs quiet and menacing. The distance between the Dark Lord and Meridian worried her, they needed them closer together for their plan to work. Aeryissa heard her thoughts. Deciding now would be a good time. She and Elfrad stepped through the throng and swaggered to stand beside Dandelion. Now every inch a Bomani. Across his robes shimmer clung. Symbols of his wizard power standing out in sharp relief. Reaching behind his back he drew his swords, the silver Aeryissa had coated them with drawing all eyes.

Letting hints of silver peek through her skin and shimmer speckle her clothes. Her eyes changed from black to red and back again. Her jaw widened as her fangs appeared. Slowly removing the collar she'd put on earlier, Aeryissa slung it to the ground in contempt. Extending her talons she let her muscles ripple, knowing that from this distance their enemies would be dazzled both by her shimmer and silver.

Squinting in the sunshine Meridian caught the glints, her gasp audible to Gilda.

Not understanding her concern, she pointed, 'what is that?'

Fafnir flew over them, as he turned his silver belly caught the sun acting like a mirror, dazzling those who looked up. Coot and Amp were trying to get the Dark Lord to move but he was rooted to the spot, wincing as each drum beat and trumpet blare burst out.

Pulling her dark magic over her like a cloak, Meridian muttered to the voices in her head.

She knew her magic was strong. She had no doubts that she could win. Something though nagged at the corners of her mind. Not helped by the incessant chatter of the dark forces also battling for a place in her head. Kingdom was bringing its full force to bear. A last stand. The question plagued her, why now? Glamour was being used, she could smell it. Silver on show for all to see. That wasn't right. She needed time to think, to really see. Her dark magic was like rain, waiting to pour across her enemies. Its constant whispering, muddled her thoughts.

Her reverie was broken as she caught sight of Katrina looking in her direction.

'Why are you here?' she demanded.

Katrina as usual when faced with Meridian's anger pulled her head down and shook. Gilda seemed amused by her question, which infuriated her more.

'Well?'

'The clan leaders have escaped,' she spluttered in fear.

'When did this happen?'

'Days ago, whoever took them had enough magic to make it seem as if they were still incarcerated.'

Dark magic crackled wanting to be let loose. The Dark Lord's acolytes surrounded him, noisy and opinionated about what they thought should be happening, scorning Meridian's magic as inferior to his.

She for her part ignored their chattering, concentrating her thoughts outwards. Pondering how her magic had not been alerted to the release of the prisoners from the castle. There, she thought. A movable shield of some sort was being used. Pushing her dark magic hard against it to find its weak spots, the magic telling her that many more magicals were on the move and headed towards them.

Gilda watched her face, brows drawn together in concentration. Blocking out the thoughts she was picking up from those around them, trying to hone in on Meridian's.

Catching the words, 'it can't be. That's not possible.'

Meridian became aware of her probe, hissing at her, 'stay out of my head.'

Guarding her thoughts, she moved away from Gilda, thinking, the game has changed yet again.

Keeping up the momentum of their revelations, the crowd parted, to reveal Fia and the king, closely followed by the Baldassare. The magicals cheered as they passed. Once again the silver and gold on their horses drew all eyes from the enemy camp.

Dandelion took a deep breath, they had to get the Maia near to the Dark Lord. With Elfrad and Aeryissa beside her she walked forward. As Fia and the king dismounted, she gave him her sword, drawing all eyes as it was held aloft.

Everyone slowly quietened, waving their weapons making it clear that they were still ready to fight. Fafnir, with the Kaimi and owls patrolled the skies. The dark witches soon sent packing, their attempts to bring them down thwarted.

Ignoring the distractions around her, Damala fought hard to concentrate on keeping her glamour in place. It had wavered at one point, sure she'd seen Meridian's eyes flick towards her.

Aeryissa kept her eyes locked onto the Dark Lord. While his were drawn to Fia. The Fadia had bathed her in special herbs and oils, heightening her allure. By the glazed look on his face they were working. They couldn't let him snatch her. For their plan to work, Meridian had to be the one to appear to give her to him. She must be seen by her action, as helping to bring him down, even if inadvertanly.

Curling his talons he beckoned Fia towards him, Dandelion dashed to her side holding her tight as she tried to pull away.

At the same time Aeryissa kept the pressure up on Meridian, unaware that she, and not her dark magic was the cause of her confusion, making her doubt herself and abilities.

Meridian's hands clenched into fists wanting nothing more than to kill them all. Yet, she was conflicted. The voices in her head battering their commands against her skull. How to achieve her aims yet still escape. Her eyes drawn to the silver owls and dragon that shouldn't exist. Her head full of shouting, she couldn't think straight, her magic useless; she was caught in a vortex of doubt.

Looking inward, Aeryissa scanned the Glasserium honing in on Eadulf's signature. Guri noticed him stop and cock his head. Excitement flooded her old body.

'Get ready Purity, the old hag will soon be coming this way.'

'Will you stop calling me that,' she spat in exasperation.

Guri chuckled, they had grown close and liked to tease each other. Both soon coming to realise that having a friend was actually a good thing.

'Are you arguing again?' asked Eadulf. Ignoring their denials he continued. 'Once I get Aeryissa's signal to release the white glass it should take effect quickly. The mirror is already much paler. When Meridian realises what is happening to the Dark Lord. I have no doubt she will make her escape. Guri your job is to keep Purity calm. Meridian mustn't realise that she doesn't have full access to the Glasserium anymore.'

'My name isn't...'

'You know you like it really,' smirked Guri.

'Will you both stop? We have one chance to pull this off. She must leave Kingdom, otherwise our chance of stopping Meridian in the future will be lost.'

They all stood as if in a tableau, each locked in their own thoughts, waiting for something to happen to break the spell. Fafnir roared his disapproval of the Dark Lord's forces. Flames shot out of his mouth, making them run. The Dark Lord ignored their cries his eyes locked onto the girl. Now joined by the Fae and their dragons. The sky filled with Kaimi and owls all diving to attack.

Dandelion heard Aeryissa's signal. Keeping a tight hold of Fia, she thrust her towards Meridian.

The Dark Lord's roar wrenched her from her thoughts. Like an electric shock her touch flooded Meridian with heat. Her dark magic screamed a warning, writhing through her body like a scalded cat. It wanted the Dark Lord dead. Taunting her that while he lived she would be second best. The dark magic demanded him gone. Give him the girl it raged.

Once again the Otley twins interfered, before she realised what was happening, a tug of war between her and them with the girl in between was in place. Her dark magic rose up, with a flick of her hand she knocked them out, sending the girl crashing into the arms of the Dark Lord. Her senses in a whirl, her anger released, she tried to comprehend what she was seeing.

'Now Eadulf,' shouted Aeryissa.

Pressing one hand into the mirror while in his other he held a fragment of white glass, he willed it to flow. The glass from under the nets poured through his body and into the mirror, quickly turning it clear. As the last of it went in. The Alvie's nets began creeping across the black mirror's surface. Binding the frame and glass, distorting their shape. With one quick twist they broke its back.

The smell of the girl was driving him mad. He wanted the core of her so bad it was an ache piercing his body. Fia burrowed closer, letting her body and mind go she turned herself in the Maia.

The Dark Lord tried to prise her off as she began melting into him. The heat pushing through his body intense and painful.

Searching in his mind for his mirror he pulled its power around him, trying to shake her loose. Realising too late that what he'd called was not his mirror, only an illusion of it. The music which earlier had held him in its thrall, blasted out, the sound penetrating right through him. His blood began to boil, he watched in horror as his skin started to slough off.

The twins, wails of anguish at his demise, joined his roars of pain and anger. He glanced across at Meridian. Instead of helping him or killing their enemies she watched him as a snake did its prey.

As the Dark Lord was being consumed, her dark magic roared through her applauding his death. Shaking her head to clear its noise, she was surprised to see that the tableau of magicals hadn't moved. The so called King still stood between the vampire and the wizard. Their army making enough noise to wake the dead. The skies full of seekers, owls and dragons. Magicals on both sides spoiling for a fight. Drawn once again to the silver creatures. Meridian desperately wanted to find out where they had come from. Where she could find them. She thought she had found Kingdom's secret, the evidence in front of her proved she hadn't. Time seemed to slow down.

Aware of Coot and Amp trying to creep up behind her, she ignored their game. Now caught in a safe bubble of her own making she scanned those at the front of the army. She knew it. She could now see the edges of the glamour being used wavering, as the person controlling it struggled to hold it in place. Turning her mind towards the vampire and wizard, she pulled back in shock on hearing a voice telling her.

'Run.'

Unsure which of them it came from, the menace in its tone evident. The silver beasts, also managed to hold her magic at bay. Ignoring her probes, flashing their silver as a warning. Finally she turned her inner eye towards the one who had pushed the girl forwards. It told her that the magician had lived through many lives, and was on the cusp of getting a new one. Meridian sniggered to herself. That wouldn't be happening, someone had to pay. It might as well be her. Reaching inside, she called her dark magic forth, letting it pour from her mouth making a bee line towards the magician.

Dandelion caught Aeryissa's, 'thank you,' before several large hooks gouged into her skin, hunting her magic. Held with her feet off the floor, she hung suspended in front of Meridian. Cackles and spittle flying from her mouth, up close she looked even more ravaged by the dark magic she used. Dandelion let her mind go blank, using the mantra Aeryissa had taught her. Meridian mustn't be allowed to rummage around in her head. It took all her will to fill her mind with only the information they wanted her to know. She cried out as the dark magic swooped inside her. Pushing the images of a great magical army towards the front, showing them getting battle ready. The clans training for the fight to come, showing the Yorkus walking again in Kingdom. The Warra letting the water flow. Stockpiles of food and fresh water. Magic alive and getting stronger. Through it all silver flashed and shimmer shone. Dandelion let Meridian see what waited for her, if she stayed in Kingdom. The dark magic invading her body was working its way around her system, making her heart beat quicker and quicker. Her natural instinct for survival began to kick in. Forcing it down, letting herself be taken over. Her last sight was of her face, screwed up in anger, lined and wrinkled. As her heart stopped beating, her only regret was that she hadn't said goodbye to Margaret.

Meridian turned her attention to the glamour being woven. Sending her dark magic to seek it out and turn it off. Now that the fog in her mind had cleared, she didn't understand why the vampire and Bomani or even the king hadn't come to the magician's aid. None of them had moved, her senses looked for a trap, sure one was ready to be sprung. Laughter was not what she had expected to hear. As her dark magic stripped the glamour away. Instead of a king and the Baldassare, a woman and warriors sat upon the horses their finery and status all gone. Even the sword held aloft, was now reduced to a dull metal. The birds and beasts also appeared stripped of their silver, shown up for what they were.

Her dark magic told her to stay and fight, put an end to them all. Meridian however knew something wasn't right. Still unsure what had actually caused the Dark Lord's death, his mirror or the girl. She'd heard the magicals chatter about the Maia, the sword held by the king which hadn't gone anywhere near the Dark Lord. Even though she had wanted him dead, she needed to understand how it had happened. Why all this showmanship. It worried her that she was missing something. The magicals in both camps were itching to fight each other. Her side kept shouting for her to get on with it.

She knew she must pull herself together and do something. Her magic was strong. The Dark Lord was dead. The king she'd shown to be false. Her magicals were ready for war. Yet, she held back. Unused to indecision or doubt she tried to decide whether to flee or fight.

Trumpets sounded, drums beat out a refrain. Everyone from both camps turned towards the sound. Bardolpf enjoyed his entrance, when the Fadia handed him the sword, even though it wasn't the true Maia, that having been absorbed by Fia, he'd still felt privileged to even touch it. Its strength gave him hope they could pull off the ruse. Even from this distance he could see the confusion on Meridian's face. She wanted to strike, but the doubts they had sown made her stay her hand. Now they had to convince her to run.

Drawing the sword, he pointed it, making it clear that he would now use it to kill her. Hoping her indecision still held, Bardolpf rode at the head of the Baldassare, like him their drawn swords all pointed at Meridian and her followers. Holding the sword above his head, he shouted.

'This Maia was created for one purpose only, to kill those in thrall to dark magic. The Dark Lord is dead. Now it's your turn to die.'

There was no mistaking that this King was real. Meridian could smell the royalty emanating from him, how was this possible? She muttered. Her dark magic hurtled around inside her head in a panic, it knew, like her that he spoke the truth. The power of light, leeching from the sword, was already looking for the dark. It shouted at her to flee. Her own magic told her that a trap was being set. But each time she tried to hone onto the thought. It felt as if it was being dragged away. Finally, her sense of self-preservation kicked in, she opened a portal dragging Gilda and Kristina with her. Falling quickly into her pure mirror, she had no time to realise that it wasn't hers anymore, before the spell she'd conjured catapulted them out into Novia and safety.

Coot and Amp melted away into the crowd, pulling their hoods low over their faces, still reeling from the destruction of their master. Both vowing that he would be avenged.

Chapter Twenty-Four

'Elfrad, collect the crystal and take the other wizards into the Akiva. Pelagias is ready with his brothers to flood the lower levels pushing anyone left back up to the surface. Detonate the bombs and make sure that there are no survivors.'

Aeryissa turned as a portal opened and the Fadia stepped through. Bardolpf stepped forward and handed the sword back to their safe keeping, a collective sigh wove through the camp as the portal closed.

'Are you ready your majesty?' asked Aeryissa, dipping her head in deference.

Bardolpf's eyes crinkled up as he laughed, 'please don't call me that, it sounds much too formal.'

Smiling in reply, she waited for him to address the crowd.

'The Dark Lord is dead. Some of you are angered that Meridian escaped. Today we weren't strong enough to defeat them both. In a war you have to pick your battles. Today's victory was won not by working alone. But by us all working in tandem. Put aside your differences. Collectively we have shown that we can win.'

Cheers filled the air, all hoping that now the Dark Lord was dead, magic would return.

'Now is not the time for celebration. We may have defeated our enemy but at the same time we have lost a dear friend. Dandelion gave her life willingly, as did Fia to help free Kingdom from dark magic's embrace. Don't let their deaths be wasted.'

Margaret heard Bardolpf's words which sounded hollow to her, cradling Dandelion's head, she crooned to her as if lullabying a child to sleep. Qiao sat next to her with his head on his knees quietly crying. Sam and Balin watched, both concerned how much Dandelion's death would affect her.

Sam for one had never seen his mother's eyes flash so hard and cruel. Not even when Barry was at his worst. Each day she spent in Kingdom changed her in some way. While his father seemed to diminish. He still hadn't recovered properly from being held prisoner. Jumping at the least little thing. Spooked by everything, his nerves on show, stretched taut ready to snap. Glancing over to Meg and Dillon, Sam smiled, his friend had also changed since spending time away, now much more alert and aware. Standing taller, more at ease with himself. As soon as Meg had clapped eyes on him she'd pulled him into a hug, Dillon prised her off keeping her at arm's length, seemingly for the first time embarrassed to show his feelings.

Elfrad joined Herwig and Fianna, they had placed the crystals in all the tunnels. Meridian's forces running away at the sound of their voices.

He had many emotions running through his body, sadness at the death of Dandelion, pride that she chose him as her successor. It hadn't taken long for his wizard self to emerge. Even after such a short time he found it hard to imagine himself as a greeter. Walking back out into the sunshine, Elfrad watched Bardolpf work the crowd smiling each time someone stepped too near and the Baldassare pushed them back.

'They're all ready,' he told Aeryissa. 'The dark magicals have tried to get out, finding the tunnels blocked, they have gone down.'

Acknowledging him with a nod, she looked inward and told Pelagias to release the water. Counting to twenty, Elfrad detonated the crystals. With one almighty explosion the top of the Akiva rose up high into the air before slamming down, making the ground shudder. As the cloud of dust dispersed it was no more, only a few trickles of water left lying on its surface.

'Margaret, it's time to release Dandelion's body, we need to prepare her for burial.'

'Why did she have to be sacrificed?' She spat, her eyes flashing their hurt and anger at losing her friend.

'She gave her life willingly. This was to be her last life cycle that's why she retired to her village. Dandelion had lived a long time, she was dying. Kingdom didn't call her, she offered. She wanted to go out on a high.'

Margaret's eyes filled with tears, letting them fall down her face.

'She was my friend,' she sobbed.

Slowly the camp cleared, the clans going back to their settlements and the Kaimi to their nests. The Yorkus waited for their orders, while the other trees took delight in having the Alvie back. The Warra busy making sure everyone was supplied with enough water for their needs.

'Bardolpf, we won't have long before Meridian regroups. Magic is still weak in Kingdom. As we saw today, hers is much stronger. Once she realises how we duped her, the next time we meet; she will not be so easily thrown. If we gained access to the Osias. Would you be able to boost our magic like your father used to?'

'Even if we could get passed the magma she has released. I'm not strong enough to walk the circle, it could make matters worse.'

'Vengeance,' pronounced Lefu. 'That's the only path we have left her with. You all saw how dark magic has taken her over. It has its claws firmly into her. That type of magic doesn't stop until all are made dark. We have to ready ourselves for whatever onslaught she will unleash. Today we fought and won. Next time, victory may not be so easily taken.'

Trees ringed the clearing, a carnival atmosphere presiding. Margaret had insisted that the celebration of Dandelion's life was full of fun and laughter. Since the Dark Lord's death and Meridian's escape, Kingdom had become even more muted. No one knew who to trust, only a few dark magicals had been captured or killed. Many others had gone into hiding, not only in Kingdom, Novia also held their fair share. The smell of their dark magic not easily shed.

Since Dandelion's death, Margaret found herself withdrawing from everyone. Even having Sam safe and with her in Kingdom, wasn't enough to pull her out of her misery. She had tried explaining to Balin, not only about the grief she felt over her friend's death, but how she felt in herself. Something in her was stirring. The door in her mind opening wider. When looking in a mirror, visually, she saw the same Margaret looking back. Inside though, she knew she wasn't. The taste of magic when joined with Aeryissa and Elfrad, hadn't really left her. She wasn't magical in the sense they were, but she had changed.

'Mum, are you okay,' asked Sam, a worried look on his face.

Bringing herself back to the here and now, she answered, 'I'm fine. Where's your father? I haven't seen him since the festivities kicked off.'

'I'm worried. Since we were taken and even more since he was wrapped, he seems to be growing weaker. Earlier, I found him sitting against one of the trees ringing the clearing. An Alvie told me he had fallen, he didn't want anyone told, so she ask the tree watch over him.'

Margaret headed towards the inner ring of trees, patting their trunks as she passed.

'There you are.'

Balin smiled, thinking, every day she got lovelier. Since circumstances had brought them together, the changes in her were now even more pronounced. Unaware of the glow she carried, lighting her skin from within or of the affect she had on others when she smiled. He loved her now more than ever, unfortunately, he also knew their time was limited. His body was failing, the trauma he had sustained had taken its toll.

Putting his arm around her shoulder he pulled her towards him in a hug, kissing the top of her head. Balin closed his eyes breathing in the scent of her.

'I sat too long in one position that's all,' he mumbled, trying to mask the pain shooting up his back.

The pine tree he'd been sitting under shook its branches in admonition at his lie. Sam and Meg waved as they emerged from the trees, both noticing how slow Balin was walking.

'Have I missed it?' shouted Dillon, racing to stand beside them.

Above their heads small lights appeared, swaying to a sound only they could hear. The ground shook and heaved, a hole appeared growing wider, sending everyone scurrying backwards out of harm's way. Hands appeared then branches, heaving himself upwards, Fingerling stood tall and proud in front of them. The cheers of the Yorkus rent the air, soon joined by all the other trees ringing the clearing, all come to honour Dandelion.

Aeryissa and Elfrad moved towards the front, the crowd moving aside to let them pass. The pounding of feet heralding the arrival of the king. Layla and Damala hurried over to join their friends. At the sight of the leaders their clans shouted their names in jubilation. The crowd swelled as more and more magicals piled into the clearing. Fingerling shook his branches, rustling leaves they couldn't see, yet heard by all. One by one the crowd grew quiet.

The sky lit up, drawing delighted oohs, hundreds of tiny stars exploded their colours making the crowd cheer as they fell like rain over them. Magicians and witches had banded together to write Dandelion's name across the sky. As each added their spell, her name shone a beacon for all to see. As the last letter faded and the sky turned dark, everyone settled down to reminisce, torches were lit, campfires blazed. Stories of Dandelion's life were dredged from memories, shared around, earning her a place in the folk lore of Kingdom.

The next day, everyone was up early, eager to get home; even if it was to prepare for war. All heard the command echo inside their heads.

'Stop and listen.'

Used to hearing Aeryissa's voice, even when nowhere in sight, none thought to disobey.

Elfrad told them. 'We gathered yesterday in celebration of our dear friend Dandelion, who gave her life willingly and honourably to stop the Dark Lord. She would be proud and probably embarrassed, at all the kind words that have been said about her. She and the Maia enabled us to kill one enemy. Kingdom though, is still under the threat posed by Meridian. She will strike, when? We have no idea, or even where or how it will happen.'

He paused, to let his words sink in.

'You proved that by working together you could boost your powers. This must continue. Our spies tell us that since she fled, she has hid herself away. Her cohorts however have been working hard to gather more to her side.'

The crowd muttered, their words laced with equal amounts of fear and anger.

'Rumours have been circulating that Meridian was the one who triggered the magma. She mustn't be allowed to gain access to the Shimmers or the tomb,' explained Bardolpf, 'we cannot abandon Novia to Meridian, neither can we take our fight there. Until she makes her move, our hands are tied. Take the time to hone your magic and skills. Practise in groups, make your magic go further. Magicals will be arriving home from Pictures. Their magic will be stronger for a while, use them wisely to practise. Stay alert, danger hasn't gone away. Pockets of wraiths are still hiding out, including many dark magicals. These still need to be rounded up and dealt with. The less she can rely on for help, the better. Go home, be prepared. When the call comes do not hesitate. If we lose the coming war; we lose Kingdom.'

The sky darkened, as the beating of giant wings caused a flurry of hats to fly off. The dragon flew over the crowd. Growing smaller as he circled, changing into his magical form as he descended. The Baldassare drew their weapons ready to strike.

'Your majesty, forgive my interruption. I need Aeryissa to come with me.'

'What's happened?' she asked.

'There's been a breech.'

'Elfrad you know what to do.'

Before questions could be asked, she grabbed Fafnir's hand and they both disappeared.

'Are you ready yet? Qiao is getting impatient,' she asked, wishing they'd hurry up.

Bilberry had sent word that Dandelion had been adamant that her home was to be given to Margaret. Still in shock at her death and from being given such a gift, she was still undecided about going back to where she felt her journey had actually started. She knew she couldn't go back to her old life, even though it would mean being separated from Sam. Too much had changed. Balin certainly didn't want to return to Novia.

Remembering the peace and tranquillity of Dandelion's home, helped make her decision final, she hoped also that it may restore Balin to better health. Persuading Sam to come with them before he returned home had been much more difficult. He wanted to leave Kingdom. Only persuaded to change his mind when Meg and Dillon said they would like to see where Dandelion had lived. Damala had also asked to join them. Having been close to Bardolpf when he was a wolf, she was finding it hard to see him as a King.

The armoury was a hive of activity, having lost the Akiva it was decided that this would be the new base of operations. Even though no one actually wanted Meridian to come back, they knew she would. None had any doubts, if not stopped, she would endeavour to clear the magma, taking control of the Shimmers and the tomb.

Elfrad watched as the walls and shelfs were stripped of their weapons, the great hall bare, only the shields remaining. The stone flagstones were muddy from all the feet which had been crossing it since yesterday. Sconces had finally arrived to fill it with light. Several times he'd had to ask them to stop moving around. So nosey they kept plunging parts of the hall into darkness, curses and bruises the result. Following each other in a line, the tables came in butting each other in their need to grab the best spot. Chairs, chose a table one minute, before flying across the hall to sit themselves at another.

Banging his staff, he commanded, 'enough, find your places and stay there. Or I will turn you all into firewood.'

Pointing his Wakanda at the great fireplace, the whoosh of the logs igniting gave them all pause for thought. In seconds, the table and chairs had settled down, mutterings whispered as a few stools tried to insinuate themselves. Pushed out, they arranged themselves around the walls, ready to grab a place if the chairs moved.

Feeling his pocket vibrate, he took out a small blue book and placed it onto a table. Flapping open to the middle pages, hands appeared, then a head. Forcing her body out, leaving her legs behind, Henty surveyed the room, before jumping clear.

'Your maps. Try not to lose these ones.'

'We didn't lose the last ones, they were destroyed.'

'That maybe so, but I believe you planted the crystals that burnt them.'

'Why so tetchy? It's not like you,' he asked, sitting on the edge of the table. Rapping its top with his wand when it groaned.

Hopping up beside him, Henty closed her eyes for a moment.

'We are tired. Flinders has us searching the grimoires for a way to destroy Meridian. Do you know how many there are in Kingdom? Let alone Novia. The writing is so small, archaic languages only some of us are expert in. Grimoires that refuse to open, those that won't close and dare to quote their words to us over and over.'

Both were startled when a voice floated out of Elfrad's book.

'There is one book that eludes us. Some believe that it is a myth, legend or make believe.' Narrabri shot out from the centre, dizzy from his quick exit. 'Every grimoire we find has a tantalising bit of knowledge concerning it. Following their path, lead us nowhere. We ignore their trails and they make us return to the beginning.'

'The weird thing is,' said Henty. 'We all feel that it wants to be found.'

Narrabri sighed, 'which of course doesn't help matters.'

'What does Flinders have to say?'

'Flinders says get back to your work and leave Elfrad to his maps.'

The voice echoed loudly around the room. Before they could form a reply or even say goodbye Henty and Narrabri where unceremoniously sucked back into his book.

Lefu cleaned his sword, it felt good to be amongst his clan getting ready to hunt. Glancing up he caught Cian staring at him, the anger that always surrounded him held tightly in check. He hoped that the hunt would give his old friend some release from its clutches. Cian hadn't confided in him the reasons for it and to be fair he hadn't asked. Yet anyone seeing him watch Margaret, soon become aware of why. Forbidden by Kingdom, even if both parties were willing, a vampire could not become close to a norm.

Silently the vampires fanned out. Their collars lay in a pile back at the hive, their senses flooding their bodies. Blood sang in their veins, turning their pale skin luminous. Faces warped by their need to kill, eyes black holes, gaping mouths with razor sharp teeth. Speckles of gold caught the sunlight making the horror of their countenance appear strangely beautiful. Trees shrunk back as they passed, Alvie blending into their trunks. Most confident they wouldn't hurt them, yet none were willing to take the chance. Kaimi, on a reconnaissance mission heard their roar as they spotted the Gork's. Not wanting to witness the slaughter, they wheeled away as fast as their wings would take them.

Harsha and Emry's ran side by side urging each other on, they were acting as the chasers. Herding their prey towards the vampires waiting on the other side of the hill. As the Gork's broke cover, their squealing and grunting heightened the vampires need. Their large bodies and warty skin slick with sweat from the chase. Crammed onto the small path that ran around the hill, pushing against one another in their efforts to break free. The vampires waited, as bad as their prey they snapped and snarled at each other. The first Gork broke free as others soon followed. Lefu brought his hand down and the hunt was on. The vampires flowed over the Gork's, biting their necks draining them dry in one fluid movement.

Lefu as the leader of the clan hunted the largest Gork. A wily old beast determined not to be caught, it had run into a dense wooded area. Immediately the trees disappeared leaving it exposed. Shrub and gorse bushes its only cover. Lefu stood perfectly still, he could hear the pant of its breath, smell the stench of its body. Suddenly it shot out of its cover, legs flying, the pounding of its heart music to his ears. In one fluid movement he was astride its back, wrapping his talons around its neck he wrenched its head off, blood spurted, he leant forwards and drank.

Covered in blood he listened for sounds of the hunt. It was over, now, only the slurping and chewing of vampires feasting could be heard.

Cian was the last to return to camp, covered in blood, still dripping as he walked, he carried the heads of four wraiths. Throwing them down in front of Lefu, he snarled.

'These are what we should be hunting.'

Not taking his eyes from Cian, Lefu commanded, 'kneel.'

Cian didn't move. In one swift movement he was down. Lefu whispering in his ear.

'Margaret will never be yours. Do not bring your anger over what you cannot have into the clan. If you ever show your opinions to me like that again. I will kill you.'

The noise level dropped away, as the vampires entered the hall.

Although showing no signs all were aware that earlier they had been hunting Gork's. All hoped that their blood lust had been sated.

Taking their seats next, Aeryissa and Elfrad scanned the crowd making sure that everyone who had been asked had now arrived.

Elfrad spoke first, 'Meridian has been holed up as suspected with her cronies in Greenwich. So far, she hasn't been doing anything, apart from killing her own magicals. This will soon change. Our spies have reported seeing dark magicals out and about trying recruit others to their cause, tempting them with offers of magic and power.'

Addressing the clan leaders, Aeryissa asked, 'what have you managed to glean from your captives?'

'We have been working with the Alvie and the Fae,' said Gawain. 'When we spot any magicals, with help from the foresters and their trees, they are herded into a group. The fairy dust ascertains if they are dark or light. If dark we hand them over to the vampires.'

Peasey sat with his arms folded over his chest a look of petulance on his face. The items in his pockets spilling out of one and returning to the other in a continuous stream. Testament to how upset and angry he was.

'Well?' she asked. Not allowing him to voice his thoughts, she continued. 'I believe you no longer wish to be the leader of the Quiryn? That you are finding the tasks set, beneath you? The real problem though, is that you personally do not want to do anything to help save Kingdom.'

Peasey looked mutinous as all eyes turned his way.

'Are you going to explain your behaviour,' demanded Bardolpf. Leaning forward, he let him feel the full force of his miss matched eyes as they raked him with their laser like gaze.

Cornered, Peasey wilted. The steady stream of objects leaving his pockets stopped.

'I'm scared.'

Quickly looking up, a red blush suffused his face, hands shaking he whimpered.

'When Meridian held me captive, being confined, unable to escape, affected me more than I would have thought possible.'

Silence greeted his words.

'With his majesties permission, we have been monitoring Peasey's communications,' announced the Scotts.

Aeryissa smiled, as his face turned white. He began to shake. The hall darkened, the shields displayed on its walls shook. The fire burst into black flames shooting up roaring its escape. The tables hummed and vibrated. Magicals ranged around the sides of the room moved closer to the centre light, aware of whisperings close to their ears, swotting at themselves as if attacked by flies. The Ambrogio touched their collars. The Fae's dust hovered. The Alvie's skin flashed colours of concern. The Kaimi rose up in their bird forms seeking the threat which had entered the hall.

Elfrad nodded at Herwig and Beadu, as the warriors approached Peasey, his eyes frantically looked for a way out, he was tripped by his own items still falling from his pockets in a mad rush, as his stress levels rose. They hauled him up, sweat glistened on his face, a foul stench emanated from his body filling the hall with its noxious smell.

Holding him tight between them, they felt him flinch as Aeryissa grabbed his head holding it still, looking deep into his eyes, slowly the room began to lighten, the fire died back down and the whispering's stopped.

Aeryissa broke contact with Peasey as did Herwig and Beadu. The temperature in the hall changed, dropping by several degrees. His eyes rolled to the back of his head the voice that emerged nothing like his own.

'This creature is mine,' rasped the voice. 'My vengeance will not be swift, but it will be painful. Sides are being taken, battle lines are being drawn. Others have joined me. Who can you trust?'

Manic laughter burst from his mouth. Falling to the floor his feet banged against the ground as his whole body shook. He clawed at his face as if to remove his eyes. The crowd held back by sentinels, could only watch in horror as black lines covered his skin. He clutched his chest as he fought for breath, giving one long agonised scream before laying still.

The hall erupted in shouts. The Quiryn unsure of what had happened. With no idea that their leader had been taken over by dark magic, they all thought they too would now be under suspicion. As Bardolpf stood, the Baldassare moved. Bringing everyone back to the present. Shocked but quiet, they waited for him to speak.

'Keekle you are to take over as leader of the Quiryn. No one else in your clan or this room has been compromised. Meridian is a sly and cunning sorceress. She is much more dangerous than she was before.'

'Why wasn't Peasey dealt with sooner? Surely allowing him to enter the hall with everyone present, was placing us all in danger?'

'It was felt, you all needed to see how far Meridian's power can reach,' replied Elfrad. Indicating to the sentinels to remove Peasey's body.

Bardolpf's voice rang out, 'you have all seen here today how dark magic can be used to infiltrate our defences. It lives inside Meridian like a beast. Our love for Kingdom gives us our strength but also our weakness. She will use anything she can against us. Stay alert and be vigilant. If you suspect someone has become tainted, no matter who it is, it is your duty to speak up. Lobes and Lens have been tasked to watch and listen. Honing in on certain key words. Those who have quickened to her call will be killed.'

Chapter Twenty-Five

Margaret held her face up to the sun glad of its warmth. Smiling to herself as she heard Sam and Meg argue over which of them was the best shot as they practiced their archery. Perical, a surprisingly good teacher once he'd got over his attitude of self-importance. Knocked out of him by Dillon. Balin the one to separate them. Bruised and battered they had given each other a wide berth. Only putting aside their differences when a couple of dark witches had risen up and tried to take Meg prisoner. Both wading in, fists flying, their magic weak but finding its mark. Hearing their shouts others came running, the witches had broken free intending to run. Caught by a large tree which had pushed its way up, its branches easily catching them. Dropping the pair into the waiting arms of a vampire, one glance at his fangs and they both fainted.

At first, when they had arrived at Dandelion's house, it seemed that the fight for Kingdom was happening elsewhere. The villagers, seemingly unconcerned with the coming war. Once they had all settled in though, Margaret soon began to notice the changes. Outwardly still a sleepy village. Ringed by trees, hills that kept moving and water that one day could be a stream and the next a raging torrent as the Warra went about their business.

Bilberry told them how all over Kingdom the same things were happening. Magicals were honing their skills. The little magic they had being pooled with others. The clans working together in groups to hunt those who were tainted by dark magic. Everyone knew they had to act as if they hadn't a care in the world. While at the same time prepare for war.

Balin mentioned the strain everyone was under each time he returned from the village. Spies were what everyone feared most. Codes were used. The Kaimi and messengers kept busy bringing news and instructions. Walking amongst the many trees that had returned with them. Always gave her pleasure. Patting them as she passed, their 'good morning,' echoing in her ears. The trees which usually surrounded the village had been beside themselves when the others arrived. No one knew why they had come. Whatever their reason, they all agreed they liked having them near.

'Anyone home?' asked Damala, waving her hand in front of Margaret's face.

'Sorry, I was lost in thought, enjoying the sunshine. How are you feeling?'

'Whatever Bilberry put in that soup, really didn't like me.'

'There was nothing wrong with it,' shouted Bilberry from the kitchen. 'Too much wine more like,' she added, with a chuckle.

Sam watched Meg making a circlet of flowers, thinking, how lovely she looked.

As if hearing his thoughts, she looked up.

'What are you smiling at?'

'I'm just happy.'

'Are you glad you came? Instead of going straight back to Novia?'

'Well I was at first until I realised nothing's changed. This may seem like a calm and serene place, but it's not. I'm fed up always being on alert. Not knowing who to trust. I have so many codes going round inside my head. I worry I'm going to say the wrong one and be accused of turning dark.'

Meg put down the flowers and picked up his hands.

'Your mother needs you. She is so happy that you're here.'

'She doesn't. Not only because she has my father by her side. She's different, and is getting more so each day. You never knew her in our realm. Scared to say anything. Always one step behind anyone else; as if apologising for even existing.'

'I do know what you mean. Not how she was before. But here in Kingdom. She is stronger, not so much physically, but in her presence. Sometimes when looking at her eyes they remind me of Aeryissa's, the way hers pin you to the spot.'

'What are you two talking about?'

Perical flung himself down beside them. Laughing, when Dillon joined them, panting from his run.

'Mum.'

'She's scary.'

Before he could ask what they both meant, Balin appeared, telling them supper was ready.

The table groaned with all the food Bilberry had laid out. The stars twinkled above them, lanterns swapped for sconces, their muted glow bathing them all with golden light. Glasses chinked as toasts were given. Bottles vying to refill any that fell empty. The conversation varied and lively, thoughts of war forgotten.

Sam looked across at Meg, at her nod, he stood up. Slowly everyone became aware of him standing glass in hand. Perical nudged Dillon, winking as he glanced towards Meg. Dillon looked at his sister's face shining with love for Sam. Gulping his drink, making himself choke, a bottle raced to fill his glass. Meg turned towards him, at the raise of her eyebrow he lifted his glass. Sam could see everyone looking at him expectantly, now the moment had come his knees felt weak. Turning to his parents he saw the love they had for each other evident on their faces. Hoping, when they looked at him and Meg they saw the same look reflected.

'Mum, dad and friends.' Swallowing, he quickly added, 'I have asked Meg to marry me.'

'Oh Sam, that's wonderful,' Margaret hugged Meg making her squeal.

'Has she said yes though?' slurred Perical drunkenly.

Cuffed round the ear by Dillon, he lunged towards his friend and fell off the bench.

'I'm glad I came back to spend time with you and dad. It's given us a chance to really get to know each other. But I want to go home. This is your life, not mine. I only entered Kingdom to find you.'

'I understand, I really do. I will miss you. Now though, as Balin's son, you will be able to visit anytime you want to.'

'Of course we'll visit. Meg will want to return and see Dillon. He doesn't want to go back yet. If at all.'

'Your still happy to have the wedding here?'

'Bilberry and Damala would never forgive us. Between all the food one wants to "create" and the costumes the other expects us to wear. I'm sure it will be a lively affair if not a weird one.'

'Charming,' said Bilberry, making Sam jump.

'Are you sure you are not a transporter like Qiao? Only every time I say something you don't like. You seem to have a habit of popping up and telling me off.'

Tapping the side of her nose, Bilberry chuckled, 'wouldn't you like to know.'

'Elfrad cannot come. He sends his regards. Since the death of Peasey, both he and Aeryissa have been busy checking the clan members for any dark magic. Word has come that Meridian may soon be on the move. Even though she hasn't been seen outside of her lair in Greenwich. Bardolpf gave me permission to attend the wedding. Then I have to go back.'

Margaret smiled at the confident man in front of her. When she'd first met Qiao he had been a hesitant boy, gangly and shy. Now with his new found fame as a transporter his confidence had grown.

'I'm glad you're here. It wouldn't be the same without you.

Bilberry has made your favourite cakes and Damala has created an outfit for you.'

'Please no,' he laughed.

Sam felt so nervous, he wanted to marry Meg. He hadn't expected though so many magicals to attend. Most they didn't know. Bilberry insisted they all come. They were old friends of Dandelion and as the wedding was to take place in her house and grounds, they had to be invited. Damala had festooned everywhere with bunting and flowers. Even the trees had given in to her demands, allowing her to "dress" them. Coloured lanterns had arrived for the occasion. Some conjured by the magicians, others turning up hearing a party was taking place. Tables and benches not happy where they were placed, constantly moved around, much to Bilberry's annoyance. She had called on the services of a Butler for the event. Who in her opinion, wasn't capable of doing his job properly; meaning, she had to supervise everything.

'You look beautiful,' said Margaret.

Dressed in a long white floaty dress, jewelled sandals and matching belt. A witch who's forte was hairdressing, had turned Meg's unruly locks into a cascade of curls. The purest white roses Margaret had ever seen adorned her hair like a crown. Her bouquet made up from wild flowers that had suddenly sprung up under the trees, adding a dash of colour. Meg blushed, feeling beautiful and lucky.

Margaret smoothed down her own dress, a mixture of blues and greens silky soft. She liked the swish of it as she moved. When Damala had announced she would be dressing them, they had all groaned at the thought. Loving her, yet knowing how often her imagination run away with her. All worried what she would dress them in. Restraint, not a word usually associated with Damala. Having partially gained her magic back, she once again took great pains with her appearance. Making them all laugh and despair in equal proportions.

Dillon stood beside Sam, he could feel him shaking every time he moved closer. The trees let their branches act as a canopy for everyone to sit under, they knew Meg was coming when their leaves rustled in excitement. Both turning at the same time, Sam felt his heart stop at the beauty of her. Dillon grinned, Meg had never looked so serious or lovely. Catching her twin's eye she smiled back, breaking the tension she felt walking down the aisle. Margaret sat down between Balin and Qiao pulling their hands into hers sighing in happiness as they watched them marry.

The band got more and more out of tune as the night wore on. Arguments between the instruments kept breaking out. Accusations of playing "flat" bandied about. The drums wouldn't stop when the song finished, wanting to do a solo performance. The cymbals joining in, making the sound a jarring barrage.

The Butler had long since called his cleaners to clear the tables. The Barmen quickly running out of most drinks. A magician was trying to cast a spell to make beer. So far what he'd made looked more like a muddy puddle. Groups of magicals had splintered off, talking in low voices about what was happening in Kingdom. Bilberry and Damala were asleep on a bench which was moaning about their combined weight.

Dillon, Perical and Qiao were dodging a gaggle of witches who had set their sights on snagging them. Margaret and Balin held hands watching Sam and Meg dance. The raucous music not heard by either of them, dancing to their own soundtrack. Dillon heard it first, the thwack of an arrow as it embedded itself. Telling Perical to shush. Hoping that he was wrong, he strained his ears to listen. Out of the corner of his eye he caught a glint. Meg and Sam the only ones dancing, lanterns bobbing in a circle around them showed the pair in clear relief against the dark. He knew that sound.

'Sam, Meg get down,' he screamed.

Another arrow thrummed into a table making it rear up, shaking glasses onto the floor.

Balin instantly understood. As another arrow flew past, he

launched himself between it and Sam. It struck him squarely in the back. Felled, he landed hard against the ground. Margaret rushed forward, Meg screamed. Pandemonium broke out, everyone thinking they were under attack. Magicians used their wands and staff's to clear the way. Witches snapped open their broomsticks each jostling to get airborne. Only the tableau on the dance floor didn't move.

Margaret held Balin, his breathing laboured, the arrow poisoned. Anger and hate flooded her body. Another door opened inside her head, something "other" stepped through. Her scream primeval.

Aeryissa and Elfrad transported in. In seconds the area was cleared. The large oak which had been sent to guard Margaret, commanded the trees to find the culprits responsible. The ground shook as they raced away, joined by several Yorkus. Alvie, Kaimi and Ambrogio had also poured into the area. Bardolpf decreeing, whoever had attacked Balin should be brought before him for punishment.

Coot and Amp pulled their hoods lower, wrapping their arms around themselves in an effort to keep warm. As soon as the arrow struck, they had moved away. Joining a band of witches telling them they were all under attack and that they needed to leave. Once away from the main body of magicals, Coot feigned he had hurt his leg. Encouraging the others to go on ahead, saying he and his brother would catch them up. Once out of sight, they headed for the small cave they had spotted earlier, burrowing their way in waiting for the furore they had created to die down.

Balin lay on a table inside Dandelion's house, barely alive as the poison raged around his body. Margaret and Sam held his hands willing him to survive. Dillon held his sister as she sobbed, Damala's hand on his shoulder. Cian walked through the door, his eyes seeking Margaret, flicking across Balin's body, he smelt death in the room. Wanting to go to her, give her comfort, the rage he felt at her distress showed on his face, eyes turning black, fangs extending.

Looking up, she held his eyes, tears falling, she mouthed, 'help me.'

'You can't, Margaret may never forgive you the consequences.'

'She loves him, surely she would be glad that he would still be alive?'

Harsha, like everyone knew how he felt about Margaret. Drawn to her like a moth to a flame.

'He wouldn't be though. Would he? Before you lose your temper. Think. If you change him, part of you will live forever inside him. Are you sure that isn't your motivation. A way of getting closer to Margaret? Rather than saving Balin.'

He stood up, towering over Harsha his face changed, ready to fight. She sat unconcerned at his display of anger, in his heart he knew that she was right.

Cian stood in the shadows leaning against a large Yorkus. Both he and the tree stood watch. Hunched over, arms tightly wrapped around her body, Margaret rocked backwards and forwards in her distress. Balin had died. Her wail at his passing heard by all. Sam had tried to comfort her, pushing him away she had ran. Cian followed, keeping his distance, letting her weep and rage her grief out.

'I know you are there.'

He stepped towards her, the query of how, she knew written on his face.

'I always know when you are near.'

Sitting next to her Cian summoned a small light enabling her to clearly see his face in the dark. Not normally lost for words, he felt tongue tied and clumsy at what he wanted to say, blurting out.

'I can make him live again. If you want him to. I can give Balin back to you.'

Margaret lost in her own thoughts, thought that she had misheard him.

'What do you mean? Give him back to me. He's dead, gone.' Realisation dawning, she cried, 'you mean bring him back as a vampire? In your thrall? How would that help me?'

Taking her hand, Cian's eyes bored into hers.

'Not like that. Yes, he would be a vampire. But not under my control. That's only if I choose to let it happen.'

Her first reaction was of horror. The thought of Cian biting Balin, trading blood made her feel sick. As his suggestion implanted itself in her psyche she stood up, pacing back and forth. Her mind in turmoil. How would she ever explain it to Sam? Balin would live forever, while she grew old. She had only met a few magicals who had been turned into vampires. Used for menial tasks they seemed happy at their choice. Not fully vampire's they appeared lessor somehow, than they once were before being changed.

That's it, she thought, choice. She would be making it for Balin. Unsure, if asked when alive, if he would ever consider it, she would have to take the responsibility for him being changed. Cian let Margaret argue with herself, content to be near her.

Harsha approached, she could tell by his expression that he had spoken to her, she appeared to be debating with herself the pros and cons of his suggestion.

'Margaret, please think long and hard about this. Once taken it cannot be altered. Has he told you he cannot predict how it will affect Balin?'

'This is nothing to do with you,' roared Cian, flowing off the bench, eyes black, talon's growing.

'Will you stop with the theatrics?' turning to Margaret she offered, 'if you really want to do this. Then I will change him.'

Ignoring his expletives at her suggestion. She looked them both in the eye.

'Love, however you interpret it; is between you both. You would be conflicted. As for you Cian. You should know better. Deception is not usually your forte. I like you Margaret. But I don't love you. That is why it would be best if I made the change and not Cian.'

After a fitful night's sleep, Margaret made her decision. Even though she knew it was going to cause Sam maximum distress, she had no doubts it was the correct one. Harsha had told her if it was to happen then it needed to be done tonight. Any longer and the core of what made Balin himself, would start to leave his body. Getting everyone to leave had been the hardest thing to arrange. Even outside, walking to relieve her anger, the trees followed her every move. She had debated whether to tell Sam before or afterwards. Unable to face what she knew would be his abhorrence, she chose to wait. Sure, when he saw the results, he would, if not straight away, in time come round to the idea.

'Soon my love,' she crooned, as she stroked Balin's hair. 'We'll be together again. Kissing his forehead she whispered,' I hope you can forgive me.'

Harsha waited for her to compose herself.

'Perhaps it would be better if you waited outside?'

Margaret shook her head, steadying herself, announcing.

'I want you to change me at the same time.'

'What. No, that's impossible. You're not dead.'

'Well kill me then,' she shouted.

Harsha felt trapped, she was only doing this to stop Cian making a fool of himself.

'No Margaret. You cannot expect me to kill you and then turn you into a vampire. It's against all the rules of Kingdom.'

'Rubbish,' she cried. 'It's done all the time. What about all your servants, those who work in your mines. They have been turned.'

'That is not the same. We don't kill them to order.'

'I will change Margaret. If that is truly what she wants.'

Peeling herself away from the shadows, Aeryissa made them both jump at her presence.

'Do you want to be a vampire?' her voice a caress.

'I want to be with Balin. I lost him once. I don't want to lose him again.'

'You would give your life up as a norm for him?'

'You cannot kill her Aeryissa. Kingdom would never forgive you,' said Harsha.

'I don't intend to kill her. There are other ways of dying.'

Taking hold of her hands she pulled Margaret towards her.

'Listen to me, if you are going to go through with this. Then I insist you tell Sam, now, tonight.'

Margaret shook her head, trying to release her hands and move away. Not wanting to hear the words. Changing her face, letting her vampire show, Aeryissa made her look at her.

'This is what you may turn into. When anyone undergoes the change. No one knows how they will be affected until the process is finished. Some magicals recover quickly, others take longer. Balin could wake before you, what do we tell him? Sam is your son, how do you think he will feel if you change and he didn't know. He doesn't have to like or understand your reasons. He is though, entitled to know that his mother and father as he knows them, will no longer be the same.'

'He will hate me,' moaned Margaret.

Roused from sleep, Sam rubbed his eyes. Aeryissa had sent Elfrad to wake him, fearing that something had happened to his mother he rose quickly kissing Meg, telling her he wouldn't be long and followed Elfrad out of the house. Leading him to the bough where his father's body lay, he could feel the questions ready in Sam's mind waiting to spill out, demanding answers.

'Mum, what's wrong?' he dashed to his mother's side, worry etched on his face. Conscious that his father's body lay only a few steps away.

'Give us a few minutes together.'

Margaret waited for them to draw away into the shadows.

'You as well Cian.'

Taking a deep breath, she plunged in.

'Tonight, both I and your father will be changed.'

'What do you mean?'

Embarrassed, she looked anywhere but at Sam.

'Mum, what are you talking about? You're scaring me,' he cried.

'To save your father's life and because I want to be with him. I too am going to be changed.'

His mother's words, their significance slowly sank in.

'You're going to become vampires,' he shouted. 'That's disgusting, you're not even dead. How would that even be possible? Is this why you have delayed his burial? Nothing to do with his family. You're mad. I won't let you do it. I forbid you to do it,' Sam raged, his anger making his face turn red. Clenching his fists, for the first time in his life he wanted to hit his mother.

'Sam I don't expect you to understand. Perhaps when you and Meg are older and have been...'

'Don't bring my love for her into the same sentence as your filthy plans.'

Margaret wiped the tears which wouldn't stop falling, the hatred reflected in her son's eyes, burning right into her soul.

'Do what you want, don't expect me to witness the result. Meg and I are leaving. If I hadn't come to find you. I wouldn't have found her. At least something worthwhile has come out of all this horror you have put me through.'

'See that Sam is okay and double the guard. No one is to enter this area without my say so.'

'Is this wise Aeryissa,' asked Elfrad, still shocked at what Margaret contemplated doing.

In answer she told him, 'the course of life flows in and around us in unexpected ways. We can choose to ignore it or we can let it take us where it will. Margaret's path was set a long time ago. All she is doing now is taking the next step.'

Kissing Balin, Margaret asked Harsha, 'will it hurt him?'

'Only when he wakes.'

Sure that before Aeryissa transported them out of the bower, she heard Harsha's fangs slide into his neck. Margaret closed her eyes, and in that moment regretted what she had set in motion.

'Why have you brought me here? I wanted to be with Balin,' she looked around the bare walls of the tower. Remembering the last time she was inside one like it.

'You will be. For you to become a vampire requires something different.'

'Because I'm not dead?'

Aeryissa indicated that she should take a seat.

'Close your eyes. Steady your breathing, listen only to my voice. Think of your heartbeat, concentrate all your thoughts on it. Now... Let... It... Stop.'

Warmth flooded Margaret, panic set in. In one part of her mind she was breathing, standing up, pulse racing, trying to get away. In another immobile, eyes staring, dead.

Small beads of silver left Aeryissa falling onto their clasped hands. Disappearing under Margaret's skin. Doors slammed and opened with equal force inside her head, it whipped from side to side as she tried to locate who had stepped through. Turning as she heard her name called. Rearing back when a face loomed out of the dark, fangs drawn, eyes black, skin glinting with silver. Then the pain came. She wanted to slough her skin off. It itched and burnt as the silver raced along her veins.

Using her talons to cut her wrist, Aeryissa produced a jug and filled it to the brim with her cold blood. Holding Margaret's head she forced open her mouth and poured it down her throat. As the blood hit her system she shook from head to toe. Lines of silver traced their way across her skin, followed by the red of the blood.

Something snarled in her head, snarling back, Margaret made a grab, falling through a door it closed with a slam, leaving her in the dark. Curling into a ball she let herself go. Aeryissa felt her go limp, knowing that the first part of the process had finished.

Transporting them back to the bower, she laid her down next to Balin, sealing the area. Only time would tell what the outcome of her death and awakening would be.

Sam was getting mightily fed up with magicals trying to convince him to stay. Anger at his mother's decision, making him snap at everyone, including Meg, reducing her to tears on several occasions, earnt him a taste of Dillon's wrath.

Now at last the day had come, surprised that both he and Damala were coming with them. Even Perical had ventured he may join them in a few days.

Still unsure how they were getting home, they waited for Qiao to bring Elfrad. Making Bilberry jump, when they appeared right next to her. He laughed as she cuffed him, telling him to watch where he was going in future. Elfrad wished Sam would stay, at least until his parents woke. Adamant that he didn't want anything to do with them or Kingdom, his pleas fell on deaf ears.

'As I explained Sam, your father's picture is now locked. Only he and your mother will be able to use it. Because of your help in bringing the ring and its contents into Kingdom. Permission has been granted for you to have your own picture. Some of your ancestors have professed an interest to be included. Leaving your fathers picture to inhabit yours. They too are not happy at your mother's decision.'

'Does this mean I will be able to use it now we're married?' asked Meg.

'Why would you want to use it?' demanded Sam.

'Damala has also been given one of her own, and you Dillon will still be able to use your parent's picture.'

Handing out miniatures, Elfrad told them, 'these are the keys to your pictures. Once you know where you are living, press both sides of the frame. Make sure all fingers touch. Stand back and your picture will arrive.'

A fanfare of trumpets rent the air, several Yorkus emerged

either side of the path like an honour guard. Their branches curled into fists, ready to fight. Dillon smiled, Bardolpf rode at the head of the Baldassare, looking every inch a king. Wanting to rush forward, he knew better than to make any sudden moves towards his friend. Dismounting, Bardolpf shook hands with Elfrad and commanded his guard to stay where they were.

'All ready?' he asked Dillon, walking him away from the group.

'Meg is concerned about Sam. He hasn't been sleeping, I'm sure Damala has told you how snappy he's got.'

'Give him time. He came looking for his mother, found a father he didn't expect, a realm he doesn't understand and is leaving parents who are to become vampires,' smiling to take the sting out of his words, he added, 'it can't be easy for him.'

Damala left Meg talking to Elfrad, she had tried to talk to Sam, but he had shrugged off her efforts to engage him. Standing morose, feeling sorry for himself, impatient to go. As she flung her arms around Bardolpf, the Baldassare drew their swords.

'Don't you get fed up with them reacting to everything around you? Isn't it wearing? I shall miss you Ammon,' she winked.

'Hello Sam.'

Before he had time to answer, they had emerged into the bower where his parents lay side by side, looking as if they were asleep. Anger suffused him. How dare she bring him here! He had expressly told everyone who would listen, he did not want to see or have anything to do with them. Ignoring his dirty look, she crossed her arms and waited. He wanted to turn and walk away. Held in place by conflicting emotions, he seethed.

'What do you want?' he shouted.

Trying not to look at his parents peaceful faces. His nightmares hadn't shown them like this. They had been monsters, drinking blood, tearing apart their victims. Revelling in the destruction they caused. Laughing at his pleas to stop. Tears fell, he wiped his eyes.

'I thought they would look different,' he whispered.

'They are in stasis, the process of change.'

'When, do they become…'

'Vampires? Even I cannot say how long it will take. Everyone is different. They may not even wake.'

'What do you mean? They could stay like this, in limbo?'

'For a while,' said Aeryissa, eventually though, they would die. Drawing his eyes back to her she told him. 'Your parent's can choose to be in your words, "monsters." She let her vampire wake. 'They can also choose to appear as they are now,' subsiding back to the girl Sam first met. 'Fundamentally, being a vampire doesn't change who they are in relation to you. They will still be your parents. Allowing hatred of your mother's decision into your heart, could allow dark magic to take you over.'

'I didn't understand. I thought once bitten, that's it. They're turned. Wake up and…'

He reached out and stroked his mother's face, bending down he kissed first his father's and then her brow.

'I'm sorry mum for the things I said. I do love you. But I cannot stay here.'

His eyes widened, as his mother's voice faint, but clear, echoed inside his head.

'I love you Sam.'

They waited beside the doors which would take them back to Novia.

'Can we take these off?' complained Dillon.

'Not yet,' a voice Sam recognised answered.

The Enabler studied him, even with the blindfold he could see how weary Sam looked. The eager young man gone, a shroud of sadness in its place.

'Please listen carefully, when the doors open you will enter a portal. It may make you feel sick and or dizzy. The feeling won't last long. Please do not remove your blindfolds until instructed to do so.'

Sam left Meg sleeping, opening the door quietly so as not to disturb her, he stepped into the corridor.

'Good morning. Did you sleep well?'

'I did actually. It was probably the best rest I have had in a long while.'

Holding up a small vial, the Enabler chuckled, 'I thought this may help.'

Sam laughed, it felt good to be away from Kingdom and all its problems.

'I see you still have your ruck sack. Did it come in handy?'

'My what? I don't understand, I didn't bring this with me. I wasn't wearing it.'

At his angry shouts Damala, Meg and Dillon all emerged from their rooms, rubbing sleep away. Concern on their faces.

'What's wrong,' asked Damala.

'Look,' retorted Sam, turning around. 'It's back, tell him I haven't been wearing it.'

'He hasn't,' said Meg, 'we thought it lost ages ago.'

'It doesn't make sense.'

Sam pulled the bag off his back, dumping it on the floor.

'I don't want it.'

Raising his eyes to stare at the Enabler in defiance. He knew by the look on his face that it wasn't going to be as easy as that.

Shaking his head, he nudged the bag with his boot.

'You can leave it here. But it will find you. There must be a reason for you to still need it. Otherwise, it would have disappeared completely.'

Like a petulant child, Sam held his ground.

Dillon swooped down and grabbed the bag, 'you never know it may come in…'

Before he could finish the sentence it vanished and reappeared on Sam's back. Enraged, he pulled at the straps.

Meg stepped forward. Placing her hands on top of his.

'Stop. It's not going to go way. Let's go home. Put all this behind us. Get on with our lives.'

'I've received a message from the Enabler that Sam's rucksack appeared before he was leaving the train.'

'Are our magicals in place?'

'We have Kaimi ensconced in the house across from his home. Magicians and witches dotted around the area. Plus a Lobe and Lens a few streets away.'

'He made his choice Elfrad,' snapped Aeryissa. 'It will have to be enough. We cannot spare more. Meridian's forces are on the move.'

Chapter Twenty-Six

Meridian gazed at herself in the faux mirror she had created. Locked inside her sanctuary the dark magic that held her in its thrall, outside, shrugged off like a cloak as she'd entered. Its rage and fury ignored, as it battered the door trying to get in. Threatening all sorts of dire consequences if she didn't accede to its wishes. She needed time alone to get her thoughts in order. Even though glad the Dark Lord was dead, she still couldn't come to terms with how it had happened.

Trying to draw strength from his mirror didn't work, if anything it seemed to make him weaker. The girl somehow had a hand in his death. Yet the sword was held by a king who shouldn't exist. While silver magicals where alive in Kingdom for all to see. Where had they come from? The vampire was an anomaly she couldn't fathom. Silver and gold speckled her skin. Power and strength surrounded her. She worried that her dark magic may not be a match for such a one. How could this be so? She continually asked herself. While her dark magic railed against her thoughts, telling her those problems are in the past. Insisting she take the Shimmers magic and open the tomb, to rule and not be someone else's puppet.

Entering the chamber, she ignored the stares and whispered comments at the sight of her hair writhing like a nest of snakes. She let them see the lines which zigzagged across her face, mottled and blueish in colour. The smell wafting from her as she passed, made many cover their nose at its pungency. Bent and gnarled hands held her staff and Wakanda, the red of her wand the only colour showing against her otherwise black garb.

Banging her staff onto the ground, she waited for the silence to become absolute.

'Take heed, many of you thought me mad or dead. I am neither. What I am is; determined. Too long dark magic has been pushed to the back. No more. The light has had its chance to shine. Look what has happened, magic is weak. Kingdom is not the lush place it once was. Those in power have hidden its secrets for too long. Now is the time to strike.'

Indicating that Gilda should follow her, they left the chamber. The noise levels going up as they disappeared. Meridian sat down, pouring a large glass of wine, she gulped it down. Her gaze never leaving Gilda's face. Knowing not to look away, she looked back.

'Meridian, it's good to see you back to your old self,' said Khalon, barrelling his way into the room. Trying to appear unconcerned at the rumours he'd heard circulating.

She cackled, unnerving them both. Her dark magic hissing inside her head.

'Don't trust them.'

They watched in horror, as black tendrils reminiscent of the Darkness wove around her body. The temperature in the room dropped. Both dare not move, waiting for Meridian to strike. The tendrils abated. Both breathed a sigh of relief. Gilda wanted to leave, the air in the room had grown cloying.

'Any problems I should know about?'

'Some over enthusiastic witches laid too many crystals. The whole it created leaked into a side seam, causing another breach in their defence systems. We had to stop and make it look like a normal shifting of earth.' Clicking his fingers, a map appeared on the table. 'As you can see by the red lines we are managing to plot the seams including the smaller ones. The green lines denote where their security is at its highest. The brown where entrances have been found.'

'They're here,' announced a wraith, appearing in the doorway.

'Gather everyone outside, then bring the prisoners.'

A courtyard had been built into the centre of the lair. Norms walked above unknowing that beneath their feet lay Meridian's domain. Magicals poured out of the tunnels and chambers all eager to see what the gathering was all about. Some jostled to get nearer, soon changing their minds when they saw the prisoners.

'These witches thought to change sides. Rejecting the dark, wanting the light.'

Murmurings broke out at her words.

The witches shook. The crowd silent. Placing a hand on each in turn, she stepped back. Raising her Wakanda she wove her magic around them. With three sharp bangs of her staff the spell was complete. At first nothing happened, the crowd craning their necks to see. A dot of light appeared on each witch, growing bigger as it covered their bodies. Making them look for all the world as if caught in sunlight. Their eyes bulged as they realised that the light was burning them. Different parts of their bodies began to light up with a small flame. Burning slowly, their clothes smoked. Moans heard from both them and the crowd.

'This is what you all craved,' screamed Meridian, bellowing around the courtyard, 'take heed. This is the only light on offer to any of you.'

With a flick of her wrist the fires grew larger. The witches howled their pain, struggling against their chains, fanning the flames higher. No one in the crowd dared move or even think, in case Meridian heard their thoughts. Numb at the sight of such cruelty. Burning was a nightmare death. A slow burning even worse.

Finally, after what seemed like hours, the fires died down, only piles of ash remaining. Meridian had made them all watch until the end. Her senses roaming the courtyard for any sign of dissent. Gilda made sure to lock her mind. Punishment she agreed with. This was different. She had caught the tail end of Meridian's thoughts before she also closed her mind shut. It was not a pretty sight. The dark magic encasing her, spurring her on to more cruelty. Revelling in their pain, wanting more.

Chapter Twenty-Seven

Margaret wondered why her back hurt. Turning her head, she smiled as Balin's eyes opened. Startling her as he jumped up hissing.

'What have you done?'

Swinging her legs over the edge of the bed she immediately felt a wave of dizziness engulf her. Balin had retreated to stand against the wall of the bower, his pale face looked luminous in the gloom.

'My love.'

Margaret tried to keep the fear out of her voice. He didn't scare her but his reaction had. She'd hoped to have a chance to talk, explain, before he became aware he was a vampire, his look of horror broke her heart.

'A poisoned arrow killed you. Turning us into a vampire's meant we would always be together.'

Clutching his head at her words, he cried.

'Where's Sam? Does he know?'

'He's gone back to Novia. He didn't like my decision. I'm sorry. I shouldn't have let this happen.'

Balin slid down the wall, Margaret watched as his fangs slid out and his eyes turn black. Scratching himself as his talons extended, his look of misery and shock unbearable. The bower started to disappear around them, the sentinels who had stood guard stepped back to let Harsha through.

'How do you feel?' she asked, noting the distance between them.

Balin snarled at the sight of her. Pulling back his lips, letting his fangs lengthen. Ignoring his weak display of power, she turned to Margaret.

'He is changed. Yet you look no different.'

'I don't feel any different. Perhaps it didn't work.'

Margaret heard Aeryissa's words before she appeared in front of them.

'You are as much a vampire as he is.'

Balin leaped. Talons ready to strike, froth at the corners of his mouth. Aeryissa swatted him like a fly. His cry of pain and anger rent the air. Bouncing along the ground. He jumped up ready again to attack. Once again she knocked him down. Harsha held tight to Margaret.

Telling her, 'he needs to learn.'

Exhausted, he finally fell in a heap, mewling like a kitten.

'Take him away. Give him a small amount of Gork blood. Then knock him out and let him sleep.'

'Shall I chain him?'

Margaret's eyes widened at her words.

'Only if he proves a problem.'

Watching Balin being dragged away by Harsha. Margaret didn't hear what Aeryissa said.

'Sorry. I'm so shocked by his reaction.'

'What about yours?'

'I'm fine. Really. In fact I've never felt better.'

Aeryissa waited for realisation to dawn.

'Somethings wrong. Isn't it?' feeling in her mouth, 'look my teeth are still the same. As are my nails. I expected my senses to be heightened. But they don't feel any different. Yet a part of me knows I'm dead. My skin is cold to touch. I cannot feel my heart beating, it's now more of a flutter.'

'You are a vampire. I can smell it on you. It only remains to be seen what kind. Balin is going to take a few days to adjust. Probably best if you stay away from him. As his sire, Harsha will look after him help him come to terms with how he is.'

'This is not what I expected to happen. I thought it would bring us together. Whereas in reality, it has torn us apart.'

Making sure all the spells and fortifications were in place. Eadulf made his way back to the main hall. Guri was regaling Purity with tales of her past adventures. He smiled, as her hands flapped trying to get the mirror to understand what she meant.

Aware of Eadulf listening, she asked, 'is it time?'

'Meridian's magicals have already left Novia and are congregating out near the wastelands. They are not hiding the fact. Those captured, happy to talk about her plans. Elfrad thinks she has taken a leaf out of our book, using them to distract us with their movements.' Patting the mirrors frame, he told them, 'nevertheless, she will have to use Purity, it is the only safe entrance for her into Kingdom.'

'Remind me, why we are letting this mad women loose in the Glasserium?' annoyance, making her voice sharp and snappy.

Eadulf ignored her tone, he knew she understood really. Naming the pure mirror, Purity, spending time inside it. Had forged a bond between them. Letting Meridian use the mirror, may possibly destroy it in the process. The last of its kind. He also wished there was another way. Unfortunately, they had to deal with Meridian in Kingdom. To do this she had to be allowed to enter, believing her entrance and exit were of her own choosing.

'Don't be angry,' whispered Purity, 'everyone has a part to play, this happens to be mine.'

'I want to stay inside,' announced Guri defiantly. 'We cannot be sure that she won't guess her access is limited. What if she tries to enter Purity's rooms? The game will be up. At least I could give a warning.'

'When I wrap Purity in glass and open the door for Meridian to slip through. The mirror will be in a void of my making. For you to survive I would have to also wrap you in glass. That part won't hurt, but releasing you from its hold will. It may even kill you.'

'Trust me, that won't happen,' snapped Guri, her face dark with anger. 'I am determined in this Eadulf. Purity is my friend.'

'Whiskey, that's what I need,' conjuring a bottle, Guri grasped it to her chest.

'That won't stop the pain.'

'It's not for the pain,' she muttered, 'it's for the memories.'

Pulling her chair into the centre of the room. Guri placed the whiskey on the side table and poured a large glass. Downing it in one, she refilled it three more times. Purity and Eadulf watched, both not understanding her need to get drunk. Finally, she tipped the bottle up and drained it dry. Hiccupping as she wiped her mouth with the back of her hand.

Eadulf drew the outline of a square box around her. As the glass outline firmed up, Guri closed her eyes. Her hands gripped the chair, the only indication of how she felt. Slowly he filled the box with liquid glass. Once full, he tapped the sides and it solidified.

Guri was encased. Her eyes snapped open. Eadulf blinked in surprise, that shouldn't be possible, he thought. With no time to wonder about it he turned his attention to Purity. Stepping out of the mirror he touched her frame and let glass flow from his body in to it. Knowing it would be hurting her he paused to let her calm down. Once the mirror was completely covered. He turned his attention to Meridian's escape route. They had left an opening which she had used to bounce her into Novia. He now needed to change it so that when she used it to get into Kingdom via Purity, she and anyone else she brought with her were directed to where he wanted them to go and not into Purity's interior.

Never again would he allow her or any of her kind to reside inside the Glasserium. Leaving Purity and Guri to their fate, he made his way to the maze which he had created. This would be the route Meridian would be guided to. Exiting through what he hoped she also believed, was her secret mirror held in the castle, but was in fact installed in a shack in the middle of a swamp.

Chapter Twenty-Eight

Taking his tea out into the garden Sam sat on the bench watching the day wake up. Ignoring the dove which sat on the tree branches over hanging his garden from next door.

'Good morning,' said Damala, cheerily.

Conjuring a small table as she joined him, teapot and cups appeared covering its surface, while hot buttered toast piled on a plate sat in the middle. Sam smiled, as Damala sighed contentedly.

'This is the best time of day even here in Novia.'

Nodding at the dove taking flight as another took its place she smacked her lips as butter ran down her chin.

'How's Meg, did she sleep much?'

'Not really, I think she should see a doctor. Something must be wrong. No one else has been sick.'

Meg, rubbed her eyes, pushing her hair away from her face. She looked at Damala, and saw confirmation in her expression.

'I believe I am pregnant.'

For a moment Sam thought that he had misheard. Jumping up, he made her sit.

'What? How? I don't understand. Are you sure?'

'Of course she's sure.'

'What's going on?' asked Dillon.

'We're having a baby,' announced Sam, a look of wonder on his face.

'Is that all.'

They stared at him, a look of shock on both their faces at his apparent indifference to their news.

'What?'

Tears formed in Meg's eyes.

'You are both so easy to wind up. Of course I'm pleased. Can we still go on our camping trip?'

'I'm not sure we should.'

'Meg is pregnant. Not ill,' waving away Sam's objections, Damala added, 'I will be here to look after her. She means the world to me. I'll take good care of her. I promise.'

'This is the life,' said Dillon, laying on his back looking at the stars.

Belly's filled, a plethora of empty beer cans littered the ground, testament to how many they'd drunk.

Sam smiled, happy to be out in the woods surrounded by trees that didn't do anything. That were only trees. Before they left he couldn't shake the feeling that something lurked, meaning them harm. Waking in the night he'd peered out of the window, dark shadows flited up and down the street. Yanking open the front door, he lost his momentum, instead of bursting through he gingerly stuck his head out. Recoiling as red eyes appeared over the gate.

Moaning in fear, when Damala touched his shoulder.

'What's the matter?'

Holding his chest as his heart hammered, he pointed to the gate. She stepped out, Sam flinched as a witch flew passed.

'Is there a problem?'

Turning around the witch landed on the path, she looked first at Sam then Damala.

'Nothing we can't handle. Best go back to bed.'

Sam woke to the worse headache he could remember, his stomach didn't feel much better. He could faintly hear Dillon retching in the bushes. Stumbling back clutching his stomach he flung himself down.

Covering his mouth and moaning as if going to be sick again, he whispered, 'I think we've been poisoned.'

Both became aware that the forest had gone quiet. Unlike the birds in Kingdom those in Novia didn't talk, but they did sing. Something they'd both noticed when making camp. The silence felt menacing, the shadows lengthening. Sam instantly aware that his ruck sack had appeared. Nudging Dillon, he pointed, they both knew it meant danger or at least that it was needed. Unsure of where the threat was coming from they both strained to hear any movement.

Sam took out the umbrella, hoping that it would work in the same way here as in Kingdom. They slowly stood up keeping their backs against the trunk. Watching where they put their feet they headed towards a low line of bushes which pushed their way down to the lake. Both had spotted a small rowing boat when they had first arrived. Thinking the water might keep them safe, they slid down the bank and manoeuvred themselves into the boat. Dillon took the oars, while Sam untied the rope, holding the umbrella over them both he pushed the boat off.

The sky had darkened even more as if a storm was coming making the air feel charged. Not sure where they were heading they set off. Determined to cross the lake and get to safety. Sam jumped as the anchor watch appeared on his arm.

'The arrow is pointing upwards, we'd best take a look in case we have been going around in circles.'

They were in the middle of the lake. The water calm. The sky dark and overcast, still with a feeling of electricity in the air. Feeling like fools, they laughed as the umbrella disappeared into the ruck sack. Both taking it as a sign that all was well.

'Let's turn back and head home,' said Sam.

They hadn't gone far when looking up, Dillon noticed two black dots getting bigger and bigger as they drew nearer, diving towards them at great speed. Both looked at each other in horror.

Yanked by the collars of their jackets. The witches heaved them aboard their broom sticks. Rising higher into the air telling them to hold tight. Side by side they flew, Sam had never felt so exhilarated. Seeing what birds saw all the time made him laugh in delight. Looking across at Dillon he could see the same expression matching his own.

'Get ready, we're going to have to crash land. When you hit the ground roll away into the bushes.'

The ground rushed up, hitting it with a thud, stunned, Sam could barely move. Punched in the leg, his witch indicated he follow her.

'I'm Frythe and this is my sister Jiera. Stay still and keep quiet.'

The witches mumbled a spell taking it in turns to complete a line. The ground beneath them began to sink. Sam and Dillon clutched each other's arm to steady themselves. Landing on a dirt floor covered in cobwebs made Sam shiver. The sides of the cave began to move, taking dirt and stones with it filling the space making a roof over their heads.

'What do we do now?' muttered Dillon.

Both witches declined to answer.

'How did you know we were in trouble?' asked Sam.

'We didn't.' answered Frythe. 'Jiera heard a commotion which stopped when we went to take a look. The quiet was unnatural so we knew something was wrong.'

'Once we caught a whiff of their stink, we knew that dark witches were aboard. It was at that moment you revealed yourself. You have a particular smell of your own ring bearer.'

Jiera laughed at his expression, 'it's a gift of mine; smells.'

Dillon smirked.

'How will we know when it's safe to leave,' asked Sam, ignoring him.

'My twin Vieno, will let us know.'

'I'm a twin, Sam is married to my sister.'

'We know,' answered Frythe. 'You should contact her let her know what has happened.'

'I can't, we have never been able to use our twin link.'

'Can you help him try?' pleaded Sam, concerned for Meg's safety.

'You need to clear your mind. Let your tension and anger go. Think of your sister, conjure her face. Once she is to the fore of your mind, hone in on her. Do not be distracted. Find your image and its narrative. Keep repeating it over and over while thinking of her. If contact is made, stay calm, otherwise you may lose it.'

Dillon took a deep breath, closed his eyes and thought of Meg. The hardest part was of thinking of something to make her realise he was trying to contact her.

Sifting through his memories he smiled.

'I'm ready,' closing his mind to everything else, he called. 'It's me Dillon. Sam and I are in trouble.'

Meg felt uneasy. Unable to sit still, Damala had suggested they go for a stroll. Breathing in the summer air, she held her arm as they walked towards the park. As they drew nearer to the pond, Meg's agitation became more noticeable.

Pulling her down onto a bench concern made her snap, 'what's wrong?'

Meg rubbed her head, she felt as if something was stabbing her brain. Closing her eyes she moaned as the pain got worse. Damala wanted to take her home.

'No, I must stay here.'

Palamo appeared beside them.

'What's the matter?'

Straining to listen, Meg thought she could hear Dillon's voice. Not realising, that she said his name out loud.

'Your twin link. Dillon may be trying to get in touch.'

'We've never...'

'That doesn't matter,' stated Damala. 'Hone in on his voice, something may be wrong.'

'Tell us what you can hear,' added Paloma.

Meg tried to slow her pulse rate and focus. Looking inward, she thought of Dillon, conjured his face. Held it to the front of her mind.

'Dillon,' she cried, 'I can hear you.'

Ignoring Damala and Paloma's questions. Meg cocked her head as Dillon's voice broke through the barriers.

'Sam and I are in trouble.'

Standing up in shock at how clear his voice sounded, she demanded, 'what sort of trouble?'

Frowning in concentration as she listened, repeating his words for Damala and Paloma.

'Tell him,' said Paloma, getting ready to change into her bird form. 'We will send reinforcements. Stay where they are. We will contact Jiera's brother for the exact location.'

'She heard,' exclaimed Dillon, excited at being able to talk to his twin. 'She says they are going to contact your bother.'

Frythe grabbed her sister's hand as the earth was scooped out, the sky showing. A face peered at them, ropes snaked down wrapping themselves around the quartet. Hauling them up, dumping them unceremoniously onto the ground. Cackles of laughter greeted them.

'What have we here?' nudging them with their staffs the dark witches crowded round.

'Is this him?' one called over her shoulder.

Shoved out of the way by a large wraith. Looking Sam up and down, he nodded.

Bolts of blue light reigned down, witches swooped using their wands to attack the dark witches on the ground. The wraith picked up Sam slung him over his shoulder and ran towards the trees. Dillon chased after them, knocked down by another wraith that barrelled into him. He jumped up fists ready to fight. The wraith laughed, punching him in the face before kicking his legs from under him. Winded and in pain, he pulled himself onto his knees.

The wraith turned to walk away. Dillon grabbed a handful of dirt a large stone in the centre.

Launching himself at the wraiths back, he shouted, 'hey you.'

As the wraith turned, he let loose the dirt, aiming the rock at his face. His luck held, the rock struck the wraiths eye, he screamed in agony, the wraith carrying Sam stopped.

'Bring him,' he commanded.

Before he realised what was happening, he was grabbed from behind by a dark witch. As he flew his broomstick, he dangled Dillon over the side, his hold vice like. He squirmed and wriggled but to no avail. Dragged into the trees, he was flung, ending up at the feet of the wraith carrying Sam.

Vieno arrived as his sisters and the others were hoisted above ground. Diving towards them he held his wand ready to attack. Screaming in his head at Jiera to run. The witches flying behind him, hurling stars and light balls. Peripherally he saw Sam taken and Dillon give chase. His only concern though, that of his sisters.

Slung over a wraiths back, Dillon bellowed, 'we've been taken, wraiths and dark witches.'

'Sit down, remember the baby. I know, I know. But there's nothing we can do. At least now you and he can communicate, be thankful for that.'

Damala signalled to Orev.

'Paloma will be too late, they have been taken.'

'Pack your bags. You have to leave now, dark witches are headed this way. Trying to keep a low profile. They are not flying in. The Benns caught the tail end of a conversation which alerted us.'

'But what about Dillon and Sam. Is anyone trying to find them?' pleaded Meg.

Hunching down, they left the house and entered the lane that ran at the back, overgrown with weeds, the stink of them making Meg want to retch. The click of a gate let her know they had entered another garden. The small lights the witches had allowed were enough to stop them bumping into things, not enough though to show where they were. Stepping through, the musty smell that wafted out showing that the house they had entered was disused. Thinking this was another hiding place, she was surprised to hear a voice she recognised.

Emerging from the gloom Hib-Hob grinned before pulling her into a hug.

Chapter Twenty-Nine

Cian had tried talking to Margaret. Each time he drew near, she sent him away. Frustrated at not being heard, he took his anger out on any who came near. Harsha came in for much of his displeasure, he blamed her for the mess. Letting it be known in no uncertain terms that if he had changed Balin, they wouldn't now have a problem. She for the most part ignored him, declining Lefu's offer to step in. Since their altercation on the hunt, Cian had tried to avoid being anywhere near him. He knew he was pushing the boundaries. Lefu as leader, well aware of all the spats which he'd caused, let him blow off steam, in the hope that as Margaret pulled further away from him, he would eventually lose interest.

Drawn like a moth to a flame, Cian watched from the shadows. Even before becoming a vampire, Margaret would know that he was around. Now changed as one herself her senses would be elevated even more. She would have no doubt that he lingered.

'How many more times can I say I'm sorry? Telling me time and again that it's not what you want. Cannot change it. I to, regret my choice.'

Balin snorted, the sound amplified by his vampire.

'Look at you. You look no different. Your face doesn't do this.'

She couldn't help but cringe. He had the usual vampire

visual features, fangs, talons, red-black eyes. But his face was also crisscrossed with broken blood vessels, leaching from his eyes running down his face. Instead of glowing, the only colour was from the blood which lay under his skin. It appeared to be getting worse, the large bulging muscles that all vampires developed, were now also covered in broken lines.

At first it all disappeared when he let his vampire rest. Each time it woke, a little bit more was left on his skin. As he walked away, still muttering, Margaret sighed. It had been her decision, which part of her did regret. If honest though, the other part, the one she kept hidden, revelled in her change.

'Go home Cian. Your presence is getting tedious,' she snarled.

'Sam,' whispered Dillon, nudging him in the back.

Groggily he gazed around at their surroundings, they were in a cell with smooth walls, light dripped in from a window set high up near the ceiling. The thought crossing his mind, no escape there. The blankets that lay over their legs, smelt of mould and decay. Pushing them off, he nudged Sam again.

Groaning in response, he sat up, holding his head as the room spun.

'What? What's happened? Where are we?' memories returning, he looked at Dillon, 'have you been able to contact Meg again?'

'No matter how hard I try, I cannot seem to break through the barrier.'

A scraping noise made them look up as the edges of a doorway emerged in the stone. Black robed figures stepped through followed by wraiths. Hauled to their feet the wizards thrust their wands out as if scanning them for weapons.

Turning as one they left the room, the wraiths dragging Sam and Dillon behind them. The passageways were dank and dark, they stumbled along, slowing down they soon realised wasn't an option. Dillon had tried to wriggle free, the wraith behind them punched him in the head. The wraith holding Sam held tighter. Thrown into another cell they breathed a sigh of relief that they were still at least together.

Dillon whispered, 'we need your ruck sack. Why hasn't it shown itself?'

'You know it doesn't work like that.'

'We're in serious trouble, surely if at any time we needed help. This is it,' retorted Dillon.

'You're supposed to be magical. Can't you do something?' snapped Sam angrily.

Dillon woke, for a moment the memory of his beating by the wraiths forgotten. Until he moved. The pain shot across his body as if playing catch. Trying to stretch his legs was agony, he could see the bruises on his arms making it appear as if a tattoo artist had gone mad. Lifting his tunic he could see the same pattern emerging on his ribs. His nose felt bunged up, when he touched it he flinched, it wasn't broken, only swollen. He wriggled his jaw from side to side, hearing it click. With his back against the wall, the effort to get there had tired him out. Closing his eyes he went back to sleep, one part of his brain telling him something was wrong. Before the thought could form, sleep dragged him back down.

With his head resting on a nice comfy pillow, Dillon sighed himself awake. Startled to find himself laying on the floor with a view of metal bars. Sitting up made his head ache.

'What happened? I feel as if I've been hit with a jack hammer.'

The silence greeting him making him remember. Jumping up, he held onto the wall as everything spun. Stumbling to the cell door he rattled it. No one came running to see what all the commotion was. Glancing over to the corner, Dillon reared back as he saw a crumpled body pressed up against the wall. His first thought Sam. Looking closer, he could see it was the guard, his eyes sightless, blood pooling around his head. Dillon flung himself onto the floor. Wincing as the bruises on his legs came into contact.

It took him a moment to understand what he was seeing. The

comfy pillow he'd been clutching was in fact the ruck sack. His heart rate went into overdrive. It only appeared for Sam. What does it mean? It's not real he told himself. Using his toe he nudged the bag, even though his boot he could feel the weight of what it held. Gingerly he prodded it. Waiting for it to disappear. He wrestled with the problem. The bottom line, he had the bag. But where was Sam? Could he rescue him using the contents? Was this the reason it had appeared. First though, he had to find a way out.

Taking a long swig of water, he popped a food pebble in his mouth. Trying to remember the last time he'd ate an actual meal. Pulling out the rope he swung the rucksack onto his back. Threading it through the bars, hoping with a spell, brute force and a lot of luck he may be able to open the cell door. No matter how much he pulled, cast and wished, the door wouldn't open.

Frustrated, his eye caught the body of the guard. Thinking, he must have the keys on him. No way could he reach him through the bars, his arms weren't long enough. He threw the rope hoping it would snag on something and bring the guard nearer.

Smacking his hand against his head, of course, he thought. A moving spell. Even I can do that. Slowing his breathing, he knew he must be calm.

Concentrating, he scanned the guard's body to get an idea about his shape. Fixing the information in his mind, he murmured the words of the spell. At first he didn't think it had worked. His eyes straining to see any movement. Then the guards head moved a fraction, the sucking sound it made as it pulled away from the blood spilled made him flinch. Holding his nerve he kept his concentration only on the guard. Inch by inch he was moving him nearer.

Wrinkling his nose at the smell of blood and decomposing flesh, the thought of having to touch him making him want to gag. Fortunately, the last movement brought the body with the key chain facing towards him. Wanting to snatch the key ring and escape. For once he held back. The keys may be spell cast. If so, only the guard could remove them from the chain. Stretching his hand through the bars trying not to come in contact with the guard's body. He placed the tip of his fingers on the keys. Immediately he felt the shock.

He couldn't give up now. He felt sick at the thought of what he had to do. Kneeling forwards he placed his hand on top of the guards. Steeling himself, he held his hand guiding it to the keys. If it hadn't been a flick lock he wouldn't have been able to remove them. Using the guards thumb on his left hand, he pushed the lock catch up, he then used the guard's right hand to release the keys.

His back ached with the strain of leaning forward, his face sore where it was squashed against the bars. He tried to stop his hands from shaking. With a sigh of relief he drew the guards hand towards him dropping the keys onto the ground. Shaking out his arms to release the tension. He nudged them with his finger. Swooping them up, his hands shaking so much each time one didn't work made him panic more. Finally the door opened. Wanting to run, instead he held back his impulse, and listened.

Edging his way along, he hesitated as he saw light spilling out ahead of him. Wondering, if this meant another opening or another cell. Thinking should he make a run for it, worrying how he was going to cross without being seen.

A voice shouted, 'who's there?'

Stepping out with a confidence he didn't feel. He moved to the next passageway.

'Let me out,' snarled a dark witch.

'Where have they taken my friend?'

'The wizards took him away.'

Suddenly, he could feel the beginnings of a compulsion spell. He flung the keys and ran. Skidding to a halt as fresh air wafted towards him. Taking out the umbrella he snapped it open. Feeling a sense of relief as he hid under its canopy.

A door stood open, moving into the room. The door slammed shut. Turning in a circle he looked for a way out. Dark wood panelling covered the walls, the creatures which had been carved onto its surface looking ready to wake at any moment. He walked towards the furthest part of the room, deep in shadow yet it didn't feel as menacing as the rest. Trying to ignore his fear, he combed each part of the panelling for a doorway. Without the Lens glasses he would never have seen it. A fine line hidden amongst magicians and witches strung up over pots that boiled underneath them. Pushing with all his might the door opened into another room. No panelling, breathing a sigh of relief, he let the door close behind him. The room bare, apart from one picture depicting a clown, its eyes downcast, yet he knew it watched him. The wide painted smile incongruous against the evil that fell from the picture covered him like a blanket.

He had to make a move, he couldn't go back and he couldn't stay here. The clown appeared to shrug in agreement at his thoughts, racking his terror up a notch. Counting in his head, one, two, three, he launched himself towards the door. The clown's face exploded from the picture.

The eyes looked straight at him as it shrieked.

'A joke? Shall I tell you a joke?'

His body began to vibrate as he shook in terror. The face was so close Dillon could see all the smudges of paint that had been applied in a hurry.

The clown flicked his tongue out as if trying to catch a fly.

'Well shall I?' he roared, preparing to step out of the picture.

Sheer terror giving him the impetus he needed. Shoving the face aside he hit the door with his shoulder, pushing the handle down at the same time. Landing in a heap, the door slammed shut. The clown screaming in anger at losing his audience. Still shaking, he found himself in another room. Using the light filtering through from window slits he once again stood in the middle and scanned each part for an exit. He nearly missed it. The outline of a mirror began to emerge. Terrified at what might step through he put his back to the wall and waited. He was stuck.

The light went, the mirror stayed. Tiredness took over, he slumped down snoring gently.

Waking with a start, he took a moment to think where he was. The mirror hang in front of him, tempting him with a means to escape which he couldn't use. Anger bubbled up, he had to get out. Sam was missing. Dillon hit the mirror with his fists pounding on it in frustration. The pounding became a tap, an S.O.S. Somewhere in his brain, he remembered, that mirror's meant Eadulf.

Standing back, he surveyed his handiwork. At last the mirror maze was finished. It had been harder than he expected to construct. The mirrors themselves not happy to be used in this way, testing his patience to the limit. When Meridian used the pure mirror to gain entry into the Glasserium, the enchantments in place would direct her to the maze. Even she would not be able to alter this magic.

Eadulf smiled, thinking of the shock they will get when they emerge. No firm ground for them, he knew it was childish, it wouldn't stop her. But the thought of them covered in mud, flailing around in a soupy swamp, would bring a cheer to his heart. Making his way back to the main hall, he could hear Guri speaking to Purity.

'Here you are. What is that noise? We thought it was you. But it can't be. Listen,' she said sharply, as if he had interrupted her.

He began to nod his head in time to the noise. Purity's glass trembled as she strained to fix the sound.

'It's coming from Novia.'

Eadulf cried, 'that's Dillon's voice, he's calling for help.'

'You'll have to go and get him,' stated Guri.

'I can't. I have to be here, if something goes wrong when Meridian enters. I have to be close.'

'That could be days away. He needs your help now,' she retorted, knowing how fond he was of his friend.

'Yes, or she could come today, now, in the next instant. I cannot take the chance. Purity, can you lock onto the mirror in case we lose the connection.'

'I will go,' announced Guri. 'I can bring him back,' she offered.

'If I thought you could. I would send you in a heartbeat.

Travelling through glass can only be done by me, as Master of the Glasserium.'

Guri removed the gloves she had taken to wearing, unwinding the scarf from around her neck. Kicking her shoes off, she waited for Eadulf to stop his pacing and look at her. Aware of a stillness around him, he looked up, blinking in surprise at what he saw.

Shaking his head to clear his thoughts, still the image remained. 'How? When? This is not possible. Only I'm…'

'Evidently not.'

Eadulf was stunned, she was becoming glass, like him.

'Rightly or wrongly I was never going to tell you. A complication. I thought you didn't need.'

Eadulf listened in disbelieve.

'I created the Glasserium, so that I could live surrounded by glass.' Opening her arms wide, she added, 'this is not the first hall of mirrors, that one was destroyed…'

'I don't understand,' interrupted Eadulf rubbing his head, his thoughts tumbling inside. 'Why have you not said before, kept yourself hidden. What does this make me? How did I become made of glass? If you are the Creator. Am I still Master?'

Patting his hand, Guri answered, 'Eadulf, you are master here and always will be. I liked being glass. But then I found magic shows and liked them better. I couldn't have both. Glass needs its master, otherwise it withers. That's when I found you.'

'Dillon has stopped calling. I can only make out a faint noise. I think he's crying,' Purity shouted.

'In the early days my magic shows featured glass. You were always somewhere around. Eyes taking it all in. Your parents were dead. I don't know if you had other family. I didn't ask. Perhaps I should have done. You seemed so alone. I took you home. You became my apprentice. You won't remember. I wiped those memories. You saw me as my glass self. Pestered me for days on the how and why. In the end I gave in. What harm can it do? I thought. You took to being glass like it was made for you. The more I stayed away from the Glasserium, the more entrenched you became. When creating mirrors, I gave them life. They liked to talk, enjoyed the company of other mirrors. The mistake I made was agreeing to the mirrors being used as punishment. It was hoped that locked away the culprits would learn the error of their ways. Most mirrors though, took on a life of their own and liked having the company, before long they were seeking out those who could be easily persuaded to commit offences. When the bell rang bringing new magicals, they'd flocked to receive them. It became a competition. That's when their darker side came out. Remember, Toti?'

Eadulf nodded, unable to forget the trouble he'd caused.

'It was only supposed to be temporary, his incarceration. In all the chaos happening in Kingdom, he got forgotten about.'

Eadulf remembered how Toti kept moving his mirror around the halls. Each time, infecting those he was near with his brand of hate. After that, they really started to change. It took a while to realise that those subjected to long lengths inside their mirrors, were turning into wraiths.

'He's getting fainter.'

'When I stayed inside Purity and you wrapped us both in glass. It woke mine up. Since then it has been gradually showing itself.'

'Hurry up,' shouted Purity at the top of her voice.

Guri stood up, touching her face she let the glass flow over it. Before he could say or ask anything more, she leapt into Purity and disappeared.

Dillon felt wrung dry. Taking a large swig of water he leant against the mirror. The room he had entered still a prison. Getting out of his cell had given him a boost of confidence. Short lived, after entering rooms which were another type of prison. This one may have a way out, only not one he could use.

Out of the corner of his eye, he felt sure that the glass in the mirror moved. He slowly turned his head. Nothing, except smooth flat glass. The next second he was flung to the floor, the glass exploded outwards, hung in mid-air and was sucked back into the frame, making it shake. Laughter was not what he expected to hear.

'That was fun. Haven't done that for a long time. Come on Dillon, get off the floor we need to get you out of here.'

Guri watched the look of amazement cross his face. She knew she struck a striking figure and that her glass would dazzle with its many facets.

'S.O.S. Good thinking, come on buck up. I'm Guri, this is going to hurt. I will try to be as quick as I can. Bit rusty though.'

Grabbing his hands, she pulled him into her arms and leapt towards the glass.

'Purity, now.'

Landing in a heap, Dillon felt every bone, sinew, in fact every part of his body burn with pain. Curled into a ball, he moaned to himself, unaware that he was now safe inside the Glasserium. His body had taken a beating from being dragged through glass. Eadulf covered him in blankets, Guri laying a pillow under his head. Eyes meeting, they both smiled. Purity breathed a sigh of relief, the last thing she wanted was her friends being at odds with one another.

Dillon opened his eyes to find two concerned faces staring down at him.

'Eadulf,' he cried. 'They've taken Sam.'

Groaning as he moved, his body feeling as if it had been pummelled to within an inch of his life. Moving to a chair he sighed as he sat, his head pounding making him close his eyes.

'Drink this.'

Guri held out a glass of golden coloured liquid.

'It will revive you. It does wonders for me.'

Downing it in one. The shock as it hit his system, making him cough and splutter.

'Did you have to?'

'It will do him the world of good, he already has more colour in his cheeks.'

'Who's taken Sam?'

Guri filled his glass, earning her a dark look. This time Dillon took a sip.

'We went camping. Escaped in a boat. Witches snatched and hid us. A wraith dragged Sam off. I gave chase and they took me too. We woke up in a cell. Wizards came. I got attacked, when I woke. He was gone.'

The distress on his face broke Eadulf's heart. He had grown fond of the band of brothers they had all become trying to enter Kingdom.

'You were being held in a maze prison. You did well to get to the last room as quick as you did.'

'Some take years to get that far, normally a wraith would have been waiting. You would have been supper,' cackled Guri.

'Are you saying that Sam could be someone stuck inside the maze? That he may have also escaped?'

'No, I believe he was taken somewhere else. Before you ask, I have no idea where that is. What I do know is, we have to get you into the armoury. Margaret needs to know what has happened.'

'I'm really grateful to this thing for helping me. But I wish it wouldn't keep appearing on my back like it does.'

'Open it,' said Guri and Eadulf at the same time, 'these only appear when needed.'

Rummaging through, he pulled out the rope, water bottle and letter. Sam's running shoes climbed out placing themselves next to his chair. The book lay on top of the rest. Pushing it to the side, it pushed back. Yanking it out of the way he dropped it on the floor.

'That's done it,' snorted Guri.

'The book is blank, look.'

He flicked the pages. Eadulf looked pained as he watched him bending the book back and forth.

'Put it on the ground.'

As soon as it touched the floor the pages whirled open in a frenzy of anger. Shouting could be heard getting louder as two hands appeared from the books centre, a head hove into view and an irate reader jumped out.

'This is what happens when you let norms anywhere near a book. Especially those who shouldn't be in possession of it in the first place. I'T'S NOT YOURS,' he shouted.

Guri looked amused at his outburst, it was a long time since she had been in contact with a Bodleian. Unsurprised to see they were still an obnoxious jumped up breed of magical as they always were.

'Monash we need your help. I cannot contact Aeryissa. She is out of range. Guri is going to take Dillon to a location in the castle.'

'Why do you need my help?'

'The ring bearer has been taken. His parents have become vampires. His wife may also be in danger. Meg, is also Dillon's sister. Someone in authority needs to collect Dillon from the castle and take him to the armoury. Then he can explain what happened.'

With a snort of disgust at being used as a messenger Monash disappeared back into the book.

'Come on,' said Guri, laughing at Dillon's expression, 'it won't hurt as much I promise.'

The look he gave her told her in no uncertain terms he didn't believe her. Grabbing his hand she pulled him into the mirror telling Purity to push. Before he could ask why. He felt his whole body shoved as if being squeezed through too small a space. Trying not to panic at the thought of being crushed, in seconds the feeling was gone. Then the pins and needles started making him groan in pain. Guri held tight to his arm propping him up as she dragged him through endless corridors. Finally they reached their destination.

'One more push and we are there.'

Shoved again by unseen hands, Dillon found himself inside a mirror facing into a darkened room. The walls rough stone shone wet with damp. Even inside the mirror he could smell the musty air filtering through from the room.

Guri pulled him back from the glass holding a finger to her lips she moved her face to within inches of its surface. The glass trembled and merged with her face. He hated to think if anyone was on the other side what they would see. Even from here it gave him goose bumps at what she was doing. Pulling her face away the glass reformed to a smooth surface.

'All clear, hopefully Monash has given the message and someone is waiting for you. Judging by what's now appeared on your back. I expect though, it is not going to be that easy.'

Dillon had felt the weight of the ruck-sack settle as soon as they had entered the mirror. Holding onto the mirror's frame and with a leap of faith he wouldn't be cut to ribbons he leapt through the glass. Landing on his feet, he jumped in fright when Guri stuck her face through the glass to wish him luck. Donning the glasses and hearing aid he waited for his senses to adjust and his nerves to steady. The mirror had now returned to its blank state, unless you knew it was there you wouldn't see it.

Sweeping his eyes around the room he could make out the outline of a door at the far end, sure that a bead of light shone around its edges. He examined the detail on the doors surface, caught out before, he hesitated to touch it. As far as he could tell it wasn't creatures that covered the surface. Only flowers. Breathing a sigh of relief his hand closed on the handle.

Inching his way along the passage his heart hammered in his chest. Stopping to pull the umbrella out of the ruck sack he felt relief as he opened it. Moving through the castles passageways he was struck by how icy the place felt, the cold going right to his bones, wrapping around him like a shroud.

He collapsed the umbrella and carefully placed his feet onto the narrow stairs stopping to listen every few steps. At the bottom, another passageway led to a large wooden door, the bar across its middle looked too heavy for him to lift alone. His only choice to exit into the smaller courtyard and make his way across open ground to the larger walkway, its arches moss covered, its interior uninviting.

Opening the umbrella, he ran, skidding to a halt before entering the dark. He nearly missed the movement. A large snake slivered towards him. Backing away slowly, Dillon's eyes widened as the snake was joined by others. Their large green and red bodies entwining together. The hissing getting louder as more and more joined. He opened the ruck-sack looking for something he could use. The water bottle fell open in his haste to cram it all back inside, splashing water onto the ground, reaching forward to grab it, he fell. His scream stuck in his throat as he realised that he was underground. He looked up, expecting to see a hole. Water hung suspended above him. Dillon had no idea what to do. He almost laughed, until the head of first one snake then another appeared, all looking down to where he was.

'Where's Qiao,' roared Cian.

'I'm here,' he said, running to catch up.

Elfrad shouted, as they came through the door, 'Dillon's in the castle. Eadulf gave us a rough idea of where he would be taken. Which normally would be of help. Unfortunately the castle has somehow developed the art of moving its walls and passageways about. Plus things have taken root there.'

'What sort of things?' stammered Qiao.

'Mainly snakes,' explained Elfrad. 'Although sightings of other creatures have been seen. Wraiths and darklings hunting, scavenging amongst the rubble. Fighting over what they find.'

Cian listened, his annoyance at the delay in fetching Dillon palpable. Elfrad ignored his impatience.

'Now that's settled, can we go?'

It wasn't Dillon he wanted to save thought Elfrad, but Margaret. As if reading his thoughts, Cian looked at him letting his eyes turn black as night.

Elfrad scanned the ground, snakes covered it except in the middle. What appeared to look like a sheet of glass lay in the centre.

'He's in the middle safe for now inside a puddle. Before we can get to him the snakes will have to be dealt with. Qiao, you stay up here. If anything appears to threaten you, transport away. I will deal with the snakes. Cian, other "things" may appear before I can get to Dillon. I will need you to watch my back.'

Cian nodded his agreement, Elfrad leapt over the wall and landed behind the largest snake. As the impact vibrated through the ground, the snakes turned as one. Flowing towards him, their tongue's flicked out, their hisses getting louder as they spied their prey. Elfrad held his staff away from his body, rapping the ground three times, a slivery blue light grew from its base to work its way upwards. Momentarily stopping the snakes as they were caught in its glow. The light covered Elfrad, making him look like a blue flame spread through with silver. He began to walk towards the snakes, they slivered away from him. As he walked his light spread across the ground towards them making them rear up ready to strike.

Cian let his senses flood outwards, quickly realising that the castle wasn't as empty as it appeared. Even with his sight he could hardly make Elfrad out within the blue flame he'd conjured. He caught the movement as Qiao shouted his name. Turning, he jumped over the parapet as a figure launched itself at him. His adversary growled looking every inch like a vampire. Before he could move to kill it several more launched themselves to land on top of him their jaws snapping trying to bite.

'Distraction, they aren't real, I've seen them before,' shouted Qiao as he appeared next to him.

'They felt real when they fell on me,' he retorted.

Elfrad's flame corralled the snakes as wraiths and darklings appeared out of nowhere, clinging to the walls they covered them like a carpet of ivy. In one fluid movement the snakes melded together becoming one large one with many heads. Still Elfrad held it in his flame.

Screaming in rage the snake disappeared. Several wraiths and darklings leapt into the courtyard. The wraiths looked insubstantial, whereas the darklings shape changed constantly. Their mouths agape, jaws snapping. Elfrad let his flame die down. The three moved to cover the puddle. Surrounded on all sides as more and more darklings poured over the walls. Their red eyes like laser beams honing in on their prey.

'Dillon,' he shouted. 'Raise your arms, Cian will pull you out. Get ready Qiao.'

Hearing Elfrad's words, shaking with fear, he expected to feel the water as his arms pushed through. As soon as he touched it, it disappeared. Cian reached down and hauled him out. Before he realised what was happening he was sitting under a tree.

Qiao peered out of the tower. Nothing appeared to be on the walkway, he knew from experience though, that wraiths could hide by flattening themselves out, blending into stonework. The screams of the darklings cut through him, high pitched and loud. Elfrad and Cian stood back to back. These darklings meant business, no sooner had they killed one another took its place. Blood and gore covered the grass, dripping from both of them. Headless corpses still writhed at Cian's feet. While Elfrad used his Wakanda to cut them down.

'Now,' shouted Cian.'

Hearing his shout, Qiao transported down, grabbed them both, startling Dillon as they appeared in front of him.

Entering the armoury, Cian was immediately aware that Margaret was near. Elfrad hurried Dillon away. A change of clothes and something to eat, would help to calm his nerves.

Walking into the great hall, they flooded back as he saw Margaret's eyes look past him searching for Sam. Elfrad and Cian walked beside him, yet even their combined strength wasn't enough in the face of Margaret's frown when she realised he wasn't there.

Several magicals began to fill the hall, all wanting to hear what had happened. Some had seen them arrive. Wrinkling their noses at the state of them, wondering why Dillon looked so bedraggled and was back in Kingdom. Margaret held out her hands drawing him towards her. He flinched at the coldness of them. She felt him shake. Smiling at him didn't help, it didn't reach her eyes.

'Is Sam and Meg with you?'

He had never felt tongue tied in Margaret's presence before.

His feelings about her, were at odds with her looks, she didn't look anything like a vampire. Yet power emanated from her. When she looked at him he felt as if her eyes bored into his soul.

Elfrad stepped in, telling her, 'wraiths took them. Dillon escaped. The whereabouts of Sam is unknown. Damala was going to bring Meg here but she wanted to go to Long Meadow instead.'

'Is she okay, what about the baby?' asked Dillon, feeling relief. He had tried to contact Meg via their twin link. Once again he seemed to have lost the knack of how to do it.

Margaret's eyes widened, 'does Sam know?'

Feeling more confident, Dillon replied, 'yes, she told him before we left to go camping.'

'Why have wizards taken him? The ring is gone.'

'They kept asking, where is it? They seemed to think that as the ring bearer Sam knew something.'

'We will find him,' declared Cian.

'Sam is my son. I will be going to find him.'

'You can't, you haven't…' looking to Elfrad for help.

'It wouldn't be wise, until the vampire in you makes itself known, you may be vulnerable, as we have seen with Balin.'

Margaret closed her eyes, holding down the anger she could feel waiting to burst forth at their words. As the silence lengthened, everyone in the hall began to fidget. Standing up, she turned to face the room. Although she spoke quietly her voice reached everyone's ears.

'I will be going to fetch my son. If anyone.' Her eyes sought Cian and Elfrad's. 'Tries to stop me. I will kill them.'

A vampire, but with no obvious change having taken place. On face value, no one could see how she could make true her promise. Yet everyone, felt her intent wash over them. All sure she could and would keep her word.

Chapter Thirty

Elfrad wished Aeryissa was here to go with Margaret. His concerns had grown over the last few days as they prepared to find Sam. Qiao was going to transport them into the maze prison. The Froade had been searching for the clown picture held there. It wasn't an ideal way to gain entry, but it was their only option.

The clown roared his rage, his face appearing through the picture. Shouting insults, cursing them. Stepping out, his head looked too large for his body. The skin on his face painted white, a red gash for a mouth, his tongue lolled constantly licking his lips as if hungry. His eyes bulged from their sockets. The red of his nose matching the red of his shoes. Black and white striped trousers held up with braces completed the picture. Normally a clown would barrage anyone in their vicinity with jokes. This one seemed to have something else on his mind. Both hands held knives, long curved blades, their steel flashing in the dark.

Before anyone could take action, owls flew out of the picture to surround the clown.

'Plant your bombs and leave,' the largest told them.

The clown hadn't moved, like a still life he stood hands raised, knives ready to slash and cut. Qiao looked back. The owls swarmed over the clown, their beaks pecking at his face. His shrieks of agony following them as they moved down the corridor.

Cautiously they descended. Cian taking the lead, Elfrad bringing up the rear. Margaret's impatience pushing them along. Signalling them to stop, he turned his head. In one fluid movement he ran down the passage, bursting through a door as a dark witch shrunk back in terror.

'Where's Sam,' demanded Elfrad. 'Dillon told us he threw you the keys. Why haven't you escaped?'

'I did try, each time going in circles until I ended back here again. Wizards took the ring bearer, he's probably dead by now,' snapped Katrina, glancing at Margaret, unsure of what she was. She looked like a norm, but smelt like a vampire.

'I may have an idea though where he is.'

Her sly tone and look, earned her a snarl from Cian.

Before anyone could react, Elfrad made a small movement of his hand flinging the witch against the wall.

'You will tell us where he is. Or I will gut you,' nodding at Cian, he added, 'and let him eat your heart. We are not here to play games.'

'There are many underground tunnels and passageways beneath us. I have never seen them, but many talk of their existence. Used by wizards for conducting experiments away from prying eyes. Especially Meridian's.'

Elfrad paced the floor, not sure using the crystals he had brought with him to blast through several layers all at once would be a good idea.

'What's the matter Qiao?' asked Margaret, seeing the worried look he kept sending her way.

Taking a deep breath to steady his nerves, he asked, 'do you have anything on you belonging to Sam? I may be able to use it to hone onto him.'

Instinctively touching her throat for her necklace. Shaking her head, her disappointment evident.

'Margaret, use your vampire to allow Qiao to feel Sam through you,' shouted Cian, exasperation making him snappy. Grabbing both their hands he placed hers over Qiao's, 'now think of Sam, only Sam,' he commanded her. 'Qiao, you think of Margaret. Both make the pictures in your heads. When you have the image sharp and clear. Then and only then look into each other's eyes.'

Qiao looked into Margaret's eyes and felt himself fall, following her in his mind's eye as she raced through the tunnels. Calling Sam's name, holding his image in her mind. Suddenly Qiao's image of Margaret started to waver.

Keeping all other thoughts out of his head he brought her back into focus. He could see something. His brain though couldn't make sense of what he was seeing. Margaret collapsed onto the floor ripping the image from his sight. He too fell to his knees, tears streaming down his face.

'We found him, he's being tortured,' wailed Qiao.

Cian roared, his vampire bursting forth. Black eyes, talons and teeth looking for prey to rip apart. Margaret's face was white, any colour gone. Something in her was stirring, she could feel it waking.

'Qiao,' Elfrad shook him, 'can you find him again?'

They all stared in silence at the horror before them. Sam was chained by his hands and feet to a blood soaked wall. Small rivers of blood ran down his body. Giving them hope that, with his heart still pumping he was alive.

'Wait,' shouted Elfrad, as Margaret moved forward to go to him.

She snarled in response, Cian standing closer as his vampire caught sight of hers. Qiao and the witch stepped away. The air charged with menace.

'Whoever has done this has used wizard's fire. There may be no doors to Sam's cell, but nevertheless he is imprisoned.'

Elfrad tested a small part, he couldn't bend it enough to enable him to walk through.

Margaret's eyes were locked onto Sam.

'He's still alive, we can save him.'

'The wizards have infected him with darklings. They are inside him, feeding on his blood,' explained the witch. 'They will let him die. Then the spell will revive him. He will start to feel better. As soon as his system has stabilised, they restart their feeding, continuing the cycle, over and over until the spell is broken. By using this method of torture, they must think he knows something of value to them. Only a dark magical can tempt them. To do this they would need something to attract the queen, so the others would follow.'

Margaret looked at Sam, the horror she felt, slowly being overridden by a new feeling.

Cian snarled at the witch, driving the glee he saw as she'd spoken from her face

Elfrad paced the room, his thoughts jumping from one idea to another, he knew they couldn't save Sam, but they could let him die in peace. Yet without being able to cross the wizard's fire, it would be impossible to do anything.

'What do you need to tempt them?'

Shivering at the timber of her voice. Now much deeper and menacing. Eyes that were cold pools of ice stared unblinking waiting for an answer.

'A heart, preferably fresh and a large glass jar to put it in.'

Qiao had noticed the change in Margaret as soon as she saw Sam. He had tried to warn Cian, but as usual he had brushed his concerns off. Blinkered when it came to her, even with his vampire sense of smell he hadn't picked up her scent which was getting stronger. Qiao had seen her eyes turn silver as they had raked across Sam's inert body. He knew she wasn't the same Margaret he had met so long ago. Without making it obvious he moved away. The air in the room felt like a storm coming, Elfrad's eyes met his and he saw the same concerns reflected.

'Qiao, take Cian somewhere he can find a fresh heart. When you return, find somewhere safe and wait for my call.'

'I'm not leaving,' shouted Cian. 'It's probably a trick, how can you believe what she says. She's a dark witch.'

'I'm not lying, anyway it doesn't matter. I have to get close to be able to tempt them, I cannot do it from this side of the fire. As we cannot cross, it doesn't matter if you believe me or not.'

Cian howled his frustration at her words, he dearly wanted to squeeze the life out of her. Margaret made him feel edgy, Qiao was an irritant he wanted to swat and Elfrad's mutterings were getting on his nerves.

'Cian, stop the dramatics. You will do as I say.'

Margaret nodded at Qiao. A few minutes later they were back, Cian's furious face evident by his black eyes and bared fangs. Holding a bloody heart he dropped it into the glass jar Elfrad had conjured.

She took Qiao to one side telling him, 'do not attempt to come back until I call you.'

'I cannot cross the fire Margaret, I have tried all the spells I know. Nothing has worked.'

'Stand behind me in a line. Follow in my footsteps. I will get us across.'

'You cannot do this,' said Cian, his arm barring her way. 'The wizard's fire could kill us all, who knows what it is made of.'

Lifting her eyes to his, he flinched as twin pools of silver bore into his own. Her lips peeled back into a snarl, fangs lengthened. Her whole faced changed. The softness of Margaret gone, replaced by the face of a killer. The air shifted, Katrina could feel sweat break out under her clothes, adrenaline coursed through her body. The atmosphere so charged it felt as if an explosion was about to happen. The warrior inside Elfrad rose up, he stood next to Margaret choosing his side. For the first time in his life Cian felt real fear.

Slowly he removed his arm, glancing at Elfrad to see his friend's face carved in stone. His staff charged and ready to be used, his wand pointed at Cian's heart. Margaret didn't say a word, the fire lit up for a few seconds as she step across the threshold before frizzling to a flicker and was gone. Elfrad followed, Katrina practically hanging onto his coattails. The glass jar heavy in her arms. Cian brought up the rear. Misery written over his face.

Placing the jar onto the table, Katrina examined Sam.

'I think she has taken up residence near his heart but I need to be sure before I begin.'

Elfrad laid his hands onto Sam's skin, trying not to show how cold it felt. Closing his eyes he pictured himself inside his body. Surprised how strong his heart still beat. The damage inside was extensive. Like borrowing animals the darklings had wormed their way inside his vital organs. To enable Sam to live with his insides torn up this way. Elfrad could only think that the dark magic spell used must be ancient. The witch was right, the queen sat amongst a mass of darklings, her shiny red body easily standing out from the black of theirs.

Opening his eyes he placed his wand above Sam's heart, 'she is here.'

Katrina could not stop shaking, Cian's look of hate was nothing to Margaret's silent stare. She had never used a siren song before. It should work. But only if the queen liked the sound of her new home. As the words of the chant left her lips the heart in the jar sprang to life. Its beat matching that of Sam's, conscious that three pairs of eyes watched her every move.

At first nothing happened. Making sure that the heart in the jar still beat in time to Sam's, she leant forwards and began again. Her voice this time lighter and higher. Margaret the first to notice movement under his skin.

Katrina concentrated. This was the tricky bit. She had to entice the queen towards the new heart. Only if she took flight, would the darklings follow.

If she emerged and didn't like the scent or sounds she picked up, she would retreat back down. She needed them to emerge from the same place otherwise he would be torn asunder. The skin under his heart started to bulge. Keeping her voice steady she put her arm out and placed her hand in the jar fingers touching the heart. Her crooning chant rose and fell its melody calling the queen.

A tear opened in Sam's skin, feelers appearing at its edge. A red scaled body appeared. Six green eyes bulged on top of the beetles head. No one moved as they scanned the room. Pulling herself fully out, blood ran down Sam's ribs. Keeping her voice at the same pitch, Katrina willed her to move. The hole from which she emerged was filled with the sound of chittering. A sound darklings only made when ready to take flight. The queen flew towards the heart and buried herself inside, in one violent burst the darklings followed like a dark cloud. Katrina kept chanting until the last one had entered the jar. Screwing the top secure, she took a deep breath.

Margaret traced her fingers down Sam's face. Elfrad examined his wound, after seeing inside him, he knew nothing could be done. Using his wand he sealed the edges and cleared the blood away.

'I can wake him, not for long, enough though for you to say your goodbyes.'

Sam coughed, his throat and lungs felt as if they were on fire. Sweat rolled down his face.

'Hello my love.'

'Mum?' opening his eyes, he thought he was dreaming. 'What's happened? Where's Meg? Is she okay? What about the baby.'

Margaret smiled, 'she's fine. You have been hurt and need to rest.'

'I thought you had turned.'

'It didn't work. I'm still the same old mum.'

Looking between his mother and Cian he could see she spoke the truth. Cian looked every inch an angry vampire.

'I'm tired, wake me when Meg gets here.'

Elfrad removed his hand.

'I love you Sam.'

Margaret kissed his forehead, her tears falling unchecked. Drying her eyes, they fell on the glass jar.

The queen had burrowed her way inside the heart, the darklings surrounding her. So many were inside it looked as if the jar contained a black mass of writhing bodies. In two strides she fell on it, smashing her way through the glass she grabbed the heart squeezing it between her fingers. The queen tried to escape, the darklings rising up to save her.

Katrina covered her head trying to block out the sight and sound of the darklings, their chittering getting more and more frantic. Margaret took a deep breath in blowing fairy dust out.

Cian and Elfrad fell back as she threw the heart onto the pile of darklings. The queen stunned but still alive began to move. Holding her hands over the heap more fairy dust fell. Next, she produced a foresters net and threw it over the mass, smiling as they all writhed in agony, Trapped by the net, burnt by the dust. Slowly the mass lay still, nothing left but a pile of ash.

'Cian, I want you to take Sam back. Please don't tell Balin. I will do that when I return.' Before he could reply or object she turned to Elfrad, 'we're going after the wizards that hurt Sam.'

'Shall I come back and collect you both?' asked Qiao.

'There's no need. I will transport us back to Kingdom.'

'But how?'

Margaret ignored his question. She knew she could.

'And me?' asked Katrina, as her eyes flicked towards Cian.

'Thank you for what you did. However, you are a dark witch and as such are an enemy of Kingdom. With one look Katrina dropped dead at her feet.

Elfrad was worried, so much had happened in a short period of time. Margaret's change had taken them all unawares. Finding Sam and not being able to save him weighed heavy on his mind. He could see that it was also taking its toll on her.

Now the others had gone, she had reverted back to being a norm. Her crying had left them both feeling wrung out. Finding the wizards may not be easy. As one himself, he knew how careful they would be to not leave any clues as to their whereabouts. Wiping their signatures, often replacing them with someone else's.

Margaret wanted to sink down into a pit of despair. Losing Balin to madness and Sam to death was too much to take in. When she had become a vampire she had expected to look and behave much like any other. Even though she knew she was dead, when the change didn't happen straight away, she tried to convince herself that it hadn't worked. Yet this feeling of "becoming" had been washing over her for a while. Choosing to ignore it, pushing it down, and denying its existence.

Aeryissa had spoken about what may happen to her. How like her, a "trigger" could cause the change to occur. She had listened with one ear, sure that as a vampire she would be well down the pecking order. Realising now that she should have listened.

Being a vampire was only one part of who she was becoming, other abilities were waking. She knew she had to make a choice, embrace the change or keep pushing it down.

Elfrad used his Wakanda to trace the wizard's fire. When they had crossed and broke the spell it had fallen back against the walls. Only a few small smudges remained just enough for him to pick up a slight signature. Muttering an incantation moving his hands over the wall slowly the fire began to flicker. Pinching it between his fingers he removed it from the wall. The cold flame felt like ice against them. Carefully with his wand he drew the flame upwards making it slightly bigger, with a slight flick of his hand he encased it in a glass ball. Suspended, it hang in the air waiting for his command.

'Ready.'

Margaret nodded in reply, concentrating her new senses listening for any sounds to indicate where the wizards may be. Using her ears like antenna she honed in on several voices all trying to speak at once. Once she had their sound locked in, she used her inner eye as a guide. Holding Elfrad's arm she transported them. Both immediately felt sick. Fortunately they had emerged into what appeared to be a small cupboard. The voices were on the other side of the door. She gave him a weak smile, he in turn covered his mouth trying not to retch.

She remembered both Qiao and Aeryissa saying how it took them a while before they could transport without feeling nauseous. Taking a few minutes to let their bodies settle. They realised that the voices had moved away. Margaret indicated that she was going to open the door. Elfrad's staffs blue light cast an ethereal glow around the room. Stepping through the doorway they found themselves in a castle like structure, reeking of dark magic and decay. Elfrad pulled the glass ball out of his pocket, the flame glowing red. With a flick of his wand it started to move.

The ball hovered, unsure which way to go left or right. They waited, still it didn't move. Margaret's arm shot out, grabbing the ball she took Elfrad's arm and they were back in the cupboard. A finger to her lips, they kept the door slightly ajar.

Determined footsteps were coming their way, their owner in a hurry. In a flash she pulled the robed figure inside the cupboard. He had tried to free his wand, Elfrad stayed his hand, placing his Wakanda on his sleeve. The scribe shook in fear, he had never been close to a vampire before, the smell of violence and power leeching from her covered him like fog.

'Where are your masters? The wizards. Tell us where they are?' demanded Elfrad.

Margaret's eyes turned silver, the scribe moaned at the sight.

'Tell me now and I will make your death quick.'

He jumped as the glass ball fell to the ground and broke, the fire instantly extinguished.

Mesmerised by her eyes he whispered, 'they're upstairs in the lessor hall.'

She squeezed his brain, making him cry out, 'you lie, no one is upstairs.'

'Sorry, yes, sorry. Outside, they should be outside. They were talking about an experiment. Safer to do it outdoors. Yes, outside that's where they'll be,' the scribe gabbled.

'What are you not telling us?'

He spluttered, 'nothing, I mean I've told you everything I know. Please, I only record what they do. I don't do anything.'

Margaret searched his memory, he could feel her inside his head, cold, dead and determined to find his secrets.

'You took the notes and watched him writhe.'

It took his brain a moment to catch up with the action of Margaret ripping his heart out. Flinging the bloody organ away in disgust, she flung open the door ready to launch herself out and find the wizards. Elfrad's loud shout rang in her ears. He didn't flinch as her silver eyes raked his face.

'Think before you act. These are not Bomani but they are powerful wizards. Collectively, which is how they will fight, gives them even more of an edge. Their magic will be boosted. We don't know how strong and powerful you are yet.'

'Don't try and stop me.'

Smiling in the face of her anger, he lowered his hands.

'Watch.'

Calling up a spell long forgotten, he drew a picture in the air. Six wizard's against one foe. He showed her how their enemy thought he could outwit them, going after each wizard. Failure at every turn. Until they had him cornered and pooled their magic to bring him down.

'I don't know who these are, but whoever they turn out to be. One thing I do know is that wizards think they are the best and that every other magical is second rate compared to them.' Smiling again at her frowning face, he added, 'I don't include myself in that assessment. When Aeryissa asked me to take over from Dandelion. I couldn't see how I would live up to her memory. She was a great leader and magical. One thing in her armoury that she always made use of was distraction. No matter how many times she used it, and even with most knowing it was her signature move. Friends and enemies alike forgot how good she was at it. So that's what I propose we do here.'

'Explain,' demanded Margaret tersely, her impatience to get going, making her fangs and talons ache to rip and bite.

Tapping his shoulder, he answered, 'I have my cat with me. These wizards may never have seen one up close, when I ride in on her. They will be surprised.'

Margaret's smirk left her face, when he added.

'Make no mistakes they will recover quickly and be on their guard. In that small window of opportunity, you must use your shadow self to attach one of these to each wizard.'

Elfrad tapped his closed hand, turning it over several small beetles nestled in his palm. She held out her hand, the beetles wary at first, then as one leaped across and sat in her palm.

'What will they do,' she asked, her voice back to normal, her anger held in check.

'They will disrupt the wizard's pooling of magic. Each beetle will cause a glitch, the longer they are attached, the bigger the glitch. I will keep them distracted. Once they run out of patience, they will get ready to strike. That is when you emerge. Distracting them enough for me to cloak their magic, slowing them down even more.'

'Then I kill them?'

A shiver run down his spine as she grinned.

Removing his cat from her sleeping pouch, Elfrad was aware that both had not really spent much time getting to know each other. Angry at being left for so long as a kitten, unable to be her true form unless called. When he'd first released her, he thought her anger so great she may actually kill him. Holding her sleeping form in his hand, he gently tapped her nose.

'Awake so we may ride, my beauty,' he crooned.

One moment a sleeping ball of fluff. The next a giant hell cat, spitting and snarling. A wealth of anger directed towards him. Swatting him with her paw he fell over backwards.

'I will let you have that one. Do it again and I will turn you into a dog.'

Shaking her fur and stretching her limbs she ignored his threat.

'Have you stopped preening?' he asked, hauling himself onto her back.

She moved as if thinking to unseat him, but pressure from his legs, made her change her mind. Rubbing her head, he made her purr.

Telling her, 'we are going into battle, another is with us. Your protection also extends to her.'

With a toss of her head the cat moved forward, confident in her own strength and power.

Margaret hid in the shadows, hearing the hell cat's thoughts. Its angry demeanour belying the love she held for her master.

Walking towards the wizard's, so engrossed in their experiment, it was the scribes who noticed them first. Crying out as the cat snarled, opening her jaws wide showing them her large teeth.

'Greetings.'

The wizard's looked at each other, moving away from their experiment, giving Elfrad a clear view of a poor wretch lying prone on a slab. Sickened at the sight, he worked hard to keep the revulsion off his face.

'How did you get in here?'

'The gates were open. I'm sorry to interrupt… your work. Your fame has spread far and wide. I decided to come and see for myself and perhaps be able to learn more about what you do.'

Elfrad knew that they didn't believe him, he could feel their misgivings in the way they held their staffs. All he needed was enough time for Margaret to attach the beetles.

Closing her eyes she sought her inner eye and thought of a veil, gossamer thin covering her body. No light could penetrate, no sense could detect. Movement would be fluid; quick. She let herself fall into the picture she had created in her mind. Somewhere distantly she could hear speaking. Ignoring the sounds, she flowed towards the first wizard, the beetle slipped from her fingers and attached itself. Six wizards stood in a semi-circle facing Elfrad, all now with beetles under their collars. Before she left she bent over the man on the slab, closing his eyes with a breath, she stilled his heart with a touch, and a flick of fairy dust dissolved him.

Standing once more in the shadows Margaret could hear the disbelief in the wizard's voices. Stepping forwards, the silver in her eyes abated, turning black. Her skin rippled as it surged instead through her veins. Knowing instinctively that she didn't need her vampire to kill, many though, found them intimidating, so she let hers have full reign. By the time she stood beside Elfrad, she looked totally different. His cat purred and rubbed her head down Margaret's arm signalling her acceptance.

The wizards were taken aback at the sight of the predator before them. Then their survival instincts kicked in. Linking wands and staffs they prepared to send a pulse of magic. The scribes scrambled to get out of the way. One thinking, where has the body gone? Before diving for cover behind the columns. Their masters were powerful, they had no doubt that they would triumph. Backs against the wall they began to record the action.

Elfrad slid from his cat's back, tapped its nose, picked up the kitten and placed her back into her pouch. The scribes fascinated by what they had seen, began to write it down. Only to be swept away by the blast that he created with his staff. Like skittles they tumbled over and over. Their books flying in all directions. The wizards expecting the attack to be directed at them were for a moment distracted.

Elfrad next aimed his wand at the walls surrounding them, the mortar started to fall from the bricks making them appear as if they were crying. The wizards sent a pulse of magic straight towards him. He smiled, side stepping the blast, pushing it away with his staff sending it into the walls. Then with a flick of his wrist he conjured a bubble of magic around himself.

The wizards conjured darklings, their hideous worm like bodies dripping in slime. They launched themselves towards Elfrad, howling their frustration they began to claw at the bubble. In the confusion the wizards had forgotten about Margaret, all their efforts directed towards him. Dismissing her as only a vampire. To bite them she would have to get near, confident that the spells surrounding them would stop any of her kind in its tracks.

Margaret waited for the outer walls to collapse, the scribes screaming as they were trapped by the falling masonry. The wizards held their staffs facing towards Elfrad. Magic pouring out of each one, joining together as they met, sending an arc of dark magic towards him. It wrapped around the bubble, squeezing trying to find a way in. Because he was looking for it, he could see where the beetles were starting to have an effect. Darklings beat on the bubble their mouths gaping wide. He could smell their stench, even from inside.

The wizards ignored the cries behind them, as one they walked towards Elfrad. He had deliberately let the bubble appear to be collapsing. Renewing their efforts as he calmly waited inside.

Margaret struck, barrelling into the wizards she swept them off their feet. Their magic link broken. Dazed by her attack they slowly stood up. Shaking their heads to clear their thoughts, they looked over to see the bubble now gone.

His twin swords gleamed catching the sun. As their eyes locked onto Elfrad, they started to mutter a spell, their wands humming as they took direction. Margaret leapt and landed in front of them. Startling the wizards mid spell.

Baring her fangs looking for all the world like a monster she flexed her talons.

'You killed my son.'

Tearing their staffs and wands out of their hands, fairy dust fell, the wands hissed and crackled as they burnt. Shouting a spell together they expected her to be blasted apart hit by thousands of shards of black rock. With only a thought, a large foresters net appeared in her hands, the shards hit the net and exploded. The blast knocking the wizards off their feet. Regaining their balance, their minds in turmoil. Each drew on their dark magic, aiming a binding spell at her. Thinking if they could tie her up, she would be easier to deal with. Hearing their thoughts, Margaret laughed.

Elfrad wished she would kill them and be done with it, she was like a cat playing with mice, this was a side to her he had never seen. The power in her, moved under her skin, like a creature seeking release. How she even knew what to do, or what she could do, he was at a loss to fathom. From finding Sam, a mother distraught, to a killer that showed no mercy; had taken less than a day.

Finally she had done playing. Wizards lay where they fell.

When Qiao had transported the body of Sam to the armoury it had sent everyone into panic mode. Trying to explain what had happened, that Margaret and Elfrad stayed back to track down the wizards, had met with stares of disbelief.

Cian had placed Sam's body carefully onto the floor grabbed him and demanded he take him back. When he declined, his roar brought others into the hall. Pulling him away before he could do any damage. Qiao felt shaken by the hate filled eyes he'd turned on him. Marched away, Lefu ordered that he be incarcerated until he'd calmed down, telling Harsha to go and fetch Balin back to the armoury.

Discussion about Margaret and what she may have become went on long into the night. No one believed that she would be able to transport. Now that her vampire had shown itself, like every other magical, she could cast a spell, enabling her to move from place to place. This wasn't transporting, only fast movement.

Qiao liked being one of the few who could do it, it made him feel special. Transporters the only magicals who could actually make themselves and others disappear and reappear. He remembered how painful it had been to navigate the voids, crossing realms. Once he had mastered the art of moving himself, Aeryissa had let him use her as a guinea pig. Jumping back and forth between places and realms to find her. Learning how to concentrate, hone onto her magical signature. Locking on and fetching her from the most faraway places. Gradually as he mastered the art, he was able to think of a person and be by their side in seconds.

Having explained numerous times how exhausted he was, finally he was allowed to go to sleep. Eyes drooping, he nodded, at being told that once refreshed, he would have to go and get them.

'I've put Balin in the east wing well away from everyone. I'm not sure how much he understands. He's gotten much worse since I last saw him,' said Harsha.

'Margaret will want him here I'm sure. It will be up to her how and when she tells him.'

'What's going to happen about Cian? Even before her change he was like a love sick puppy. Now that her vampire is awake he will be even worse.'

Before he could answer, Elfrad and Margaret appeared.

'I will deal with Cian.'

Aeryissa emerged beside them, 'a word in private.'

Closing the door, wrapping a spell over it to prevent others from hearing anything, she bade them sit.

'How do you feel? In yourself?'

'Different…' Remembering to speak out loud so Elfrad could hear, she added, 'I wish I had listened to what you'd told me.'

'Do you feel that you are fully changed?'

Elfrad chuckled, 'she is. Whatever that may be.'

Sounding more like the Margaret Elfrad first met, she told them.

'I have to speak to Balin before I see Sam.'

He sat facing the wall, his body constantly twitched as if poked. Margaret watched him, he hadn't turned as she'd opened the door a sure sign his senses were shutting down.

'Balin,' she called gently.

Approaching slowly, so as not to startle him, she tapped his shoulder. When he turned, she tried not to gasp. His once handsome face was now pitted and scared. His eyes not the black of night or red of fire, but a washed out yellow. His fangs broken, even she had winced, when Harsha told how he had repeatedly hit them with anything he could find. Now the stumps caught his lips making blood run down his chin. Instead of the muscle and power that other vampires have. Balin's body was weak with a greenish hue. A smell hung around him like rotting meat.

Margaret had to dig deep for the love she had once felt for this man. Knowing that she was the cause of his distress and state, a part of her wished when Cian had suggested the idea, she had gone straight to Lefu. Instead of thinking by changing herself, they could be together, when in fact her actions have driven them further apart than when they had been separated.

Something in her voice must have penetrated his thoughts. His lopsided smile nearly broke her heart. Reaching out, he flinched at the hardness of her skin.

Margaret kept her voice low and even, 'you need to listen,' his eyes searched her face. 'Sam is dead, murdered by dark wizards,' she felt his hand loosen as he pulled away. She blurted, 'Meg is pregnant, Sam told me before he died. We're going to be grandparents.'

Balin looked at her in horror, thinking, how matter of fact she seemed. Yet he knew he loved Sam. She used to love him. Then she did this to him. His jumble of thoughts easily heard by Margaret.

'Kill me,' his voice steady, his manner polite. 'Please, kill me. I hate what you did to me. Now Sam is dead, and you? What are you? Certainly not the Margaret I fell in love with. What have you done with her? Where is she?'

His shouts rang in her ears as he lost control. Charging towards her, his cracked hands and dirty talons reached for her face. She flicked him away like a fly. Falling, hitting the wall, drawing strength from somewhere he launched himself at her. Stopped mid-flight by the appearance of Aeryissa.

'I'm sorry Margaret. I told you it may come to this.'

She snapped his neck. Placing her hands on his forehead she filled his body with silver, washing it through his system, killing any chance of resurrection. Calling it back to her, she laid his body gently down.

Stuck like a statue. The guilt overwhelmed Margaret at what she had done to him. Then not done. Allowing Aeryissa to kill him, when the responsibility should have been hers.

Margaret was grateful that Bilberry had taken the trouble to return home to be with her. In a plot next to Dandelion, Sam and Balin now were together as they had never been in life. Her thoughts repeatedly coming back to the same thought over and over again. How they would both be still alive if she hadn't entered Kingdom. Their deaths were the direct result of her actions.

Bilberry, as if hearing her thoughts, patted her arm.

'You mustn't blame yourself. Our journey through life, has a funny way of taking us to the place where we are meant to be. Regardless of our efforts to steer a different path.'

'If I hadn't come here... maybe.'

Shaking her head, Bilberry told her, 'when actions are taken and you feel responsible. Stepping from your path will give you respite. In time though, you will be drawn back.'

'Are you saying, that no matter what I do, or where I go, something other than me, is in charge of my life?'

'To some extent, yes. Dandelion, used to say there are three paths in life, the right, the wrong and the other. Most magicals are on the right path for them. Those who choose or cross to the wrong, will have lives that are out of kilter. Only those with a purpose can walk the other path. Given by whom and for what. Dandelion failed to mention.'

CHAPTER THIRTY-ONE

'She's entered the mirror,' shouted Eadulf, as he opened the link between him and Aeryissa, hoping she was back in Kingdom. Relieved when he heard her reply.

'We're ready, let her through.'

The three of them waited, for Purity it would be a test of her nerve and strength. She hadn't forgotten Meridian's use of her and would dearly have loved to toss her into the void. Only Guri and Eadulf's friendship stayed her hand. In them she trusted. The unpleasantness she would feel when Meridian and her army touched her mirror, would be short lived. Bounced by spells into the mirror maze, they all couldn't wait for her exit into Kingdom.

Meridian, felt the pure mirror shaking, she hissed in response feeling a delicious thrill in its terror. She let herself be drawn forward. Surprised to see so many mirrors had survived the expulsion of the black mirror. Catching a glimpse of herself as she passed through, gave her another thrill.

When she had left the Glasserium to bring the Dark Lord forth she had already began to wither and age. The dark magic she carried, eating away at her. Now though, thanks to her elixir she was young and vibrant again.

The magicals following behind also checked themselves out in the mirrors. Many had never been inside the Glasserium, or seen so many in one place.

Eadulf watched their antics, the smell of the dark magicals through the glass, rank and bitter. Little did they know these mirrors were fake's. Once they had gone through, he would destroy the maze, now tainted by their dark magic. It would cling to the glass and frames trying to worm its way in. Never again would mirrors be used for anything other than what they were created for.

Guri joined him, it had taken some getting used to, seeing another made of glass. Like him, she too preferred to be in her magical form. Once changed completely to glass, it had taken her an effort to be able to revert back.

They waited a few minutes to make sure no stragglers were coming through. Guri returned to Purity, worried about her friend surprised to find her in remarkably good spirits. Eadulf joined them.

Climbing inside, he told her, 'this is it, never again will anyone be able to use you.'

Looking inwards, he sent his mind to find the patch put in place to allow Meridian entry. Ripping it off, he felt Purity's joy at once more being whole.

Gilda whispered to Khalon, 'you believe she knows?'

'Stop ferreting about in my mind. Of course she knows. The real question is. What are we going to do about it? Our miners have only scraped the surface of the new tunnels they are digging. This seam appears to be the best one we have found so far. I have received word. Her spies may be unaware of the breakthrough. We must return to Novia.'

'How can we? For now, we will have to put everything on hold. She suspects us of something, but still needs our help. Let's show her a united front.'

Watching Khalon and Gilda walk into her chambers, gave Meridian pause for thought. Their demeanour open. Thinking perhaps her spies had wrongly interpreted what they had saw and heard.

Gilda the first to speak at Meridian's nod, told her, 'everything is being done to find the source. Until now, as you know, we have had only a few small successes. Unfortunately, as a large fresh seam appeared, the tunnels caved in. The miners killed have been found and revived and are starting to dig it out again. Before it collapsed they managed to bring this out.'

Reaching into her pocket she held the ball of silver in the palm of her hand. No bigger than a small pearl it shone and pulsed. Meridian was by her side in a moment. Snatching the ball she rolled it around with her fingers. As small as it was she could feel its power. Dark magic flowed to her hands, seeking what it craved. The ball began to vibrate as it drew near.

Exploding, it sent small specks of silver into the air, flying away as if a wind had entered the chamber and taken them. Meridian's disappointment was as explosive. Her dark magic raged inside her, its anger at losing what it wanted distorted her features.

The spell she was using to maintain her looks, wasn't strong enough to hold the dark magic at bay. In an instant she went from a beautiful woman to an old hag. Her anger directed inward. Her body fell to the ground, writhing as if at war with itself. No more a magical, instead, a creature of the dark fighting itself.

Meridian's gaze swept across the room, daring anyone to mention her earlier loss of control. Coming to rest on Khalon she nodded at him to speak.

'We have been keeping the magicals busy, burning everything we come across. Fanning the flames to make sure all is destroyed. Many have fled into Pictures. Several have escaped into caves and tunnels, we have caught many in this way. Filling the entrances, blocking their exits,' he explained. 'The trees have gone. So has the water. The only cover we have when crossing open ground is what we conjure ourselves. Skirmishes are still breaking out, both sides sustaining losses. Kingdom's magicals want to survive to fight another day. Those who we have sent, are expendable. They don't retreat, they keep on until they are dead.'

Gilda pushed through the throng dragging two magicals in her wake, crowing, 'look what I've found.'

Meridian stared at the twins, licking her lips at the thought of what she had in mind for them. With one flick they hung suspended, their heads lolling against their chests. Poking Amp with her staff she commanded.

'Kill him.'

Confusion crossed Coot's face, as a cold breath of ice began to swirl inside his head. The intensity of the cold getting worse. Shaking his head trying to dislodge the feeling only made it worse. It moved through him, tremors racked his body as he tried to keep warm. His veins filled with ice, fingers and toes turning blue.

He tried not to turn, his body ignoring his command. Coot stared into his brothers eyes as Amp had done to him. While cold and ice took over his body. Amp's face began to turn red. Inside his head he was busy lighting fires, sending the heat through his brother's body as he sent the cold through his. Meridian watched fascinated. She had never tried this before, unsure if it would work.

Coot was turning blue, Amp was smouldering. Both locked in their own horror. The crowd gasped to see Coot crackle and explode, disintegrating before their eyes. While Amp slowly burnt, his body twisting out of shape, his mouth open in a scream, until only ash was left.

'Well that was interesting,' she murmured, poking at the mess before her.

Chapter Thirty-Two

'They're coming again, more of them this time, everyone get ready.'

Stars fell. Their explosion's making everyone flinch. Balls of blue light conjured by the magicians flung like grenades, lit the sky. Filled with pebble like creatures that clung to clothes, looking for skin to bite. The Bomani, fired flaming arrows into the sky, trying to avoid hitting any Kaimi flying low, hunting for prey. Falk landed. Shrugging of his bird form, he shouted.

'There's a large group of them over the ridge. They have crystal bombs. I could see them glinting.'

Hafren jumped, caught a falling star in his net, swung it around above his head and flung it back. Laughing as his wife Tairlaw did the same.

'The Yorkus are coming,' he cried. 'Can't you hear their singing?'

No one answered, all eyes on the battle in front of them. The dark magicals had poured out of the caves surrounding the Osias. Lobbing spells and stars in equal measure, calling up all manner of strange darklings. Black pits for eyes, mouths stretched across their faces, looking drunk as they stumbled across the ground, arms outstretched, wailing like banshees. As soon as they were knocked down, up popped another one. Cian was busy ripping them apart, like a one man vampire killing machine.

Swooping down Zekia and Yries encouraged their dragons to let their fire loose. The dark magicals screamed as their hair caught alight. Fairy dust fell in clouds, making it hard for them to see, making them cough, burning, when it touched their skin.

Several dark witches took to the skies, as if flying away. Before anyone realised, they turned around and in formation flew kamikaze straight at them. Crystal shards rained down, everyone dived for cover. Ears ringing, they crawled out of the mess the witches had created. Several were injured, two magicians had been killed. Paloma and Orev had had their feathers singed and were unable to change into magical form. Yries dragon had been hit by a star and was bellowing in pain. Out of the chaos appeared the Yorkus, the ground shaking as they emerged, dirt falling around them in small mounds.

'Captain,' said Mercia, speaking to the largest tree. 'We need these magicals clearing.'

'It will be our pleasure.'

Everyone pulled back to give them room. Some trees disappeared back underground, others pulled their roots up and ran full pelt towards the magicals. The astonishment on their faces at the sight of the Yorkus in battle charge was a wonder to behold.

The ground shook as they pounded towards them. Trying in vain to flee, witches who thought to take flight, were grabbed by branches and flung towards the ground. Trampled into the dirt by the tree roots. Magicians threw spell after spell at them, but were not a match for the onslaught. Shrugging of stars and light balls as if nothing. Squashing the creatures conjured by the dark witches. Those trees which had gone underground, forced their way up pushing the earth skywards, sucking any magicals back down with them. Repeating the action, until all were gone. Quiet descended, the destruction total. The ground, a mass of earth churned up into small hills. Broomsticks, wands and staffs the only remains of those that a few moments ago had inhabited it. Not many magicals had ever witnessed the Yorkus in battle. Formidable in size, not prone to speaking much or mixing with other trees. Since they had returned to duty, most gave them a wide berth. Now they would be the stuff of legends, mentioned over campfires, brought to life in all their glory. Some humbled, others scared by the violence they had reeked, all glad though to have them on their side.

'Falk has sent word, she's entered Reception,' Elfrad told the packed hall. 'They have cleared her dark magicals from the caves and are patrolling the skies. She has drawn a barrier around the entrance, which is in the process of being cleared.'

'Is Meridian powerful enough to take the Shimmers magic and open the tomb?' voiced Bardolpf.

'The answer is we don't know,' said Aeryissa, 'she is riddled with dark magic, if she can and does would she emerge the victor or would it consume her and escape into Kingdom? Either scenario would be catastrophic for all of us.'

'Before they died the Kaimi spying on her base managed to send back information. Wizards have been placed in the first corridor. She intends to clear the magma and open the Osias. That's when we make our entrance. It may be best Bardolpf, if you stay here, having you there will give her even more of a boost if she takes you too.'

'She and her kind are responsible for the death of my family and my exile. I will go with you as Ammon. She hasn't seen me as a wolf, only as a king.'

Meridian focused on the magma that filled the space in front of her. The dark magic inside her, melded its power with hers. All felt the movement under their feet. A slight shifting, an easing. Holes appeared, small at first, then enlarging as the magma shifted. Gilda picked up a faint flutter, signalling everyone to be quiet, she strained to catch it again.

Only the first corridor had been filled. Meridian hadn't wanted to destroy the Osias or kill the Shimmers, only stop anyone else from having access to them. Once inside, everyone would be able to see her subterfuge. They'd assumed she'd filled everything with magma. She had done nothing to disabuse them of this idea.

The wizards were stiff from their hunched position. Using the adapted crystal's they placed each one a hands width apart. The explosion lifted them bodily before slamming them back down.

The doors hung momentarily by their hinges, falling, making the ground tremor with the weight of them. Dust clouds blocked their view. Moving forwards they carried on until all the doors were open except those of the Osias.

'They are through,' spoke Gilda, still surprised that it had worked.

So close now to her dreams, Meridian took a moment to calm her senses. Shushed to silence, her stare making everyone nervous. As the words leaving her mouth grew in strength, the magma exploded, with a final thunderclap it disappeared. Sweeping along the corridors, she stood before the doors to the Osias.

In a semi-circle sat the Shimmers. Doorways heavily carved, hinted at the chambers beyond. The light spilling out, adding to the overall effect of brightness.

Ignoring all the beauty, in the middle was what Meridian had come for. The Shimmers hadn't made a sound or a move at their entrance, their eyes staring in front of them.

She and her more senior wizard's cast their magic, searching for any traps. None detected, they moved into the chamber. Dark magicals flooded the passageways. Empty of any other life they returned to the main chamber, as the witches began to search the heights.

At any other time, Meridian would have paused to wonder why they were not better protected. As excited as her cohorts, spurred on by the dark magic inside her, she threw caution to wind and accepted that all was as it seemed.

Fanning out as instructed, the chamber was soon filled with

magicals and wraiths tasked with hiding in the shadows to secret themselves away. Darklings adding to their number clung to the walls, the black of their bodies camouflaging them from sight.

Her most powerful magician's began to conjure a veil. Quickly taking shape, it covered them like a dome. Her witches cast a locking spell knitting it all together making it stronger. Once complete, Meridian and the wizard's used their staffs to further strengthen it.

She turned her attention to the Shimmers. Still they hadn't moved. Their glazed eyes stared fixedly.

The shimmer on their skin danced. She could feel the need reaching out from her dark magic to taste it. Finding it hard to contain herself. She had to remain calm and focused. The spell she had been using on herself, the foul potions she had drunk. All now culminated in her being able to summon the Shimmers magic and draw it into her own body.

Swords at the ready, they entered the first corridor. Climbing upwards, Aeryissa and Margaret searched the walls for those hiding in the crevasses and on rock ledges. While below the Alvie and the Fae worked together to clear those on the ground. Margaret's eyes began to turn silver, waiting for Aeryissa to get in position, her equally silver eyes like twin probes across the chasm.

Elfrad exploded into the air, the twin blades of his sword's cutting through the dark witches flying on their broomsticks, raining stars down on those pouring into the corridor. Alvie forester nets landed across their prone bodies, the fairy dust making them scream as it burnt their skin. Margaret heard Aeryissa's words, both leaped towards the glut of dark elemental witches preparing to reign fire down on those below. Silver flooded their bodies, making them shine in the dark.

The witches screamed in fear as the apparition's bore down on them. One braver than the rest, pointed her wand and threw a spell towards them. The others soon joined in. Fire shooting from their wands gathered strength. Aeryissa grabbed the flame, with one flick she fired it back, aiming it at their wands and staff, distracted, they didn't see Margaret creeping underneath the ledge they were perched on. Holding herself upside down she used the power of her legs to smash the rock.

To break their fall the witches tried to conjure their broomsticks. Before they had a chance, Aeryissa tore out their hearts, flinging their bodies towards the empty space that had opened up on either side of the path.

Dark wizards had conjured hundreds of darklings all shapes and sizes. Those wraiths still able to function were also throwing themselves into the fray. As they moved towards the Osias they left a massacre in their wake.

Cian's nerves like everyone else's were stretched taut. He had wanted to go with Margaret. One look from her had changed his mind. Since she'd returned, he hadn't been able to get near her. Desperately wanting to talk. So far she had ignored all his advances. Anger and despair was making him a laughing stock. Lefu didn't trust him to obey his commands. The other clan members avoided him as much as possible. Determined to make his mark, he pushed and pulled everyone, hurrying them up. Finally, his part of the assault were in and were immediately attacked by dark magicians their hissing arcs of light wrapped around their bodies, acting like chains to drag them down. So busy with trying to maintain their hold they didn't hear the wizard appear behind them. With one thrust of his staff their magic was broken. Screaming as the vampires fell on them, their ripped and torn bodies pushed over the edge into the dark.

The large doors blown off now used as a bridge over the rubble. The next corridor was a bit trickier. Whatever the wizards had used to gain entry had done a lot of damage, earth and stone still falling sent up dust clouds into their eyes. Out of nowhere dark witches appeared, dirty and dishevelled, flashing their wands, they conjured strips of light, using them like whips they flailed Cian's team as they ran. Liking nothing better than to rip them apart, he ignored the blood thumping through his veins and bellowed for an elemental.

Earth rose up covering the witches filling their mouths with dirt. A geyser of water flew over the top turning the earth to mud as the Warra sucked earth, water and witches into the ground.

Cian didn't stopped to see if the threat had been dealt with. His focus on getting to the chamber. A sentry lay smashed, magnificent in life, now a jumble of metal fused together by the magma. Felled by a thump on his back, he tumbled over as several wraiths threw large boulders. A wizard pushed passed, pointing his staff it crackled with light, blasting them into pieces. Darklings rose from the shadows throwing themselves at anyone they could find. Shouts and screams, thuds and crashes all wove into one as the melee spilled over into the next corridor. The Ambrogio were ripping them apart as fast as they appeared.

A voice from behind them shouted, 'stand back, stand back, all down, NOW.'

Without even thinking why they should, they all dropped to the floor. Several wizards were walking the path, their staffs blazing together, lighting up the dark.

The cries of the darklings as they were caught in their beam, setting everyone's teeth on edge. Silence, the light from their staff's flicked and went out. Plunged into darkness, only the vampires could see where to go. Calling for sconces and candles, the magicals followed their lead and rushed towards the Osias.

Meridian began her chanting, ignoring the small nagging doubt that kept poking her senses. Choosing to believe that whatever drug the Shimmers had taken, had dulled their reactions. Her dark magic wanted her to get on with it, its impatience drowning out her natural caution. Curling her hands she started to gather in the shimmer. As more and more of it left them the paler they became. Their hands gripping the sides of their thrones the only indication of the pain they were in.

The power hitting her system was like nothing she had ever

felt before. Mixing with the powerful dark magic already inside her made it a heady mix. Sure now her decision not to give this power over to the Darkness was the right one. Those nearest fell back. Power thrummed and whirled around her no one wanted to catch her eye.

Turning her attention to the circle, she muttered the names of each Shimmer now held inside her. The outer began to move, as it stopped, the pentagon moved upwards in the opposite direction, for the first time everyone in the Osias saw the real meaning of Darkness as the mass became visible to all. So entranced by the sight, she was oblivious to anything happening on the other side of the veil.

Approaching the dark centre her nerves finally kicked in. Stepping into the unknown was not a new experience for her, not having a planned outcome was. The Darkness surged towards her, it caught a scent and chased it. Shimmer. Silver also fizzed inside this body, it drank it all in. Meridian let it infiltrate her. The dark magic she carried, blazing at its touch. Confident that she could control it, she in turn used her own magic to search for its secrets.

For those watching, it appeared for a moment as if there were two Meridian's standing side by side. Unsure if the spell would be enough, worked on in secret, she could hear the roars from her dark magic as it beat inside her head seeing what she had done as a betrayal. Taking power, without being consumed. The satisfaction she felt at her plan coming to fruition, held back by the feeling that something was wrong. The dark magic that lived inside her had gone quiet. The feeling was persistent, filled with the Darkness yet at the same time she felt empty.

Her body began to vibrate, the humming heard earlier was back with a vengeance as was the smell. As Meridian's blood curdling screams rent the air, her forces rose up from their hiding places. The mass of Darkness poured from her body turning the veil black.

Like a switch being thrown everyone moved at once. Margaret and Aeryissa sprung. Elfrad's swords flashed. Ammon's jaws opened ready to bite. Hit by fairy dust, secured by nets. Tossed to the vampires who tore out their hearts groans of the dead and dying filled the air. The wizard's managed to stop the darklings chances of resurrecting, getting in everyone's way as they cast their spells, complaining when they got hurt from flying fist's and feet.

Elfrad was covered in blood, the leather of his clothes hanging in shreds, he'd forgotten what it felt like to be a warrior. His eyes scanning the shadows for more dark magicals to vent his anger on. Margaret brought him back to earth, her voice in his head calling his name. Leaving the smaller chambers to others to continue clearing, he made his way back to the main chamber. Seeing him enter, she beckoned him over.

'It's Eldora, she's still alive.'

The explosion knocked them off their feet sending them flying into the rock face. Buried under the falling stone. Margaret the first to emerge, bruised but unhurt, covered in dust and dirt crawled towards Elfrad, his face bloody and lacerated, his moans a joy to her ears.

Aeryissa had taken the brunt of the explosion, flinging herself over Eldora, her back was ripped to shreds. The Alvie had tried to throw up nets as a shield, but the blast was so powerful it had tangled them and the Fae into a bundle. The witches released them, even managing a smile as the forester's nets tried to nip them.

The veil and the dark magicals were gone, scooped up when the Darkness flew upwards heading for the surface and freedom.

'Now released from its prison,' said Aeryissa, 'it will be hungry. It knows what we have. It will come.'

Chapter Thirty-Three

Exhausted, Margaret and Aeryissa could do no more. With Qiao only able to do short trips, it had fallen to them to transport magicals into Pictures via a meeting point set up by the Froade. Kingdom was now a dead place, where not even the air moved, charged instead with dark magic that crackled and lit up the darkened skies, only weak daylight able to push through. Many had been caught, the lucky ones dying in battle, those taken, drained and discarded like rubbish.

The Darkness covered the land, everywhere it went it blocked out the sun, growing bigger day by day spreading its rank smell over everything. Swooping down destroying anything in its path, the earth thrown up in great mounds of dirt, leaving in its wake jagged rocks the only cover in a bare landscape.

Buildings didn't stand in Kingdom any more. Villages had been flattened, the Darkness pouring into the homes snatching magicals, draining their essence. Leaving them to roam, mindless and vacant. The trees all gone, shrubs and flowers dead, the smaller animals diving for cover deep underground. Helped by the forest creatures quickly making holes to aid their escape. Larger animals including horses and cattle, starved. With no one to care for them or scrub to eat, they roamed Kingdom, dying where they fell. Scavenged by

Gork's, their bones littered the ground. The once constantly moving landscape of Kingdom now stilled. The magic that had been woven through its fabric; gone.

Mountains and hills collapsed. The earth itself churned up as it was pushed skywards by the explosions beginning as small ripples, quickly turning into full scale blasts. Some of those hiding underground, were flung out, their bodies broken. Water long gone, leaving the earth arid and dusty. Instead, replaced by bubbling pools of poison. Their noxious stink wafting even without any breeze.

Fingerling took a last look at his home. Verlimusa was under attack. The ancient magic of Kingdom used to weave its construction proving for the moment, too strong for the Darkness to break through.

Enraged at being thwarted, it covered the veil protecting it with a poisonous membrane, scorching the land where it dripped onto the ground. Stopping light from filtering through and anyone from entering.

He cast his mind outwards. Receiving confirmation from Argonorth. He sank slowly into the earth. Tasking the creatures living underground to start work. The last thing he saw before he pulled himself under the earth, were millions of creatures filling Verlimusa, crawling up inside the veil. The Darkness had cut off the light from outside, now the creatures hid what lay inside.

All the dark magicals left in Kingdom, eventually made their way to the wastelands, something inside them thrilling to the call of the dark. Jagged rocks greeted them, thrusting up from the earth like giant fangs. The Darkness clung to the heights, plunging down filling the magicals with its breath. Retreating, it took part of their core with it. Collapsing from the brutality of the taking, they lay where they were tossed. Recovered, they roamed the barren landscape, trying to find themselves. Called back time and again, their fate, now only sustenance for the Darkness.

'Eadulf has finally sent word, the spell Flinders located has worked.

Guri and Eadulf between them have woven a thick cloak around the Glasserium. It may not keep anyone determined out but will act as a warning should anyone try to enter. He has removed and hidden the inner sanctum, also cloaked, this one though is much more substantial. Eadulf is hopeful, unlike Meridian's usage of the Glasserium, the core of the Darkness may not have any knowledge or need of his halls,' explained Aeryissa. 'Every picture magical or otherwise has been moved to the vaults. Access not allowed, even using miniatures. The Froade have started the cleansing. It may not work, the Darkness has renewed its efforts to gain access. Our pictures have also been confiscated and locked away in a vortex. Entry for us not an option. Concerned the Darkness would be even more determined to enter Pictures if it thought we were inside.'

After weeks of being chased all over Kingdom rescuing those caught outside of Pictures. All three realised they could do no more. This Darkness was nothing like the others which had come before it. Those left in Kingdom used as fodder for the dark. Roaming the desolate landscape, half alive, half dead. The Darkness didn't differentiate between light and dark magic, it took. Never sated, it wanted more.

Craters dotted the landscape as the Darkness scourged the earth looking for its treasure. Turning its attention to the three of them every time they were caught out in the open. Their bodies like a beacon drawing it forth. Several times, only saved by their ability to transport away. Many refused to leave Kingdom, wanting to fight to the end. Seeing Pictures as a last resort.

Zekia had commanded her clan to take their dragons into it for safe keeping. Even though she knew it would limit some of what they could do. Flying no longer an option. Too many dragons and witches already dead from being caught out in the open. The Alvie, bereft at the loss of the trees nevertheless were the only magicals able to blend in against the barren land. Often using their bodies to hide those they had found until they could be transported away.

The Ambrogio lost all their mines of Obsidian, the Darkness

recognising it from its imprisonment. Going to great lengths to destroy every part of it. Letting it rain down on anyone caught in the open. The vampires were at the fore front of the war. Many had been killed, drained and discarded. Their home destroyed, their clan decimated.

Lefu had finally lost patience with Cian when he put Harsha and several witches in danger. Instead of helping to get them to the meeting point he'd been more concerned with what Margaret was doing.

Before he could deal with the situation. She stepped in. Drunk and belligerent, bellowing out his anger to any who'd listen. Seeing Margaret enter, silver glowing under her skin all left the chamber. Lefu, unable to meet her eyes walked quickly away.

Aware of the silence, Cian turned around.

'Where have you been?'

Ignoring his question, she told him, 'you have two choices. Enter Pictures or death.'

'I haven't seen you for weeks. I don't know where you are. Or what's happening. I thought we had something.'

'We never had anything. It's all in your mind.'

'I love you, I always have, from the first moment I saw you.'

'I'm not that norm anymore. I'm, Well, I still don't know what I am,' looking him straight in the eyes, she let hers turn silver.

Saying goodbye, had been hard on all three of them, knowing there was a good chance this was it. The end of everything. Kingdom was dying, everything destroyed; tainted by the Darkness. For Margaret it had been Qiao's face when he realised she would not be able to join him. With his wounds healing he had wanted to help both her and Aeryissa. Given smaller transports he'd still managed to play his part. Finally though, even he had to stop. Nearly caught. He and the Alvie he was transporting only managed to evade the Darkness as it swooped in to take them. She felt better knowing he was safe. Gone with Ammon and Layla to Long Meadow.

Bardolpf no longer wanted to be king, explaining he never had. He'd been trying to live up to the expectations of others. Many tried to tell him of the dangers of continually staying as a wolf. He chose to ignore their words. Happy to be with Layla and the friends he had come to love.

Margaret had desperately wanted to see Meg. She hadn't seen her since they'd all left to go to Novia. Hearing from Dillon she'd lost the baby. Felt like a dagger to her heart. Like losing Sam all over again.

Waiting at a meeting point where she knew Margaret was due to bring a batch of magicals. Damala felt overcome with sadness. So much had happened since she had first met Meg and Dillon, she looked on them both as the family she never had. Qiao, had also found a place in her heart.

'How are they?' she asked, shooing the magicals forwards.

Damala, couldn't help a chuckle breaking free, in full vampire mode, Margaret looked incongruous as she assured them all would be fine.

'Everyone's scared. Dillon pretends he isn't as usual, Meg jumps at the least loud noise. I'm still not sure why she has been so affected, it's not only losing the baby. She reminds me sometimes of how Balin was, after being wrapped by the Warra.'

Margaret stared into the distance, her eyes catching a movement, feeling a change in the air. Turning to enter the picture, Damala caught a glimpse of her expression making her wonder who she feared the most; her or the Darkness.

For Aeryissa, being with her father again, fighting beside him had given her immense pleasure. So long by herself, with only Eadulf for company. It had been good to be with someone she felt an affinity with. Now as they said goodbye, she could see the strain of the last few weeks showing clearly on his face. Pulling her into a hug, he kissed her forehead. Those watching, unable to look away at the sight of two predators with tears running down their faces.

'Take care Aeryissa. I know...'

'Father, even if I could enter Pictures, I wouldn't leave Margaret.'

'What is it about her that draws such loyalty? I had much the same conversation with Elfrad. He also told me he wouldn't leave her side.'

'We have to see this through to the end; together. The Darkness wants all three of us. It won't stop until it gets what it wants. We are linked somehow. Together we stand or fall.'

In the process of escorting several norms found hiding out in tunnels. Surprisingly untouched by dark magic. Elfrad had expected to find only Hib-Hob at the meeting point. To his great delight, Dalil, followed by Guido stepped out. Bringing a smile to his face when they told him how all Mr Culpepper's Emporium's were filling up with unused pictures. So much so they'd had to be fortified to stop them bursting open.

Not so funny though, when they explained they and several other greeters were to stay in Novia. The norms being called were still turning up. No one as yet could figure out how it was possible they even knew where the Emporium's were situated.

The only possibility was that the pictures inside had somehow remained active. Saying goodbye to his friends, brought home to Elfrad how alone he Aeryissa and Margaret were going to be.

With the last of Kingdom's magicals now safe inside Pictures. They began to lay their trap. They had kept Eldora in hiding, Hafren and Tairlaw had volunteered to take care of her, sealed in a tunnel under the armoury, when Elfrad went to fetch them he could immediately see that she had worsened considerably. Scooping her up into his arms she felt as light as a feather. Smiling at him as she placed her head on his shoulder, the deep sigh leaving her body an indication that she didn't have long.

Aeryissa transported the Alvie to their meeting point with Mercia. Making sure that she zigzagged back through Kingdom before returning. She wanted to leave a trail. At the same time they were not ready to be found yet.

Several times the Darkness had entered the armoury. Margaret and Elfrad had done a good job of fooling it into thinking only dark magicals resided within its confines. After nearly being caught themselves trying to rescue Herwig and Beadu. Elfrad wanted to kill the dark magicals on the spot, in retaliation for what they had inflicted on his friends. Margaret stilled his hand.

Instead, brought back, she used their blood to smear the walls with their taint. Sealing others in the lower tunnels. Making it appear as if they had set up camp. Also stationing some of them around the armoury, chained, waiting for the Darkness to drain them. It made him realise how focused and cold bloodied the vampires were. The dark magicals to them a means to an end. Telling him sentiment was a luxury they couldn't afford.

Moving quickly and with purpose they weaved their scent. Touching everything that still stood, making sure that when the Darkness came it would think the walls ran with shimmer and silver.

Exhausted from tearing all over Kingdom, it took all their remaining strength to complete the task. Taunting the Darkness, letting their glow shine. The only bright light to be seen in the gloom of Kingdom, sending it a message, come and get us.

'It's coming,' shouted Aeryissa.

The sky darkened, the humming which always preceded it growing in pitch. Out of nowhere, the earth beneath their feet erupted. Like angry bees searching for nectar, the Darkness flew upwards. Separated by the explosion, each avoided attracting its attention.

Eldora pulled herself up. The movement making the dark cloud turn in her direction. Giving the performance of her life she stood facing their nemesis. The shimmer that both Margaret and Aeryissa had washed her in earlier, shining on her skin. The silver she had drank, flowed through her veins, its siren call permeating the Darkness's conscious.

More and more of it poured in, blasting the remaining outside wall, the inner only holding up because of the bedrock behind it.

Hunting its prey all over Kingdom. Finally, cornered. Nowhere else to run. The Darkness struck. As the dark cloud retreated, weak daylight began to filter through the gloom. Nothing stirred.

The magic, the very fabric of the land, taken. Magicals, its life blood, dead or in hiding. Its last hope; gone. Kingdom, finally let go...

PART III

CHAPTER THIRTY-FOUR

Exploding out; tumbling over and over, they slammed into a pile of rocks before coming to rest at the bottom in a jumbled heap. Bruised and battered, the only sound their panting. Aeryissa rolled over onto her knees, shaking her head, trying to clear the ringing in her ears from the force of their entrance. Margaret pulled herself up, her clothes hung in shreds. She too found her ears filled with a cacophony of sound, trying to filter it out only made it worse. Holding her head she moaned. Elfrad had taken the brunt of their fall, his face cut and bleeding, a large wound to the back of his head. Grabbing his hands they hauled him to his feet.

'Where are we?' he asked groggily, feeling himself sway.

They all looked up as the sound of beating wings filled the air. Blotting out the sunlight, the dragon circled, folded its wings, landing in its magical form.

Fafnir hurried towards them.

'Kingdom?'

'Taken. Everyone who could, has settled in Pictures, some have chosen Novia. Kingdom is now the Darkness's domain. We fooled it enough to allow our escape. When it regroups it may realise its mistake and come looking.'

Still feeling dizzy from his fall, Elfrad stared at the landscape before him. After the shock had worn off at finding himself somewhere he hadn't even known existed, his senses flooded outwards. Used to Kingdom's barren dry land, the sun hidden by the Darkness. He revelled in the warmth of Eirian's on his face, his gaze drawn to the trees which were everywhere, all shapes and sizes. He could hear water and see it sparkling in the distance. The cottages were picture box pretty. The grass lush looking like an endless green carpet. Flowers waved in the breeze. Their scent wafting towards them, bringing back memories of a happier time.

Surreal, came unbidden into Elfrad's thoughts, one moment they were fighting for their existence. Next, they were catapulted into a land, seemingly untouched by dark magic.

Once clean and donning fresh clothes, they emerged to find a feast waiting for them. While they ate, Aeryissa spoke of their last days in Kingdom. Elfrad kept glancing across at Margaret noticing how silent and preoccupied she had become since entering Eirian. He watched as her head moved from side to side, listening to something only she could hear. Her skin he noticed had taken on the glow of shimmer while her eyes changed repeatedly from blue to silver.

'Are you okay?' He asked gently. 'You really should try to eat and drink something.'

Turning towards him, her eyes held a vacant look, as if she had gone, leaving her body behind. Elfrad frowned, something was wrong. He glanced at Aeryissa who also looked worried.

Resting their backs against a large oak, the peace and tranquillity surrounding them like a balm to their senses. Elfrad still found it hard to fathom, that only a few short days ago they had been in a realm where Darkness ruled.

'How is it, I have never heard of Eirian?'

Ignoring his question, Aeryissa told him, 'over time it has been forgotten.'

'You obviously knew about its existence did Margaret?'

'My ancestors came from here, as I believe do yours. She has only known for a short while. She mustn't be influenced in anyway. It isn't finished Elfrad. The battle for Kingdom, for Eirian; is still ongoing. With the Darkness released, it will act as a beacon, drawing demons to its call. If they should…'

'We couldn't stop it from rising, how on earth can we stop demons? Are you suggesting that we use the magicals here? There aren't enough of them to make even a small army.'

Margaret stretched, now that her thoughts had stopped wondering, she felt more rested than she had in days. She still didn't understand where they were. When Aeryissa told her about it, for some reason she had got it into her head that it was a safe place in Novia, not a totally different realm.

Since entering Eirian the silver and shimmer in her had drawn even more to the surface of her skin. The silver speckled eyes which stared out of the mirror, looked other worldly against her norm features. Remnants of dreams passed through her mind, tantalising her, blowing away when she tried to catch them. She smiled as the door opened. Both Aeryissa and Elfrad glad to see her looking more alert.

'I'm going to try a little experiment. Perhaps you'd like to come along?'

Aeryissa grinned, at the look Elfrad threw her.

Walking together, all three enjoyed the feeling of movement around them. Glad to be out of the confines of the manor house. The breeze wafting through the branches made the trees rustle. Margaret felt the need to pat each one she passed, smiling when they sighed at her touch. They hadn't gone far when the Calmans started springing up either side of her.

Laughing loudly she stopped, wary of treading on them when so many popped up to surround her, their colours vivid and bright, making them stand out even more against the green of the grass. Bending down she caressed a large yellow daisy like flower.

'Hello,' she whispered, her breath washing over its petals.

Immediately the flower started growing, stopping only when it was on a level with her face. Reaching forward the flower brushed its petal's against her skin.

'Welcome home.'

Fafnir appeared in front of them. Margaret's vampire and Elfrad's wizard senses reacted instantly as if to a threat. Aeryissa pulled them back.

His dragon ready to emerge, Fafnir held up his hands.

'Sorry, I didn't think.'

Glancing at Margaret, he couldn't suppress a shudder. For a moment he'd felt the full force of her magic.

Aeryissa faced Elfrad, 'in front of us is a veil. Unlike the one that Meridian created in the Osias, this one cannot be seen. The Darkness chased you for a reason. This may be it.'

Nudging Margaret they walked forwards, followed by Fafnir. Taking a leap of faith, Elfrad moved to follow, his mouth gaping open in wonder at the sight before him.

Aeryissa's arms swept wide to take in the gathered throng.

'Changelings,' she announced, the pride in her voice evident. 'This is Eirian's army.'

Dragons, bears, wolves and owls, all touched with silver filled the landscape.

Bursting through the ground hands appeared, they all grinned as Fingerling pulled himself up. Shaking his branches as if he'd been squashed in a box. Sighing with pleasure as he stretched upwards towards the light. His booming voice echoed around them in greeting.

Water began pooling around his trunk, splattering of droplets as Pelagias emerged.

'Can you have a word with the Yorkus? Since they emerged ready for battle. That's all they talk about. They are drinking too much water. If they take on anymore they will be water logged. We tried keeping it from them, but the din they make when deprived, is getting on everyone's nerves. They are also stealing rations.'

Fingerling roared, the ground trembled before splitting open, allowing a large oak to spring up.

'Captain. Deal with the Yorkus. Tell them if they don't calm down their drinking. I will personally tie a knot in their roots.'

The ground trembled again as the tree disappeared. The earth moving quickly to fill in the hole.

Kebale, the leader of the bears began introducing them to the council.

'You have already met Fafnir and know that his changeling is a dragon.' Chuckling, he added, 'I am of course a bear.'

Two large powerful wolves, reminding them of Ammon entered next, their eyes raked across Margaret, startling her when they dipped their heads in acknowledgement.

Pointing to the wolf with the darkest fur, Kebale told them, 'this is Lype, and his brother Raul.'

Next to step through were the owls, their feathers bristling as they argued.

'Bena, Veda, some other time perhaps for a domestic.'

'Why have I never heard of Eirian? Or the power of silver, until I met Aeryissa.'

Used to hearing her voice in his head, Elfrad didn't react when she told him.

'Be patient, all will be revealed.'

'The Darkness in Kingdom is not the first of its kind to emerge,' explained Kebale. 'It is though, the only one that has managed to sustain its hold. If it hasn't already done so, it will soon begin to call its master. When. Not if. Then it will come for Eirian.'

'Have we endangered you all by coming here?' asked Margaret, worry etched on her face.

'This is your home,' said Bena.

Aeryissa glared at the owl.

Memories of the meetings held by Dandelion flooded back to Elfrad. This felt the same, everyone on edge. Knowledge of things known by some, hidden to others. He had thought Eirian, a sanctuary, now it seems they had entered another realm of uncertainty and fear.

The talk went on long into the night, Aeryissa and Elfrad each recanting the story of Kingdom's last month's. Margaret once again sat oblivious locked inside her own thoughts.

Keen to blow off steam, Aeryissa decided to join one of the patrols sent out to check the veil. After months of fighting she was finding it hard to relax. The strain beginning to show from having to keep things to herself. She thought of both Elfrad and Margaret as not only friends, but as family too. They had been through so much together, facing the end game side by side. Since entering Eirian she was conscious of a split beginning to occur between them.

Hearing Fingerling give strict instructions that all must watch what they say and discuss in front of Elfrad and even more so with Margaret. Questions of any sort to be ignored or glossed over. It made her feel she was colluding in keeping them in the dark. Drawing her even more into the collusion, when Fingerling asked her to impress on Vedi and Bena the need for caution. Having set themselves up as her companions. Trying to find ways to keep her entertained, they didn't mind her silences, her vague countenance. Margaret for her part, found their constant bickering acting as a backdrop to her thoughts.

Eager to see Eirian and meet the changelings Elfrad had taken up Raul and Lype's offer to show him its wonders. Aeryissa watched him go, since the meeting with the council they hadn't spoken much. Their conversations short and to the point.

'His memories are buried deep, he needs to face them before he can go forwards.'

'I'll speak to him, Kebale, I promise. I'm more concerned with how Eirian is affecting Margaret. Sleep seems to be drawing her down. When she is awake, she hardly seems so. It's more than pre-occupation. Whatever it is though, my senses cannot penetrate it.'

'I too have felt her difference. When you first emerged, you both had the same aura around you. Now though, while yours is still bright. Margaret's blazes out. Her "otherness," is more apparent each day. Magic is drawn to her. Something I haven't seen in a long time.'

Aeryissa chuckled, 'ever since I've known her she has been changing. The process seems set to continue. What she will eventually become, is anyone's guess.'

'So we wait,' said Kebale. 'That's all we can do. Margaret will be the driver to any action that occurs. Until then our hands are tied.'

'How do you feel?' asked Raul, as they walked side by side. He and Elfrad had quickly struck up a friendship. Finding they had the same sense of humour and way of looking at things.

'That's a good question,' he answered. 'Unsettled, would best describe how I feel. When I was in my greeter persona, I knew what was expected of me. Now, from one day to the next I have no idea. As a Bomani I feel the need to always protect those I am close to. Yet, those I stand beside, dwarf me in both power and magic.'

'I feel that way when I stand next to Kebale and Fafnir,' chuckled Raul. 'Not because of their size, rather it's their bearing. As changeling's our magic is different to magicals our strength and power is in our changeling form. Without that carapace some of our magic can be weaker, we appear less fearsome. Whereas even out of changeling form bears and dragons still manage to exclude both power and strength.'

'There you are,' shouted Lype, bounding towards them, changing from wolf to magical in the blink of an eye. 'Where shall we start?'

As Raul and Lype left to return home, Elfrad found a quiet spot in the shade. Wanting to think about all that had happened, put it in perspective. Lost in his own thoughts he took no notice as Aeryissa sat down beside him.

'Elfrad.'

Turning at the sound of her voice, he waited. Determined to hold his tongue.

'You mustn't share anything I tell you with Margaret.'

'Why all this secrecy surrounding her. Why is she kept ignorant of what is happening or happened? Haven't you seen how withdrawn she's become since we entered Eirian? But it's more than that. I don't understand why Margaret is held in such regard. She is no more fragile than you or me. Yet we handle her with kid gloves and constantly watch what we say around her. With no real reasons given why we should do so. It's getting tedious.'

Aeryissa also wished everything could be out in the open and their speech not so guarded. Whenever her doubts assailed her, Fingerling would remind her of what was at stake.

'When I was growing up,' Aeryissa told him. 'I knew that I was different. Even as a child magicals were wary of me. Mach and his gang kept telling me to show myself. Getting so bad that it seemed as soon as I stepped outside the door. Someone would be goading me to react. Fingerling stepped in. He told me what my problem was and would be. That my ancestors had silver magic and were part of a vampire guard, how some also attained clan abilities and shimmer to add to their repertoire and that one day I might need these skills for the greater good of Kingdom.'

'I thought Lefu was your father?'

Aeryissa smiled, 'he is.'

'Then how come.?'

'Silver, apparently goes where it will and in varying degrees. Hence, not all vampires have it. Those still in Eirian do, others in Kingdom may. As you have seen, not only do Margaret and I have silver and shimmer but everything else as well. Both triggered awake by violence. Fingerling spoke to me on many occasions until finally he convinced me about my heritage. Once I accepted what I may become. I immediately wanted to go to Eirian. This he was adamant was not possible, unless in a dire emergency. I decided if I couldn't go there then I would hide myself away and the greater good could look after itself. That's when I met Eadulf, he too was running away. The Darkness had taken over the Glasserium, dark magic stalked its halls. Like lost souls we both ended up in the same place as if drawn together by unseen hands.'

'So where do I fit in? My family have never mentioned anything about Eirian or silver. I know that both my father and grandfather were Bomani, my wand and staff passed down to me from them. I know there was some controversy years ago. But it was never openly talked about and certainly never made it into any tales to be told around the camp fires.'

'Fingerling told me the split between the wizards caused problems for many families,' explained Aeryissa. 'In some cases pitting siblings against each other. Even their ancestor's pictures had to be separated. When wizards returned from battle, their warrior side would abate. No one really knows why some choose not to let it. Retaining their hell cats, wearing their swords and armour. Generally seeing themselves as different. Even their attitude, way of thinking changed. At some stage silver entered their bodies. They became bigger, swaggered more. Always quick to take offense, now they were able to back it up with strength and power. They chose to be called Bomani to separate them even more. Especially when some wizards were found to be dabbling and sometimes using to full effect, dark magic.'

A memory stirred, dredging it up, Elfrad murmured to himself, 'my uncle, something about my uncle or was it my cousins?'

He frowned, remembering as the memories surfaced, the shouting and fighting. Cowering under the table, making himself appear as small as possible. His grandfather trying to split his father and uncle up.

Flinching every time he heard a punch land. Magic bouncing from the walls as spells were thrown. Finally, his grandfather had blasted them both. Using his staff he'd called forth a binding star. As it exploded, it locked on, holding them both still. Their eyes burning with their hatred of each other and their father for stopping them. Elfrad didn't dare move, holding his breath, sure that his grandfather knew he was there. Frightened to emerge, not wanting to see his father bound and helpless. The door crashed open, all he saw were legs and boots.

'Take him,' shouted his grandfather. 'He is riddled with dark magic and is no longer a son of mine.'

Elfrad jumped out from under the table, his uncle was shouting and cursing as he was manhandled out of the house. His father lay where he'd fallen. His arms rigid as the binding star held him tight. Wanting desperately to go to him, one look from his grandfather stilled his action.

'You are lucky Will, that I believe you. Not everyone is so understanding of the action you took.'

Snapping his fingers he released his father.

'I didn't know what to do.'

'You should have come to me first and not tried to take matters into your own hands. Because you did, an innocent life was nearly taken.'

Elfrad listened to words spoken by his grandfather, not understanding what they meant. Surely he didn't mean that his father had tried to kill someone.

As if hearing his thoughts, his grandfather turned to Elfrad, 'your father is going away. You will not be joining him.' Seeing the look on his son's face, he told him, 'you've been playing at being a warrior, now it's time you learnt how to become one for real.'

As the memories settled around him, Elfrad remembered the feelings of loss after his father left. He loved his grandfather but he was much stricter and expected a lot more of him. As he got older he had wanted to follow in his father's footsteps. The few times that he had come home, he had been equally impressed and frightened by how much his father had changed. He always arrived atop his hell cat, swords heavy on his back. His eyes never still, always scouring the land around him, as if potential enemies surrounded him.

Wanting to show his father how hard he'd worked the next time he came home. Elfrad threw himself into his training. A few months later his father returned unexpectedly, days later he lay on his death bed, dark magic threaded through his body. Elfrad sat by his side, falling asleep, waking to find his grandfather had covered him with a blanket and watched over him while he'd slept. His words hitting him like a sledgehammer.

'I'm so sorry.'

He realised that the hand he held had grown cold. The fingers stiff. His father in death, didn't look anything like the warrior he once was. The dark magic had stripped him of his power. Elfrad's heart broke. Even though he didn't see his father often, he still loved him.

'Who did this to him?' he demanded of his grandfather.

'He's gone, they all have.'

His anger burned inside him. Answers to his questions would now have to wait. His uncle and cousins had done this to his father. Clutching their grudge to them for years, waiting for the right time to strike. Now like the cowards they were, they'd fled.

'I can see by your demeanour that your thoughts are of revenge. You have to let it go, otherwise the hatred will never stop. It will consume you, as it did them.'

A few days later he hoisted his pack onto his back checked his father's wand was secure holding tight to his staff he opened the door. His thoughts of avoiding his grandfather useless.

'Where will you go?' he asked, standing in front of him blocking his path. 'I shall miss you.'

He wanted to push past. His eyes locked with his grandfathers. In them he saw an old wizard who had now lost everything. Taking a deep breath, he tamped down his anger.

'I don't blame you. But I cannot stay here. I have promised I will not search the killers out.'

His grandfather flinched at the harshness of his words.

'If however they cross my path. I will kill them.'

'How did you go from being a Bomani to a greeter? I wouldn't have thought one leant itself to the other.'

'Once my training had finished. I tracked my uncle and cousins down. I killed them all. After the slaughter, and that is the only way to describe it. I lost my way. My conscious was clear. My thoughts though, were unsettled to say the least. I had heard about the greeters on one of my many forays to drown my sorrows. Seemed like a good idea at the time, a way to disappear. Reinvent myself if you like. I found that I liked and enjoyed meeting the norms. Especially at the start of their journey when everything they saw was through fresh eyes. It helped to put any thoughts of being a warrior to the back of my mind.'

'Why bring it back? You had a choice. You could have declined Dandelion's request that you take over her mantel.'

Elfrad chuckled, 'you of all magicals should know Aeryissa, that our true selves have a way of working themselves to the fore whether we like it or not. We all like to think we are in control. You may not, but I feel that I have been manipulated by Kingdom and possibly now Eirian to do exactly what I'm supposed to. Free will to follow my own destiny seems to be in short supply in both realms. The silver running through me may help in the coming battles. I hope so. The Darkness must have seen it as a threat, it chased me enough times seeking it.'

Chapter Thirty-Five

G etting up, Margaret was surprised to see that it was still dark. Feeling for the first time in ages that she had actually slept well. Wanting to stretch her legs, she opened the door and stepped outside into the hall. Letting her ears extend, she swept for sounds of anyone else before setting off to explore. The hall seemed endless, no doors were visible, yet she knew they were there. Finally, she came to the end where a large set of doors barred her way. Plain unadorned wood, the sort you didn't often see in Kingdom, proudly guarding what lay behind.

'You've turned into a right old sleepy head,' said Vedi, as her sister Bena drew the curtains, letting the sunlight flood the room.

Her reaction was not what they expected. She flew off the bed, her vampire on full show. The owls reared back in fright. It was a long time since they had seen one emerge in such a violent way. The door crashed open, Aeryissa strode in pushing the owls out. Elfrad shut the door behind them. Margaret's eyes burned silver, her breath came in pants as she tried to make sense of how she felt.

'Something's not right,' she shouted, confusion written across her face. 'I was awake. I went for a walk. The doors… I stood. I don't understand how I got back into bed.'

Standing once again in front of the large wooden doors, Margaret was determined this time to find what lay behind. She brought all her strength to the fore. Placing her hands onto the wood, she pushed not only with her body but with her mind, as the stale air wafted out she was sure she heard a sigh. Stepping inside she was delighted and surprised to see that it was a library. The stacks disappearing into the dark, the books old and tired, like the trees she felt the need to pat each one she passed.

At her touch, shelves straightened, books stood upright, covers gleamed as dust fell from their jackets. Her feet barely made a sound, her eyes like silver twin orbs probed the dark corners. Hidden books waking as she went by, her body singing to be near so many.

Aeryissa followed Margaret, her instincts correct, a siren call was being used. Standing in the corridor she too had felt its tug, recognising it for what it was. The walkway between the stacks stopped as a set of doors appeared blocking the path.

Deciding to make her presence known she took Margaret's hand and broke the siren call.

A voice announced, 'welcome to the Scriptorium.'

Out of the dark a magical made his way slowly towards them. Banging his staff hard onto the ground after each step he took as he tried to keep himself upright.

'Who are you?' demanded Aeryissa, stepping in front of Margaret.

'I am a changeling. My name is Zosio. I was put in charge of the Scriptorium many years ago to await the return of the guardian.'

Beckoning them forwards he shuffled off towards another set of doors. These even more elaborately carved opened as they approached.

'You must call the book, it is both a tale and a guide and will help you understand what you have to do.'

Both were at a loss as to what he meant. Thinking to call a Bodleian, Aeryissa pulled a book from the nearest shelf giving it a tap.

The changeling watched, amusement crossing his lined face as her impatience grew and her taps become harder.

'The Bodleian won't come. They can't. They were set free on the proviso that they never return. You don't need them or me to find it. The Afsaneh will only come for you.'

Zosio leant across and touched Margaret's arm.

'You are the Guardian. Therefore only you can call the book.'

'Me?'

Zosio laughed, the sound like nails on a blackboard, ending with him coughing enough to turn his face red.

'Remnants of the original are inside you. It has got stronger since you entered Eirian. Whether by hereditary or design, I cannot say. But as such, only you are able to call the book and only you can become the Guardian,' he explained. 'You must call the Afsaneh and read it from cover to cover. The door won't open until you have read it all. Time in here is different. Don't be afraid, she is part of you as you are part of her.'

Feeling as if she'd been transported, Aeryissa found herself outside the closed doors. Ignoring her growl, Zosio conjured a chair, glad that his time was nearly over, weariness like a cloak around his shoulders.

'What happens if Margaret is unable to call the book or if it doesn't come to her?'

'Then she will stay locked inside the room until she can and it does.'

Aeryissa's face began to change at his words.

'It won't matter how much power you have or can control. Only two can enter that room and you are not one of them.'

Placing her hands onto the desk Margaret closed her eyes. After a few minutes she opened one eye, all she could see was the bare desk in front of her. As she looked up the room appeared to be getting darker. Even her vampire sight finding it hard to penetrate the gloom. A swirling mist detached itself.

'My name is Eshe. I need to merge with you so that my magic will be yours to command. Only then will you be able to call the book.'

Margaret didn't like the sound of that.

'You cannot leave this room. Your destiny is set. Reading the Afsaneh will show what is expected of you. By stepping over the threshold you have given your agreement to this happening.'

'Zosio never mentioned anything about merging, only that I had to read the book.'

'His only directive is to open the door and let you in, standing guard until you have completed the task. Then he will disappear, his life over.'

Eshe watched her expression's change as she played out what she was thinking of doing to get out of the room.

'No scenario which you can come up with will work. Your path written many years ago. You can delay it, but you cannot change it.'

Margaret's claws began to lengthen, digging into the desk making it groan.

'How does it happen?' she asked, resignation clear in her voice, as she let her vampire subside.

The swirl of mist settled over her like a cloak. She could feel her skin tingle, her blood rush through her veins. Her mind began expanding with magic so strong, the force of its entry knocked her out.

Coming to, her head resting on the desk, thinking at first she'd fallen asleep and it was all a dream. As her senses fully awoke, she knew it wasn't and that she was changed once again. Recognising the feeling from when she had become a vampire. She had known instantly that she was dead. Now she felt alive again.

Thanks to whatever Eshe had given her she could see the room clearly. Bookshelves soared to the ceiling their gold and silver covers shining like the sun. Even the ceiling was covered. As she watched they began to rearrange themselves.

Placing her hands onto the desk, she felt it move as it adjusted its position, becoming even sturdier. Even with the power now running through her veins she couldn't stop a nervous giggle escaping.

'Afsaneh.'

A large blue book slammed onto the desk making it groan and sag. Creatures roamed its cover, her vampire hearing bringing their wails of anger at being woken to the fore. The centre pictured a smaller book its surface smooth. She pressed it thinking it may be the key to its opening. Immediately the creatures attacked. Pulling back her hand they hung onto her fingers biting and clawing. Trying to shake them off only made them cling harder. She went to stand, but found she couldn't, her legs as if stuck to the chair. She took several deep breaths trying to regain control, all the while the creatures dangled from her fingers. At a loss as to what to do, she slammed them down onto the book. In a flash they were gone.

'If you don't open. I cannot read you,' she snarled.

The cover fell back. For a few moments the page in front of her stayed blank. Her anger flared. The paper quickly filling up as if the letters were in a hurry to find their places. The words settled, the air in the room changed. The desk stopped creaking. She could move her legs. Getting comfortable, the first words brought a smile to her lips and memories of Sam. Once upon a time...

Chapter Thirty-Six

With the last of her strength, Bayu leapt, holding tight as Orara took to the skies. Exhausted, she lay down against the dragons back, safe in the knowledge that she would take her home. By the time she slid to the ground, Orara had changed into her magical form.

'You must rest and regain your silver.'

Letting herself be led away, Bayu thought not for the first time that life was becoming a chore. Closing her eyes, her thoughts wouldn't quieten, the demons that had risen this time were much more tenacious that those that had come before.

Silver flooded her body repairing the damage she had sustained, running through her system reviving her flagging spirits, energising her body for the fight still to come. Its magic wrapping her in a cocoon of safety as she finally slept.

Keeping her face still so as not to show any reaction, Eshe listened in horror as Bayu explained how grave the situation actually was.

Pausing for a moment to gather her thoughts, aware of the panic her words would cause, Bayu turned to face the crowd.

'The realms of Cala, Neg and several smaller ones are gone.

The magicals dead, or taken. The lands destroyed. Only Idona and Tarian are left.'

Shouts of disbelief rent the air, many in the crowd had never heard of Tarian or the others, Idona however, was their home.

'The demons that were responsible were found to be in the thrall of others of their kind. Brothers, two enemies, but with a common purpose.'

All eyes were locked onto Bayu her words filling them with fear and dread.

'When we fought in Cala we injured them badly. The lessor demons they were using had set up rolling fires filled with poison. While we were engaged in trying to stop their spread, they fled. The Ambrogio tracked them to one of the uninhabited realms. The Minns listened to their chatter. They are determined to carry on the fight before any other demons can join the hunt. The only way to stop them, is to let them have what they want. Me.'

Eshe's shocked face at Bayu's proposal, echoed across the gathering. A voice shouted.

'Then we will be truly lost. There's no guarantee once they have you, they won't still destroy Idona and Tarian.'

'It has to end otherwise there will be no peace. Unfortunately the demons know of our whereabouts, leaving me no option except to move you all into another realm. I have found two voids. My intention is to lead the demons across one, while everyone else led by Eshe, goes through the other.' Looking at the clan leaders, she told them, 'your task is to make sure that everyone goes. Many will not want to. If I fail, no one must be left here for the demons to use.'

Everyone wanted to have their say. Her mind already made up. Nevertheless Bayu listened patiently to all their suggestions and objections.

'It is the only way. Something is different about these demons. They have clearly shown with their destruction of the other realms that they won't stop. I will have to rip the fabric of the voids apart. There is no time to open them slowly. In doing so I will cause a vortex to be created. You must all have entered the realm before it begins. If you get stuck inside it I will not be able to help get you out.'

'Could we not move everyone using a portal?' asked Eshe fearfully.

'It would leave a magical signature which the demons could follow, besides, we are moving a whole realm. I'm not sure even I could create a portal that big, or sustain it for long enough to get everyone through.'

Bayu watched the conflicting emotions cross Eshe's face. She wished there was some other way of defeating the demons which didn't involve them losing their home. Even sacrificing herself, was no guarantee they wouldn't still pursue them out of anger at losing their prize. She hoped that with the loss of the magic they craved and the inevitable pull from the Soul Lost land, it would be enough to send them back.

For herself, she craved release. Ever since the demons had become a problem. She had been swamped by a feeling which nagged at her. Flicking across her mind, dredging up memories long kept hidden. Silver letters, melting and reforming, shaming and accusing her all at the same time.

'This is the last of the potions.'

Bayu passed Eshe a large goblet filled to the brim with more foul smelling liquid. Gulping it down as quickly as possible she began to choke.

'The small amount of silver and shimmer inside you isn't enough for you to do the tasks set you. You need much more. If I do not come back, you will be queen.'

'The wizards will never accept that.'

'They will have no choice, even as we speak my power, magic and authority is flowing through your veins. Like everyone else they too will soon recognise its scent,' stated Bayu.

Snapping her fingers maps appeared across the table. Eshe tried to keep her eyes from blurring as the details moved quickly around them, looking for where they should settle. She thought at first they showed the position of the new realm, when in fact what they showed was the void in between.

Most voids were now dead spaces, used only as a means to cross between realms. The occasional vortex would start up, mostly though they fell apart without causing anyone any harm. These voids though, thought Eshe, looked much more threatening. Even the paper they were noted on, appeared cowed by them. Trying to curl its edges and creep away. Only Bayu rapping her knuckles against the table made them stop.

'When I rip into these, you and everyone else has to be ready. Take only what's really needed. Everything can be conjured and remade when you're settled. Don't waste time or space.' She pointed at a long thin black line that wriggled as it faded in and out. 'This is the void that you need to follow. At its end will be our new home. It shall be called Eirian.'

Eshe stared at the wriggling line. Hoping that following it would be as easy as Bayu was making it sound.

'Once settled there will be much to do. A word of warning, choose wisely those you ask to help with the task.'

She had been preparing Eshe for days for her new role. Voicing instructions and planting others deep inside her head. The doors hiding the messages, barred until needed.

While she slept, unbeknown to her, Bayu filled her with more silver and shimmer. Each morning she looked for signs of change. The day Eshe's eyes flashed with silver, Bayu knew her transformation was complete.

Stepping away, letting the guardian drive their exodus, her role now to safe guard their escape.

Entering the cave, she called her dragon.

'Is it time?' asked Orara, changing into her magical form.

'This is a lot to ask of you…'

Orara smiled, 'We have discussed the risks. You are taking as many, if not more.'

'This new realm, I know nothing about it except that it is flooded with silver and shimmer. The place I have found you to stay is buried inside a mountain, surrounded by a deep valley filled with trees. They are not like ours, they do not move or talk. But they are sturdy and are a barrier. Once you're in place, I will call my silver to add to what is already there.'

Seeing her falter, Orara, smiled, 'you have to chain me. I understand. So does my dragon.'

Entering the uninhabited realm, Bayu could immediately smell the demons. Surprised that they were both still together. She read their minds and their intent. Both appeared to want her power for their own. Banding together out of necessity, rather than brotherly love. Her probes had also found another presence buried deep in the recesses of their minds, one she vaguely recognised. With no time to investigate further, she climbed the hill top and stood in full view, her skin glowing with silver, specks of shimmer rising from its surface with a life of its own. The runes and silver woven into her clothes a siren call to the demons. Even her long brown hair was dressed in silver beads, letting them trail down its length. Her boots shone, her swords blazed. She knew she was a sight to behold and a beacon for those who were drawn to her magic.

The demons had been sleeping, burying themselves deep underground the smell of silver hitting them like a drug flooding their senses, its call irresistible. Following the scent they emerged into bright sunlight, to see a sight that thrilled and scared them at the same time. Bayu tracked their progress as they caught sight of her. Their long skinny bodies at odds with their large heads and bulging eyes. Slimy skin, even from this distance she could see was covered in warts and growths. As they loped to the bottom of the hill their thoughts were easily read.

Her instincts to transport herself down and confront them, held in check. They had to bring the fight to her. They had to chase, believing they were winning and could take her. The doubts rising to the surface she pushed away. The nagging voice beating like a drum inside her head gave her no peace. Payment was due, it was time to make amends. She had to engage and she had to appear to lose.

Wielding her swords, Bayu slashed the first demon as he turned to snarl at his brother. So intent on taking the prize for themselves, they were making her job easier for her.

As if hearing her thoughts they turned as one and launched themselves at her. Their talons growing to razor sharpness as they raked them down her arms and legs. Kicking out, making them falter she flew down the hill. Allowing herself to stumble at the bottom and drop her swords. In an instant they were on her. Their foul breath enough to make her want to gag.

One grabbed her hair, wrapping it around its claws trying to pull her towards him. His brother incensed at losing his prize grabbed her arm, like a tug of war they pulled her between them. She couldn't make it too easy for them, so she transported a short distance away. Leaving them unsure at what had happened.

Making it seem as if she were running away she stumbled across the stones and rocks, leaving traces of silver on everything she touched. As one they roared, butting heads, attacking each other, blood flew as they gouged. Bayu couldn't believe her eyes, if they carried on the way they were they would kill each other, let alone her. She needed them to stop.

Sending a blast of blue light she swept them off their feet. Tossing them up in the air she slammed them back down. Sending stars to reign down onto their bodies, the explosions as they hit, lighting up the sky. She let her silver blaze out, their skin fizzing as it touched them.

Like a wakeup call, their heads whipped round. Their lips pulling back as they growled. Tendrils of darkness began to form around their bodies turning into lessor demons. Bayu ran. This time they followed. One of the brothers managed to get in front of her. The other stayed behind. She could see and feel how much they wanted to hurt her. How focused on her silver their thoughts were. They attacked, the lessor demons wrapping around her legs, pulling her down. Her silver recoiling at their touch. The demons wanted her heart, her core, she could hear their thoughts as they clawed at her, both wanting her power. Poison dripped from their skin, as their anger grew.

Bayu let her power burst forth, the explosion of it flung them all away. Getting onto her knees, she hung her head as if in pain. The lessor demons had retreated back into the brothers.

She ran, zig zagging, letting her breath sound ragged, moaning in fear. Acting exhausted, she led them on towards the voids entrance. Although she didn't want to take them into another's realm, she had no choice. It would soon become obvious that she was playing a game.

At last all the magicals had crossed. Eshe could breathe a sigh of relief. All had felt the vortex coming. Its waves undulating through the void, making them hurry. With a snap the entrance closed. The vortex battered and whirled against the barrier. Making camp everyone was quiet. This new realm smelt different from Idona, making many worry what daylight would bring. Others too tired to worry, settled down, some using their Narla's others conjuring soft beds. All weary, snores and sighs soon the only sounds to fill the night sky.

Eshe set up patrols of vampires, blending into the dark even her keen eyes found it hard to see where they were.

Hearing her name called, she opened her eyes, her joy at seeing the face of Bayu hovering in front of her, making her smile.

'There is a door in your mind, it shines. Can you see it? Open it and enter.'

Eshe walked forwards, the door opened. In the middle of the

room sat a table. Two books lay on its surface. Bayu held herself steady. She had heard the demons enter the cave lower down. She had to get Eshe to cast the spells before they reached her.

'Touch the book on your right, it will open on the page you need.'

Even in her dream state Eshe wondered if a Reader would pop out.

'Clear your thoughts. Think only of me. Read the spell,' commanded Bayu, wanting to hurry her up, but knowing that the spell couldn't be rushed. It had to be done correctly or it wouldn't work and all her efforts would have been for nothing.

Eshe began reading the spell, if awake and not compelled, she would have refused. One part of her mind screamed at her to stop, the other relentless in making her carry on.

On hearing the words, part of Bayu also wanted her to stop as she began to feel its affects. The silver in her body moved. Like a snake wanting to escape, the pressure under her skin grew. She tried not to cry out, the pain of losing it too great, not only physical but mental. It was part of her and now it was leaving. The links she held in her mind began to break. She heard and felt their snaps. The pain sustained in her fights with the demons now flooded her body. Unused to the feeling, she moaned, clamping her hand over her mouth to deaden the sound.

'Eshe,' croaked Bayu, her voice strained with the effort of staying in control.

'Touch the other book, think only of me. Read the words.'

As the last link to her magic began to unravel, Bayu realised for the first time with clarity what she had done. Shame and fear fought for ascendance. Hearing Eshe repeat the words of the spell that would bind her. She nearly cried out, telling her to stop. Knowing she would remember nothing of her previous life as a queen or ancient. The use of magic would no longer be an option. Hot tears of regret and self-pity fell down her face. As the last words fell from Eshe's lips, she collapsed. Spell bound, her links to silver and shimmer destroyed. Her shame gone. Her mind began to retreat. Only a shell of her former self now left, her silver raiment's started to fade, turning a dirty grey, their shine all gone. Before her mind finally closed down, somewhere in her consciousness she heard the words.

'She's over here.'

CHAPTER THIRTY-SEVEN

E she had to think for a moment where she was, her head ached, while her mouth felt dry. She couldn't shake the feeling that something had happened while she'd slept. As she became more awake, the sounds of the camp waking up assaulted her ears. Shouts emerged, adding to the general hubbub.

Deciding she couldn't put off the moment any longer she emerged from her tent. As far as her eyes could see magicals filled the land. Before she had taken even a step, a group of wizards bustled up demanding an audience. Suddenly joined by witches and magicians. All speaking at once, wanting to know what she was going to do about... Everything!!

The magic Bayu had given her reacted before she could stop it, her eyes flashed silver in anger. They all took a step back not sure if they had really seen it happen.

'The land has to be surveyed. Bayu only had time to scan it. I have yet to see what it has to offer. For now, everyone should take the opportunity to rest and take stock. Eirian is going to be our home. There is no rush to conquer it.'

Walking away, Eshe realised that Bayu's vampire guard were dogging her footsteps. These unlike other vampires had silver running through their blood. Captain Torrens nodded his head in acknowledgement and continued to follow close behind her.

Bayu had instructed her repeatedly over many days on what she had to do to make Eirian into a proper home for the magicals. First on her list was water. No one liked to conjure it unless in an emergency. Always leaving an aftertaste that often lingered, spoiling the taste of any food eaten after drinking it.

In Idona the rivers, lakes and streams were controlled by the Warra. All who had carried the jars were honoured to be carrying such precious cargo. Everyone gathered, turning it into a game, each taking a cup of water and sprinkling it onto the hard ground. The dry earth drinking it down. Everyone hoping that the Warra had come with them and now would wake and work their magic in Eirian as they had in Idona.

Eager to see all aspects of the new realm, she transported herself and Torrens all over its landscape, weaving Bayu's magic into every part. Bringing it to life. When she saw a range of hills collapse and reform, she knew it was starting to work.

Deciding she couldn't put it off any longer, Eshe called her council, the wizard Wyong forcing his way to the front. Closely followed by his cronies. Their cloaks adorned with enough wizard symbols to make the cloth appear non-existent. They waddled to their seats, their faces screwed up in distaste at the plainness of the wood, conjuring sumptuous cushions before sitting down.

Eshe couldn't help a smile break out as Coomba walked in, the magician's pockets bulging at the seams. Items falling as she walked, leaving a trail behind. Wyong snorted at the sight. Clicking her fingers Coomba's mess quickly disappeared. Starting the whole process all over again. She often wondered how magicians didn't trip over all the stuff that continually fell out of their pockets.

Undowah, and Merri came next, followed by, Paroo, Huon, Narren and the Minns. Karugh and Berrima the last to arrive.

'When can we build our settlements? Our position in Eirian dictates we should have first pick of any land,' demanded Wyong.

For a second Eshe's eyes flashed silver, damping down the

power that she could feel rising to the surface, she turned to him and smiled, 'all in good time.'

Incensed, his face contorted as his anger overtook him.

'How long will it be before the trees are woken?' asked Narren.

'Fingerling is still recovering from the loss of his family destroyed in the battles of Cala and Neg. Those who survived need to rest, especially the Yorkus, only a handful remain. Have the animals survived?'

'The majority of them did. Unfortunately some of the smaller ones didn't survive the shrinking,' said Narren.

'The Calmans made it,' added Merri, her wings fluttering, stirring the air. 'My dragon nearly stood on a bunch that had emerged. He won't be doing that again any time soon,' her laughter like a bell chiming. 'Thankfully our dust has settled down and stopped flying off by itself for no reason' she added.

Eshe asked, 'and what about the Kaimi?'

'Until the trees wake and we have their permission to build our nests, we are helping with the vampire patrols,' replied Paroo, glancing at Huon.

Merri clapped her hands, her laughter infectious to the majority in the tent.

'In a few days our settlements will be complete.' Her frown at odds with her smile, she added, 'Noosa informed the Fadia of our choice. She hoped that you wouldn't mind.'

Eshe returned her smile, 'thank her for me.'

'Why should the Fae get to settle first before anyone else?' and what have the Fadia got to do with it?' demanded Wyong, his anger at the news barely held in check.

Eshe knew what she was about to say would unsettle the council except him and his cronies. For them it would appear as the perfect opportunity to make mischief.

'Bayu tasked me with creating a veil. That is the reason the Fae have been allowed to choose their settlement first, and why the Fadia have been called. They are the only ones capable of conjuring such a large one. Once complete it will allow only myself and my guard to enter.' Eshe ignored the look of contempt on Wyong's face and the questions she could feel everyone else wanted to ask. 'I am not an ancient like Bayu. Therefore every now and again I will have to undertake a dead sleep. When this will be required and for how long, I truly have no idea. When I am indisposed, you as the council will oversee Eirian.'

All saw Wyong's smile burst through, practically rubbing his hands in anticipation of her being out of the way.

'Remember though, I will wake. If in my absence anything has been done contrary to my instructions and laws. Those who flout them will be punished.'

Eshe entered the veil. The quiet instant. Picking up the scents of vanilla and apple. Turning at the sound of footsteps, Torrens strode towards her.

'The inner chambers are all prepared. The Fadia doubled the veil around your sleeping chamber.'

'Have they added enough space for it to grow?'

'They have, both the external one and the majority of the inner ones. They advise though, that you should fix your sleeping chamber once you have prepared it and secured the silver.'

Letting her senses flow around her Eshe set them searching. Immediately the answer came back. Silver. A vast lake of it right under where she was sitting and where the Fae had made their camp. She walked the perimeter of the veil. Then the inner chambers, chanting spells as she walked, sprinkling the ground with silver beads.

Guri become aware of the earth beneath her feet shaking. One new mirror fell, the glass shattering, not old enough yet to withstand the fall. A roaring started as if from the bowels of the earth. With one almighty heave, the ground inside her Glasserium began to fall away. In its place a thin gauze like substance appeared. Half of the glass hall disappeared. The veil between blocking her sight.

When Eshe entered what was going to be her sleeping space she didn't understand why there was glass scattered all over the floor. A larger piece of glass began to vibrate drawing others to it. In a trice it was whole again. She had seen glass in Idona move or ripple at some time or another. No one took any notice. This though was different. A voice shouted.

'Stop. You're destroying my home?'

Eshe reared back as a magical stepped through the glass.

'Who are you,' she snarled, as her magic flared.

Guri stared back not liking her tone, undaunted by her silver eyes. While Eshe for her part was astonished to see someone so indifferent to the sight of her magic.

'I am the Guardian of Eirian. Only those with silver in them should be able to enter the veil,' said Eshe in a gentler voice.

The magical hesitated, it had been a long time since she'd had any interaction with anyone. Unbeknown to the magicals of Eirian, she had listened to their chatter. Learning about their flight from their home Idona. Deciding to keep herself apart until she understood them more.

'My name is Guri. I live in my Glasserium in deep caves underneath here. The construction of your veil has split my halls in half, destroying most of them in the process.'

'I have never heard of a Glasserium. What do you mean?'

The glass shone, the frames sparkled. Eshe saw herself from all angles. The silver under her skin reflecting in the glass. Bouncing back from the mirrors ranged everywhere.

'It's beautiful.'

Sensing something had changed, she whirled around and truly felt her heart had stopped. Where a magical had stood before, now was a many faceted glass figure. Stunned, Eshe had never seen or heard of such a magical, couldn't even remember Bayu in their many talks mentioning one.

Guri smiled at her response, explaining. 'I loved glass. I felt drawn to it, would spend days staring into a mirror. Others thought me vain, whereas I was trying to understand its workings. I longed to reach inside. I would press my face against it trying to push through until one day I did. To this day I'm still not sure what happened. Perhaps my longing to be inside it made the difference. Gradually, I started to change. Every mirror I passed I felt a pull. Until one day I was literally sucked inside. Scared, but excited I began to explore. The more mirrors are used the more rooms they can make. Being able to turn myself into glass was a shock the first time it happened. I was scared that I wouldn't be able to turn back, but as you can see, I can.'

'You must have silver as well as glass in you? Otherwise you wouldn't be able to enter the veil.'

Eshe didn't know what to do. It appeared that Guri would be able to come and go at any time. She couldn't move the veil. The silver was ready to be drawn. Not only in her sleep state. But any time she would be vulnerable.

As if hearing her thoughts, Guri handed Eshe a piece of glass.

'Place this onto the wall, the mirror it will become, will only ever be a mirror. You should have no fear that I lurk in its depths. I propose that you see me as another layer of protection. Your vampire guards are on display for all to see. I however won't be. No one else need know of my existence.'

Eshe gave the all clear for the magicals to start spreading themselves throughout the realm. She watched with amusement as they argued over boundaries. All wanting to put their stamp on the land they had chosen to build their homes and villages on. Most clan members stayed together in the same settlement, others who preferred to mingle, sort their leader's permission to integrate. She made sure to keep a low profile, observing them from the side lines, some busy conjuring everything they needed, while others happy to use both magic and their own labour to construct their homes.

Wizards, who had decided to fully embrace the warrior part of their nature were now calling themselves Bomani and had distanced themselves from the lessor wizards as they now saw them. Discarding the usual wizard's robes they chose instead leather threaded with runes depicting their status. Their lethal crossed swords a reminder to everyone that they were warriors first and foremost.

Much to the delight of everyone else, the vampires set up their homes close to the outlaying borders. Eshe didn't understand the magicals fear of the Ambrogio, they never attacked anyone unless commanded to. Everyone though, felt much better when they weren't in their vicinity.

The magicians who had once again built a ramshackle village were the first to notice the lake near to them was on the move letting everyone know that the Warra had survived.

With this news it meant Fingerling could wake the trees properly. Hearing him order his captains to show the new recruits how to move and disappear. Introducing them to the Alvie, telling them they will be their companions. Eshe was pleased at last to see and hear him sound much more like his old self. Finding a forest full of trees stripped of their leaves, their branches curled like fists. Reminding him of the Yorkus, made him boom with laughter. Eshe had watched in delight as he woke them, both knowing he had made the right choice when they roared with anger. Those who had survived the crossing were put in charge of teaching the new trees to fight.

His next task was to allocate the forest's that could be cut for wood. The Kaimi buzzing around him, waiting for him to issue them with their new homes. Fed up with them following him everywhere he nominated some of the most docile of trees for them to build their nests in. His only proviso that they should spread them out through Eirian and not try and build them all in one place as they did in Idona. The Kaimi on Cala and Neg, died mainly as a result of their nests being too near each other.

Eshe, had grown weary of the wizard's continual moaning. Losing her patience with Wyong when he voiced his objection at where the Lobes and Lens intended setting up their village. He wanted them as far away as possible, preferable right at the edges of Eirian. Concerned, they would see and hear things that he didn't want them to.

She sent Torrens to deal with the matter. Escorting the Lobes and Lens to their chosen site. Wyong and his cronies soon dispersing when he saw them arrive with the vampires.

The witches after many weeks of searching finally settled on a place for their coven. Once they moved in, Undowah requested a private audience.

'Why so worried?'

'Since we came to Eirian something has been happening, some of us are changing.'

Eshe stilled her from saying anything more. Transporting them away, she brought her to a rocky outcrop with views over one of the more spectacular valleys.

'You don't seem surprised.'

'Bayu once told me about the witches of Neg. They were called Elementals and to some degree could control what they were aligned with. Why some witches could and others couldn't was never known.'

'Why has this started to happen here? Why not on Idona?' the confusion Undowah felt, echoed in her voice.

'That I can't answer. They must practice, become proficient, gain an understanding of their ability and learn to control it. There must be a reason for these gifts, even if at the moment we cannot see why they may be needed.'

In Idona, Eshe as guardian had the use of Bayu's private sanctum inside the Scriptorium. Filled from floor to ceiling with gold and silver books. Her desk was made from old oaks, coming to the end of their lives they had willingly allowed themselves to be used in its construction. It sat like a giant beast, alert to any who didn't have permission be inside the room. Many a Reader on the hunt for a book or a grimoire had fallen foul of its temper, so intent on the chase they forgot where they were.

They had been constantly moaning and grumbling, no matter how much Eshe tuned them out. Somehow they seemed to manage to get passed her defences. Fed up with being consigned to a corner of her tent. They wanted to create their library, set up the stacks and start filling the books with words again. The problem she had tried explaining was the veil. Unlike in Idona, here in Eirian, the inner sanctum and parts of the Scriptorium, had to be inside, while the other part which included their libraries had to be outside of it.

Guri came up with the solution. Since first making herself known to Eshe, they had become firm friends. More importantly, Eshe trusted her. Often spending time together either in the Glasserium or inside her sleeping chamber.

She found it comforting to be able to speak to someone about the queen. Telling her how she had met Bayu by chance as a young child. Her parents, her mother a witch and her father a magician, had been part of a group who had been taken prisoner by several dark magicals.

Lost and wondering, she remembered the vision of silver floating towards her. When Bayu looked into her eyes, Eshe knew she was found.

The only other magical to know about Guri was Torrens. Hearing her shout he had rushed into the chamber to find them laughing, getting louder on seeing his expression, his vampire on show, ready to kill. Eshe explained who Guri was, informing him that she would also be acting as part of her guard. His look of disbelief, sent them off into another fit of giggles. Once they had composed themselves, Guri told her.

'I've been thinking about your problem and may have come up with a solution. A mirrored portal between the Scriptorium and the libraries. Let me explain.'

Guri manoeuvred the last of the mirrors into place, aware that Eshe still didn't believe it was possible. Everything in the

Scriptorium was back in place, if Bayu came back now, she would instantly recognise it. The only difference, the stacks housing the books had the walls behind them lined with glass. Dead glass, Guri had been at pains to explain. Eshe still unsure what it meant.

'Walk towards the last stacks, don't hesitate, keep going.'

Eshe walked forwards and disappeared. Returning the same way, she smiled at her friend.

'Will I be able to enter and return from any of their libraries or will it only be this one?'

She needed every library to lead back to the Scriptorium. Their libraries wouldn't be static and could be anywhere. She also needed to be able to return from any of them. She had tried transporting, that proved impossible. The Scriptorium would not allow it. Each time she tried, she hit a wall, ending up back where she started.

'The dead mirrors will bring you back wherever the libraries are situated. Even if you were in another realm.' She chuckled at the look on Eshe's face. 'I call them dead because they have no rooms behind and cannot make any. Their purpose only as a conduit to pull or push you through the portal. The silver you gave me, enough, that they will recognise only your signature. Others with silver in them can enter the main Scriptorium, but not the portal.'

Satisfied all was in place, Eshe placed her book onto the table. With a flurry it opened to show its middle.

'Don't start your nonsense now,' she snapped. 'You've been pestering me for weeks.'

Hand's appeared, then a head, hair sticking up. Yarra, looked at his surroundings before hauling himself out of the book, rubbing his hands in anticipation, his impatience showing as he hopped from one foot to another.

'Come on, hurry up. We've work to do.'

More hands appeared, launching themselves out, the Readers bowed at Eshe, their eyes drinking in the sight of their side of the Scriptorium and its empty shelves.

Dubbo, snorted his dissatisfaction at having to wait so long, stuck inside small books, with no room to get away from his wife Kewa and his brothers Pinjarra's incessant chatter.

Eshe tried unsuccessfully to hold back her grin. All small in stature, as round as they were tall. She always wondered how they never fell over. Wobbling as they walked around the Scriptorium examining the stacks waiting to be filled. While the women had masses of curly hair, Yarra and Dubbo's bald pates were in complete contrast. Pinjarra and Kewa she understood to be sisters. Judging by how much they looked alike she thought they may even be twins. Both with large green eyes, small noses and wide generous lips. Dimples at each corner, she understood why their constant giggling got on Dubbo's nerves. Each sentence ended with one, no matter what subject they were talking about.

'Please let me know when you have completed the first phase.'

'Why? Our libraries are not your concern.'

Her eyes flashed silver. Pinjarra and Kewa clutched each other, their giggling finally stilled. Dubbo stepped away from Yarra.

'I am the Guardian. As such every part of Eirian is under my control. That includes your libraries. If you find that difficult to comprehend. I can always rescind your permission to create any.' Tapping the book on the table, she added, 'perhaps you would prefer a life of containment?'

Now that the veil was in place, Eshe had taken down the tent and replaced it with a large wooden structure. Creating inside a meeting place for the council, with a great hall, big enough for any gatherings to now take place. Her family picture removed from the archives was the first to be copied and reanimated.

'May we enter?'

'Permission granted.'

A large white owl flew out of her picture, quickly changing into her magical form.

'We are finished. Everyone's pictures have been completed. The archives are locked and secure. All ancestors are settled, only a few moans and groans about the state of their rooms. It seems in our haste to leave, that a few of the pictures lost part of their space inside. Rooms got squashed, furniture damaged, always a problem when we have to resort to miniatures for transport.'

A deputation of clan leaders had raised concerns to her about the safety of Pictures. They wanted it to be a separate entity. A place in its own right. Where dark magic could not thrive and would be rejected if it tried to enter. Having nearly lost access during their flight from Idona. They wanted to make sure that no matter what happened their ancestors would be safe. Vidya had added her concerns. All the Froade had seen how vulnerable and unstable at times Pictures had become.

'If Pictures were now to be treated as the separate entity it always was, then as leader of the Froade I should make any future decisions. It is after all my creation, not Bayu's. She took it upon herself to claim it for her own,' stated Vidya, letting her eyes grow even larger in size, mesmerising Eshe with their stare.

Although she had always respected Bayu, at the same time she knew that she believed ownership of all things in her realms belonged to her. Eshe was only now finding out exactly what that meant. Showing Vidya she meant business, she followed her back into Pictures and began sweeping her magic through its rooms and corridors, like a new broom it sought out anything dark.

'From now on Pictures will exist as a place in its own right. As guardian, I acknowledge it as your creation and your rightful domain.'

Chapter Thirty-Eight

Huon and Nowra, crept slowly forwards, several Gork's were rooting around the bottom of a small hill. Their noise an assault to their ears. Breaking cover they attacked. Huon easily bringing down the biggest Gork, wrenching its head back, his jaws clamped onto its neck. Drinking deep, once drained, he tossed the carcass away.

Looking around for Nowra, confusion crossed his face. Not only could he not see her. But he couldn't feel her either.

'Huon, quick, follow me.'

He turned to see her waving at him from behind a low rock fall.

'Where did you go?' he shouted, worry making him snap.

Her vampire flared at his tone.

'I've found a void. Or rather I fell through it.'

He stepped over the rocks and found himself in a dead space. The silence like a thick black cloud descending. In seconds they found themselves in a land much like Eirian. As far as their eyes could see, Gork's in their hundreds filled the landscape. With a shout they were off, unused to anyone chasing them they hesitated, then their senses woke to the threat, running much to Huon and Nowra's delight. Fully sated, they crossed back into Eirian. Both keen to tell the guardian what they had found.

Eshe called the council. Waiting for them to take their seats. She once again blocked out Wyong's litany of woes. Indicating that Huon should speak.

'Nowra and I have found a void that took us into a realm much like Eirian. We didn't enter the interior, faced with such a large number of Gork's we got distracted.'

Wyong, snorted.

Huon turned, 'something you would like to add,' he asked, showing his fangs as his eyes turned black.

'I think we should send a recognisance party, before anyone else stumbles across it,' said Eshe. 'Paroo, could you nominate one or two of your strongest and fastest seekers. Narren, a couple of foresters will also be required. Those better equipped for rough terrain. Speak to Fingerling, see if he wants to send any trees to survey the land, or rely on the Alvie you send.'

'Would it help if a Lobe and Lens also took part?' asked the Minns in unison. 'The Wilds, as their name suggests, are particularly good over long distances. If there are any inhabitants in this new realm. Between them they should easily be able to pinpoint where they are.'

'That's an excellent idea. The sentinels will guard the party, plus Huon and Nowra have both offered their services.'

'We don't know enough about Eirian to bother about sending magicals wondering around an unknown realm,' blustered Wyong, tapping his staff in annoyance.

'Perhaps you could do us all a favour and keep your unwanted comments to yourself,' snapped Eshe, for once letting his negativity get to her.

Incensed, he bristled at her attack, vowing one day she would pay for her words.

Torrens moved to stand behind him. The only thing stopping him from replying. Huon's vampire also reacted to the anger in the air. Merri's fairy dust shifting on her skin as it picked up on the threat. While Undowah tried hard to keep her new elemental skill under control. She could feel it wanting to burst forth and envelope Wyong in the heat of its fire.

Months later another void came to light, found by magicians who had been practising new spells. After complaints about the noise and the mess they were making they had decided to head out in search of somewhere they wouldn't be disturbed and could practise to their hearts content.

Fingerling had also given them short shift, when one of their spells got out of control blasting the trees in the vicinity with such a bright light they had seared their branches and damaged their trunks. Their screams had alerted the Yorkus. Fingerling having to bellow at them to put the magicians down and step away.

So busy with their experiments they hadn't taken any notice of where they were or how far they had come. Totally lost, in trying to find a way out of the forbidding landscape they had come across the void. Unsure where it may lead, they marked the place and set up a distress call. After many hours a seeker flew within a few miles of them, their continual thanks at being found ringing in her ears as she guided them home.

Returning to the centre they asked for an audience with the guardian. Still in her dead sleep she couldn't be disturbed. Seeing their agitation, Wyong advised as a member of the council they should tell him and he would pass it on. Tired and hungry, the magicians were easily swayed into spilling the details.

Contemplating what he'd been told, he decided he would check this one out for himself. Taking, Tarago and Walcha he followed the magician's directions. Unsure where the void would lead them they were hesitant at first to enter. Assaulted by the sounds and smells, the amount of people milling about. They soon realised they stood out in what they wore and how they looked. Conjuring clothes to help them blend in, confident in their magic to protect them they set out to explore. Not sure what to do as the place and populace was so different from where they come from. Wyong decided to return and think about the knowledge they had gained. Crossing back into Eirian, his thoughts filled with how they could keep it a secret for a while longer before informing the guardian. Tarago was the first to spot her surrounded by vampires and warriors.

All three tried to defend their actions. Eshe ignored their rantings, sending a party of magicians and witches to cross the void. Turning her attention back to the wizards, she demanded to know what they had seen. Walcha couldn't help himself, always the bragger, earning him dark looks from both Wyong and Tarago.

On returning, the magicians and witches confirmed what the wizards had said. All shocked when Eshe told them that she would enter and see for herself.

Changing her appearance and that of Torrens, like those entering before them the noise was the first thing she noticed. The inhabitants didn't appear magical, although magic did exist. Then her senses picked up the smell and feel of silver. The land was infected with it. She could feel it beneath her feet calling to her. She closed her eyes, stopping the change which was beginning to happen.

Returning, she told no one of what had taken place. She knew in future she would have to go there. Once word got out about a non-magical land unlike either Idona or Eirian, all wanted to see. The tales of what was there would be too strong a draw for some to ignore. She decided it would be better to give her permission, otherwise everyone would be up in arms if she denied them access only to be found using it herself.

She announced the new realm would be called Novia. Permission granted to cross the void, on the understanding that they blended in and didn't use their magic in front of a norm as those who inhabited it soon begun to be referred as. Some magicals immediately began looking for its darker side. Many like the wizards, thought by being in another realm, they were outside of her control and could plot against her without her knowledge.

Word began to filter in from the far reaches of Eirian about a large contingent of beasts who were making their way across the planes. The Kaimi on patrol noticed the mass moving at a slow pace towards a protected valley surrounded by hills. Swooping lower they spied scouting parties way out in front made up of bears and wolves. They broke off at the sight of a large dragon rising from behind a mountain, flying over the mass guarding their flank.

Eshe despatched sentinels, she would have preferred to have sent the vampires but they were busy rounding up Gork's who had managed to cross the void. Until they had finished the hunt and their blood lust sated, they couldn't be approached or sent.

Wyong immediately offered to go with the warriors and find out who and what they were and why they were here. Eshe couldn't help wonder why he and his cohorts were so eager to help.

The wizards were excited, eager to flex their muscles, especially as the Ambrogio couldn't come. Viewing the sentinels as being lessor magicals than they. All three were confident they would be able to manipulate them to do their bidding.

As they drew nearer they could see an encampment of sorts was in the process of being set up. Bristling at the nerve of them, entering Eirian without permission, doing as they pleased. Commanding the sentinels to draw their weapons, they in turn, armed their staff's as they rode towards the mass.

Everyone was drained, tired and bone weary. They had fallen into a vortex and had only just managed to crawl their way out. Not sure at first if they hadn't fallen into another, the land they entered; hostile. It was only as they got further into it, did the landscape start to; if not welcome them, at least stop making them go round in circles.

The dragon was aware a group of magicals were on their way. The owls had already spotted them in the distance. Ryu, hoping they could have at least got some rest before anyone found them. They all needed to sleep. Telling everyone to hunker down as best they could, he and several bears and wolves went to meet the party.

The ground shook as he walked, conscious not to let his wings batter anyone as they drooped.

The wizards couldn't believe their eyes, these were beasts. Animals not magicals. Wyong made up his mind they would have to leave. Now, straight away. He didn't like the way the bears were looking at them. As if they wore a sign round their necks saying dinner, thinking how they would get on extremely well with the vampires.

The wolves howled, answering howls echoed back.

Wyong rode forward. He didn't bother asking who or what they were.

'You must leave. Turn around and go back to where you came from. This is not your land.'

Ryu wished his dragons fire wasn't so depleted, Tarra standing next to him, placed her paw onto his leg, knowing instinctually his thoughts. Raking the wizards and warriors with his eyes the dragon's voice rumbled towards them as soft as he could make it.

'We ask for asylum, to enable us to rest and recuperate. Our realm has been destroyed by demons.'

'That is not our problem, you should have gotten permission before you entered.'

The bears laughed, as the sentinels smirked.

'How were we supposed to have asked for permission? We fell out of a vortex,' one wolf bellowed, his anger barely contained.

Ryu was too tired to ague. Everyone was worn out, sleep would soon come upon them. Then it wouldn't matter who wanted them gone then.

'Take me to whoever is in charge. I will seek their permission.'

The bears and wolves shook their heads, the dragon like them was near his time. If he went and didn't come back, they were not sure how the rest would cope. He had kept their spirits up. Keeping them going, making sure they stayed together. They thought they had got to safety. It seems though, they had given up one nightmare for another.

Wyong didn't know what to do. A message could easily be sent. But he wanted the kudos of taking the dragon back.

Tarago, whispered, 'the Fae have their small dragons, but nothing on this size has ever been seen before.'

Before Wyong had a chance to say anything, Tarago shouted.

'You will have to be chained.'

The bears and wolves roared and howled their disapproval. The owls relayed the message back to the others. Equally incensed at their proposal. All too tired though, to do much about it.

'If I go with you. Will I be assured that everyone else will be left alone to rest?' asked Ryu, his head drooping the need for sleep hard to ignore.

Wyong let a smile spread across his face. Pleased at how easy it had been.

'We will need to leave a guard. But yes, for the moment they will be safe as long as they do not roam from this designated area.'

Getting the sentinels to wrap the chains around the dragon's neck and wings made him look an even worse sight. The changelings watched in horror to see Ryu being led away at the end of them, tugged along, the wizard's smug expression a goad many wanted to react to. All relishing thoughts of the revenge they would wreak upon him once they had their strength back.

The whole of Eirian was awash with the news. The size and danger of the dragon had grown at each telling. The Fae were eager to see it. They hadn't told their own but somehow they must have known. Their excitement palpable. Threatening to muzzle them if they didn't stop breathing fire every few minutes singeing everything in sight. Eshe knew an instant affinity with the dragon as he walked into view. The chain around his neck an insult to his race. Her fury held in check.

Wyong let the chain fall with a clang. The dragon didn't look up but collapsed onto the ground. Making it shake and shudder. Nobody looked impressed. Yes it was big, but they had expected a ferocious fire breathing dragon. This one looked like it wanted to go to sleep. Its eyes kept closing, some adamant they even heard it snore.

Wyong planted his feet, his stance that of a conquering hero as he announced.

'Behold, this beast and other's entered our land without permission. Told they had to leave. This dragon insisted it be brought before you to seek permission for it and the other beasts to stay in Eirian. It claims sanctuary.'

'Why did you chain him?' asked Eshe, keeping her voice light.

'It's a monster. With one breath he could burn you, with a flick of his wings kill you. I couldn't take the chance that so dangerous a beast could put you or anyone else in danger.'

Someone shouted from the back of the crowd, 'he doesn't look dangerous, are you sure he's not asleep?'

Wyong ignored the heckler. Pumped with his own self-importance, convinced he had saved Eirian from being overrun by ferocious beast's intent on killing all. Now she would see sense and reward him for his efforts.

'Release the chains.'

'No, no, you mustn't,' he cried, sure the dragon once released would take to the skies.

Turning her head towards him, she showed him her silver eyes. Wyong stayed pinned to the spot, too scared to move, like a snake ready to strike Eshe stared at him.

'Everyone leave,' at first no one moved. When her guard emerged from the shadows, she commanded, 'make sure they all go home.' Pointing to the three wizard's she ordered, 'lock them up. Remove their staffs and Wakanda's. I will deal with them later.'

Turning her back as the vampires moved in, she walked towards the dragon. He was nearly asleep and she knew why, not only through a battle fought and a journey made, but because like her he needed to. She could see a faint flicker of silver under his scales.

Placing her hand gently onto his head, she told him, 'I know what you are.'

At her words he opened his eyes.

'Changeling. You are safe now and so will your people be. I need you to follow me. I know it will be an effort. But I will find a place where you can safely sleep.'

With great effort Ryu hauled himself up and followed Eshe, each step an agony of effort. His body wanted to pull him down into sleep, forcing it to keep moving was taking his last reserves of strength.

Eshe opened her link.

'I need your help. Could you make a sleeping chamber big enough to hold a large dragon? Somewhere secure.'

Preparing the cave, Guri, blasted away the rock to make a nest where he could lay stretched out and rest. She dabbed small amounts of glass over the walls. If anyone other than Eshe or herself were to enter the cave they would coalesce together shielding the dragon from view.

'The Changelings?' he asked, the effort to speak nearly too much to bare.

'Do your leaders always wake first after you?'

'Yes,' he managed to answer, his eyes starting to close.

'I will inform them you are safe. When they wake they can tell everyone else. They must stay where they are until you come to them.'

Ryu could barely open his eyes to acknowledge her words.

'This will help.'

Eshe placed her hands under his scales feeling for his skin, the cold from it immediately leeching into her hands. Sleep was taking him, but if she didn't give him silver, he may not wake. The warmth from her hands, trembled through Ryu's body as silver began to flow into his blood, his heart slowed, his scales dulled. With one great sigh he was asleep.

'I know you'd rather not leave the safety of your Glasserium.' Seeing the fear on Guri's face, she coaxed, 'Only you can help. Will you come?'

Arriving at the camp, the first thing that hit them was the silence. Everyone was asleep. Jumbled together for warmth, they lay where they fell. Eshe's heart broke at the sight of them battle scared, dirty and bedraggled. In sleep they looked weak, awake would be a different matter.

If they woke and found their leader taken and not returned, there would be a bloodbath in Eirian. While she sought out the leaders, Guri, began securing the site, a wall of glass began to emerge. Fortunately they had their backs to a large hill, she had been worried they may be scattered for miles. Seeking comfort with each other making her task easier. Eshe found the leaders, touching them in the same way as the dragon, she left a message in their minds. When they woke, they would immediately know what had happened. Before Guri sealed them up. Eshe sent a waft of magic and silver into the air letting it fall over them to feed them strength while they slept.

Weeks later when Ryu finally woke, he found Eshe watching him. Smiling to see his scales shining first with splashes of silver before turning to their natural black, while his underbelly kept its slivery sheen. Snorting to clear his nose, small puffs of fire fell around him. She watched him in amusement, sure that when she woke, she must look just as dazed. Finally the dragon took notice of her.

'We are the same?'

'Similar,' she smiled. 'I apologise for your welcome. Or rather lack of it. It appears that Bayu ruled both our realms. We managed to safely cross the void she directed us towards. Whereas you must have got caught inside the vortex. Otherwise I'm sure we would all have arrived more or less at the same time. As such all of you are welcome to make your home here. My name is Eshe. I am the Guardian.'

For answer, he let his dragon disappear and his magical form show. Bowing low he told her.

'My name is Ryu. On behalf of the changelings I thank you for your offer of a home. You have assured me we are welcome, however that is not the impression we got from your wizards. Tarian, has been destroyed by the same demons as your realm Idona would have been. We want to make a home. We have had enough of fighting and death.'

Eshe was struck by Ryu's air of authority. His magical form was as impressive as his dragon one. Taller than average, his skin glowed with the silver running through it. His eyes a cross between green and violet. Held her own without looking away. He must be high up in the hierarchy of Tarian, she thought, yet he hadn't been appointed guardian like her. She wondered how he and the rest of changelings would take to her being in overall charge of them.

As if hearing her thoughts, he asked, 'what happened to Bayu? Did she defeat the demons?'

Unsure how much she should tell him, Eshe answered, 'we believe she must have defeated them. We have lived in peace for a long while. As to what happened to her, we don't know. I personally live in hope that one day she may return. I fear though, as time goes by. The magicals are forgetting her and her sacrifice more and more each day.'

Eshe transported Guri and Ryu to the camp, releasing the glass the changelings cried out at seeing him returned. She waited to be introduced. The leaders stepped forwards. Ryu sent his voice outwards so the whole crowd could hear his words.

'Forget the welcome we first received. A misunderstanding.' Nodding at Eshe, he told them. 'The guardian welcomes us to Eirian. The magicals that already inhabit this realm were like us ruled by Bayu. Eshe, appointed by her. You are to obey the rules as laid down by her and only her.'

Mutterings soon filled the air. Many changelings angered by his words. Having been ruled by a queen. They objected to being ruled by a magical who they didn't know.

Although Eshe didn't agree with the wizards action's and was still angry at the way they acted, she could clearly see the problem Eirian's magicals would have with the new arrivals. Her main concern was the silver magic running through their veins. The knowledge of its existence was to be guarded at all cost. Bayu's directive like a pulse beating under her skin.

Cutting through her thoughts, Ryu began introducing the other leaders. A large black bear silver threaded through its fur, changed into her magical form as she stepped forwards.

'My name is Tarra.'

Followed next by the largest wolf, Eshe had ever seen. Wolfric stayed in his changeling form, seeing no need to appear as anything other than what he was. His deep voice rang out with one word, a wealth of meaning hidden behind his tone.

'Guardian.'

Pokana had no such problem, changing from an owl to her magical form in a flurry of feathers. Her large owl eyes replaced by equally large brown eyes, as she giggled like a child.

Eshe smiled as she addressed the crowd, 'somehow, we have to find a way to be able to live together. You have silver, while our clans have magical skills many of you may not have come across before. However, Bayu impressed on me the need to keep my silver magic secret.'

Eshe took a moment, letting the implication of her words sink in, deciding that unless she made them aware of the differences between them and the magicals. Problems between the two would soon occur. The only way to make them see was show them.

Silver flooded her body, adding a touch of shimmer made her shine, caught by the sun's rays she blazoned out, the changelings all stunned at the sight before them. Many had never even seen the queen in all her glory. To see someone who wasn't one, appearing as if she were, made them all sit up and take notice.

Guri couldn't hold back a laugh, she knew Eshe didn't get much chance to show of her sparkly self.

'I want you to see Eirian as your home, as the queen would have wished. My one proviso, the silver which adorns you, must remain hidden as much as it is possible for you to do so. Only I, and my guard have been gifted with it. We try not to advertise the fact unless necessary. Magicals can be a jealous bunch, especially some of our wizards.'

'Do you really think they will accept us?' asked Pokana, making Ryu dizzy, as one moment she was an owl, the next in her magical form. 'Sorry, you know what I'm like when I'm anxious.'

Her sister Empley muttered, 'don't we all.'

'It's the question many are asking,' added Nadgee, remembering how the wizards reacted when she had been in her bear form. She didn't trust them. The guardian perhaps, she like them had silver flowing through her veins. The rest, only time would tell.

'We must have always been meant to come to this realm. When Bayu told us to leave and cross the void. We knew there was a chance of encountering a vortex. She herself told us that she had never ripped one apart before. If it hadn't happened then we would probably have been here at the same time.'

'How come they have a guardian in place? We never had one in Tarian. Why should she be in charge of us?' demanded Surat, 'dragons don't like anyone telling them what to do. You should know Ryu,' he laughed, to take the sting out of his words.

Since they had arrived Eshe had made sure they had a secure home, given them silver to repair the damage to their magic. Ryu believed that her attentions were honourable. They had spoken extensively about Bayu and her battle with the demons. It soon became clear to him how high a regard she held Eshe in. Aware of some wizard's animosity towards them, she nevertheless didn't let their views sway her to treating the changelings differently to anyone else in Eirian.

'She is the queen's representative and holds the key to our survival. I trust her. I don't however trust all the magicals around her. Cutting ourselves off behind the wall of glass Guri made for us, was helpful when we first arrived. Now though, I believe we should move towards making our homes within the various communities.'

Seeing the look of disdain on Wolfric's face, Ryu ignored his mutterings.

'We have been asked to join the next council.'

'I bet that went down well with all those obnoxious wizards,' retorted Pokana.

A few days later upon returning from meeting Fingerling, Eshe was greeted with the sight of the changelings now in their magical form mingling with others in Eirian. With their silver hidden no one could really tell the difference. Some possibly had a more air of menace or impatience, most though, appearing much the same as everyone else.

Only Wyong and his coterie of wizards still resented the fact that the changelings had been allowed to stay. Finding out their leaders had been asked to join the council, put him on the defensive, then to be told that a chamber had been created inside the veil for their dead sleep, was the last straw. Eshe heard all their rumblings, checks were kept on them by the vampires. Owls followed them, the Minns adding their comments to the reports. Their words and deeds all reported back to her.

Chapter Thirty-Nine

A dream started to invade her sleep. Eshe dreamt constantly of a book. When she tried to concentrate, she couldn't bring it into relief, instead it hovered on the fringes of her mind. To the chagrin of the Readers, over the next few weeks she spent much of her days and nights in the Scriptorium moving between both sides of the portal. They kept an eye on what she was doing, diving inside those she'd read once back on the shelves. She knew they were there. They thought that hiding in books made them immune from her senses. Little did they know that she could see them as clear as day.

On one of her many forays she overheard a row taking place. Dubbo worked up and shouting. Rai, a changeling, looking unconcerned and even surprised at the veracity of his outburst. Asking what the problem was? Brought forth another tirade. So incensed, Dubbo's words jumbled together making them run into each other. Gradually as the silence grew, he realised that it was Eshe asking the question. Deciding that attack was still the best policy. He pointed his finger at the changeling.

'He has been entering without permission. To make matters worse he has been caught reading the books.'

Eshe was confused. Only Readers should be able to call any forth. Seen as precious words were able to do good, equally able to harm and cause trouble in the wrong hands. The ordinary part of the library was open to all. The inner part, controlled by the Readers, access granted only to a few magicals they deemed worthy.

'Leave us, I will deal with this.'

A book thumped open onto the table, Dubbo dived head first inside.

'Firstly how have you been able to enter without permission?' demanded Eshe.

'I wanted something to get my teeth into. I like reading. Before I knew what was happening I was inside here.'

'Show me.'

Rai, glanced at the stacks, a book dropped onto the table. Book of Names, boldly written across the cover. Picking it up Eshe flicked through the pages, filled with names the words staying still.

'I was so engrossed in reading I called automatically for the next book in the sequence. Apparently, someone else had called it at the same time. A tug of war started. Dubbo came to investigate, found me holed up. The sight of the opened books, the words static, incensed him so much he lost his temper.'

Deciding to call a meeting to discuss Rai and what he could do, the Readers pre-empted her.

'This cannot continue. Never has anyone been able to access the inner library without our express permission. To think that this changeling believes it is his right to come and go as he pleases will not be tolerated,' said Dubbo, in his most pompous voice.

'How does he even do it?' asked Pinjarra. 'No magical has ever been able to,' smiling at Eshe, she added, 'except of course you and the queen.'

'We didn't give permission for him to enter. It can only have been you,' spluttered Dubbo.

'I realise this is not something that you condone or want to happen. Now that it has though, we should at least make use of him.'

Each of their faces told her that her suggestion had not gone down well. Her next one she knew, would shock them even more.

'I want you to create an Afsaneh.'

Stunned at her suggestion, their mouths gaped open at her effrontery to request a Once Upon a Time book. She may have the authority of the queen, but underneath she was still only a magical.

Dubbo told her, 'with no disrespect, you would never be able to open or use it.'

'Nevertheless I want you to create one. I also want links added.'

'Really,' they all blustered, 'that is going too far. Surely this must exceed your authority?'

Eshe was incensed, it was bad enough the wizards trying to ignore her commands.

'Do as I command or I will block access to the Scriptorium and your libraries. Blank books will be your new homes.'

The all froze. The silence in the room absolute. All heard the threat in her voice. Over the next weeks the Readers poured all their efforts into creating the Afsaneh. Finally it was complete. Sure that Eshe would not be able to open it. They waited in anticipation of its return. A space made ready in the bowels the Scriptorium where it would lay until it faded away.

The Afsaneh lay on the desk, its blue cover, dull and sinister looking.

'This is your last chance to change your mind.'

Rai glanced at the book, unable to stop the feeling bubbling up that it was also waiting for his answer. He lived for words and books. Before they had fled Tarian, Bayu had given him a token for safe keeping. Once awake it would enable him to activate all the scribe's memories before the demon attack killed most of them. Those left, so traumatised, their minds were left virtually useless. Losing all sense of where they were or what they had been. Too frightened to venture anywhere in Eirian. Happy to live out their days in seclusion.

Lost in his thoughts, Rai jumped nervously when Eshe spoke.

'Leave nothing out. Everything is of value. If not now, then in the future. I have reanimated the token once you put it on it will be linked only to you.'

'Both the libraries and books know not to obstruct you. I have instructed them to wipe the details of your searches from their records. The Readers cannot be told. This will make them want to find out what you are doing even more.'

'I have evaded their efforts so far,' he replied smugly. 'I'm sure I can continue to do so.'

'Don't under estimate them. That has been many a magicals downfall. Let them see you as an oddity, rather than a threat. Many of them like flattery, but don't take it too far or they will become suspicious.'

Rai smiled, it was like the sun coming out. Eshe had never seen him look so happy.

'Our scribes were a bit like that on Tarian. Sadly many died and the others are lost. This task you have set me. I shall do so in their memory. No one will deter me from that path.'

Eshe smiled in return, she could hear the steel in his voice. Sure once again that she had made the right choice of chronicler.

'Once the histories of the realms are complete, start collecting information from other sources. Anything you find to do with demons or darkness is to be written on separate pages. Dark magic has started to flourish in some places more than others. Find out why. Write only in the book I will give you, even if you are only jotting down your thoughts. The words will find their way to the Afsaneh. Be clear in what you write. Facts are important. Equally, a possibility, a suggestion could show others the way.' Pausing to let her words sink in, she continued, 'once the next step is taken. There will be no going back. Only if the book is called, will the spell release you from its hold.'

Rai nodded his agreement. Placing her hands onto the book, silver began to flow, with her finger she drew a picture of a smaller book onto its cover. Touching the centre it began to firm up. Taking it out, the hole it had left behind quickly filled, making it whole again. She placed her hand on top of the smaller book as Rai placed his on top of hers.

'Afsaneh.'

Rai immediately felt a tingling run up his arm racing towards his heart, making it quicken. Arms appeared on each side of the Afsaneh clasping it tight. Before melting into the books surface. Creatures appeared over its cover. Roaming over the top and down the sides as if on guard. Locks could be heard turning. The silver bursting from inside lighting up the room. With one final blaze of light it disappeared.

Eshe told him, 'you are bonded to the Afsaneh, beholden to keep its secrets. If you tell anyone about your task it will imprison you. Death will seem like a treat compared to the fate that will await you.'

Rai paled at her words, already he could feel the pull of the book inside him. Its thirst for knowledge. The underlying threat that lay in wait if he deviated from his chosen path.

Leading him through a corridor, opening a heavy wooden door, she announced.

'This part of the Scriptorium is yours to use.'

His eyes lit up, a room of his own, the stacks filled with books waiting for the words to be called, he could feel their impatience matching his.

'The Readers know me only as guardian, choosing to forget or act in ignorance of the powers which are mine to use. They won't have expected me to be able to wake the book. Let alone be able to link others to it. Do not tell, or show them or anyone else that you have one. If any suspect or search, it will simply disappear back into the main book until the danger has passed.'

'What do I say when they ask? Which they will. What if they ask about the Afsaneh?' asked Rai, worry etched for the first time on his face.

'In time their thoughts of its calling will recede. You can let it be known that due to the loss your scribes, you are researching the changelings history. By the time you are finished and have started on the magicals history, their knowledge of the Afsaneh ever being called will have disappeared from their memories.'

CHAPTER FORTY

Having gotten used to crossing the void into Novia, many magicals began discussing the possibility of exploring the one found by the vampires. The Ambrogio had pushed the Gork's into the wastelands leaving the borders free. Safe crossing places were beginning to emerge. Keenly aware of the discussions taking place across Eirian, Eshe ventured into the interior of this new realm, seeing a land rich and vibrant with plenty of space. She called it; Kingdom.

Her sleep time had once again crept up on her. No matter how often it happened she was always taken unawares. Glancing at Eshe, Ryu had seen the flicker behind her eyes, the movement across her skin. His own body and those of the other changelings were also showing signs of needing to sleep. This time they were all in sync and would dead sleep together.

Leaving the care of Eirian and now Kingdom, in the hands of the council, did not bring her any comfort. All her previous dead sleeps had taken place with Torrens and the changelings still awake. With all of them out of action, she knew Wyong would see it as an opportunity to seize control. Each time she slept he took more and more on himself. Always forgetting that she would wake and he would have to explain his actions.

Removing Wyong and his band of brothers as Ryu suggested, wouldn't solve the problem, someone else would soon take their place. At least this way they knew who their enemy was.

Before her dead sleep finally overtook her, Eshe decided if the majority of magicals were going to make Kingdom their home, then she would have to make sure it could sustain them and their magic. Pouring a glass of water onto the floor, she called Pelagias. Shaking himself like a dog he sprayed water all over her.

'I'm so sorry. You caught me playing waterfall.'

'I need you and your brothers to make sure all water sources in Kingdom are checked and adequate for the magicals needs. I have no idea why so many want to leave Eirian. All I can do is make the transition as easy as possible.'

Eshe knew that magicals and changelings were all unaware of how much their magic relied on what she gave to the land. She had spent many days weaving her magic through Kingdom's landscape, unlike when she had done the same in Eirian though, her enthusiasm this time had to be worked at.

As she finished her last circuit she felt her sleep pulling at her, slowing her down, making her mind foggy. Fingerling, chuckled to see her eyes keep closing when she told him he could now wake all the indigenous trees of Kingdom. Like the Warra he was enjoying the challenge of new pastures. The Alvie happy to be where ever trees wanted to live and like him wanting a new challenge, also left, only a few stayed to look after the trees who were too old to move.

The Kaimi already used to flying in both realms gradually moved across into Kingdom, abandoning their nests, as more and more trees also decided to leave. The Fae one of the last clans to leave, did so reluctantly. They too though, couldn't forget how their dragons enjoyed Kingdom. When their friends the Kaimi decided to go. Eshe knew they wouldn't be far behind. For whatever reason Eirian was being abandoned, even the Readers had requested permission to set up libraries in Kingdom, citing the fact that permission had already been granted to set up several in Novia.

With a quick blast around the landscape she let her magic fall where it will. Transporting back, as soon as she emerged, she flinched as the noise inside the veil hit her senses. With the decision taken for all changelings to stay inside its confines for their dead sleep. The veil had grown to accommodate them.

Making room for the dragons had seemed a bit problematical at first, undecided which form to stay in when they slept. Usually it would be their changeling form. The veil as if hearing their discussions on not enough room, expanded their quarters. Now all could stretch out without feeling cramped.

Ryu once again voiced his concerns to Eshe, his scouts only managing to return to Eirian before the voids closed. Informing him both Kingdom and Novia appeared to be riddled with dark magic. Much more so than first thought. While in her dead sleep this could make her and them vulnerable to attack. She dismissed his worries, reminding him they had been changing and evolving for many years and would continue to do so.

Finally, to allay his fears and stop his nagging, she asked Guri to construct a cover for the veil, and to keep watch over them and Eirian.

Waking, Eshe knew instantly ice had covered the land while they'd slept. Stepping through the veil, the glass which had protected them lay shattered at her feet, breaking when the ice melted. She could hear and feel others stirring from their long hibernation. Once Torrens and enough of her guard were awake she transported them all to Novia. Disguised to look like everyone else they soon blended into the crowds. The odd person stopping for a second look, usually those with a faint hint of magic living inside them.

Before her sleep had taken hold she had capped the reserves of silver in Eirian. Putting measures in place to make sure no one found or tried to use it while she slept. Here in Novia it flowed beneath her feet. She could feel its pull in each step she took.

As she walked deeper into the mine her eyes glowed red, small lights followed her progress clinging to the walls fading as she passed. She paused, listening, hearing the rush of silver as it began its way towards her. Feet planted she waited for its attack. For that's what it was, it assailed her body pushing itself through and over her until she was covered in silver.

Writhing and twisting into her skin, snaking along her veins, no longer red. She made no sound as it engulfed her. Power thrummed through her body and back into the earth. Some she sent back to Eirian, to dissolve the cap she had put in place. The silver bubbling and moving in response to her command. Once the assault had finished, she waited to make sure it fell back into the depths of Novia.

On her return to Eirian most of the changelings had woken up. Only the younger bears still asleep. Safe in her quarters, she let herself be drawn into the black room created in her mind by Bayu, a place where she could view what had occurred while in her dead sleep. Often jumbled together, it would be up to her to make sense of what it showed. Remembering what Bayu had said about not making any judgements until all had been shown or she may mistake what she sees and react incorrectly. She let her breathing slow. Chanting words the she had told her to use, she let the scenes slowly emerge.

She was immediately disturbed to find that the ice had started in Kingdom. Appearing to have been called forth from the depths of the Soul Lost land. Stilling her anxious thoughts, she concentrated, the images becoming clearer, showing her a time before the ice came.

A powerful magician, named Zador, had begun to place himself above all others. Helped along by several wizards. Her thoughts flew to Wyong, suspecting he may be involved somewhere. Bringing herself back to the moment, Eshe let the images play out and the story unfold.

He and many others had been hiding in Novia. Escapees from Cala and Neg. Zador, the first to see the norms potential, sought out those who had even a drop of magic, turning them into slaves, some with a much darker side to their nature rose in the ranks. Once magicals started to cross the void into Novia, he set about converting them. Forced to take part in rituals that would bind their magic to the darker ways.

Gradually his army in Novia began to grow. Once Kingdom opened up and started to become populated. He turned his attentions to its magicals. Using a witch he'd turned, enabled him and cohorts gain entry into Kingdom. Slipping in unnoticed he ordered they all lay low until sure no one was paying them any attention.

Eshe now understood how pockets of dark magic had been springing up all over Novia before spreading into Kingdom. In her never ending quest to find silver and Bayu, she had allowed it and this magician to rise unchallenged. By dismissing what was happening in Novia as not her concern, she had allowed the magician to get a foothold in Kingdom. Pulling her thoughts away from what she should have done. She stilled her anger and once again let the story unfold.

Zador's influence and power grew as norms and magicals cleaved to his side. Wanting more, he sought out the darkest magic in search of an incantation which would conjure a demon. Even though the spell went wrong, payment was demanded, the demon making his anger plain. Panicked, Zador offered to supply him with several wizards instead. He saw it as the perfect solution, the demon would get more than he asked for. While he would get rid of his brother and those who were beginning to become a problem. The demon agreed to the deal. Now all he had to do was manoeuvre them into summoning it.

He told them that he needed their help with a spell which would allow them to cast dark magic more effectively. Zador laid out the benefits careful to gloss over what the payment would be. Convincing them it would cement their fellowship even more, binding them together with the darkest magic possible. Omitting to tell them only their part of the spell would work, while his part wouldn't.

They cast the spell, all except Zador surprised to see a demon emerge. It pounced. Forcing their bodies through the void. Placed together in a cage, it took several days before they were awake enough to notice that he hadn't come with them.

Eshe sighed once more in annoyance at herself, watching as the images played out it was obvious with no real leader in Kingdom to give direction. It had been ripe for some nefarious magical to take it over, making her feel she had really let Bayu down. All her concerns had been about Eirian and finding silver. Hoping by maintaining one and searching for the other she would eventually find Bayu. Sighing again, at her own foolishness, she brought her concentration back to the task in hand. Her anger and fury at what had been happening, plus her own lack of awareness, fuelled her feelings of rage, making the silver inside her flare.

The sleep she and the changelings had awoken from had been the longest so far. So much had happened in Kingdom. It had gone from a place of peace to a landscape torn apart by conflict and violence.

Zador used all the power at his disposal to make it hard for the magicals to rest. Wanting them on the back foot, they never knew when his cohorts would attack. Several clans had banded to together managing to disrupt his plans. In the process killing several of his leaders and decimating his forces. With the many losses he suffered in his latest battle all hoped he would stop.

The repercussions when they came were the most violent and savage anyone had ever seen. Magicals of all ages taken from their homes, children and babies separated, families never to be seen again. Staff's, wands and broomsticks, destroyed in a great bonfire, their wailing heard for miles. Screams rent the air as the magicals were whipped and pummelled by unseen hands. Given no rest.

Exhausted, they fell. Then it would start again. Driving them mad not knowing when it would happen.

Hiding was not an option, whatever spell had been cast followed them. The trees who had tried to help, now chained and docile. Some having their branches loped; again by unseen hands. After the dragons were attacked and several hacked to death. The Fae took the rest and hid. Using their dust as a thick barrier allowing no one to enter the caves.

To combat the strength and threat of the vampires, Zador conjured hundreds of darklings, sending them to wonder the borders. Harassing the Ambrogio, keeping them busy in the outlying areas and away from all else that was going on. Cut down, they reformed and got back up again. A few vampires who had been in the interior when the fighting started had caused problems. Their ferocity, matched by Zador's intellect to quickly adapt to changing situations. He set free hundreds of Gork's, the vampire's blood lust at the sight of so many could not be contained. Any magicals dark or light that were caught between them and their prey also paying the ultimate price.

Feeling her concentration slipping again. Eshe shook her head, focusing again on what was being shown, taking a deep breath, she immersed herself once again in the past.

In seconds her anger flared, as she was shown Wyong's efforts to inveigle his way into Zador's orbit of power. Making sure his voice was heard over everyone else's. Throwing out suggestions on the most outlandish ways to torment magicals. Working hard to integrate himself and his cronies into everything which was going on.

For his part Zador took no notice, Wyong to him was a magical to be used for his own ends. He had already ascertained he was one to be watched, recognising someone who couldn't be trusted.

Seeing an opportunity to shine, Wyong told him about Eirian, a land filled with beasts and a few stray magicals ruled by a lone woman. Demanding to know where her power came from, gratified to see him taking an interest in him at last, Wyong blurted out that it lay behind a veil, where no magical was allowed to go. Zador remembered when enslaving magicals hearing mention of this realm, unsure of the power he may be able to take and wield, he'd put thoughts of it aside.

Now with his hold secure he decided to send a reconnaissance party, they quickly reported back that as far as they could see no one lived there, a silent land, which many of them had found unsettling, especially at night. The sentries put in place while they slept, made jittery by the feeling of being watched, even though they saw no sign of beasts or magicals.

Over the next few months several more forays were undertaken with still nothing found. Zador began to wonder if this woman and veil, really did exist.

Accused of lying, Wyong quickly produced others to back up his claim. Those reluctant to talk encouraged by a spell to loosen their tongues.

Guri walked around her creation covering the veil making sure all was well. Alerted to a noise, she peered out, moving across the landscape an army slowly approached.

Zador had crossed the void ready for battle, so far the only thing he'd encountered were Gork's roaming the borders as they did in Kingdom. The Ambrogio had seen the magician and his army as soon as they emerged. Normally they would have fell on them, either taking them prisoner or ripping them apart. With so many dark magicals flooding Eirian and the guardian still in her dead sleep. Their only concern to maintain the belief that nothing of any interest was being guarded. Melting away, they let their vampires fade as they disappeared into the caves.

Guri knew those outside would not be able to see her unless she let them. The glass and the veil both barrier's they couldn't cross, the outside appearing as a smooth stone wall.

Zador drew his horse to a stop, they had travelled the lands from end to end encountering no one. Villages and settlements abandoned, the magicals long gone. One settlement on the outskirts had held his attention, a place of waifs and strays, their minds gone. Leaving in disgust when the sound of their wailing and moaning reached a crescendo at the sight of his army.

Disappointed not to feel magic in any part of the land, Zador was determined to come away with something for his troubles. Drawing on all the dark magic he and the others with him possessed, they tried to breach the wall.

Guri watched their efforts, smiling every time they were thwarted. Tasked with keeping watch, she didn't know what to do when she overheard the magician order a camp to be set up. In the morning he would return to Kingdom, those left behind were to watch for any signs of movement by anyone inside.

Hearing his words, she realised he was not going to give up. When Eshe woke she would find them camped outside. This wouldn't be a problem for her to deal with. But she had been adamant that no one should truly know what Eirian contained. This was why the veil was in place.

As night fell and those outside made camp. Guri fretted about what to do. She couldn't wake Eshe or anyone else. Until the process of their dead sleep was complete, nothing could be done. If she didn't do anything they definitely wouldn't go away and the problem would escalate. Decision made, she waited for the sun to rise knowing the sight of her glass would be more effective with the light shining on to it. Taking a deep breath, praying she had made the right decision, she allowed the glass to show.

The sun caught the movement perfectly, bouncing its rays around Eirian. The army dazzled by its many facets. Zador left his tent at their cries, his mouth gaping open at the sight before him. The glass stretched endlessly into the distance, lighting up the land, reflecting it back in all its glory.

Magic, ready to be used in the case of attack, they waited for a door, something to open. They didn't expect to see a face appear in front of them. Guri leant towards them, making the glass bulge outwards.

'Hello.'

Stupefied they stood looking at the apparition in front of them.

Zador stood straighter and answered, toning his voice down, making it as soft as silk.

'We have come from Kingdom to offer our friendship. May we enter...?'

Replying in an equally soft voice, Guri told him, 'if only it were possible.'

She let the glass show its sharp side. It pushed out shards, they offered razor sharp blades, ready to cut ribbons into soft flesh.

'Perhaps,' wheedled Zador, a crafty note entering his voice. 'If we cannot come in, and you cannot come out. Our people could occupy this land. It seems such a waste, for one magical to inhabit.'

Realising, he was wilier than she thought, she laughed, hoping it didn't have a forced ring to it.

'If you wish to live here. Then as you can see I cannot stop you. You won't however be able to survive.'

'We have magic,' shouted a voice, others joining in. 'We can make this land into anything we want.'

Zador watched as she spoke, trying to read her expression not made easy by the planes and dips of the glass framing her.

'I can only warn you. I cannot make you listen. You must choose your own destinies. My only advice, do not return to Kingdom at night. If any are to leave, it would be safer to go now.'

Feeling she'd done all she could, Guri let the glass fade to appear again as stone. Watching closely as the army shuffled and muttered at her words.

The magician didn't move, his eyes trying to bore through the glass. Guri could almost hear his thoughts. He had been so sure this was a land full of magic instead all he'd found was her.

Zador had never felt indecisive before, the search for power and magic his life blood. Yet he couldn't doubt his own eyes, they had searched everywhere and found nothing, except a glass magical sitting like a spider in the middle of her web while unseen monsters patrolled her borders.

'Pack up,' he commanded, we return to Kingdom.'

Guri watched them go, dark magic following them like a cloud of angry bees.

Shortly after returning, several small groups of magicals had been sighted heading towards the void's entrance. Knowing what awaited them on the other side he let them go through. Some who crossed managed to escape the Gork's and return. Using what happened to them as an example, he made it known only in Kingdom under his rule would magicals be safe.

Wyong's anger and hatred gained in intensity when Zador wanted to know why he'd sent him on a wild goose chase, making him look like a fool. Knowing he must do something and quick, trying to make up for his failure. He brought an ancient grimoire to his attention, taken from a witch during a raid on his village.

When the demon had taken his brother into the Soul Lost land, Zador had expected that their twin link would be broken. Realising it was still open, he lived in fear that using his brother the demon could drag him down into its domain. The grimoire detailed a spell that could sever their link for good. At first, all went well, he'd read the instructions many times and was confident he knew the incantation off by heart. It wasn't until the afternoon of the second day when he realised things were starting to go wrong. Jumping after each chant, thinking he heard his brother's voice calling him. The feeling of being watched, slowly began to creep up on him. He missed a chant and had to repeat it. Sweat trickled down his back at his mistake. Nothing must go wrong. He must be free. His future secure. Taking a deep breath he continued. A touch was all it took. He stumbled, a dish spilled to the floor. Liquid disappeared between the cracks in the floorboards. He saw a shadow out of the corner of his eye, growing larger, darkening the room. He ordered the sconces to brighten, they ignored him.

'Hello brother.'

Zador realised too late the spell had opened a gateway between them.

Fear made him shake, he couldn't go. He wouldn't go. Drawing on all the dark magic he had taken over the years, he directed it towards Cillian. Standing firm, tamping down his fear, focusing on the words he must say. Keeping them in order. As he spoke, his brother began repeating his words line for line. Trying to ignore the echo, he soon began to notice the cold, his breath making clouds as he spoke. The walls of the tower started to turn white. He pulled his eyes away. His brother was trying to distract him.

Stamping his feet which were turning numb, ice creeping over them. Zador carried on, still his brother repeated his words back to him. Something was wrong, the ground beneath his feet had started crackling; turning to ice. He couldn't stop now, compelled to continue he rushed the rest of the words.

'Welcome brother.'

Turning towards the sound. Cillian laughed at the expression of shock on Zador's face.

'You used me and the others. Did you really think that we would do nothing to avenge that?'

'What have you done?'

'We are cleansing Kingdom of your dark forces. The ice will wipe it clean, and you will return with me to face your punishment.'

Zador wove his hands, drawing magic symbols, aiming them like arrows at his brother, watching in amazement as they shot straight through him. Realising Cillian wasn't actually out of the Soul Lost land spurred him on. This wasn't real. He must be dreaming. Suddenly the air was rent with a creaking as if something large was being pulled asunder.

'We know you went to Eirian. That too is being covered. The sound you heard was the ice crossing the void. You could of course go to Novia, our influence only extends to parts of it. I knew you would try and keep me imprisoned for ever. I and the others you discarded for your own needs, banded together. Now you reap the rewards. Not only have we covered everything that you covert with ice. We have stifled your magic, you will soon start feeling the effects of being spell bound.'

Using every last bit of magic he processed, Cillian dragged Zador down into the Soul Lost land to face his accuser's.

Guri had heard the sound of the ice coming, unsure what was happening. Thinking it was the magician returning. As it had in Kingdom it pushed across the land, turning everything white. Bitterly cold, everything froze in seconds. Creeping towards her glass, the light began to fade. Her world becoming a tomb. She returned to her Glasserium. The maze she was constructing would keep her occupied while she waited for Eshe to wake.

CHAPTER FORTY-ONE

E she tuned out, everyone wanted to voice their opinion. The owls as usual wanted to help. While the bears and wolves wanted to leave well alone. Ryu's thoughts only of turning into his dragon form and soaring high into the clouds. Fingerling waved his hands trying to bring the meeting to order. Resulting to bellowing when no one would take any notice.

She had nothing but admiration for those magicals who had managed to survive the ice in Eirian and Kingdom. The scouting parties had found them hiding in deep caves in both realms. The majority, thankfully, had managed to flee into Pictures, safe with their ancestors. The Ambrogio had also survived. The vampires were the first to hear and see the ice coming. They too took refuge deep underground, obsidian on both sides of the void acting as a barrier.

With Kingdom remaining a cold dark place still gripped by the hold of ice, magicals began returning to their old villages and settlements in Eirian trying to get their lives back into some sort of order. Eshe took on many guises. Admiring their bravery and skill to survive. She helped unseen where needed, giving advice to those who sought her out, believing that she was a wise women. Torrens or another member of her guard, their vampires hidden, observed those who came near and listened for their intentions. Dark magic as predicted had returned with the magicals.

She moved amongst them wary, but engaged. Disguising herself as a crone, gave her more scope to integrate. To see their true ways and feelings. Even with her disguise, some magicals she felt sure had known who she was. When talking to her their glance kept flicking to what stood behind her, aware that a vampire was in their midst, easy for them to appear just magical, not so easy to disguise the smell of their raw power and strength.

It took many months for Kingdom to recover but once it had, magicals were once again eager to return. As she travelled through Eirian, bolstering its magic, Eshe could see and feel their restlessness. The homes they were making, temporary. Some seeing the changelings were reminded once more of their old fears of being attacked. It soon became obvious, magicals couldn't settle. Reluctantly, she opened the borders.

The changelings had hoped that the magicals treatment of them would change after the ice came. Happy to accept their help at the start, soon though, the mistrust started. Wyong, once again at the fore front of the accusations. Seeing her dismissal of his help as another way to undermine him in favour of the changelings. He still fumed to find they had access to what lay behind the veil whereas he didn't. It played on his mind, imaging treasures and magic beyond belief hidden and kept only for a pretend queen and her pets.

Her question. "How had he got on with Zador?" The last straw. Wyong quickly realising, that somehow, she knew exactly what he had been doing while she'd slept.

As the push to move back to Kingdom got stronger, Eshe decided this time they must have someone to rule them. With this in mind she sort out those that proved themselves worthy of the honour. She was going to create a King to rule Kingdom. Someone who would guide the magicals and not subjugate them.

The one she chose was a strong and just magical. His ethos to help others. Nothing was too much trouble.

When approached, Conan didn't want to do it. Telling Eshe how at times he struggled to get his sons to do as they were told. Let alone getting a whole realm to follow his lead. She assured him it would be so. She would use her magic and influence to make it possible. Over time though, her influence would gradually wear off. It would then be up to him to establish himself as their leader and king before this happened. He would also have to choose advisors. Making no favourites, keeping his distance and perspective.

She tasked Fingerling and the Warra to bring the trees and water back to Kingdom. The vampires herded the Gork's roaming far and wide back onto the borders. Once Kingdom was in order and ready she began spreading the word, before long everyone was talking about the king who was taking them home.

Eshe's blue book lay open in front of her, lost in her own thoughts, she was surprised to look down and see words appearing. A formal request from the Readers for a meeting to discuss the future of their libraries. Tapping the book, she waited as Yarra pulled himself out from its middle. Speaking as soon as his feet touched the floor.

'Now most magicals are moving back to Kingdom. The majority of us feel that we should be allowed to do the same.'

'You do realise that if none of you are to live in Eirian, then access to the Scriptorium will be closed.'

Yarra blanched at her words. This they hadn't bargained for.

Seeing his distress at her words, she softened her tone, telling him.

'Relinquishing allegiance would not be all bad. Released from your oaths, would mean you could run your own libraries.'

Eshe knew they had never forgiven her for allowing the changeling Rai to be given a task they were not involved with. Or her for requesting the Afsaneh to be created. Even more furious when they realised it hadn't returned. Meaning she must have been able to open and use it.

Yarra had conflicting emotions, without allegiance to the Scriptorium they would be cut off from its works. It contained the most priceless grimoires, the most interesting ones and the oldest. Many were favourites. On the other hand the thought of being in charge. Not answerable to her would please many of them. Their nature of in fighting and jealousy meant she had always overseen them. Being independent they would be able to choose a clan name, Yarra couldn't help the smile cross his face, he would call them Bodleian.

Eshe had allowed her ears to pick up Yarra's thoughts. Putting himself forward as overall leader, one who wouldn't now have to wait for her approval, would cause friction amongst some of the others.

'To soften the loss of all you know and love, I will allow each one of you to select a grimoire to keep.'

Approached soon after by the Ambrogio for permission to leave, put Eshe in a quandary. She agreed on the proviso that they maintained their border patrols in Kingdom. Her intention once all those who wanted to go had left was to close the voids between Eirian and Kingdom.

When Conan heard about their request, he contacted Eshe, immediately fearful that he wouldn't be able to control them without her influence. In Eirian this had been the task of her royal guard. Like the rumours about the changelings, the Ambrogio had to put up with similar ones. She had never known a vampire attack a magical unless in times of conflict. There had been the odd occasions when one went rogue. That though, was the exception rather than the rule. Gork's were their preferred prey. Fortunately, these seemed to repopulate quicker than the vampires could kill them.

She discussed the problem with Torrens, his suggestion of how to rectify the situation surprised her. Once all was prepared, she called Huon to a meeting, for what they had in mind they needed the leader of the Ambrogio to be if not happy, then at least in agreement.

'Is something wrong?'

Ignoring his question, Eshe asked, 'how is the move going?'

'I and Nowra are making sure we haven't forgotten anything. Once we have sealed the obsidian safely in Eirian as you requested, then we shall also leave.'

Nodding at his words, she murmured, 'there may be a problem with your clan living in Kingdom.'

'I don't understand, you gave your permission as did the king.'

Torrens stepped forward, Huon couldn't help it. He flinched, as the large vampire appeared to loom over him.

'What we are trying to determine is, can your clan be trusted?'

Huon was now really confused, he didn't know what to answer. Eshe smiled. It didn't make him feel any better, in their presence somehow he didn't feel like a leader. Rather though as someone accused of something he wasn't aware of he'd done; or was going to do.

'Vampires. As we all know are a powerful race,' Eshe let her eyes flick towards Torrens. 'Some of you more than others. Nevertheless your clan will be one of the most powerful if not in terms of magic, then in strength and power that will inhabit Kingdom. Here, as you know,' once again her eyes flicked to Torrens. 'It would never be a problem. Your desire to leave. I understand. Somehow though, we have to balance this with the needs and fears of everyone else.'

Letting her words sink in, Eshe could see Huon's play of emotions cross his face and hear the confusion in his mind.

'Those rumours are untrue. Yes, there was a fight and a magician and a witch did get hurt, so did the vampire. They blasted him with so many small stars he is still recovering. It was an ongoing argument between friends which got out of control. He didn't attack or try and bite them.'

It was the opening Eshe needed.

'Torrens informed me this was the case. Surely you can see the problem. Magicals love rumours, growing out of all proportion to the action taken. I want to put their minds at rest. At the same time, safeguard your clan from any unfounded accusations in the future.'

Torrens held out a golden collar, 'this has been created for the Ambrogio to wear.'

Both Torrens and Eshe heard Huon thoughts.

'It is not a shackle,' she told him.

'Really, because that's what it looks like. What is it supposed to do? Kill us if we do something it doesn't like?'

Huon let his disgust show on his face, his vampire flaring.

Torrens reacted to the threat. Eshe held her hands up stilling them both.

'They will not stop you hunting and killing Gork's. If however without permission to remove them, a magical is killed by a vampire, then yes, the collar will kill.'

Now with a king in place and magicals showing for a second time their preference to live in Kingdom. Eshe felt it was time the changelings looked upon Eirian as their proper home.

Ever since they had entered the realm, they had been confined to only showing their true selves either behind the veil or in their original settlement. Calling a gathering, she smiled to see the puzzled expressions on both the magicals and changelings faces.

'I decree that from now on the changelings who share our realm, shall no longer hide their true forms. Many of you have at one time or another, seen the other side of them. What you won't have seen though, is this.'

Nodding to Ryu, he changed into his dragon form and took to the skies. Letting the silver under his scales and on his belly flare out. The other dragons quickly following suit.

Stunned, the magicals stared in wonder. The owls let loose their bonds. Soaring upwards, their silver feathers reflected the light from the sun. The wolves and bears changed together, Lype's fur glowing as the silver caught the light. His eyes staying bright blue, adding an ethereal contrast. The bears silver claws and snouts shone, the silver in their fur a contrast to the black. Finding their voice the magicals cheered and clapped. Seeing their reaction Eshe knew that she had made the right decision.

Disguised once again as an old crone, Eshe travelled through Kingdom making sure that the magic she'd woven into the landscape was still active. The magicals she spoke to on her journey appeared content, when asking for their thoughts about Novia, most referred to it as a place of wonder and noise, somewhere they liked to visit but not stay. Eirian she was glad to note had become a land of myth and legend, another story told around the camp fire. With the king in place, the magicals settled and the land flourishing, her search for Bayu could now begin in earnest. Hoping that by mapping the silver riven through all three realms it would eventually lead her to the queen.

Even though life in Kingdom and Eirian had settled down, both enjoying a peaceful phase. Something kept nagging at Eshe, not sure what it meant or what it was. She'd woken from her dead sleep and felt immediately under threat. Troubling stories were relayed to her by the Froade. Dark magic was on the rise. Magicals and norms being turned to its ways especially in Novia. She decided to go in search of any large gatherings. Interested to hear what was being discussed, making sure the information she collected was sent back to the Afsaneh.

Rai had told her via their link that several grimoires had been targeted, before they could be taken, he'd changed all their words to nonsense. He'd also heard that many magicals and norms were heading to celebrate the solstice and those looking to source dark magic would also be putting in an appearance. Whisperings about Kingdom were also being bandied about. So far he hadn't been able to make sense of them. Snippets of information he'd gleaned from left over remnants of thoughts attaching themselves to the books he'd sent out as bait.

Eshe tagged onto a group of witches all chattering over each other in their exictment. She was astounded to see so many together in one place. Tuning out the excited chatter, she wove her way through the crowds. The smell of dark magic unable to hide its tell-tale stink even surrounded by so much light magic.

Deliberately she sought out the larger pockets of it, interested to see those who had chosen its path. Surprised at how ordinary they looked, mostly made up of magicians and witches with the odd wizard on the fringes. Several norms obviously compelled, judging by the vacant looks on their faces appeared to be acting as a buffer between the dark and the light. Making sure to keep her power, especially any hint of silver hidden. She used glamour to change her appearance. Allowing herself to appear frightened when she strayed into their area. Scuttling away, making a few of them laugh.

Standing towards the back of the crowd, still in the guise of an old crone, she let her senses slowly trickle out. Noting where dark magic was at its strongest and tracking those who were moving through the crowd. Making a map in her head, once she had their positions fixed, she took out her book and wrote the details. By the time she had finished writing the last sentence the Afsaneh had already started claiming the words, the paper flashing, impatient for her to be done.

Earlier she had noticed several witches moving as one through the throng. Stopping to talk, their smiles lighting up their faces, hugs were exchanged by many. It seemed they couldn't walk more than a few paces before being caught up in conversation. Noticing how each time they were stopped, they automatically reached out to touch those they spoke to. Several waited, before rushing forwards as a group to claim their attention. Letting her senses flow like a ribbon towards only them, she quickly detected a difference in their magic.

During the process of gifting her silver magic, Bayu told her how in the early days of her friendship with Athanasia, they decided to cast a two part spell, the first, to enable them to recognise their signature in others. The second, enabling them to use small amounts of each other's magic to mix with their own. For some reason the second part of the spell didn't work for Athanasia. Whereas Bayu gained more than limited access to Athanasia's shimmer.

Unfortunately this caused a falling out between them. Bayu's assurances, that she had no intention of using anymore of Athanasia's magic than what the spell should have cast, held no sway with her. The fact that shimmer would always be eclipsed by silver, Athanasia already resented, having given away access to her magic, without recourse to Bayu's, made the situation worse and the divide between them grew.

Only joining forces once more when demons became a problem for them both to deal with. Demons preferred conflict, unlike magicals who wanted to enjoy life. A leader began to emerge. Pik began by moving the demons into the villages and settlements. He knew the queen's had been alerted to their presence, so he made sure they behaved and fitted in with the magicals. The watchers soon relaxed, convincing everyone that the demons were integrated, settled and not a threat. When they rose, many villages were destroyed overnight. Demon's revelling in their destruction and the violence and mayhem they caused.

Both queens came down hard, showing no mercy. This was exactly what he wanted. He needed them to be constantly engaged in fighting. He conjured darklings, cut down, they would reform, wearing out the magicals, making them careless. The demons would then sweep in and finish them off.

Pik wanted them to feel they had nowhere to turn as they watched their realms destroyed and magicals killed. He'd soon come to realise that although both were powerful, they were not of equal statue. Bayu ruled more realms and wielded the stronger magic and controlled the vampires, these powerful magicals once let loose could be as merciless as the demons ranged against them. After suffering a massive defeat at their hands, coming close to being killed himself, Pik decided to change tact.

Lulling everyone into a force sense of security, he moved his demons back to the edges of the wastelands, making it seem as if they were worn out and licking their wounds. Beaten back into submission as the lowest in the realms.

After a few months of relative calm, he began to seek out those close to Athanasia, bending them with dark magic to obey his will. It didn't take him long to find out how much she resented the fact that the stronger magic had gone to Bayu, believing it should have been hers to control. Finding out that on more than one occasion she let herself be drawn towards the darker side of magic, he realised that he had made the right choice of who to target.

After her magicals latest skirmish with a clutch of demons. It was brought to Athanasia's attention, that Pik's brother Neo, had been taken prisoner. Expecting him to remain silent on the whereabouts of his brother, he quickly offered him up as a prize. With the realms in chaos and no end in sight, she decided listen to what he had to say. In exchange for his brother he wanted her to create a realm for demons where he could rule and his brother could be imprisoned. Selling it as benefit to both of them.

Like Bayu, Athanasia was an ancient. Pik wasn't. He should by rights be dead, caught in a barrage of stars, crystals and her shimmer. Somehow he'd managed to crawl away. Injured, but not dead. She had fought many demons over the years, none so tenacious though. Many tried to settle as the magicals did. But it didn't last. Arguments would soon arise. Sleights imagined and real were acted on. The violence escalated until all involved either fled or were killed.

Bayu had gotten wind of what she was contemplating, making it known in no uncertain terms that it was much too dangerous. A chain reaction could occur and not stop. Interpreting her interference as another way to show her control. The more Bayu railed at her, the more convinced Athanasia became that she should at least attempt it. Neo had assured her on numerous occasions that his plan would work, and that once his brother was in his clutches, he was never getting out. She had scanned his thoughts many times, searching for deceit, each time hitting a blank wall. Then an opening would appear letting her in to seek the truth of his words. Each time she searched, took her further along the path to believing that opening a realm was her only option.

Creating the vortex she found relatively easy, not getting sucked into its centre not so. It took all of her magic to keep herself in place. Spinning faster and faster, mesmerised, she felt its pull wanting to suck her inside. The void she had chosen was the thinnest she could find, the realm began to emerge, the split getting wider, the vortex slowing as the forces pitted against it pulled it apart. From the grimoires she'd read, the land should keep on expanding until it couldn't do so anymore. Only then would the realm be stable.

Her mind flitted from one possibility to another. Before she could think of putting any of her thoughts into actions, she had to deal with the inevitable fallout from Bayu. Finally, the land stabilised. The earth stopped moving. Pleased with her creation, bare at the moment, she could however envisage how it would look once filled with demons.

'What have you done? I told you not to?'

Athanasia was incensed, she was a queen, not a lackey to be spoken to in this way.

'This is none of your business. Your realms are not constantly attacked day and night. Your magicals safe in their homes. Mine on the other hand are hurried like sheep. The threat of death hangs over them like a sword waiting to strike. Demons are never satisfied with what they have. A realm of their own, something they've never had may make them settle down.'

'I understand where you are coming from. What I don't though, is your choice of who is going to oversee this demon realm. How can you trust what Neo says? Once in place…'

Athanasia had had enough, before thought could watch her words, she snarled.

'This is my creation. If it worries you so much, I can always choose to oversee it myself.'

'Demons are a contrast, a counter balance. You may have dabbled on the fringes of dark magic, they are riddled with it. Spending time with them will taint you, I forbid it,' snarled Bayu.

'Do not propose to tell me what to do. You are not above me. Perhaps you are jealous that I have come up with a solution to the problem, that you ignore as not worthy of your time or interest to pursue.'

Bayu flinched to see the hatred Athanasia felt for her laid bare on her face. Her posture combative, her stance ready to attack. Without starting a war between them there was nothing she could do. Keeping her tone light, she pleaded.

'Make this right. Reverse your spells.'

'And if I choose not to?'

'Then I fear you will come to regret it.'

Eshe's musings made her wonder how much shimmer Athanasia still retained and how much of it she had distributed amongst the magicals before she was taken prisoner. The witches, were obviously recipients. She couldn't remember coming across anyone else that held it inside them, although to be fair she hadn't been looking. Rai had made a vague references to others he had come across, but she had dismissed them out of hand. She knew silver's core was held underground but had no idea where shimmer's was held.

The king knew Eshe was still angry over the Pictures fiasco. The doors that had been created, had quickly become part of the problem. Even the Froade didn't appear to have as much control over their own creation as they used to. Deciding that he had no choice but to contact her he opened his link, after regaling her with the misdeeds that some of the magicals had been undertaking both in Pictures and Kingdom, he was relieved that she could see the sense of what he proposed.

As he didn't know of Guri's existence, his suggestion surprised her. Leaving him with the impression that it wasn't something she couldn't do. Eshe told him she would have to give some thought to how she would achieve it. With the power of silver inside her, she thought she may be able to create the prison, whether she could make it accommodate magicals was the part she wasn't sure of.

She lightly tapped the frame of her mirror, letting Guri know that she wanted to speak to her. Busy inside her maze, she smiled as Eshe's face appeared on each of the mirrors.

'I have received a request from Conan. He wants to create a place for those that require punishment. I wondered if a Glasserium of some sort would serve that purpose.'

Guri was astonished. Why would Eshe think it a place of punishment when it was created as a thing of beauty? Letting her annoyance show, she touched the mirror nearest to herself, collapsing the maze.

As the last mirror folded she stepped out into the chamber, her glass covered body sending beams of light in all directions. She shook her head and in an instant had changed into her magical form. It still fascinated Eshe to see Guri sparkling in her glass carapace, the next looking like any other magical.

Realising she had upset her friend, she smiled.

'It's becoming a real problem, otherwise I wouldn't ask. Do you think you can help?'

'You appear to have a short memory,' retorted Guri, the irony in her voice not lost on Eshe. 'The last Glasserium I created. You set about destroying most of it.'

'I was unaware that your home was underneath where the veil was to be built. To be truthful, once called, its construction cannot be stopped. Drawn by and to the silver in the earth. I'm sorry that you resent me still for what happened. I had thought us friends.'

Relenting at Eshe's obvious distress, Guri explained.

'I can do a temporary facility to help in the short term. Building a Glasserium will take time, meaning that I would have to make it my new home.'

Peace had settled on both Eirian and Kingdom. Eshe was busy keeping a watchful eye on the rise of dark magic. Her travels in Novia searching for Bayu, had taken her to too many places seemingly riddled with it. Lost in her search, she ignored the stories about the king's brother trying to summon a darkness. Wanting to become a Dark Lord and rule Kingdom. She remembered Tassach, how he had shown signs of jealousy towards Conan right from the start of his reign. She dismissed what she heard as wishful thinking. Fingerling alerted her to the seriousness of what was happening, how Conan had his brother killed before the change could happen. The darkness had been contained using fairy dust and forester nets. The dark magicals killed or captured.

Angry at herself once again for being so distracted in her search for silver and Bayu, she knew this time she would have to intervene.

Opening her link, still distraught over the killing of his brother, his garbled words poured out in a steady stream of woes. She listened patiently. Finally he pulled himself together.

'We have contained the Darkness, unlike a demon we cannot kill it and are at a loss as to what to do.'

'I cannot be seen to be interfering in Kingdom's decisions.'

'If you cannot help, then what is to happen to if it gets loose? The nets and magic we have used may not be strong enough to hold it indefinitely.'

'I didn't say I wouldn't help. Kingdom needs to see its king take charge,' retorting, 'especially as it was a member of your family that caused the problem.'

Eshe transported into Kingdom. Her disguise an old grizzled magician. When called forth, she could hear the magicals all wonder who she was and how she knew so much about what needed doing.

A few days later Eshe contacted Conan telling him that after studying the spell used by the dark magicals. Even she didn't recognise its origins. Recommending the only available option was to cast them into the most severe binding mirrors, before placing them into the far reaches of the Glasserium.

A solution on what to do in the future to safe guard Kingdom and its magicals, Eshe found even harder to solve. She didn't want to stifle his rule. She debated the quandary of what to do back and forth in her mind, until she had grown weary and angry. Going back to Eirian to search the Scriptorium for answers, she realised this time he should be the one to deliver its actions.

She transported back to Kingdom, before Conan had time to think what was happening she emerged into his rooms. Took his hand and transported them straight out again. Dizzy from the motion of travel, he sat on a bench, while Eshe poured him a large glass of wine.

'I have read every grimoire I could find for an answer. All point to the same conclusion. The tomb must be guarded by those of a pure heart, those chosen, will be named Shimmers after the magic for which I will endow them and you with. As far as anyone else is to know, including your family. Shimmer stems from you. Something you have acquired as King, from Kingdom. The knowledge of where it comes from must be guarded at all costs.'

He listened, trying to take it all in. His thoughts wondering to what type of magic it was. Each time she replenished Kingdom she also gave his magic a boost. Perhaps, he thought it would be more of the same, but stronger. Realising, when she had stopped speaking that he had allowed his thoughts to wonder. He smiled sheepishly, while she frowned at him in annoyance.

'The names of the guards should be etched into the outer circle as another layer of protection against the dark held within the centre.'

Conan tried to keep his attention on what she was telling him, his thoughts though, kept slewing away to the magic she was going to give him and them.

Eshe held her anger in check, as once again he failed to listen to what she was saying. She knew by his thoughts that he had honed in on only one part of what she'd been explaining. Sharp with annoyance she snapped.

'All royals will have to take part in an Ashbala. The Darkness contained in its tomb, cannot merge with anyone. It will however, try to turn any who draw near to it. That is the test. Walking the outer circle will assure all watching that they have a pure heart, for some a gift of magic will be given.'

'Would it not be better if I were to step down? My brother has…'

Eshe felt sorry for Conan, he was a good man, and had proved a good king. Easy to see though how he could easily be taken advantage of. If though he and his descendants were to continue to rule, then measures to safeguard Kingdom even against them, had to be taken.

He turned as a contingent of men marched into view.

'These are the Baldassare. Their task, to obey and protect you and any future kings. If however, any should move towards the dark. My command will be activated, and they will kill.'

As the seriousness of her words sunk in, Conan looked even more defeated.

'What happens if it does get out? Finds a host, will your magic be strong enough to put it back?' he blurted.

He had been listening and if he were honest he didn't like what he was hearing. Wishing in some way he could go back to being himself. Unlike his son who couldn't wait to take on the mantel of king.

'You have done nothing wrong, your brother Tassach is to blame. Do not, doubt yourself as anything other than a good king. Magicals have to not only understand, but see the measures being taken to safeguard them.' Pausing to let her words sink in, she continued. 'The Fadia, are creating a sword, endowed with the skill of each clan, including magic from me. Should the Darkness escape its tomb, find a host and create a Dark Lord, the Maia will be able to destroy it.'

465

Deciding, for the moment to keep the secret of what Fadia were really creating to herself.

CHAPTER FORTY-TWO

For many years Kateb had been searching libraries both big and small reading dusty tomes old grimoires and anything that may contain information on the seven witches. He'd spent many hours listening to magicals drunk on wine and beer tell stories of what they knew. He travelled far and wide in search of answers. Noting down everything he found out.

Overhearing a witch talk about the solstice and how it seemed to be filling up with more and more dark magicals. Also caught his attention. Amazed at the size of the crowd gathered, Kateb made his way through the throng. He too could feel dark magic in the air. Pulling his cloak tight around him, he found a seat behind a group of magicians. Taking out his note book, he scanned those nearest, making sure no one was taking any notice of him. Each group that appeared he scrutinised to see if they were the ones he sought. Hearing laughter, he saw a group of witches moving as one through the crowd.

These he thought could be them. His eyes locked onto their faces, committing them to memory. Hugs and kisses slowed them down. He saw a magician approach, dark magic speckled around him. Turning as one they hissed a warning. Rearing back, the magician scuttled away.

Back in his rooms, he wrote up his notes, drawing pictures of the witches faces proved more of a problem. Each time he began, his vision blurred, blinking to clear his eyes. Nothing was noted. The page bare. Kateb realised he may actually of found them. Trying one more time he began to draw. In seconds his eyes blurred and his pencil broke. Deciding to have his supper, as he ate he flicked through an old grimoire looking for a spell that would be able to determine magic that was different to either dark or light.

Finally, written in the smallest print as if the words were hiding, he came across something that he may be able to try. Reading the details of the spell again, Kateb realised that to cast it, he would need help. Loathe to tell anyone why he wanted it, he racked his brains for who he could ask.

Rising early, he picked up his staff, changing its appearance to that of a walking stick. Pulled his satchel over his head. Hiding it under his baggy coat, he set out. Walking through the country lanes, Kateb could easily believe that he was in Kingdom. The one bug bear to living in Novia was the noise and the norms that were forever scurrying about. No time to dawdle, or take in their surroundings. To him they always appeared to be in a hurry. Only in their parks and countryside did they take a bit more time to relax, and then for only short periods. He missed Kingdom's much slower pace of life and it's quiet.

Having exhausted his search there for any information about the witches. He'd turned his attention to Novia, soon finding that likeminded norms liked to gather together. When he had first started attending, dark magic had only appeared on the fringes. Now though, it was on the rise. Each time he entered a gathering, especially a new one, he made sure to cover himself with a spell to dumb down his magic, making it appear not worth bothering about. His appearance as an old magician, tottering along minding his business, had stood him in good stead. Anyone taking an interest in what he was writing soon left him alone. Acting as if they were a captive audience he started reciting poetry. Finding it the quickest way to deter anyone's interest.

The cottage he was looking for was at the edge of the village. Ramshackle and dilapidated looking, many passed it by thinking it uninhabited. The witch who lived inside had spelled it to look this way. Her family had been one of the first to move from Kingdom to Novia. She liked the fact that any norms, plucking up the courage to pay a visit, thought of her as an old witch. Her pills and potions something secret and dangerous they could take away. Believing they had been given a little bit of magic. When they left, her laughter often followed them down the path. The joke on them, she was a witch and her magic was real.

Kateb hesitated before stepping through the open doorway, the dark inside uninviting.

'You may enter,' a voice called out from the depths.

Making sure not to touch any of the walls, he followed the sound of singing.

Looking him up and down, Prisca, asked, 'why do you want this spell?'

Kateb was taken aback, he hadn't yet broached the subject of what he wanted. Two black cats appeared from the garden to sit either side of her, making her appear as the quintessential witch that norms usually described.

He couldn't stop the smile from crossing his face. Rearing back, as both cats hissed at him, before showing him their claws.

Placing her hands onto their backs, Prisca crooned, 'there, there my lovelies, Kateb has been here before. You should recognise his scent.'

Indicating that he should take a seat, the witch shooed the cats away telling them to go hunt for better prey.

'The eagerness surrounding you tells me you are concocting another experiment.'

'I want to find out if anything exists between.'

The silence made him feel as if a weight was pressing down on him.

Prisca aware of what he was feeling, studied his face as her mind searched for the real reason he wanted the spell. Not completely convinced by what he had told her, but having dealt with him before, she trusted him and knew his experiments were nothing to do with dark magic.

'I will concoct it, however, you must be careful how you use it. Only a few drops. If anything exists between, it will be enough for you to see.'

This time Kateb was ready. As soon as he arrived at the gathering he scouted around the crowd. Listening to the chatter from both norms and magicals. Keeping away from the edges were those of a darker persuasion waited. Finding a good vantage point, he glanced around making sure that no one was taking any interest in him. Turning away, he quickly let a few drops of the concoction fall into his eyes, they immediately blurred. For a few moments he was unable to see anything. As they cleared, he searched. He didn't have long to wait, catching sight of movement, several different groups began to make their way through the crowd. The witches he sought the only ones to stop and chat. Each time hugs were offered and taken. Arms, faces and hands stroked, making all those they touched smile. Making slow progress, enabled him to see the small lights dancing above their heads, golden with a few brighter specks sprinkled through. No one else in the crowd had anything like them. Kateb sure now, that these were the witches he'd been looking for. Transfixed, he blocked out all other sights and sounds. Everyone waited, their eyes fixed in the distance while he watched the seven. Like everyone else they became bathed in the sunlight, as soon as it faded, they began to make their way back through the crowds. Determined to see where they went, he packed up his book and followed.

He heard them shout their goodbyes and chasing each other like young girls, they ran towards a belt of trees. Sitting down, pretending to be more tired than he was. He fanned his hat in front of his face, his eyes locked onto where they had gone. A faint flash confirmed his suspicions. They had used a portal.

Over the next year he managed to follow their progress. Each time, noticing more and more how touch played a huge part in their travel through any gathering. Details all added to his notebooks as he built a picture of their ways. Coming to the conclusion, that there was more to their touch than friendliness. Waiting was agony. His thoughts only of the witches, losing himself in his research gave him his only interest. His friends long tired of his excuses on why he couldn't visit. Meant that most days and nights he spent alone. A few days before the solstice was due to take place, Kateb made his camp in the clump of trees where he had seen the flash of the portal.

Hunkering down, determined to see the witches emerge and return. He nearly missed them coming through. Tired from all the writing he'd done, his eyes closed and he fell asleep. The portal startled him awake, making a loud booming sound as it appeared, before settling down to a low gentle humming. Keeping still, he peered around the trees, thankful that they were not the same as in Kingdom, otherwise they would have announced his presence. They stepped out laughing and smiling as always and set off towards the gathering.

While he waited for their return, he took the opportunity for something to eat and drink, being still careful to remain hidden. As they got nearer to the portal he could see its blue outline more clearly, as if it were calling them home. One by one they disappeared inside. Before he could think what he was doing he leapt forwards. Tumbling over and over banging his head on the cave walls before coming to a stop.

'Well, well, who do we have here?'

'Kateb,' he answered groggily.

Poking him with her staff Eshe told him, 'come on then, get up, unless you want to be caught.'

He got to his knees, everything spun. Kateb held his head, which was pounding fit to burst. Then the feeling of sickness washed over him. Groaning, he looked up and stumbled through the door.

'Sit down,' ordered Eshe. 'Drink this, it will take the pain away and make you feel better.'

Handing him a golden goblet filled with a foul smelling concoction he pulled a face at the thought of drinking it. The magical watched him as if daring him not to. Taking a deep breath he downed it in one. Wiping his mouth with the back of his hands he flinched as the moisture stung his lips.

Surprisingly he did feel better. Looking around they were in some sort of cave. The walls lined with tapestries depicting woodland scenes showing creatures he'd never seen before. Sconces held their own against tall candles both vying to light the space. Hissing at each other in their efforts to burn brightest. A fine bottle of wine appeared in front of him banging the table in impatience waiting for a glass to appear. Filling it to the brim it raced to the magicals glass, putting her hand over it, the bottle screamed its annoyance. With a click of her fingers she stopped its nonsense, sending it back to the shelves.

Kateb took a cautious sip. Eshe stared at him, her eyes taking in his shabby clothes and unkempt appearance. The large strap across his back pulled down with the weight of the attached bag. She noticed that his eyes looked too big for his face and that he wasn't blinking. Realising, that was how he had been able to see the shimmer which hovered above the witches.

'Who gave you the seeing spell?'

Kateb thought about lying but seeing the look on her face decided not to.

'Prisca's not a dark witch,' he cried, 'I wanted to be able to find the seven. I don't want to get her into trouble. She has always been kind to me.'

'What makes you think the magicals you followed, are those you seek?'

Pulling off his bag he delved inside and brought out several tatty leather books.

'These tell me so. My notes. For years I have read every book and grimoire I can find. Tantalising snippets, about seven witches that have special magic.'

Showing Eshe the pages of his books, his writing small and cramped, each page filled with his musing's.

'Do the Readers know what you're doing? I'm surprised they haven't tried to confiscate your words. What do you intend to do with them?'

His laughter, not what she expected to hear.

'My notebooks may seem tatty, but that is for a reason. Many years ago when I started my quest. Prisca found a spell that could circumvent them from taking my words, or even reading them, as long as I only wrote in these notebooks. I'm not sure if the spell still works. No word though, has ever disappeared from them, not even when I have been writing inside a library.'

'Tonight you can stay here,' calling for food, she bade him stay seated. 'We will talk again later. Replenish and rest.'

Distracted by the logs in the hearth crackling as they burst into flames. When he'd turned back she had gone. The door locked and barred, with a sigh he drew a plate of stew towards him and filled his bowl. The bottle that filled his glass earlier flew off the shelf poured him a drink, landing on the table with a self-satisfied bang.

Eshe entered the Scriptorium, since created by Bayu out of her love of books, like most things magical, it had taken on a life of its own. Walking through the stacks, small pink lights followed her, displaying themselves whenever she ventured inside. Sitting at her desk she allowed her senses to drink in the smell of the books. Head back she closed her eyes.

'I'm busy.'

'You always say that. You're getting to sound more like a Bodleian each day.'

Rai smiled as he sat down.

She tapped Kateb's books with her fingers.

'I need you to investigate these. Tonight. Find the source

material, bring it to me. Replace it with something else. Then do a search to make sure nothing else has been missed. Although, he has been thorough.'

'I'm not...'

'Tonight. No arguments. A witch called Prisca has a spell that can allow people to see things they shouldn't. She must have access to an old book. And has also found a way to use a Reader's block. Remove these from her grimoires, make sure they do not exist anywhere else. One last thing, see if anyone other than Kateb has been seeking the same knowledge.'

With all the words now safely hidden in the Afsaneh. Eshe pondered on what to do. Even Rai had been impressed by the amount of knowledge Kateb had gained. He hadn't managed to dig up anything much about her or a queen. Only vague tales about one who died as a result of fighting a demon. No names were mentioned, meaning he could be referring to either Athanasia or Bayu.

Many years of patient work had gone into his notebooks. This she admired. At the same time, if he a lowly magician could find the information then so possibly could others. Rai confirmed that others had been looking. Nothing yet appeared to exist as detailed as Kateb's writings, or contain details concerning her or Eirian. Rai, often in his searches could see that notes had been taken, when asked if he should wipe and replace with nonsense. Eshe said no. It would alert whoever they were that someone was taking notice of what they were doing. Checks were to be put in place, anything from now on that was sought or noted, to be copied and sent to the Afsaneh.

Eshe let her thoughts wonder, the paths suggested by Bayu, had been clear. One in particular though, had stood out sharper than the rest. Worried that this may be the true path of the future, Eshe made her plans.

Kateb awoke to the smell of frying bacon. His nose twitched as the delicious smell wafted his way. Eyes unfocused, he carefully sat up pushing back the blankets that covered him.

'Please, join us.'

Eshe introduced him to Rai. Kateb was in his element. He loved books, he loved history. He had gained great knowledge as he searched for the witches. Rai, much to Kateb's delight, listened avidly.

After a few days had gone by, Eshe told him that it was time for him to return home. Sitting with her on his last night he realised how contented he felt. All his life he had been searching for something indefinable. His hunt for the witches kept him busy and his brain sharp, seeing them as a puzzle he must solve. Now that he had, he didn't know what he was going to do with his time.

Aware of his thoughts, Eshe waited until they finished their meal before broaching the subject she wanted to talk about.

'I would like you to work for me. You have already proved that you are adept at finding obscure information. Determined and thorough in your investigations. History hides in many places. One day it will be needed, brought forth and shared. I want you to take this book with you, continue to follow the witches. Record what happens. What you see and what you hear. Especially if it concerns dark magic. Only write in this book. Your words will disappear and hide themselves amongst the many books written.'

'Why do you need me? Surely Rai is more than capable of keeping records?'

'I need someone who can be physically present in Novia. Who knows what to look for, and has a feeling for when somethings not right and is good at rooting out information.'

'You want me to be your spy?'

She laughed, 'I want you to find someone for me. She may be drawn to magic, especially gatherings. You may have already seen her. She may appear lost, confused.'

Placing her hands either side of his head, she showed him a picture of a face in his mind.

'You may not have noticed me at the gatherings but I have noticed you. I have watched you follow the witches with your eyes, at the same time it's obvious you are still conscious of what is happening around you. You have showed us your book about them. What about the other one you keep in your pocket, the red one? What do you write in that?'

'Rai told you? Has he taken my words?'

Pulling out the book he could see that his words were still inside. Although looking at them closely, they looked faded, as if ready to leave at any moment. Glancing down he could see that as they were speaking they were disappearing.

'He's taken them.'

Picking up the book from the table she opened it showing him his words now filling the pages.

'Anything you write that concerns what we have discussed is not to fall into the wrong hands, it may be taken. Anything that is deemed okay to be found by someone else, will be copied, but stay written.'

'I still don't understand why you need me to do this.'

'Our futures are unknown. The paths we take unclear. Something is stirring. It is evident in yours and others writings. Precautions need to be taken. An Afsaneh, has been created, the words it contains, a guide, a history, a light. It grows with knowledge and has taken on a life of its own. Aware that it is not yet needed, it hides itself everywhere and nowhere. Your words will be added to this book.'

'Why me? Flattered as I am. Surely you must know a magical that is much more suitable for the task.'

'Because you know who I am or at least you suspect. Yet you have not mentioned this to me or to Rai. You also haven't written it down anywhere. Rai has searched. Why?'

'I have always had a strong feeling that I shouldn't,' explained Kateb. 'Even though faint, I could at times see silver and gold speckling around you. The first time I thought it might be just something you wore, caught by the sun. I picked up a rumour from an old wizard. As I watched the witches, I kept you in my eye line. When I looked at them and then looked at you, it became obvious.

When you are concentrating on them you look different. You stand different. Your aura shines. It clicked into place, as if you had told me yourself. You are the Guardian.'

Satisfied that she had made the right decision, Eshe gave Kateb the gift of second sight, and the title Finder. No longer would he need to use a spell to follow those he sought. His eyes would automatically be able to spot them. The book would enable him to write his words and for the Afsaneh to take them.

In her many travels through Novia, Eshe soon came to realise that norms were a fickle race. Their actions and deeds often bloody and violent. Many were greedy, wanting riches, willing to take from those who they deemed victims. She had seen for herself, how easily they succumbed to a dark magicals influence. Rai had made her aware of a wizard who had been careless enough to note down details of her existence. He had gone on to share the details with a few others. All with the same view as him of removing her.

A dream they still held, even knowing that without entry to Eirian, they wouldn't get near enough to try. Eshe wasn't surprised, she told Rai to only copy the words for the Afsaneh to take. Leaving them in place so as not to alert the wizards that she knew who they were.

The majority of magicals had put any thoughts of her and Eirian long to the back of their minds. Only their ancestors really remembered a time before Kingdom and Novia. Unlike in the past when the ancestor's stories were treasured, now magicals hardly listened to them.

Fate leant the wizards a hand. Others like them in Kingdom also drawn to the darker side of magic. Set out to conjure a demon, thinking they could control it to do their bidding. No one involved spoke of what they intended, everything was done by the passing of runes depicting the action each should take.

Disappointed, at the puny dead looking thing they had conjured the witch's left it were it lay, unaware they had been tricked.

CHAPTER FORTY-THREE

E she was exhausted, she had been fighting the demon for many months. Kingdom and Eirian were both now clear of his influence. Chased into the voids between, before he gained enough strength to flee into Novia, she would have to find and kill him, if she didn't, then it would all have been for nothing. If the demon won, he would be able to let through many others to roam and destroy. Novia unaware that a war may soon rage within its midst.

Their battles so far, violent and bloody. Many magicals including the king, dead, his son, thrust onto the throne in the midst of war. The clans decimated. Eshe had fought a long side his father, as a protector and warrior. Keen to keep her real title hidden, she moved among the people of Kingdom in many guises, as she used to in Eirian.

A few wizards who still remembered tales of a different realm told over the campfires, couldn't be so easily fooled. They watched her like a hawk. Some seeing it as a chance to kill her, believing that they could take her power for their own. With Eirian abandoned while she was in Kingdom. Who knew what riches it may contain?

Changelings surrounded her. Vampires walked by her side. Eshe aware of their thoughts, dismissed their ravings as wishful thinking. She was more concerned with the real threat the demon posed to the realms.

The air around her started to move. Eshe readied her staff, her silver flaring as she called for her guard. Torrens and his vampires flooded the cave, eager to reap violence on any who came near.

Seven witches stepped through the portal, before the vampires could react, they were stopped in their tracks.

Eshe showed no fear. Waiting for the answers she was sure would come. If these were her enemy they would have attacked her first. Besides, she recognised them from the solstice.

Bowing to her in deference the witches conjured seats and sat facing her.

'You have done well, your power though, is diminished. You may not even have enough to send the demon back to where he came from.'

She listened carefully, even though they were telling her something she already knew.

'We can help, we want to help. But there is a price.'

Eshe waited, the silence stretched. She wouldn't ask what their price was.

'We wish to live in Eirian. We also have shimmer, mixing ours with your silver you should be able to defeat the demon and send him back. Without our help, you may die, even with it, you still might.'

'What makes you think that I possess silver?'

The witches laughed at her question. They too could wait.

Seeing that they weren't going to answer. Eshe asked, 'why don't you fight with me?'

At this the witches all shuffled in their seats looking uncomfortable.

'We cannot. The shimmer we hold was gifted to us by our queen. Like all magic it can be used as a weapon. For us though, we are unable to use it in this way. It has always been so. We lost her a long time ago. Betrayed and taken by demons into the Soul Lost land which she had created for them.'

Eshe had followed these witches, both Rai and Kateb had gathered information on them. Racking her memory, she couldn't remember any details of their association with Athanasia being found.

Kateb had been unable to find or write anything about her or Bayu, perhaps thought Eshe, it was the same for Athanasia. Breaking into her thoughts, the witches continued.

'We have lived in many places. With all the dark forces swirling, the harmony between realms doesn't exist anymore. We crave stability. If we do not help and you lose, we all are threatened. Even if you win. You may be depleted of magic, weakened. It has come to our attention that certain fractions, would be glad of this. You, like us, understand that sending the demon back. May be only a temporary solution, others will stir again, looking for ways to break through. Dark magicals are everywhere, they do not know what they wish for. Only seeing the power they may gain. Not the life they will have.'

'How would this work? Those living in Eirian may not accept you. Many are different. You would have given your power away for nothing.'

The witches nodded at the same time, as if they had spoken inside their minds.

'When we merge our magic, all that is yours will flow to us, all that is ours will flow to you. We do not take your magic as you do not take ours. We share it. Magicals will soon see how we can work together, for the good of all. The demon will be gone. Peace can have another chance to grow.'

'Why should I, or my magicals trust you to keep your word?'

'We want a home, somewhere we can feel safe. Finding out how powerful our shimmer is would be a boon to certain magicals. That's another reason why we would like to live in Eirian, wizards have started to take an interest in us. So far we have managed to play down anything we may have done to help you.'

Eshe raised her eyebrows in question.

'The battle of Telin.'

She searched her memory.

'That was you?'

'Don't forget the magicals hiding in the Drogma Hills,' spoke another witch, 'we managed to pull them out before they were blown apart. We have always worked at the edges, over the years we have helped in numerous ways. You know we speak the truth when we say that here now before us, you do not need our help. But going up against the demon you do.'

Eshe spoke first to the changelings. They too were tired. Unable while in Kingdom to use their animal and bird bodies. The strain was beginning to show. Without the added benefits of utilising the changeling side of their natures, even though silver still traversed their bodies, it made the whole process of battle much harder to undertake.

Until they found that they had no choice but to confront the demon in Kingdom, many had never left the safety of Eirian. With no desire to go to Novia, they knew nothing about Eshe's knowledge of the witches.

'I first became aware of them when I began attending the many gatherings that happen all over Novia. The seven are always seen together and are popular. Even though many attend, I felt particularly drawn to these witches,' explained Eshe. 'They have a similar role to mine, while I hold and guard silver for our queen. They hold shimmer between them for theirs. To help defeat the demon they are offering me the use of it.'

'And in return?'

'They want to live in Eirian.'

Ryu, frowned, 'that's all they want?'

'That's the words they used,' smiled Eshe. 'Reading their thoughts though, they would like me to step aside and for them to act it in my place.'

The room erupted.

'They believe that in fighting the demon even with their shimmer. I may not survive. We all know something is wrong in Kingdom. The last time I replenished it, before the demon came. I could smell dark magic's foul stink seeping in to it and its magicals.' Sighing deeply, she added, 'there are still a few intent on mischief, plotting how best to dispose of me.'

Eshe knew she couldn't tell them everything, some things even she didn't yet understand. This though, she knew was the right path. Like a door opening in her mind, a suggestion, a hint kept flaring. Nudging her along.

Looking at all their faces turned towards her, she realised how fond she had become of the changelings and how much she missed the magicals left behind in Eirian. With the witches offer though, she would be able to continue her search for Bayu without the incumbency of either realm to worry about. She could easily manipulate the scenario to appear as if they had replaced her, it would suit her purposes for all to do so. Allowing her the opportunity to keep to the background, making it easier to keep an eye on those of a more nefarious nature. The white room had shown her the truth yet to be written depending on which paths she and others took. Kateb and Rai were still investigating any information they found appearing first in her book before being transferred to the Afsaneh. She brought her thoughts back to the here and now.

'The demon must be defeated. The witches want a safe haven. Like me, they were given power. Unlike me, they have never ruled. I will not be stepping down, only away.'

'How will it all work? Do we guard them or you?' what will we call them?' asked Torrens, showing his distaste.

'When, not if, I send the demon back. Even with their added shimmer, as the witches so forthrightly told me, I may be depleted and require a lot of rest to recuperate. It could also tip me over into a dead sleep.'

Everyone nodded in agreement, this was something they had

debated earlier before the meeting. Many of the changelings could already feel their time was imminent.

'The witches taking up residence in Eirian shouldn't cause too many problems. Welcome them, make them feel they have gained a home, a refuge even. If they want to play at being me, let them. Unless I'm killed by the demon.' Seeing the look on their faces, Eshe let a chuckle escape. 'Don't look so worried. I have no intention of losing. I will still be in the background. The witches used all the right words, yet they still gave me the impression of being a bit naïve. Besides, it won't be a bad thing for those who remember me, to believe that I am no longer a threat.'

The majority of magicals were unaware of the part played by Eshe and the changelings in removing the demon from Kingdom. Hunted across the void, she had tracked it as it hid at the edges of the wastelands. Wolfric thought he had caught its foul stink, instead they came across a clutch of dark magicals taking part in a ceremony.

The first demon had caused only minor damage and disruption, its puny body didn't appear to hold much magic. Exhausted from being chased over the realms it had fallen into a deep pit, mewling as it tried to claw its way out, a warrior jumped down and run it through with his sword. Eshe knew the real problem lay in the information it had sent back.

The demon emerging next wasn't so easy to deal with. This one was wilier, disguising himself to blend in, starting with a small group of magicals, he set them off one against each other. This soon escalated, until fights were breaking out all over Kingdom. None could remember who had started them or even why they were fighting. Words were whispered, stories told, families set against each other.

Once the magicals turned to more extreme measures of hurting each other, all soon became aware that something was seriously wrong. The king declared curfews. Sending in the vampires to maintain control. The demon managing to flee each time Eshe and her small army drew near to it. Calling forth darklings who set about burning everything they came across. The trees fled underground as the Warra sprayed water constantly trying to put out the fires.

A whole village of mainly women and children were caught unawares, the majority got away, those caught in the deadly flames died, their screaming seeming to echo across Kingdom. The demon was ramping up the violence and damage he was causing. Eshe was sure dark magicals must be hiding or at least helping him. Too many times they had come close to capturing him to be left empty handed. Frustrated, she came up with a new strategy.

She commandeered a small village. Changelings and wizards took up residence acting as if they lived there, witches and magicians turned up pretending they had come for a celebration. All was in place, Eshe could only hope that not only had the demon heard about the celebration, more importantly that he believed it to be true.

The party started low key. Everyone enjoying each other's company, then they began to get rowdier and more vocal towards each other. Shouts rent the air as they let off steam. Pushing and shoving, a few small stars were released, none would hurt, only sting. Staffs were shook, Wakanda's readied.

Torrens smelt it first, the demon was on his way drawn by the atmosphere of anger. Eshe's senses flared, it was in their midst. A scruffy magician was leaning against the side of one of the cottages, she had caught the dull gleam of his red eyes, before he blinked and they changed to brown. Nodding at Wolfric, she began to thread her way towards him. She camouflaged her scent by copying the demons.

Her arms shot out, she grabbed him around the throat. Torrens immediately joined her, between them it took all their strength to hold him. Squirming and spitting in his fight to get away. The dark magic poured from his skin trying to subjugate them. Both shook it off. As soon as they were a safe distance from everyone else, Eshe transported them into a void. One moment she and Torrens had the demon between them, the next it had gone.

Making sure the voids into Eirian and Kingdom were sealed. They could do no more and would have to wait until it resurfaced again. This time the only place left for it to go was Novia. Wanting the demon gone none questioned where the stronger magic used against it had come from. Many surmising that it must be from an outside force, unconcerned who had given it, glad only that it had worked.

Eshe, soon realised that she wouldn't be able to keep her presence secret from the king's council any longer.

The wizards were incensed at not being made aware sooner. Over the years many had dreamt of getting into Eirian and take her magic. If that meant killing her for it, then they would do so. If they had known she was in Kingdom, there may have been a chance to realise their dream.

'How do we even know that these witches, who have seemingly appeared from nowhere, have enough power to help her? How is it that no one has heard of them before?'

The king knew in his heart that no matter what evidence was shown, the wizards would object to the witches help, even though everyone else was willing to listen.

The wizards left the meeting, now they knew she was involved, their feelings were torn, they wanted to stop the demon from returning to Kingdom. At the same time, they also wanted her to lose. Blind to what a demon really meant. All they could see was the power they could take if the guardian wasn't around.

Eshe knew that she was running out of time. She had thought long and hard about what she had seen and heard in both the black and white rooms. Sure now that something other than this demon would eventually come. Her thoughts often turning to Athanasia and how she was taken. Even Torrens had pointed out that the demon appeared to be targeting her, drawing her out into the open, make her follow its path. The decisions she made now would have repercussions for both Eirian and Kingdom, possibly even Novia.

Before she could change her mind she began to put her plans in place. Not convinced, that even with the witches help that she was going to survive the battle. So far all her efforts had been in driving the demon out of Eirian and Kingdom. She could see now that it had been the demon's plan all along. To draw her away and into the void, the real battle would be between him and her. For days now, she had been hearing the echo of Bayu's words. Failsafe.

She trusted few magicals. Having learnt early on in her guardianship that they often showed one side, while thinking another. Although the witches had Athanasia's magic in them. It had not been given in the same way that she had received hers. Whereas Bayu had freely given the use of silver to her and the changelings. Athanasia only used magicals as repositories for her shimmer. Eshe was still convinced that somewhere, Bayu was waiting to be found. Her task to make sure that her silver was kept secure.

Eshe let her body settle, the witch's still looked drowsy after the merging. Slumped together, in a drunken huddle. Before they joined their magic, Bayu's words had once again rebounded around her head. With that in mind she put a cap on the amount of silver the witches would be able to access.

Their shimmer had started moving through her body as a trickle, believing the witches had also capped their magic, she was stunned when it quickly turned into a torrent. Bursting through in waves, looking for hers. At one point she felt as if it was trying to drown her silver, so much of it flowed into her body.

Gradually the witches woke, their mouths gaping open. Where they speckled, she shone. The shimmer, sparkled and flared as the silver beneath pushed through. Her eyes had also changed, one minute gold the next silver. Before settling down into her normal blue. She saw the query in the witch's eyes.

The shimmer inside her pulsated, she had always stood beside power. Now she was that power. Guardian not Queen. But with both queen's magic flowing through her body.

CHAPTER FORTY-FOUR

Fighting the demon had truly taken its toll, her dead sleep was imminent. Eshe couldn't take the risk of transporting to Eirian, it was all she could do to stay upright. The Enabler hadn't been sure at which station she would board from, alerts had gone out to all of them, detailing trusted magicals to be on the lookout. A group of magicians had spotted her, standing off to the side, they didn't know who she was, her aura of magic though easily spotted. Crouched over, she tried to blend into the background, making herself appear as small and insignificant as possible to the norms entering the platform.

Spotting a dark magical making his way determinedly towards her. The magicians as one surrounded Eshe, sweeping her up into their group, the train stopped, as one entity; they entered the train and disappeared. Once inside, they melted away. The magic emanating from her, making them feel uncomfortable.

Recovering from her battle with the demon, her sleep ended, Eshe disguised herself to appear as a magician. She'd nearly tripped over as the items in the pockets of her coat, fell out of one and climbed into the other. Halting their progress would have brought her to the attention of other's. All she could do was threaten to seal them up if they didn't slow themselves down.

Before her battle with the demon she had replenished Kingdom with silver. This time she replaced it with shimmer. She wanted to make sure to keep her two powers as separate as possible. In future any silver found in Kingdom or Novia would be redirected to Eirian and shimmer likewise directed to Kingdom.

Before she went to visit Fingerling and spoke to the Froade, she decided to go and see Guri. Since she had left Eirian to build the Glasserium, she had not been in contact. Eshe missed their discussions, the only real friend she'd ever had. Tapping, she waited. The faint noise, immediately recognised by Guri as the glass she had given to Eshe.

Astonishment at the sight before her took away the anger she still felt.

'You're,' she stuttered, 'you're all a glow.'

'I'm still getting used to it. My silver is quick to react to my commands. Shimmer however, seems to have a mind of its own. I've missed you. I truly am sorry.'

Guri sighed in annoyance at herself, as soon as she'd left Eirian and entered Kingdom she realised what a fool she'd been. Eshe hadn't destroyed her Glasserium out of spite. Intent on keeping herself apart from other magicals, she should have made her aware of the position of her home once she realised a veil was being created.

'It's amazing, the mirrors are so beautiful. I hope the king, appreciates all your efforts.'

Eshe was surprised at how big the Glasserium was. Sure that it hadn't been so large in Eirian.

As if picking up her thoughts, Guri answered, 'once again magic seems to be taking on a life of its own. As he wasn't able to tell me exactly what he needed, we decided on an ante hall, a main hall and then others off to the sides.'

Eshe laughed, 'it all sounds so efficient and a bit cold. Your mirrors have always been full of warmth and beauty. Has it changed them in any way having magicals inside?'

Guri's faced expressed sadness in both her eyes and voice.

'They are not the same. The Glasserium has grown out of all proportion to what was envisaged. I cannot stop it. Mirrors are begetting mirrors. Only in my private quarters are they still the same,' a frown crossed her face.

'What is it, what's happened?' demanded Eshe.

'Some of the inmates, have used their mirrors here, as a way to peer out of those held in Kingdom and Novia, so much so, the king has commanded all mirrors are to be locked.'

Guri stood back and waited to see if Eshe would be able to sense silver. Eshe knew as soon as she drew near, placing her hands onto the wood, it thrummed beneath them, drawn to the silver inside her. Stepping through the doorway it was even more potent. The mirrors lining the walls were wreathed in its glory. Even Guri's face showed her astonishment as they flared all reacting to her touch.

'It followed you.'

'When I created these rooms, there was a flash, seconds that's all. I thought I may have imagined it.'

Eshe smiled, 'you didn't Guri, silver is here and more than a touch of it.'

Having walked her inner sanctum to assess the extent of it, Eshe was sure that it hadn't leeched out into the halls. Closing her eyes and letting her mind clear, she stood in the centre of Guri's home and called the silver. Reluctant at first to obey her bidding, finally unable to resist her command, it left the walls and mirrors, sinking down into the earth before flowing back into her body. She blazed it out, her whole body going rigid with the force she expelled. Silver drowned every surface, Guri stood immobile as it rained down onto her and her home. As the torrent finished, Eshe searched for signs of its existence, now hidden properly, only someone like her would be able to see or find it.

Eshe hated saying goodbye, having seen a few of the mirrors that contained the magicals, she wasn't sure that it had been a good idea to use them in this way. She also sensed Guri's unease with her creation. Unlike the Glasserium in Eirian, the one in Kingdom appeared darker. The shadows in the corners deeper. Something wasn't right with the halls. Dark thoughts abounded.

'They are here?' she asked, her eyes raking the bare landscape.

Fingerlings booming laughter swiftly bringing a smile to her face. A sound she never thought to hear again. The ground began to shake, Eshe found herself faced with a half circle of trees. As soon as they had settled into position the arguments started, all vying for the best place, wanting to be noticed first. The largest rustled his branches stilling the others to silence. They had all been stunned when the call came.

'These are the famous Trip Trees. Known far and wide for their tricks, or should I say trips?' once again Fingerling boomed, laughing at his own joke.

Eshe studied them, smaller than most, their branches strong and whippy, she could see how they could easily bend them to the ground, or wind them around an unsuspecting magical. Like eager puppies all straining at the leash to find out why they were here. Eshe had to hold back a smile as their thoughts all tumbled together in their excitement.

'I have been assured by Fingerling that I can trust you.'

The trees all held their branches still. Something in her voice unsettling them.

Eshe felt their nervousness.

'I have been looking for a repository. A safe place. Somewhere I can leave magic and draw on it when needed. Fingerling has assured me that you would be able to fill that role.'

Now they really were worried. Their questions ready to burst forth.

Eshe let her silver show. It snaked over her skin, catching the sunlight, her silver eyes, making the trees shudder. In an instant she turned from silver to gold. It shimmered over her whole body, making it hard to look at her. Colours danced inside, unaware that this was Eshe's emotions showing, the trees watched in wonder at the spectacle before them. None understanding how they could help such a powerful magical.

Letting it abate, Eshe walked towards the trees, she and Fingerling both saw them flinch as she placed her hand on each of the twelve in turn. Only a small amount of shimmer left her hand to travel through their trunks and branches. It was enough. As soon as it hit their system there leaves curled and their branches retracted.

'It's a natural reaction to something foreign hitting their system,' said Fingerling.

It took a few more minutes before all the trees had regained the use of their branches and for their leaves to once again be green and verdant.

'What happened?' they cried in unison.

Eshe ignored their question.

Their top most branches caught the sun, the shimmer inside flaring before disappearing. Eshe felt for the first time that she was back in control of her destiny.

'Fingerling has told me that you are seen as mischief makers. That role should continue. As the repository of my shimmer, no one must know that you hold it within you or that it is hidden inside the land given to you by him. If I need to draw on it, he will be alerted first.'

She once again touched each in turn, lighting them up against the night sky. The shimmer would flow through their trunks and down into the earth in a continuous cycle. She read their thoughts, worried that they would be stuck in one place unable to move. Eshe laughed, telling them that they were not prisoners. They could still and should play.

Since Pictures had become a separate entity she didn't transport inside anymore. The miniature she was supposed to receive had not materialised. The Froade deciding to await the outcome of her battle with the demon. When they made their announcement, she had tried not to smile at the seriousness of their tone. She let them continue to believe that she would need one to be able to enter their domain. When in fact, she didn't.

They, like most magicals were still unsure of how much power she wielded. Because she was known as guardian, they assumed that her magic was of a lessor strength. When in fact she had as much, if not more magic at her fingertips than Bayu had ever done.

Sitting in the sunshine, she became aware of a faint tapping over her shoulder. Turning, she could make out a small blueish dot hovering in the air, like a mini portal. Exploding outwards it settled and steadied into a picture. A large owl, followed by several smaller ones flew out, shaking their feathers.

'Guardian.'

Amused at the short greeting, Eshe smiled. The tension surrounding the Froade lessoned.

Vidya offered Eshe her miniature, depicting a scene from Idona that she had asked for. Memories of happy times flooded her thoughts.

'You do know that I don't actually need it. I will though, respect your preference of my entry into your domain. Have no doubt now or in the future, that I go where I will.'

The smaller owls hissed.

'You would test my resolve?'

'Apologises. My brothers and sisters mean no offence.' Vidya broke off to glare at the owls. 'Pictures have once again begun changing. We are at a loss of what to do. It was bad enough when it created the doors into Kingdom and Novia. All pictures hanging in either realm have now become replicas of themselves. The true picture residing inside Pictures. Endless amounts of them. First it allowed magicals to enter and then travel through. Now some have even set up home in them, others holidaying. Opening doors, upsetting ancestors. A few have fallen foul of the voids between the pictures and the frames. Unable to be released. We can but hope that it may serve as a lesson to others,' Vidya gushed, her anger and distress in equal measure.

Listening to her tirade, Eshe wondered again what it was about the realms that appeared to cause all these changes. Pictures was only supposed to be a place for a magicals ancestor's to reside in, and for theirs to enter when their life cycle ended. She thought that once the magicals left Eirian the changes would stop. The same influence must be what had affected the Glasserium.

'What measures have you put in place?' she asked, still trying to make sense of their news.

'Those who can split themselves into two magicals were approached and have agreed to police the pictures and corridors, act as guides. They are calling themselves Picture Players.'

Vidya snorted in disgust at their vanity, striding about as if they were in charge and not the Froade.

'One leads and the other follows behind those they are guiding, magicals safe in between. A boon many have gained comfort from. Those who thought using them unnecessary, soon regretted their decision. Seeing Pictures as a place of fun, soon finding out that not all pictures were happy to have visitors and could become violent.'

As the other owls joined in with a litany of complaints, Eshe tuned out. What they saw as a problem, she saw as a possible solution.

'We wanted you to know about the situation and the problems it is causing,' spat Vidya, letting her anger at being ignored show in her voice.

Eshe dragged her thoughts back.

'Would you be able to create a picture, one that can recognise magic in norms, even if they have only been touched by it?'

Vidya's large eyes blinked rapidly as she searched the archives. On a dusty shelf pushed to the back she saw in her mind's eye, a small blank picture.

'What would you want it to show?'

'Blue skies and a beach.'

'Are we allowed to ask its purpose? Or is this something else we have to accept,' Vidya retorted.

Not used to explaining her reasons, but knowing she needed their help. Eshe softened her tone. Keeping her answer vague.

'I'm looking for someone.'

Vidya waited, she too could hold her nerve when required. Sensing, there was more to this request than what was being asked.

Keeping her temper, Eshe told her, 'once created, the pictures should be distributed around Novia. Not all norms will be called or attracted to them, even so, there could be an influx of them that do. This is also where I need your help. Once identified, I want them brought into Kingdom,' she smiled, trying to lessen the command in her voice.

Vidya could hear the screech from her fellow owls as their objections filled her mind. By the look on Eshe's face she also could hear their thoughts. Sure that she wouldn't make this request unless she had a good reason. Stepping aside, to save Kingdom, nearly dying in the process, was something that many had quickly chosen to forget. Decision made, she snapped the owls to attention. Eshe's grin, her reward.

'Something will have to be set up in Novia, a place where the pictures can be held. Only appearing when needed. The pictures design will be the same for all, although variables may be needed if the scene fails to attract. For the safety of Kingdom, the norms should in the first instance, only be able to gain entry into their picture.' Vidya's eyes held Eshe's, keeping her tone light, she asked, 'once inside. What will happen to them? Where will they go? Someone will have to be deployed to help them.'

CHAPTER FORTY-FIVE

Each time the witches attended a gathering or a solstice Eshe followed in the guise of a magician. To make sure that she blended in, her pockets were given strict instructions that they could play, but not to the extent that they tripped her up. Damping down her silver and shimmer was the only part of staying in the background that she found hard. Once again the magic appeared to have a mind of its own. She could feel it wanting to flare out at the most awkward of moments. Even with her strong will it had caught her unawares, transporting herself away until it settled down.

Looking out for Kateb, catching his glance. He like her followed the witches path through the throng. She knew Torrens wanted them to stop the visits, saying that it wasn't safe for them to attend without a guard. Novia was becoming a volatile place. Many dark magicals attended the solstice. Leaving them vulnerable to attack and therefore Eirian. The witches wouldn't listen, saying it was part of who and what they were.

Eshe continued to put her plans into place. The white room had shown her what the future may hold. She wasn't as spent as most thought. Stepping away was easier than she thought. She began by passing on magic to many without their knowledge. Some would come to fruition, others not. Only those special enough would be able to use it.

Her vampire guard already had silver flowing through their bodies, since living in Eirian some had also gained other clans abilities, she now added shimmer to enhance their magic even more. Only one of them would retain all, to pass along to future generations. The knowledge of who it would be, hidden, even from her.

When Torren's informed her the witches had given silver to the magicals of Eirian so that they could cross the veil. She wondered if they had somehow found out what she had been doing.

Kateb glanced quickly at the trees, his sight enabling him to see the faint blue of the portal clearly. The witches emerged, flowers adorning their hair, smiles wreathed across their faces. Eager to meet anyone and everyone. A sad looking figure followed behind them, the straw hat she wore, crammed on top of her head. The over large staff banging into the ground as if she were summoning something. Kateb, held back a smile, the sight, bringing her into sharp focus. Eshe glanced over, a wealth of meaning in her look. Her words thundering through his mind.

'My future has arrived.'

A feeling of dread crept over him. Scanning the gathering everything appeared normal. There were plenty of dark magicals in the crowd, none though, that appeared that much of a threat. Yet somehow Kateb knew that that was what her words meant. Unlike the witches who always touched and hugged people as they made their way to the summit. The guardian usually kept to herself, only on a few rare occasions had Kateb seen her interact with other magicals. Surprised to see that this time, she stopped several, touching their arms, holding their hands, making them laugh. They in turn reacted as if they knew her. Patting children's heads, stroking cheeks, Kateb had never seen her so engaged with those around her.

Finally, she moved away to stand alone, her face as if carved in stone. Turning to watch the witches Kateb saw them raise their arms holding each other's hands. Waiting for the sun to bath them in its light. Seven white clad figures passed behind them. Like dominos the witches fell one by one. For a moment he didn't understand what he was seeing as they lay on the ground unmoving. Screams rent the air. The witches were dead. Black lines covering their bodies as the dark magic moved under their skin.

The crowd moved away in fear. The culprits swallowed up. Kateb sought the guardian. Shaking, as he spotted the small black bundle, straw hat discarded, laying as if asleep. This couldn't be happening. His instincts were to run. Instead he strolled over to where she lay.

Sitting down he reached forward to pick up her hat, before gently gathering her up. A witch turned, eyebrows raised.

'The shock, it made her faint,' he told her, moving slowly away.

He didn't know what to do. Unsure, if she were dead or not. She had no outward sign of blood or black lines under her skin. Yet she appeared lifeless. His only thought to take her back through the portal. Before he entered the trees he glanced around to make sure no one was paying attention. All eyes were on what had happened. Seven had been killed while surrounded by hundreds of others. His sight enabled him to see the dark magic still woven through the crowds, a thicker patch was pushing its way through, leaving the scene of the murders.

There was nothing he could do for the witches, his only concern now what to do with Eshe. He knew that he must never enter the portal unless called to do so. Yet he couldn't just place her inside, she may not be found.

Laying her gently onto the ground. He took his book out and wrote in large letters, HELP. The witches have been killed by dark magic. The Guardian is affected. HELP ME PLEASE. His hand shook so much, he nearly tore the pages in his haste to send the message. His thoughts a jumble, he could do nothing but wait.

Magicals and norms were leaving, all subdued at what had

happened. Determined, that if anyone looked to be coming their way he would drag her through and worry about the consequences later. So concerned with keeping watch, he didn't realise the portal had faded. Now he was frightened. Eshe hadn't moved, her skin looked waxy, her eyes closed and still.

He bent close to see if he could hear or feel her breath. He kept checking the book. Nothing. Night began to fall, he pulled her cloak around her and covered her with his own.

A deep powerful voice made him jump.

'Keep still Finder. Dark witches are aboard.'

As his eyes adjusted to the dark he could make out a large shape. He reared back when a vampire's face appeared in front of him. Its fangs extended, eyes black. What really made him scared though, was its smile. The vampire looked as if it was pulling itself up taller, towering over him and Eshe, spreading his cape open like a fan. Kateb felt the air turn cooler, get darker, a mist appeared creeping first along the ground then rising as it met the trees. Aware of sounds coming closer, he stiffened hearing voices calling to each other.

'It must be somewhere over here, there's nowhere else it could be, we should have looked for it earlier.'

As if hitting a wall, the voices stopped. Then he heard them whispering.

'Something's here. Is it the portal?'

He nearly laughed when the vampire purred.

'Dinner's arrived.'

Making himself known, the magicals shrieked their terror. His hands shot out.

'Who shall I eat first,' he asked, letting them see his fangs.

Their screams rent the air, wriggling to get out of his grasp. He let them fall. Laughing, as they jumped up and ran, flinging spells over their shoulders at him. Letting his vampire settle he turned back to Kateb.

'There isn't much time. Once they get over the shock, they will return. Go back to your life, record the details as instructed.'

The portal opened, the vampire picked up Eshe and snarled.

'Do what she commanded. Write what you see. Find the one she seeks.'

Kateb made his way home. Jumping and twitching every time he heard a noise. A few days later slumped in his chair after a particularly busy day he fell into a fitful sleep. His senses brought him awake with the overwhelming feeling that someone was in his room.

'Who's there,' he shouted, trying to make his voice menacing.

'It's only me.'

Rai stepped out of the gloom, the changeling's sad face told Kateb all he needed to know.

'When we first met, I got the impression that you never left the Scriptorium.'

'I don't normally. However this is…'

'Exactly,' pronounced Kateb.

They sat in companionable silence, enjoying their wine, letting their thoughts go where they will.

'Guri told Torrens that it appears to have been a coordinated attack on the witches to coincide with the killing of the king and his sons, and whether by luck or design their deaths affected Eshe. No one knows why she cannot wake. Everyone is subdued and wary. Dark magic is still doing the rounds. Magicals are closing ranks.'

Hurrying to open the door, Kateb nearly dropped one of his precious books. His excitement held in check. A smile lit his face, his thoughts flying to Eshe, wishing he could tell her what he'd found. Writing the details for the Afsaneh to take, he couldn't help feel that it was a bit soulless. If she didn't wake, who would read about his discoveries?

Slow down, he told himself. Take a deep breath. Shrugging off his coat. He emptied his bag, placing the precious book on top of the pile. Underneath his hand he felt it move, it too was eager for him to begin.

Humming to himself, it took all of his self-control to walk away. Preparing his supper, laying the table, pouring the wine, he knew were all delaying tactics. Nevertheless he took his time, savouring the flavours, before he realised, he'd finished the bottle. Sleep wanting to claim him. His eyes closing of their own volition. He stumbled into his comfy chair, thinking, he would gather his thoughts, put them in order, then he would write. With a sigh he let his body and mind relax.

When Eshe had asked him to find the person she was looking for, letting him see the image of her face in his mind. Kateb felt sure that amongst all the norms in Novia his chances were slim to none. Like her he attended many gatherings, while searching for the witches so too did he search for the face. Since the attack he hadn't returned to the place where it had happened. Realising, that by not doing so he could be missing an opportunity, he steeled himself to attend.

Serendipity must have made him bump into her. Busy writing in his book, realising the time he gathered everything pushed it into his bag, jumped up and nearly knocked her over. In his rush to apologise, his words dried up, as her face swam into view. Nearly choking at the sight before him.

'Are you okay?' her voice was strong, her smile wide, reaching out to grab him, before he lost his balance.

Stuttering, 'it's me that should apologise. I was so engrossed. Didn't look where I was going.'

Laughing at his rush of words, she told him, 'I'm Penny. You are?'

He could do nothing but stare, as the image in his head was mirroring the face before him. 'Kateb,' he answered, with a chuckle. 'Could we sit? I feel a bit wobbly.'

'Off course.'

Penny took his arm moving him through the crowd to find a clear spot where they could sit down.

Not knowing what to say, Kateb blurted, 'is Penny short for Penelope?'

'I'm always asked that. No, I'm called Penny. Because…'

He waited. He was good at waiting.

Penny glanced down at her hands, without realising it she had been wringing them over and over while they sat.

He saw the frown and the worry flick across her eyes. Eshe had told him that if he found her, she may be conflicted. Unsure of herself. The sight she had given him allowed him to see the faint aura surrounding her. It wasn't a part of Penny as most magicals was, rather as if it stood to the side. In a flash of insight, he realised that she have must have been spell bound. Now he understood her reticence. The spell would keep her from saying anything out of place. Whereas her mind wanted to break free. The conflict inside her must be intense.

This always happens, thought Penny. Her mind became scrambled, the words wouldn't come. Her name had been given to her by the person who'd found her. A caver group were on their way out, worried, they followed her. At one point they thought she had disappeared into thin air. Then one of the group heard a low moaning sound. Apparently she then began calling out, her words jumbling together. Making no sense. Stanley who eventually found her lying curled up on the ground, thought she was in fancy dress. The dull silvery outfit she wore, dirty and torn, shredded beyond repair.

When asked her name at the hospital, for some reason he'd blurted out Penny. With no identification on her, they decided to use it until her real one was known. She remembered waiting to be discharged from the hospital. No one had come forward to claim her. She didn't know where she was going to go or do. The staff were amazing, rallying around to donate clothes for her to wear. Her biggest surprise though was finding Stanley waiting outside for her.

Smiling sheepishly, he gabbled, 'my sister has offered you a room. Until you get on your feet. Find out who you are…' He frowned as his words tailed off. 'Sorry that was a bit insensitive. I mean. Only if you want to. She would be glad of the company. Rose has cats, is that okay? You're not allergic are you?'

Penny laughed, 'thank you Stanley. You are both kind. I don't really know what to do. I feel... Lost.'

'Rose dear, do you want me to unpack these boxes? There seems to be an awful lot of them.'

Once again, Penny removed the large tabby cat who insisted on following her everywhere. If she didn't know better, she would think it was trying to talk to her.

'I didn't realise my mother had kept so much of my stuff.'

Rose, wiped her hands, making the once white towel she held, turn black.

'I suppose I ought to look through each one.'

Her defeated tone, made Penny laugh.

'Surely if you haven't looked inside them in the last ten years. You don't need to now. Why not take them to the fair, put them next to the stall. Sell them sight unseen.'

Rose looked shocked.

'You mean not even a peek. What if something amazing is hidden inside?'

Penny's look said it all.

Rose chuckled, 'let's do it. I'll ask Stanley, he'll be happy to help.'

At the sound of the bell, Penny turned, several tourists entered, eyes agog at the displays of jewellery on offer. She loved working in the shop. They mostly sold silver necklaces and rings, with the odd bracelet thrown in. All lovingly hand made by Rose.

She had tried to get Penny interested in the creative side of the business. It hadn't worked. The lump of silver Rose had given her to fashion she'd kept it in her pocket instead, rubbing it like a talisman. She began to find leaving the shop difficult, using any excuse to stay, when the tenants in the flat above moved out she pestered Rose to let her move in.

Putting the finishing touches to the table, Penny smiled to herself, this would be the first time Rose had been allowed to see the completed transformation of the flat into her home. She loved its new look, sure that Rose will be equally impressed. Hearing the outer door open, she rushed down the stairs.

'Let me take your coat. Are you ready?'

Opening the door. She stepped aside. Rose hadn't known what to expect. Everywhere had been painted a silvery grey colour. The soft furnishings mirroring the look. Something about it made her feel odd. Aware that Penny was waiting for her reaction. She forced a smile.

'It's so, so...' Lost for words, Rose's eyes caught the sight of the picture over the fireplace. 'This is really lovely,' she enthused.

'I got it from that new antique shop in the village. Once it caught my eye I had to have it.'

Penny touched the frame, her eyes closing for a second.

'I don't remember a new shop opening.'

The golden sand and bright blue sky of the picture was also making Rose feel uncomfortable. Noticing that Penny's eyes had taken on a faraway look, before she replied dreamily.

'It's where the sweet shop was before it moved.'

On her way home, Rose walked back through the village high street. There was no new antique shop. Over the next few weeks she noticed a marked change in Penny. Usually she would be fully engrossed in the activity of the shop. Customers always gravitated to her wanting her advice. Now she appeared unable to settle. Constantly looking over her shoulder, nervous and edgy. When she heard Penny snap out a comment to a customer. She knew something must be wrong.

In one part of her mind, Penny knew she was being asked questions, at the same time she heard a voice calling to her. The pull from it was getting stronger. Today, she had found it especially difficult to concentrate. Each customer breaking into her thoughts. Stopping her from honing onto the sound she could hear. Her thoughts constantly flying to her picture, the golden beach and blue skies. Sure at times she could even feel the heat of the sun on her skin.

CHAPTER FORTY-SIX

Margaret read the passage, her mind in a whirl. She had taken in so much information it felt as if her brain would explode. Closing her eyes she let her thoughts unscramble. The Afsaneh was directing her where to look, or rather who to look at. Still Margaret didn't believe what it was telling her. How could Penny be the queen? She cast her mind back to their one and only meeting. How strange she had acted, obviously nervous and on edge.

Deciding to reread the last few pages, the book was having none of it, disappearing in a cloud of silver. The desk groaning as the weight lifted.

Stepping out into the corridor, his task complete, the changeling's seat was empty. As she walked through the Scriptorium, the books shuffled themselves upright as if to stand at attention.

Elfrad and Aeryissa turned at her entrance, their mouths gaping open in amazement at the change that once again she had undergone. Her skin glowed from within, speckled like her hair and eyes with silver and shimmer, making her look ethereal. Looking in the mirror, she murmured, 'oh…'

Everyone gathered around. Their eyes locked onto Margaret. She exuded so much power and magic, none doubted that she was now the Guardian.

'I have read the Afsaneh as instructed. I won't quote it word for word,' she told them. 'To summarise the salient points. Eshe, the previous guardian, had been instructed by Bayu of what to do in the event that she didn't return from killing the demons. Eirian was to be their sanctuary. Many though, once Kingdom was discovered, wished to leave. In the end only those magicals with silver and the changelings stayed in Eirian. Living out their lives behind the veil. Safe but effectively imprisoned. We are all more than aware of the history of Kingdom and its fate when the king died. At the same time witches were killed in Novia, linked by their magic, it caused Eshe to sink into a coma, this wasn't the same as her dead sleep. This apparently was one of the failsafe's she'd put in place. As was my ascendant to taking her place. The Afsaneh was used to write the history of the changelings and magicals and to note anything to do with dark magic or anything that may affect the realms. It also tells how Eshe set out to find her lost queen. If here now Bayu would be in control of the silver we have flowing through our bodies and the shimmer that used to flow through Kingdom.'

Margaret looked at the faces all turned towards her, stunned, didn't do it justice. She could easily pick up their thoughts of disbelief.

Glancing at Elfrad, she continued, 'I was introduced to a norm. I was told Penny couldn't cope and that her picture would become a Watcher. Eshe was told to sever Bayu's links and to then spell bind her. Hoping this would deter the demons enough to allow the magicals and changelings to get safely into Eirian. Reinstating her power, would mean we have a real chance of fighting and more importantly winning.'

'Surely,' Fafnir said with exasperation, 'as the guardian, you already have all this power. Can't you take on the fight? This norm may turn out to not be the queen. What happens then?'

'If I'm right it will make her much more powerful than I can ever be.'

Raul, snorted, 'have you looked at yourself lately?'

Margaret's silver eyes raked his face. She let the silence lengthen.

'You really need to keep your emotions in check. Your vampire, is scaring everyone. The magic in you doesn't help. The silver is bright enough, the shimmer changing colour is giving everyone including me, a headache,' said Aeryissa, adding with a smile, 'I know more than most how difficult this is for you. In the meantime though, spare a thought for the rest of us.'

For the first time Margaret saw real fear directed towards her.

'I'm sorry. When I became a vampire, my heart stopped. After merging with Eshe and taking on her mantel. Once again it beats. Not in the same way. I can't really describe it. My body at the moment has a life of its own, my thoughts and it have become out of sync.'

Ever since Margaret had mentioned Penny's name, Elfrad had been racking his brains to think who she meant.

'Was she the one who wouldn't stop asking questions?'

'That's her.'

'We need to make contact with the Froade,' said Aeryissa. 'Get them to do a search of the archives and pull together her details. Fortunately we have a time line to give them which should help to narrow down the field.'

They huddled together waiting for Margaret to arrive. When she appeared, they all did a double take. Gone the vampire predator. Her skin showed no trace of silver or shimmer. Her eyes once again blue. Dressed in simple tunic and trousers. No ornamentation to denote who she was. All surprised how ordinary she looked.

Elfrad and Aeryissa had gone to great pains to advise what those coming with them should wear and how they should behave. Still though if you looked closely enough other magicals would be able to tell that they were of the same ilk. Margaret though, had somehow turned herself into a norm. Not even a faint smell of magic anywhere near her could be detected. She laughed when she saw their faces.

'I tested myself on Raul's excellent nose. I've left him trying to work out how he is unable to detect my scent.'

Their trip into Novia was twofold, find Penny and the dragon. When Margaret had spoken of Orara, Fafnir's ears had pricked up. He remembered the tales of the famous dragon who chose to subjugate herself to Bayu. Their friendship legendary. Finding Orara, meant they would also find the silver.

Margaret transported Elfrad and Fafnir. While Aeryissa transported sisters Nyx and Heng, vampires with some of the same abilities as she possessed. Crouching down at the sound of voices. The small group waited. Their senses straining to hear if anyone had noticed them arrive.

Kateb had tracked Penny to a village on the outskirts of a small town. Not wanting to draw attention to themselves. Margaret and Elfrad went to find her, while the rest went in search of the dragon. Kateb had written that Penny apart from going to gatherings never left the area. Something had been keeping her anchored to the place. It may be because this was where she was found. If not, then the silver and the dragon must be somewhere in the vicinity.

They found a bench and sat in the sunshine to wait for the shop to open. Margaret could smell the silver. It was wrapped around this valley like a collar. She breathed in its aroma, making sure not to let any of her own rise to meet it.

Opening the door its bell reminding her of another shop. Before her thoughts could take her there. She stared at Penny, shocked that it could be this easy. Elfrad whispered.

'You're unnerving her.'

'I'm sorry, you reminded me of someone I used to know. The resemblance is remarkable.'

Penny looked wary, for a moment she felt a sense of unease as a memory tried to surface.

'Could you show us some necklaces, Margaret lost one a while ago. We kept meaning to replace it, but wanted to wait until we could find something more individual.'

At Elfrad's words, her face lit up.

'I'm sure you will be able to find something in our collection. Rose, the owner of the shop is also the creator of the pieces on display. She can also make bespoke items if that is what you would prefer.'

They all turned as the bell tinkled.

'Sorry I'm late. Mum was having a moment.'

The woman who entered looked as if she had been dragged through a hedge backwards. As she spoke, she ran her hands through her wild hair which instead of helping, made matters worse. The bright yellow kaftan she wore drained the colour from her skin, making her look ill.

'Can you help these people they wish to look at the necklaces?' smiling, she told them. 'Brenda will help you with anything you want to look at.'

Turning back as she opened the door, Penny called out, 'I won't be long.'

Oblivious to the tension in the air, Brenda began opening the glass cases and drawing out items reverently laying them down onto the counter.

By the time they left the shop they had gained more than an insight into Penny's life or in Brenda's words, lack of one. It didn't take much persuasion for her to start talking. Elfrad had cast a spell making anyone wanting to enter walk away. Left in peace, they had a better understanding of what they were dealing with. Penny was a loner, she was pleasant enough, according to Brenda. Not snooty, keeping herself to herself. Didn't socialise. Although, she often went on trips. A bit of a hippy, Brenda smirked, tapping her nose. Making Margaret smile while Elfrad looked bemused.

Elfrad helped Brenda to put the jewellery back, while Margaret transported into Penny's flat above the shop. Her senses had already told her that no one was inside. Letting them flood out, she sensed no magic. Not even a whisper. Her mission to find the picture. Without it, they wouldn't be able to get Penny into Kingdom, let alone Eirian. She emerged back into the shop as Elfrad was saying his goodbyes. Brenda's eyes had a faraway look. Margaret clicked her fingers, by the time the door closed she had forgotten all about them.

Making their way to the meeting point, they were both lost in their own thoughts.

'Is it her,' asked Aeryissa, as Heng and Nyx joined them. Fafnir following closely behind.

'Definitely, she hasn't changed a bit, well not in looks, calmer in herself. I searched her flat. It isn't there.'

Elfrad chimed in, 'to get her to Eirian we're going to need it.'

Aeryissa and Margaret had the same thought, saying together, 'Damala.'

'Who's that?' asked Nyx.

Aeryissa laughed, 'our secret weapon.'

'Will the Froade allow her out, and more importantly will they allow her back afterwards?' As much as Elfrad wanted her help, he was worried that if it all went wrong she would be left in Novia.

When Margaret spoke, they all heard the determination in her voice.

'The Froade will comply. They know this is our last chance to make a difference. The Darkness has once again turned its attention to gaining entry into Pictures. That cannot happen.'

'Our luck was a little better. We spread out and so as to cover more ground. This area has an enormous concentration of silver. We think we may have found the hotspot.'

'So why are you here,' interrupted Margaret.

'Equally short in his tone of voice, Fafnir snarled, 'if you let me finish. There are dark magicals in the area. They have been digging test tunnels.'

Heng took up the story, 'I let myself blend in with the surroundings. The magicals were so busy shouting at each other. I'm not sure they would have noticed me if I had stood in front of them. They spoke of someone called Khalon.'

'Was he there?' asked Margaret, making sure to lower her tone.

'No, that I am sure about. They were scared of him and what he would do when they told him they couldn't get any further in.'

'Go back there tomorrow. Set up a camp, use it as your base. Find this tunnel. It may be our way in. I'll contact the Froade, Qiao can transport Damala here. Using her glamour she can make herself look like Brenda, Penny's assistant. We need to find that picture.'

Damala had been spending her days in Long Meadow trying to keep Megs spirits up. Since losing the baby she had become even more withdrawn. Dillon was no help. The last time he'd told her it was about time she pulled herself together. Like a she cat, she flew at him, her nails raking his face. Splitting and snarling the violence of her attack left him shaken. He'd never seen his sister lose her temper in that way before, only the intervention by her and Ammon saved him from any real injury.

Layla suggested he go off traveling for a while, let things calm down. For Damala, this made her feel even more like a spare part. Most days she was at a loss at what to do with herself, the call when it came was both unexpected and welcome.

Her senses told her she wasn't alone. Opening her eyes, two owls sat perched on a log at the base of a tree.

'You have been granted permission to leave Pictures and enter Novia, you will also be allowed to return,' they announced in unison.

Before she could ask what was going on, or say a word, Qiao appeared.

'Come on,' he yelled. 'No time to lose, we're needed.'

She felt her senses whirl, rocking backwards and forwards as they emerged.

'Qiao, wait a minute, I don't understand. Who need's us?'

A sick feeling began to wash over her, Damala covered her mouth. It had been a long time since she had been transported. As her head burst into a pounding headache, she closed her eyes and groaned.

'There was no need to bring her quite so fast Qiao.'

Lifting her head out of her hands. She looked up to see Elfrad, Aeryissa and Margaret all smiling at her.

'I thought you had been killed,' she wailed, unable to stop the tears from falling down her face.

'Drink this,' said Elfrad, thrusting a cup into her hands. She knew from experience it to be a disgusting concoction, one though, which would immediately make her feel better.

Once she got her first look at Brenda, Damala let her glamour take over, while Margaret compelled the real one. Nyx had found a derelict barn tucked at the end of a farmers field, Qiao was tasked to watch over her. His annoyance at not playing a bigger part soon abating after one look from Margaret, finding her silver eyes particularly unnerving.

Aeryissa and the vampires had left early to continue their search for the silver. Elfrad and Fafnir decided to find out who the dark magicals were feeding their information back to. Margaret, alone for once wondered the village, as she enjoyed the sunshine she thought how strange it felt to be in the realm she was born into and yet not feel any affinity with it. The changes she had gone through, had taken her on a fantastic and dangerous journey, the path she was following, pre-determined, set by others many years ago, she couldn't stop a sigh escaping.

Damala watched Penny deal with the customers, with her engaging manner all responded with warm smiles and thanks as they left clutching their boxes and bags.

'Shall we have a break? A cup of tea?'

Turning the sign round, Penny locked the door. Damala didn't know if as Brenda, she was meant to make it. Unsure what to do, she smiled.

'That's a lovey idea, shall I put the kettle on?'

Penny's answering smile was all the instruction she needed.

'What sort of pictures do you like? To hang on the walls. I like seascapes myself,' mused Damala, dunking her biscuit, catching it before it fell into her tea.

'Oh I see. Well yes, I must say, I do find those cheery. Are you thinking of buying one?'

Ignoring her question, Damala murmured, 'it has to be the right one though. One that calls to me. Making me feel that I could simply step through and onto the beach.'

Penny looked startled, she had never heard Brenda talk so fanciful before. She had always thought of her as a more practical sort of person. The mention of a beach, stirred a memory long buried. She tuned out, as her mind began searching. Brenda's voice fading into the back ground as if coming from far away.

Damala headed away from the shop, as she passed a passageway, Margaret grabbed her arm and transported them away. Not feeling so sick this time, her body adjusting to speed of movement. Nevertheless it still made her feel wobbly. Elfrad sat her down, passing her a drink, this time only water.

Holding out the glass for a refill, she told them, 'I've planted the seed. Her mind wondered and her eyes glazed over, obvious she had tuned me out.'

'How did you all get on?'

'We have found the tunnels,' said Aeryissa. 'Evidence of their progress easy to detect. Whatever failsafe's Bayu put in place, have held. As far as we could tell they have only been able to find faint veins of silver. Enough to keep them digging. But not enough for them to do any real damage with.'

Elfrad jumped in, 'I can confirm it is Khalon, Meridian's old cohort who is directing the new searches. He must have already been in Novia when the Darkness was released.'

Aeryissa added, 'Heng and Nyx are to follow their progress and report back.'

As she finished speaking Fafnir appeared. His satisfied smile lighting up his face.

'I've found her. Well not physically. But I'm pretty sure I know where she is. Orara.'

Entering the shop, the first thing she saw was Penny standing by the counter lost in her own thoughts.

'Good morning.'

She jumped as if scalded. Looking so startled, Damala thought her glamour had worn off.

'Sorry Brenda, my minds all over the place. Shall we start again? Good morning. I've unpacked the delivery but haven't yet put it away. Would you mind doing that for me? I have to go out.'

Before she had a chance to reply Penny once again lost herself in her thoughts. Shaking herself like a dog, she half-heartedly smiled.

'I'm doing it again aren't I? Rose has my picture, apparently I asked her to store it. I've been racking my brains as to why.'

Pretending not to know what she was talking about, she raised her eyebrows in enquiry

'The seascape, Brenda. I have one. If I can find it you can have it. Drove me crazy last night, every time I dropped off to sleep. My mind kept coming back to it.'

Without further ado she opened the door and left. Damala didn't have a chance to sort the delivery, an influx of customers kept her busy. She found herself actually enjoying selling things. Getting as much pleasure from it as those that bought the jewellery. Finally getting a break she decided to make a cup of tea, turning away from the back of the shop, on hearing the bell ping. She stopped dead on seeing Penny's face. Clutching a picture to her chest as if it was a life preserver.

'I found it,' she blurted, looking uncomfortable.

Damala could see that now she had a hold of it, she was reluctant to let it go. That was a good sign. Even as a Watcher it should still be tied to her. Penny unwrapped the brown paper, falling open the picture appeared to shine. The sky bright blue, the sandy beach inviting. Small waves could be seen breaking on the shore. Three beach huts in the distance. Doors all closed.

'I'm not sure...'

Penny wiped her hand over the frame and onto the picture, stroking the glass, her eyes glazing over. Damala barked out, breaking her trance.

'It's nice. Mind you I prefer a bit more than some old huts and a bit of beach. A boat or two would be nice.'

Once again Margaret was waiting, whisking Damala away as soon as she left the shop. No one wanted to speak until Fafnir and Aeryissa returned.

Nyx and Heng were on tender hooks ready to blurt out what they had found as soon as they entered the camp. Elfrad had grown weary of keeping them in check. Finishing their meal, calling for lights as the darkness descended. All heard Fafnir's groan as he and Aeryissa emerged. Waiting for them to eat and drink put them on edge, all wanting to speak. Margaret indicated that Damala should go first.

'Penny found her picture. I'm glad to say she and it are still attached to each other. The bond is still there. However, when the Froade releases the watcher and turns it into a portal again, how will we get her to agree to enter it?'

Elfrad added, 'plus it will take her into Kingdom and we need her in Eirian.'

'We're going to have to drag her through,' said Margaret. 'We haven't got the luxury of waiting. Elfrad you will have to reprise your old persona as a greeter.'

'What do I do with her once in the picture? The Darkness will know we are there as soon as we open the door into Kingdom.'

'Eadulf may be able to help. We need a distraction.'

Fafnir announced with a flourish, 'we have found Orara, once we went deeper I picked up her dragon scent. We didn't enter the cave. We both also felt a strong pull from the silver stored with her.

It's no good trying to wake her until we are sure that Bayu is safe in Eirian.'

'We too have been busy,' chimed in Heng and Nyx together. 'Dark magicals have been gathering a few miles from here. We picked up their sent, easy enough as there are so many of them. Nyx compelled a couple. They were travelling like many others who had heard rumours of a large cache of special magic which is to be distributed to those lucky enough to be thought worthy.'

Deep in the confines of his home Eadulf and Guri dozed in companionable silence as Purity watched over them, safe inside the inner sanctum, all three were conscious that what was once thought of as their sanctuary, had now become their prison.

Jerking awake. A voice Eadulf never thought to hear again, whispered in his head.

Guri opened her eyes, 'what's wrong?' she mouthed.

Purity picking up tension from both of them moved closer.

Eadulf held up his hand, cocking his head as he listened. Honing in on the voice he was sure he could hear.

'Hello old friend.'

'Aeryissa,' cried Eadulf. 'The others? Are they with you? Or…'

She chuckled, 'all are well. Margaret and Elfrad both send their regards. I have a task for you. It will be dangerous. Elfrad is going to open a door into Kingdom. The Darkness will react. I need a distraction so that I can transport him and the magical with him away.'

'Away where?' asked Eadulf, shaking his head at Guri as she waved her hands in front of his face, wanting him to explain what was happening.

'Who is this magical?'

'Bayu. Speak to Guri, she will tell you all about her. Once we are all in place, Margaret or I will send the signal. I have linked all three of us together.'

'What is it? What's happened?' demanded Guri, hating to be left out of the most exciting thing to happen to them in ages.

Eadulf was still processing the fact that his friends were alive and well. Although he had agreed to help, he was unsure how he was going to achieve it. His mind already thinking of what he could do that would be enough to attract the Darkness's attention for long enough for Aeryissa's plan to work.

'What is happening?'

'Elfrad is bringing someone into Kingdom she said you know her.'

'Well don't stand there looking gormless, who is she?'

'Bayu.'

Guri sank down into her chair, her thoughts turned inward to the last time she had spoken to Eshe, still convinced that the queen was out there somewhere. It seems her instincts were correct after all.

They had talked long into the night trying to come up with a plan that they thought at least had a chance of working. It wasn't enough to emerge shouting. "Here I am. Come and get me."

Purity had in the end come up with the solution. Fed up with their bickering about who was going to go, she snapped.

'If large glass shards are placed as far afield as possible, then in your glass form you project your reflection towards them, it will give the impression of an army of glass magicals. The Darkness will come.'

CHAPTER FORTY-SEVEN

Elfrad opened the door to the shop as Margaret transported into the flat above. The picture hung in pride of place over the mantel piece. Grabbing it, she transported into the shop as Penny emerged from the back. Elfrad had changed the sign on the door to say closed.

'How can I help? What are you doing with that? How did you…?'

Before she could continue, Margaret propped the picture up against the wall, tapping the frame, it immediately began to grow. Elfrad grabbed Penny's arm and pulled her towards it.

'Get off me. What are you doing? Who are you? Help. Help.'

Elfrad didn't hesitate, he walked towards the picture as if it was a normal doorway. Penny tried to wrench herself away, he tightened his grip.

Once they disappeared inside, Margaret sent her signal to the Froade. They confirmed that Elfrad and Penny were indeed on the beach. The picture would now be destroyed. Without further ado, it crumbled away to nothing. Transporting away, Margaret grabbed Brenda, leaving her rocking on her feet from the speed of their travel. Damala's glamour already starting to fade.

Aeryissa waited for Eadulf's signal telling her it was safe to enter

Kingdom. Penny had flung herself down onto the beach, sobbing and wailing. He'd tried talking, now back to being a Bomani, he found it hard to be sympathetic, his patience thin. Deciding to leave her to settle, she couldn't after all go anywhere. Thinking that he may have to gag her if she didn't stop her noise by the time they were ready to open the doors.

Guri ran low to the ground, Kingdom had an eerie feel. Nothing stirred. No sounds rent the air. A dead place. As she ran she scattered the shards, the spell she cast fixing her image, ready to flare up when called. Pausing, she heard a sound like angry bees off in the distance getting closer.

Opening the link between them all, she whispered, 'it's coming.'

Moving slowly, she began changing into her glass self. The weak sun unable to compete with her dazzling shine. Eadulf had remembered a spell they'd used in their early days of magic shows, sure he could adapt it to enhance even more the depth of colours held within her glass body.

As the last part of the spell left Guri's mouth the shards woke. Standing before her was a glass army, or at least what appeared to be. The Darkness circled. Guri held her ground.

'Now,' she told Aeryissa.

Hearing a shout of, 'open the door,' Elfrad wove the spell before kicking the door inwards, sending Penny into a paroxysm of screaming. Drawing one of his swords, she instantly shut up. Holding her arm he marched her inside. The door in front of them had also to be opened. This is why they needed the distraction. Aeryissa's magic could break the seal. But it wouldn't be instant. Penny hung limp, all the fight had going out of her. Elfrad strained to listen.

Aeryissa could hear and smell the Darkness, its drone and foul stench both now a part of Kingdom's fabric. Conscious, she had to work quickly before it picked up the scent of silver otherwise no matter what diversion Guri was attempting, it wouldn't be enough to stop it coming for her.

Guri stood in the maelstrom of the Darkness. Its tendrils snaking their way towards the various shards dotted around.

Aeryissa could feel the door vibrating through her hands. The seals used to keep it closed, fighting her all the way. At last her magic began to override their grip. She could feel the difference in the wood each time another breech occurred.

'It's hesitating. It may have picked up your scent. Hurry,' Guri's voice trembled, as the Darkness swooped towards her.

Elfrad pulled the door inwards, Aeryissa smiled in greeting, forgetting that her vampire was on show. Penny screamed. The Darkness halted its attack.

Guri gathered herself, glass shards exploded from her body making it appear as if silver rain was falling onto Kingdom. The Darkness's attention was once more directed towards her. In a frenzy it dived to attack, boiling and writhing, its tendrils searching for the treasure that had already begun to sink into the earth. Before she had a chance to realise what was happening, Margaret scooped her up and dumped her unceremoniously in front of Eadulf and Purity before promptly disappearing. At the same time, Aeryissa transported Penny and Elfrad before the Darkness realised that what it sought, had gone.

'I felt the shift,' snapped Aeryissa, 'why take the risk?' her annoyance showing in her voice.

Margaret ignored her tone and her question, she had eyes only for Penny curled up on a chair, her eyes roaming between the pair of them.

Seeing that she wasn't going to explain, Aeryissa changed the subject.

'Fafnir has sent word that they have broken through.' Nodding at Penny she added, 'before you reinstate her magic we should make sure that the silver she will need, can in fact be harvested.'

As soon as Margaret emerged at the tunnel entrance, her eyes immediately began to turn, the blue fading as silver and gold took over, even the lights they'd conjured were unable to match her eyes for brightness. The deeper they walked inside, the more they shone. Aeryissa also felt herself begin to change, noticing how her skin glowed and speckled the nearer to the mother lode they got. Fafnir, Heng and Nyx all stared as the two vampires walked into view. Predators they maybe, but all three thought how beautiful they both looked. Aeryissa and Margaret both smiled, picking up their thoughts breaking the tension between them.

'She's this way,' said Fafnir, his excitement palpable.

The dragon was magnificent, even with her scales dulled by years of being unused and underground. Her wings lay folded against her body while her head hung between her front legs. Eyes tightly closed, no movement to show whether Orara was alive or dead. All of them now felt the silver beneath their feet. Its energy calling to each of them in varying degrees.

The dragon's neck was circled by a metal collar, her legs encased in bands equally as thick. Over her wings longer chains had been slung weighing them down, pressing them tight against her body. Margaret was at a loss, the Afsaneh had made no mention of what type of spell had been used to contain Orara. If she used the wrong one to reverse it, she could instead kill her. One thing the book made clear though, if they wanted to access the silver, Orara had to be woken.

Moving to the back of the cave, Margaret sat down with her back to the wall needing time to let her mind settle. Guardian she may be, but as yet she had no idea how much power she could wield. Changed once again, she hadn't had time to get used what it really meant. Her eyes detected movement. Standing before her was a black haze. Slowly it coalesced together and a magical began to emerge. She felt her body engulfed. A heaviness stole through her limbs, weighing her down. Doors opened and closed in her mind before she could catch a glimpse of what lay in side. Warnings given. Fail safes reiterated. Memories lodged with her own, mixing together becoming joined. One stayed hidden, out of sight. Her body thrummed with the pull of the silver beneath her, while shimmer danced through her body like a summer sun. Sure she must have blacked out, Margaret shook her head to clear her thoughts. Standing with purpose, she brushed down her clothes.

Laying her hands onto the dragon's side she commanded.

'I am the Guardian and you will wake for me.'

Touching each link in the chains she spoke words in a language none of them had ever heard before. Standing back as the metal began to glow, Margaret lifted her clasped hands, as she wrenched them apart, the chains snapped, falling from Orara to settle on the ground before disappearing beneath the surface. At first nothing happened. Then Fafnir noticed a slight twitch. Her wings lifted and settled. Small puffs of air blew from her nose. A faint glimmer of silver flashed under her scales.

'Wake Orara, the Guardian commands you.'

The ground shook as the dragon tried to stand. Her legs going from under her. Too long in one position had stiffened her joints. Finally her eyes opened fully. Fafnir stepped into her line of sight, reassuring her that all was well. Recognising Margaret's words if not her countenance, Orara forced her eyes open.

'She needs to be in her magical form,' said Fafnir. 'Her silver is all but depleted. If you could…'

Margaret stepped forward, Orara knew instinctively what she carried within her. Allowing her into her mind, she only flinched once as the sealed door locked so long ago was opened. Laying her hand over Bayu's hand print, she felt it pulse beneath hers making her catch her

One moment Orara's dragon filled the cave, the next she stood in front of them in her magical form. Fafnir catching her as she swayed. Sitting her down, Margaret approached, kneeing down she clasped Orara's hands. Letting silver flow between them. Laying her gently down, she turned to Fafnir.

'When she wakes, make sure she stays in her magical form. Her body needs to repair its self and for her to get her strength back.'

All four vampires snarled, fangs extended, ready to pounce. The air shifted as Damala and Qiao emerged.

'What are you doing here?' shouted Aeryissa, letting her vampire recede.

'You forgot about us,' retorted Qiao. 'We've been stuck here since you left. I honed in on your transports. The Froade won't let me transport back into Pictures.'

Both Aeryissa and Margaret felt bad, after asking for their help they had both forgotten their friends in their eagerness to get Penny into Eirian.

'I'm. We're sorry,' smiled Margaret, wanting to make amends.

'It's been a bit tricky,' said Damala. 'We had to hide. After you left, several dark magicals arrived in the village. Some went to the shop, Qiao transported into the flat upstairs to listen in. They questioned Brenda, fortunately they soon got fed up with her chatter. A few have left, the others though, seem set to stay.'

'Khalon,' snapped Qiao. 'Remember him, well I also heard him speaking about how he is near to finding what he seeks.'

Margaret took Qiao's hand, the power moving under her skin, a warning, giving him no choice other than to calm down.

'I will contact the Froade.'

'Can't we come with you? I know you're not staying here. Kingdom is dead. Where do you go?'

A slight pressure and Qiao stilled. Placing her other hand on top of his. Margaret told him, 'the Froade have opened the way. Go now. Thank you. I'm sorry…'

Damala chuckled, 'don't apologise it's been the best of times. You cannot imagine how bored we've been. That's why Qiao's cross. That our adventures are over.'

Scowling at her words. He pulled free from Margaret, touched Damala's shoulder and transported them away.

Fingerling clapped his hands bringing the meeting to order. Kebale and Fafnir the last to stop talking earning them a tap on their heads.

Lype and Raul loped into the hall, changing from their wolf form before sitting down. Vedi and Bena had left Bayu asleep, the door sealed, sitting between Heng and Nyx they listened avidly as they told them about Novia. Aeryissa, Margaret and Elfrad moved away from their huddle in the corner drew out chairs and sat down.

'Now that we have found the silver,' said Fingerling, 'it's time to reverse the spells that bind her.'

Vedi spoke up, 'she's skittish. Jumping at anything and everything.'

Bena adding, 'I'm sure though part of her recognises... I mean, sometimes it seems as if she is totally aware of where she is and understands that we are magical. Then she'll go blank again.'

'We have another problem, when I read the Afsaneh it didn't state which spells were used. The separation of her silver was done first, then she was spell bound. I have searched Eshe's memories. She cast them, they should be there. Yet, each time I think I have found them, they slide away. To stop her reversing them, Bayu must have added a lock somewhere within the spells.'

'The Bodleian?' suggested Elfrad, 'they must surely be able to find them.'

'Eirian has faded from their memories. The Scriptorium is different from other libraries. Bringing them here, letting them loose inside may not solve the problem.'

'If he won't let you in. You will simply have to do it by force,' muttered Fingerling.

'Can you do it?' asked Aeryissa, 'more importantly, will he survive if you do?'

'I'm lost,' said Elfrad, 'what are you talking about?'

'Mind walking,' said Kebale.

Fafnir explained, 'It was a little known skill on Tarian. Only used once to my knowledge, when our history was removed from the minds of our scribes and placed inside a token. Many never recovered.'

'We have no choice,' Fingerling stated firmly.

Margaret entered Bayu's room. This time when she sat at the desk, it welcomed her like an old friend. Letting her mind's eye see into the books that surrounded her, she searched for the one that would give her the best chance of making contact. Pushed to the back a small blue book waited. Wanting to jump onto the desk in its eagerness to be called. Margaret's inner eye had passed over it on her first glance. Drawn back, in her mind she picked it up, flicked open the pages and saw them fill with words. Snapping her eyes open, the book pushed its way to the front of the shelf and fell onto the desk. Margaret felt sure she heard it sigh. Placing her hands on its cover, she let go and entered the book, it tingled as she walked through its pages. Its excitement palpable. Wanting to please her.

'Quick, somethings happening, all the books are moving, quick, come on,' shouted Henty, leaving the room.

Flinders could now hear others calling out, the fear in their voices evident. They stood mouths agape watching as the books took flight. Rearranging themselves, before a few seconds later flying again across the room. As if changing their mind about where they preferred to sit.

'Stop them Flinders,' cried Narrabri.

'It's not only this library,' shouted Gerringong. 'All the others are acting the same, it must be dark magic.'

A small blue book emerged from the maelstrom above them, floating down to land at their feet. None dare move. Flinders, as leader, knew he must take charge but was at a loss at what to do. Before he could act, the book opened showing its middle, hands appeared, then a head. Margaret pulled herself out, smiling at the worried faces before her.

'I think I prefer transporting,' she chuckled, as the book disappeared.

Flinders found his voice, 'how, what are you doing here. We thought you were...'

'Dead,' chuckled Margaret. 'Been there, done that.'

None of the Bodleian appreciated her humour, angry instead, that she had caused so much mayhem.

'Why didn't you transport. How have you managed to travel through a book?' snapped Flinders.

Ignoring his questions, Margaret clapped her hands, commanding, 'go back to your rightful places.'

They looked on in astonishment as the books began once again changing places, making the Bodleian even angrier at this interference in their domain.

'Sit.'

Margaret ignored the dark looks thrown her way.

'I need some information. Which I believe you personally hold. What I require isn't inside your physical books.'

Letting her words sink in, Margaret was still unsure if they would know what she meant. She saw Flinders eyes widen as realisation dawned.

'How can you... You're not powerful enough... You can't...'

'What does she mean,' demanded Narrabri.

All eyes turned to Henty, as she announced, 'she's talking about a mind walk.'

Margaret sat back and let them bring the subject to the fore.

'What are you talking about,' shouted Narrabri, the fear straining his voice.

'You can't,' retorted Gerringong.

'What is it you think we know,' Flinders finally asked.

Margaret was fully aware that she could take what she needed with or without their permission.

'It would take too long to explain everything that has happened since we escaped from the Darkness. I believe that you have knowledge hidden deep inside you that could help save Kingdom.'

Deciding that unless she showed them her true form they would remain unconvinced. Yes, she could force her way in. As in most things though, acceptance, went along way to easing the path taken. Her vampire as the dominant part of her, flared. The Bodleian had seen plenty of vampires before, their reaction stayed muted. Then silver and shimmer fought to cover her skin. Her eyes first blue, then gold, before turning to silver. Magic crackled around her like lightening in a dark sky. The glow lighting up the room, the books sighing, as it touched their spines. The Bodleian felt it through the soles of their feet. Vampire, Norm, Magical none of those words could describe what they were seeing before them.

Letting it all abate, Margaret once again, waited. Henty was the first to find her voice

'You can search me.'

'Thank you for your offer. As leader of the Bodleian, it's Flinders I will have to search.'

Resigned to the fact, his smile more of a grimace, as he waited for her to pounce.

'I understand. Do what you have to.'

'Can we stay?'

Henty looked at the others for support.

Flinders nerves were stretched taut. Margaret looked so innocuous sitting in front of him. The fact that she would soon be walking through his mind, he found hard to take in. He closed his eyes, willing his legs to stop shaking. Feeling comfort as Henty pulled his hand between hers.

With no idea if what she was going to attempt would work. She imagined his mind like a set of rooms. Finding the door that would open the corridor between them. Unaware that she was turning her head from side to side. There, she'd found it. Locking her thoughts on opening the door, she let go.

The Bodleian all gasped as she disappeared. Flinders groaned as his body went limp. Henty still holding his hand placed her other over the top, crooning to him like a mother to a child. Margaret was astonished to find herself actually inside Flinders mind. Orientating herself, she followed the passage towards a door marked with runes. This should open into a corridor. Each room off it would have to be searched, how many there would be, she had no idea. She could feel her impatience start to build, her vampire pushing to show itself.

Unsure what she was looking for, she had rummaged in Flinders mind with no thought to how it may make him feel. Aware of a low keening, she let herself settle. As she calmed, so did Flinders mind.

Like a light bulb moment, she raced back along the corridor, the first room she had entered had been from his childhood. That's what she'd overlooked, the Afsaneh was a, "Once Upon a Time Book." In Novia this would be a fairy story, a tale, not real. The door wouldn't budge.

Speaking gently, she told him, 'Flinders, I'm sorry for the mess. I will make it right before I leave. Now though, I need you to trust me. Open the door.'

Margaret didn't want to force it, if she did she would rip his mind apart, knowing though, that if he didn't or couldn't comply she would have to. The door swung open. Unlike when she'd entered earlier, now every item in the room trembled as her gaze swept over them.

Something was different, moved. The picture she was seeing wasn't the same. Flinders mind was still trying to stop her finding what she needed. Closing her eyes she thought back to when she had first opened the door. The books and toys still adorned the shelves, clothes piled in a heap on the floor in the corner. That's it, the clothes. Earlier they had been on top of a small wooden chest not on the floor. Margaret scanned each corner of the room. It had to be here. Then she noticed that the bookshelf behind the door, wasn't lying flat against the wall anymore. Looking behind it she was surprised to find the chest had elongated and flattened itself to slide between. Pulling the shelves away, the chest popped back to its original shape and made a run for it.

Margaret was quicker, holding it down as it tried to wrench itself from her grasp. With no idea how she knew what it contained, she lifted the lid and let the whispers out. Their scratchy sound filled the room. Each time she honed onto one, it became so faint even with her vampire and Lobe hearing she couldn't decipher the words. The whispers surrounded her, taunting her hearing. Knowing for Flinders sake she must remain calm. Ignoring them, as they butted against each other mixing up their words. Making it even harder to understand what they were saying. Breathing slowly and deeply she let them come to her. They fell on her like rain. Sinking into her skin. Each one sighing as it disappeared inside her. A picture began to emerge. The details of the spells used long ago taking shape.

Making sure not to withdraw from Flinders too quickly. Remembering her promise. She walked the corridors of his mind, scattering silver droplets, healing him, making good the damage she'd caused.

'Take care of him Henty.'

Before she could reply, Margaret dived into her book and disappeared. Rushing through, no time to waste, she exploded back out.

'For the severance spell to work the silver has to be directed to a repository, apparently this is me,' announced Margaret.

'How will that work?' Elfrad asked, the concern on his face mirrored by Aeryissa.

Fingerling explained, 'as Guardian, Margaret will be able, if she wants to, use, control and call every bit of silver there is. To all intents and purposes she already is the repository. The silver will need someone to link with until Bayu can take over.'

Everyone waited on tender hooks, as the last words left her mouth, it took all her strength to keep the silver under the earth. Kebale roared as he felt it move beneath him. While Raul and Lype changed into their wolf form and howled. Bena and Vedi, clutched Elfrad's arms, much to his annoyance. Their claw like hands digging into his skin as they screeched their fright. The only changeling unconcerned was Fafnir as for a brief second silver flared across his body. Quickly dying down as he forced his changeling to stay inside him. Fingerling's trunk turned silver, while Aeryissa's vampire flared. Margaret, the one with all the power, literally at her feet, the only one not to be affected.

Bena and Vedi collected Penny, she trembled when all eyes turned towards her.

'Please do not be afraid. No one here wishes you any harm,' said Margaret gently.

'If you really mean that, then let me go.'

Her eyes widened to see a tree inside the hall, its branches pressed against the high domed roof. Lype and Raul changed back to their magical forms. Penny's scream echoed around the hall.

At Fafnir's scowl they both mouthed, 'sorry.'

Margaret ignored Penny's wailing. If the spell to reverse the binding works, then Bayu should emerge. Taking a deep breath in, she grabbed Penny's head between her hands.

'Quiet.'

Once again speaking in a language none of them understood, Margaret began chanting. The explosion of power knocked them all off their feet. Fingerling's roots bursting through the floor to hold them down, all could feel the shockwaves nudging them as they slowly dissipated.

'Where did she go?' asked Elfrad, his ears still ringing.

Margaret and Aeryissa used their vampire and Lobe skills in tandem, both couldn't detect any trace of the queen anywhere in Eirian.

Fafnir was the first to feel it. Detecting the scent of another dragon, he walked outside, the others quickly following. Now released from her bonds, silver hers to command, all traces of Penny had gone. Bayu was now clad head to toe in clothes made of silver cloth. The runes running across her coat, speckled with shimmer. Her hair shone with silver beads woven into its length. The sword she held aloft, caught the sunshine, reflecting the silver and shimmer it contained. Her boots studded with lethal barbs tipped with silver, their points eager to sink into her prey. Bayu walked with purpose towards them, her smile genuine.

'Sorry to leave so quickly. As soon as you released my bonds, the shift would have started rippling out into other realms. The silver Orara was guarding, had to be secured. We have a war to fight, Darkness or demon it makes no difference. I'm going to destroy them all.'

CHAPTER FORTY-EIGHT

Used to being in command, Aeryissa and Margaret both found it strange to be taking second place to Bayu. Fingerling the last to arrive, bowed his branches to her in deference.

'For now we have to put any thoughts of rescuing Kingdom on hold. The Darkness that covers it, is not the real threat.' Letting her words sink in, she asked, 'what do any of you know about the Soul Lost land?'

Margaret answered, 'That Athanasia was duped into creating it, then was betrayed and taken prisoner'.

'There was a time when demons walked the realms,' explained Bayu. 'They loved mayhem and conflict. Fighting amongst themselves as much as with anyone else. None could be trusted. Some magicals used them to threaten anyone they were having problems with. After a while the demons took their actions further, whether asked to or not. Using dark magic and violence against their adversary's. Caught, they were severely punished or killed. It didn't stop them, in fact, it made them worse. Resentment set in. When the Soul Lost land was created, it was supposed to be a realm, in the same way as Kingdom and Eirian are. Something happened, perhaps the vortex created was too strong, or the spells weren't strong enough to hold it open. The void closed, the land created gone. Somewhere below it must still exist. Demons may no longer walk the realms, yet we all know that they have and are still being conjured if only in their shadow form.'

'How do we find this land if it is buried?' snarled Aeryissa. 'And stop whoever controls it.'

'When it disappeared, the area was scanned many times to find an entrance. Nothing was found. If the realm has survived, traps may have been put in place to stop anyone burrowing beneath the earth to find it. Athanasia like me, is an ancient. Somewhere inside the demons lair, she will still be alive.'

'Surely those who tricked her are long dead?' asked Elfrad, confused that someone with so much powerful magic hadn't been able to escape.

Aeryissa stated, 'when the Darkness chased us across Kingdom. It was obvious that it did so because of the silver we hold inside of us. How would it have known that we have it? Or that its power even exists? Unless someone in there is controlling it and holds the knowledge of its existence.'

Bayu heard the frustration in their voices and saw it in the faces turned towards her. She feared that, if not a prisoner, then Athanasia must be in control as she had threatened to do.

Vidya had been resistant at first to the releasing of magicals from Pictures. Bayu brooked no opposition. She transported, taking Margaret and Elfrad with her, setting off all their alarms. The sirens and bells so loud in their panic, everyone's ears rang for days afterwards. The Froade's inner sanctum had never been breached in this way before. When the door crashed open Vidya and her sisters and brothers thought the Darkness had found its way in. Shocked and surprised to see Margaret and Elfrad stood beside a magical they didn't at first recognise.

'Quiet,' Bayu shouted, as the owls all began to speak at once.

'I never thought to see... I what...'

'Sit down Vidya, sorry for the dramatic entrance. Time is of the essence.' Clapping her hands Bayu shouted, 'all is well.'

Immediately the alarms and bells stopped their racket. Turning to Margaret and Elfrad, she told them, 'find who we need, take them back to Eirian. I'm going to stay here for a while. Now that we are all linked, let me know when everyone is in place and I shall return.'

Margaret closed the door, unsure where to find those they needed in the many labyrinths of Pictures. Before they had taken a step, a player appeared.

'I'm Fy-Finn. Vidya has asked me to help make your task quicker.'

Cian knew she was there before the knock came on the door. Wrenching it open, he couldn't stop a gasp escaping. Margaret shone. Sensing that once again she was being drawn even further along a different path to him. When she spoke, he could hear the authority in her voice.

'We need your help.'

Elfrad stepped through the door followed by Lefu and Harsha as several others filled the corridor.

The Alvie missed the trees, the ones in Pictures weren't the same, shadow trees they called them. They spent more time with their friends the Fae, whose dragons also missed the freedom of Kingdom. The Froade had set up areas where they could fly and stretch their wings but it wasn't the same. Restrictions on where they could go were in place for them as they were for everyone. With Pictures being so overcrowded space was at a premium.

Fy-Finn wobbled, trying to keep on her feet. She had never transported before, sure that Vidya hadn't meant this mode of travel when she'd suggested her help.

'What's happened to you? Right old rag tag bunch you all look.'
'Elfrad!!'

Tairlaw bounced over, hugging him before he could say another word.

'No one was sure if you were alive or dead. It's so good to see you.'

'Put him down,' laughed Hafren, 'you're embarrassing him.'

Mercia hearing all the kerfuffle raced over. Elfrad was squeezed into another hug, at this rate he thought, there'll be nothing left of me.

'As you see I'm alive, so is Aeryissa and... Well see for yourselves.'

They all looked at Margaret in wonder. All had seen her as a norm and changed into a vampire. None understood how she had become the creature now standing before them. Fairy dust and shimmer hovered above her skin, before sinking underneath and reappearing again. Blue, silver or gold eyes none could tell, the black of her vampire dulled by their glints. None doubted the power emanating from her, all surprised at how her voice had taken on a resonance that reached into their very beings, drawing them to her.

'Gather your clans, we need your help,' the voice of Margaret told them, as the Guardian held their gaze.

Qiao had heard the news that magicals were leaving Pictures. Thinking at first it was wishful thinking, he knew how bored they all were. Imprisoned yet not in prison.

Picking up her trail, emerging in haste he bumped into Zekia's dragon, landing on his back he groaned as his head struck the ground. Margaret leant down and heaved him upright.

'I hadn't forgotten you. Your job is to start taking everyone who is ready back to Eirian. Don't tell them where they're going. Aeryissa will explain once they get there. Lock on to her signal.'

Rubbing his head, he winked. Making her blink in surprise.

'I won't let you down,' he laughed, to see her for once caught out.

To Fy-Finn, she said, 'we need to find the seekers and the elementals next.'

Elfrad had to stop a smirk, as she tried to stop Margaret from touching her.

From high up above, Orev could see movement in the field

below. Magicals were walking across the picture, this was unusual in itself. This area had been designated for the Kaimi's use. Falk and Gawain had also noticed. Then they spotted Usoa and Palamo walking to meet whoever had entered their lands.

Folding their wings all three landed together. Changing as they did so into their magical forms. Falk was the first to spot Elfrad. Palamo and Usoa were talking to a magical they vaguely recognised.

Margaret turned at their approach, all three stopped dead. Their words of greeting dying in their mouths. Surprised and glad to see that Elfrad was still alive, was nothing compared to their shock at seeing the changes that had happened to her. Instinctively they knew she held more than just their clan abilities inside her.

'It's good to see you all,' said Elfrad breaking the silence.

'We need you.'

Each nodded their heads in acknowledgment, even though they had no idea what Margaret meant.

'Gather your clan. Qiao will come to transport you. Aeryissa is waiting. She will explain.'

Fy-Finn held herself ready, fixing the position of the Hecate clan in her mind. As soon as Margaret touched her they transported.

Witches and elementals lay on the grass looking up at the sky. A few on their broomsticks, hovered mid-air, enjoying the sunshine. All wishing they could be somewhere else, other than in this false realm. The elemental side of the clan especially felt trapped. Their extra skills could not be used. The Froade adamant they would not let the balance inside Pictures be thrown into chaos by them playing with the elements.

Reacting to the ripple in the air, the witches not only stunned to see them still alive, they all felt the pull of their magic as it flowed through Margaret. Always hard to get a word in edgeways with a witch at the best of times. Seeing the two of them again after so long, all their questions poured out.

Fy-Finn tried hard to keep a straight face. Not only were the witches firing questions at Margaret and Elfrad, but also amongst themselves, all wondering how they'd survived, the changes in Margaret and why are they here? Realising that both were staying silent, the witches began to quieten down.

'We know you all want answers. We don't have time for explanations. Kingdom is still in the thrall of the Darkness. We have another enemy to fight before we can release it from its grip. We have come to take those with elemental skills back with us.'

'What about us?' the other witches retorted.

'Why can't we help? We may not have their skills, but we're...' Sansu tailed off, unsure what extra skills, they could bring to the fight.

Elfrad glanced at Margaret, she too could see their resolve, and their boredom. Left behind, the Froade wouldn't be happy if they started causing problems.

'Who's left?'

'Only the wizards,' explained Elfrad. 'The Scotts are gathering the Lobes and Lens who are willing to come. Keekle got wind of what is happening and has already taken it upon himself to organise the magician's ready for transportation.'

'Do you want me to go alone to speak to them?' asked Margaret, knowing that confronting them may be difficult for him.

Elfrad shook his head, 'not all wizards have turned. I know that.'

'If you're sure.'

Before they were allowed to roam free all wizards including the Bomani, had to be incarcerated away from the other magicals. Listening to their complaints, Vidya told them crossly, it wasn't her fault that out of all clans, the wizards were the only ones to have so many turn towards dark magic.

Having read the Afsaneh, Margaret knew that it wasn't something that was only happening now. It had always been so. Once the split between wizard and warrior took place it became more evident that some couldn't be trusted.

'We thought you were dead,' cried Herwig.

'I've heard that a lot today,' muttered Elfrad.

'We went a bit mad when we were released. The Froade weren't best pleased, our cats caused a bit of damage. Now though we have explored, talked ourselves silly and spend our days picking fights with each other to relieve the boredom.' Sighing she added, 'please say you've come to rescue us? Take us back to Kingdom.'

Margaret and Fy-Finn were ignored by the wizards. They had had their fill of players telling them what to do. Dismissing Margaret, who had reverted to her norm self to allow Elfrad to take command. As the warriors clustered round, they were joined by a few wizards. Hesitant at first, their curiosity brought them nearer. As one stepped forwards, Herwig and the other warriors stepped aside. Elfrad looked into his eyes, letting his wizard senses gauge the others intent.

'My name is Bermudo, these.' He indicated the other wizards now ranged behind him, 'are my friends.'

Herwig snorted. 'Wizard's, cannot be trusted.'

'We.' Once again he indicted the others. 'Cannot be held responsible for what others do. We're as loyal as the Bomani, who often conveniently forget that they are also wizards. We like them, have fought the Darkness and Meridian, losing in the process family and friends. Do not underestimate us. We are as capable of killing dark magicals as any warrior is.'

Before Herwig could make any reply. Margaret stepped forward.

'Your offer is welcome. Each side has something to offer in the fight against dark magic. Those of your clan who have chosen that path have at times made it awkward for any wizard be they warrior or not to be thought of as trustworthy. All of you here now, have been proved uncontaminated and therefore should equally be given your due respect.'

Nodding at Elfrad to continue, Margaret ignored the stares and mutterings thrown her way.

'All the clans are being asked to take up arms again. The fight this time will not be in Kingdom. That is one we will have to save for later. This time we fight a different enemy. Will you join us? And I do mean you all.'

The first thing they noticed as they emerged in Eirian was the noise. Spread out before them was a vast army. Margaret picked out the sound of Aeryissa's voice as she shouted a roll call of names. The magicals stared at the changelings as the silver in their fur and wings caught the sunlight. As Fafnir took to the skies, the Fae's dragons roared their approval, excitement making them snort small puffs of fire.

Striding towards them, Aeryissa's smile lit up her face as she turned to indicate the crowds.

'Confinement in Pictures has obviously been a chore. I've never seen so many magicals keen to take up arms. Especially when they have no idea who or what they will be fighting.'

'They were pretty keen to get out,' chuckled Elfrad.

'For us,' added Margaret, the fight hasn't stopped. For them one minute they were in the throes of a war. The next, confined in a place many had only visited or passed through, never lived in. I know which I'd prefer.'

'Have they been briefed yet?'

'Not fully,' replied Aeryissa. 'At the moment we are moving them into groups like we did in Kingdom, made up from various clans to utilise all their skills.'

Bayu emerged into the sunshine, silver speckled her clothes and hair drawing all eyes. Whisperings rolled across the crowds all wondering who she was. Hearing their thoughts, understanding their concerns, she cleared their worries from her mind.

'The explanations you seek will have to wait. Know this, I am your queen and all will obey my commands. I need your strength, resourcefulness and loyalty if we are to save Kingdom and stop the Darkness. Those who believe they are unable to follow without question should leave now and return to Pictures.'

Bayu's eyes raked the crowds, all silent, none moving.

'There is a realm called the Soul Lost land, it is a land of demons. When dark magic is used to conjure darkness or a demon, this is the pit they crawl from. I intend to destroy it.'

Bayu paused to let the mutterings abate, the magicals and changelings asking each other if any had known of its existence.

'Something else you should be aware of, this realm was created by another queen. Her name is Athanasia. She, like me is an ancient.'

Fear flooded through the crowd, none had ever met one before, their existence myth and legend only. Ignoring the interest her words provoked, she continued.

'Athanasia was duped into its creation. That was a long time ago. Taken prisoner? Or in control? Before we can destroy the demon realm we will have to ascertain what her position is. Fighting an ancient, is not the same as fighting demons or dark magicals.'

'As used in Kingdom, smaller fighting groups taken from each clan will be deployed,' explained Margaret. 'Bayu's group and ten others will enter the Soul Lost land first. It may not be stable. Once secure. Aeryissa will lead the next ten groups through. Her task to find Athanasia and relay her status to me. Depending on what circumstance's they find her in, will depend on what happens next.'

A voice shouted, 'how are we going to get in without them knowing we are coming?'

'Quickly,' shouted Elfrad, breaking the tension, making them laugh.

Standing in front of Bayu, her eyes looking them up and down, the groups shuffled their feet.

'Once an opening is made big enough for us to enter, you must all fan out. The demons will not be the same as when conjured, that is their shadow form. Inside their own realm they will be much more powerful. Speed is of the essence, don't go in blind assess the situation before you attempt to take them on. What you see and hear may not actually be real.'

'Once Bayu has the entrance secure. My group can enter. Followed by the others. Not before. When the void collapsed, it may have remained unstable, you could all be pulled into a vortex.'

The groups nudged each other, excitement lighting their faces at the thought of the coming fight. Bayu, locked eyes with Aeryissa.

'If Athanasia is not a prisoner, do not try and tackle her yourself. Use our link. I will come. Somewhere inside the Soul Lost land lies its power. Be it queen or demon, this is what my group will be looking for.'

The desolate landscape stretched for miles, the ridges steep, the valleys pitted and scarred. No trees or water marred the bareness. The scrubby earth dry and dusty the nearer the perimeter they got. Bayu called a halt as her senses flared. Orara changed quickly into her dragon form, climbing upon her back they took to the skies. Flying low, both scanned the ground. Orara the first to spot the difference in colour. White lines, had begun to leech across the ground, a sign that an active void was near. All the others they had come across so far had been closed, dormant.

'Follow me and stay in my footsteps unless I tell you otherwise,' commanded Bayu.

Falling in behind her, realisation dawned that they were to enter a realm both foreign and dangerous. One, even she appeared to know little or nothing about.

Cian, waved in acknowledgement as he moved passed Aeryissa. His thoughts for once not focused on Margaret. Harsha walked beside him, she like Lefu, had stayed away from him when they had been forced to enter Pictures. His morose attitude and sense of betrayal colouring all his friendships.

Meeting her again, reacting the way he did, had stood him in good stead. He knew the only way Lefu and the rest would accept him back into the fold, was for him to prove himself worthy to be part of the clan again. More importantly he needed to show them that her influence no longer had any bearing on his actions or thoughts.

Harsha's snarl brought him out of his reverie. His vampire also flaring. Balrath roared, the silver in her fur seeming to bristle. Zev the large black wolf which had been loping along beside her, lifted his snout and howled to the sky.

Bayu bent down, her fingers trailing along the ridge of white they could now clearly see.

'It's here.'

She drew back her arm and punched her fist into the ground. Disappearing up to her elbow. All felt the tremors under their feet. Standing with feet apart looking straight ahead, she turned. Her whole body spun. Faster and faster. Like a drill, the hole beneath her feet grew wider. None had been able to watch her. The speed too great to hold in their minds. The pit she had created dark and forbidding. All feeling the malevolence emanating up from its depths.

Without waiting to see if they followed Bayu let herself fall. Landing on her feet, the others made the descent anyway they could. The cave smelt of sulphur and something else, a tang none could describe but all found noxious to smell.

Conjuring lights, they followed as she cautiously made her way along the shaft. They hadn't gone far before Gawler darted in front, his net held ready. Her mind occupied with what and who they would find had nearly caught them out.

'Alvie,' she called.

Pushing their way to the front, Gawler told them, 'the floor is alive with something. I don't think it's lethal. More like to make us ill than anything. I'll go first and cast my nets, each of you do the same with your group. Make sure they understand to stay in the middle and only walk on them.'

Bayu indicated that he should lead. Gawler slung his first net, confident it would hold, still he gingerly placed his foot, as he waved his group forward. Each time they laid a net, the ground boiled in anger. Once everyone was sure the nets would hold, they stepped onto them with confidence. All wanting to get out of the tunnels and into the open air as soon as possible.

Deryn flew towards the light, Bayu listened to his running commentary to the other owls. Perching on a small rock fall he swivelled his head, his enormous owl eyes scoping the landscape. Nothing moved, yet his senses told him that others shared the space.

'The opening is clear but not secure. Something is hiding. I don't think its demons. The presence is more...'

'They will be using darklings,' Bayu explained. 'A lessor form of demon. Pass the details along, tell the groups to be prepared to be overwhelmed as soon as we break cover.'

Bayu stepped out first, the air locked underground for so long, lay still and heavy, waiting. When the void collapsed it had been dragged downwards pulling the land created with it. Rocks and earth hung overhead seemingly without support, creating a roof instead of a vast expanse of sky.

Running across the open ground, she could smell the darklings even if as yet she couldn't see them. This space had been deliberately left to appear empty. Half way across, they emerged, renting the air with blood curdling shrieks.

Cian and Harsha quickly waded in to rip them apart, no sooner had they put them down then others sprung up in their place. Zev clamped his jaws onto any that moved, shaking his head, raking his claws along their bodies. The other wolves joined him to herd the darklings into the centre before attacking them.

Deryn hovered with the other owls, once they understood the darklings movements they directed the magicals and changelings to where they were likely to appear. The Kaimi also took flight. As soon as Feeny and Orev spotted one rising, they dived in formation, changing at the last minute into their magical forms. Knives drawn, ready to rip them apart.

Bermudo, glad of the opportunity to at last lead his wizards into the fray, hacked at the darklings with their staffs, moving determinedly towards where Bayu was fighting several larger ones, each reforming as soon as she put one down. Tanika, like the other Fae hadn't brought her dragon, instead, using Balrath and the rest of the bears, they sat astride their backs sprinkling fairy dust, making the darklings fizzle and pop as the bears attacked them with their teeth and claws.

Their backs against the wall, the darklings still reforming and advancing in front of them. With nowhere obvious to go, all wondered how they were going to get out of the realm, let alone, find a way to enter further into its interior. Bayu wasn't worried, drawing the magicals and changelings to her side had always been part of her plan. This corner was from where the first darklings emerged, this the entrance they needed to use. She'd allowed herself and them to be backed up in front of it, as if all were lost.

Like a black wave, the darklings rose walking over the bodies of those already slain. Bayu felt the air move behind her and knew that many more were going to emerge.

'Drop to the ground. NOW.'

All except Bayu and the wizards lay prostate, using their staffs they banged hard against the ground, before charging them with magic, the words chanted in unison. Linked together they created a ring around them all, magic flew outwards as a pulse of blue light. The darklings caught in its beam screamed and squirmed as they burned.

Silence, made everyone aware that for now the fight was over. Raising their heads all were surprised to see that the quadrangle was empty.

CHAPTER FORTY-NINE

G lad the wait was over, used to being at the vanguard of any
action, Aeryissa and Margaret were finding it hard to take a
back seat. The trust and respect they had for each other hadn't yet
translated over to Bayu. Finding out that both queens were ancients,
set alarm bells ringing. If Athanasia had turned, did that mean Bayu
could also succumb?

Adjusting her swords, her silver on full view brought a smile
to Lefu's face. Changed since last he saw her, he marvelled at the
strange but beautiful creature she'd become.

'Keep our personal link open,' whispered Margaret.

Before she could stop him Lefu jumped into the pit first. The
lights Bayu's party had conjured sprang into action. The Alvie's nets
still lay on the path. In case any damage had been done she called her
foresters to lay theirs on top. Boomi stepped in front, she could see
that those already laid had begun to sink into the ground, rendering
them useless. Flinging her own outwards, her satisfied smile lit her
face while her changing colours lit up the tunnel. Unlike Bayu's
party they made swift progress.

The entrance gaped open like a giant mouth waiting to devour
them. Fanning out, they moved across the quadrangle. Even though
Bayu had assured her that all had been cleared. She and the rest of

them kept their eyes peeled. The Kaimi and owls flew overhead, swooping at the least change spotted. The scarred hole in front of them gave them pause. A low humming emitted from its depths, unsettling all.

Lefu waited for Aeryissa go first, he'd heard and felt the sharpness of her admonishment when telling him that she didn't need his protection.

The air felt heavy, like a weight pressing down, sapping their energy. As soon as they emerged, the weight lifted. Trees dotted the landscape, these though were dead, the Alvie's colours flashing as soon as they spied them.

Kaimi and owls took flight, looking for any opening or structure where Athanasia may be held. The witches conjured broomsticks, offering the Fae a ride. Used to the broad backs of their dragons they giggled as they tried to stay on.

As they flew the wolves and bears loped along underneath them, senses on high alert. Kebale stood on his hind legs and roared. Everyone stopped. The seekers, owls and witches drawn back towards the sound.

'What's wrong?' demanded Aeryissa.

'She's here,' puzzled he added, 'there are bears.'

Aeryissa asked the wolves, 'what can you sense?'

'There are bears and although it isn't strong. There is a definite scent of Athanasia.'

She was at a loss, she couldn't do what Bayu had done to create an entrance. The ground they stood on seemed firm and bare. If an entrance was here, she couldn't think how it managed to stay hidden from sight. Killykeen approached.

'If the magicians are happy to help, boosted by their magic, we may be able to shift the earth and find the entrance.'

The witches stood side by side, Naddle and the rest of the magicians behind them. They held hands and started chanting, as soon as they stopped the magicians placed a hand on the shoulder of the witch in front of them. They too began to chant, the witches joining in a beat later. Many felt mesmerised as they listened. The chant Aeryissa realised, had the same rhythm as a siren song. The ground in front of them began to move. The earth churned as it was forced apart. Like a hand clenched tight it didn't want to give up its secrets. In a tug of war, the witches and magician's pulled one way the earth another. She placed her hand onto Dromore's shoulder and let her silver flow. Like an electric currant it filled their bodies, the surprise on their faces matched by the strength of their magic. With her help the ground couldn't resist their call. Large gaps started to appear, until with one great heave the ground split asunder. In front of them sat a flight of stairs going down. Once again the sulphur and tang they'd smelt earlier burst out washing them all with its foul stink.

They descended the stairs, pausing to let their senses fan out, the low humming still heard, as an irritant to their ears. Aeryissa didn't like the feeling she was getting, something wasn't right. So far no one had seen any demons, not knowing where the threat was going to come from was putting them all on edge.

The humming was getting on everyone's nerves, even those without the added benefits of vampire or Lobe hearing. The stone walls of the corridor were covered in mildew and moss. The wolves moved forward their snouts lifting and falling, smelling both the ground and the walls. Shimmer. A hint, but enough for their super senses to follow its scent.

Everyone felt the excitement, picking up the pace they surged forward. Stopping before the corridor opened out. Naddle used his wand and staff to check the opening. The Alvie flinging nets forward making sure the ground was secure. Palamo flew out of the entrance, surprised to find that the ceiling height soared above them. Aeryissa listened as they relayed back to her what they could see. Small glints of shimmer twinkled as they flew past, stirring the air.

The chamber was empty of demons, they were both convinced though, that someone or something was hiding. Calling them back,

Aeryissa directed Lefu to take the right side she would take the left. Spreading out with their groups behind them, weapons drawn, they entered the chamber. Now they were inside shimmer did more than twinkle, it positively glowed in places. She could easily pick out the clusters.

As the others explored, she stood in the centre and let herself settle. The humming had been replaced by a slow pulse, like a faint heartbeat. She was aware of the sounds around her, the shouting of, 'clear,' penetrating her mind each time an area was checked. Still though, she stood.

Lefu paused in his searching, Aeryissa looked like she had left her body, her face blank of all expression. Worried something had happened to her, he waited by her side. As she came back to herself she smiled on seeing his concerned expression.

'I'm alright father. I know where Athanasia is.'

Placing small mounds of their fairy dust around the chamber Zekia hoped that they had got the ratio's correct. Using it had seemed like a good idea to be mooted, assuring Aeryissa that they could create an opening, without all the explosive force and noise that crystals would make.

Naddle snorted in derision, crystals at the ready, he argued that magicians were best suited to creating anything explosive. Ignoring him, Aeryissa told the Fae to go ahead. Turning to face the chamber, they clapped their hands. Small puffs filled the air, the noise hardly detectable. The magicians laughed, sure that they would now be called upon to do a proper job. Counting in their heads, the Fae giggled as the ground began to gently fall away, the noise and mess minimal, as if the earth had been brushed aside by unseen hands.

Peering over the crater, Aeryissa was even more certain they were headed in the right direction. Many like her leapt off the side, those not so brave, conjured ropes and abseiled down. Drawn like a moth to a flame she made her way across the piles of rocks and dirt. A small opening, its dark centre gaping open like a mouth was where she could hear the pulse coming from. Without thought of what may be waiting for her she began to crawl through.

Lefu bade everyone else follow, the look on his face closing down the mutterings that arose at the sight of where they had to go.

Sliding out, Aeryissa was almost afraid to look up. This chamber was smaller, covered in vein like structures that ran over every surface including the floor. At the centre was Athanasia. Arms and legs extended, she was attached to the wall by heavy chains, a metal Aeryissa didn't recognise. A cage of the same metal made her prison complete.

That would have been bad enough but when she really looked, she could see shimmer was being leeched out into the veins that ran away from her body disappearing into the Soul Lost lands structure. Held upright by her bonds, eyes closed. Ancient, yet dead.

As the others filled the chamber all eyes turned, many gasping at the sight. Aeryissa's first thought was to release her, surprised as the wizards stood to block her path.

'The bars and chains have been created with wizard's fire. Even you may not be strong enough to break the sequence.'

They had to find out if Athanasia was friend or foe. Opening her link to Margaret she told her what they'd found.

'How did you cross the fire? To get to Sam.'

Painful memories made her flinch, felt by Aeryissa, she apologised for bringing them up.

Mentally shaking her head, Margaret told her, 'I walked through and it broke. I knew I could. To this day I don't know how.'

'Do you think that I can do the same?'

'Honestly, I have no idea. I was so determined to save Sam, I don't think anything would have stopped me.' She added, 'there is another way. If you trust me.'

'Of course I trust you.'

'Enough though, to let me inside you, take control of your body. For you to appear as me?'

Silence greeted her words. Aeryissa had seen with her own eyes how powerful Margaret had become after each change she went through. She did trust her. Nevertheless, the thought of someone even a friend invading her body, using it to make her step aside from herself made her shiver.

'I'll only stay long enough to break the fire and the chains. No harm will be done. You will still be as you are now,' promised Margaret.

Lefu watched Aeryissa's face, aware that his daughter was having a conversation with someone inside her mind. He had seen that look before, never before though tinged with fright.

'We have no choice. Do it. Give me a moment to explain to Lefu and move everyone back. I don't know how much they will see or understand. I'd prefer it though, while you're inside me that no one reacts and tries to interfere.'

Quickly explaining, his shocked expression matched by her own. She dismissed his fears. Reinforcing to him and herself that she trusted Margaret.

Moving everyone back proved problematical. All knew something must be happening, all wanted to see. Lefu worried at what Margaret and Aeryissa were going to attempt, brooked no questions. His face doing the answering.

Aeryissa had no idea what to expect. She only knew Margaret had entered her body and mind by a faint tickling sensation flaring over her skin.

Speaking gently as if to a child, she told her, 'I have opened a door, enter the room and stay there until I call you back.'

Margaret could smell the dark magic woven through the metal, the shimmer still retained in the walls. Striding forwards, she grabbed the bars and pulled them apart, fizzling and popping the bars swung about like snakes with their heads cut off. As the chains fell to the floor, she turned, Lefu gasped. Aeryissa had gone. The Guardian stood in her place. He blinked and she disappeared.

Bayu strode into the chamber, brought up short at her first sight of Athanasia in years.

'The power source we have been following led us here. I can smell demons, so far we have not located any. Nor has any sought us out. Something isn't right.'

The voice when it came, rasped. Croaky from being unused, sore from the poisons flooding her body.

'They think me useless, unable to do anything. My shimmer drained, my body weak. They took my eyes, using my body to experiment, knowing I wouldn't die. Gloating over their findings, be they poor or great.'

'What are they going to do?' asked Bayu, keeping her voice gentle, as she leaned towards Athanasia, trying not to flinch at the sulphurous smell surrounding her.

'The demons hope that when you find me, or cannot find them, you will blast the realm apart.'

'That's exactly what I plan to do,' snarled Bayu.

'You mustn't,' she croaked. 'By doing so you would enable them to escape and call the Darkness.'

Athanasia sagged, her chains may have gone but she was still attached to the wall by vein like strands that covered her arms and legs. Talking had taken strength from her body that she didn't have to give. He head hung down, defeated, her body twitched.

'Why can't they leave?' demanded Cian, trying to tone down his belligerence. He added, 'they must do when they're conjured.'

Bayu's eyes swept the group, her muddled thoughts unlocked by Cian's question.

'They can't leave. Athanasia must have added a retaining spell when she created the realm. That's why their shadow forms can be conjured. But their real selves have to stay behind.'

'Ripping the land apart will allow them to escape the spell,' muttered Aeryissa.

'Exactly,' explained Bayu. 'They must believe her shimmer has all gone. Silver is what they want now. The Darkness is also part of their plan, it was conjured from here. Once out they will need a power source to draw on.'

'It still begs the question,' muttered Cian, 'where are they?'

'Down, underneath, in the subterranean caves that's where they're hiding. Unless you blast them out. You cannot get to them. If you do, you will have played into their hands,' croaked Athanasia.

'We can't leave them,' Aeryissa spat, her anger welling over.

'I agree,' said Bayu, 'otherwise we won't know a moment's peace.'

Chapter Fifty

Margaret made her way back to the Scriptorium, Elfrad appearing as she opened the outer doors.

'What's wrong?' he asked, concerned etched on his face.

The communication between them had been getting stronger each day. Both only having to think of each other and their link automatically opened between them. Ignoring his question until the doors closed. She tapped the nearest stack.

'We're here.'

A large fat book fell from the shelves landing on the floor at their feet. Opening with a flourish, Flinders catapulted himself out, his words running into each other, making no sense. Elfrad stepped forward, grabbing his arms holding them down by his sides.

'Slow down.'

'Sorry. I found it. Here look. It doesn't want to open, what are we going to do?'

Elfrad looked from Flinders to Margaret, asking, 'what's going on? What does he mean?'

She sighed with annoyance, once again nothing was as it seems. Each time they appeared to find a solution, up popped another complication.

'Can I stay? Perhaps hearing you explain to Elfrad will make it seem real.'

The book opened at her touch. Filled with small neat writing that kept rearranging itself on the page. Margaret closed her eyes and let herself go, shocking them both.

Flinders could feel her walking the pages, Elfrad could see them move as if something was in the paper. He had seen many wondrous things, this though, mesmerised him. Thinking, even magic didn't explain how Margaret could do the things she did.

As the pages settled, she appeared in front of them again, her expression grim as she told them.

'Eshe made me aware of the Gedeon's, the name of a series of books written long ago by magicals called Catien's. Cryptically telling me she hoped I wouldn't, yet at the same time feared, that I would need their help. She spent her life searching for Bayu believing that if found she would put an end to all the dark magic that was running rife in the realms.'

'Why do I get the feeling, that isn't what she's going to do?' stated Elfrad.

Flinders shook his head, 'she can't. She doesn't control enough power to enable her to do so.'

'She's the silver queen, of course she has enough power,' retorted Elfrad.

'From the witches Eshe received full control of all shimmer and then passed it on to me.'

'Your point is?'

Looking him in the eyes she added, 'in the same way Eshe got shimmer. I got silver.'

He didn't understand.

'When the spells were broken, Bayu got some,' continued Margaret. 'Enough to make her believe she has control. I on the other hand, do have control, of it all.'

Elfrad smiled, 'Surely as long as someone can wield the magic, in the circumstances does it matter which one of you can?'

Flinders anger got the better of him, 'if only her finding out she doesn't, was all we had to worry about,' he snapped, 'it wouldn't be so bad.'

'Why don't you go home Flinders, there's nothing more you can do.'

'I think I will. Call if you need me. I know we haven't always seen eye to eye. Please take care, both of you,' with a final bow he dived into his book and disappeared.

'Athanasia is the power in the Soul Lost land.' Margaret explained. 'When I entered Aeryissa, I knew straight away that she wasn't what she seems. Bayu may also become a problem when she realises that silver is not hers to control.'

'How will... They are both ancients. You are not.'

'This Gedeon, gives instructions on how to kill them.'

Athanasia listened as Bayu and the others discussed how they could free her and get to the demons hidden below. The retaining spell she'd cast to keep demons inside had also worked on her. Unable to draw on her shimmer so easily she pretended to be knocked out, allowing the brothers to chain her. As soon as Neo realised that none of them could get out, he decided to change tact and befriend her.

On hearing his thoughts, she held back a smile, judging the time to be right, she let a groan escape her lips, while fluttering her eyelashes.

'She's waking up,' cried Pik, nervously.

'Why have you chained me?' she asked, holding back her anger, keeping her voice even.

'For your own safety. The demons wanted your blood for trapping them. We decided that if they saw you being held prisoner it would calm them down.'

'And has it?' she sneered, before she could stop herself.

'Once you open the void releasing them, they will quickly come back to heel.'

'I cannot. My magic isn't strong enough. The vortex and therefore the void, must have been more unstable that it appeared. We are all trapped. Only from outside can we be released.'

As she broke the chains, Pik moaned deep in his throat, rubbing her wrists she stared at him.

'In good faith, I created a realm for you and a prison for your brother, then you betrayed me.'

When Neo had been deciding who to target, he soon become aware that like him, Athanasia wasn't what she seemed or portrayed, her heart was as dark as his.

'Be honest,' he told her, 'this is what you wanted. You used us, as much as we used you.'

Neo smirked, seeing the look cross her face, his arrow hitting home.

'Why don't we put aside our differences? With your magic and our devious minds, surely we can find a way to make this work?'

Pik wished his brother would stop taunting Athanasia. Her magic may have waned but it wasn't gone, he could see bursts of shimmer flaring as she fought to keep control of her anger. Neo's problem was liking the sound of his own voice without really looking at or listening to those he was trying to convince.

'I accept. On the proviso you remember that I am a queen. While you are only demons.'

After listening surreptitiously to Neo once again working a crowd, Athanasia decided that now was the time to show herself and make her mark. Stepping into the open arena, letting her gaze sweep across the demons, aware of a hush descending Neo turned. The demons were wary. Nevertheless, Pik could see how impressed they were, their eyes turning away from his brother, their attention rapt as they listened to what she had to say.

'Trapped inside the Soul Lost land unable to leave, could seem like a punishment. Instead, I propose we use it to our advantage. This is your realm. And now mine.'

Neo stiffened at her words, opening his mouth to interrupt, he was held back by the demons response. Shouts and yells filled the air, not in anger but in agreement.

'Since the void closed, I have been working to refine a spell that will allow your shadow forms to leave our realm. Depending on how strong your core is, will depend on how long you can maintain your freedom. Eventually, the pull from your bodies will be too great to resist and you will be snapped back. Those given the chance to leave will be tasked with spreading dark magic, bringing magicals over to our side and encouraging them to conjure more demons.'

Athanasia knew they would cleave to her side. Any release they saw as a benefit compared with being stuck underground. The thought of causing mayhem and murder while spreading dark magic had encouraged them all to listen to her. Neo had offered them a realm but not much else. His solutions all falling by the wayside as unworkable. Their interest soon waning. Now energised by what they may gain, she knew that she wouldn't have to force anyone to try her spell, they would be lining up to do so.

She began to show her more trusted demons how to detect anyone with even a hint of shimmer, making sure that these were targeted first. Interrogating them as soon as they snapped back into their real forms. Quickly taking whatever magic and information they had managed to collect. Those who complained were swiftly reminded of her power.

The idea of sending them to go up against Bayu came like a bolt out of the blue. Several demons upon their return told her that she had taken over Cala and Neg, realms which by right, belonged to Athanasia. Upon hearing this news she let her anger engulf her. Tearing through the Soul Lost land, any demons that didn't get out of the way quick enough were killed. Her rage like a wild beast driving her on. Collapsing in a heap, she wept not in fear but in anger at her situation, at not being rescued, at being abandoned. Once calm, she did what she did best, she began to plot.

Over the coming weeks she put all her energies into training and honing the demons skills. Their mission to destroy the realms. At the same time they were to target Bayu. Relentlessly, she sent waves of demons and darklings. Allowing them minimal rest, before making them start all over again. Neo and his cohorts kept well out of her way lest they also be sent. When the news filtered through that Cala and Neg had been destroyed, the magicals killed or fled. Her delight that Bayu was being harried, spurred her on to do more.

The next wave of demons had one specific purpose, capture Bayu. Athanasia knew there was no way that they would be able to take an ancient. What she wanted was for Bayu to track the demons to their source, hoping that she would then blast the Soul Lost land apart releasing her.

Idona and Tarian were next to be targeted. These realms she knew were close to Bayu's heart. Especially her beloved changelings. Everything went well, the realms were overcome, the magicals and changelings fleeing. All she held dear was being systematically destroyed. She wanted Bayu pushed into a corner, until retaliation become her overriding need.

The demons sent to do battle with her, were the best of the best. They were supposed to lead her towards the void, where other demons would be waiting. Athanasia hoped that seeing them disappear inside she would blast her way in to get at them. Bayu foiled them all. She was the one that drew them on. She knew instantly that Bayu had been spell bound, something shifted, unaware though that she had also been severed from her silver, she called the demons back. Whereupon she tore them apart before turning them into dust.

Neo's resentment at the way Athanasia had taken over was growing. He thought about her constantly, wanting revenge for taking what he deemed to be his realm.

Athanasia's demons sole purpose was to find a way for them all to leave. At the same time making sure that when they emerged, there would be whole realms of dark magicals waiting to welcome them. Towards this end she had gotten her most trusted demons to search for the darkest grimoires. Making sure that they kept their endeavours secret, unable to bring any back with them, she had devised a memory spell that upon their return only she could unlock.

Neo knew she was up to something when informed that her demons had been seen slinking inside libraries. When approached, they declined to say what they were up to, threatened, they laughed. Sure, that when Athanasia found out their interest, she would make them pay. His demons were loyal to him, but not stupid. They backed off, making sure to tell him what had happened as soon as they returned.

Confronting her was not something Neo enjoyed, he knew that behind her words she was laughing at him. Listening to Pik's advice for once to tone down his attitude he requested an audience. Something else that made his anger flare. When she wanted to speak to him she flounced in, ignoring anyone he was with or what they were doing. Demanding his instant attention.

'What are you searching for?' he asked, hoping his voice didn't betray his thoughts. 'My demons.'

He nearly lost it when she raised her eyebrows, her voice dripping venom.

'Your demons.'

Choosing to ignore her tone, he continued, 'what spell are you trying to find? What will this one do? I thought we were in this together,' forcing himself to smile, to take the bite out of his tone.

Athanasia was getting tired of their exchanges. Why she kept him alive she still couldn't fathom.

'There is a book that detail's how in certain circumstances, a darkling can be turned into pure Darkness. It also tells how this can be manipulated into taking a host and if successful, become a Dark Lord, possibly even an entity in its own right.'

She saw this as a possible way to escape from her underground prison. If all the stages worked and a Dark Lord emerged, once he'd gained enough power, under her instructions, he should be able to blast the realm apart.

Neo listened with mounting horror, he liked living underground. It had taken a while to getting used to being snapped back into his body when he left or when occasionally he let himself be conjured.

The rewards though, were worth the pain. He quickly realised that it was his one advantage over her. She couldn't leave.

'This system you set up offering demon services. I think we can take it to the next stage.'

Neo didn't like the fact that she had been monitoring what he did so closely. For once keeping his expression neutral and his mouth shut, he showed Athanasia that he too could wait.

'Few magicals who take up your offers renege on their deal. So the rewards remain small. I propose that we start targeting untainted magicals. We look for those who sit on the fringes of dark magic. Those who like the thought of dabbling, but don't. Who get a thrill by thinking they are close to its source. Everyone has someone or something that they would like to influence. Find what it is, use it to convince them that the services offered are a way of levelling the field. Assure them that the demon will be doing the work, their hands will be unsullied.'

Neo could see the benefits, their magic would be purer and all the sweeter for it; but not how to convince a magical who didn't use dark magic to give a piece of themselves away to a demon.

'We won't be taking a piece of them. Instead they will be joining us here in our realm.'

'What you're proposing doesn't make any sense. How can they get in? If we cannot get out?'

Neo looked at Athanasia as if she were mad. Seeing the self-satisfied look on her face, he knew; she had once again found a way around the problem.

The first few times hadn't gone according to plan. Once a demon had singled out a magical to target, they were supposed to cast the spell she had concocted and wait for the magic to take effect. So eager were some that they tried to bring the magicals back with them before the magic had fully entered their systems. The spell made their bodies pliable and wraith like. Their minds open, enabling a link to be forged between them and the demon. Each demon bringing them was supposed to use the link to tether them to themselves. When they were snapped back, the magical came with them. Once the spell wore off they reanimated. Ready to be drained of their magic and core.

The demons eagerness, meant that several magicals weren't ready. Tethered, they couldn't get free, the demon was snapped back and the magical shredded in the void. Athanasia's anger was like a wild fury whipping through the realm. All fled. Those not quick enough ripped apart, trampled, her demented screams cutting through them like a knife.

When they finally managed to bring magicals safely through without mishap. Neo had once again wrongly believed that these would be shared out amongst them all. Giving everyone a boost of magic.

Demons had been sent out to explore the new realms that had sprung up since Bayu was spell bound. Quickly finding, that no matter how many of them tried to enter Eirian they were rebuffed. Magicals also talked of a non-magical realm called Novia, she dismissed it at first, until she found out that its norms as they were called, often showed signs of violence and greed. Two things with which her demons could work with. Kingdom however was perfect, rife with magicals, many drawn to the dark. Information quickly began to flow back to her concerning a magician called Zador who had cast himself as its leader.

On hearing the terms of the contract offered, Zador realised that he hadn't thought it through. Ignoring what he may have to give away, thinking only about what he would gain. Wanting to cancel his request, the demon laughed, reminding him that payment was due.

'What if, in return for a well spring of magic, I could get you a clutch of magicians all ripe for the taking,' he offered.

'I'm listening,' snarled the demon.

Incensed, when she heard his proposal, Athanasia first thought to drag him down and make him suffer for his effrontery. Changing her mind, when it was pointed out to her that they may be able to use him to get into Eirian.

Dareh kept track of Zador's progress. With his new found magic and the obstructions to his leadership banished, he took to ruling Kingdom, like a King. He conveniently forgot where his powerful magic had come from. Carried away by his own quest for power, he decided to use his magic to sever the twin link between him and his brother. Dareh's informants told him all about Zador's proposal.

'You don't look like twins,' she snapped. 'Yet your brother is in the process of casting a spell to sever your twin link.'

Cillian hated Athanasia, her cruelty knew no bounds, her sense of entitlement the same as his brothers. They would have gotten on well, he often thought.

'We are not identical, but we are twins. Zador locked the link between us a long time ago. I have tried since to open it. Perhaps that is why he is intent on severing it once and for all.'

'My informants tell me he thinks of himself as King and acts like one,' spat Dareh. 'He needs to be punished.'

Cillian seeing his chance to get back at his brother and possibly Athanasia told them.

'I could fool him. Let him think the spell has worked. Let him see me, think I've escaped and have come for him. Perhaps the others he cast aside could also play a part.'

Anger suffused Athanasia's face, retorting she cried, 'what makes you think I need this charade.'

Cillian saw his chance at revenge disappearing.

'I agree he deserves the ultimate punishment. He may though have information that we could still use. Let his brother and his cohorts play their games,' said Dareh. 'Once here, I will extract his knowledge bit by bit, as painfully as possible. Leaving his core and magic intact for you to take.'

Athanasia wrenched the link between the brothers open. Cillian gained a foothold and didn't let go. Zador was dragged back into the Soul Lost land.

What, she hadn't bargained on, was Cillian being able to cast a rolling spell at the same time. That was not in his remit to do. Unable to stop the spread, ice covered both Kingdom and Eirian. Athanasia was incandescent with rage. Dareh didn't get a chance to interrogate Zador. She ripped him, Cillian and the other magicians apart with her bare hands, her fury so great none would come near for days. Her anger festered and grew. With the realms covered, no demons could leave and none could be conjured. More importantly, no unsullied magicals could be taken for her to feed from.

Settling herself into the fabric of the Soul Lost land. With fewer magicals to work with, Athanasia found a way to use the shimmer and the magic she collected to fill the walls, wrapping it around her like a cocoon, the vein like growths leeched across walls and floors. She started to extend her range, using magicals who still contained shimmer to line the walls. Pressed into its surface, like a tap it flowed from them into her.

Being queen of the demon realm, brought out the darkest part of her nature which she had kept hidden even from herself. Her resentment at being unable to leave; the driver in anything she did. Her only thought, escape, to wreak her vengeance on those she blamed for leaving her imprisoned.

The brothers hadn't slept for days. Banded together, the chamber they occupied was covered floor to ceiling in runes. All dedicated to keeping out anything that tried to cross their surfaces. She waited until nightfall to strike. Defiant to the end, Neo, refused to make a sound as the veins streaked across the floor to cover him.

She set his demons to work setting up a network enabling them to keep track of those who were being conjured. Any demons wanting to leave of their own accord could do so only with permission. Any caught flouting the rules were killed. She gave no second chances. Whereas in the past they could use their shadow forms to leave, only snapping back when the strain became too great to bare. Now they could only go with a specific task and timetable in mind. Athanasia put demons loyal to her in charge of their movements. Many resented this curb on the only freedom they had. Those who spoke out were swiftly dealt with.

The spread of dark magic was one of Athanasia's goals. This was one way she knew that she could undermine the realms. Still she wanted more. Even with everything she was accomplishing she was no nearer to escaping her prison.

Athanasia's impatience was legendary. Waiting for news she paced her chamber, making the air around her crackle as her anger flared. When the demon entered he did so with fear in his heart. The news wasn't good, the magicals using her instructions had managed to create a black mirror and conjure the Darkness. The king's brother a willing host. Unfortunately, killed before he could enter. The Darkness captured and entombed. Anger left her like a hurricane, all those caught in its wake, dead.

Her rage so great she scoured the walls of magicals ranged behind her severing them. Only the collapse of their bodies falling untethered bringing her out of her manic state. The veins that snaked across the walls broken, shimmer sparkling at their ends. Demons lay trampled and broken, the silence eerie as all others hid away from her wrath.

Slowly Athanasia began to calm down. Telling herself that she couldn't keep on losing her temper in this way. The destruction she caused, had cost her dearly in lost magicals. Finally, once she had herself under control, she called for the demons to return. Reluctant at first, they knew they had no choice. All hoping that her anger was spent.

Choosing to see it as another setback in a long line of them. None looking at her now would place her at the central cause of the carnage that lay about her. Smiling was not her forte, for once she allowed herself to do so. The demons unsure what this meant much preferred it when she barked out orders.

Thanks to the spells she had created, her spies informed her that unable to kill some of those involved, they had been incarcerated. She decided to change tact. For the moment the Darkness was no use to her, nor were the dark magicals while imprisoned.

Demons were still being conjured and still leaving the Soul Lost land to capture magicals or to gain information. Dark magic was spreading, her tentacles, unseen and unknown were everywhere. An army waited, when she escaped she would need one, loyal, ultimately to her and her alone. The demons in fear of a painful death were not allowed to mention her in any of their dealings. As much as she wanted her name shouted from the rooftops, common-sense told her the time wasn't right.

Working in the shadows, although imprisoned, gave her a degree of freedom. Dark magic not laid at her door, but at some mythical entity with several different names depending on who was telling the story. To this end she made her plans.

A King may rule where he shouldn't, she would however, make his reign and those that came after him, as uncomfortable as possible. Demons that in the past had complained about not getting out enough, even as their shadow forms, now often wished for those days of peace and quiet. Where they could fight amongst themselves without fear of Athanasia looking over their shoulders, demanding they get back to work. When news filtered through that part of the Darkness had escaped and that it was hiding in the same place where the dark magicals were being held. Athanasia's roar of triumph reverberated around the realm. Now, she would rise.

All else was forgotten, the Darkness would need a new host and a black mirror. Each time she thought she'd came up with a workable plan, the fact that demons couldn't get inside the Glasserium made it useless. Once she heard though, how some had found a way to leave their mirrors by enticing magicals to swap bodies. She soon realised, this would fix another piece of the puzzle.

Her demons began haunting mirrors, high jacking any magicals or wraiths that left them. Turning them towards dark magic, while those already looking in that direction they used to convince others. Gradually, dark magic was gaining ground. The Glasserium turning darker. The magicals inside the mirrors were turning into a better sort of fodder than she had at first thought possible. Those of a more demon like nature she singled out. Enabling them to leave their mirrors and the hall permanently. The only thing she couldn't influence was their wraith like visage.

It had started slowly at first, magicals intent on being on the outside as much as possible noticed that each time they returned they appeared to be fading. Even those not venturing out but who had been imprisoned for a long time were being affected. Some revelling in their misty forms, those still able to retain their magical forms shunned them.

Co-ordinating from afar was not ideal, Athanasia, didn't really trust anyone. But to achieve her goal she had to put aside her natural caution and rely on others to do her bidding. Fachnan and Itachi eager to perform. Dareh, the steadying hand between them.

'The Darkness that escaped, is not the mass, only its tendril form. This we assumed would complicate matters, expecting that the whole of it would be required. I'm glad to say that isn't the case. The tendrils have entered the king's nephew. He carries a dark heart, a perfect host for the Darkness to take,' crowed Fachnan.

Word finally came, that the dark magicals imprisoned had been released by the Kai. The host's father using Iwatoke's was ready to kill the king and his sons. Athanasia found it hard to sit still, as she waited to hear. Knowing that as her creation she would feel a shift in the magic released by his actions.

Only Dareh, dare approach her, confident in her need of him, the demon saw by her eyes that she'd guessed.

'Tell me,' she spat.

'The sons were killed. The king lived. His anger his undoing. He wouldn't wait, he entered the mirror. As he struck Abaddon's head from his shoulders, the Darkness managed to flee back into a mirror. Most of his more powerful dark magicals escaped into Novia.'

'And the king?'

'In destroying the mirror, a piece entered his body, the poison killing him. Leaving Kingdom ripe for the taking.'

Foiled once again, her anger simmered. The demons, expecting her fury to erupt were all surprised when she dismissed them with a wave of her hand.

She had nearly given up all thoughts of rescue after the last debacle, now, offered another chance of escape, she was finding it hard to concentrate, the thought of being disappointed again at the fore front of her mind. Realising that there was a major fault in her plans which she had chosen to ignore. For her to call the Darkness she had to be released. To be released she needed someone powerful enough to blast the void. If it became an entity in its own right, control of it would be harder, especially if the host it chose was strong. These fears she kept to herself. Doubts were for others to worry about, she would escape and she would rule.

'How far along are we with the first phase? Has enough been done to make it appear a search is taking place for the remains of the black mirror?'

'It has been kept it as furtive as possible,' crowed Itachi. Seeing her look, he added, 'the bait has been taken.'

Once again her dream was a possibility. The Darkness had taken a host. The dark witch Meridian had finally given herself over to dark magic, in exchange for more power. Like those before her, all eager to drink from its well, forgetting to read the small print. Using the witch meant, that Athanasia had someone close to the Dark Lord in her thrall, even though her power was turning into something more than what had initially been given away. Because she didn't yet have full control of all dark magic, she set her demons to finding the source of this extra magic Meridian was drawing on.

Athanasia was getting good at waiting. Over the years she had finally learned patience. The Dark Lord had left the Glasserium. Battles were taking place all over Kingdom. Her only niggle, Meridian. She worried that someone else was also manipulating events.

'Well,' she demanded.

'They were working together. Now they're at odds. She released the magma, not the wizards,' replied Dareh.

'How does he seem, is he able to harness power easily?'

'You have to tell her,' interjected Fachnan.

Athanasia looked with annoyance from one demon to another.

Dareh explained, 'we have known something isn't right in Kingdom for a long time. We have caused plenty of problems all aimed at undermining the magicals. Softening them up. Here inside our realm our magic is as strong as it was when we first entered. In Kingdom, we knew as our shadow forms our magic would be less, but not by how much and it's getting weaker.'

'The magicals say the same,' added Itachi.

'How does this matter where the Dark Lord is concerned. He is ultimately my creation.'

'Because whatever is the cause, is also affecting him. When he emerged he was violent, strong and after his first taste of freedom, focused. Now at times he appears diminished, lost, unsure of what to do next.'

Athanasia raged inside, once again her plans were going awry. When the news came that the magicals of Kingdom were rising up. She thought this would galvanise the Dark Lord into action. She had her demons keep a close watch on Meridian, her power growing, her mind nearly gone. She was like a bomb waiting to go off.

The Dark Lord was dead. Meridian had escaped to Novia. None dare enter her chamber. Her rage like an animal, feral and uncontained.

When she had finally brought herself under control on being told that Meridian was on her way to release the Darkness from its tomb, Athanasia found it hard to applaud her actions. The news when it came that she also was dead, didn't surprise her. Released, the mass would be untethered. With no one to give it direction it would spread out and continue to cause destruction until called or stopped. With the whole of the Darkness released, one part of the problem was solved. The next not so easy. She still needed someone powerful to blast the land apart.

When she felt the shift in magic, she knew Bayu had been released from her spell bound state. She willed her thoughts to turn to the Soul Lost land as the source of the Darkness, blasting it open to find its master.

The thought galvanised Athanasia into action. Her best chance of escape was to play the victim. Now all she had to do was keep up the act long enough to be released.

Chapter Fifty-One

Aeryissa kept her expression neutral not wanting anyone to suspect she was talking and listening to someone else.

'The reason Bayu felt drawn to where Athanasia is being held is because she and not the demons are the power.'

Careful not to show her surprise and shock at how Margaret knew this. Aeryissa listened. 'She wants the Soul Lost land blasted, then she will call the Darkness. It's been her all along. Have you actually seen a demon?'

'Only darklings. She's saying they are hiding down below in the depths, ready to emerge.'

'They may already be dead, if not they will be her army. Don't believe what you see. You must make sure that Athanasia believes we are on her side.'

'Has Qiao finished moving the trees?' muttered Margaret, her mind distracted by what she was proposing to do.

'He's transporting the last of the Yorkus, as usual they are proving a problem.'

'When he's done, tell him to meet me in the Glasserium. Eadulf is expecting him, he won't bounce off this time.'

Fingerling boomed with laughter at the expression on Qiao's face when he told him her command.

'It's not funny,' he retorted.

'Eadulf is expecting you…'

'Like the last time you mean. He was supposed to let me through, got distracted and forgot. When I eventually got inside. Not a word of apology. Only Guri laughing, while my head felt like a hammer was thumping around inside it.'

'I can hear your thoughts Elfrad.'

'I know you can. That doesn't take away the fact that I'm worried about what you propose to do. How powerful are you? Are you powerful enough?'

'Why are you smiling?' he asked in exasperation.

'I have changed so much from when we first met. I'm glad that, sometimes, when you look; you are still able to see. Just me.'

'That was better than last time,' Qiao chuckled, emerging in a flurry. 'Those trees, I tell you, they are a nightmare to move. Moan. Moan. Moan! They may be fighting trees but they sure are frightened when it comes to being transported. The fuss they made. Fingerling is still trying to get them to calm down and stop charging about looking for something to hit.'

As Qiao paused for breath, he realised that only Purity was listening to him. The others had moved away and were bent over a table with a map stretched across it.

'Charming,' he told her.

She let her glass ripple in agreement.

'Stop whinging,' said Guri, over her shoulder. 'I saw that,' she added, as he pulled a face behind her back.

Argonorth sat proudly in the middle of the map. Small moving dots denoting the trees that had been caught, when the Darkness emerged. Bound by dark magicals, abandoned to their fate, the creatures beneath had chewed through their bonds. Margaret pointed to a patch of ground near to a clearing in front of the trees.

'This is where I believe the first black mirror was constructed.'

'Wasn't it destroyed?' queried Elfrad. 'All the stories told of those days are adamant that it was. What makes you think otherwise?'

'The Afsaneh and Eshe. Those involved as we now know were very powerful. It wasn't smashed like Abaddon's. Or overcome with white glass as the last one was.'

'You think it's still out there?' asked Guri. 'If that's the case why hasn't the Darkness been searching for it?' seeing Margaret's expression, she answered her own question. 'The mirror needs a host, and all that's left in Kingdom are mentally unstable magicals and wraiths.'

'If Athanasia is the real power in Soul Lost land.'

'She is,' stated Margaret.

'Okay,' continued Elfrad. 'How is she going to call the Darkness? If she does. When she does. What then? How will she draw power from it?'

'She doesn't need to,' sighed Guri, wearily. 'She created the Soul Lost land, therefore once out, she would be able to control the Darkness and the demons.'

'Why are we here?' asked Qiao forcefully, impatient to get going on whatever adventure was being taken on next.

'If the black mirror can be located, then I propose to enter it and wait as bait for the Darkness to take me.'

Stunned into silence, no one knew what to say. Before they found their voices, Margaret continued.

'Eadulf can you create a glass box? It needs to be large enough to accommodate both myself and Elfrad. Guri, as creator of the Glasserium do you think that you would be able to find and unwrap the black mirror.' Before she could form an answer, she told Qiao, 'you will be needed to transport us to Argonorth. Elfrad, I'd like you to stay with me as my anchor.'

All looked puzzled at her last words, it was Purity who asked, 'if you are locked inside a glass box here. How are you going to go to Argonorth?'

Guri, cackled her disbelief, 'you're going to split? Aren't you? Is there nothing you're not capable of? Like the players, Margaret is going to split into two people. Why do you need an anchor?'

Elfrad blurted out his annoyance.

'What happens when the Darkness enters you? The power you have surely will make it even more so. Won't it change you? I don't like this. It's too risky, both to you and to everyone.'

'That's why I need you to be my anchor. What will go with Guri is only a splinter of me. The Darkness may not come. I'm offering it another alternative. Become a power in itself or bend to Athanasia's will. If it takes my offer, I will be able to confront her without her knowing who I am. It's the only way I can see to stop her gaining more power.'

'Why do you need a glass chamber?' asked Eadulf.

'To keep my stronger part separate. If it goes wrong then only a part of me will get hurt. Or die.'

'This is madness.'

'If I am to confront Athanasia, I need to gauge her strengths and weaknesses before I reveal myself. Plus, we don't know where Bayu stands in all this.' Looking at Guri and then Qiao, she added, 'I cannot transport this part of myself. If the Darkness accepts me as its host. I will need to get near to the Soul Lost land. Would you both...'

Guri smiled in support, 'we'd be delighted,' nudging Qiao, who nodded grudgingly, like Elfrad, he wasn't happy with what she proposed.

Margaret opened her link, keeping her voice interested, but not eager. Listening carefully to the tone used by Bayu, letting her senses flow gently towards her words. As sure as she could be, they told her she was genuine in her concern for both Athanasia and what would happen if they gave the demons the release they wanted.

'There may be another way,' she told them. 'Aeryissa, do you remember when Damala contacted you using beetles?'

Shaking her head, before remembering that Margaret was speaking inside their minds and couldn't see them, she answered. 'That was to send a message.'

'Well this is a message of sorts. I've spoken to her and she has started the call to arms. Everyone should pull back. Once the ground has collapsed, you will be able to enter and attack the demons. Reinforcements are also on their way.'

As Cian and Orara directed everyone to return to the surface, Bayu spoke to the queen. Aeryissa kept her private link with Margaret open for her to hear the conversation between them.

Slowly lifting her head Athanasia worked hard to keep a look of triumph from her face. Her ruined eyes turned towards Bayu, the veins standing out on her skin as shimmer moved underneath, its glow weak and broken.

'We're leaving to go to the surface.'

'Don't worry about me. Kill them all.'

Margaret listened carefully, detecting an undercurrent from Athanasia's words, Aeryissa also picking it up. Only Bayu appeared oblivious to the lie being told.

'What happens if your plan doesn't work?' asked Qiao, worry etched on his face. 'If you're not as powerful as you think you are.'

Ruffling his hair as she used to, Margaret once again was astounded at how far he had come since they'd first met. Refusing to call her guardian, telling those who tried to correct him that she was Margaret, his friend, and always would be. Even when he questioned anything she asked of him, in the next breath, he volunteered to do whatever she wanted.

Elfrad too felt anxious, he more than Qiao, had often been present at each point of her changes. This though, she was attempting, worried him on several levels. Mainly, would she be able to resist the call of the dark magic she was going to allow to encase her. Even split she still held considerable power. Easy enough to snap back into one body. His job as anchor, he still didn't understand. He had silver inside him and was powerful. But nowhere in Margaret's league. As usual she hadn't chosen to explain what his presence in the glass box would make in keeping her grounded and her magic secure from the Darkness.

Eadulf and Guri had created the box together, in better times they would have taken great pleasure in doing so. Now they both kept their concentration on making sure that it would be strong enough to contain Margaret if anything went wrong.

She knew what she had to do. Thinking herself into the mind of a player, she encouraged her body to split itself into two separate magicals. With a loud pop, making Qiao step back, two Margaret's stood in front of them.

'Well I never,' said Guri, chuckling to herself as she held onto Purity's frame.

Qiao's eyes had widened, making him look like a startled deer as he stared at his friend, wondering which one was the real one.

Margaret's voice said in unison, 'we both are.'

'Which of you does Elfrad go in the box with?'

Both Margaret's raised their eyebrows.

Eadulf pointed, 'that one, she has the power.'

Sealing the glass, he stepped back as first shimmer then silver began to cover its surface blocking them both from view.

'Fingerling has instructed a large oak to allow you both to hide in his trunk. If the Darkness takes my offer and I emerge. You must transport me to the coordinates I have given you. Do not touch me Qiao, only touch Guri, when glass she cannot be contaminated by the Darkness. Transport away, do not linger or wait to see what happens. If the Darkness doesn't take my offer...'

Guri announced, 'we find another way. None of us are giving up now. As for the Darkness not wanting such a juicy morsel as you. Your problem will be shrugging it off, not attracting it in the first place. If all else fails,' she cackled, 'we can always drown our sorrows in whiskey. I have plenty stored away.'

Eadulf shook his head at her levity, knowing that she too was as fearful of what the outcome would be. He sat down leaning his back against Purity's glass. All they could do now was wait. Inside the box, Elfrad held Margaret's hand, her face immobile as she concentrated.

They emerged into a silent dark land. Argonorth held its breath. Fingerling had sent the message far and wide telling all to help anyway they could. All three wore the capes that Margaret had made. The forester net light yet strong enough to conceal their magic. How long they would remain undetected was the issue they were unsure of. The ground beneath their feet began to churn and move sideways. Small beetle like creatures appeared.

Qiao never a lover of anything that scuttled, clamped his hand over his mouth to stop the shout he wanted to do from being heard. Earning him a scornful look from Guri. Bending down Margaret held out her hand. A larger beetle was pushing her way to the front. Settling in her palm, she lifted the beetle up towards her face.

'I'm seeking the spot where a black mirror was created.'

The beetle listened, hearing the truth behind her words. Even though Fingerling had instructed all to help, she wanted to make sure herself that this wasn't another trick. Several times the Darkness and its followers had tried to engage the small creatures that inhabited the earth. Both wheedling and threats used to get them to show themselves. For some reason, even with all its power it couldn't penetrate their homes. Sure, that it didn't need or want them, the fact that they didn't bend to its ways, enough for them to be of interest to it.

Guri glanced at Qiao, his eyes frantic as his feet were being covered by beetles of all colours and sizes, Margaret with her acute hearing easily picking up their chirrups as they worked. Soon a patch of black dry earth began to be exposed. No beetle would cross it. Surrounded by hundreds of them it sat in the middle, bare.

'This must be the spot where it was created and hung. Can you pick up anything that says the mirror may still be here?'

Guri didn't want to, yet she knew that unless she stepped into the black centre she would have no chance of locating the mirror. Taking a deep breath she turned into her glass form. The instant she stepped into the centre she felt it. A slight tremor, enough though to know that it was still here.

'It's here.'

Qiao jumped, his nerves stretched taut as the oak Fingerling had detailed to hide them appeared. Shaking out its branches, it began opening its trunk wide enough to accommodate them.

Guri didn't like the feeling she was getting from the mirror's glass. Even after all this time the evil it had briefly contained still resonated. She began her call, as soon as the words started to form, the mirror woke. She could feel its hesitancy in the planes of the glass, she had no way of acting like a dark magical. As creator of the Glasserium she hoped that it would accept her power over glass and come. She could feel it moving, still attached to the ground where it had been created, nevertheless she could feel that it was ready for release. Margaret knew it was coming, Guri had warned her that her glass may change colour.

The black came as a shock, she heard Qiao gasp. Ignoring him, concentrating, she couldn't stop the sigh escaping as her glass once again turned clear. The mirror had sprung up at the same time she changed colour. Margaret readied herself to leap into it as soon as it was fully formed.

The smell hit them all at the same time, sulphur and a tang they recognised from Meridian. The mirror hung above the ground its surface flat and dead, no light penetrated in or out. Guri stood out in sharp contrast to the pit in front of her.

Backing away slowly, hoping that she wasn't its anchor. Bad enough hiding inside a tree trunk if the Darkness comes, let alone being out in the open for it to see. Stepping onto the grass, Guri immediately felt a sense of relief. Her part wasn't over yet, the next as dangerous. Still though, she couldn't help but feel pleased that she had managed to do what she'd been asked. Margaret nodded, before leaping inside the mirror.

Joining Qiao inside the trunk, Guri grasped his hand, giving and receiving comfort as they waited to see if the Darkness would come.

Margaret was clothed in dark magic. The black outside matched by the black within. Although it had never been used in the way it had been conjured for, the mirror still retained the taint of the Darkness. Coiled like a snake, waiting for a host to enter and be taken.

'I'm in,' she told Aeryissa.

Settling down, all she could do was wait and hope the Darkness took the bait. Trees started pouring in. Bursting through the ground, shaking their branches at the dark gloomy sky, acting as if the sun shone. Making sure to make plenty of noise the Yorkus glad to be doing something at last, added their bellows to cacophony of sound now rolling around Argonorth. Not wanting to put any magicals in danger, the trees had offered to act as a distraction. Cooped up for so long they relished the chance to play. None were taking any chances; adhering strictly to what they had been told by Fingerling, even the Yorkus listening avidly for once. Commanded that, at the first sign of the Darkness they were to leave, all hoped it would take its time, giving them a chance to stretch themselves and meet up with those they hadn't seen for a while.

Guri and Qiao listened to the trees helloing each other, the tree they were hiding in shooing away anyone that got to near. Both conscious that when Margaret emerged they will have only seconds to get her away.

Margaret knew instantly it was coming, she remembered what it felt like when they had waited in the armoury for it to swoop. When Eldora sacrificed herself to save them. Like angry bees disturbed in their hive. The drone was getting louder. Then the smell hit her, making her eyes water.

As one the trees disappeared. The one hiding Guri and Qiao, pulled its leaves inside, letting its branches appear gnarled and dead. The mirror thrummed as the Darkness drew near. Out of nowhere dark magicals began flocking towards the mirror. Without recourse to Fingerling, the trees burst forth again, blocking their way. Up ending them, as the Yorkus wrenched open the ground, burying them, before they could make a sound. All done in silence, not wanting to draw attention away from the mirror.

Margaret let small amounts of silver and shimmer speckle her skin. The Darkness reared back, twisting as it tasted her remembered scent. Hungry for it, throwing caution away. It dived inside. She let a few more beads of silver fall, allowing her shimmer to flare. That was all the temptation the Darkness needed. Going rigid as it entered her, filling her body with its cold, dark magic. Looking through the corridors of her mind. It searched for where the magic was hiding. She let one door open as if it were unable to resist the pull of the Darkness's will. It pushed forwards filling the space, revelling in the magic it found. She let it bask for a few moments in the power it craved. Then she started the whispers.

Follow me. Become. Relentlessly, saying the refrain over and over again. The Darkness tested the strength of her body. Margaret allowed herself to be manipulated. Satisfied that she was strong enough, it flooded her system. Her eyes snapped first black then red. She worked her jaw, feeling the change as it settled inside her.

As Athanasia's creature, it should by rights only obey her commands. Herded into a room in her mind, she began the process of bending it to her will. It didn't take her long to realise, although the links between the two of them had withered, if Athanasia managed to leave the Soul Lost land they could soon be reinstated, enabling her to call the Darkness, and take the magic it had collected. Margaret enforced the understanding that only by obeying her will, would it be able to throw of its shackles.

Left alone for so long without proper direction from its creator, it was ripe to be used. Meridian had left it with a craving for the magic and power of silver and shimmer, something she had in abundance. As the Darkness flooded her senses, trying its best to break down her barriers, she scanned its workings. Dismantling the spells put in place by Athanasia, using new ones to bind it to her instead. She promised it a new host, one where it could remain forever. All it had to do was obey her command and the magic and power it craved would be it's for the taking. Instead of covering Kingdom as a black cloud, it would be able to walk its landscape and rule the realm. All she asked in return, was that it carried out her instructions without hesitation.

The Darkness listened to Margaret's words, it waited for the threats to begin. When none were forth coming, it began to consider what she was saying, unaware that her magic was working its way into every fibre of its being.

When it had escaped the confines of its tomb, it had revelled in its freedom. Drawing magic from anyone it came across. The landscape of Kingdom was littered with magicals, husks of their former selves, barely alive, they roamed, their minds gone. Their only purpose to answer its call. Once it had drained everyone dry, scourging the land looking for any it had missed, it didn't know what to do. It had found a veil, sure that the silver it craved was hidden inside. Nothing it did could penetrate it. The reek of dark magic brought the Glasserium to its attention. Once again it was thwarted. It knew by those it drained that there was a place called Pictures full of magicals. Like the other places it had tried to enter this also denied it entry. With no new magic to plunder, its strength began to wane.

Catching Margaret's scent, it remembered chasing its host. Swooping in to claim its prize, only to find a dead magical wearing a carapace of silver and shimmer, not real magic. Frustrated at losing again, it had let its anger reign down on Kingdom. Churning up the earth, barrelling through hills and mountains, forcing upwards caves upwards to the surface. Destroying any buildings, ripping them apart, pulverising them to dust. Like a child denied a toy; its temper lost. Its mission to destroy everything in its path. Kingdom now nothing more than a land full of pits and craters. The ground stony and dry. One day scorching sunshine, the next endless rain. Electrical storms filled the night skies, making a display that no one saw. Margaret heard its thoughts, letting it know that, all that could change. With the power it would wield it could force magicals to return.

Guri and Qiao both felt a nudge, Margaret's emergence was

imminent. Discarding their cloaks, both exposed, the tree that had hidden them, gone. Qiao held Guri's hand as she readied herself. The shock of seeing Margaret transformed once again, nearly made her forget what she had to do. Qiao's hard pinch, bringing her back to herself. When the mirror exploded into dust behind her. Guri grabbed Margaret's arm, even through the glass of her hand, she could feel the dark magic that now engulfed her.

Chapter Fifty-Two

Emerging from the shaft, Aeryissa was amazed to see how many magicals and changelings had answered the call. To leave the safety of Pictures was no mean feat. She watched Bayu's face as her gaze swept over the crowds.

'Will you address them?' she asked.

She shook her head, Bayu could hear their conversation's, splattered with excitement and fear in equal measures. Many didn't even know of the Soul Lost lands existence as anything but a myth told around a campfire. Making her realise, that in her absence the realms had moved on. Only Eshe had continued the search for her. To step in now and claim them as her subjects, she knew wouldn't work. No matter how much power she wielded they hadn't come for her. Drawn by their loyalty to Kingdom, their desire to go home. Once again they showed themselves ready to face the Darkness or anything else dark magic may throw at them.

The shouts brought her back into the moment. The ground beneath their feet had begun to move. Everyone started to move backwards as the opening they were standing next to begun to churn. Millions of beetles big and small were scurrying back and forth, rolling the earth, pulling it down creating a bigger opening, the earth sucked from below.

The witches took to their broomsticks, hovering above the pit, watching as it grew bigger and bigger, sending back a running commentary on the beetle's progress. The magicians sent wave after wave of pulses to search for the demons hiding underneath the soil.

Orara had also taken to the skies, her keen dragon eyes scouring the pit for the first sign of them. Attuned to her, Bayu was the first to hear her thoughts. Aeryissa and Lefu picking up their scent moments later. The beetles were still moving through the earth, darklings were the first to emerge. The Ambrogio jumped into the pit, ripping them apart, flinging them up for the Fae's dragons to set them alight. Aeryissa and Bayu both ran, launching themselves into the opening, magicals and changelings following.

The demons were slow at first to react, exposed to the light, they needed time to adjust. Using this pause to get into the main clutch of them. Aeryissa and Bayu drew their swords, hacking at any that moved, searching for those in charge.

The Fae used their fairy dust in conjunction with the Alvie. As soon as they threw their foresters nets, the dust clung to the mesh. Locking the demon into a burning cage. Several demons had corralled a dozen witches, taking their broomsticks, snapping them before using them to beat them to a pulp. Spells were thrown, stars ignited, shouting, screaming. Blood curdling howls from the wolves rent the air as they downed a demon making everyone jump.

Cian, Lefu and Harsha worked as a team, barrelling their way through. Leaving the others of their clan to clear any demons they missed. Relentlessly the demons attacked, interspersed with waves of darklings, with no let up. Exhausted, those who were injured left the pit, as others took their place.

Aeryissa could feel Bayu's frustration as they worked together clearing a path. Both had seen the tunnels entrance now cleared by the beetles. Bayu sure that whoever was leading the demons this was where they would find them.

She kept her thoughts guarded. Bayu's earlier mention of Athanasia catching her unawares, stopping in time from voicing her fears that she was the one they sought. Conscious, that Margaret was risking everything to stop her, worrying that in the melee she would miss her signal to set off the crystals Kebale had laid. Magicians followed them into the tunnels, using their staffs to light them up.

Bayu, placed her hands onto the walls, letting her mind search. Concern crossed her face, she had been stopped. Only another ancient had the power to do so. Trying again she came up against another wall. This time she had no doubt. Athanasia was the power.

Screams rent the air, magic used as weapons lit up the sky. The fallout, fell like rain. The demons now exposed, unleashed the full force of their violent natures. Unlike the magicals and changelings who wanted to survive the fight, they didn't care, crazed, their bloodlust up, they took on all comers. Even attacking their own darklings as the frenzy took them over. Their dark magic like a miasma around them, hate filled eyes, razor sharp teeth, claws that could cut like knives, made them formidable.

Most had never encountered demons on this scale before. Seeing their comrades injured and killed spurring them on to keep going against the seemingly overwhelming odds.

Athanasia's prison was soon exposed to the light. Still feeding from those imprisoned below her chamber. She could feel the air move, her eyes hidden behind the mask she had created watched the battle. Attached to the walls by her vein like tendrils had seemed like a good idea at the time. Giving weight to her capture. Something had gone wrong. She had used the veins numerous times in the same way, her preferred way of feeding from the magicals. Unable this time to break free from the magic that held her, brought her anger to the fore. Willing Bayu to blast the Soul Lost land apart, releasing her from its grip and her prison.

Kebale fought his way to Aeryissa's side, shouting, 'the smell of bears is getting stronger.'

Using his claws he swung round behind her as a large demon lifted a hammer like staff, ready to bring it down onto her head.

With one swipe Kebale ripped his throat out, black blood spraying everyone nearby. Aeryissa quickly hacked another demon with her knife, paused, sniffing the air. Lefu, plunged his hand into a demon's chest that jumped in front of her, pulling out his heart, kicking the body away.

'I can smell them.'

Kebale stood on his hind legs, his head moving from side to side, nose receptors on high alert.

'This way,' he growled.

The beetles hearing Aeryissa's call directed their efforts to moving the soil. Pulling Kebale back. Sure now she had heard Athanasia hiss as the earth began to move. Beneath her now lay another pit, those inside also chained to the walls. Kebale roared his fury, bears, magicals and demons were being drained. Some had died where they hung, others driven mad by fear and terror. Those still alive, barely able to lift their heads. All wondering what knew torture awaited them.

Lefu spotted the veins snaking down, Aeryissa shook her head, whispering in his mind, to ignore what he'd seen. Kebale only had eyes for the bears. Without thought of what would happen, he used his claws to slice through the veins, the bears instantly going rigid. Some fell, unable to take the shock of being released. Others, panting in pain, saw who had saved them grimaced with relief that help had finally come. Joined by other bears and vampires they worked quickly to release them all. Cian had wanted to leave the demons to their fate, Aeryissa insisted they too should be released, obvious that they also had been used.

She had shut her mind to the thoughts she could feel drifting from Athanasia as they worked, her anger felt like a physical blow each time another captive was released.

Moving them all towards the surface, while trying to fend off the attacking demons, tested all their reserves of strength. The magician's came to their rescue, adapting small stars they used old fashioned sling shots to pulverise the demons with. Raining down like arrows, the spells they had cast making sure that they only exploded when hitting demons. Assailed from all sides, nevertheless no sooner had they been beaten back, than they surged forward again. Now their blood lust was up no demon would be able to stop. Only death would put an end to their assaults. Denied uncontrollable violence for so long, even if they had wanted to stop and surrender, their nature gave them no choice. Death or victory their only options.

'Can you contact Margaret? something must be wrong, my link with her isn't working.'

Unsure how to answer, Aeryissa ignored Bayu's question. Leaving those they rescued to be cared for, she and Kebale returned to the fight.

Incensed at being ignored, Bayu, transported so close in front of her that she killed a demon by default of it being in the way when she emerged.

'What aren't you telling me?' she demanded. Her silver flaring as her anger took over.

The noise of battle, the screams and cries of the injured and dying, a back drop they were both aware of.

'I'm not in league with her. If I'd have thought before acting, I would have guessed sooner that she is the power, not the demons.'

Bayu waited, she had never been in the position before of feeling subservient to someone else. She may be ancient, but Aeryissa held much more power than she currently did.

'As you've guessed, Athanasia is controlling what is happening. When Margaret stepped inside of me to break the wizard's fire. She saw her for what she is. She is the one who needs the land blasting open. Margaret believes it is the only way she can escape from her own retaining spell. Releasing her from its grip will also allow her to call the Darkness.'

'Where is Margaret? Why can't I contact her?'

'She's here. Haven't you seen her? She's been helping with the reinforcements and getting the injured away to safety.'

Bayu knew she was losing control, if she'd ever had any in the first place. When first awakened from being spell bound, she had once again felt all powerful. As silver flooded her body and her senses came back to her, she truly felt alive. Seeing the magicals and changeling's of Eirian all come to pay homage had brought back memories of old. Now though, she wondered if she had been a curiosity to be seen and picked over, rather than someone to be followed. Both Kingdom and Eirian had had to take care of themselves for a long time. They didn't appear to need or want someone to rule over them.

Margaret could easily hear her chaotic thoughts as they chased each other. Eshe had given her much more than magic and power. She had given her memories, stories and secrets.

'I know this is hard for you. Eshe was determined to find and wake you. I think she hoped that all would go back as it once was. Reading the Afsaneh, it was clear in how much regard she held you. I was directed to find you because she believed we needed you. We have kept you out of the loop...'

'In case you couldn't trust me,' she looked Margaret square in the eyes. Defying her to deny it.

'Both of you are a threat to all. Athanasia has turned to dark magic. She was I believe once your friend. Even though I have Eshe's memories of you. I do not know you. When I entered Kingdom I came only for a new life. I didn't ask for any of this. But it is what it is. My role is to make sure that neither Kingdom nor Eirian, are ever in thrall to anyone, ever again. Whether they call themselves queen or ancient. Athanasia has given us no choice, she will have to die.'

'Even I cannot kill another ancient,' Bayu retorted, shocked at Margaret's suggestion, that it was even possible.

The void gaped open, what was once the land of the demons, now a pit of despair. Bodies littered the landscape. Demons injured, were ignored by other demons, enjoying killing each other as much as anyone else, even those who lay dying weren't saved from their fury.

The witches and the Fae had been swooping down when finding injured magicals or changelings, taking them to the first aid stations set up. While Qiao transported those too bad to climb aboard the broomsticks or dragons, the sickness of travel, forgotten, in the comfort of being safe.

'Are you okay?' asked Elfrad, as Margaret clung to his arm.

Gathering herself, she smiled, 'yes, a bit of a wobble, that's all.'

When Eadulf had released them from the glass box. Margaret had felt her body waver, as if someone had struck her behind the knees. Elfrad, held onto her as she sagged. His strength for once propping her up. Once she began to move around, gotten used to the feeling of being cut in half, colour started to return to her face.

Guri the one to ask, 'so what's it like. The Darkness?'

'Cold.'

Although separate, she could feel what was happening. Something she hadn't bargained on feeling so much.

The crystals blew, the ground heaved upwards. Demons, free at last from the spell that bound them, poured out. Darklings also surged, flowing over the top looking to escape. The magicals and changelings had pulled back, now they also surged forward. Yelling and shouting, roars and clashes of steel rent the air. Bodies flew as they were hacked and slashed.

The dragons raced across the sky, using their breath to set fire to the fleeing demons. Revelling in their screams as they burnt. The battle making many forget who they were fighting. Stopping in time from killing their friends, the magicals and changelings didn't have time to pause as the next round of demons were upon them. The magicians reigned stars on anything that moved. Cian's vampire raging at them to stop and think where they were throwing them. Caught by a flurry, small burns pockmarked his body.

Out of the chaos arose Athanasia. Golden, no more sightless, her black eyes roamed across the fighting. The veins that had held her captive trailing down like stems of ivy. Taking advantage of her distraction, the demons surged. Overwhelming the forces against them. Evening the score as they in turn hacked at the magicals and changelings too slow to get out of their path. Everything stopped, as if an unheard command had been spoken. Silence ruled.

The Soul Lost land gaped open, the void it had been made from now ripped apart. Laid bare its stench wafted, the dark magic that it had held for so long now free. Athanasia basked in the glory of release. Turning her eyes towards Kingdom, she called. The demons understood her action, raising their arms high they whooped and shouted. Turning their gaze on the enemy before them, their eyes glowing red as they thought of the massacre to come.

Bayu stood next to Aeryissa who in turn stood with Margaret and Elfrad. He holding onto Margaret's arm as if keeping her from falling. Aeryissa noted the action.

The magicals and changelings ranged behind them all stared up in wonder at Athanasia glowing above them. Turning her now seeing eyes towards the group, she floated gently down, landing on her feet, inducing a sigh from the demons, heard by all.

'You left me, Bayu,' she announced, her voice firm and in control. Gone the wavering croakiness she had earlier used. 'This may have been my creation. You alone knew, that I was tricked into making it. Yet, you never came to find me. For that you will pay.'

The demons on hearing her words bellowed their agreement, wanting to set to and attack. With one look Athanasia silenced them.

'You and your puny army are no match for me and mine,' she spat, her words an act of fury. 'For years I have been funnelling shimmer. My demons have brought me tasty morsels that have boosted my magic. The Darkness in Kingdom has felt my release and heard my call. Once I have taken the magic and power it has collected, I intend to be the only one to rule the realms. I may not be able to kill you. But I can make the rest of your life...' Licking her lips, she added, 'interesting.' Her laughter rang out to the delight of the demons. 'Nothing to say. The vampire especially has been vocal. What are you anyway? I can see the way your skin catches the light that you have both shimmer and silver inside you. How is that possible? Did you give them to her Bayu? I know you stole shimmer from me.'

Elfrad held tight to Margaret's arm, feeling the tremors racking her skin. She'd told him that this might happen when her other self was drawing near.

Athanasia saw the direction of Bayu's gaze.

Shrieking, she cried, 'it comes.'

The noise of the Darkness recognised by all except the demons. The drone, once again as if millions of angry bees were flying straight towards them, the smell of sulphur hot on their tail. Athanasia lifted her arms skywards, ready to receive it. Her face transformed as the need for power made her appear almost beautiful. Aeryissa clamped her arm across Bayu as she went to move forwards. She raised her eyebrows in query. Aeryissa mouthed.

'Wait.'

The Darkness, blotted out the weak sunlight. Bringing a coldness to the air. It whirled around Athanasia's head as if working out where to settle, what to do. What was a mass of dense blackness, slowly began to form into a shape. Athanasia closed her eyes, willing the Darkness to fall on her, ready to receive its magic. She couldn't help the smile as she felt its movement brush over her. Standing with her feet planted, her mind open, she waited. Hearing shouts from the demons made her open her eyes.

Bayu and her group still stood in the same place. No one had made a move against her. Once again the sky was clear. Surely, she thought, that wasn't it. Taking in the Darkness even for her, should be a brutal intrusion into her body. Peripherally she saw something move. Turning her head she looked over her shoulder. The Darkness had coalesced into an entity.

Athanasia could see by Bayu's expression that she too didn't understand. The voice when it came dripped with sarcasm.

'You are not as powerful as you think you are.'

The entities features were hard to make out, as if the Darkness hadn't fully engaged with its host. Bayu felt Aeryissa's nudge, interpreting it as an instruction to stay still and silent. Athanasia was incensed that her creation may have turned against her. She created it. Its only purpose to serve her needs.

Margaret's trembles were getting stronger, Elfrad held on tight. She made the decision to concentrate on Athanasia, Bayu wasn't showing any signs of wanting to change sides. In fact, she looked scared, as if cornered like an animal. She had to be careful not to let Athanasia hear her command, the Darkness although now bent to Margaret's will, was still her creation, its loyalty not yet tested.

The miasma of darkness launched itself, they fell, Athanasia quickly jumping back onto her feet. She brought her hands together with a clap. Like thunder, the sound echoed around the land a pulse of magic tore through Margaret's other form. The pain unimaginable. The Darkness tried to retreat but there was nowhere to go.

Elfrad held his Margaret, Aeryissa moving to stand close beside her. Both worried about the heat emanating from her skin. Before they could stop her, Bayu placed a hand on her back. Instantly her body began to cool. Unsure what this signalled. Did it mean she was on their side? Or like Athanasia had, was she playing them. Seeing Margaret start to settle, both their thoughts were the same, they would worry about her reasons later. At the moment they were grateful that she'd helped.

Athanasia stood over the entity. Mewling like a kitten, curled into a ball, she was shocked to see how easily it had been brought to heel. Using her wand she let small beads of magic drip from its end, convinced that the magic contained in the host was still usable.

'What you have taken. Is mine. It belongs to me,' she snarled.

Her hands like claws, she plunged them into the dark mass that was Margaret's other body. Drawing the Darkness from her, making her scream in agony.

Elfrad got ready to run, timing was crucial, she would have

only seconds to snap back. They hoped that in her delight at having retrieved the Darkness Athanasia wouldn't notice her escape. Elfrad ran, Margaret snapped back.

Bayu stopped her from falling backwards with the momentum of her entrance. Aeryissa grabbed her arm, pinching her hard as Margaret had told her to do. Elfrad returned to take his place by her side.

Athanasia drank the Darkness in, letting it flow through her body. Filling her up with its magic and power. Now she would make them pay. As the last remnants of it died down. She turned her gaze to the spot where it had been. Her surprise at not finding a host evident. Whoever it had been she wanted to rip apart for daring to take what was hers by right. Bayu's group hadn't moved. The demons also hadn't taken anyone. Perplexed she looked around, a bad feeling starting to emerge as she realised that something was wrong.

Margaret's body settled. The two halves joined once more. Her experience of the Darkness inside her not something she wished ever to do again. Its taint, locked away in the recesses of her mind and body was a part of her she would have to cut away. Sure now that Bayu would not be a problem. Her steading hand had been what she'd needed. Athanasia though she would deal with, her death warranted.

She stepped forward as near to appearing as a norm as she could make herself now look. Athanasia turned, her glance insolent and sneering. All could see the magic begin to crackle around her. Small sparks of shimmer flaring out, making the demons retreat so as not to be touched by its rays.

'Because of you,' stated Margaret, making sure that her voice was strong and steady, 'we have all lost those we love. I don't believe that you were completely tricked into creating the Soul Lost land. At first maybe, once you realised though that you could manipulate everyone from a place of safety, a place many had never heard of. You took over.'

Athanasia clapped. The demons laughed, the noise raucous and sarcastic.

'Some would think that revenge was at the heart of your actions. Whereas the truth is you have always been riddled with dark magic. Hiding your true nature, working in the shadows. If you hadn't used such a powerful retaining spell things may have turned out differently. Instead, you made a prison not only for demons but yourself. Try as you might to escape. You have been foiled repeatedly.'

'Until now,' roared Athanasia. 'Now I am free and so is my army. Weak, that's what you are. Using magic as if it was a tool and not a power. It's wasted on all of you. Kingdom, Eirian and not forgetting Novia under my rule will reach their full potential. You do know what I am?' searching out Bayu, she pointed, 'don't forget her. When you are all dust. We, or rather I, shall still rule.'

'That's not going to happen,' grinned Margaret. 'I'm going to kill you.'

For a moment Athanasia's face registered shock. Then her arrogance took over, bolstered by the Darkness inside her and the demons at her back. Shaking her head, at this creature who dared threaten her. Making sure that her voice also travelled over the crowds, she retorted.

'Even if you were strong enough to overpower me, a prisoner you could make me. But not kill me. That is outside of anything you think you can achieve.'

Athanasia bored with the conversation, readied herself to kill this magical. The change in Margaret stilled her hand. The demons gasped, the sound reverberating as their fear took hold.

Bayu's face was as stunned as Athanasia's, Margaret's transformation was complete. Gone was the norm incarnation of herself. Now a warrior stood at the front of her army. Silver and shimmer speckled her skin. Her vampire on full view. Her eyes golden one minute and silver the next. Their original blue a backdrop making them sparkle even more. The frayed and dirty tunic and trousers she had worn, replaced by the thinnest leather, pale grey, the runes woven across their surface adding to her shine. Boots studded with spurs of silver, their blades honed to a razor sharpness. Margaret let every part of her guardian show. Power and strength oozing from every pore. None that saw her would ever forget the sight. This was magic in all its glory, making them stand straighter, want their magic, thinking no more that it was weak and feeble. Feeling a strength many hadn't felt for a long time fill them. While others who had never experienced a boost of magic freely given before, laughed in delight, as it flowed across their skin.

The ground began to shake, many moving backwards knowing what it signalled. The Trip trees burst forth, shaking out their branches. Arranging themselves behind Margaret. None could believe the sight they were seeing. The trees sparkled, shimmer dripped from their branches. Behind them came the Yorkus, their fists raised to the sky, their bellows making everyone glad once again that they were on their side.

Fingerling the last to burst through.

'Oh my.'

Smiling at her old friend's reaction, Margaret dipped her head in acknowledgement. Behind the magicals and changelings, much to the Alvie's delight trees were springing up all over the place. While this was going on Aeryissa hadn't taken her eyes from Athanasia, Bayu also held her in her sights. Only Elfrad was distracted by all that was happening.

Athanasia didn't know what to think. This creature before her obviously had control of silver and shimmer. But she and Bayu were queens, these gifts belonged ultimately to them. Whatever this magical thought she could control would soon prove false. A show that's all this is. Somehow they meant to capture her. That she told herself would not happen. She had no intention of being hidden away ever again.

Glancing across at Bayu, Athanasia tried to penetrate her thoughts. Surely she wasn't in league with this vampire. She must be biding her time. Fooling them she was on their side. No ancient would stand aside, for a mere magical to take her place. Athanasia decided that she cannot simply stand here and wait to be attacked. The demons had fallen back as the vampire exposed her magic. She must rally them to her call. Failure wasn't an option.

The trees when they appeared had been the last straw, they dripped with shimmer. Who in their right mind gives it to a tree? Those who showed signs of silver only had it in small quantities compared to what Bayu could call. Yet each time she looked at her she appeared more and more diminished. Her glow getting weaker.

Everyone looked up as flocks of elemental witches flew in formation. Landing behind the Yorkus, they pushed to the front. Margaret smiled in relief. Now it ends.

Without any warning she dived headfirst into Athanasia and disappeared. Stunned and shocked in equal measures. The demons fell further back, their courage waning. The trees held back the magicals and changelings from surging forwards. Elfrad couldn't help the shout, calling her name as she sprung. Aeryissa, their link open, heard the oomph as she entered Athanasia's body.

Bayu fell to the ground, landing with a bump as her legs gave way beneath her. When she created the role of guardian, she had never given her this much power. Eshe's concern, that she wouldn't know how to wield it still a memory Bayu hadn't forgotten. Her shock at taking access and control of the witches shimmer was nothing to Bayu's now as she realised that somehow Margaret had taken her silver. None of the spells she had used would have enabled any of this to happen. For the first time in her life she felt as if she was being manipulated by unseen hands.

Athanasia's body went into shock at the invasion by the powerful force that was Margaret. Frantically she tried to close her mind, draw her dark magic into a safe place.

Margaret didn't stop, she barrelled her way through Athanasia's blocks, knocking them down like skittles. Wrenching open the doors in her mind she blasted each room with silver and shimmer. The dark squirming to get away. As each room was cleared. Athanasia grew weaker. The magic she had relied upon was being erased. Her defences went into overdrive. She had to expel her visitor. Still convinced that she couldn't be killed. Athanasia started to fight back. In the dark reaches, she called forth the Darkness, letting it loose. It enveloped Margaret recognising her scent. Trying to invade her body as she was invading Athanasia's. The tussle for supremacy a battle to the death. Margaret let the Darkness in.

Sensing victory, Athanasia let it surge forward. Margaret opened her mind. The blinding light she created, began to eat into the Darkness, trapped inside her it had nowhere to go. Realising it had been tricked it fought back against both of them.

The elementals caught Margaret's signal. Holding hands, each drew on their power, the earth beneath Athanasia's feet began to churn as small flames licked along her legs, moving upwards, the air rushing in to fan them. Athanasia was obvious to what was happening, concentrating all her efforts on ousting Margaret.

Elfrad wanted desperately to stop the witches. The force of Aeryissa's glare holding him back. Now the wind got up, buffeting them all as they watched Athanasia burn. The rain fell only on Athanasia, small droplets at first, turning to fat ones that pounded her body, putting out the flames. All gasped, as she remained untouched.

The Darkness was getting weaker. The last tendrils holding fast, before Margaret's magic consumed them. Athanasia's fury knew no bounds. Carelessly she opened the doors of her mind, sending everything she had towards her. Wanting her out. Wanting her dead. Silver and shimmer surged forwards to meet the darkest magic Margaret had ever known. At its core, death and destruction, hate filled it ripped into her. Like a dog with a bone it shook and worried at her magic, trying to tear the fabric of it apart. Athanasia had lost control, her madness let loose had no direction. She tried hard to call it, but to no avail. Margaret let her magic build, as it reached its peak, she exploded out of Athanasia's body taking her magic with her.

The Trip trees enveloped her within their branches. Hidden from view, she let them feast. They had trained for this. They didn't let her down. Athanasia's magic was drowned by their goodness.

Athanasia stood like a puppet whose strings had been pulled. No one though, believed that she wasn't still a threat. They had seen dark magic too many times make a comeback to go anywhere near her.

Opening her eyes, she sneered, 'you, think you've won? Taking my magic won't kill me. I can always get more.'

'Did you feel the fire?'

'Your witches paltry attempts to burn me were pathetic,' brushing her arms down her body. 'Not even a mark.'

'That wasn't the point. Ancients, have many layers of magic protecting their bodies. Repairing them if injured. The fire wasn't to burn you. It was to set up a chain reaction in those layers. Even now the elemental's magic is working through your system. Peeling them back, exposing your vulnerability, will allow me to kill you.'

Bayu couldn't help her thoughts leeching out.

'I thought it was a myth,' she whispered.

'Stop her. If you don't you'll be next,' cried Athanasia in desperation.

Now that she had been made aware, she could feel herself become lighter as each layer disappeared. She gathered herself to transport away, and nothing happened. Margaret watched amusement on her face as Athanasia nearly managed to do it, then was stopped. Frustration and fear made her want to lash out, this vampire who Bayu must have brought into their midst was the cause of all her problems. Unsure which one of them she wanted to kill the most.

'It's done,' called out each elemental as they stepped back beside the trees.

Athanasia's eyes frantically sought a friendly face. All stood not in fear but in disgust and remembrance in all that she had made them lose. Bayu didn't want to look, sure that Margaret was going to rip her apart.

'You are no longer ancient. Under my command, the Darkness has disconnected you from your past cycles.'

Magicals and changelings pressed forward as the trees struggled to hold them back. Athanasia looked into Margaret's eyes and saw no mercy. Her face closed and cold. Every inch a queen. As the thought formed, Margaret shook her head, speaking loud and clear so all heard.

'Queen I will never be.' Looking over to Bayu, she added, 'or you.'

Athanasia legs buckled, she fell to her knees.

Margaret pulled her head up, looking into her eyes she commanded.

'Die.'

Athanasia tried to hold on, but the will now inside her body was too strong to ignore. Her organs began shutting down, her blood stopped flowing, her breathe caught in her throat. Those watching turned away, what Margaret was doing seemed particularly cruel, many preferring that she had slain her quickly with her own hands. As Athanasia lay on the ground, Margaret repeated her command.

'Die.'

Bayu, surprised by the tears flowing down her face, turned away. Athanasia's eyes closed, her mind quiet, her magic gone, ancient no more. Now just a body distorted by dark magic. As her true form was revealed, many took back the pity they had first felt. Margaret waited. When she rose, all fell away in shock. Athanasia once again hovered above them. Her gloating smile a goad to their anger. Demons hearing her cry returned to the fray, ready to take up arms in her name.

'Sorry to disappoint,' she cackled. 'Nice try.'

Margaret leapt, entering Athanasia again, the shock tumbling her over. Realising what she was going to do, she cried out.

The Darkness had shown her where to look, curled as if asleep, lay a smaller core, plucking it from its root. She felt the shock bounce around Athanasia's body.

A tear ran down Bayu's face as Athanasia's skin started to whiten before cracking open and crumbling into dust.

'Is this to be my fate?'

Margaret didn't have a chance to answer, the demons attacked. With no thoughts of surrender they threw themselves head first into battle.

Chapter Fifty-Three

Drawing Aeryissa aside, Margaret held onto Bayu, transporting the three of them a short distance away from the melee.

'I'm leaving.'

'What do you mean? We need you to stop this bloodbath in its tracks.'

'The magicals and changelings have to fight this battle themselves. If I step in, they will never feel strong and safe on their own merits. It's time everyone stopped relying on someone else's power and looked inwards to their own.'

Aeryissa's anger made her bolder, spitting, 'you're leaving us? Taking your magic and what…? Rule?'

Bayu waited as the friends glared at each other. What fate Margaret had for her she tried not to think of. One thing she was sure of though, she had no intention of ruling anyone. Her defences were the strongest Bayu had ever come up against, even so, she had still managed to catch snippets of her thoughts.

'Margaret is right. I should have allowed the magicals of Idona and the changelings of Tarian to stay and fight for their realms. Instead, I made them leave and I took on the task of killing the demons. If I had a bit more faith in their abilities, then maybe all that has happened as a result, could have been prevented.'

'That's not all you did though, is it?' snapped Margaret. 'If you both hadn't been so greedy for power, taking what wasn't yours to take. Then all the deaths that have happened as a result of your actions, wouldn't have occurred.'

'What do you mean?' demanded Aeryissa, her impatience at being away from the fight, and anger at Margaret leaving, showing in the cutting tone of her voice.

For the first time Bayu looked at Margaret with hatred in her eyes.

'Are you going to kill me the way you did Athanasia,' she snapped, 'the last of the ancients. None to stand in your way.'

She surprised them both by laughing.

'Your anger, is the result of the actions you took long ago about to be laid bare. You've deceived yourself into thinking all that has happened, is someone else's fault and that you had no hand in its creation. When in fact you were instrumental in its cause.'

The ground beneath their feet began shaking, the earth moved, sucked downwards. Hands appeared, then branches. Fingerling heaved his body upwards. His trunk forcing itself through the hole he'd created. Every branch and hand shaking in anger.

Next, a puddle appeared, the water rising higher as the shape of a man began to form. Pelagias's eyes locked onto Bayu.

'Am I supposed to guess what this is all about?' she demanded. 'Or is someone going to tell me?'

'Have you really forgotten, or are you pretending to yourself that you don't remember?' snapped Fingerling.

Turning to Margaret, Bayu told her, 'if you're going to kill me. Then get on with it. All this… Is meaningless.'

'If you won't explain for her,' chimed in Aeryissa, her annoyance growing by the minute. 'Then perhaps you can tell me? Only in case you've all forgotten there is a battle going on.'

'A long time ago,' explained Fingerling. 'Many ancients walked the realms. None ruled. Magicals, changelings and demons lived together. Most in harmony, those that didn't, were banished to the fringes of the realms. The use of dark magic, rarely seen. As in all things though, life doesn't stay the same. Their powerful magic had been handed down to them. None, could remember who had given it or why it was they who had received it. In doing so, it enabled some of those chosen to wield enormous power and live long lives.

Unfortunately, the gift of magic wasn't given in equal quantities. Most were content with their lot. Overtime a few came to resent what others had, wanting more for themselves. Shown the error of their ways, they settled down, thankful for the magic that they did have. All, except two of them. These two craved more, expected more. Athanasia had always been drawn more to the darker side of life. Bending towards those who were always in trouble. While Bayu enjoyed the feeling of pure power magic gave her.'

She stared at him daring him to continue.

'It was her idea. She swept Athanasia along. Getting her to learn more about the dark arts. Convincing her that with its help, they could take our magic for themselves. A spell was made. In her defence, Bayu did finally come to her senses, realising what she had proposed, tried to renege. It was too late. The deed was done, the spell cast.'

'I did try to get her to reverse it. But she wouldn't listen.'

'That maybe so, yet you still walked away. Athanasia with shimmer and you with silver,' raged Pelagias. 'She may have knowingly imprisoned us, but you still took our magic for your own. Worse still, you never wondered what happened to us. Where we were? What had become of us? Wiped from your mind, as if we never existed.'

Aeryissa looked from Fingerling to Pelagias.

'You're the same?'

'We are,' boomed Fingerling, as Pelagias nodded in agreement. 'As are Guri and Vidya.'

'Bayu, took silver from me, and Athanasia took shimmer from Fingerling. Athanasia also tried to commandeer Guri's Glasserium on Neg, destroying it in the process. While Bayu, took Pictures for her own. Ignoring the fact that it is Vidya's creation.'

Aeryissa's astonishment, made her cry out, 'why did I not know any of this?'

'I did try to make amends,' sighed Bayu, trying to justify herself by adding, 'I worked hard to make sure that I only used silver for fair purposes.'

Margaret retorted, 'you still took what wasn't yours. Then set yourself up as a queen. All that has happened has stemmed from the spell both you and Athanasia cast. All the misery and death occurring, caused by your lust for power.'

Bayu spat, 'all this talk of past deeds. What do you hope to achieve. I cannot change the past. I did try to make amends. If I could go back and put things right, I would. I can't. So what happens now?'

'Can the spell be reversed?' asked Aeryissa.

'No,' Pelagias and Fingerling said together.

'Speaking for myself, I have been in this form for so long. I doubt that I would enjoy the confines of standing on two feet, besides I would miss my friends, the Warra.

Fingerling shook his branches in agreement.

'I too would find it strange to once again walk the realms in that way.'

Bayu straightened her shoulders, lifted her chin.

'I am sorry. I don't know what else to say. If it's any consolation, all magic has left me. I can still feel its pull, but it's weak, no longer powerful. Margaret controls it all now.'

As interesting as all this was, Aeryissa wanted to get back to the fight.

'Why don't you spell bind her, this time permanently,' she suggested. 'Unless you think she should be killed in the same way as Athanasia.'

'I don't think she should be killed,' explained Margaret, 'neither did Eshe. The details she left for me in the Afsaneh, were clear, even though Bayu started out as one of the instigators in all that has happened. Over the years she has done many good deeds. Eshe also made it clear, even when she found out what Bayu had done, she still trusted her. At the same time she demanded that when the time was right, as much as it pained her to say, Bayu should be punished, while silver and shimmer should go back to their rightful owners. Magic will always be at my command. Unless I need to call on their power, silver will once again flow through water and shimmer will again live inside trees.'

Seeing the look on Aeryissa's face, she smiled, 'I'm not an ancient in disguise.'

'You must be something though…?'

'Margaret is descended from those who came before. She embodies all that we were supposed to be and more,' pronounced Fingerling, unable to keep the pride from his voice.

If asked, all would swear, that for a moment, overlaying her face was that of another.

Leaving Aeryissa to return to the fight, Margaret transported Bayu to Eirian. Fingerling and Pelagias following.

As soon as they emerged inside the veil, Bayu asked, 'once you spell bind me. Could I be taken back to Novia? To where you found me.'

'Why,' asked Fingerling, his thoughts of imprisoning her somewhere dark and remote, waning.

'Before all… I was happy. In my ignorance.'

No structures stood in Kingdom anymore, all flattened long ago as the Darkness tore them apart looking for magicals to drain. Only Gork's had somehow managed to survive the chaos. Margaret honed onto Lefu's signature and transported as near as she could get to him. Busy ripping apart demons. She didn't ask his permission before snaring several vampires, making them roar in anger, as her ropes of shimmer wound around them pulling them from the battle to her side. Before they disappeared she caught the look Lefu cast her. Deference for her position hanging by a thread. Her absence noted and not liked.

When they emerged into Kingdom, the vampire's anger was to the fore, turning on her forgetting who she was, showing their fangs, eyes black with fury.

'The battle will be finishing soon,' she told them, ignoring their posturing. 'Gork's are roaming Kingdom. Kill or contain them. It's up to you just don't get in my way.'

'Does Lefu know where we are? He is our leader,' shouted a large vampire, his bloody axe a testament to how many demons he'd killed.

Margaret's eyes locked onto him. Her gaze coming to fall on the rest letting them see and feel a glimpse of her power. Without another word they turned away and set off, all feeling diminished in the face of such raw magic. Margaret watched them stomp away, anger in every line of their bodies. Once out of sight, she turned her gaze to the once beautiful landscape. The Darkness had scoured the earth, pits and craters abounded. Boggy ground a death trap. Jagged peaks instead of hills and mountains soared sky wards. A foul smell still clung over many parts of the land. Its miasma swirling like a mist. Dazed and broken magicals wandered. Their minds gone, their magic taken. Like zombies they roamed.

While the vampire's took care of the Gork's. Margaret rounded up the magicals, transporting them to the far reaches of Kingdom and putting them out of their misery whether they be dark magicals or not. The wraiths were harder to put down. Now, even more hazy than they were before the Darkness used them. Appearing to evaporate before reappearing again. Unable to hold them in one place long enough, she cast a herding spell. It flew around Kingdom, drawing the wraiths together into one solid mass.

Once sure that she had gathered them all. She cast a dissolving spell. Bound together by cords of shimmer, they wailed and screamed as her silver fell upon them like rain. As soon as the droplets landed, they shrieked all the more. Once they were all extinguished, she called the Warra. Cleansing the ground, they washed the wraiths into oblivion.

The demons which inhabited Kingdom, had managed to somehow stay hidden. They had used the state of the land, to tunnel underneath. Used to keeping to the shadows, the dark magic they wore like a cloak helping to deflect interest from the magicals.

Margaret transported into the heart of the still raging battle, demons that were surprised by her appearance, quickly attacking. With no time to engage, she blasted them by razing her hands, shimmer and silver flew in an arc. Burning any within her range. The magicals and changelings who saw it happen. Cheered, to see the Margaret at last enter the fray. Ignoring their cries of jubilation, her mind sought Elfrad.

Using his two swords at the same time, he was barrelling his way through a crowd of larger demons. Manically shouting at the top of his voice, his battle cry lost in the noise from others with their own refrain. Breathing hard, he turned to find Margaret in front of him, without a word she grabbed his arm and transported them out of the battle and into Kingdom. Rocked by the speed and surprise of her entrance. Elfrad returned his swords to the sheaths on his back.

'Where have you been?' he yelled. Realising where he was, he added, 'why are we here?'

As usual Margaret didn't explain.

'I'm clearing Kingdom. The demons are the last. I need you to be my anchor, while I split again. My other self still retains the Darkness's taint. I need this part of my body to convince the demons to come out of hiding. Once out, I can deal with them.'

Because this other self couldn't transport, but could still climb, Margaret had positioned herself on top of a hill, its flat top gave a perfect three hundred and sixty degree view of the surrounding landscape. Her senses had told her that the biggest concentration of demons was hidden in this area.

She conjured a soft wind to swirl her scent, pushing it outwards, encouraging it to seep into the crevasses dotted around. To travel underground, tempting the demons to appear. Her eyes caught the first movement, this was no demon, only a darkling sent out to scout the area. Sitting still she let it get nearer, the hazy cloak of darkness she wore, making it unsure what it was looking at. She knew though that it recognised the Darkness's taint. Its hole for a nose twitched, drawing in the smell. Scuttling back to the hollow it had emerged from, she waited for the demons to come.

Slowly they began to appear, cautious and wary they climbed out of the tunnels. Sniffing the air, looking towards the hilltop. Muttering, as they noticed the cloud of Darkness waiting for them. Scrambling towards her, Margaret knew she may not get all of them here right now, setting up a chain reaction spell would be the only way she could make sure that eventually, they would all perish. She needed a few to cast it on, then like a virus it would spread. Leap frogging to any demon it came into contact with. Even when the demons were dead, it would lie dormant inside the earth ready to claim another victim as soon as any set foot in Kingdom or Eirian.

The nearer they got the more wary they became. She didn't move, letting the cloud of darkness she had conjured move around her, even replicating the Darkness's drone and smell. Urging the demons to come closer, believing that their master had returned. The spell flew outwards, the black cloud descending on the demons. Unworried at first, they revelled in the touch of their master. Then the spell began to bite. Speeding through their bodies, turning their insides to mush. Burning their magic, wiping every bit of dark knowledge from their minds. Like an empty box they staggered, mindless, until, with no strength left they fell. Their bodies disintegrating before turning to dust.

Margaret called to Elfrad, letting go of her arm, she snapped back into her body, the force making her yelp. In seconds he was back in the thick of the fight. Demons attacking from all sides.

Aeryissa felt the shift of Margaret transporting, reaching out with her mind, she was ecstatic to hear her answering words.

'Kingdom is ours.'

CHAPTER FIFTY-FOUR

The celebrations went on long into the night, spilling over into the next day. All reluctant to leave. Magicals and changelings slept where they fell, exhaustion from fighting for some, too much drink for others. For once, none worried about sleeping with one eye open.

The vampires had enjoyed hunting the Gork's. Once their hunger was sated, they began corralling them ready for the others of their clan to arrive. Knowing what a feast awaited them, went some way to allaying their fears at what Lefu would say to them for leaving the fight.

Margaret, Aeryissa and Qiao all felt drained, encouraging each other to keep going, as in relays they transported magicals and changelings long into the night. Margaret directed them to the large clearing she had found when travelling around the realm. The only real piece of flat land left. But it was filling up fast.

No one wanted to go back to Pictures, all wanted to be in Kingdom. Not even the state of it putting them off. For the changelings it was somewhere they had heard of, yet many had never visited. Margaret's plan to take them directly back to Eirian was shot down quickly by Kebale.

Telling her, 'they had fought together. Their friends and family had died together. Now they would rebuild Kingdom together.'

Cheers rang out at his words. Both pleased to hear such passion echoed back by the crowds. This is what Kingdom needed. Unification. Everyone coming together.

Already tales were being woven around the campfires, all telling their part in the battle. Margaret let her shadow-self emerge, blending into the background she listened as the stories unfolded around her.

When she had left the fight and Aeryissa returned. Many looked for her to take a stand, end the fighting in one fell swoop. With no time to wonder where she was or why she didn't act, anger at all that had happened to them sharpened their will to win.

As she would have expected the vampires were at the forefront, tearing into the demons and darklings, matched only by the power of the bears and wolves. Lefu was held up by many as a true leader, directing everyone, his cool demeanour even within the midst of battle, now legendary. Joined with Aeryissa they made a formidable team. She able to utilise all the clan skills at her disposable, many thought of her as some sort of whirling dervish. Able to fly and swoop without need of a dragon, her diving skills only matched by those of the Kaimi and the owls.

Magicals were in awe of Fafnir and Orara, in their dragon forms they looked like silver streaks flashing through the sky. Their roars telling everyone to run, heeded straightaway, the demons left wondering why they were retreating, soon burnt to a crisp as the flames from the dragons engulfed them.

Margaret smiled to hear how the Fae's dragons hearing the bellowing of the changeling ones. Set up their own roars, wanting to join in the fight with them, the Fae normally in full control, had to use their fairy dust to calm them down. Directing them to smaller groups of demons, instead of the dragon's fire burning them, Zekia and her sisters used their dust to good effect.

Elfrad also had emerged as a hero, wielding his two swords as if an extension of his hands. His hell cat appearing and disappearing in the blink of an eye. He had invoked feelings of awe. The tales of his fighting, embedded forever into the folk lore of Kingdom. Finally in the thick of things, where he was always meant to be. His greeter self, sloughed off like an old skin. A warrior, a Bomani, in all his glory, made her proud to know him as her friend. Standing in the shadows of a tall oak, it cheered her to listen as the wizards and warriors at last put aside their differences. Coming together in adversity, standing shoulder to shoulder they had fought, protecting each other from the demons onslaught. Each of their tales of daring do getting more and more fantastical as each one added their part. By the ease of their tones and the smiles on their faces she could easily see the competition between them for so long had been replaced by nothing more than friendly banter.

As the trees began springing up on the edge of the clearing, the Alvie left to sit amongst their friends again, swapping tales and remembering those they had all lost. The Kaimi had already put in a request to Fingerling allowing them to start building their nests. Shaking his branches telling them to have patience. Kingdom still needed to be cleansed before anyone could start setting up homes.

Margaret let her shadow-self recede, finding a cairn of rocks she listened to the hubbub all around her. The happiness of the magicals and changelings flowed over her as she drank in their laughter. Her thoughts turning to those held deep in her heart who she'd lost as Aeryissa emerged beside her.

'Celebrations are hard, nothing brings back memories of those we miss more.'

Margaret smiled, their link, like Elfrad's more often open. To close them down she had to really force the issue. Eventually, she had given up. Whatever was driving her, obviously wanted them to stay in contact. They sat in silence, each lost in their own thoughts.

As the sun began to rise and the populace began to stir, Margaret turned to Aeryissa.

'It's time, one last mission. Once we are sure that all has been destroyed. Only then, will I cleanse Kingdom.'

Fingerling waved them off, each time Aeryissa looked at him

she tried to see the man behind the tree. When he'd caught her staring at him, he'd boomed.

'This is who I am now and have been for aeons. Nothing is left of the man I once was.'

His laughter making her smile and feel ashamed all at the same time.

Emerging in Novia, all stood for a moment, the same thoughts in everyone's mind. The norms had no idea of the battles that had been raging, or that, if lost, their realm would have also been taken. Obvious to the magic surrounding them, often ignoring what was right in front of their faces. Wrapped up in their own troubles and worries they never seemed to see further than the end of their nose.

Margaret and Aeryissa could both smell the dark magic that still weaved itself under the earth. Following the directions Bayu had given her before being spell bound, they headed towards the hills that surrounded where she had been found and once again chosen to live. Climbing down the side of the hill, the rocks and shale piled up at the bottom gave them their first hint of tunnels being excavated. The opening hadn't even been hidden, a few brambles pulled across.

Tairlaw and Hafren constructed net cloaks, damping down everyone's magic. The nearer they got without detection, the easier it would be in making sure that all were caught. Lefu and Harsha went in front, the Alvie following. Next came Keekle, Margaret had commanded his pocket contents to stay inside and not tumble out as he walked. He patted them constantly, whispering nonsense only he and they could understand. Zekia kept throwing him dark looks. Her dust lifting from her skin in warning, which he chose to ignore. Elfrad and Aeryissa brought up the rear. Both had wanted to go with Margaret. Shaking her head no, as soon as they entered the tunnel, she transported away. As they walked, voices began drifting towards them, all looked surprised at the drunken sound.

Rounding a bend they halted, Lefu and Harsha holding up

their hands, talons extended, ready to fight. Aeryissa and Elfrad moved forwards, both had heard Margaret tell them to proceed with caution and not be deceived by the merriment they will come across. Elfrad nodded to Lefu, he and Harsha tore round the bend and into the chamber, the sight that met them stopping them in their tracks. Several dark magicals lay over the floor, all laughing manically to themselves. Their skin had taken on a greenish hue, their eyes fiery red. All looked as if they hadn't slept in weeks or washed, the smell lifting from them, hitting the back of their throats. At the sight of the vampires they pulled themselves up from the floor, some staggered as soon as they were upright, others fell down again.

Keekle muttered, 'they are magic drunk, look at them, their minds have gone. These are no threat.'

Hearing his voice the dark magicals began to hiss, unknown words and sounds pouring from their mouths. Babbling, they grouped together and began chanting. Elfrad and Aeryissa joined by the vampires leapt forwards, cutting them down. Blood spurted and poured, the ground soon slick with their blood. Hafren and Tairlaw dashed forwards, nets ready, they swung them over the bodies. Instantly, they ate into the mass until with a last shudder all were gone, the chamber cleared.

'What did you say?' Lefu asked, sardonically.

The magician staggered by the violence that had taken place, shrugged, his voice locked in shock.

Once again they picked up the sound of voices, leading them forwards enticing them to enter. This time they were more prepared. Keekle stayed outside, avoiding the carnage until the forester's nets had done their work. Feeling that out of all of them he was the most useless. After several more skirmishes all were getting weary of the path they were following. Margaret appeared, Aeryissa feeling the shift before she emerged. Without a word said, she transported them further into the depths and conjured a box around them.

'Khalon is here. He is letting the dark magicals drink from the tainted silver, that's why they appear drunk, it's poisoning them.

They have been trying to separate it out into its two component parts. Wanting to siphon off the pure silver from the dark. I didn't want to say too much in Kingdom. Some discussions are better taken out of the realm. It's not over. Kingdom is not yet fully safe.'

'I don't understand,' barked Harsha. 'I thought you had cleared everything dark out before we all entered.'

'When I read the Afsaneh, Eshe made it clear that when searching for Bayu and the silver, she had come across a lode that wasn't pure. Curious at first, she quickly realised that it was tainted with dark magic. Since speaking to Bayu myself, she told me that when she took the silver from Pelagias. Somehow, once in her, it started to splinter. Unlike Athanasia who was drawn to the dark. Bayu wasn't. She found a way to separate it. The pure silver she kept mainly in Eirian, the tainted she wove around these hills, with Orara in the middle sitting on another pure stash. She thought, if someone found the tainted lode, they may not look any further for the pure. It worked. Over the years there were a few minor breaches, those looking, soon diverted to the tainted lode.'

'That's where Meridian must have been drawing her darker magic from,' said Aeryissa. 'Even Athanasia didn't know where it originated. Shimmer had not been affected in the same way, it always remained pure. Now Khalon thinks to use it against us.'

'And you want me to kill it?' asked Keekle, once more patting his pockets.

'With Elfrad's help. Yes.'

'Me? What am I supposed to do?'

'You are still my anchor.'

'Khalon like Meridian, is descended from the wizard Wyong who Eshe wrote about in the Afsaneh. He has been immersing himself in the silver ever since escaping from Kingdom. Like his ancestors before him a sly and powerful wizard. I'm sure since our last encounter he has been honing his skills even more.'

'Surely he is no match for you?' asked Harsha.

'All silver magic is under my control, including the dark side of it.

You are right Khalon represents no threat to me, a fly to be swatted. The dark silver however does. I have destroyed the Darkness, not a speck of it remains. Its taint though, is still within my body. This is what I used to summon and kill the demons. Silver knows that I am its master. Killing Khalon without the darker side of silver destroyed first. May open the way for the tainted part to attach its self to me.'

Keekle stepped forwards, 'you may not all know that I am an experimental magician.' Looking to Zekia, he added, 'don't be fooled by the mess that follows me.' Glancing at Lefu, he retorted, 'or my apparent abhorrence for violence.'

Margaret nodded for him to continue. 'Unsure what help I could be. Once I realised why my presence was requested, I have been giving the problem some thought. Elfrad as the anchor, blocks dark magic, deflects it away from Margaret.' Before Harsha could speak, he snapped, 'no, I don't know how it works. Be thankful it does.' His turn now to raise his eyebrows, 'may I? Khalon will want Margaret to attack. Elfrad is the block to her actions, while I draw the silver away. It won't be able to resist my siren song. I won't though be able to hold it forever, enough to push it off course, make it confused, unable to detect Margaret's scent. That's when we will need forester nets and fairy dust,' Keekle glanced at Zekia, seeing new respect in her eyes, he straightened his shoulders. 'As I reel it in, you all have to work together to cover it first with the nets, then with the dust.'

'Khalon is not going to be quiet, while all this is going on,' said Elfrad, as Lefu and Harsha nodded in agreement.

'He may not even be alone,' added Aeryissa. 'Do we fight? What do we do?'

The decision was made for them, exploding out of a tunnel off to their right, several dark magicals launched themselves towards the group. Aeryissa standing shoulder to shoulder between Lefu and Harsha, chopped and slashed until a pile of bodies lay in front of them.

Keekle ignored the screams of the dying and the snarling of

the vampires. Keeping his thoughts clear and focused. This was his time to shine. Taking over from Peasey he hadn't yet really made his mark as leader. A couple of chances had come his way and he had managed to deport himself in a good light. This mission though, would be the pinnacle of his career. He was determined not to let anyone down.

The walls began to move outwards, Khalon was coming, Margaret could feel the dark silver magic flowing through his veins. He didn't glow like her, his silver flat. His entrance, made them all stare. Like Meridian, using the magic had not been kind to him. Not vain like her, he let its presence show. His face distorted out of shape, jaw askew, eyes flame red, lines of black leeching outwards, giving him a clown like appearance. His hair hung down his back, grey and straggly, his beard equal in match. Like the Darkness, a sulphur smell hang around him like a hazy cloud. When he spoke a foul stench wafted towards them.

'Welcome, to my humble abode,' he croaked, banging his staff onto the ground, causing shockwaves to ripple out.

Elfrad held Margaret's arm keeping her close. She had once again let all her power abate. Back to her norm self, she kept her eyes averted.

'I've been waiting for you. I knew you'd come,' Khalon tried to catch her eyes.

Silver began snaking along the ground, climbing the walls covering the chamber. Not bright and shiny, instead grey and dirty looking. He stepped forwards, Aeryissa, Harsha and Lefu, matched him.

Khalon laughed the sound off key with a slight manic edge to it.

'You think to pit yourselves against me? I'm not a witch like Meridian. I am though a wizard. Come any nearer and I will burn you where you stand.'

Aeryissa couldn't help it, she laughed, 'you, really are insane. Aren't you? Have you looked in a mirror lately? The dark magic you are so fond of is killing you. We've come to put you out of your misery.'

Margaret moved backwards by one step, Elfrad holding her tight in his grip. The movement pulling Khalon back to her presence. Ignoring the vampires as not worth the bother.

'It's in you. I can feel it. You want to succumb. Together we can rule. Let yourself awake.'

She kept her eyes down, ever since the dark magic had entered the chamber she could feel its pull through her body. Seeking the part of her that was tainted.

Keekle had started his siren song as soon as Khalon appeared. Zekia, thought he had frozen, her nudges, pushing his focus. Raising her elbow to give him another push, Tairlaw stopped her. Her senses told her he was in the midst of his song and it was working.

Slowly at first, the silver snaking across the floor began to coalesce together, like a snake seeking its charmer. Hafren, Tairlaw and Zekia began to fall back, following Keekle. He'd told them that once the silver was fixed within his song, he would be running away. The silver should follow.

Once out of Khalon's orbit the vampires would strike. Using themselves as a distraction. All he needed was a good coil of the silver once that was caught, the nets and dusts could get to work. The song once set would keep calling the silver. Unable to resist, it would snake to its doom. As soon as Margaret felt it was under control and not a threat to her anymore, she would be able to deal with Khalon.

So convinced of his own power, he laughed to see the silver flee. Because he was drowning in its grip he couldn't understand why she ignored its call. Launching himself at her, wanting to drag her away from her body guard, his actions took them all by surprise. His appearance as old and infirm at odds with his quickness of movement.

Wrenching Margaret from Elfrad's grip, immediately her vampire flared. Silver flooded her body, she shone like a beacon in the dark.

Khalon stared in wonder at the creature now before him.

Envious of her power, this is what he wanted. Had expected to get. Seeing how she shone, feeling the power emanating from her, brought all his anger and jealousy to the fore. He struck her with his staff, a glancing blow, hardly felt. Except that it was riddled with dark magic. She felt the change in the air immediately. The snaking lines of dark silver stopped leaving the chamber.

'It's coming,' he crowed. 'Even you can't stop it. You will become a Dark queen and I will rule by your side.'

Keekle also felt the tug and then again as his siren song broke. The silver not trapped by the nets and dust, turned and fled back to the chamber. Margaret the only call it would obey. Her greatest fear realised. She knew that if she couldn't contain it. All their efforts, all those lost and injured would be for nothing. Reaching deep inside herself, looking for what controlled her. Knowing it was hidden deep inside her core, she called. The answer when it came was like a soft breeze on a summer's day.

'Leave,' she shouted, at Aeryissa. 'Take them and go.'

Margaret's face wasn't her own, something else stirred just below the surface, without thought of disobeying, Aeryissa transported them all out of the dark and into the light. Khalon was so lost in his dreams of power, he didn't recognise what pure power looked like. When he finally looked at her, his eyes widened. Over laid across her face, was something out of a nightmare. The hatred and violence contained in that one look, set him running. Fleeing for his life. Each way he turned there she was. Standing, staring with her hate filled eyes.

With a flick of her finger he was drawn towards her. Pain like no other racked his body. The dark magic was being pulled out of every fibre of his being bit by bit. Heart racing, he could do nothing but stare into her unforgiving eyes. Empty, she let him fall. Others hiding, were prised out and dealt the same fate. The bodies piled up. None dared move. So great their fear of her. Hoping she would leave them, forget they existed. Let them live.

The dark silver waited, coiled ready to spring back to its source.

The part that was still Margaret sent a warning to Aeryissa and Elfrad, telling them to get as far away as possible. Erupting out of the tunnels, her body drew the silver towards her. Thunder rolled around the skies, darkening as lightening crackled. Norms fled inside their homes. The air thick with a tang, none could abide, yet all knew it was powerful and dangerous.

Silver began running across the hills, along the valleys, moving over the water. From above it looked as if the ground shone with a millions of lights. Intertwined in places, a darkness showed, trying to grab more of the silver, turn it towards the dark. Margaret hovered above the ground, her body so bright, if any had looked, none would be able to see if it was her or a nova exploding out of the sun. The pressure of so much silver was building, those who had crossed into Eirian felt the ground tremble as it was called.

The dark silver began to climb, desperate to reach the source and be reunited. Like tendrils waving they clung to the pure silver wending its way towards Margaret's body. Finally, they began to wrap themselves around her, ready to sink into her skin, bury themselves deep within her. The more that came the more they drowned her shine. Margaret exploded. Every bit of silver at her disposal called, the dark overwhelmed by the light. The sky lightened, the storm calmed, the air became fresher.

She woke, every part of her body ached. Sitting up, she was amazed to see the destruction around her. The hills had been ripped apart, the earth thrown up. Rocks and boulders piled on top of each other. Nothing stirred, nothing moved. She knew instantly that someone other than her had done this. The magic that lay inside her quiet. The taint of the Darkness gone.

Emerging into Kingdom, she smiled as her friends rushed forwards. Keekle apologising for not being able to hold onto the dark silver. Elfrad annoyed with her as usual. Lefu and Harsha disappointed to have missed the fight. Zekia had only got started on the silver, as to had Tairlaw and Hafren. Aeryissa the only one to see the peace on Margaret's face, understanding that at last, it was over.

CHAPTER FIFTY-FIVE

A s the ridge she stood on began to move, Orara swooped down, jumping upon her back Margaret joined Fafnir as they raced across the skies. Kingdom was waking, alive once again. Moving over the land, for the first time she felt the real freedom to laugh out loud. The magicals and changelings all eager to start making their homes. The borders between Kingdom and Eirian; open. Those who had never travelled to Eirian before, seeing it as an adventure while they waited for Kingdom to be cleansed.

The destruction caused by the Darkness and all that had happened previously, was too much to clear it in small projects. Standing on a high ridge that once was a valley floor, she drew on the magic held deep inside her. Casting her view all around she raised her hands. Words that she had never spoken before and which she didn't understand the meaning of, poured out. Bending down she touched the earth, grabbing a handful she let it run through her fingers. The chant she spoke echoing across the land like the peel of bells.

All over Kingdom the ground began shifting, the only parts not moving were those that surrounded Verlimusa and the ring of boulders shrouding the entrance to the Glasserium. A soft breeze sprang up, the scent of flowers wafted. Grass appeared, rolling out like a carpet. Hills flattened, mountains grew. Valleys and ravines appeared again. Water began flowing. The Warra hearing her command, quickly filling the lakes and streams. Rushing into the rivers, filling the reserves.

Fingerling also answered her call. Trees burst through the ground, shaking their leaves in delight in being free at last. The Yorkus battle cries heard all over Kingdom as they let off steam. The Kaimi waiting patiently flew across the skies, joined by the owls, they whirled and swooped, each wanting to pick the best spot to build their nests. Trees that liked having them perched atop, calling out, encouraging their competition.

Gawain and Orev had become firm friends with Sephora and Deryn. The owl's silver feathers a sharp contrast to the Kaimi's dark ones. The wolves and bears were some of the few who looked set to stay in Eirian, they liked the emptiness of the landscape. Kebale especially felt more at home there, while Balrath couldn't make up her mind, constantly moving between the two. Ulf and Curragh had taken their pack of wolves and were busy searching the boundaries. The wolves not convinced that demons weren't still hiding out waiting to pounce.

In the process of listening to Keekle's diatribe, Margaret's eyes were drawn to the myriad of objects falling from his pockets.

'They mean well. It's when I get agitated they do too.'

'Elfrad is aware of the problem, he's spoken to the wizards. Wu is in the process of creating a more secure enclosure for their hell cats to reside in.'

Before she could say anymore, a deputation forced their way past Keekle.

'We're losing our elemental skills.'

The angry tone of their voices, made Margaret looked at each witch in turn before showing them the elemental skills she now held.

'Do not demand what isn't yours to keep.'

The witches saw the fury in her eyes, the silver flare across her skin. Bowing their heads in deference they each felt a stab of pain as a door in their minds was securely locked.

Mercia led her clan towards the trees, their smiles and cheers a boon to all that saw and heard them. Hafren and Tairlaw the first to claim their oaks. These they had saved from the wraith bindings, their trunks still bearing the scars, but their dispositions still sunny. The sounds of laughter as they made their camps echoed back to Zekia and her sisters. The Kaimi and the Fae bonds of friendship had been strengthened by the battles they had fought together side by side. Fairy dust and forester nets the perfect combination used against the demons and dark magicals. Several trees had even volunteered to let their dragons use them as their scratching posts. Rubbing their backs against them, small puffs of fire falling from their mouths as their itch was relived.

Over many months the magicals and changelings began to settle. More left Pictures and Novia to return home. The Froade sad to see them go. When the magicals had first escaped in such vast numbers and Pictures had been overwhelmed. They had rued the day the Darkness had ever been let lose. Over time though, they like the pictures, came to enjoy having so much company.

The Lobes and Lens had been the last magicals to leave, staying to enjoy Pictures bare of visitors, the silence and stillness a boon to their senses. For so long assaulted by all the sights and sounds that only magicals confined together can make.

After saying their last goodbye's, the Froade were surprised to come across Margaret walking through the corridors and pictures, taking time to talk the ancestors, reassuring them that all was well.

Damala pounced, 'there you are, I've looked all over. Every time I get near to speaking to you. You're off,' she squealed in delight.

Ignoring the changes to her friend, she acted as if Margaret was still the same.

'Bit of rough time lately?' laughed Damala loudly, making heads turn.

For Margaret it was like the sun coming out. Pulling her into a hug, she laughed loudly.

'It's good to see you. Have you spoken to them?'

'Dillon has suggested that he bring Meg to see you away from Long Meadow. Meg sees it as her sanctuary. If she was set back by the meeting, Dillon didn't want it tainted by her fear.'

The meeting didn't go well. As soon as Meg saw Margaret coming towards her, she started a low keening sound in the back of her throat. Her body began to tremble, her eyes frantically looking for escape.

'Take her home, Dillon.'

Margaret watched them walk away, a sadness in her heart. She knew if Meg would only let her near that she could help her.

'Her heart is broken,' sighed Damala, 'she fears everything. I think if she hadn't have lost the baby, she may have had a chance of happiness. Now though, she barely exists, while Dillon watches her fade.'

Entering the picture where Bardolpf and Layla had taken up residence, Margaret smelt the wolf in them first before she saw them. They emerged from behind a tree, holding hands they both looked hesitant as they walked to meet her. She knew instantly. Her face broke into a broad grin.

'Congratulations,' she beamed. Damala realised what she meant and joined in her laughter.

'That is good news. When are you due? How do you feel? Can I help? She spluttered, showing her eagerness for all things baby.

Bardolpf ignored Damala's chatter, turning to Margaret he bowed his head.

'Guardian.'

'King.'

Bardolpf laughed.

'Those days are long gone. We seek permission to live in Kingdom.'

'You are my friends, as I hope will your children be. Before coming to meet you, I re-scanned Kingdom. The Baldassare won't rise. They are no more. The Darkness destroyed them. That's all you need to know.'

Damala added 'it's safe to go home, whether as Bardolpf or Ammon, the choice is yours. One day I also hope to return. My brother is dead. My form restored. At the moment Meg still needs me. Although, if you need a baby sitter, don't forget me.'

'Damala,' chuckled Layla. 'Once met, no one can ever forget you.'

'That's because she can't stop talking about herself,' roared Bardolpf. 'I had to endure years of her chatter.'

'You may have been a King.' Looking to Layla, she added, 'in some eyes you still are. To me though, you'll always be a big shaggy wolf, my companion and my friend.'

Bardolpf drew Damala into a hug, smiling over his shoulder as her tears fell.

Lefu was still counting the cost of all the clan members killed in the battle. At the forefront of any fight, his clan had suffered more than most. Harsha had taken a near fatal blow to the head and had since been laying as if in a dead sleep for days. When Margaret heard that nothing could wake her, she sat by her side and smoothed her brow, whisperings words as if to a child.

Harsha at last opened her eyes. Unsteady, she insisted on being taken outside. Asleep while Kingdom was being revived, her senses were overloaded with all the activity and happiness she could hear and feel.

When Margaret had come, Cian had hung back at first, unsure if he should say anything or let sleeping dogs lie. The decision was taken out of his hands when she sought him out.

Still covered in blood from hunting Gork's, he was surprised to find her waiting for him.

'How was it? What I mean is, how are you?'

Cian didn't answer. He wasn't going to make it easy for her.

Guardian she may be. He knew though, without looking into her eyes that she was speaking to him as a woman.

'I'm sorry.'

'For what?' he retorted.

'I don't know, but I am.'

He crowed, 'at last she feels.'

Wiping the blood from his knife, he sat down, patting the seat for her to join him.

'Long ago you made it clear that we walked different paths. As Kingdom wakes and peace reigns, a chance may come for us to walk the same one. I am content to wait.'

Margaret reached out, taking his hand, they sat, their thoughts for once united. Their hearts content.

The flow between Eirian and Kingdom of those who couldn't decide where to live was constant. It seemed as if the sun shone every day. Magic once again wove itself throughout the lands. Everyone feeling its pull, enjoying the small surges of magic received, helping them all get back to full strength. The sound of building filled the air. Some used magic to construct their homes, others who liked and wanted to build, took longer. All though happy to see each home evolve. Another family arrive. Laughter, was forever the sound that overrode all others. All helping those who still suffered.

For some, the fear of dark magic, wouldn't go away. Margaret aware that not everyone could easily put aside their worries, tried to visit them privately. Several had been helped by holding her hand, feeling her strength and power. Understanding that as their guardian, she would keep them safe.

It was decided after much discussion and argument that the majority didn't want to wait to celebrate their victory. Preparations began in earnest.

Entering the Scriptorium, Margaret immediately became aware that something had changed. The doors to Bayu's room stood open, she picked up mutterings and curses as pages were rifled. A scene of chaos lay in front of her, open books covered every surface, their pages scattered. The most precious laid bare. The Bodleian were frantically trying to gather the pages together.

'We didn't do anything,' cried Henty at the sight of her.

Flinders, near to tears, told her, 'a wind howled through the stacks. Books fell, pages were torn out and flung aside. Narrabri tried to cast and hold them still. The spell flung back at him, knocking him down.'

'The doors to your room crashed open,' he added taking up the tale. 'Before we realised, we'd run inside. The books started falling, whirling around the room, as if unseen hands were shaking them loose.'

'Precious books, destroyed,' mourned Flinders. 'Their words disappearing, their pages blank.'

She felt the presence inside her shift and settle.

'Call your families. Bring them here.'

Margaret pushed the books unceremoniously off her chair and sat at her desk. Rubbing its surface, the wood purred at her touch. Lifting her hands together before pulling them apart, as she did so, the walls of her room began to move and expand. Unsure and wary, the Bodleian watched in fascination as the Scriptorium was once again made whole. The division's put in place, removed.

Margaret announced, 'no more will this room be out of bounds. Our most precious books hidden away and that includes the Afsaneh.'

Flinders couldn't help the sharp intake of breath. He like the other Bodleian had thought it gone, hidden. To be able to read what was past, what was foretold and possibly what will be. Would be a dream come true.

Margaret and Aeryissa, walked the length and breadth of Verlimusa. The creatures that had hidden it from the Darkness, all gone. The land lush and green. Fingerling stood surrounded by the Trip trees. His and Margaret's visit to Argonorth a poignant one. Hers because she felt that it was the place where the Darkness's fate and that of Athanasia was sealed. Fingerling because what was once full of dead looking trees, now flourished. Returned to their full glory, reaching to the skies, their branches sturdy their leaves green and abundant. The taint of evil and death gone. Rebirth and renewal the only scents that lingered.

'Shall we start?'

Rustling their leaves in acknowledgement. Margaret and Aeryissa stood side by side. Shimmer lifted, it left Margaret's skin in a fine cloud. Aeryissa's flew upwards. The Trip trees leaves blew it away, taken by a gentle wind Margaret had caused.

The shimmer gathered together, each wisp potent but different. Flying up and outwards it sought the veil above Verlimusa. Clinging to the membrane it started to eat away at the magic that held it together. Slowly small gaps began to appear, instead of seeing the sun through a filter, it burst through.

As the veil came down, magicals and changelings poured in, this would be where the celebrations would take place. In the heart of Kingdom.

'Are you making your home here?' asked Margaret, as she and Aeryissa emerged inside the Glasserium.

'No he's not,' snapped Guri. 'In fact. Take him away. A nuisance he's become since Eadulf dismantled his shields.'

'She doesn't mean it,' he chuckled. 'It's her way.'

'Did much get damaged?' asked Margaret.

Stepping out of Purity, where he'd being doing some repairs. Eadulf answered, 'no, we were lucky. Only a few halls have been blocked, but with Qiao's help they should soon be clear.'

Heads together they began discussing his and Guri's part in the upcoming celebrations.

Guri drew Aeryissa to one side, 'what's the matter?' she raised her eyebrows, 'well?'

'I'm not sure. I've been busy in Eirian and Novia. Coming back to Kingdom was a shock. It looks more or less as it used to.'

'And that's wrong? Why?' asked Guri, making sure to keep her tone light.

Aeryissa didn't really understand herself how she felt. Since young she had either been in hiding or fighting. Now with peace assured, she felt lost, adrift. Margaret was in no need of a guard she was capable of looking after herself and everyone else. Her role? She was lost as to know what it now was.

Finishing her conversation with Eadulf, Margaret touched Aeryissa's arm and transported them away.

'You heard? Of course you did.'

She smiled, 'never doubt your place by my side. You saved me long before I could save myself. I have something I want to give you. Hopefully, it will go some way in showing you how much I trust and esteem you.' Reaching into her pocket she took out a small book. 'I'm not an ancient. Chuckling, she added, 'well not in the sense the others are. I am though, something, other...' Changing her tone, she counselled.

'This Gedeon, will show you alone, how, if I were to turn to the dark, you could kill me.'

Aeryissa didn't know what to say. To hold something so powerful over another was not something she wanted to do.

'I can't. I wouldn't. Why me?' she spluttered.

'You are my friend. I trust you. The dark side of life is not my way. Eshe however, is still a part of me. She wants a failsafe in place. She nags. I've listened.'

Aeryissa took the book. Immediately she could feel the weight of the words trapped inside. As a thought formed, Margaret answered.

'Cian would kill you first.'

Aeryissa whooped with joy.

'At last.'

'Not yet, but soon. I say again. I trust you. This book is...'

'Something I'm sure I will never need to use. Now enough doom and gloom. We need to celebrate. Will Cian call you Guardian or Margaret,' she joked, making kissing noises.

As the sounds of the celebrations drifted through the open window, the magic displays of old revived. Margaret thoughts settled. In private moments she still felt unnerved by what she had become, the many changes, she had gone through. Coming to terms with her "otherness" had been the hardest. Peering into the mirror Eadulf had crafted for her, so far removed from the norm she once was, faded memories began to surface, of another time and place.

She smiled on seeing Elfrad standing in the doorway, looking every inch a Bomani. Their friendship an unbreakable bond. Her anchor against the dark.

Pausing on the threshold, he announced with a flourish.

'I've found him.'

Moving aside, her guest stepped forward. Astonishment at her transformation writ large over his face. Like everyone else he knew that she was the guardian, what he hadn't been aware of though, was how much she had changed since their first meeting. Rumours had abounded, everyone discussing how powerful they thought her magic actually was. The stories growing wilder at each recanting. Seeing her in the flesh, he didn't doubt now that all he'd heard was true, magic fairly crackled around her.

Dalil, couldn't stop the flinch as she grasped his hands, or the surprise from showing on his face, when she asked.

'What are your memories of Margaret?'

For exclusive discounts on Matador titles,
sign up to our occasional newsletter at
troubador.co.uk/bookshop